LE PASSAGER DU POLARLYS

Paru dans Le Livre de Poche :

GEORGES SIMENON

Le Passager du Polarlys

PRESSES DE LA CITÉ

1

Le mauvais œil

C'est une maladie qui s'attaque aux bateaux, dans toutes les mers du globe, et dont les causes appartiennent au grand domaine inconnu qu'on appelle le Hasard.

Si ses débuts sont parfois bénins, ils ne peuvent échapper à l'œil d'un marin. Tout à coup, sans raison, un hauban éclate comme une corde de violon et arrache le bras d'un gabier. Ou bien le mousse s'ouvre le pouce en épluchant les pommes de terre et, le lendemain, le « mal blanc » le fait hurler.

A moins qu'il ne s'agisse d'une manœuvre loupée, d'un canot qui vienne se jeter étourdiment sur l'étrave.

Ce n'est pas encore le mauvais œil. Le mauvais œil exige la série. Mais il est rare qu'elle ne suive pas, que la nuit, ou le lendemain, on ne constate pas un nouvel avatar.

Dès lors, tout va de mal en pis et les hommes, mâchoires serrées, n'ont qu'à compter les coups. C'est le moment que la machine, après avoir tourné trente ans sans une panne, choisira pour s'enrayer comme un vieux moulin à café.

En dépit des notions les mieux établies, des tables météorologiques et de l'expérience, les vents se tiendront pendant vingt jours s'il le faut là où ils n'eussent jamais dû souffler à cette saison.

Et la première lame venue emportera un homme à la mer ! Il y aura de la dysenterie, si ce n'est de la peste !

Encore heureux si on ne va pas s'échouer, sur un banc qu'on avait évité cent fois auparavant, ou si, en pénétrant au port, on n'accroche pas la jetée.

Le *Polarlys*, amarré au quai 17, dans un des bassins les plus lointains et les plus sales de Hambourg, devait appareiller à trois heures de l'après-midi, comme l'annonçait un panneau accroché à la boîte aux lettres de la passerelle.

Il n'était pas deux heures que le capitaine Petersen sentait déjà confusément rôder le mauvais œil.

C'était pourtant un petit homme énergique, trapu, costaud. Depuis neuf heures du matin, il arpentait le pont en surveillant l'embarquement des marchandises.

Un brouillard exceptionnel, jaune et gris, chargé de suie, crachotant une humidité glacée, pesait sur le port et, de la ville, on ne voyait que les lanternes des tramways, les fenêtres éclairées comme en pleine nuit.

On était à la fin de février. A cause du froid, ces nuages, où l'on se débattait, vous laissaient sur le visage et les mains une sorte de verglas.

Toutes les sirènes marchaient à la fois, en une cacophonie qui couvrait le grincement des grues.

Le pont du *Polarlys* était à peu près désert : quatre hommes au-dessus de la cale avant, pour guider les palans, décrocher les caisses et les barriques.

Est-ce à l'arrivée de Vriens, vers dix heures, que Petersen avait commencé à flairer le mauvais œil ?

Le navire n'avait rien de prestigieux. C'était un vapeur d'un millier de tonneaux, sentant la morue, le pont toujours encombré de fret, qui faisait le service de Hambourg à Kirkenes en longeant la côte norvégienne dont il desservait les moindres ports.

Bateau mixte. Il y avait place pour cinquante passagers de première classe et pour autant de passagers de troisième. On emportait à destination de la Norvège des machines, des fruits, des viandes salées. On ramenait des barils et des barils de morue ainsi que, de l'extrême Nord, des peaux d'ours et de l'huile de phoque.

Jusqu'aux Lofoten, le climat était quelconque. Puis, tout à coup, on tombait dans les glaces et dans une nuit de trois mois.

Les officiers étaient Norvégiens. Des bons garçons, qui savaient d'avance combien de barils on prendrait à Olsen et Cie, de Tromsö, et pour qui étaient les machines-outils chargées à Hambourg.

Le matin même, Petersen avait arraché son dernier galon, qui ne tenait plus que par un fil.

Et voilà que la compagnie lui envoyait avec des kyrielles de recommandations, comme troisième officier, un Hollandais de dix-neuf ans, un gamin maigre et étroit qui en paraissait seize !

Il sortait la même semaine de l'école navale de Delfzijl. Il s'était présenté la veille, pâle, ému, dans un uniforme d'une ahurissante correction, s'était mis au garde-à-vous.

— A vos ordres, mon capitaine !

— Eh bien, *monsieur* Vriens, lui avait dit Petersen, je n'ai pas d'ordres à vous donner pour le moment. Vous pouvez disposer jusqu'à demain. En qualité de troisième officier, vous vous occupez de l'embarquement des passagers.

Vriens était parti. Il n'était pas rentré de la nuit. A dix heures du matin, le capitaine le voyait descendre d'un taxi, vacillant, avec un teint de papier mâché, des paupières gonflées, un regard peureux.

Lorsqu'il traversa la passerelle, c'est tout juste s'il ne titubait pas.

Petersen lui tourna le dos, l'entendit joindre les talons pour saluer avant de s'éloigner dans la direction de sa cabine.

— Il est malade comme un chien ! venait dire

10

le steward un peu plus tard. Il m'a demandé du café très fort. Il est étendu, tout raide, sur son lit, et il parvient à peine à parler. On mettrait le feu à son haleine avec une allumette !...

Bien sûr que ce n'était pas catastrophique ! Mais, quand on a l'habitude de vivre en famille avec ses officiers, on n'aime pas voir surgir un garçon de ce genre-là, surtout si une lettre de l'administrateur l'a précédé, recommandant de faciliter ses débuts.

A dix-neuf ans, Petersen, lui, ne sortait pas de l'école, mais il avait fait trois fois son tour du monde !

Il aurait pu l'annoncer d'avance. La série commençait. Tout en faisant le tour de son bateau, les mains dans les poches, la pipe aux dents, il avise un grand type roux adossé au bastingage et roulant une cigarette. L'homme se contente de le saluer d'un vague mouvement de la tête, cherche des allumettes dans ses poches.

Un rat de quai, c'est clair ! Un de ces vagabonds du Nord qui ne ressemblent à nul autre vagabond de la terre.

Un garçon de moins de quarante ans, grand, fort, l'air sain en dépit d'une barbe de huit jours et de ses joues un peu creuses.

Il s'est installé comme chez lui. Il fume à petites bouffées, en bombant la poitrine sous une ancienne tunique de la Landwehr dont il a changé les boutons.

— Qu'est-ce que tu fais ici ?

Du menton, l'homme désigne le chef mécanicien qui traverse précisément la passerelle. Et ce dernier explique au capitaine :

— Hans vient d'avoir sa crise de malaria. Je dois le laisser à terre. Alors, j'ai avisé ce type-là, sur le quai, et je l'ai embauché comme soutier. Il est solide...

— Il a des papiers ?

— En règle ! Il sort de la prison de Cologne...

Et le chef mécanicien rit en s'éloignant.

— De deux ! grommela Petersen

Cela lui était parfaitement égal d'avoir un soutier sortant de prison, car on trouve les soutiers que l'on peut. Mais l'individu lui déplaisait de la tête aux pieds. Tout en faisant les cent pas, il continua à l'observer à la dérobée.

La plupart des vagabonds allemands ont cet air de confiance en soi, cette absence de honte et même simplement d'humilité.

Celui-ci avait en plus quelque chose d'ironique dans le regard. Il se sentait examiné. Il continuait à fumer, collant parfois d'un coup de langue le papier humide de sa cigarette, puis regardant la fumée qui s'échappait de ses lèvres et se mêlait au brouillard.

— Comment t'appelle-t-on ?

— Peter Krull...

— Qu'est-ce que tu as fait pour aller en prison ?

— La dernière fois, je n'ai rien fait ! C'était une erreur judiciaire...

Il parlait posément, d'une voix traînante, et ce fut le capitaine qui abandonna la partie.

D'ailleurs un câble cassait au même moment et un tracteur agricole, enfermé dans une énorme caisse, dégringolait de six mètres de haut au fond de la cale.

Un premier passager arrivait, dont Petersen ne vit que la malle verte et le pardessus gris.

— Où est Vriens ? demanda le capitaine au steward. J'espère que je ne vais pas devoir m'occuper de l'embarquement !

— Il est installé au salon, devant ses registres.

C'était vrai. Il avait sans doute l'estomac chaviré, le crâne douloureux, mais il était à son poste. Il reçut le passager, transcrivit les indications de son passeport, lui désigna une cabine.

Les deux dernières heures, comme toujours, furent désordonnées. Les camions qui amenaient le fret arrivaient en retard. Les grues ne pouvaient fonctionner plus vite.

— Tant pis ! On laissera ce qui ne sera pas embarqué à temps !

Une menace traditionnelle, qui ne fait peur à personne. Une passagère monta à bord, suivie d'un porteur. La police discuta avec Vriens, qui avait oublié de remplir une partie des formulaires.

Au premier coup de cloche, la route était libre

en face du *Polarlys*. Mais, quand on largua les haussières, cinq minutes plus tard, un gros pétrolier anglais avait trouvé le moyen de se mettre en travers et il fallut exécuter des manœuvres compliquées.

Une péniche à moteur allait son petit bonhomme de chemin, au ras de l'eau, avec un seul marinier appuyé à la barre et fumant sa pipe.

On la heurta de flanc. La moitié de son pont s'engagea dans l'eau et ce fut miracle si elle put continuer sa balade parmi les coques noires des cargos qui se dressaient autour d'elle comme des murs.

Sur l'Elbe, c'était une procession. Trois files de navires se suivaient en chapelet, dans le brouillard qui empêchait de distinguer la ratière du précédent, et les sirènes engageaient des discussions rageuses.

Des bateaux plus rapides s'acharnaient à trémater les autres. Des voiliers se faufilaient et on voyait soudain leur misaine blafarde se dresser à moins d'une encablure de l'étrave.

— *Doucement... Stop... Arrière... Stop... Doucement... Demi... Stop...*

Le *télégraphe*[1] cliquetait et on avançait à hue et à dia, par saccades, dans la crasse glaciale.

A sept heures, on était toujours sur la rivière et on n'apercevait pas encore le feu de Cuxhaven qui annonçait enfin la mer.

1. Instrument servant à transmettre les ordres du pont aux machines.

Le capitaine descendit de la passerelle où il laissait son second en compagnie du pilote et se prépara à une autre corvée : présider le repas des passagers.

Le steward promenait son gong dans les couloirs, avec insistance, sachant par expérience que, le premier jour, les voyageurs ne sont jamais pressés.

— Cinq couverts ? remarqua Petersen.

— Une dame et trois messieurs... Voici la dame...

Elle s'avançait avec aisance, un fume-cigarette de jade aux lèvres. Elle avait fait toilette comme pour dîner à bord d'un transatlantique de luxe et semblait nue sous sa robe de soie noire.

Une étrange petite créature, mince, nerveuse, aux mouvements lascifs, qui, par tous les artifices de la mode, s'était donné un type très souligné.

Elle avait les cheveux aussi blonds qu'un bébé, et d'une même finesse. Séparés par une raie centrale, ils retombaient sur ses joues avec une seule ondulation, soulignant l'ovale allongé du visage.

Ses prunelles étaient sombres. Et, pour que le contraste soit plus violent encore, les cils étaient noircis à l'aide de rimmel.

Une bouche mince. Des seins très hauts, très petits.

— Capitaine... ? murmura-t-elle sur un ton interrogatif.

— Capitaine Petersen...

Il s'était à peine débarbouillé. Ses cheveux drus avaient besoin d'un coup de peigne.

— Si vous voulez vous asseoir...

Elle le fit avec désinvolture, choisit la place qui lui revenait, à la droite du capitaine.

Un passager entra, serra la main de Petersen, prononça machinalement :

— Sale temps !

C'était Bell Evjen, le directeur des mines de Kirkenes, qui faisait le voyage à Londres et à Berlin tous les ans et que le *Polarlys* avait amené un mois plus tôt. Il observa la jeune femme avec intérêt. L'instant d'après un autre voyageur s'inclinait sans mot dire devant chacun ; un grand garçon au crâne rasé, sans cils ni sourcils, qui portait des lunettes aux verres si épais que les yeux en étaient démesurément grossis.

— Servez, steward ! Vous frapperez ensuite à la porte du cinquième passager...

Car il restait un couvert libre. Le repas commença, à la mode scandinave : potage, entrée chaude suivie d'une multitude de plats froids, charcuteries, salaisons, poissons en conserve, compote et fromages.

— Le 18 ne répond pas.

— Dites au troisième officier de s'en occuper.

Deux fois Petersen monta sur le pont, inquiet du ralentissement brusque des machines. C'était toujours la même situation : brouillard, cargos en file indienne, clameurs de sirènes, de trompes et de sifflets.

A table, on se taisait. Entre deux plats, la jeune

femme alluma une cigarette à l'aide d'un briquet qui était un chef-d'œuvre d'orfèvrerie. Petersen supposa qu'elle était Allemande, ainsi que le passager au crâne rasé.

— On vous servira le café au fumoir ! dit-il enfin, en se levant, selon une formule qu'il répétait depuis douze ans à chaque voyage.

Il était en train de bourrer sa pipe dans le couloir, devant sa cabine, quand la voyageuse passa près de lui et s'engagea dans l'escalier raide conduisant au fumoir. Tout le temps qu'elle monta, il regarda ses jambes que la soie noire rendait très voluptueuses, ses genoux déliés, et même l'éclat d'un peu de chair.

— Eh bien, *monsieur* Vriens ?

Le jeune homme s'était mis machinalement en position. Ses lèvres frémissaient. Il se raidissait comme s'il eût été jeté soudain au cœur d'un drame.

— Le passager est introuvable. Et pourtant ses bagages sont dans sa cabine...

— Qui est-ce ?

— Ernst Ericksen, de Copenhague... Je l'ai encore aperçu moins d'une heure avant le départ !...

— Un homme en pardessus gris, avec une malle verte ?

— C'est cela !... J'ai cherché partout...

— Il sera retourné à terre pour acheter des journaux et il aura raté le départ...

Evjen et le jeune homme aux lunettes avaient pénétré dans leur cabine. La passagère était seule au fumoir. Or Petersen l'entendit pousser un petit cri. Une porte claqua. La robe de soie noire parut au haut de l'escalier.

— Capitaine...

Elle paraissait émue, s'efforçait néanmoins de sourire, contenait des deux mains les battements de sa poitrine.

— Que se passe-t-il ?

— Je ne sais pas... Je n'aurais pas dû avoir peur... Je venais d'entrer au fumoir... J'ai trouvé le café sur une table, ainsi que les tasses, et j'ai commencé à me servir... A ce moment, il m'a semblé entendre du bruit derrière moi... Je me suis retournée et j'ai vu un homme que je n'avais pas encore aperçu... Je suis sûre qu'il a été effrayé car il s'est levé et s'est enfui en courant...

— Par où ?

— Par cette porte... Elle donne sur le pont-promenade, n'est-ce pas ?...

— Il portait un pardessus gris ?

— Gris, oui... J'ai crié... Pourquoi s'est-il sauvé ainsi ?...

Tandis qu'elle parlait, Petersen avait l'impression qu'elle s'adressait plus à Vriens qu'à lui-même.

— Allez voir ! commanda-t-il à l'officier.

Celui-ci eut une hésitation marquée, surtout au moment de passer devant la voyageuse qu'il devait frôler pour sortir.

— Tranquillisez-vous, madame... Tout ceci va certainement s'expliquer...

Elle esquissa un sourire, articula avec une moue coquette :

— Je vais rester seule au fumoir ?

— Vos compagnons ne tarderont pas à monter...

— Vous ne prenez pas de café, capitaine ?

Il sentait son parfum, très sourd, et il eût même juré qu'il percevait la chaleur émanant de sa chair. Tandis qu'un peu plus tard elle versait le café, il détailla ses lignes et, lorsqu'elle se retourna, elle le trouva plus rouge, occupé à tirailler sa cravate.

Evjen entrait.

Lorsque Petersen quitta le fumoir, conçu pour cinquante personnes, confortable mais un peu froid à cause de ses boiseries de chêne très clair, Evjen, dans un coin, annotait des documents commerciaux qu'il avait extraits de sa serviette. Dans l'angle opposé le jeune homme aux lunettes lisait le *Berliner Tageblatt*.

A égale distance de l'un et de l'autre, la passagère avait étalé sur la table de menues cartes à jouer et commençait une réussite.

— Voulez-vous me donner du feu, capitaine ?

Il dut revenir sur ses pas. Elle tendait vers lui son long fume-cigarette, en se penchant de telle sorte que le regard de Petersen plongea dans le corsage, glissa sur la naissance de la gorge.

— Merci... Nous arrivons en mer ?...

— Nous approchons de Cuxhaven, oui ! Il faut que j'aille sur la passerelle...

De près, il remarqua qu'elle avait, comme Vriens, les paupières battues, les traits las de quelqu'un qui a passé une ou plusieurs nuits sans dormir. Comme Vriens, aussi, elle avait parfois un frémissement inattendu des lèvres.

Sur la passerelle, il trouva le troisième officier qui le cherchait, le visage si défait qu'il avait l'air d'avoir pleuré.

— Vous l'avez retrouvé ?

— Non... Il se cache, c'est certain... J'avais pourtant pris trois hommes avec moi... Mais ce n'est pas cela...

Petersen le regardait d'une façon peu engageante.

— Eh bien ?

— Je voudrais vous dire, capitaine... que... que je regrette infiniment ce qui...

Sa voix se cassait. Des larmes lui montaient aux yeux.

— Je vous jure que c'est un hasard... Je n'avais jamais bu... Cette nuit... Je ne peux pas vous expliquer... Mais cela m'est intolérable de penser que vous...

— C'est tout ?

Il devint si pâle que son interlocuteur eut une bouffée de pitié.

— Allez vous coucher ! Demain il n'y paraîtra plus ! ajouta-t-il moins durement.

20

— Vous croyez que je suis encore ivre ?... Je vous donne ma parole...

— Allez !

Et Petersen, endossant sa peau de bique, s'approcha du pilote, tandis que glissait à quelques mètres le feu vert d'un cargo qui faisait route en sens inverse.

— Pas encore arrivés ?

L'homme montra la nuit de sa main gauche.

— Cuxhaven ! grommela-t-il.

C'était un pilote de l'Elbe et il devait, sous le feu de ce port, s'embarquer dans un petit bateau à moteur qui l'attendait.

Le capitaine lui servit le *schnaps* traditionnel dans la chambre de veille tout en échangeant quelques banalités. Il remplissait un second verre lorsque les machines ralentirent, puis stoppèrent tout à fait.

Bientôt on aperçut une luciole dans le brouillard à ras de l'eau. Elle semblait lointaine et pourtant, la seconde d'après, elle se transformait en une lampe à acétylène dont on distinguait tous les détails. Aussitôt on entendait un heurt contre la coque, en dessous de l'échelle de coupée. Poignée de main.

— Bonne nuit...

Le steward achevait de mettre en ordre la salle à manger. Au fumoir, les trois personnages, séparés les uns des autres par plus de huit mètres, continuaient à s'ignorer, bien qu'Evjen regardât souvent la jeune femme.

Le pilote avait à peine mis les pieds dans l'embarcation qu'il appelait :

— Ohé, capitaine !... Quelque chose pour vous...

Penché sur la lisse, Petersen distingua dans le canot une silhouette inattendue : un homme, en ulster, qui tenait une volumineuse valise à la main.

— Qu'est-ce que vous désirez ?

— Je vais vous expliquer...

On dut aider l'homme à gravir l'échelle. Une fois sur le pont, il regarda autour de lui avec inquiétude.

— Conseiller de police von Sternberg ! dit-il. Je n'ai pas pu prendre le bateau à Hambourg et j'ai fait la route en auto...

C'était un personnage d'une cinquantaine d'années à qui une barbe en pointe et d'épais sourcils donnaient un air d'autant plus étrange que l'ulster de teinte indécise déformait sa silhouette.

— Je prendrai mes repas dans ma cabine ! ajouta-t-il comme le *Polarlys* se remettait en marche. Si des passagers vous interrogent...

— J'en ai trois en tout !

— Si des passagers vous interrogent, vous répondrez que je suis malade et que je garde le lit... Donnez-leur un autre nom... Wolf, par exemple, Herbert Wolf, négociant en fourrures... Je paierai la traversée...

— Vous êtes en mission ? questionna Petersen

dont la mauvaise humeur s'était accrue. Il y a quelqu'un à bord qui... ?

— J'ai dit *conseiller* de police ? Je n'ai pas dit *inspecteur*...

— Pourtant...

Le capitaine n'ignorait pas tout à fait que le titre de conseiller de police est, en Allemagne, un titre prestigieux et que la fonction ne consiste pas à courir après les malfaiteurs.

Mais qu'il fût question de police, cela suffisait à le rendre hargneux. Il était capitaine et il prétendait rester le maître à bord de son bateau.

— Après tout, vous ferez comme il vous plaira ! grommela-t-il. Au fait ! si c'est un certain Ernst Ericksen qui vous préoccupe, j'aime autant vous dire tout de suite qu'il est insaisissable... Disparu !... Il se cache Dieu sait où, bien qu'il ait payé son passage et que ses bagages soient dans sa cabine...

Il appela :

— Steward ! Vous conduirez monsieur dans une cabine libre... Vous l'y servirez... M. Wolf !...

Et, tourné vers l'homme en ulster :

— C'est bien cela, n'est-ce pas ?

Il prenait son quart à six heures du matin et il eût déjà dû être couché depuis longtemps. Il rentra chez lui, se mit au lit, mais inconsciemment il resta attentif aux allées et venues du couloir.

Il entendit ainsi Evjen et le voyageur au crâne rasé pénétrer dans leur cabine. Il était plus de minuit que la porte de la jeune femme ne s'était pas encore ouverte. Il sonna le steward.

— Tout le monde est couché ?

— Pas tout le monde... Il y a la dame...

— Elle fait toujours des réussites ?

— Pardon ! Elle se promène sur le pont avec...

— Avec ?

— Avec M. Vriens !

— Il a eu le culot de la relancer au fumoir ?

— Non ! Il était dans sa cabine... C'est elle qui m'a prié de l'appeler...

Le capitaine se retourna lourdement sur sa couchette et gronda quelque chose d'inintelligible à l'adresse du steward, qui attendit encore un moment et se retira.

2

Le passager saugrenu

Le lendemain, il était neuf heures et le capitaine montait son quart depuis longtemps sur la passerelle, quand le premier passager se montra.

C'était dimanche. En principe, la vie était la même à bord du *Polarlys* que tous les autres jours.

Et pourtant il y avait ce jour-là, dans l'atmosphère, quelque chose d'indéfinissable qui le distinguait des autres.

Le thermomètre, vers la fin de la nuit, était tombé à zéro et même un peu au-dessous. Lorsque Petersen, non rasé, non débarbouillé, avait endossé sa peau de chèvre pour prendre le quart, il y avait encore dans l'air une sorte de pluie pulvérisée.

Elle s'était cristallisée avec le jour et le soleil avait bientôt fait disparaître la couche de minuscules grains blancs déposés sur le pont.

Un drôle de soleil, qu'il était impossible de regarder en face et qui, pourtant, ne chauffait pas, n'égayait même pas. La brise était fraîche et les scintillements de l'eau avaient la crudité de reflets de fer-blanc.

On longeait le nord du Danemark, assez au large pour ne pas voir la côte.

Le premier passager levé était le jeune homme à lunettes, qui portait des culottes de golf, un pull-over, et qui tenait son veston sous le bras.

Arnold Schuttringer, ingénieur à Mannheim, lut Petersen, qui avait emporté le registre.

Schuttringer, après s'être rendu compte de la disposition des lieux, opta pour la plage avant, posa son veston sur le cabestan et commença une série de mouvements de gymnastique rationnelle, sans hâte, sans ennui, le front têtu.

Il avait retiré ses lunettes et ses yeux étaient

25

d'une grandeur normale. C'était donc la convexité des verres qui les grossissait d'habitude.

Le capitaine était seul sur la passerelle. Dans une cage de verre, derrière lui, le timonier se tenait immobile, les deux mains sur la roue de cuivre, le regard rivé au compas.

Un garçon de cuisine, en bonnet blanc, traversa le pont pour lancer des épluchures à la mer, aperçut le jeune Allemand et resta un bon moment abasourdi, car le passager, couché de tout son long sur le dos, s'étirait et se redressait comme un automate à une cadence régulière, avec des « han » de satisfaction.

Il y avait un autre personnage à suivre des yeux cet exercice et, en l'apercevant, Petersen esquissa une grimace de contrariété.

C'était Peter Krull, le soutier, assis près de l'écoutille du poste d'équipage, une cigarette collée à la lèvre inférieure.

Il n'avait que deux heures de liberté. D'habitude, les hommes des machines ne se donnent pas la peine, pour si peu de temps, de se laver, ni surtout de changer de vêtements.

Or il avait troqué son bleu de chauffe pour sa vieille veste d'uniforme. Sa poitrine était nue, couverte de poils roux, et il avait gardé le calot de toile sur la tête.

Aucun règlement ne l'empêchait d'être là ou plutôt, l'hiver, alors que les passagers sont rares, c'était une tolérance. Plus que la veille encore, sa physionomie frappa le capitaine, le gêna à proprement parler.

Une gêne assez semblable à celle qui nous fait détourner la tête quand nous croyons lire de l'intelligence dans les yeux d'un animal d'ordre inférieur.

Peut-être gardait-il trop de désinvolture, d'assurance, voire d'élégance dans sa dégradation ?

Il ne quittait pas Schuttringer du regard. L'Allemand le remarqua au moment où il terminait ses exercices et où il endossait sa veste. Le capitaine crut discerner un certain malaise et, en tout cas, le jeune homme s'éloigna à grands pas, sans se retourner.

Un peu plus tard, Evjen, selon son habitude lorsqu'il était à bord, gravit l'échelle de la passerelle pour serrer la main de Petersen.

— Bien dormi ?

— Pas mal... Il paraît qu'il y a un passager malade ?

— Un malade, oui ! gronda le capitaine entre ses dents. Qu'est-ce qu'il y a, *monsieur* Vriens ?

Car le troisième officier surgissait à son tour, à peine moins défait que la veille, prononçait très vite :

— Je traversais la cale, il y a un instant, quand j'ai entendu du bruit derrière les caisses... J'ai entrevu le passager...

Il y eut un silence. Evjen regardait le capitaine pour savoir ce qu'il fallait penser de cette histoire.

— Dites donc, Vriens !

Celui-ci tressaillit, eut même un sursaut, comme quelqu'un qui pressent un danger.

— A quelle heure vous êtes-vous couché, cette nuit ?

— Je... je ne sais pas...

— Je vais vous renseigner, moi ! A deux heures, vous étiez encore à vous promener sur le pont ! Et vous n'aviez pas dormi la nuit précédente ! Et vous aviez voyagé toute la nuit d'avant...

— Que voulez-vous dire ?

— Que je commence à craindre que vous n'ayez des hallucinations ! Prenez les hommes que vous voudrez et mettez-moi la main sur ce passager fantôme ! Compris ?

Cela recommençait déjà. Durant ses premières heures de quart, Petersen n'avait pu s'empêcher de penser aux événements de la veille. Et, mal éveillé, un bol de café noir dans l'estomac, maussade dans le petit jour glacé, il en avait fait une sorte de cauchemar où son troisième officier, le soutier de Hambourg, cet Ericksen dont il n'avait vu que le pardessus gris et la jeune femme apparaissaient tour à tour sous un aspect fantastique.

Qu'il y eût quelque chose d'anormal à bord, c'était évident. Sinon un haut fonctionnaire de la police ne se fût pas donné la peine de courir après le *Polarlys* jusqu'à Cuxhaven et de prendre tant de précautions.

Quelque chose de grave ! Comme Sternberg

l'avait dit lui-même d'un ton cassant, il était conseiller et non pas inspecteur.

Etait-ce Ericksen qu'il cherchait ? Il n'avait pas sourcillé quand le capitaine lui en avait parlé. Il n'avait posé aucune question.

Peter Krull ?

Celui-ci s'en allait justement en traînant la jambe pour reprendre son travail dans la soute.

Et quel besoin avait la jeune femme de faire appeler Vriens à minuit, de se promener sur le pont avec lui jusqu'à deux heures du matin ?

Evjen dressait sa haute silhouette racée, à côté du capitaine, fixait l'horizon de ses yeux gris.

— Vous croyez que nous aurons une bonne traversée ?

— Vous avez déjeuné ?

— Pas encore...

— Vous ne savez pas si la passagère est dans la salle à manger ?

— Elle ne s'y trouvait pas quand je suis passé. Allemande ?

— Allemande, oui ! Katia Storm... Mais, d'après ses papiers, elle est domiciliée à Paris, rue Vavin...

— Elle se rend à Bergen ?

— Justement non ! A Kirkenes ! Schuttringer aussi ! Tout le monde, cette fois-ci, descend à Kirkenes, où d'habitude il n'y a que vous à aller !

— Voyage d'agrément, bien entendu ?...

Evjen s'intéressait à elle. Il avouait qu'il avait regardé dans la salle à manger en passant. Sans doute même avait-il remis son petit déjeuner à plus tard avec l'espoir de le prendre en même temps que la passagère.

Ils la virent arriver sur le pont, qu'ils dominaient. Elle mettait timidement le nez dehors à la façon de quelqu'un qui sort du bain et qui craint d'être saisi par le froid.

Elle avait changé de toilette et portait un ensemble gris et rose qui, comme la robe de la veille, sortait d'une grande maison de couture. Elle était fraîche. Ses cheveux gardaient encore les traces du peigne.

En levant la tête, elle aperçut les deux hommes, leur sourit.

— Bonjour, capitaine...

Puis, pour Evjen, elle esquissa un petit salut plus réservé.

— C'est le beau temps ?

— Je le souhaite.

Le steward montra dans l'entrebâillement de la porte un visage désespéré parce que personne ne se décidait à manger et qu'il perdait sa matinée à attendre.

Evjen descendit, après une phrase banale. Petersen le vit faire les cent pas en ayant soin de se rapprocher insensiblement de Katia Storm qui suivait des yeux un vol de mouettes.

Le capitaine eût été incapable de dire pourquoi l'atmosphère lui donnait une angoissante sensation de vide. Vide le ciel, qui était sans nuages et pourtant d'un gris lugubre. Vide le navire où les gens allaient et venaient sans but, sans entrain. Vide lui-même...

Il lui semblait qu'il attendait quelque chose et il ne savait pas quoi. Il vit trois matelots qui sortaient de la cale avant en compagnie de Vriens, leur cria :

— Rien ?

— Rien !

Parbleu ! Il y avait des montagnes de caisses et de colis de toutes sortes qu'on ne pouvait déranger, car ils étaient arrimés dans l'ordre des ports auxquels ils étaient destinés. Un homme, là-dedans, pouvait échapper, plusieurs jours durant, aux recherches.

Soudain il ne vit plus personne. Evjen et Katia Storm devaient manger. Vriens s'était dirigé vers le carré des officiers. Seul le garçon de cuisine venait de temps en temps lancer quelque chose dans l'eau.

Deux heures passèrent ainsi, à regarder l'horizon, puis le compas, puis encore l'horizon, en même temps que l'esprit de Petersen échafaudait des suppositions sur la mission de Sternberg.

La cloche piqua le quart. C'était au tour du troisième officier à prendre place sur la passerelle où il se présenta, tout raide dans sa tunique trop mince mais galonnée, la casquette ornée d'un large écusson.

Le capitaine le regarda des pieds à la tête, faillit recommencer une discussion, se contenta de grommeler avec lassitude :

— Gardez le cap... Nord-nord-ouest...

Il mit une heure à se laver et à s'habiller. Il avait

vu en passant ses trois passagers au fumoir : Bell Evjen et Katia Storm à la même table, Schuttringer dans l'autre coin en train de lire un album illustré qu'il avait trouvé sur le radiateur.

Quand il fut prêt, il erra un moment dans le couloir bâbord. C'était le seul occupé. La première cabine était la sienne, plus grande que les autres, avec un recoin formant bureau. Puis venait celle d'Evjen, suivie d'une cabine vide. Ensuite le fameux 18, qu'Ericksen avait abandonné pour se cacher dans la cale. Enfin les cabines 20, 22 et 24, occupées respectivement par Katia Storm, Arnold Schuttringer et le conseiller de police.

Le reste était vide et, tout au fond du couloir, une petite plaque désignait les lavabos et les salles de bains.

Le steward dressait la table, passait et repassait, les bras chargés de vaisselle, devant le capitaine.

— M. von Stern... je veux dire le 24... M. Wolf... il ne vous a pas encore sonné ?

— Pas encore.

— Le déjeuner est prêt ?

— Dans un instant...

Et, en effet, après avoir posé les serviettes à leur place, le steward s'empara du gong qu'il alla mettre en branle à la porte du fumoir.

Un rayon de soleil pénétrait par les hublots, faisait rutiler les petits pavillons de la compagnie posés sur les tables.

Rasé de frais, sentant encore le savon, Petersen

avait endossé un complet de ville en drap qui le rendait plus gros et un peu gauche.

Il attendit, une main sur le dossier de sa chaise, que tout le monde fût installé. Evjen et la jeune femme arrivèrent ensemble, achevant une conversation sur les sports d'hiver à Chamonix et au Tyrol. Schuttringer avait exactement le même visage que le matin, lorsqu'il accomplissait ses mouvements de culture physique.

Le capitaine, avant de s'asseoir, se tourna vers le couloir avec la sensation qu'il manquait quelque chose et il devait se souvenir par la suite de cette angoisse imprécise.

Car, juste à cet instant, on entendit un cri étrange, qui commença sur un mode étouffé pour finir par une note aiguë. On eût juré un cri d'agonie !

Katia Storm se tourna vivement vers le capitaine. Evjen, qui disait quelque chose à sa compagne, s'interrompit au milieu d'un mot. Schuttringer, lui, reposa la serviette qu'il venait de saisir, demanda :

— Que se passe-t-il ?

Petersen fit quelques pas dans la direction de la porte, distingua la veste blanche du steward qui se tenait debout contre la cloison, dans le couloir, en face de la porte ouverte du conseiller de police.

Le steward se couvrait la figure de son bras replié, se tassait sur lui-même, semblait faire un effort pour repousser le mur. C'était lui qui avait crié. Mais il n'était plus capable de le faire. Ses jambes mollissaient.

Le capitaine franchit le reste du chemin en courant. Arrivé à la porte, il s'arrêta net, les poings serrés, les mâchoires dures.

Est-ce qu'il ne s'était pas attendu à quelque chose de semblable ?

La couverture avait glissé du lit sur le sol. Le matelas était de travers, les draps roulés en boule, tachés de sang. Il y en avait un sur le visage de Sternberg, comme si on eût voulu le faire taire.

Et, au milieu de la poitrine découverte par le pyjama déboutonné, deux ou trois entailles, des taches rouges, des traces de doigts sanglants.

Un pied nu dépassait du lit, livide, que Petersen n'eut besoin que de frôler pour avoir la certitude de la mort.

Le steward n'avait pas bougé. On entendait claquer ses dents et il s'obstinait à tenir son bras replié devant son visage. Les trois passagers s'avançaient, encore hésitants. Evjen marchait le premier.

— Qu'est-ce que c'est ? questionna-t-il.

A ce moment, le capitaine remarqua que la jeune femme, qui n'avait pas encore vu le cadavre, mais qui avait dû apercevoir des taches de sang, crispait les doigts de sa main droite sur le bras de Bell Evjen.

Ce fut à cet instant aussi qu'il eut l'impression que Schuttringer, malgré ses lunettes, ne voyait pas très clair. L'Allemand avançait toujours. Il se tint un bon moment sur le seuil, les sourcils froncés, après quoi il prononça :

— Qui est-ce ?

— Calmez-vous, disait Evjen en tapotant la main de Katia Storm. Ne restez pas ici...

Car, peu à peu, elle se laissait aller à son émotion, et on pouvait prévoir le moment où la crise de nerfs éclaterait.

— Emmenez-la donc ! cria furieusement le capitaine.

Il repoussa Schuttringer.

— Et vous, laissez le passage libre !

La porte du fond, qui communiquait avec les cuisines, s'était ouverte et on apercevait des silhouettes curieuses, encore hésitantes.

— Entre, commanda Petersen au steward.

— Non !... Pas ça !... gémit celui-ci.

Peu après, le capitaine ne s'expliqua pas comment il avait saisi son interlocuteur par le bras pour le faire pirouetter dans la cabine 24 dont il referma la porte d'un coup de pied.

— Il a sonné ?...

— Non !... Mais... quand... quand vous m'avez parlé de lui, j'ai eu l'idée de frapper... Il était tard... Je n'avais pas encore entendu de bruit... On n'a pas répondu... J'ai ouvert doucement... Laissez-moi partir...

Il poussa à nouveau son cri peureux parce que, tout en bougeant, il avait frôlé de la main le pied nu du mort.

— Oui, va !... Fais venir...

— Qui ?...

— Personne !... Je ne sais pas...

A qui pouvait-il s'adresser ? Il était capitaine. Il n'y avait aucune autorité à bord en dehors de lui.

— Va !... Referme la porte...

Le cadavre ne lui faisait pas peur et même, comme ce pied qui dépassait gênait ses mouvements, il le posa sur le lit, à côté de l'autre.

A tout hasard, il toucha la poitrine. Le corps était déjà raide, glacé. Le crime avait dû être commis pendant la nuit. Pas une goutte de sang qui ne fût complètement coagulée.

La valise de Sternberg avait été retirée du filet et posée sur le sol au beau milieu de la cabine. On l'avait ouverte. Son contenu bouleversé jonchait le tapis.

C'était du linge, un complet de rechange, des cols empesés et des cravates. Il y avait aussi des souliers en chevreau verni.

Petersen évitait autant que possible de toucher aux objets. Mais il ne se décidait pas à sortir, persuadé que la cabine contenait une indication quelconque sur l'assassin. Il n'apercevait aucune arme. Par contre, en bougeant un tant soit peu l'oreiller, il vit des journaux français et allemands qui dépassaient.

Il y avait eu lutte. Sinon, il n'eût pas été nécessaire de couvrir la tête de Sternberg avec un drap roulé en boule. Les traces de sang sur la poitrine, il les avait faites lui-même, dans l'agonie, de ses doigts qui étaient encore gluants.

Il se dégageait de l'aspect de la cabine et du corps une impression saisissante de sauvagerie, en même temps que d'inexpérience, de maladresse.

La scène avait dû être atroce. Le conseiller de police était vigoureux. Surpris dans son lit, il s'était débattu. Et l'autre avait continué à frapper au hasard, en essayant par tous les moyens de faire taire sa victime.

On n'avait rien entendu ! Les passagers qui occupaient les cabines proches prétendaient avoir dormi à merveille.

Le veston pendait au portemanteau. Petersen glissa la main dans les poches, qui étaient vides, mais, dans l'ulster, il trouva un portefeuille. Il contenait cinq mille marks, des cartes de visite au nom de Sternberg, des lettres et un titre de parcours gratuit sur les chemins de fer allemands.

Après coup seulement, le capitaine sortit d'une pochette le portrait d'une jeune fille d'une quinzaine d'années, aux grands yeux noirs, aux cheveux bouclés, presque crépus.

Il n'avait pas pensé à fermer les yeux du mort. Il hésita à le recouvrir d'un drap.

Quand il sortit, il trouva Evjen et Schuttringer qui arpentaient le couloir, séparément, et qui levèrent la tête vers lui au même instant.

— Je n'ai rien à dire ! répondit-il à leur interrogation muette. Nous arriverons à minuit à Stavanger. La police s'occupera de cette affaire. Où est Mlle Storm ?

— Dans sa cabine ! Elle demande qu'on la laisse seule...

Il faillit rentrer chez lui aussi, mais il se ravisa, jeta en passant journaux et portefeuille sur sa couchette et alla prendre place à table.

Après quelques instants, les deux hommes se décidèrent à l'imiter.

Le steward, bouleversé, encore pantelant, les servit sans savoir ce qu'il faisait.

Ils mangèrent, mais ce fut par contenance que Petersen se leva avant la fin du repas, car il songeait soudain qu'il avait oublié de se laver les mains.

3

La morte de la rue Delambre

Petersen lisait l'anglais et l'allemand sans peine, mais il dut se servir du dictionnaire pour déchiffrer tant bien que mal l'article du journal français qui, seul, pouvait avoir un rapport avec la présence de Sternberg à bord.

Le journal était daté du 17 février. Le *Polarlys* avait appareillé le 19, à trois heures de l'après-midi, c'est-à-dire à peu près au moment où les quotidiens de Paris du 17 étaient distribués à Hambourg.

« Un crime à Montparnasse », annonçait le titre. Et le sous-titre précisait : « Encore les stupéfiants ! »

Le hublot de la cabine était glauque. Le capitaine y colla un instant le visage, constata qu'avant la nuit le brouillard serait à nouveau aussi épais que la veille, tendit l'oreille aux bruits de la machine et finit par s'asseoir devant son bureau.

Sur la cloison il y avait un portrait agrandi de sa femme, joyeuse et bien portante, non dépourvue de joliesse.

Plus bas, une photo d'amateur était épinglée : Petersen, en bras de chemise, jouant avec ses deux enfants dans le jardin d'un bungalow, sur les hauteurs de Bergen.

Tout en feuilletant le dictionnaire, il répétait, en les déformant, les mots français qu'il cherchait. Et *grosso modo* il reconstitua le sens de l'article :

« Une affaire particulièrement pénible vient à nouveau jeter un jour cru sur la vie cosmopolite de Montparnasse, dont les mœurs ont de moins en moins de rapport avec les vraies mœurs parisiennes.

» Au 19 *bis* de la rue Delambre, à deux pas des

trois ou quatre brasseries qui retentissent du matin au soir de palabres dans toutes les langues du monde, le peintre munichois Max Feinstein occupe depuis plusieurs années déjà un atelier qui, situé au rez-de-chaussée, possède une entrée particulière sur la rue.

» Max Feinstein, qui a acquis une certaine notoriété, voyage beaucoup et chaque hiver, entre autres, passe deux ou trois mois sur la Riviera et sur les plages de l'Adriatique.

» Lors de ces voyages, il a l'habitude de laisser sa clef à quelque camarade qui profite ainsi du logement vide.

» Cette année, il partit vers le 1er janvier en annonçant à la concierge que des amis viendraient de temps à autre chez lui et en la priant de donner à l'occasion un coup de balai.

» Nous avons dit que l'atelier avait son entrée particulière. Ajoutons qu'au fond d'un petit réduit transformé par le peintre en salle de bains, une porte, qui communiquait jadis avec la loge de la concierge, a été condamnée.

» Ce n'est que grâce à cette porte, permettant d'entendre les bruits de l'atelier, qu'on a, à l'heure actuelle, une vague idée de ce qui s'est passé.

» La concierge a bien voulu nous répéter ce qu'elle a déclaré à la police. Nous reproduisons textuellement son témoignage :

» — De M. Max, je n'ai rien à dire. C'est un bon locataire, assez sérieux pour un jeune homme, mais beaucoup trop bon. Cent fois il a ramené ici des compatriotes dans la misère. Parfois il en a gardé pendant des semaines et il les faisait coucher sur le divan de l'atelier.

» C'est le dimanche après son départ que, pour la première fois, j'ai entendu du bruit. Je ne me suis pas inquiétée, vu que j'étais prévenue. J'ai seulement remarqué qu'il y avait au moins six personnes, dont deux ou trois femmes, que tout le monde parlait allemand et qu'on débouchait des bouteilles de champagne.

» Le lendemain, je suis allée mettre de l'ordre et j'ai failli écrire à M. Max, car ses amis avaient transformé l'atelier en une véritable écurie. Il y avait des verres cassés et des bouteilles dans tous les coins. La baignoire était pleine d'eau sale ; on s'était essuyé les mains aux rideaux. Et je ne parle pas du reste !...

» Bref, ils sont restés quelque temps sans venir. Puis, un mercredi, je crois, j'ai entendu des voix. Mais ils n'étaient que deux, un homme et une femme, qui ont passé la nuit dans l'atelier. Vers le matin, une telle odeur d'éther m'arrivait par-dessous la porte que j'ai été sur le point d'aller les mettre dehors. Mais cela ne me regardait pas, n'est-il pas vrai ?

» C'est dimanche dernier qu'ils sont venus pour la dernière fois, à cinq ou six. J'avais ma belle-sœur d'Argenteuil à la maison, si bien que je n'ai pas fait attention. Mais j'ai tout de même reconnu des voix que j'avais entendues le premier dimanche.

» Ils ont dû partir très tard. Le lendemain, les ouvriers commençaient le ravalement de la cour et je n'ai pas eu le temps de jeter un coup d'œil à l'atelier. Mardi, c'était mon jour de sortie.

» A dire vrai, j'étais dégoûtée d'avance à l'idée de la saleté que j'allais trouver et ce n'est que jeudi que je me suis décidée.

» La police vous a dit le reste. Moi, je me suis enfuie en courant et j'ai attrapé par le bras le premier passant venu, tellement j'étais effrayée.

» Une femme était couchée sur le lit sans un vêtement ! Une toute jeune personne, qui avait dû être bien jolie, mais qui avait des taches bleuâtres sur la figure et sur le corps.

» Il traînait du champagne et du whisky partout. J'ai marché sur une seringue en verre, sans le vouloir, mais les experts ont pu faire quand même l'analyse.

» Les lâches, n'est-ce pas ? Quand ils ont vu qu'elle était morte, ils se sont sauvés ! Et ils l'ont laissée là, toute seule ! »

Petersen regarda l'image de sa maison norvégienne, en bois peint, aussi pimpante qu'un jouet, et il se sentait mal à l'aise comme un homme qui découvre pour la première fois certaines maladies particulièrement répugnantes.

L'article continuait :

« Ces derniers mots de la concierge résument assez bien la situation. La police judiciaire a ouvert une enquête, mais, si celle-ci a donné des résultats quant à la victime, elle n'a rien appris sur les coupables.

» L'examen du cadavre a révélé tout d'abord que la jeune fille, âgée de vingt ans, saine et sans tares, a, dans la soirée de dimanche, absorbé une forte dose d'alcool et de stupéfiants.

» Mais la mort est due à une piqûre de morphine dont on a retrouvé la trace sur la cuisse gauche.

» La photographie publiée hier dans les feuilles du soir a permis son identification. Il s'agit d'une nommée Marie Baron, née à Amboise, vendeuse dans un magasin de la rue de Clichy et vivant seule dans un meublé du boulevard des Batignolles.

» Sa famille habite l'Indre-et-Loire et c'est une amie qui est venue reconnaître le corps à l'Institut médico-légal.

» Cette amie a déclaré en outre que le dimanche précédent, comme les autres dimanches, elles devaient aller ensemble à Luna-Park. Mais, le samedi soir, Marie Baron lui dit qu'elle avait rencontré des jeunes gens *très rigolos* et qu'elle préférait les suivre à Montparnasse.

» Il n'est que trop aisé de reconstituer les faits. Une bande d'intoxiqués, comme il arrive souvent, a trouvé piquant de s'adjoindre une jeune fille n'ayant jamais usé de la drogue.

» Ainsi pimentée de la présence de Marie Baron, l'orgie a commencé à grand renfort de champagne, d'alcool et d'héroïne.

» La jeune fille manifestait-elle encore trop de résistance ? Il est certain, en tout cas, qu'étant donné son inexpérience, *elle n'a pu pratiquer elle-même la piqûre à la cuisse.* C'est donc un de ses compagnons qui a dû s'en charger, peut-être par surprise.

» Le docteur Paul affirme que la mort, par inhibition, a été à peu près instantanée.

» Effrayée, la bande s'est enfuie, en ayant soin, toutefois, de ne rien laisser sur les lieux pouvant permettre d'identifier les personnes présentes. C'est un trait de caractère à noter, car il révèle que l'affolement, du moins pour certains, n'était que relatif.

» Une enquête dans les milieux internationaux de Montparnasse n'a donné aucun résultat. Seul le peintre Max Feinstein pourrait dire à qui, en partant, il a confié ses clefs.

» Hélas ! c'est en vain qu'on a télégraphié à Nice et à Cannes. Aux dernières nouvelles, il se serait embarqué voilà huit jours pour une plage de l'Adriatique, mais on ignore laquelle.

» Aucun détail, dans cette affaire, qui ne soit particulièrement odieux.

» Quant aux vieux parents de Marie Baron, on imagine leur stupeur, leur incrédulité, puis enfin leur désespoir devant la révélation de pareils faits.

» La police fait diligence. Elle ne craint pas

moins, avec juste raison, que les coupables soient loin lorsqu'elle sera parvenue enfin à établir leur identité. »

Petersen parcourut des yeux les titres du journal allemand sans y rien trouver qui pût se rapporter à l'affaire.

Il était pâle et le malaise qu'il ressentait était aussi physique que moral.

Depuis l'âge de treize ans il vivait en mer. Il avait assisté à des batailles dans les bouges des ports. Une fois, un matelot ivre lui avait raconté ses crimes.

Alors qu'il était capitaine, la police avait procédé à son bord à plusieurs arrestations. La première fois, il s'agissait d'un escroc international, la troisième d'un Polonais qui, dans une crise de jalousie, avait étranglé sa femme et ses deux enfants.

Tout cela l'avait laissé presque froid. En bon protestant, il faisait la part des bons et des mauvais instincts qui se disputent l'âme humaine.

Or, maintenant, c'était plutôt une sorte de honte qui l'étreignait. Il n'avait jamais vu Paris. Il essayait d'imaginer ce Montparnasse dont parlait le journal, puis l'atelier du peintre, l'atmosphère d'orgie, le cadavre nu sur le divan...

Il fut longtemps sans se demander si l'affaire avait un rapport quelconque avec le meurtre du conseiller de police von Sternberg, et pourtant, dès lors, et presque à son insu, ce fut pour lui une certitude.

Malgré lui, il passait en revue des visages, des silhouettes : cet Ericksen en manteau gris, dont il n'avait vu que le dos et qui se cachait dans la cale ; le soutier Peter Krull et son sourire inquiétant ; Vriens, avec ses paupières rougies, sa nervosité maladive ; Schuttringer et ses yeux en billes, sans cils, ni sourcils...

Il se souvint avec gêne du sang plus chaud qui lui était monté au visage à la vue des jambes de Katia et il s'avoua à lui-même que, par deux fois au moins, en passant près d'elle, il s'était arrangé pour la frôler.

Ce qui dominait ses pensées, c'était l'impression qu'il y avait quelque chose de détraqué dans son univers. Et cela le déroutait à tel point qu'il se prit la tête à deux mains, sursauta, beaucoup plus tard, en entendant piquer six heures.

Jusqu'à son bateau qui n'était plus le même ! Une fois hors de sa cabine, il lança au long couloir un regard méfiant, remarqua que le steward se tenait tout près de sa porte.

— Où sont-ils ? questionna-t-il d'une voix soupçonneuse.

— Qui ?

— Les passagers... Evjen... Schuttringer...

— Là-haut... Au fumoir...

— Et la jeune femme ?

— Elle est allée les rejoindre...

Il gravit pesamment l'escalier, ouvrit la porte du fumoir et resta debout sur le seuil, les traits durs.

Les passagers étaient à la même place que le matin : Bell Evjen et Katia attablés ensemble devant une bouteille d'eau minérale ; dans l'angle opposé, Schuttringer qui jouait aux échecs, tout seul.

Les lampes venaient de s'allumer. Trois visages s'étaient tournés vers le capitaine. Evjen, plus familier que les autres, ouvrit la bouche pour parler.

Mais Petersen referma brusquement la porte et continua à monter jusqu'à la passerelle. Il distingua la silhouette étroite de Vriens, qui venait de passer la consigne au second officier.

Pourquoi, arrivant sans bruit par-derrière, lui mit-il tout à coup la main sur l'épaule ? Le jeune homme en trembla de tous ses membres, montra un visage décomposé.

— Cap... capitaine !... bégaya-t-il en essayant de reprendre son sang-froid.

— Qu'est-ce que vous avez ?... Vous grelottez...

— Rien... je... je ne m'attendais pas...

— Allez !

— Il paraît qu'il y a un... un mort, capitaine ?

— Un mort, oui ! Peu importe ! Allez !...

Sa voix était si sèche que le second officier, qui le connaissait depuis des années, s'en étonna. C'était un garçon de trente ans, qui n'avait pas de brevet et qui suivait patiemment la filière, sûr d'être capitaine vers quarante-cinq ans. Il vivait avec sa mère, à Trondheim.

— Une vilaine affaire ! dit-il quand Vriens se fut

éloigné. Il faudra quand même qu'on mette la main sur l'homme qui se cache à bord...

— Où sommes-nous ?

Ils se penchèrent sur la carte. Petersen grommela :

— Avec ce brouillard, nous n'arriverons pas à Stavanger avant une heure du matin. Et on doit en repartir à deux heures et demie ! Si seulement nous avions la T.S.F., comme on nous le promet depuis deux ans...

Il n'était bien nulle part et c'était la première fois que cela lui arrivait à bord de son bateau. Pour regagner sa cabine, il devait traverser le pont-promenade où s'alignaient les hublots du fumoir. Il y jeta un coup d'œil, constata l'absence de Katia Storm.

Au dîner, il ne desserra pas les dents. Il était visiblement préoccupé par la place vide de la jeune femme.

— Elle mange dans sa cabine ? demanda-t-il au steward.

— Non ! Elle n'y est pas...

Il avait le front barré d'une ride profonde et soudain il se leva, marcha vers l'avant du navire où était installé le carré des officiers.

Il allait atteindre la cabine de Vriens quand la porte s'ouvrit. Katia sortit précipitamment, s'arrêta net en voyant le capitaine à moins de deux pas d'elle. Un moment, elle en eut la respiration coupée. Puis elle reprit son sang-froid, prononça :

— On n'est pas encore à table, n'est-ce pas ?...
Ce n'est pas moi que vous cherchiez ?...

— Non... On vous attend dans la salle à manger...

Il feignit d'avoir à faire dans la cabine du second, qui était vide. Mais, dès que Katia se fut éloignée, il ouvrit la porte de Vriens, qu'il trouva étendu sur la couchette, la tête dans ses bras repliés.

Le jeune homme se redressa avec une hâte maladroite, sans parvenir à effacer tout à fait les traînées humides qui luisaient sur ses joues.

— Capitaine...

— Rien ! Restez couché !...

Et Petersen s'en fut, plus sombre que jamais, sans savoir lui-même ce qu'il pensait. A table il retrouva la jeune Allemande qui parlait d'abondance, d'une voix pointue, et qui se tourna souvent vers lui.

Mais, comme il feignait de ne pas prendre pour lui ce qu'elle disait et que Schuttringer restait aussi absent qu'à son habitude, force fut à Katia de s'adresser à Evjen.

Elle s'inquiétait de l'escale de Stavanger.

— Croyez-vous que la police va nous retarder ?... Moi, il me semble que, si on fouillait le bateau une fois pour toutes, on finirait par mettre la main sur cet homme... Comment s'appelle-t-il encore ?... Ericksen ?... C'est peut-être un faux nom...

Et le capitaine sentait qu'Evjen, un peu gêné, surtout devant lui, qui était l'hôte régulier de sa femme, à Kirkenes, eût préféré que la conversation devînt générale.

A cinq milles du port, on embarqua un pilote qui accosta dans un petit cotre. Le brouillard était si opaque, dans ces parages semés de récifs, qu'il fallut mettre tous les hommes en vigie.

Ils étaient une grappe sur le gaillard d'avant, criant vers la passerelle des indications fiévreuses.

Le *Polarlys* était, dans l'obscurité, comme un nuage phosphorescent. Mais, de la passerelle, on ne distinguait même pas l'arrière !

La sirène criait sans discontinuer et on essayait de repérer la direction d'une autre sirène dont, par intermittence, on percevait la clameur comme un lointain gémissement.

Les passagers avaient le visage collé aux vitres du fumoir. Ils virent ainsi des disques blanchâtres cerner le navire. Puis, tout près, on entendit des voix avec une netteté hallucinante.

On pouvait se croire à des milles du port. On ne percevait même pas l'éclat du phare. Et on était à dix mètres du quai ! Les matelots lançaient déjà les aussières !

Il pluvinait. Le sol gardait dans les creux de grandes traînées de neige molle.

Quand la passerelle tomba, une vingtaine d'hommes se précipitèrent vers les cales ouvertes pour procéder au déchargement. Un fonctionnaire de la police, en uniforme, salua militairement Petersen et questionna :

— Beaucoup de passagers ?

De la ville, plantée à flanc de montagne, on ne voyait rien que l'amorce d'une rue en pente où les réverbères éclairaient quelques façades de bois peintes en vert et en ocre foncé.

— Il faut aller chercher votre chef tout de suite ! prononça le capitaine. Un crime a été commis à bord...

Il était plus d'une heure. Les règlements norvégiens sont stricts : pas un café n'était ouvert.

Pas un passant non plus ! Pas une ombre sinon celles des débardeurs qui avaient mis les palans en action et qui extrayaient des caisses des deux cales.

Il y eut quelques instants de flottement, de stupeur. Enfin le policier se décida à frapper aux volets d'un hôtel proche, afin de téléphoner.

Du côté du quai, le brouillard était comme déchiré par les allées et venues et on pouvait distinguer à peu près gens et choses.

Mais, vers le bassin, c'était une nuée blanchâtre, impénétrable, d'où arrivaient des bouffées glacées. On ne voyait même pas l'eau sous le flanc noir du bateau.

Ce fut là, soudain, qu'il se passa quelque chose. On entendit, malgré les grincements des poulies et le heurt des caisses contre les dalles du quai, le bruit d'un corps assez lourd crevant la surface liquide.

Petersen, que rejoignait le fonctionnaire, enjamba

des barils pour atteindre la coursive tribord. Comme il y arrivait, il bouscula Vriens, qui haleta :

— Là !... Vite !... Je l'ai vu sauter...

— Qui ?...

— L'homme en gris... Ericksen...

Le policier ne pouvait rien comprendre. Le capitaine se pencha sur la lisse, mais ne vit rien, n'entendit rien.

— Vous êtes sûr ?...

— Quelque chose est tombé dans le jus !... vint confirmer un débardeur qui travaillait à six mètres de là. Mais quoi ?...

— Je n'ai vu que du gris... répéta le troisième officier.

— Un canot !... Ouste !...

On n'avait pas le temps d'en mettre un à la mer. Petersen courut vers le quai, largua une barque qui s'y trouvait amarrée, au pied d'un escalier de pierre.

Le fonctionnaire de la police l'avait suivi. Les hommes, au-dessus des cales, interrompaient leur travail et on devinait la veste blanche du steward qui se penchait sur le bastingage.

Les avirons clapotèrent. Le capitaine cria :

— Un fanal !...

Et quelqu'un en fit descendre un le long du bord au bout d'un filin. Mais tout ce qu'on put voir alors, ce fut, à travers les lambeaux de brouillard, la surface noire de l'eau qui s'étirait mollement.

Est-ce que l'homme avait eu le temps de s'éloigner à la nage et de gagner une des échelles du quai ?

Le capitaine maniait les avirons à petits coups rageurs. Le policier en shako écussonné se penchait avec conscience, fouillait l'obscurité du regard.

Les lignes du *Polarlys* se découpaient comme dans un décor de féerie, avec des saillies lumineuses et des grands pans d'ombre. Dans un des disques de lumière, Petersen distingua les épaules de Vriens, sa tête penchée et, derrière lui, la silhouette claire de Katia Storm qui avait la main posée sur l'épaule du jeune homme.

— Allons ! grommela-t-il.

— On n'entend rien, n'est-ce pas ? Sans doute a-t-il coulé à pic...

— Sans doute, comme vous dites !

Jusqu'au policier qui regardait avec une certaine stupeur le capitaine dont il ne comprenait pas l'humeur farouche, les décisions trop promptes, contradictoires, les gestes saccadés !

Le chef de la police arriva en auto, n'ayant passé qu'un pantalon noir et une pelisse sur son pyjama. C'était un homme maigre et aristocratique qui semblait toujours évoluer dans un salon, s'adresser à des gens du monde.

— On m'apprend qu'un crime...

Petersen l'entraîna dans sa cabine, après avoir déclaré à l'agent en uniforme :

— Je crois qu'il vaut mieux que vous ne laissiez sortir personne.

Il était si catégorique qu'il apparaissait comme le vrai maître.

— Asseyez-vous... Je vais essayer de vous mettre au courant en aussi peu de mots que possible... L'horaire prévoit l'appareillage pour deux heures et demie... Il est plus de deux heures... Dans vingt-cinq ports norvégiens, toute la population nous attend à un moment donné... J'ai le courrier à bord, le ravitaillement, les machines, les journaux... Seulement, j'ai aussi un homme assassiné...

Il s'enfiévrait en même temps que ses allures devenaient plus calmes. Il ne bougeait pas, ne gesticulait pas, mais une frénésie sourde s'affirmait dans le son de sa voix.

Tout en arpentant sa cabine, où le chef de la police s'était assis, il raconta les événements depuis le départ de Hambourg, sans oublier de résumer l'article du journal français qui était toujours sur la tablette.

Deux fois il s'interrompit pour grimper sur le pont, surveiller le déchargement, recommander aux hommes de se presser.

— Qu'est-ce que vous allez faire ? questionna-t-il enfin, en se laissant tomber au bord de sa couchette et en se prenant le menton dans la main.

La côte norvégienne est constituée par une chaîne de montagnes que deux ou trois routes seulement traversent, dans le sud. A partir de Trondheim, ces routes n'existent plus et il est encore moins question de chemins de fer.

Ce sont des vapeurs côtiers, dans le genre du *Polarlys,* qui doivent assurer toutes les communications, les relations postales et le transport des vivres.

Dans le nord, par exemple, la seule production naturelle est la morue, le phoque et le renne.

Que les bateaux viennent à manquer et voilà la population séparée du reste du monde, avec dans le dos la montagne inaccessible et, en face, les houles de l'Atlantique.

C'est pourquoi les compagnies de navigation sont subventionnées par l'Etat et assument un service officiel.

Le chef de la police était soucieux.

— Vous me dites que cet Ericksen vient de se jeter à l'eau ?

— J'ai dit que quelque chose était tombé à l'eau et que mon troisième officier a vu une silhouette grise ! précisa le capitaine.

— C'est tout comme !

— Si vous voulez...

— Les autres passagers ont des papiers en règle ?

— Les passeports ont été vérifiés à Hambourg, comme d'habitude, par la police allemande...

— Je vais les faire examiner à nouveau. Je ne vois qu'une solution : téléphoner à Oslo. J'aurai la communication d'ici une vingtaine de minutes. Pendant ce temps, un médecin viendra examiner le corps et un spécialiste prendra des photographies de la cabine, essayera de relever des empreintes digitales. Les passeports seront épluchés. Enfin, le bateau sera visité de fond en comble. Cela vous fera environ une heure de retard, que vous regagnerez sans peine... Si tout laisse supposer, comme je le crois, que cet Ericksen est l'assassin, si aucune charge n'est relevée contre les autres voyageurs, je n'ai guère le droit de les retenir...

Et le chef, en se levant, poussa un soupir qui disait combien ces décisions, si simples en apparence, étaient difficiles à mettre en pratique.

Lorsqu'il quitta le bord, il répéta au policier :

— Que personne ne sorte !...

Les hommes de peine déchargeaient les derniers colis, suivis des yeux par le steward qui ne savait où se mettre et qui aimait encore mieux prendre froid dehors qu'errer seul dans le bateau désert.

L'auto s'éloigna en vrombissant, escalada la côte. Moins d'un quart d'heure plus tard, six hommes en tenue prenaient possession du *Polarlys*, pénétraient les uns par la cale avant, les autres par la cale arrière, et promenaient partout le jet de leurs lampes électriques.

Schuttringer, une petite casquette *jockey* sur la tête, en veston, arpentait le pont au pas de gymnastique, en homme soucieux de son hygiène physique.

Bell Evjen, l'air ennuyé, cherchait à s'approcher du capitaine et à le questionner.

Et tandis que Petersen arrivait à l'arrière, où l'ombre était plus dense que partout ailleurs, un chuchotement partait de l'abri formé par le gouvernail de secours, un baiser bruissait.

Le capitaine fit encore quelques pas en silence, devina deux ombres enlacées, distingua, dans le noir, la tache laiteuse de deux visages accolés lèvres à lèvres.

Il n'avait pas besoin de distinguer les traits. Les galons neufs de Vriens scintillaient. Et, à hauteur des épaules, sur la tunique sombre, on voyait le bras nu de Katia.

4

Les deux tickets

Quand les passagers et les officiers furent réunis au fumoir, le chef de la police, avec une bonne grâce parfaite, leur tint ce petit discours :

— Madame, messieurs, vous êtes au courant du

tragique événement qui explique ma présence à bord de ce navire. Jusqu'ici tout nous fait supposer que le coupable n'est pas parmi vous, mais qu'il a sauté par-dessus bord dès l'arrivée à Stavanger. Il reste néanmoins un certain nombre de formalités à accomplir et croyez que je veillerai à vous les rendre aussi légères que possible. Veuillez n'y voir aucune marque de suspicion, mais le seul souci de permettre au *Polarlys* de poursuivre sa croisière. Que chacun ait l'obligeance de regagner sa cabine afin d'assister à la visite qui va avoir lieu...

Un commissaire avait adressé des phrases un peu moins longues aux membres de l'équipage et fouillait déjà les cadres, les sacs de marins et les valises.

Les palans s'étaient immobilisés. Le bateau n'attendait plus que l'autorisation de la police pour appareiller.

Dans la cabine 24, deux experts avaient relevé la position du corps et pris un certain nombre de photographies. Puis le cadavre, étendu sur une civière, avait quitté le bord et s'était enfoncé dans le brouillard.

Il était difficile d'user de plus de tact et de rendre l'atmosphère moins pénible. Et pourtant, même après les paroles du chef de la police, surtout après ces paroles, il y eut une même expression artificielle sur tous les visages, aussi bien sur celui d'Evjen que sur celui du second officier.

En définitive, puisqu'on n'avait arrêté personne, chacun était susceptible d'avoir commis le crime.

Et chacun s'observait, essayait de paraître aussi naturel que possible. Petersen était peut-être le plus gêné, parce que le policier l'avait prié de l'accompagner dans les cabines. Il exigea qu'on commençât par la sienne, afin de donner l'exemple, ouvrit sa malle, les tiroirs du petit bureau, souleva même sa paillasse.

— Je vous en prie... protestait le chef.

La cabine suivante était celle d'Evjen qui attendait, debout au pied de sa couchette. Tous ses gestes furent ceux d'un voyageur au cours d'une visite de douaniers. Il avait déjà retiré ses valises du filet et fait jouer les serrures. Deux ou trois fois, il s'efforça de sourire, entre autres lorsqu'il montra une série de menus objets inattendus.

— Une clarinette... Pour mon aîné, qui a douze ans... Ce nécessaire de couture est pour ma fille, qui va avoir sept ans... Voici les derniers disques parus... J'en fais provision chaque année... Des livres... Ceci ?... une petite commission dont ma femme m'a chargé : de la toile cirée pour le lit du dernier bébé...

— Passons... Je vous en prie !... protestait le chef de la police.

Mais Evjen étalait trois complets, un smoking, du linge fin, marqué à son chiffre, ses notes du *Savoy*, à Londres, et du *Majestic*, de Berlin.

— Je vous remercie ! Vous serez tout à fait

aimable en remettant votre passeport à l'inspecteur qui est resté là-haut... Une simple formalité, n'est-ce pas ?... Naturellement, vous n'avez aucun soupçon ?

— Aucun ! répliqua Evjen avec une certaine sécheresse.

La cabine suivante était vide. Puis venait celle où étaient déposés les bagages d'Ernst Ericksen, le passager disparu.

— Je les saisis ! déclara le policier. Faites-les porter à terre... Voyons... Un seul sac... Un vieux complet... Deux chemises...

C'était maigre. Les vêtements, de bonne coupe, étaient usés. Il n'y avait même pas de chaussures de rechange.

— Passons au suivant...

Katia Storm avait imité Bell Evjen. Ses effets étaient étalés sur sa couchette et, comme le chef de la police hésitait à fouiller parmi ses robes et son linge, elle le fit elle-même, les mains frémissantes.

Petersen était resté à la porte. Il se sentait humilié, avec, en même temps, une pointe d'anxiété indéfinissable. Ce fut lui, pourtant, qui ramassa un petit éventail de papier mauve et qui lut à mi-voix : *Kristall-Palace*, *Hambourg*.

— Ma dernière nuit à terre ! dit Katia en riant. J'ai passé une heure au *Kristall,* car j'avais envie de danser.

— Seule ? questionna le policier.

— Seule, mais oui !

60

Elle avait pour le moins quinze toilettes, toutes d'une qualité et d'un goût aussi raffinés. Son linge était du linge de grande coquette.

La trousse était d'argent ciselé. Et le moindre objet, le plus petit bibelot, appartenait à la même classe.

On relevait le nom de maisons de l'avenue de l'Opéra, de la rue de la Paix, ainsi que de commerçants londoniens et berlinois.

Un seul détail choquait : un petit parapluie tompouce, acheté à Bruxelles, et qui ne devait pas coûter cent francs. Elle rit encore, expliqua avec enjouement :

— J'ai été surprise par la pluie, en Belgique, et je suis entrée chez le premier marchand venu...

— Vous vivez habituellement à Paris ?

— A Paris, à Berlin, à Nice...

— Vous connaissez le peintre Max Feinstein ?

— Non ! C'est un compatriote ? Sans doute un juif ?...

— Quand êtes-vous arrivée à Hambourg ?

— Jeudi soir... Je croyais qu'il y avait un bateau pour la Norvège, vendredi...

— Vous veniez de Paris ?

— Pas directement... J'ai passé huit jours à Bruxelles et deux jours à Amsterdam...

Elle s'efforçait de garder un air dégagé, regardait son interlocuteur dans les yeux. Mais, en pareil cas, il est dangereux de juger du naturel des attitudes, car l'innocent qui se croit soupçonné est parfois plus troublé que le coupable.

La cabine était parfumée, le tapis jonché de bouts de cigarettes. Sur la tablette on voyait un flacon de liqueur à moitié vide.

— Je vous remercie, madame...

— Mademoiselle ! rectifia-t-elle.

— Vous comptez rester longtemps en Norvège ?

— Quelques semaines. Le temps de visiter la Laponie...

Petersen fut sur le point d'intervenir, de poser une question.

— *Combien avez-vous d'argent avec vous ?*

Mais il rougit d'y avoir pensé.

La dernière visite, à Arnold Schuttringer, fut la plus brève. Peu de bagages. Des vêtements confortables, sans luxe. Des objets de toilette comme on en vend dans les bazars, à peu près neufs. En somme, il s'était équipé pour ce voyage.

Calme et lourd, un peu renfrogné, il assistait au va-et-vient du chef de la police sans intervenir, sans provoquer les questions. Il répondit par le strict nécessaire de mots.

— En résumé, tous les passagers ont leurs papiers en règle. Il n'y a pas la moindre charge contre l'un d'eux. L'assassin, affirme mon inspecteur, était ganté, si bien qu'il est inutile de prendre les empreintes digitales...

» Les hommes qui ont fouillé la cale n'ont rien trouvé, et il semble probable que cet Ericksen se soit jeté à l'eau, peut-être avec l'espoir de gagner le quai à la nage.

» Vous avez confiance dans votre troisième officier ? Car c'est lui qui a vu plonger le passager, n'est-ce pas ?

Petersen évita de répondre. Il était plus de trois heures. Les formalités étaient terminées. Et on n'avait obtenu aucun résultat.

— Je vais me mettre en rapport avec la police allemande, ordonner des recherches dans le bassin et dans la ville.

Le chef cachait l'inquiétude que lui donnait cette affaire sous une fausse assurance.

— Encore une fois, je ne puis pas immobiliser le navire jusqu'à ce que l'enquête soit terminée. Et, si je devais garder quelqu'un à la disposition de la justice, il n'y aurait aucune raison que ce soit l'un plutôt que l'autre... Il me faudrait arrêter équipage et passagers...

Le capitaine ne disait rien. Il attendait, sombre, renfermé, en esquissant parfois, par déférence, un signe de tête affirmatif.

Dans le brouillard commençaient à papillonner de fins flocons de neige. Des courants d'air froid traversaient le bateau dont les portes étaient sans cesse ouvertes et refermées.

— Je vais vous laisser un inspecteur à bord, à

tout hasard, afin de dégager ma responsabilité et la vôtre...

A trois heures et demie, Petersen et le chef de la police faisaient les cent pas le long de la coursive, tandis que l'équipage prenait les dispositions d'appareillage. Les deux pilotes, qui se relayeraient sur la passerelle tout le long de la côte norvégienne, s'étaient embarqués, en bottes à semelles de bois, en vêtements de fourrure, leur coffre de bois noir sur l'épaule.

Il y avait encore, sur le quai, quelques silhouettes obstinées. Un inspecteur avait pris l'auto du chef pour aller chercher des vêtements de rechange. On l'attendait.

Comme les deux hommes n'avaient plus rien à se dire, ils cherchaient des phrases quelconques qu'ils prononçaient sans conviction.

— Votre passagère doit avoir du succès, seule parmi tant d'hommes ! Surtout qu'elle est... comment dire ?... piquante !... Une drôle de petite créature...

Le premier officier, aussi lugubre que son capitaine, était déjà à son poste, sur la passerelle, adossé à la rambarde, le regard perdu dans le brouillard.

Bell Evjen, après la visite de la police, était resté dans sa cabine, ainsi que Schuttringer. Mais on aperçut Katia à travers un hublot du fumoir. Elle étalait ses cartes à jouer sur la table, tout en maniant son long fume-cigarette de jade.

Enfin, on perçut un bruit de moteur. La voiture

64

stoppa en laissant deux traînées noires dans la neige, qui commençait à former une couche régulière.

Pendant que l'inspecteur montait à bord, Petersen et le chef se serraient la main.

— Bon voyage !... dit ce dernier, tandis que le visage du capitaine se durcissait.

Trois coups de sirène. Quelques commandements. Des piétinements. L'aussière qui tombait à l'eau dans le sillage du *Polarlys*.

— Vous demanderez au steward de vous désigner une cabine ! fit Petersen à l'adresse de l'inspecteur, qui était un homme d'une trentaine d'années, poli, effacé, faisant plutôt penser à un employé de bureau qu'à un détective.

Et il arpenta le pont, sans savoir ce qu'il avait envie de faire. Deux fois il mit la main sur la poignée de la porte du fumoir. Puis il faillit se diriger vers le poste des officiers, avec l'arrière-pensée de s'assurer que Vriens était couché.

Mais le jeune homme passa soudain à moins de deux mètres de lui sans le voir, colla son visage au hublot du fumoir, y entra.

Le capitaine n'avait jamais épié personne. Pourtant il n'hésita pas à s'approcher à son tour du hublot. Il vit Katia Storm qui levait la tête, s'adressait à son compagnon.

Il distinguait le mouvement des lèvres, mais n'entendait aucun son, à cause de la clameur naissante de la mer.

Vriens s'assit près d'elle, très près, parla avec plus de véhémence, comme s'il l'eût suppliée.

Son émotion à jet continu devenait crispante, finissait même par faire mal à voir, car on se demandait comment il pouvait supporter si long-temps une telle tension nerveuse.

Ses traits étaient d'une mobilité fébrile. Et son corps tout entier s'agitait. A chaque instant, il chan-geait les jambes de place, gesticulait, et ses pru-nelles ne se fixaient nulle part.

Pour comble, il devait avoir attrapé un rhume de cerveau car, pendant l'entretien, qui dura une dizaine de minutes, il se moucha quatre ou cinq fois rageusement.

Katia Storm ne le voyait sans doute pas avec les mêmes yeux que le capitaine. Tandis qu'il parlait, elle lui mit soudain la main sur la bouche, et, d'un mouvement qui révélait un attendrissement d'aînée, se pencha pour lui baiser les yeux.

Elle riait, d'un rire déroutant, plein de choses confuses, d'ironie, de désir, de tendresse, peut-être d'un rien d'effroi ?

Quand elle se leva, Vriens la suivit et Petersen les vit se diriger ensemble vers le couloir des cabines. Sans descendre, il entendit une porte se refermer. Après quoi, il n'y eut plus de bruits de pas.

Le jeune homme était rentré avec elle.

Le steward était malade de fatigue. Pourtant il venait jeter un dernier coup d'œil au fumoir, ranger les fauteuils et éteindre les lampes.

Il trouva le capitaine penché sur le sol près de la place de Katia et occupé à ramasser deux petits bouts de carton rose qui étaient tombés de la poche de Vriens alors que celui-ci en tirait son mouchoir.

— Vous savez, capitaine, je suis content qu'on l'ait emporté ! Je crois que je serais devenu malade, rien que de le savoir là... Vous avez remarqué sa bouche ouverte ?...

Petersen n'écoutait pas, maniait les papiers roses qui étaient des tickets de vestiaire du *Kristall*. Il finit, en soupirant, par les glisser dans son portefeuille.

— Vous restez ici ? s'étonna son compagnon.

— Non ! Tu peux éteindre et aller te coucher...

— Vous croyez que cet Ericksen a vraiment sauté à l'eau, vous ? Dites ! S'il était encore caché à bord...

Mais il n'obtint pas de réponse. Le capitaine s'éloignait en haussant les épaules, jetait, du pont-promenade, un coup d'œil vers la passerelle, où il distinguait la cigarette du premier officier et les larges épaules du pilote dont le bonnet de loutre couvrait presque tout le visage.

Il y avait un feu blanc à peine visible, quelque part dans la brume : une barque de pêche, sans doute. On passa si près qu'on entendit les voix de deux hommes qui conversaient paisiblement, assis sur le banc de quart.

Jamais Petersen n'avait été aussi mécontent de lui-même, aussi dérouté, et pourtant il n'eût pas pu dire pourquoi. Cela ressemblait aux cauchemars imprécis qu'on fait certaines nuits d'indigestion. Il ne se passe rien d'effrayant. On ne court aucun danger. Mais les moindres objets évoqués par le rêve prennent un visage revêche. L'édredon devient monstrueux, écrasant. On va et vient à travers un monde hostile, sans comprendre, et l'on a confusément la volonté de se réveiller, sans y parvenir.

Le *Polarlys* était changé. Et il n'était pas jusqu'à cette présence à bord d'un policier, pourtant bien gentil et bien effacé, qui ne pesât au capitaine.

Des houles plus fortes soulevèrent l'étrave. Le bateau, sorti des passes, prenait sa vitesse normale en donnant, par principe, deux coups de sirène à chaque minute.

Parfois l'aile blanche d'une mouette dessinait un trait mouvant dans le brouillard.

Petersen fit soudain volte-face, se courba pour franchir la porte de fer donnant accès à la chambre des machines. Sous l'échelle, dans la lumière crue des lampes sans abat-jour, il vit le chef mécanicien qui réglait la pression d'huile tandis qu'un homme en bleu sommeillait près du cadran du télégraphe.

Il descendit. Le chef le salua d'un grognement.

— C'est fini, ces histoires ? Ça redevient tranquille, là-haut ?

— C'est fini, oui...

Et le capitaine se faufila le long des arbres de transmission qui lui lançaient des gouttelettes d'huile, passa par une porte plus petite et reçut au visage la lueur rouge de la chaufferie.

L'homme qui pelletait le charbon, torse nu, ne se retourna même pas, se contenta de porter sa main noire à son visage noir.

Et Petersen continua. Maintenant, il devait marcher le corps plié en deux. Le charbon croulait sous ses semelles. La sueur commençait à gicler de tous les pores de son visage.

Enfin, il fut dans la soute, où un être méconnaissable sous son barbouillage le regardait venir, assis dans la houille et mangeant une tartine.

C'était Peter Krull. Les poils dorés de sa barbe perçaient la couche de suie dont il était couvert. Ses yeux blancs avaient un éclat plus ironique que jamais.

Il ne se leva pas, ne salua pas. Il continua de manger et c'est la bouche pleine qu'il articula d'une façon à peine perceptible :

— Alors, on l'a trouvé, ce fameux Ericksen ?...

Il riait silencieusement, pour lui seul. Il se pencha vers la chaufferie afin de s'assurer qu'on ne réclamait pas de charbon.

— Tu le connais ?

— Parbleu !...

— Que veux-tu dire ?

— Que si vous voulez, je vais vous en fabriquer un tout de suite ! Et ressemblant, hein !...

Il avait achevé sa tartine, dont la dernière bouchée était aussi noire que ses mains. Il se leva sans se presser, ramassa un sac vide dans un coin, y jeta une dizaine de briquettes.

— Voilà ! annonça-t-il.

— Explique-toi !

— C'est Ericksen !... Enfin, c'est le même que celui qui s'est jeté à l'eau tout à l'heure... J'avais remarqué en route qu'un sac avait disparu... Quand on est arrivé à Stavanger, c'était mon tour de repos et je prenais le frais sur le pont... J'ai vu mon sac dans la coursive, prêt à être balancé par-dessus bord...

— Qui l'a poussé ?...

Mais l'homme se tournait une fois de plus vers la chaufferie.

— Attention !... Le chauffeur réclame du charbon, là-bas... D'ailleurs, je ne sais rien de plus...

Et, courbé en avant, il enfonça sa pelle dans le tas de houille, commença son travail à un rythme puissant et régulier.

Le capitaine l'observa quelques instants, ouvrit la bouche pour parler, puis s'en fut, maussade, sans avoir rien dit, refit en sens inverse tout le chemin parcouru avant de respirer l'air glacé du large.

Au-dessus de sa tête, le pilote et le premier officier, immobiles dans l'obscurité, se passaient l'un à l'autre une blague à tabac et des allumettes.

Cornélius Vriens

— Allez me chercher Vriens !

— Il est de quart...

— Peu importe ! Du moment que le pilote est là-haut...

Petersen, le visage soucieux, s'était enfermé dans sa cabine dès le départ de Bergen, où les trois heures d'escale avaient été remplies par des allées et venues, de multiples soucis, des poignées de main, des formalités à remplir.

Au siège de la B.D.S., à qui appartenait le *Polarlys*, on avait dit au capitaine :

— Bah ! Vous n'y êtes pour rien, n'est-ce pas ? Et du moment qu'il y a désormais un homme de la police à bord...

Mais celui qui parlait de la sorte était un administrateur et non un capitaine. Il ne pouvait pas comprendre. Ce même administrateur avait signé la lettre recommandant Vriens et il donna à Petersen des renseignements complémentaires.

— Je ne le connais pas personnellement, mais un ami, qui dirige l'école navale de Delfzijl, m'a écrit six pages à son sujet. Il me le représente comme un garçon travailleur, d'une droiture exceptionnelle.

» Son père est quelque chose comme directeur adjoint des services météorologiques à Java. Dès l'âge de dix ans, Vriens a dû quitter les Indes à cause de sa faiblesse de constitution, si bien qu'il a passé toute sa jeunesse dans des pensions hollandaises...

» Il n'a guère connu la vie de famille. En neuf ans, il est retourné deux fois en vacances chez les siens. Voilà deux ans, sa mère est morte à Java et, bien entendu, il n'a pu la voir sur son lit de mort.

» Depuis lors, il travaille avec plus d'acharnement et le dimanche, à Delfzijl, il fallait user de ruse ou d'autorité pour le faire sortir du bateau-école...

Le *Polarlys* commençait la deuxième partie de son voyage. De Hambourg à Bergen, c'est encore le sud, parsemé de grandes villes.

Mais désormais, surtout lorsque, le lendemain, on aurait fait escale à Trondheim, le vapeur ne s'arrêterait plus guère que le long de pilotis, en marge de bourgades composées de quelques maisons de bois.

Déjà à droite du navire, les flancs des fjords étaient tout blancs. Des eiders volaient au ras de l'eau, où plongeaient parfois des hirondelles de mer.

Le capitaine avait commencé par porter au livre de bord les mentions journalières. Puis, les coudes sur la tablette d'acajou, il avait laissé errer la plume sur une feuille blanche.

Peu à peu, ses préoccupations s'étaient transcrites en une sorte de diagramme ingénu : un gros point d'abord, puis un trait fin, simple traînée d'encre, et un autre point ; encore un trait, un point... un point... un trait...

L'ensemble était une figure géométrique irrégulière, une ligne brisée avec une tache noire à chaque angle.

Le premier point représentait le conseiller de police von Sternberg, tué dans sa cabine. Venait ensuite Ernst Ericksen, qui existait malgré tout en chair et en os, au fond du port de Stavanger ou dans quelque recoin du *Polarlys*. Puis Peter Krull...

Le trait devenait plus long, plus étiré, et on arrivait à Katia Storm, près de qui Petersen plaçait directement Vriens.

Etait-ce tout ? Il hésita, laissa traîner sa main, fit du bout de la plume un sixième disque noir : Arnold Schuttringer.

Pourquoi pas ?

Sans le vouloir, le capitaine avait donné à la figure la forme d'un polygone, mais il manquait une ligne pour le fermer.

Il ratura avec mauvaise humeur, se leva, alluma sa pipe, et c'est alors qu'il sonna le steward pour l'envoyer chercher le troisième officier.

Ce qui le troublait le plus, peut-être, c'était le sentiment qu'entre ces six points, ces six personnages, existaient des affinités, des points de contact, voire des complicités qui lui échappaient.

A cause des formalités, il n'avait pas eu le temps,

à Bergen, d'aller embrasser sa femme et les gosses, et son humeur s'en était encore assombrie.

— Entrez ! grommela-t-il soudain en se rasseyant.

C'était Vriens, en tenue de quart, qui arrivait de la passerelle, du givre sur les épaules.

— Vous comptez monter tous vos quarts dans ce costume ?

Et il toucha un des boutons dorés de la capote bleue, galonnée comme la tunique, beaucoup trop mince pour le climat.

— Capitaine, je...

Mais non ! Il avait la respiration coupée ! Il ne trouvait d'ailleurs rien à dire. Il n'avait que ce costume-là ! Quinze jours plus tôt, il n'était qu'un élève et portait l'uniforme de l'école. Il avait eu juste le temps d'aller à Groningue commander les vêtements dont, maintenant, on lui faisait grief.

— Asseyez-vous, *monsieur* Vriens !

Petersen était d'autant plus bourru qu'il ne savait pas au juste pourquoi il avait fait comparaître le jeune homme. Son regard tomba sur la feuille où deux des six points se trouvaient tout près l'un de l'autre, mais les paroles qu'il prononça n'eurent aucun rapport avec cette image.

— Vous me ferez le plaisir, quand vous serez de quart, d'emprunter le manteau d'un de vos collègues ou d'un pilote ! Compris ?

— Oui, mon capitaine...

— Capitaine tout court, je vous l'ai déjà dit ! Je vous ai prié aussi de vous asseoir...

Pourquoi avait-il une telle envie de le prendre aux épaules et de le secouer ?

Il rageait, malgré lui, devant cette silhouette correcte, aux épaules maigres, et surtout devant ce visage blafard, ces yeux fiévreux, ces narines pincées qui l'impressionnaient peut-être davantage que le cadavre de Sternberg.

— Je dois avant tout vous rendre ceci...

Il tendit les tickets roses du *Kristall*, tandis que Vriens ne pouvait maîtriser ses nerfs et sursautait.

— Bien entendu, une fois à terre, vous vous amusez comme vous l'entendez. Je préférerais cependant que ce ne soit pas en compagnie de nos passagères...

Petersen sentait qu'il avait tort. Jamais il n'avait fait une observation de ce genre à un de ses hommes ! Au contraire ! L'été, lorsque le *Polarlys* transportait jusqu'à cent touristes, il y avait à chaque traversée des aventures que les officiers se racontaient en riant pendant les heures de veille...

— Qui vous a dit... ?

— Que vous étiez au *Kristall* avec Mlle Storm ? Vous le niez ?

Vriens s'était levé. Il était devenu plus pâle encore, si c'était possible. Ses lèvres étaient sèches, décolorées.

Et tel quel, il se dressait, tout raide, révolté, avec un effort douloureux pour garder son sang-froid.

— J'attends la suite, articula-t-il d'une voix contenue.

— Vous connaissiez cette personne avant de rejoindre le bateau à Hambourg.

Il avait à peine dix-neuf ans. Petersen était deux fois large et fort comme lui. Et pourtant, tendu comme un jeune coq, il prononça en regardant ailleurs :

— Il y a des questions auxquelles un gentleman n'a pas à répondre !

Le capitaine devint tout rouge, se leva à son tour et fut à deux doigts de retourner d'une gifle la figure du gamin.

— Et depuis quand un gentleman ment-il ? riposta-t-il âprement. Depuis quand un gentleman jure-t-il, devant la police, qu'il a vu un homme se jeter à l'eau alors qu'il n'a vu qu'un sac de charbon passer par-dessus bord ?

Il regretta presque son emportement, tant le visage de Vriens, à cet instant, fit mal à voir. Le jeune homme ouvrit la bouche sans parler, sans pouvoir respirer. Ses prunelles étaient rivées à Petersen avec une expression d'angoisse affreuse. Et ses doigts blêmes s'agitaient dans le vide.

— Je... je...

— Quoi ?... Vous avez vraiment vu Ericksen sauter à l'eau ?

Des gouttes de sueur ruisselaient sur le front du troisième officier. Sa pomme d'Adam montait et descendait à une cadence rapide le long de sa gorge.

— Je n'ai rien à dire...

Et pourtant il était sur le point d'éclater en sanglots ! Le capitaine en était sûr. Si sûr qu'il faillit
frapper l'épaule de son compagnon, lui crier :

— Ne vous mettez donc pas dans cet état-là,
imbécile ! Croyez-vous qu'une femme, qu'une
Katia Storm, en vaille la peine ?

Il ne le dit pas et il s'en repentit par la suite. Il
regarda son polygone inachevé, rapprocha encore
en esprit les deux points qui figuraient les amants.

Il était trop en colère pour n'être pas mal ins-
piré.

— C'est cela qu'à l'école de Delfzijl on appelle
un garçon d'une droiture exceptionnelle !... grommela-t-il, assez haut pour être entendu.

Alors, Vriens, hurlant presque, la voix cassée, des
larmes au bout des cils, de lancer :

— Est-ce que, en Norvège, la droiture consiste
à trahir une femme ?

Il n'en pouvait plus. Il était prêt à faire n'importe
quoi. On entendait sa respiration forte.

Le capitaine, un instant, avait suffoqué.

— Si cette femme est une vulgaire...

— Taisez-vous ! Je vous défends...

Oui, Petersen se tut ! C'était tout ! Brusquement,
sa fièvre tombait ; il comprenait le ridicule de cette
scène, et surtout ce qu'avait d'odieux pareil dialogue.

Est-ce qu'il n'aurait pas fini par en venir aux
mains avec ce gosse fiévreux dont les lèvres étaient
agitées d'un tremblement convulsif ?

Odieux ! Avec, comme toujours en pareil cas, des questions de nationalité qu'on se jette à la tête.

Le silence plana. Le capitaine se mit à aller et venir le long des trois mètres de la cabine.

— Il n'y a rien d'autre à vos ordres ? balbutia péniblement Vriens.

Petersen ne répondit pas, continua sa promenade, saisit la feuille de papier au polygone et la déchira.

— Il y a un mort... prononça-t-il à voix basse.

C'était une façon de s'excuser sans faire d'excuses à proprement parler. Vriens le comprit autrement.

— C'est moi que vous accusez de... ?

— Vous lisez le français ?

— Un peu...

— Eh bien ! Voyez...

Il lui tendit le journal trouvé sous l'oreiller de Sternberg, s'assit devant son bureau et feignit, pendant que Vriens déployait la feuille, de se plonger dans son livre de bord.

Il n'était pas fier de lui. Tout cela était mal parti.

Et, premièrement, pourquoi était-ce à Vriens, avant tout autre, qu'il s'en était pris ?

Certes, il y avait ces tickets du *Kristall* et l'éventail de Katia Storm. Il y avait l'arrivée du jeune homme, à dix heures du matin, à bord du *Polarlys*, et sa tête de papier mâché.

Il y avait... Le fait encore que, le premier soir, l'Allemande l'avait fait chercher et s'était promenée avec lui deux heures durant sur le pont...

Et cette nuit de Stavanger, enfin : les deux amants dans la même cabine !

Mais après ? Est-ce que Katia Storm avait esquissé le moindre geste permettant de la soupçonner ? Le journal français ne parlait pas d'elle, ni même en particulier d'une femme. Et une femme n'aurait pas été capable de tuer Sternberg avec une telle vigueur et une telle sauvagerie.

Petersen rougit en se souvenant que, le premier jour, comme elle gravissait l'escalier conduisant au fumoir, il avait regardé ses jambes, et surtout un éclair de chair, avec insistance.

Est-ce qu'il était tout bonnement jaloux de son troisième officier ? Furieux de voir celui-ci, sans coup férir, lui souffler une aventure ?

— Ce n'est pas vrai ! s'affirmait-il à lui-même. Je sens bien qu'il y a *quelque chose*...

Mais il était incapable de dire quoi ! Et il se rongeait ! Il était humilié, mal d'aplomb.

— Qu'en dites-vous, Vriens ?

Cette fois il abandonnait le *monsieur* Vriens ironique qu'il avait adopté. Le jeune homme, qui avait terminé la lecture de l'article, continuait à lire machinalement le journal qu'il tenait à la main.

Son visage s'était brouillé. Sa silhouette avait perdu sa raideur. Il questionna, anxieux :

— Pourquoi m'avez-vous fait lire cela ?... Quel rapport ?...

— Je vais vous le dire ! Autant qu'on en puisse juger par les apparences, le conseiller von Sternberg était à bord pour suivre l'assassin de Marie Baron et peut-être ses complices... N'oubliez pas qu'il y avait des femmes, rue Delambre...

Vriens était décidément l'homme des contrastes. Son attitude changea, une fois de plus, du tout au tout. Il devint d'un calme glacé. Il questionna :

— C'est tout ?

Et pourtant n'y avait-il pas de l'égarement dans son regard ?

— Cela ne vous suffit pas ? L'homme qui a tué cette gamine... Il est à bord...

— Et vous supposez que c'est moi ?

Il dit cela avec un pâle sourire, plus douloureux qu'un sanglot. Petersen était à bout de patience.

— Filez ! gronda-t-il. Allez reprendre votre quart ! J'ose espérer que le grand air vous fera du bien...

Il souhaitait que Vriens ne consentît pas à s'en aller ainsi. Il le guettait du coin de l'œil. Mais le jeune homme fit demi-tour, sortit.

Le capitaine, une fois seul, ramassa le papier où il avait tracé des points et des traits d'union, le déplia puis, une fois encore, le roula en boule et le lança dans la corbeille.

A table, ce soir-là, Katia Storm demanda deux fois du feu à Petersen, lui adressa sans cesse la parole au sujet des curiosités naturelles qu'on admirait au cours de la croisière.

Le policier de Stavanger, un certain Jennings, avait proposé lui-même de prendre ses repas à part, si bien qu'il y avait toujours la même pincée de personnages à un bout de table, avec la veste blanche, les cheveux blonds et le timide sourire du steward derrière eux.

Le capitaine présidait, Katia Storm, à sa droite, avait Evjen comme voisin, Schuttringer comme vis-à-vis.

Si la jeune femme ne parlait pas, il arrivait qu'on fît tout un repas en silence. Après quoi il n'y avait plus qu'à se traîner jusqu'au fumoir où l'Allemande avait pris l'habitude de servir le café, car le steward se contentait de poser la verseuse et les tasses sur une table.

— A partir de quand aurons-nous très froid ?

Ce fut Evjen qui répondit.

— A cette saison, vous ne connaîtrez que le froid moyen : douze degrés sous zéro à hauteur des Lofoten ; dix-sept ou dix-huit dans l'océan Glacial...

Et Petersen remarqua avec ennui qu'Evjen, lui aussi, était troublé par sa voisine. C'était d'autant plus significatif qu'il lui arrivait de faire une traversée entière sans adresser la parole à ses voisins, qui regardaient curieusement cet homme glacé, aux gestes mesurés, aux prunelles du même gris que la mer, capable de rester des heures sans bouger, sur le pont ou au fumoir, à fixer un point dans l'espace.

— Est-ce que tout le monde va se mettre à tour-ner autour d'elle ? songea le capitaine en observant Schuttringer.

Mais l'Allemand rasé, qui, depuis deux jours, se mettait à table en chandail, se contentait de manger avec une application qui frisait la gloutonnerie.

Parmi les charcuteries servies chaque soir, il y avait de la langue qui devait être son plat préféré car, régulièrement, il s'en coupait jusqu'à dix tranches, qu'il enduisait de beurre avant de les avaler.

Encore les taillait-il si épaisses que le steward ne manquait pas de lancer un coup d'œil inquiet au capitaine, avec l'air de dire :

— Nous n'en aurons jamais pour tout le voyage !

Au moment où Petersen se levait, Katia l'interpella :

— A-t-on des nouvelles du passager qui s'est jeté à l'eau à Stavanger ? La police de Bergen a dû se tenir au courant...

Le capitaine la regarda dans les yeux, trop longuement, car il remarqua qu'Evjen devinait un soupçon dans ce regard et détournait la tête.

Katia ne broncha pas. Elle avait aux lèvres son fume-cigarette qui n'avait pas loin de trente centimètres de long. Et elle était vraiment extraordinaire !

Comment expliquer cette ambiance voluptueuse qui l'entourait, émanait d'elle ? Comment la concilier surtout avec l'air enfantin de sa physionomie ?

Car elle donnait l'impression d'une enfant. Mais

d'une enfant perverse ! Plus exactement encore perverse avec innocence !

Deux mots contradictoires qui s'appliquaient pourtant à elle, non pas tour à tour, mais à la fois.

Jamais, lorsqu'on la regardait, elle ne détournait les yeux. Jamais non plus, dans ses prunelles, on n'eût pu lire une provocation. Et pourtant...

Evjen lui-même, l'homme de l'extrême nord, le directeur des mines de Kirkenes, dont le teint à force de vivre dans la lumière froide était devenu neutre, avait des instants de trouble si flagrant qu'il tentait de cacher son visage au capitaine.

Qu'elle fût habillée de noir ou de rose, couverte de drap ou de soie, on devinait ses formes et on croyait percevoir la chaleur et le parfum de sa chair.

Si elle se penchait, le regard allait machinalement à la naissance de la gorge. Quand elle marchait, on suivait des yeux ses jambes au galbe plein, aux chevilles à la fois fines et charnues.

Petersen la détestait et subissait son charme.

— Vous avez peur de ce passager ? questionna-t-il.

— C'est un assassin, n'est-ce pas ? Alors...

— Vous seriez heureuse d'apprendre qu'il s'est noyé ?

— Qu'il n'est plus à bord, tout au moins...

Même la peur, chez elle, devenait voluptueuse, parce qu'elle faisait frémir la chair de ses épaules.

— Eh bien...

Il hésita. Il regarda Schuttringer, qui semblait

réprouver cette conversation retardant l'heure du café, puis Evjen, puis Katia qui lui offrait l'eau fluide de ses prunelles.

— ... rien ne prouve qu'il n'y ait pas un assassin à bord !

— Vous voulez m'effrayer, n'est-ce pas ?

— Peut-être...

— Expliquez-vous, capitaine... Du moment qu'on l'a vu se jeter à l'eau.

Petersen se sentit pris d'une vilaine petite rage contre elle, car soudain il la revoyait pénétrant avec Vriens dans sa cabine. Et, tout en regardant ses épaules, il ne pouvait chasser l'image du troisième officier, qui, dans l'ombre de la plage arrière, à Stavanger, avait la tête posée dans leur creux.

— Ne craignez rien !... Il sera certainement arrêté avant d'avoir pu tuer à nouveau...

Evjen montrait quelque impatience. Schuttringer, pour tuer le temps, avait repris des abricots confits et les mangeait avec l'application qu'il apportait à toutes choses.

— Vous me faites presque peur, capitaine !... riposta-t-elle avec un petit frisson le long de la nuque. Vous êtes méchant, ce soir...

Il se leva, laissa passer les passagers devant lui, s'attarda comme d'habitude dans le couloir où il bourrait sa pipe.

Il vit s'approcher le steward, qui demanda d'une voix hésitante :

84

— C'est vrai, ce que vous venez de dire ? L'assassin est...

— Mais non ! Mais non !

— C'est bien ce que je pensais ! Sinon...

— Sinon ?...

— Je descendrais à Trondheim... Rien que de penser...

Petersen entra dans sa cabine, en ressortit, aperçut le policier qui venait dîner à son tour et qui, de loin, lui adressa un salut aimable et déférent.

Le vent se levait. On le sentait aux mouvements du bateau. Des vagues assaillaient l'étrave, un peu à bâbord, à un rythme progressif.

Est-ce qu'il allait monter au fumoir, ou bien jeter un coup d'œil dans la cabine de Vriens, qui avait fini son quart, ou encore avaler quelques gorgées de bon air sur la passerelle ?

A force d'avoir le front plissé et de se ronger comme il le faisait depuis trois jours, il ressentait à hauteur des tempes une douleur sourde, obstinée.

Il pouvait voir l'inspecteur Jennings, qui, tout en mangeant, parcourait les journaux illustrés, achetés à Bergen.

Il se surprit, en place de points d'encre, à aligner des noms :

— Vriens... Katia... Schuttringer... Peter Krull... Bell Evjen...

Oui ! Maintenant, il ajoutait même Bell Evjen, qu'il connaissait depuis huit ans !

Il entendit une sonnerie. Le steward passa en disant :

— On m'appelle au fumoir...

Quand il redescendit, il annonça avec un étonnement mêlé de respect :

— Six bouteilles de champagne !... C'est la demoiselle.

Elle apparaissait au haut de l'escalier, s'écriait :

— Montez un moment, capitaine !... Mais si !... Je viens de me rappeler que c'est aujourd'hui mon anniversaire... Je veux le fêter, car je suis très superstitieuse !

Une fois de plus, de bas en haut, il voyait ses jambes, ses genoux. Le faisait-elle exprès de se pencher, d'en découvrir davantage ?

— Tout le monde doit en être... Vos officiers aussi...

Petersen se mit à gravir l'escalier lentement. Et il évoquait toujours des points noirs, qu'il rapprochait ou écartait les uns des autres selon les instants.

Dans le fumoir, Bell Evjen et Schuttringer étaient pour la première fois assis à la même table, échangeaient des phrases banales pour lier connaissance.

— J'ai toujours été persuadée, disait Katia Storm avec une animation joyeuse, que si je ne m'amuse pas le jour de mon anniversaire, c'est une année triste qui se prépare... Donnez-moi du feu, capitaine !... Non !... Avec votre pipe... Nous allons nous amuser, n'est-ce pas ?... Il n'y aura pas trop de vent cette nuit, dites ?...

— Allez chercher les deux officiers qui ne sont pas de quart ! commanda Petersen au steward, qui arrivait avec six bouteilles de champagne et des coupes.

Tout seul, dans la salle à manger, le policier, que personne ne servait, se levait de temps en temps pour aller chercher un plat trop éloigné.

Comme Schuttringer, il commença par montrer un certain penchant pour la langue écarlate, mais, plus compliqué, il en couvrit chaque tranche de compote de prunes.

Quand le steward revint en s'excusant, il déclara avec un gentil sourire, la bouche pleine :

— Ça va... Je me suis servi moi-même... Pourquoi font-ils tant de bruit, là-haut ?...

6

L'anniversaire de Katia

Le second, qui ignorait pourquoi on l'appelait, arriva dans sa tenue de tous les jours, en gros drap usé et gras, au moment où Katia Storm tendait des coupes à la ronde. Il en reçut une, se tourna vers le capitaine comme pour lui demander conseil, remarqua que Petersen avait l'air à peu près aussi embarrassé que lui.

Il faillit boire trop tôt, par contenance. Heureusement que la jeune femme, tournée vers la porte, prononça :

— Il manque encore quelqu'un...

Et Vriens arriva enfin, s'arrêta un instant sur le seuil, décontenancé par tous les regards braqués sur lui.

— Venez boire aussi à ma santé, cher !...

L'atmosphère manquait de chaleur et l'entrain n'était pas encore né. Il n'y avait que l'Allemande à s'agiter, à parler, à sourire, et c'était inouï qu'elle ne se décourageât pas en voyant que sa gaieté restait sans écho.

— A la russe ! s'écria-t-elle en élevant sa coupe à hauteur de ses lèvres. D'un trait...

Elle renversa un peu la tête en arrière, avala jusqu'à la dernière goutte le vin pétillant, demanda à Evjen :

— Ouvrez une bouteille, voulez-vous ?...

Et, à Vriens :

— Allez chercher dans ma cabine le phonographe et les disques, cher...

Le capitaine s'était assis ainsi que Schuttringer, mais les autres étaient debout et le second officier avait l'air de n'attendre qu'une occasion de s'en aller.

Evjen, empressé, avec une pointe de gêne, secondait la jeune femme comme elle l'en priait, débouchait les bouteilles d'une main habile, emplissait les coupes.

— Il fait très froid, ici, capitaine ! Est-ce que le radiateur ne marche pas ?...

Petersen se pencha sur l'appareil caché par une fausse armoire, ouvrit tout grand le robinet qui laissa gicler un petit jet de vapeur. Dès lors, on devait entendre sans cesse un sifflement qui se noyait le plus souvent dans les autres bruits.

— Votre verre, capitaine !... Ce n'est pas du café ! Donc, vous pouvez boire, n'est-ce pas ?...

Vriens revenait avec un phono portatif et deux mallettes de disques qu'il posa sur une table.

— Très bien ! Vous êtes un amour... Jouez maintenant un tango... Vous dansez le tango, capitaine ?

— Je ne danse pas...

— Jamais ?

— Jamais... Excusez-moi...

— Et vous, monsieur Evjen ?...

— Je danse très mal...

— Cela ne fait rien... Dansons !... Non !... Buvez d'abord... Cher, vous remplirez les coupes pendant que nous danserons...

Ces derniers mots s'adressaient à Vriens, qui avait mis l'appareil en marche. L'atmosphère devenait un peu moins froide. Les phrases du tango s'étiraient mollement, soulignées par la voix d'un ténor allemand.

— Vous dansez très bien... Pourquoi disiez-vous...

Le reste de la conversation se perdit. Katia, souple et lascive, se serrait contre la poitrine d'Evjen, qui était beaucoup plus grand qu'elle et qui, raide, un peu solennel, se penchait d'une façon contrainte.

Vriens dut passer devant le capitaine pour s'approcher de la table où étaient les verres.

— Pardon... balbutia-t-il en regardant ailleurs.

Sur la banquette, Schuttringer ne bougeait pas, regardant droit devant lui, à travers les lunettes qui déformaient ses yeux. Katia riait, à la suite d'une phrase que son cavalier avait murmurée.

Elle était surexcitée. Mais Petersen, qui ne cessait de l'observer, eût juré que cette excitation était artificielle.

— Alors, personne ne boit ? lança-t-elle, comme la danse finissait.

Et, non sans un rien d'impatience, elle prit des mains de Vriens une bouteille que celui-ci ne parvenait pas à ouvrir, fit sauter le fil de laiton, tandis que le jeune homme rougissait.

— Mettez donc un autre disque... Qu'est-ce que vous faites ?...

En d'autres circonstances, Petersen n'eût pu s'empêcher de sourire. Depuis qu'il avait mis les pieds au fumoir, Vriens était envoyé d'un côté et de l'autre. Il obéissait, mais avec une mauvaise grâce visible.

— Non !... Pas cette vieille rengaine !... Il y a un très bon *blues* dans la mallette rose.

Et elle s'approcha du second officier qui ne savait quelle contenance prendre, lui dit d'un air câlin :

— Dansons...

Comment et à quel moment jaillit l'étincelle ? Toujours est-il que ce fut long. Le steward, sonné par Katia, apporta une seconde fois six bouteilles.

— Pourquoi ne buvez-vous pas ? se lamentait-elle. C'est mon anniversaire ! Je veux que tout le monde soit joyeux !...

Elle y mettait une bonne volonté inlassable. Elle dansa avec Arnold Schuttringer, qui apporta à cet exercice la même application patiente qu'à ses mouvements hygiéniques du matin et qui ne desserra pas les dents.

A certain moment, elle laissa tomber sa chaussure de satin.

— Donnez, cher... dit-elle à Vriens, qui dut s'agenouiller.

Elle riait, avec peut-être une sourde envie de pleurer. Elle buvait plus que les autres parce que, à chaque instant, elle s'approchait de quelqu'un, deux coupes à la main.

— *Prosit*... Ensemble...

Et le contenu du verre y passait, son teint devenant plus rose, ses yeux brillants.

— Je ne peux pas aller me coucher, maintenant ? questionna le second, à voix basse, après une heure.

Le capitaine lui fit signe de rester. Le radiateur

commençait à chauffer avec exagération. L'air était épaissi par la fumée des cigarettes. Comme la jeune femme ouvrait son étui vide, Evjen lui tendit le sien, mais elle refusa.

— Elles sont trop fortes... Vriens ira chercher la boîte dans ma cabine... N'est-ce pas, cher ?...

C'étaient des cigarettes de grand luxe, à bout de rose, qu'elle posa parmi les bouteilles et les coupes. Le phonographe marchait toujours. Bell Evjen, à deux ou trois reprises, avait engagé la conversation avec Schuttringer, mais celui-ci répondait avec un tel laconisme qu'il avait fini par y renoncer.

La seule chose que fît le jeune Allemand rasé c'était boire. Il vidait les coupes les unes après les autres comme, à table, il avalait les tranches de charcuterie. Son visage luisait, reflétait une satisfaction béate.

Petersen buvait aussi, parce qu'il n'y avait pas moyen de faire autrement et que Katia lui tendait sans cesse une nouvelle coupe.

Combien en avait-il déjà bu ? Il n'eût pu le dire. D'habitude, il était sobre. Et l'été, lorsque les touristes organisaient des parties de ce genre, il prétextait le règlement du bord interdisant à l'équipage et à l'état-major les boissons alcooliques.

Cette fois pourtant, il y prenait un certain plaisir. Peut-être parce que, la boisson aidant, il sentait avec plus d'intensité ce que l'atmosphère avait d'étrange, de sourd, de grinçant.

Souvent, on avait joué du phono dans ce même

fumoir tandis que la masse noire du *Polarlys* se poussait à grands coups d'hélice à travers les houles et que le pilote, là-haut, se balançait d'une jambe à l'autre dans la bourrasque.

L'antithèse amusait les touristes. Des femmes s'extasiaient en entendant l'appel rauque d'un goéland à la fin d'une ritournelle de jazz.

Aujourd'hui, il n'y avait même pas d'antithèse. L'extérieur n'existait pas. Personne ne s'en préoccupait. Nul visage ne se collait aux hublots pour apercevoir la barrière neigeuse des fjords.

Tout se passait dans le fumoir. Et on n'eût même pas pu dire ce qui se passait.

Une femme jeune, belle, voluptueuse riait aux éclats en renversant la tête en arrière, devenait à chaque instant un peu plus ivre, essayait d'entraîner ses compagnons à sa suite.

Et Petersen cherchait le rapport !... Les six points noirs sur la feuille de papier, avec les traits indécis allant de l'un à l'autre...

Le rapport avec Sternberg, qui était mort, avec le petit corps nu de Marie Baron trouvé dans un atelier de la rue Delambre, le rapport avec l'assassin...

Pas une fois il ne put rencontrer le regard de Vriens, mal à l'aise dans le rôle qu'on lui faisait jouer.

— Qu'est-ce que vous attendez pour ouvrir une autre bouteille ?

Encore un qui avait envie de pleurer ! Elle dut

s'en apercevoir ! Et, comme elle avait déjà beaucoup bu, elle lui mit soudain un baiser au coin des lèvres et murmura :

— Tu es un drôle de petit chéri... Dansons tous les deux !... Je veux...

Petersen compta les bouteilles vides. Il y en avait huit. Et ils étaient six à boire !

Personne n'était ivre. Mais Evjen, déjà, suivait les allées et venues de Katia d'un regard trop éloquent, Schuttringer sommeillait, ronflerait sans doute lorsqu'il aurait bu deux ou trois verres de plus.

Il n'y avait que Katia à soutenir le train, à garder un peu de nerfs. Elle le sentait. De minute en minute elle trouvait une plaisanterie à lancer. Ou bien elle éclatait de rire. Ou encore elle esquissait un pas excentrique.

— Vous ne vous amusez pas ! soupira-t-elle cependant. Et je voudrais tant, moi, que l'on s'amuse !... Ce n'est pas gentil, capitaine !... Dansez avec moi, dites !...

Elle faisait presque pitié, tant sa voix était suppliante. Et n'y avait-il pas dans ses yeux, par instants, comme la peur du silence qui s'abattrait dès qu'elle cesserait de remuer ?

Il dansa, gauchement, suivi des yeux par Vriens qui se tenait debout, tout seul, dans un coin.

— Pourquoi êtes-vous si sérieux ?

— Mais...

— Tout le monde est sérieux ! Et moi, je ne puis

pas vivre comme cela... Venez boire !... Si !... Je veux !...

Elle l'entraîna vers la table qui servait de buffet.

— Viens aussi, chéri... dit-elle à Vriens. Mais viens donc !... Je ne veux pas que vous soyez tous ainsi... Ce n'est pas possible...

Cette fois, elle exagéra... Elle vida trois fois son verre, coup sur coup, se passa la main sur le front.

— Donnez-moi une cigarette... Non ! Pas de celles-là... Les miennes sont quelque part... Eh bien, Vriens !

Et elle frappa le sol du pied avec impatience.

— Il n'y a personne pour remonter le phonographe ?...

Pour la première fois depuis qu'on était au fumoir, elle s'assit, regarda en haussant les épaules Schuttringer qui était à peu près aussi vivant qu'un bloc de pierre.

— Venez vous installer ici, capitaine... Toi ici, chéri...

Elle voulait mettre Petersen à sa droite, Vriens à sa gauche. Le jeune homme hésitait à s'avancer.

Alors elle éclata.

— Mais qu'est-ce que vous avez donc tous ?... On dirait que nous sommes à un enterrement... Donnez-moi à boire... Si !... Je veux !... Je boirai toute seule... Tant pis...

— Calmez-vous... intervint gauchement le capitaine.

— Pourquoi voulez-vous que je me calme ? Est-ce que votre bateau est une cathédrale ?... Qu'on fasse de la musique...

Ce n'était plus la même femme. La nervosité latente, qu'on devinait d'habitude en elle, prenait le dessus. Et c'était une créature désordonnée, incapable de se refréner, de ressaisir son sang-froid.

— Qui est-ce qui boit avec moi ?... Personne ?...

Vriens se pencha, balbutia quelques mots qu'elle put seule entendre et qui étaient évidemment un appel à la sagesse.

— Toi, laisse-moi... Si je veux boire, cela me regarde, n'est-ce pas ?...

La crise de nerfs n'était pas loin. Le capitaine la sentait poindre, s'en effrayait et s'en réjouissait tout ensemble.

N'allait-il pas enfin découvrir quelque chose, à la faveur de cette atmosphère de serre chaude ? Déjà, peut-être, il comprenait mieux le récit de la concierge de la rue Delambre, peuplait, en pensée, l'atelier de femmes qui ressemblaient à Katia.

— Donnez-moi du feu...

Elle regarda les trois bouteilles encore pleines. Schuttringer venait d'allumer un gros cigare noirâtre qui répandait une odeur âcre. Evjen prenait un air aussi dégagé que possible.

Brusquement, elle se leva, fit rouler les bouteilles par terre, d'un geste violent, se dirigea en courant vers la porte. Arrivée là, elle marqua un temps d'arrêt, se retourna, aperçut Vriens qui marchait derrière elle.

— Non !... Pas besoin... bégaya-t-elle d'une voix hachée.

Et elle descendit l'escalier si vite qu'elle ne garda l'équilibre que par miracle.

Le jeune homme hésita un instant, finit par sortir à son tour.

Petersen regarda ses compagnons. Ils étaient aussi embarrassés l'un que l'autre. Le second murmura :

— Je peux aller me coucher ?...

Quant à Evjen, il se mit à arpenter le fumoir d'un air sombre. Le capitaine marcha jusqu'à la porte, où il faillit se heurter au steward.

Il l'attira sur le pont-promenade, où ils furent enveloppés tous deux de flocons de neige que la bourrasque naissante faisait tournoyer.

— Où est-elle ?

— Dans sa cabine... Que s'est-il passé ?... Lorsqu'elle est passée près de moi, elle avait les joues pleines de larmes...

— Vriens ?...

— Elle lui a fermé la porte au nez... Il lui parle au travers... Je n'ai pas pu entendre ce qu'il disait... Elle est ivre ?... Une question, capitaine : est-ce sur son compte que je dois porter les bouteilles ?...

— Bien entendu... Va...

Petersen venait d'apercevoir une silhouette, dans l'ombre. Ou, plus exactement, il n'avait vu d'abord que le petit disque rouge d'une cigarette. Il s'avança vivement, dut mettre son visage près du visage de l'inconnu pour reconnaître Peter Krull.

— Qu'est-ce que tu fais ici, toi ?

Posément, le soutier retira le rouleau de tabac de sa bouche.

— Vous voyez ! Je prends l'air...

— C'est ton heure de repos ?

— Non ! Mais j'ai donné une couronne au camarade pour prendre ma place... C'est mon droit !... Du moment que le chauffeur a son charbon...

Il ne faisait rien pour expliquer sa présence à cet endroit, ni même pour paraître naturel. Au contraire ! Ses petits yeux pétillaient d'une façon plus malicieuse que jamais.

— Nerveuse, la petite dame ! ajouta-t-il comme le capitaine se demandait ce qu'il devait faire.

— Tu as regardé à travers le hublot ?

— Tout le temps, oui !

Et Peter cracha par-dessus le bastingage, essaya, malgré le vent, de rouler une nouvelle cigarette.

— Tu l'as déjà rencontrée ailleurs qu'ici ?

— Pas nécessairement elle ! Mais des femmes du même calibre ! J'en ai eu une à mon compte...

— Dans les bouges de Hambourg ? riposta Petersen pour remettre le soutier à sa place.

— A Berlin... Vous connaissez le quartier Ouest ?... La Jacobstrasse ? Une rue tranquille avec de grosses villas modernes entourées de jardins...

Il fouillait ses poches pour y trouver des allumettes.

— Qu'est-ce que tu faisais là ?

— Pas grand-chose de bon... J'étais inscrit au barreau, comme stagiaire, mais je ne mettais pas les pieds au Palais... J'avais une grosse voiture... Tenez ! une des premières autos sans soupape...

Et toujours ce regard ironique, ce flegme voulu qui déroutaient Petersen.

— Et la femme ?

— C'était la mienne... Une divorcée... Elle avait d'abord été la femme de Breckmann, le grand métallurgiste de la Ruhr... Maintenant, il paraît qu'elle vit en Egypte, où elle a épousé une sorte de consul ou d'ambassadeur anglais...

Le capitaine jeta un regard à travers le hublot le plus proche, vit Evjen quitter le fumoir et Schut-tringer qui, toujours somnolent, vidait deux coupes encore pleines.

Ce que Krull venait de lui dire le gênait à l'égal d'une incongruité. En bon Norvégien de classe moyenne, il préférait ignorer les situations équivoques qui existent fatalement de par le monde.

— Qu'est-ce qui prouve qu'il ne me ment pas ? se disait-il pour se rassurer.

Mais en même temps, il regardait le soutier de travers, se souvenait des premières impressions ressenties devant lui, comprenait qu'en tout cas l'homme n'avait pas toujours été rat de quai.

D'instinct, il ne le tutoya plus.

— Pourquoi êtes-vous monté sur cette passe-relle ?

— Pour voir...

— Voir quoi ?

— *Eux !*

On passait à ras d'une montagne blanche où un feu rouge marquait la place d'un écueil. Au bas de la côte, il y avait une petite maison de bois, toute seule, qu'on ne fit qu'entrevoir l'espace de quelques secondes.

Des gens vivaient là, à des dizaines de kilomètres de tout village ! Et il n'y avait même pas de route ! Rien qu'un peu de terre au pied de la falaise à pic, de quoi nourrir quelques chèvres ou quelques moutons.

Dans le fumoir, Schuttringer s'était levé, s'étirait comme un homme accablé de fatigue, avisait le verre de Petersen qui contenait un reste de liquide doré et le buvait.

— Ça n'a l'air de rien...

Le capitaine faillit sursauter en entendant la voix de Krull s'élever ainsi tout à coup. Car cette voix était moelleuse, nostalgique.

— Qu'est-ce qui n'a l'air de rien ?

— C'est du champagne !... Il n'est pas fameux, mais c'est du champagne !... Vous ne pouvez pas comprendre... Allons !... Il est temps que j'aille remplacer le camarade, sinon il me réclamera une seconde couronne... Un bon conseil, capitaine : laissez *tout ça* tranquille...

Il s'éloignait déjà. Il eût fallu le rappeler et Petersen jugea que ce serait contraire à sa dignité. Il préféra attendre que le soutier eût disparu. En passant devant le fumoir, il s'aperçut qu'il était vide.

En bas, le couloir était vide également, à part le steward assis à la place où il veillait jusqu'à minuit.

— Vriens ?...

— Il est parti en voyant qu'elle ne lui ouvrirait pas...

— Les autres ?

— Dans leur cabine... M. Evjen m'a commandé une bouteille d'eau minérale...

Petersen resta un moment immobile. C'est alors qu'il constata avec mauvaise humeur que, s'il n'était pas ivre, ses jambes n'avaient pas leur solidité habituelle.

— Le soutier ne vient jamais rôder par ici ?

— Quel soutier ?...

— Rien !... Ça va !... Mon café à cinq heures et demie, comme toujours...

Il lui sembla que du bruit arrivait de la chambre de Katia Storm. Mais, en présence du steward, il n'osa pas aller écouter à la porte.

Quelques instants plus tard, il se déshabillait et se surprenait à grogner :

— Qu'est-ce qu'il a voulu dire ?

C'était la phrase de Peter Krull qu'il ne digérait pas.

— *Un bon conseil, capitaine : laissez tout ça tranquille...*

Cette nuit-là, il rêva que Katia, qui était la femme

d'un consul anglais, l'invitait à danser dans le salon de première classe d'un paquebot à trois cheminées.

Elle avait une façon étrange de river ses jambes à celles de son cavalier et soudain, devant tout le monde qui riait, elle l'embrassait sur la bouche tandis qu'un maître d'hôtel, qui ressemblait comme deux gouttes d'eau à Peter Krull, circulait à la façon d'un marchand de cacahuètes et criait :

— Qui en veut ?... Qui en demande ?... C'est du champagne !...

7

La journée des portefeuilles

La journée du mercredi, qui commença par une escale de deux heures à Trondheim, fut d'un calme si absolu qu'il ne paraissait pas naturel.

Depuis le départ de Hambourg, Petersen avait trop peu dormi et, le champagne aidant, il se sentait mou, tant au physique qu'au moral.

Quand le steward vint lui dire sur la passerelle que Katia Storm, malade, ne voulait pas quitter sa cabine, il se contenta de hausser les épaules et de fumer sa pipe à petites bouffées plus rapides.

Il ne vit pas Vriens de toute la matinée. Il est vrai que le pont, balayé par une tempête de neige fine comme du sable, qui semblait vouloir s'incruster dans la peau, était désert.

On approchait du cercle arctique. Les maisons, à flanc de montagne, devenaient de plus en plus rares. Trois fois, ce jour-là, le *Polarlys* desservit des bourgades d'une dizaine de maisons où des hommes en bonnet de fourrure chargeaient les caisses et les barriques sur des traîneaux.

Dans le troisième port, la couche de neige atteignait près de soixante centimètres et les gamins circulaient en skis ou en patins.

Le ciel était gris. La mer était grise. Si bien que la lumière semblait émaner de la blancheur crue des montagnes dont le navire suivait toutes les découpures.

Au déjeuner, il n'y avait à table que le capitaine, Evjen et Schuttringer. Evjen prononça deux ou trois phrases, par acquit de conscience, puis la conversation tomba à plat.

En sortant, Petersen serra la main du policier discret qui se montrait aussi peu que possible.

— Si cela continue, il ne se passera rien et le voyage sera excellent ! se félicita Jennings. Je suis persuadé que l'assassin erre par quelques brasses de fond dans le bassin de Stavanger...

Le capitaine évita de le détromper.

— Que fait-elle ? demanda-t-il à la stewardess qui sortait avec des plats de la cabine de Katia.

— Elle est étendue sur son lit, la tête tournée vers la cloison. Elle n'a presque pas mangé. Elle ne parle pas...

Vers trois heures, après avoir sommeillé une heure environ, Petersen grimpa sur la passerelle où Vriens était de quart. Tandis que le jeune homme joignait les talons, il se contenta de le saluer de la main, s'adressa au pilote, avec qui il avait fait plus de cent voyages.

— Vous croyez qu'il faudra farder les panneaux ?

Jusque-là on avait navigué à l'abri d'une ligne presque continue d'îles et de récifs. Cette ligne reprendrait aux environs des Lofoten mais, vers le soir, on serait à découvert, avec, sans doute, un vent assez violent.

— C'est prudent... répondit le colosse engoncé dans ses fourrures et planté sur ses énormes bottes à semelles de bois.

Vriens se tenait, selon la coutume, dans l'angle de la passerelle, tandis que le pilote, au centre, indiquait de temps à autre, au timonier, la direction à suivre, de sa main gonflée par une mitaine en peau de renne.

Le capitaine, un instant, les compara, haussa encore les épaules. Il hésitait à adresser la parole au jeune homme. Il sentait que celui-ci, gêné, osait à peine regarder de son côté.

Pourtant ce fut Vriens qui s'avança soudain et murmura :

— Je voudrais vous dire, capitaine...

Petersen attendit, en regardant par-dessus son épaule.

— ... Bien entendu, dès le retour, je vous offrirai ma démission...

Il n'obtint qu'un grognement en guise de réponse et le capitaine descendit l'échelle, jeta un coup d'œil au fumoir où Bell Evjen avait étalé ses papiers commerciaux.

L'après-midi fut morne. Le dîner ressembla au déjeuner, à cette différence près qu'on entrait dans la région découverte et que le roulis faisait glisser verres et assiettes. Evjen tint bon, encore que son sourire fût un peu forcé.

Mais on vit soudain Arnold Schuttringer, qui depuis quelques instants avait les mâchoires serrées, se lever d'une détente et gagner la porte à grands pas maladroits.

— Elle est vraiment malade ? questionna Evjen.

Petersen esquissa un geste évasif.

— Drôle de créature !... Hier soir, j'ai bien cru que cela finirait mal...

Le capitaine avait l'oreille attentive au heurt des lames contre la coque. Il entendit une masse d'eau qui s'écrasait sur le gaillard d'avant et, déposant sa serviette, gagna la passerelle après avoir décroché au vol sa peau de bique.

Il trouva deux silhouettes appuyées à la rambarde. A travers le nuage de neige fine, on distinguait les feux d'un petit port où l'on devait faire escale. Petersen examina un instant le profil blafard de Vriens et remarqua que les mâchoires avaient la même crispation que celles de Schuttringer.

— Malade ? questionna-t-il d'une voix bourrue.

— Non !

Le jeune homme criait cela en se raidissant et on le sentait frissonner des pieds à la tête dans ses vêtements trop minces.

— Endossez ceci !

Il lui jeta son manteau et, après quelques phrases échangées avec le pilote, il descendit se coucher. Il n'avait pas aperçu une seule fois Peter Krull de la journée.

Quant à Katia, il l'imaginait recroquevillée sur sa couchette, en proie au mal de mer aussi, sans doute, mais s'obstinant à n'appeler personne.

Les meilleurs moments de la journée du jeudi furent, pour Petersen, les heures du matin, alors qu'il montait son quart à côté du pilote.

On avait passé Bodö. Le *Polarlys* se faufilait entre les Lofoten, piquant du nez, d'heure en heure, dans une tourmente de neige.

Pendant quelques minutes, on ne voyait plus rien, et il était impossible de garder les yeux ouverts. La poussière de glace s'infiltrait dans les moindres coutures des vêtements et des chaussures.

Les deux hommes battaient la semelle, se rapprochaient parfois pour se tendre une blague à tabac ou un briquet. Le thermomètre marquait douze degrés sous zéro et, pendant les éclaircies, tandis que luisait un pâle soleil qui permettait d'apercevoir deux ou trois grains à divers points de l'horizon, les montagnes blanches surgissaient, sans une tache, sans une maison, sans une herbe, sans un être vivant.

C'était immense. On reconnaissait les contours de certains pics à plus de trente milles.

Et, soudain, passait presque à ras du navire une barque de pêche longue de huit à dix mètres, les haubans grossis par la glace, le pont lourd de neige, avec deux hommes déformés par quatre ou cinq couches de vêtements qui se penchaient sur la lisse et pêchaient la morue.

L'air glaçait les poumons. Mais Petersen l'aspirait quand même avec avidité, comme si l'oxygène pur, en le vivifiant, allait chasser le cauchemar de la gamine nue sur le lit de la rue Delambre, de Sternberg avec sa poitrine déchirée et le drap roulé en boule sur le visage.

Il regarda avec une réelle indifférence le policier de Stavanger qui, ne sachant que faire, s'était collé contre une cloison, à l'abri du vent, et contemplait le paysage.

Ce fut en entendant tousser derrière lui qu'il tressaillit, fronça les sourcils et demanda à Schuttringer qui venait de surgir :

— Que désirez-vous ?

Un avis, au bas de l'échelle, interdisait l'accès

de la passerelle où les passagers n'avaient rien à faire.

— Je voudrais vous parler confidentiellement, capitaine !

Il n'en avait jamais tant dit à la fois. Il se montrait compassé, hésitant. Il avait retiré sa casquette de voyage et son crâne nu faisait un effet inattendu dans l'atmosphère glacée.

— Couvrez-vous ! Qu'est-ce que c'est ?...

L'Allemand désigna le pilote.

— Vous pouvez parler devant lui.

— Je viens d'être victime d'un vol...

— Vous dites ?

— Quelqu'un a pénétré dans ma cabine, hier au soir ou ce matin, et a emporté deux mille marks et quelques centaines de couronnes qui se trouvaient dans ma valise... Je suis désolé d'ajouter à vos soucis... Mais il faut absolument que je retrouve cet argent car c'est tout ce que j'avais pris avec moi pour mon voyage...

Le pilote s'était retourné et regardait le passager avec curiosité.

— Vous êtes sûr que cet argent a disparu ? questionna Petersen, les traits durs.

— Certain !... Par prudence, je ne l'avais pas placé dans mon portefeuille, mais dans une simple enveloppe de papier bleuâtre glissée sous mon linge...

— Qu'avez-vous fait ce matin ?

— J'ai pris mon bain à huit heures. Ma cabine

108

est donc restée vide. Puis je suis allé dans la salle à manger et je me suis promené sur le pont arrière... C'est à l'instant que...

Le capitaine se tourna vers le pilote :

— Vous ferez bien sans moi un moment ?

Et il descendit l'échelle le premier. Comme il passait devant la salle à manger, il se heurta au steward.

— Vous n'avez vu personne entrer au 22 ce matin ?

Le steward sursauta comme un pantin à ressort, balbutia :

— Au 22 aussi ?... M. Evjen vient justement de me demander si personne n'avait pénétré chez lui...

Evjen, dont la porte était ouverte, se montra. Il avait entendu.

— Capitaine !... Voulez-vous venir un instant ?...

Il était nerveux, mais il gardait son empire sur lui-même. Il n'y avait guère que ses mains longues et très soignées à s'agiter.

— On vous a volé quelque chose ?...

Mais Evjen regarda Schuttringer avec méfiance.

— Entrez un instant, voulez-vous ?

Il referma sa porte.

— Vous savez que je ne descends dans le sud qu'une fois par an... C'est à ce moment que je me munis des sommes nécessaires à l'exploitation pendant au moins six mois de l'année... Nous n'avons pas de banque à Kirkenes... Dans cette mallette en porc il y avait, hier soir encore, cinquante mille couronnes en billets et quelques pièces d'or que j'ai l'habitude d'apporter à ma femme...

— Disparu ?...

— La mallette est vide... Je m'en suis aperçu à l'instant... Je travaillais au fumoir quand j'ai eu besoin d'un document enfermé, lui aussi, dans cette mallette... On a fait sauter la serrure de la malle où elle se trouvait cachée sous mes effets...

Schuttringer, dans le couloir, faisait les cent pas avec impatience.

— Voulez-vous n'en pas parler pour l'instant ?...

— Qu'allez-vous faire ? Pensez que...

Petersen sortit sans en écouter davantage, recommanda de même le silence à l'Allemand qui répéta :

— Il faut *absolument*... vous comprenez ?... Je n'ai plus rien et...

Le capitaine retrouva Jennings à la même place, sur le pont, et le policier prépara un aimable sourire dès qu'il l'aperçut.

— Bonjour, capitaine !... Quel beau pays !... Les gens du sud ne se doutent pas que...

— Venez avec moi...

Il l'entraîna dans sa cabine, dont il referma violemment la porte.

— Deux vols viennent d'être commis à bord, l'un dans la cabine 14, voisine de celle-ci, où on a enlevé cinquante mille couronnes, l'autre au 22, où deux mille marks environ ont disparu.

— Ce n'est pas possible ! s'écria l'inspecteur qui n'en revenait pas. Ici, à bord !...

— Hier soir ou ce matin, oui ! Il y a trois démarches que je voudrais que vous accomplissiez sans perdre de temps : visiter à fond la cabine de Katia Storm, d'abord...

— Vous croyez ?...

— ... et, s'il le faut, la faire fouiller par la stewardess... Ensuite, visiter la cabine de mon troisième officier... Enfin, si cela n'a rien donné, jeter un coup d'œil du côté d'un certain Peter Krull, qui travaille dans la soute...

— Je croirais plutôt, en effet, que c'est dans ce sens que...

— Je préfère, si vous n'y voyez pas d'inconvénient, que vous commenciez par l'Allemande... Elle est chez elle...

— Je dois lui dire ?...

— Que quelque chose a disparu et que votre devoir est de fouiller tout le navire...

— Vous m'accompagnez ?

Petersen hésita, décida soudain, avec une véhémence mal contenue :

— Je vous accompagne, oui !

Il rencontra Evjen dans l'escalier.

— Voulez-vous aller attendre des nouvelles au fumoir en compagnie de M. Schuttringer ?

Et, au steward :

— Empêchez qu'on ne passe dans le couloir jusqu'à nouvel ordre...

En apparence, il était très calme. Mais, au fond, il bouillait. Ce fut lui qui frappa à la porte de Katia et il se passa quelques instants avant qu'on reçût une réponse.

— Qui est là ?

— Le capitaine... C'est urgent...

— Je ne veux pas me lever aujourd'hui...

— Je suis forcé d'entrer, madame ! Veuillez nous excuser...

Comme dans la plupart des bateaux, les cabines du *Polarlys* ne fermaient pas de l'intérieur. Il tourna la poignée, fit signe à l'inspecteur d'avancer.

Une forte odeur de tabac blond et de parfum prenait à la gorge et la fumée était si dense qu'il fallut un instant avant d'apercevoir la jeune femme, en pyjama, étendue sur sa couchette.

Elle avait les cheveux en désordre, le corsage entrouvert, mais surtout la peau moite, le visage fatigué. Elle recula d'un geste instinctif, chercha à se couvrir du drap sur lequel elle était étendue et qu'elle ne put attirer à elle.

— Un vol important vient d'être commis à bord et...

— Et vous me soupçonnez de... ?

— Je ne soupçonne personne. Néanmoins, le devoir de l'inspecteur est de fouiller tout le navire...

Elle rit, d'un rire pointu, méchant, bondit de son lit sans plus se soucier de sa tenue.

— Eh bien ! cherchez... Je ne croyais pas que la coutume, en Norvège...

C'était la deuxième fois qu'une question de nationalité intervenait. Vriens n'avait-il pas prononcé une phrase à peu près semblable avec les mêmes intentions insultantes ?

— Je ne dois pas sortir ?... Est-ce mon lit que vous voulez fouiller ?...

Avec des gestes saccadés, elle arracha les draps, la couverture, fit tomber un roman allemand qu'elle avait dû commencer à lire.

Petersen était frappé de la différence entre son attitude et celle des jours précédents. Jusque-là, à part la scène d'ivresse, elle avait été maîtresse d'elle-même, sans jamais se troubler, sans donner prise au soupçon.

Et voilà que son indignation maladroite cachait mal une véritable panique.

Elle ricanait, elle s'agitait, elle avait envie d'injurier. Elle fit tomber une valise du filet et en éparpilla le contenu au milieu de la cabine.

— Mon linge !... Je suppose que cela vous intéresse, n'est-ce pas ?...

Le fait qu'elle n'était pas en toilette et qu'elle se montrait sans poudre, sans fards, avec des moiteurs sur la peau, contribuait sans doute à souligner son désarroi.

— Qu'est-ce que vous voulez voir encore ?... Au fait, l'argent est peut-être caché sous mon pyjama... Dois-je l'enlever ?...

Elle en déboutonnait la veste.

— Vous êtes convaincu, maintenant, capitaine ? Ou peut-être ne désiriez-vous que surprendre une

·femme au lit ?... Attention ! Vous avez oublié mon carton à chapeau...

L'inspecteur, rouge jusqu'aux oreilles, esquissait des gestes gauches.

Mais Petersen, qui était resté debout devant la porte, était sombre, de sang-froid, et se remémorait les phrases du soutier.

— Laissez *tout* ça tranquille...

Est-ce qu'il ne commençait pas à comprendre le sens de ces paroles ? Cette Katia Storm ne lui était-elle pas plus étrangère, plus mystérieuse qu'une Lapone du Finnmark transportant ses enfants sur le dos à travers la toundra ?

Mme Petersen était la fille aînée d'un pasteur protestant. Pendant un an, il lui avait fait la cour, dans le jardin du temple de bois peint en vert pâle où les amoureux étaient toujours entourés des cadets dont le plus jeune avait six ans.

Elle jouait de l'orgue. Il l'accompagnait au violon. Et il n'était rien resté en lui de tous les ports traversés, des scènes brutales auxquelles il avait assisté sans même chercher à en pénétrer le sens.

Son second était fiancé. Le chef mécanicien avait huit enfants.

L'été, quand le bateau était plein de touristes, qu'on faisait du phono et que des flirts s'ébauchaient dans tous les coins, il lui était arrivé de passer la nuit dans une autre cabine que la sienne.

Mais le lendemain c'était oublié. Il s'efforçait d'effacer le souvenir d'un visage. Et il rapportait

114

de Tromsö, pour ses gosses, quelques jouets fabriqués par les Lapons.

C'est tout juste s'il avait appris de la sorte qu'il existe des femmes d'une nervosité excessive, effrayante même, incapables de passer leur vie dans un bungalow coquet et confortable. Certaines ne l'avaient-elles pas gêné par leurs transports au point qu'il n'avait qu'une hâte : échapper à la moiteur des étreintes et se caler bien d'aplomb sur la passerelle !

Katia devait être de cette race-là. Et Petersen la regardait avec obstination, persuadé qu'il finirait par comprendre.

L'odeur de la cabine le choquait, comme ce pyjama ouvert sur des seins à peine bombés. Il notait maints autres détails : la bouteille de chartreuse verte, les cigarettes tarabiscotées, de la lingerie dont sa femme ne soupçonnait même pas l'existence.

Un instant, il essaya d'imaginer Vriens dans cette même cabine, la nuit où le couple s'y était enfermé.

— Rien ! murmura le policier d'une voix honteuse.

— C'est fini, vraiment ? Je ne suis pas une voleuse ? Vous ne croyez pas qu'il serait prudent de découdre le matelas ?...

Sa gorge était si serrée qu'on s'attendait plutôt à entendre éclater un sanglot que des syllabes. Elle resta là, toute droite, les mains sur les hanches, jusqu'à ce que les deux hommes se fussent éloignés.

Et c'est seulement lorsque la porte se fut refermée sous une poussée violente que Petersen s'avisa qu'il avait oublié de s'excuser.

— Chez Vriens !...

— Vous la soupçonniez ? questionna l'inspecteur.

Et son embarras, ses oreilles rouges, son regard fuyant disaient clairement qu'il était troublé, lui aussi, attiré, en quelque sorte, par cette simple visite, en dehors de l'orbe normal de son existence.

C'était comme une échappée sur un autre monde, sur un domaine nouveau d'émotions, de sensations.

Un matelot polissait les cuivres du carré.

— Le troisième officier est chez lui ?

— Non ! Je ne l'ai pas vu...

Petersen poussa la porte. Au-dessus du lit, la première chose qu'il aperçut fut une grande photographie du bateau-école de Delfzijl, noir et blanc, avec une nuée d'élèves en grande tenue gantés de clair, sur le pont, sur la dunette et même — les plus jeunes — perchés fièrement sur les vergues.

Sur la table, les *Instructions nautiques* norvégiennes, encore ouvertes au chapitre des balises et signaux.

— Je dois fouiller ? soupira le policier.

Et son interlocuteur haussa les épaules avec une certaine lassitude.

— Faites !...

Dans la valise, c'était encore le trousseau de l'école, avec les marques au gros coton rouge. Il y avait une autre photo, prise au cours du bal de la promotion : des guirlandes de papier, des accessoires de cotillon, des jeunes Hollandaises bien portantes parmi les uniformes.

Vriens, coiffé d'un bonnet de papier plissé, se tenait dans un coin, honteux, eût-on dit, de son accoutrement, et le magnésium lui avait fait fermer les yeux.

Jennings changea de place trois dictionnaires, au fond du sac de voyage, découvrit un fin mouchoir de femme qui répandait le même parfum que Katia, puis, sous un cahier, une liasse de billets de banque.

Petersen l'avait vue en même temps que lui. Tous deux se regardèrent.

— Comptez ! articula le capitaine d'une voix qui n'avait pas sa résonance habituelle.

Pendant deux minutes, on n'entendit que le froissement des billets presque carrés de mille couronnes.

— Quarante...

— Vous êtes certain ?

— J'ai compté deux fois.

Des pas retentirent. La silhouette de Vriens se profila dans l'encadrement de la porte.

Il avait à peu près le même air ennuyé que sur la photographie du bal. Il regarda le capitaine, puis Jennings, et alors seulement aperçut les billets.

La transformation fut d'une rapidité saisissante. Ses traits déjà las se burinèrent en l'espace de

quelques secondes, tandis que les épaules se tas-
saient comme celles d'un malade.

Il ne dit rien. Les bras ballants, le regard rivé
aux quarante mille couronnes, il attendit, frappé
d'hébétude.

8

La fortune de Katia

Vriens n'attendit pas d'être questionné pour se
laisser tomber sur le bord de la couchette qu'encom-
brait la valise ouverte.

— Voulez-vous nous dire d'où vient cet argent ?
fit le capitaine d'une voix qui, à son insu, fut presque
affectueuse.

Le jeune homme eut un mouvement accablé des
épaules. Il fixait le linoléum de ses yeux vides.

— Je n'ai pas volé.

— C'est-à-dire que quelqu'un vous a demandé
de cacher l'argent chez vous ?

— Je ne savais même pas qu'il fût là... Ce matin,
à sept heures, il ne s'y trouvait pas...

Il parlait d'une voix morne, sans faire un effort

pour convaincre ses interlocuteurs. Et, dès lors, on ne put rien lui tirer d'autre, sinon :

— Je n'ai pas volé... Je ne sais rien...

Jennings et le capitaine étaient à peine sortis qu'ils entendaient derrière la porte des sanglots déchirants, de vrais hurlements de désespoir, et l'inspecteur, troublé, ému, regarda Petersen.

— Vous croyez que...

— Je ne crois rien ! répliqua son compagnon avec une impatience inattendue.

— Il manque dix mille couronnes...

— Et les deux mille marks de Schuttringer, oui !

Le capitaine hâta le pas. Le gong résonnait encore dans les couloirs et Bell Evjen venait de s'installer dans la salle à manger. Schuttringer, qui arrivait, aperçut le premier la liasse dans les mains de Petersen.

— Mon argent !... dit-il, en faisant rapidement quelques pas.

— Je ne l'ai pas. Jusqu'ici nous n'avons retrouvé que quarante mille couronnes, qui appartiennent à M. Evjen...

— Quarante ? répéta celui-ci en comptant curieusement les billets.

— J'espère que l'inspecteur Jennings mettra la main sur le reste.

— Qui peut bien avoir eu l'idée de...

— Ne m'en demandez pas davantage, voulez-vous ?

— Pardon ! intervint Schuttringer d'un air têtu.

Le voleur de monsieur est certainement mon voleur. Par conséquent, j'ai le droit de savoir...

— Servez, steward ! Mme Storm n'est pas sortie ?

— Je ne l'ai pas vue.

— Elle n'a pas sonné ?

— Non, capitaine...

— Voulez-vous mettre cet argent dans votre coffre jusqu'à la fin de la traversée ? demanda Bell Evjen qui était embarrassé de l'épaisse liasse de billets.

Et l'Allemand à lunettes grommela :

— J'aurais dû en faire autant tout de suite. Ce sera gai à Kirkenes, si...

Petersen n'entendit pas la suite. Il était à peine dans sa cabine, où il fit jouer la serrure d'un coffre-fort portatif, que deux cris de sirène retentissaient. Il saisit sa peau de bique, dit au steward, en passant :

— Vous me servirez à déjeuner tout à l'heure !

C'était Svolvaer, avec les trois à quatre mille barques de pêche en sapin clair qui, en février, affluent de tous les coins de la Norvège afin de participer à la saison de la morue.

Un fouillis de mâts. Une forte odeur de résine.

Et dans la ville qui, normalement, ne compte pas plus de deux mille habitants, un grouillement de traîneaux, d'hommes en fourrures ou en cirés. Des piles croulantes de morues déjà salées, maniées à la pelle.

120

Un petit vapeur noir, au milieu du port, était entouré d'un essaim animé de barques. On y achetait le poisson qui ainsi ne touchait même pas terre et s'en allait le soir même à Aalesund.

Petersen dut serrer des mains, entendre des histoires et des chiffres, tandis que l'inspecteur montait la garde d'un air aussi discret que possible au bout de la passerelle.

Trois barques avaient disparu la veille, emportées vers le Maelström. Par contre, en moins d'un mois, on avait pêché quarante-cinq millions de morues.

Il écoutait, distrait. Son regard errait sur un décor et sur des visages familiers : des maisons de bois, la plupart peintes en teintes pâles ; des rues en pente, invariablement couvertes de neige, et des gamins en skis qui s'élançaient, se faufilaient entre les traîneaux, les caisses, les barils.

Quelques vapeurs de cinquante à cent tonneaux étaient amarrés au même quai que le *Polarlys* et portaient sur une ardoise le nom de la localité des îles qu'ils desservaient. De partout, des voix partaient à l'adresse de Petersen, qui essayait de garder sur ses lèvres un pâle sourire.

Il voyait Evjen et l'Allemand face à face dans la salle à manger. Un Lapon en costume bariolé, en bonnet à quatre pointes, se tenait debout à un angle du quai de pilotis et semblait s'emplir les yeux du mouvant spectacle, tandis qu'au loin, par-delà le bras de mer, on devinait les montagnes blanches d'où il était descendu.

C'était coloré, trépidant, sans nervosité. C'était gai, avec pourtant un fond de gravité nordique qui, d'habitude, enchantait l'âme du capitaine.

Alors qu'il essayait de s'identifier avec le décor, une idée le frappa soudain, parce qu'il venait d'évoquer Katia, moite de la chaleur du lit, debout dans sa cabine en désordre, à l'atmosphère si lourde d'odeurs.

Au flanc du *Polarlys* glissait une barque où deux hommes aux gestes précis, émergeant des morues qui leur arrivaient aux genoux, tranchaient la tête des poissons, arrachaient les langues qu'ils lançaient dans un baquet, fendaient la bête en deux dans le sens de la longueur et laissaient retomber deux filets égaux, tandis que l'arête et les entrailles passaient par-dessus bord.

Petersen les suivait des yeux sans les voir davantage qu'une toile de fond, évoquant par contre les moindres détails de la silhouette de la jeune femme.

— Il n'y avait pas d'argent dans sa cabine !

Il se rappelait tous les mouvements de Jennings. Il revoyait la lingerie fine et, entre autres, des chemises de soie noire qui l'avaient étonné.

Mais pas d'argent ! Pas de portefeuille !

Il essayait de reconstituer la première fouille, dans le brouillard de Stavanger, et sa mémoire ne gardait aucune trace de billets de banque aperçus.

L'inspecteur était adossé au bout de la passerelle que des débardeurs traversaient en file indienne.

Plus loin, Petersen vit Krull qui ne s'était toujours pas rasé et dont le visage était couvert d'une broussaille rousse. Il sembla au capitaine que le soutier l'observait, et il détourna la tête.

— Donne le premier coup de cloche ! commanda-t-il, dix minutes avant l'heure prévue, au second officier.

— Dites, capitaine ! C'est vrai, ce qu'on raconte ?... Vriens ?...

— Je n'en sais rien !

— Il prendra son quart ?

— S'il ne le prend pas, tu le prendras à sa place...

Il y avait comme des nuages de poudre de soleil qui passaient un moment dans le ciel, éclairaient un groupe de voiles, une proue luisante, un clocheton d'ardoises et qui faisaient place aussitôt à la grisaille et à la neige.

Le Lapon, après avoir hésité, monta à bord et prit un billet de troisième classe pour Hammerfest. Mais il refusa de descendre dans les cabines, s'assit sur le cabestan où Petersen devait le retrouver, tel quel, trois heures plus tard.

— Le second coup !...

Les palans furent rentrés, les panneaux tirés sur les cales qui commençaient à se vider.

Et, malgré la forte odeur de poisson qui régnait

dans le port et dans la ville, le capitaine gardait sur la langue comme le goût âcre de la cabine de Katia.

— Vriens est là-haut ?

Car c'était le quart du troisième officier. En levant la tête, on put le voir, inouï, inhumain, raide comme un fétiche nègre, dans un coin de la passerelle.

Tous les objets devaient tourbillonner devant ses yeux, les sons se mêler en une cacophonie. Et pourtant, quand le pilote lui adressa un signe il s'approcha de la cheminée, tira par trois fois la poignée de la sirène qui déchira l'air.

L'eau bouillonna à l'arrière. Les barques fuyaient comme des moutons pris de panique. Un nuage de mouettes entourait l'étrave.

— Vous déjeunez, capitaine ?

C'était le steward, et ses cheveux blonds, son visage éclairé d'un éternel sourire timide, sa veste blanche.

— Pas encore...

Petersen se raccrochait au spectacle du port. On passa devant une usine qui, dix ans plus tôt encore, travaillait la baleine, mais qui ne faisait plus que l'huile de foie de morue.

Puis, brusquement, comme on virait de bord, ce fut une mer d'un vert pâle, des montagnes neigeuses qui ruisselaient de soleil.

Apothéose qu'il fallait se hâter de saisir car la lumière dorée fondait et un voile d'un gris de cendre s'étendait sur l'eau comme un rideau.

Trois minutes plus tard, les montagnes n'étaient plus que des icebergs livides.

Petersen passa devant le policier sans rien lui dire, et, comme Evjen, après déjeuner, s'attardait dans le couloir, il feignit d'avoir à faire dans sa cabine.

Aussitôt que le chemin fut libre, il en sortit, s'arrêta une seconde devant la porte de Katia Storm et, après un claquement énervé des doigts, l'ouvrit sans frapper.

Rien n'était changé dans la cabine depuis la visite du matin. L'air était toujours aussi doux et parfumé. Un drap de lit pendait par terre et un bout de cigarette y avait tracé un petit rond brun.

Il n'y eut pas un mot, pas un mouvement. L'Allemande en pyjama, pieds nus, cheveux défaits, était assise sur son lit, le dos au mur, et regardait l'intrus de ses yeux auxquels le khôl délayé donnait des reflets plus troubles que jamais.

Le capitaine referma la porte, dut enjamber une valise qui faillit le faire tomber.

— Je suis venu vous poser une question, dit-il.

Elle l'écoutait avec indifférence. Sa fièvre du matin était tombée. Elle était sans nerfs, sans coquetterie, avec un pli découragé au coin des lèvres.

Il voulait parler doucement. Et même il eût aimé

lui faire comprendre que cette visite, sans l'inspecteur de police, n'avait pas un caractère agressif.

Il se passait en lui le phénomène contraire de tout à l'heure. Dans la cabine, c'était le va-et-vient du port qui s'obstinait sur sa rétine et la jeune femme s'y dessinait comme en surimpression.

— Voulez-vous me dire combien d'argent vous aviez sur vous en quittant Hambourg ?

Elle sourit, d'un sourire à la fois amer et sarcastique. Mais ce n'était pas à son interlocuteur que s'adressait le sarcasme. C'était à elle, ou bien au sort.

— Cet argent, se hâtait-il d'ajouter, vous devez encore l'avoir, car vous n'avez rien pu dépenser à bord, les comptes se réglant en fin de traversée...

— Eh bien ! le mien ne sera pas réglé...

Sans changer de place, elle s'était contentée de lever un bras. Son sac en crocodile, signé d'un des meilleurs maroquiniers de Londres, se trouvait dans le filet, au-dessus de sa tête.

Elle en tira la poignée et il tomba sur le lit.

— Tenez !... Comptez... Donnez-moi d'abord mes cigarettes...

Comme il ne saisissait pas le sac, elle l'ouvrit, le poussa vers lui, fit jaillir la flamme d'un briquet d'or ciselé.

— C'est tout ce que j'ai... Vous n'osez pas ?...

Elle fermait à demi les yeux parce que la fumée de sa cigarette l'aveuglait. Elle tira un mouchoir du sac — un mouchoir tout pareil à celui qu'on avait trouvé dans la valise de Vriens — puis une boîte de métal travaillé contenant du rouge, de la poudre et du noir pour les yeux.

Enfin, elle éparpilla sur le lit une petite pincée de billets.

— Comptez... Voici dix marks... Cinquante francs belges... Trois coupures françaises de dix francs... Ah !... une pièce de deux florins et demi...

Elle jeta par terre le sac vide, se cala davantage contre le mur, répéta :

— C'est tout...

Peut-être y avait-il encore une certaine fièvre dans sa voix. Mais une fièvre assourdie. Et tout son visage était beaucoup plus humain que d'habitude, plus proche des visages que Petersen connaissait.

Un jour, une voisine de seize ans, avec qui il jouait dans la montagne, s'était foulé un pied en heurtant une souche de sapin. Elle était coquette. Quelques instants auparavant encore elle se moquait de lui.

Elle n'avait pas voulu pleurer. Elle avait souri. Mais elle montrait une pauvre figure brouillée, au teint irrégulier, rouge par plaques, où les lèvres ne savaient quel pli adopter.

A cet instant, Katia ressemblait un peu à la jeune Norvégienne et, de son côté, elle dut sentir que son compagnon la regardait d'une façon nouvelle, car, d'un geste inattendu, furtif, elle ramena son pyjama sur sa gorge.

— Voilà !... Je ne pourrai même pas payer le

champagne que je vous ai invité à boire... J'avais juste de quoi prendre mon billet... Six cents marks, je crois... Et la monnaie qui me restait, je l'ai dépensée, la dernière nuit, à Hambourg...

— Avec Vriens, au *Kristall*...

Il eût été plus à l'aise assis. Mais il ne pouvait s'asseoir qu'au bord de la couchette, c'est-à-dire trop près d'elle. Et il devait tenir les pieds écartés, à cause des objets qui encombraient le sol.

— Que comptiez-vous faire à Kirkenes ?

Elle ne dit rien, le regarda d'un air presque apitoyé, en haussant les épaules.

— Laissez-moi ! A quoi tout cela nous avance-t-il ?... Voulez-vous me donner mon sac ?

Elle y prit un petit miroir dans lequel elle se contempla avec ironie. Ses doigts saisirent le bâton de rouge, puis le laissèrent retomber.

— Vous avez des parents ?

— Peu importe, n'est-ce pas ? A Kirkenes, vous n'aurez qu'à me remettre entre les mains de la police, pour n'avoir pas payé mon champagne et le vin que j'ai bu aux repas... Le steward ne recevra pas de pourboire...

Elle eût crié, elle se fût montrée échevelée que Petersen n'eût sans doute pas ressenti une telle impression de désespoir, d'irrémédiable dépression morale.

Il demanda, pour dire quelque chose :

— Vous avez déjeuné ?

— Non...

128

Les ongles de ses pieds, qui frôlaient le capitaine, étaient aussi roses et polis que ceux des mains.

— Vous savez qu'on a retrouvé une partie des billets volés dans la cabine du troisième officier ?

— Vriens ?

Elle venait enfin de sursauter. Elle jeta sa cigarette sans se soucier de l'endroit où elle tomberait.

— Qu'est-ce que vous dites ? C'est impossible !... Vous cherchez à savoir et...

— Quarante billets de mille couronnes ont été saisis dans sa valise...

— Mais c'est impossible !... Ne comprenez-vous donc pas que c'est impossible ?...

Elle s'était soulevée et, comme elle ne pouvait se mettre debout dans la cabine trop étroite, elle était maintenant agenouillée sur la couchette.

— Ecoutez-moi, capitaine !... Je vous jure que...

Mais ses bras retombèrent. Elle se tut d'un air las. Comme elle baissait la tête, Petersen remarqua, à la racine des cheveux, un petit bouton de fièvre qui tendait la peau.

— Allez-vous-en... Vous ne me croirez quand même pas... Mais il faudra bien que tout cela s'arrange...

— Vous étiez à Paris, rue Delambre ?

Elle ne tressaillit pas, comme il s'y attendait. Une fois de plus, elle haussa les épaules et répéta :

— Allez-vous-en...

Puis soudain :

— Où est Vriens ?

— Il monte son quart sur la passerelle...

— Laissez-moi ! Il faut...

Elle s'était levée, en dépit de la valise dans laquelle elle marcha. Elle arracha une robe du portemanteau.

— Vous voulez rester ici ?

On sentait qu'elle avait pris une décision. Brusquement, elle retira la veste de son pyjama, passa sa robe à même la peau.

Petersen battit en retraite, sans rien trouver à dire pour prendre congé. Le steward l'attendait à la porte de la salle à manger, où son couvert était toujours mis.

— Vous déjeunez, capitaine ?

Mais il grimpa jusqu'au fumoir où Evjen faisait les cent pas, tandis que Schuttringer entreprenait une nouvelle partie d'échecs qui ne l'empêcha pas de lever la tête et de questionner :

— Mes deux mille marks ?...

— Pas encore...

— Ce que je ne comprends pas, commença Bell Evjen qui avait réfléchi longtemps à la question, c'est l'absence des dix mille couronnes et des pièces d'or. Le voleur n'avait aucune raison de diviser ainsi l'argent en deux parts inégales... Si nous avions fait escale quelque part on pourrait croire...

— Il a pris toutes ses précautions ! gronda Schuttringer en avançant le fou du parti noir et en examinant la situation, le menton dans la main. Si bien qu'à l'heure qu'il est il n'est pas dépourvu...

Petersen vit une ombre passer devant les hublots, ne reconnut pas la silhouette, mais eut l'impression très nette que c'était Peter Krull.

— Quelle est l'opinion de l'inspecteur ? reprit Evjen. Vous croyez, vous, capitaine, que c'est un policier intelligent ? Il me fait l'effet... Comment dire !...

— Comme tous les inspecteurs ! intervint une fois de plus l'Allemand à lunettes.

Et, la langue passée entre les lèvres tant son attention était concentrée, il avança une tour de trois cases, articula pour lui-même :

— Echec et mat !...

Le soir tombait. Il n'y avait plus que la neige des montagnes à garder une luminosité qui paraissait artificielle. Les flots étaient d'un noir d'encre et se confondaient, à l'horizon, avec le ciel, grâce à la transition fournie par des gris dégradés.

Au moment où le capitaine sortait pour s'engager le long de l'échelle conduisant à la passerelle, le soutier en descendait, un bout de cigarette éteinte collé à la lèvre. Il se montra contrarié à la vue du capitaine.

— Qu'es-tu allé faire là-haut ?

— C'est mon heure...

— Tu ne sais pas lire ?

Et Petersen lui montrait l'avis interdisant l'accès de la passerelle de commandement.

— C'est bien le premier bateau où...

— A qui as-tu parlé ?

— A personne ! Ils sont muets comme des morues...

Le capitaine eut la sensation désagréable que son interlocuteur essayait de lire dans sa pensée. Et cela lui était d'autant plus pénible à ce moment que cette pensée était plus vague.

— File ! prononça-t-il en s'engageant dans l'escalier.

Debout devant le compas, le pilote l'accueillit en étendant une main vers le couchant et en annonçant :

— Du froid pour cette nuit... Si cela continue, il faudra casser la glace dans la baie de Kirkenes, comme en plein hiver...

Vriens avait le visage coupé par la bise. Il existait, à chaque angle de la passerelle en plein vent, un abri fait de deux panneaux vitrés où l'officier de quart pouvait se tenir.

Mais le jeune homme, encore qu'il n'eût qu'un maigre manteau de drap sur les épaules, restait à découvert. Il n'avait pas détourné la tête en entendant parler le pilote. Ses lèvres étaient bleues et ses mains sans gants serrées sur la rambarde.

— Qu'est-ce que j'avais ordonné ? l'interpella Petersen.

Vriens le regarda avec stupeur, chercha dans sa mémoire.

— D'emprunter une capote à un collègue pour monter le quart. Et des mitaines !

— Bien, mon capitaine...

Il ne bougea pas.

— Combien de tours aux machines ?

— Cent dix...

— Combien de brasses de fond ?

— Quatre-vingts...

Il était à gifler — ou à priver de confiture ! — tant il avait l'air gosse dans ses vêtements tout neufs, avec son galon doré qui manquait de patine, sa poitrine creuse qu'on voyait se soulever au rythme de sa respiration et ses yeux cernés, ses mâchoires qu'il serrait à grand renfort de volonté pour avoir l'air crâne.

9

Le neveu de Sternberg

La nuit tombait plus vite que d'habitude. Il n'était que trois heures et déjà il fallait allumer les lampes. Le capitaine commanda :

— Qu'on commence à farder les panneaux... C'est prudent...

Il s'attardait sur le pont en observant Vriens à la dérobée quand il vit arriver l'inspecteur Jennings, un papier à la main. Le policier se montrait agité.

— Lisez !... Il faut que nous causions, mais ailleurs qu'ici... Le postier du bord me remet ce télégramme à l'instant, alors qu'il l'a dans son bureau depuis une heure.

Vriens, qui avait forcément entendu, ne s'était pas retourné, n'avait pas tressailli. Le capitaine poussa la porte de la chambre de veille, tout en lisant :

Police Stavanger à inspecteur Jennings, à bord du Polarlys.

Sûreté Paris nous avise qu'assassin de Marie Baron est identifié : Rudolph Silberman, de Düsseldorf, ingénieur, neveu du conseiller Sternberg. Stop. Connexion évidente entre les deux affaires. Stop. Probable Silberman embarqué Polarlys Hambourg sous faux nom. Stop. Dragages bassins Stavanger sans résultat. Stop. Resserrer surveillance navire car affaire retentissante en Allemagne.

— Qu'est-ce que vous en dites ?

Jennings était complètement démonté par cette dépêche.

— Est-ce que vous croyez que l'homme puisse encore être caché dans les cales ?

Petersen relut le message, marcha jusqu'à la porte, parce qu'un coup de roulis l'inquiétait.

— Non ! Il n'y a plus d'Ericksen ici. Premièrement, le bateau a été fouillé par deux fois, dont une avec toutes les précautions possibles par la police de Bergen. Secundo, le fret presque tout entier est débarqué et les cales n'offrent plus d'abri... Tertio, cet Ericksen n'a jamais été vu, à bord, que par Katia Storm et par Vriens...

— Mais vous ?...

— J'ai aperçu, deux heures avant l'appareillage, le dos d'un homme en manteau gris... Le troisième officier m'a dit que c'était Ericksen... Mais, à partir de ce moment, il a eu tout le temps de quitter le *Polarlys*...

— Pourquoi ? Son passage était payé, ses bagages à bord...

— Oui, pourquoi ?... Et il y a bien d'autres pourquoi dans cette affaire...

— Pour quel port était son billet ?

— Stavanger.

Une fois encore, le capitaine marcha jusqu'à la passerelle, le front plissé, demanda au pilote :

— Les panneaux sont fardés ?

L'homme lui montra sur la mer une vilaine tache claire, d'un gris glauque, à l'horizon.

— Vous avez pourtant examiné tous les passeports ! reprit Petersen en revenant sur ses pas.

Le policier commençait à se montrer inquiet, lui aussi, non qu'il pressentît la tempête, mais parce que le roulis s'intensifiait, et faisait naître une vague angoisse dans sa poitrine.

— Il ne faut pas nous arrêter à la question des passeports ! répliqua-t-il. Il est à peu près impossible de reconnaître un faux passeport d'un vrai... Dans toutes les grandes villes, et surtout dans les ports comme Hambourg, il existe des boutiques de papiers d'identité. De faux papiers qui sont parfois vrais, soit qu'ils aient été volés à leur titulaire, soit que, par tout un jeu de complicités, ils proviennent de bureaux officiels...

— Si bien que Silberman... ?

— Peut être n'importe qui : Ericksen, Vriens, Evjen, Schuttringer, Peter Krull.

— Mettez Evjen à part. Il y a huit ans que je le connais...

— Restent quatre...

— Moins Ericksen qui, j'en jurerais, n'a jamais existé...

— Alors, pourquoi Katia Storm et votre troisième officier se sont-ils obstinés à faire croire à sa présence à bord ?

— Et pourquoi le sac de charbon ? fit Petersen sur le même ton. Et pourquoi ce vol ? Pourquoi ne retrouve-t-on que quarante billets dans la valise de Vriens, qui disposait de cent cachettes sûres dans tout le bateau ?

Une première lame passa par-dessus l'étrave et s'écrasa sur le gaillard d'avant, tandis que l'inspecteur essayait de sourire.

— Ce n'est pas une tempête ?

— Pas encore !

— Vous croyez que... ?

— Si vous alliez jeter un coup d'œil sur les effets de Krull ?

— Tout en bas ?

— Oui. Sa couchette est à gauche de la chambre des machines. Le chef mécanicien vous conduira...

La température fraîchissait avec une rapidité déconcertante, au point qu'en sortant le capitaine tourna deux fois son écharpe autour de son cou.

En se penchant sur la rambarde, il vit quatre hommes occupés à tendre de fortes toiles sur les panneaux. Mais il était déjà trop tard. On contournait une île et soudain on reçut le vent par le travers avant.

Le *Polarlys* fit une brusque embardée et la lourde glacière, qui n'avait pas encore été arrimée, brisa les crochets la maintenant sur le pont, glissa à bâbord.

Un homme faillit être écrasé. Il y eut une courte panique, car l'instant d'après le navire se couchait sur tribord et le meuble, qui avait deux mètres de haut, autant de large, et qui était en chêne épais, doublé de plomb, recommença sa promenade menaçante.

Petersen descendit en courant, saisit le bout d'un filin et se mit, comme les quatre hommes, à la poursuite de la glacière. Comme ils allaient enfin l'immobiliser, elle s'échappa une dernière fois et, après avoir heurté un hauban, passa par-dessus bord, disparut dans les remous.

On ne s'aperçut de l'accident qu'en entendant des hurlements tout à l'avant du vapeur.

Le hauban, sous le choc, s'était brisé net. Faisant fouet, il avait atteint le Lapon, toujours assis sur le cabestan, et lui avait cassé une omoplate.

Le malheureux lui-même n'avait rien vu et était d'autant plus affolé qu'il ne comprenait pas ce qui lui était arrivé.

— Portez-le dans une cabine ! Vite !... Prévenez Evjen...

Car à Kirkenes, où il n'y a pas de médecin, il arrivait souvent à Bell Evjen de donner les premiers soins à des ouvriers blessés.

On naviguait dans un couloir étroit, entre deux îles. Les lames étaient courtes mais, à quelques encablures, c'était la mer libre, sans abri, où on apercevait des creux vertigineux.

Petersen rencontra le premier officier que les chocs avaient arraché à son sommeil et qui accourait.

— Voulez-vous vous occuper du blessé ?... Je monte là-haut...

Vriens n'avait pas bougé. Le dos collé à la cloison ripolinée de la chambre de veille, il regardait droit devant lui. Sa casquette s'était envolée et la bise ramenait ses cheveux blonds sur son front.

Il devait clore à demi les paupières, pour empêcher la poussière de glace dont le vent était chargé de l'aveugler.

— Que se passe-t-il ? murmura le capitaine en observant le compas.

Une fois de plus, comme à Hambourg, c'était la

série ! La glacière d'abord ! Le Lapon blessé ensuite !

Et voilà que la petite ampoule électrique éclairant la rose du compas se ternissait. Peu à peu les filaments apparaissaient, rougeâtres, puis bruns. Et enfin on ne voyait plus rien !

Il se pencha pour s'assurer qu'il en était ainsi de toutes les lampes. Le halo lumineux qui entourait habituellement le navire avait disparu.

— Ralentissez les machines... Soixante tours. Tant que l'on sache...

On fut bientôt renseigné. Le premier officier arrivait en courant.

— Ce sont les accus qui se sont vidés d'un seul coup. Un court-circuit a dû se produire quelque part...

— Et les dynamos ?

— Le chef y travaille, mais il prétend qu'elles ne sont pas en ordre.

Petersen descendit au fumoir où le steward allumait les deux lampes à pétrole montées sur cardan. Katia était assise dans un pan d'ombre, toute seule. Elle se tenait la tête à deux mains et il était impossible de saisir son regard.

— Le Lapon ? demanda le capitaine au steward.

— Dans la première cabine de tribord. M. Evjen est près de lui...

Il s'y rendit, entendit des hurlements à plus de vingt mètres. Evjen, manches troussées, palpait l'épaule du blessé de ses longues mains blanches qui avaient des gestes adroits de chirurgien.

— Grave ?...

— L'omoplate cassée net... Et je ne peux rien faire qu'immobiliser le dos par une planche... Il faudra le conduire à l'hôpital de Tromsö... Quand y serons-nous ?

— Vers minuit...

— Vous n'avez pas de morphine ?...

Petersen tressaillit, sans se rendre compte tout de suite de la raison de son malaise, regarda Evjen d'un air soupçonneux, s'en voulut de ce rapprochement machinal avec l'assassin de Marie Baron.

Jamais l'atmosphère à bord n'avait été aussi trouble. Les couloirs étaient à peine éclairés par des lampes à pétrole. Dans les cabines, il n'y avait que des bougies.

Et le Lapon qui criait éperdument, le dos nu, ses vêtements bariolés jetés par terre, constituait un spectacle d'autant plus pénible qu'à chaque coup de roulis l'homme était lancé contre la cloison et que tous ses traits se tordaient de douleur.

Pour bien faire, le capitaine eût dû aller encore jusqu'aux machines afin de s'assurer que la dynamo était hors d'état. Mais il n'était pas tranquille à l'idée que Vriens restait seul avec le pilote sur la passerelle.

Son esprit était partout à la fois.

— Pourvu que Jennings ne dégringole pas en bas

de l'échelle et ne se blesse pas à l'arbre de transmission !...

Et Schuttringer ? Il ne l'avait pas vu.

Est-ce que Krull était à son poste ?

Tout cela à l'instant précis où la vérité était sur le point de se faire jour, où, en tout cas, on possédait enfin quelques données positives.

Le second officier l'appelait sur le pont.

— Nous ne pouvons pas continuer à marcher à soixante tours... La mer nous drosse...

— Je monte...

Il n'avait pas encore déjeuné. En passant devant sa cabine, il y prit ses bottes à semelles de bois, car il pressentait que ce n'était pas près de finir.

Il demanda au steward qui passait :

— Schuttringer ?

— Je l'ai vu tout à l'heure sur le pont avec quelqu'un...

— Avec qui ?... Le soutier ?...

— Peut-être... Je n'ai pas fait attention...

Tant pis ! Petersen ne pouvait s'occuper à la fois de son bateau et de l'assassin.

— Quatre-vingts tours... Cent... commanda-t-il en arrivant près du disque du télégraphe. Où sommes-nous au juste ?

— On doit voir apparaître le feu de Lödingen...

De telles bourrasques déferlaient que Petersen dut imiter Vriens et le pilote, se coller à la cloison. A chaque coup de roulis, les trois dos, avec ensemble, se détachaient, oscillaient un instant, puis heurtaient la tôle peinte.

— Rudolph Silberman... L'assassin de Marie Baron... Le neveu et le meurtrier du conseiller von Sternberg...

Le capitaine, pour la vingtième fois peut-être, regarda Vriens à la dérobée. Car il pouvait être Silberman ! Personne, à Hambourg, ne l'avait vu auparavant.

Un jeune homme arrivait de Delfzijl pour prendre le poste de troisième officier à bord du *Polarlys*. On ne le laissait pas arriver à destination. Par un moyen ou par un autre, Silberman adoptait sa personnalité et se présentait à sa place...

— Non ! gronda soudain le capitaine à mi-voix, en évoquant la photographie du bateau-école.

Et pourtant, de tous ceux qui pouvaient être Silberman, Vriens n'était-il pas celui qui avait eu la conduite la plus étrange ?

D'abord, il était l'amant de Katia. Et Katia, elle aussi, pouvait être soupçonnée d'avoir assisté à la tragique orgie de la rue Delambre.

Etait-il devenu son amant à bord ? L'était-il auparavant ?

Et pourquoi, tous deux, avaient-ils imaginé cet Ericksen fantôme, qu'ils avaient d'abord fait aller et venir sur le *Polarlys* pour le supprimer ensuite, sous la forme d'un sac de charbon, à Stavanger ?

Katia n'avait pas un centime et un vol était commis à bord ! Et la plus grande partie de la somme volée était retrouvée chez son amant !

— Un feu, capitaine...

— Un quart tribord... Il vaut mieux passer au large de la Pointe-des-Baleines...

Il essayait de reprendre le fil de ses idées, s'impatientait de se sentir incapable d'un raisonnement serré.

Ses yeux, comme ceux de ses compagnons, scrutaient l'obscurité pour y découvrir les balises.

Car on naviguait à l'estime. Tout le long de la côte, qu'on longeait à deux milles au large à peine, il y avait des îles et des récifs qui ne laissaient que des passes étroites où bouillonnaient des courants contraires.

La question était de découvrir à temps les feux verts, rouges ou blancs qui clignotaient au sommet des balises.

Les trois hommes restaient un quart d'heure, une demi-heure, sans desserrer les dents. Puis quelqu'un montrait un point de l'espace où les autres ne tardaient pas à voir poindre une lueur. Alors un nom était prononcé :

— Stokmarknes... Sortland...

— Si Vriens est Silberman... reprenait le capitaine.

Et les sourcils froncés, le front barré de rides profondes, il tentait de récapituler les événements et de les expliquer à la lumière de cette hypothèse.

Malgré ces préoccupations, il ne ressentait aucun malaise de la promiscuité du jeune homme, que parfois un coup de roulis lançait contre son épaule.

— Si Krull...

Mais pourquoi Krull avait-il révélé le coup du sac de briquettes ? Est-ce que, par hasard, il aurait menti ? Est-ce qu'un certain Ericksen, ou se donnant pour tel, avait bien sauté à l'eau à Stavanger ?

On n'avait pas retrouvé son corps, mais, dans les ports, c'est chose fréquente. Les cadavres s'accrochent à de vieux filins traînant au fond de l'eau, à une ancre, ou sont emportés vers le large par les courants de marée.

— Capitaine...

Arraché à ses pensées, Petersen tressaillit, aperçut le steward qui s'avançait prudemment, effrayé par les soubresauts du bateau et surtout par le spectacle de l'eau qui courait le long des flancs, blanchâtre, animée, eût-on dit, d'une vitesse insensée.

— C'est l'inspecteur...

— Où est-il ?...

— Dans sa cabine... Il est malade... Il demande à vous parler tout de suite...

Le capitaine s'assura du cap, regarda le pilote et Vriens, puis l'homme de la timonerie qui n'était qu'une ombre blafarde dans l'ombre de sa cage de verre.

Il descendit l'échelle, aperçut Katia, toujours à la même place, dans un coin du fumoir où le verre d'une des lampes s'était noirci.

C'était crispant, cette atmosphère irréelle ! Toutes ces ombres anormales peuplées de mystère...

Que pouvait-elle bien faire là ? Est-ce qu'elle pleurait ? Est-ce qu'elle se moquait du monde ? Avait-elle le mal de mer, elle aussi ?

Jamais le *Polarlys* n'avait été aussi morne, aussi inquiétant. Jusqu'à cette glacière qui avait mis une véritable perfidie dans ses sursauts !

Quatre-vingt-dix-neuf fois sur cent le hauban brisé n'eût atteint personne ! Il fallait que justement un Lapon, malgré le froid, la bise, les embruns qui gelaient à mesure qu'ils tombaient sur le pont, allât s'asseoir sur le cabestan !

Et il ne comprenait pas un mot de norvégien ! On ne pouvait rien lui dire ! Il lançait des regards hargneux autour de lui comme si tout l'équipage l'eût pris en traître !

Est-ce que cela n'avait pas commencé dès Hambourg, avec ce câble qui s'était cassé, lui aussi, ce brouillard crasseux, le retour d'un Vriens ivre mort et la péniche qu'on avait failli envoyer par le fond ?

— A l'autre, maintenant !

Et Petersen ouvrit la porte de la cabine de l'inspecteur, trouva celui-ci penché au-dessus de la cuvette de carton destinée aux passagers atteints du mal de mer.

Il n'y avait plus que trois centimètres de bougie. Elle éclairait un visage défait, des yeux larmoyants, une bouche amère.

— Si seulement je pouvais vomir !... C'est une terrible tempête, n'est-ce pas ?...

— Jusqu'ici, ce n'est rien...

— Vous croyez que... ?

— Vous m'avez appelé ?...

— Oui... Attendez... Je ne sais comment me mettre... Quand je suis couché, il me semble que c'est encore pis... Il n'y a vraiment pas de remède ?... Attendez, capitaine !... Je suis allé en bas... Je crois bien que j'ai failli me tuer, avec ces échelles de fer... J'ai fouillé le sac de Krull... J'y ai trouvé ceci...

Il montrait quelques pièces d'or qui se trouvaient sur la tablette, près d'une serviette mouillée.

— M. Evjen les a reconnues... Ce sont bien les siennes...

— Krull vous a vu ?

— Il n'était pas là... Il paraît qu'il venait d'aller respirer sur le pont... A Tromsö, il faudra l'empê-cher de s'enfuir... Je ne sais pas si je serai en état... Voyez !...

Il resta un moment immobile au-dessus du baquet. Sa poitrine fut tiraillée par trois ou quatre spasmes tandis qu'il ouvrait la bouche.

— Voilà !... Impossible !... Et la tête me tourne... Qu'est-ce que c'est ?...

Il avait sursauté, l'oreille tendue. On entendait un vacarme continu sur le pont.

— Une vague...

Petersen, lui aussi, était soucieux, car il compre-nait que cette vague-là avait atteint la passerelle.

— Ne vous agitez pas...

— Non... Je...

Il hésita à remonter là-haut, se dirigea vivement vers la chambre des machines où le chef mécanicien travaillait toujours à la dynamo.

— Réparée ?

— Rien à faire tant qu'on ne sera pas au port...

— Krull est à son poste ?

Le chef se tourna vers la chaufferie, transmit la question. Le chauffeur montra un instant sa tête noircie dans l'entrebâillement de la porte de fer et se répandit en invectives.

Il y avait plus de deux heures que Krull avait disparu, et cela alors qu'on avait besoin de plus de pression que jamais. Le second soutier ne pouvait suffire. Le chauffeur réclamait un homme, n'importe qui, pour charrier de la houille.

— Il n'est pas dans sa couchette ?

— Il n'est nulle part...

— Je vais vous envoyer un matelot de pont...

La salle des machines n'était pas l'endroit le moins sinistre, ainsi éclairée au pétrole, avec les hommes qui devaient faire des prodiges d'équilibre pour ne pas être happés par une transmission.

Au moment où il remettait les pieds sur le pont, Petersen jura, d'énervement, comme si une kyrielle de gros mots eût pu le soulager.

Il attrapa au vol un homme qui passait.

— Va donner un coup de main dans la soute !

— Moi ?... Mais il faut que je...

— Va !

Ce n'était pas le moment de discuter. En se penchant, il aperçut une balise rouge qui annonçait les récifs de Risotyhamm. Bell Evjen le cherchait. Il n'était pas fort d'aplomb, lui non plus. Ses narines étaient entourées de ce cerne jaunâtre et luisant qui annonce le mal de mer.

— Un instant, capitaine... Il vient de se passer un petit incident... Comme je vous l'ai annoncé, j'ai fait une piqûre au blessé, qui n'aurait pu supporter la douleur... Le steward m'avait apporté la pharmacie, que j'ai laissée dans la cabine...

— Il s'est empoisonné ?

Petersen s'attendait à tout, aux malheurs les plus invraisemblables. Du moment que la série était si bien engagée !...

— Non... Il y avait une boîte de six ampoules de morphine... Elle a disparu... Je n'ai pas non plus retrouvé la seringue...

— Qui est entré dans la cabine ?

— Il n'y aurait que le Lapon pour nous l'apprendre... Et il ne comprend rien de ce qu'on lui dit... Il est persuadé qu'on veut le tuer et il se tasse au fond de sa couchette à la moindre approche...

— Le steward n'a rien vu ?

— Il était sur la passerelle, dit-il...

— Bon !

Petersen gravit lourdement l'échelle, arriva trempé près du pilote et de Vriens, car une vague l'avait atteint en plein dos à mi-chemin.

Sans mot dire, il se cala entre eux deux, contre la cloison, suivit des yeux, avec une étrange ironie, une vague qui arrivait de travers, si haute qu'elle cassa une des deux amarres d'un canot suspendu sous la cheminée, entre les portemanteaux.

A minuit, il était toujours à la même place, transi, la bouche hargneuse, à guetter les balises.

Il y avait trois heures qu'il ne fumait pas, parce qu'il eût fallu retirer ses mains de ses poches, ouvrir son manteau et entrer dans la timonerie pour frotter l'allumette.

Des stalactites pendaient aux haubans et à l'étai du mât de charge et, sur le gaillard d'avant, les lames successives avaient laissé un iceberg luisant, bleuâtre, arrondi comme une méduse monstrueuse.

10

Tromsö

— Vriens !...

Le jeune homme se retourna lentement, encore que cet appel, après un silence de plusieurs heures, fût inattendu.

— Peter Krull est introuvable... Peut-être s'est-il enfui à Svolvaer...

Ce fut Petersen qui eut honte de son regard scrutateur devant le visage du jeune homme qui était buriné par la fatigue, plus triste qu'anxieux, avec, peut-être, quelque chose de mâle qu'on y sentait pour la première fois.

L'intention du capitaine avait été d'arracher à son compagnon un aveu quelconque, une phrase révélatrice. Mais il comprit que ce n'en était ni l'heure, ni le lieu. A sa droite, le pilote emmitouflé dans ses fourrures tendait le cou vers l'obscurité où c'était miracle qu'à force de vouloir voir des lumières il n'en vît pas en imagination.

Dans sa cage, le timonier, épuisé, se cramponnait à la roue de cuivre, sans quitter le compas du regard.

Et toujours, de dix en dix secondes, ces grands chocs qui ébranlaient le *Polarlys à* en briser les membrures, cet effort de chacun pour garder son équilibre.

Trois vagues, coup sur coup, atteignirent le sommet de la cheminée à bandes rouges et blanches, et la troisième arracha le canot de sauvetage qui ne tenait plus que par un palan, l'emporta dans son bouillonnement.

— Capitaine !

Le pilote concentrait visiblement son attention.

— Vous comprenez ce qu'ils disent, là-bas ?

Et il désignait des feux mouvants qu'il fallait quelques instants pour distinguer.

— Déjà Tromsö ? s'étonna Petersen.

— Tromsö, oui ! Mais je jurerais qu'ils nous ordonnent de filer au large... Vous n'avez pas vu ?... Attendez !... Ils recommencent... Trois blancs... Un rouge... Un blanc...

— Deux blancs ! rectifia Vriens d'une voix mate.

— Mais après ?... Vous avez vu ?...

Le capitaine s'était avancé jusqu'à la rambarde qu'il tint à deux mains, ce qui ne l'empêcha pas de chanceler tout en recevant une gerbe d'embruns au visage.

— Stoppez les machines !... commanda-t-il. Je ne suis pas encore sûr, mais...

Le sémaphore, là-bas, dans la nuit, répétait inlassablement le message à l'aide de lumières intermittentes.

— Il faut leur répondre... Je parie que nos fanaux ne sont pas prêts...

Il regretta ces mots, car Vriens, de lui-même, était déjà dans la timonerie où il allumait les lampes.

— Envoyez-leur : compris !

Et, au pilote qui l'avait rejoint :

— Ils nous disent de stopper en rade. La passe est obstruée par un chalutier qui a coulé ce soir même en plein travers...

Il saisit la manette du télégraphe, transmit aux machines :

— *En avant... Demi...*

151

On ne voyait à nouveau plus rien. Puis on distingua un vague halo lumineux et le *Polarlys* lança trois longs hurlements de sirène.

Tromsö était là sur la gauche, derrière une ceinture de roches entre lesquelles la passe était juste assez large pour un vapeur de moyen tonnage. On devait s'agiter sur les jetées, autour de l'épave. On entendait le grincement d'une grue.

Et le courant, insensiblement, drossait le navire vers les récifs. Il fallut remettre en marche, stopper, battre arrière, stopper encore, ce qui n'empêcha pas le vapeur d'être pris de travers et d'avoir toutes les peines du monde à se remettre en ligne.

Le second officier était accouru.

— Ils vont nous envoyer une vedette avec les sacs postaux ! lui dit Petersen. Parez l'échelle de coupée... Qu'on débarque le Lapon aussi doucement que possible...

Il était presque satisfait de ce nouvel avatar, car, à Tromsö où il connaissait tout le monde et où l'agent sédentaire de la B.D.S. était un gai compagnon, il lui eût fallu parler, serrer des mains, alors qu'il n'en avait nulle envie.

On entendit bourdonner le moteur de la vedette à pétrole bien avant de voir son feu blanc glisser de l'arrière à l'avant. Et ce fut toute la série des manœuvres ennuyeuses : *Avant ! Stop ! Arrière ! Doucement ! Avant...*

Dix fois la vedette fut à quelques centimètres de l'échelle. Dix fois le flot la repoussa.

Enfin on put l'amarrer. Deux hommes en ciré sautèrent sur le pont et Petersen marcha à leur rencontre, leur serra la main.

— Comment est-ce arrivé ?

— Un chalutier tout neuf, avec un magnifique *Diesel,* qui allait pour la première fois faire la morue au sud du Spitzberg... Naturellement, pas de pilote à bord !... Pas un homme connaissant les parages !... Les Allemands ne se fient qu'à leurs cartes... Ce qui ne les a pas empêchés de se mettre au sec dans la passe...

— Des morts ?

— Un mousse de quinze ans, qui s'est jeté à l'eau au moment du choc... On discute, là-bas, pour savoir si on va faire sauter le bateau à la dynamite...

Le postier apportait les sacs. Trois hommes transportaient le Lapon avec précaution. Mais l'homme, à qui il était impossible de faire comprendre ce qu'on faisait, se débattait de toute sa vigueur, poussait des hurlements inhumains.

— A l'hôpital, hein !... Tout de suite...

Ce furent d'autres difficultés pour le descendre dans la vedette.

En fin de compte, tant il se débattait, il y tomba de deux mètres de haut, la tête sur le plat-bord, et s'évanouit.

— Vous savez qu'on ne distingue pas vos feux de position à une encablure ?

— Je sais ! grommela Petersen.

— Attention ! Il y a deux charbonniers anglais qui descendent de Kirkenes et qui sont annoncés pour cette nuit...

— Oui...

Il avait hâte d'en avoir fini. Le *Polarlys* se rapprochait dangereusement de la ville dont on voyait les lumières à travers le brouillard de glace.

Une neige fine recommençait à tomber, piquant la peau comme des fléchettes, s'infiltrant dans les bottes et dans les habits.

Le capitaine n'avait cessé d'observer les allées et venues autour de la vedette. Au moment où elle larguait ses amarres, il compta les ombres à l'intérieur, donna le signal du départ.

C'était Vriens qui dirigeait la manœuvre sur la passerelle, et Petersen tendit l'oreille avec une certaine inquiétude. Mais l'hélice commença à battre l'eau correctement. A peine éloigné de l'embarcation, le navire prit deux quarts à tribord, puis le télégraphe commanda quatre-vingts et enfin cent vingt tours aux machines.

Il devait être pâle, là-haut, la main sur la manette, le regard planté dans l'obscurité où l'on ne distinguait que les crêtes laiteuses des vagues les plus proches !

Au lieu de monter tout de suite, Petersen entra dans la salle à manger, trouva le steward étendu sur une banquette, livide.

— Ça ne va pas ?...

— Vous savez, moi, c'est toujours la même chose... Je supporte un peu de roulis... Mais ça !...

— Tu n'as vu personne ?

— M. Evjen m'a sonné pour demander de l'eau minérale...

— Malade ?

— Un peu !... Il tient quand même... Il allait se coucher...

— Les autres ?

— Je ne sais pas... Tout à l'heure, l'inspecteur a essayé de sortir, mais il a dû rentrer aussitôt... Il est encore plus patraque que moi...

Le verre de lampe était cassé, la flamme en veilleuse. Le capitaine regarda le couloir à peine éclairé et se dirigea soudain vers la cabine d'Arnold Schuttringer. Il fut sur le point de frapper, mais il haussa les épaules, ouvrit.

L'Allemand, qui avait retiré ses lunettes et dont les yeux, vus ainsi, étaient d'une grandeur normale, était assis sur le bord de sa couchette, le front en sueur.

Un regard suffit au capitaine pour s'assurer qu'il avait eu recours au baquet de carton huilé qui traînait encore au milieu du chemin.

— A quelle heure serons-nous à Tromsö ?... Quelle manœuvre vient-on de faire ?...

— Tromsö est dépassé.

— Vous dites ?

Il s'était levé d'une détente, le visage presque menaçant à force d'être hargneux.

— On a dépassé Tromsö ?... Sans faire escale ?...

La bougie éclairait mal. Et pourtant on pouvait voir les gouttes de sueur gicler une à une des pores de la peau, sur le front irrégulier de Schuttringer.

— Un chalutier a coulé ce soir dans la passe...

— Mais alors ?...

— Le courrier a été apporté à bord... Le fret sera débarqué au retour...

C'était bien la première fois qu'il perdait son sang-froid, manifestait une agitation aussi intense. Il gronda :

— Je serais curieux de savoir jusqu'à quel point la Compagnie a le droit...

— Vous vouliez descendre à Tromsö ?

— Télégraphier...

— Si vous l'aviez dit, l'employé de la poste est venu à bord. Peut-être était-ce pour demander des fonds en Allemagne ?

Le jeune homme ne répondit pas.

— Dans ce cas, je crois pouvoir vous affirmer que votre argent ne tardera pas à être retrouvé... Déjà on a mis la main sur des pièces d'or cachées dans la paillasse de Krull, le soutier... Il se terre lui-même dans quelque coin du bateau...

— Merci ! dit sèchement Schuttringer, en faisant un geste pour saisir la poignée de la porte et la refermer.

Petersen s'éloigna tête basse, avec un tressaillement chaque fois que son bateau recevait un choc plus violent. S'il eût eu des hommes sous la main, il eût donné l'ordre de retrouver Peter Krull, coûte que coûte, car il avait la certitude qu'il était encore à bord au départ de Svolvaer.

Il gravit lentement l'escalier qui le conduisit à la porte du fumoir, distingua, dans l'ombre, un visage tourné vers lui.

— Capitaine...

C'était la voix de Katia, encore hésitante. Il ne répondit pas, resta debout dans l'entrebâillement de l'huis.

— Ecoutez-moi... Il faut que je parle à Vriens, rien qu'un instant... Il est là-haut, n'est-ce pas ?...

Et, comme il ne disait toujours rien :

— Je vous en supplie... Il n'a pas volé, je le jure !... Il faudra que tout cela s'explique... Est-ce qu'on a quitté Tromsö ?...

— Dépassé, sans y faire escale...

Alors, elle se leva, fit vivement quelques pas vers lui. Elle était impressionnante ainsi, dans sa robe noire qui se confondait avec l'obscurité, le visage déformé par l'étrange éclairage.

Petersen remarqua que le bouton sur le front était violacé. Les lèvres sèches, gercées, trahissaient la fièvre.

— Ce n'est pas possible !... Dites !... Pourquoi ?... Quand s'arrêtera-t-on à nouveau ?...

— Demain soir, à Hammerfest...

Elle s'était agrippée à lui et il la sentait trembler.

— Mais alors...

Elle se passa la main sur le front. Les traits douloureux, elle gémit, suppliante :

— Qui est encore à bord ?

— Tout le monde... Ou plutôt il n'y a qu'un soutier qui ait disparu... Un certain Peter Krull.

Il ne la quittait pas des yeux. Et ses jambes vacillaient d'impatience à l'idée que d'une seconde à l'autre il pouvait être appelé dehors. Sa place était sur la passerelle. Est-ce que Vriens et le pilote verraient le feu de Skjervoy, un des plus difficiles à distinguer ?

En même temps, il sentait que c'était une minute unique. Son interlocutrice était à bout. L'angoisse, la tempête avaient usé ses dernières forces de résistance.

Mais il ne fallait pas prononcer une phrase maladroite. Elle était encore capable de se raidir, de recouvrer toute sa présence d'esprit.

Il dégouttait d'eau, empêtré dans sa peau de bique détrempée et dans ses grosses bottes qui lui faisaient des jambes comme des colonnes.

— Je puis me charger de votre commission pour Vriens... Par le fait des billets retrouvés chez lui, il est virtuellement en état d'arrestation... A Hammerfest, il sera transféré à...

— Non ! Non ! s'impatienta-t-elle. Taisez-vous... Laissez-moi lui parler, moi... ou plutôt...

Elle regarda autour d'elle comme pour se raccrocher à quelque chose.

— Il sera poursuivi pour vol d'abord. Il aura à prouver ensuite qu'il n'a rien de commun avec un certain Rudolph Silberman...

Elle recula d'un pas, le regarda durement dans les yeux.

— Qu'est-ce que vous dites ?

— Je parle de l'assassin de Marie Baron, du meurtrier et du neveu du conseiller von Sternberg... Rudolph Silberman, ingénieur à Düsseldorf, embarqué sur le *Polarlys* sous un faux nom.

Elle s'assit. Chose étrange, elle se montrait soudain d'un calme tel que le capitaine s'en effraya.

Elle était à deux mètres de lui, un coude sur la table où il y avait encore une bouteille vide et, le menton dans la main, elle fixait le plancher.

— Qu'est-ce que vous savez encore ?...

Elle rejeta en arrière ses cheveux qui lui tombaient sur le visage, chercha machinalement son sac pour y prendre une cigarette. Mais elle avait dû le laisser dans sa cabine.

Il y eut à ce moment un tel mouvement de roulis qu'elle fût tombée avec sa chaise si elle ne se fût retenue à la table et que Petersen lui-même dut saisir le chambranle de la porte.

La sirène se mettait à hurler. Le capitaine avait envie d'être là-haut. Il gardait sur la rétine la hantise de l'océan noir où il eût voulu chercher le feu de Skjervoy.

— Un instant encore... s'accorda-t-il à lui-même.

Et, à haute voix :

— Silberman, accompagné d'une femme, a fui de Paris à Hambourg, a pris passage sur le *Polarlys* en faisant l'impossible pour brouiller sa piste, en inventant même un passager...

Elle rit nerveusement.

— Et puis ?...

— Depuis Hambourg, il ruse, s'évertue à fausser les données du problème... Et sa compagne n'a pas cessé de l'aider... Il a tué Sternberg... Peut-être, maintenant qu'il se sent traqué, va-t-il encore essayer de...

— Taisez-vous...

Et déjà c'en était fini de son calme. Elle déchirait du bout des ongles un petit mouchoir bleuâtre.

— Laissez-moi parler à Vriens, capitaine !... Ou plutôt... Non !... C'est inutile !... Tout est inutile, *maintenant*...

— Silberman est votre amant, n'est-ce pas ?

— Taisez-vous !... Partez !...

— Répondez...

— Mais non !... Vous n'avez rien compris !... Allez...

— Qui est-ce ?

Elle était si nerveuse qu'un attouchement l'eût fait bondir. Ses lèvres rugueuses s'agitaient à vide.

— A quoi bon ?... Il est trop tard...

— Et si vous évitiez un nouveau crime ?...

— Laissez-moi, je vous en supplie !... De grâce !... Je vous jure que je ne peux pas... Dites à

Vriens... Il est innocent, même du vol, vous devez le croire... Dites-lui que...

Elle cherchait les mots en regardant autour d'elle avec égarement.

— ... que c'est fini... qu'il peut...

— Qu'il peut ?...

— Rien ! Je ne sais plus ! Vous ne voyez donc pas que je suis à bout, que j'ai mal partout, que... Partez !... Tant pis !...

Et d'un mouvement inattendu elle se coucha sur la banquette, de tout son long, la tête dans ses bras repliés, et se mit à sangloter convulsivement.

La sirène hurlait toujours, avec une insistance inexplicable. Petersen regarda les cheveux blonds de Katia, sa silhouette noire, hésita encore.

Mais il ne pouvait plus rester là. Du moins eût-il voulu laisser quelqu'un, Evjen, par exemple, auprès d'elle, car elle l'inquiétait.

Il n'avait pas le temps de descendre dans le couloir des cabines.

Il gagna la passerelle et reçut en passant deux paquets de mer. Comme il arrivait près de la timonerie, Vriens, sans qu'il fût besoin de le questionner, haleta :

— Ecoutez !... Par là...

Il montra l'espace.

— Un bruit de machine... Sans doute un des charbonniers... Il a répondu deux fois... On n'entend plus rien...

Il avait encore les doigts crispés sur la poignée de

la sirène. Les deux bateaux étaient enveloppés d'un tel nuage de neige qu'ils n'apercevraient leurs feux respectifs que quand il serait trop tard pour s'éviter.

— Soixante tours... Quarante !... commanda Petersen.

Le pilote lui-même, qui faisait la ligne depuis trente ans, laissait percer de l'anxiété.

— Ces Anglais se fichent des règlements !... Où peuvent-ils bien être ?...

Sans la tempête, les Anglais l'eussent entendu car au même instant un feu rouge glissait à moins de trente mètres du *Polarlys*. On distingua un as de pique sur une cheminée blanche, une dunette brillamment éclairée.

Indifférent à l'eau qui ruisselait sur ses vêtements, et comme si la sueur eût été moins supportable que les embruns, Vriens s'épongeait d'un mouchoir tout mouillé, tout en esquissant un pauvre sourire.

Petersen, qui était tout près de lui, devina un sanglot étouffé et il comprit, fut remué dans les meilleures fibres de lui-même, celles du marin.

C'était sa première traversée ! Et il était resté tout seul pendant plus d'un quart d'heure, les nerfs tendus, à guetter ce monstre de charbonnier filant vingt nœuds quelque part dans l'ombre.

Le feu rouge était passé comme un météore.

Et maintenant, Vriens devait avoir les jambes molles. Par un phénomène que Petersen connaissait bien, il était pris d'une peur rétrospective.

Un petit sanglot...

Il remettait son mouchoir dans sa poche, s'adossait à la cloison de la chambre de veille, cherchait à nouveau les feux dans la nuit.

— Vriens...

Petersen regretta d'avoir appelé, car il devinait le visage blême, nerveux, tiré, qui se tournait vers lui avec méfiance.

Et il eût voulu trouver quelque chose de gentil ! Non, d'apaisant...

Il n'avait pas encore tout compris. Mais il pressentait confusément le rôle du troisième officier.

— Capitaine ?...

La voix était rauque.

Alors Petersen poursuivit avec lassitude :

— La sirène !... Toutes les trente secondes... Il y a deux charbonniers d'annoncés... Donc il en reste un !

Sur ce terrain-là, il était trop maladroit et sa maladresse l'humiliait.

Mais aussi, c'est tellement difficile de dire à brûle-pourpoint, surtout dans de pareilles conditions, à un gamin :

— Vous savez... J'ai confiance en vous...

Surtout qu'il eût été capable d'ajouter :

— Pardonnez-moi d'avoir été si dur, mais...

Non, en mer, la capote ruisselante, les pieds gelés, on prononce plus facilement :

— La sirène !... Toutes les trente secondes...

Elle hurlait à déchirer les tympans.

La nuit de Hambourg

Il était huit heures, et un jour équivoque dessinait les contours des montagnes en blanc sur gris quand la détente se produisit. Déjà, depuis un certain temps, les bourrasques étaient moins violentes. Mais l'Atlantique restait houleux, couvert de grandes traînées blanches.

Le *Polarlys* virait enfin de bord, pénétrait dans un couloir abrité.

Et, bien que le vent sifflât encore dans les haubans, on avait une impression de calme plat.

Les nerfs, les muscles, les os étaient moulus. Les trois hommes, sur la passerelle, avaient les paupières qui picotaient et une douleur sourde à la nuque et dans les reins.

Le premier soin du capitaine fut de bourrer une pipe qui, dans sa poche, s'était remplie de petits cristaux de neige.

— Le second officier a dormi. Il va prendre notre place ! dit-il à Vriens qui, jusqu'au bout, avait fait appel à toute sa volonté pour ne pas tomber d'épuisement.

— Bien, capitaine...

Petersen jeta un coup d'œil au compas, au compteur de tours, au bateau entier qui émergeait de la nuit, plaqué de glace sur toutes ses faces.

Puis il fit quelques pas, suivi du jeune homme, s'arrêta pour le laisser passer le premier.

— Capitaine... commença alors Vriens en détournant la tête.

Il sentait évidemment que le regard de Petersen était cordial, encourageant, et cela semblait le mettre mal à l'aise.

— C'est vrai que Krull est descendu à Svolvaer ?

— Je ne le pense pas ! Il se cache à bord... Tout à l'heure, je le ferai rechercher...

Et soudain, en posant la main sur l'épaule de son compagnon :

— C'est son amant ?... Son mari ?...

Vriens baissa la tête, la redressa pour regarder le capitaine avec anxiété.

— Son frère... articula-t-il enfin à voix basse. Elle est innocente...

— Venez !...

Petersen lui fit descendre l'escalier, ouvrit la porte du fumoir. Et ils eurent honte l'un comme l'autre du spectacle qui s'offrait à eux. Une des deux lampes à pétrole brûlait toujours et tachait de jaune la grisaille de l'aube.

La bouteille d'eau minérale était tombée par terre et s'était brisée.

Sur une banquette, enfin, Katia dormait. Si on n'eût pas entendu les vibrations de son souffle, on eût pu croire qu'elle était morte.

Toute joliesse s'était envolée de ses traits que la fatigue avait durcis. Des cheveux collaient à ses tempes humides. Sa main droite pendait par terre.

Et, même dans le sommeil, elle gardait une expression douloureuse, inquiète. Ses lèvres avaient ce pli saumâtre que donne le mal de mer.

Vriens détourna la tête. Ce fut Petersen qui l'entraîna dans sa propre cabine, où la tempête avait fait quelques dégâts, renversant entre autres une bouteille d'encre qui avait taché le linoléum.

Le capitaine sonna.

— Asseyez-vous...

Il sentait encore des velléités de résistance chez son compagnon, mais de plus en plus faibles et, une fois assis sur la couchette, Vriens poussa un soupir de lassitude.

Le steward frappa à la porte, arborant déjà une veste propre. Ses cheveux gardaient les traces du peigne mouillé qu'il y avait passé.

— Allez dire au premier officier de mettre la main sur Krull, coûte que coûte...

Et au jeune homme, une fois la porte refermée :

— C'est fini, n'est-ce pas ?... Il a senti lui-même qu'il était traqué... Je pense qu'il a voulu quitter le *Polarlys* à Tromsö où, par le plus grand des hasards, nous n'avons pas fait escale... Sa sœur l'a compris...

Il lui tendit sa blague à tabac, et machinalement Vriens répondit :

— Je n'ai pas de pipe... Je ne fume que la cigarette...

Une lumière froide, qui soulignait l'affaissement des traits, tombait du hublot.

— Vous pouvez parler, maintenant, Vriens !... Je sais que vous n'avez pas tué, que vous n'avez pas davantage volé l'argent d'Evjen, ni celui de Schuttringer... Et pourtant, lorsque nous toucherons au port, je serai obligé, si les choses en restent là, de vous remettre entre les mains de la police... L'assassin s'est débattu jusqu'au bout... A l'heure qu'il est, il a perdu... On va nous l'amener d'un moment à l'autre...

Il s'était assis en face du jeune homme et un mince filet de fumée montait de sa pipe.

— C'est à Hambourg que vous l'avez rencontrée ?... Vous ne la connaissiez pas auparavant ?...

— Est-ce qu'on l'arrêtera aussi, elle ?... Dites ! Est-ce un crime de vouloir sauver son frère ?...

L'un et l'autre étaient hantés par le souvenir de la jeune femme qu'ils venaient de voir, ayant renoncé à toute coquetterie et même à toute féminité, littéralement écrasée par les événements.

— Je l'aime !... déclara Vriens, tandis que ses cils battaient précipitamment.

— C'était au *Kristall* ?...

— Non ! Je venais de descendre du train. Il était tard. Ne connaissant pas le port, je m'étais dirigé vers un hôtel... Je ne l'ai pas remarquée tout de suite... Le portier de nuit était un Hollandais et il m'a questionné pour remplir ma fiche, puis par curiosité... Nous avons causé... Je lui ai dit que je devais rejoindre un bateau où j'allais remplir les fonctions de troisième officier... Ce n'est qu'à la fin que j'ai vu qu'elle était assise sous le hall et qu'elle écoutait... Elle m'a demandé du feu...

Vriens se tut, esquissa un geste vague.

— Vous ne pouvez pas comprendre...

Cette fois, le sourire du capitaine fut franchement affectueux.

— Vous avez fait connaissance... Vous êtes sortis tous les deux...

— Ce n'est pas une femme comme les autres... Je ne sais pas comment vous dire...

Petersen l'imaginait si bien, à peine hors de l'école, entraîné brusquement dans le sillage d'une femme comme Katia ! Comment n'eût-il pas perdu la tête !

— Qu'est-ce qu'elle vous a demandé ?

— D'abord de céder ma place à son frère... Il serait venu à bord, sous mon nom... Elle m'a avoué qu'il avait eu un malheur, à Paris... Il s'adonne aux stupéfiants... Vous savez le reste... Une jeune fille est morte, au cours d'une séance. Alors, il fuyait... Bruxelles d'abord, où un ami leur a donné de l'argent... Puis Hambourg... Mais je ne pouvais pas, n'est-ce pas ?... J'ai dit que c'était impossible... Je me suis presque enfui... Je ne voulais plus la revoir, pour ne pas être tenté...

— Et elle est arrivée à bord, comme passagère ?

— Oui... Je n'avais pas vu son frère... Je pensais bien qu'il était, lui aussi, sur le bateau... Quand

Ericksen a disparu, j'ai eu la certitude que c'était lui...

— Katia vous a détrompé...

— Elle m'a avoué que c'était une ruse imaginée par son frère, un moyen, si une dénonciation arrivait de Paris au dernier moment, de faire tomber les soupçons sur un passager inexistant... C'est un camarade qui est venu le matin, en pardessus gris, prendre un billet pour Stavanger, sous le nom d'Ericksen, et déposer quelques bagages dans la cabine... Ensuite, il s'est éclipsé...

— Et Sternberg ?

Vriens avait à présent la tête entre les mains.

— Je ne sais pas... Elle ne voulait pas croire elle-même que c'était son frère qui l'avait tué... Elle m'a supplié de faire en sorte qu'on soupçonne Ericksen de s'être jeté à l'eau... Vous comprenez ?... Pour que l'enquête ne continue pas à bord... C'est moi qui ai rempli le sac de charbon... Je voulais fuir avec elle... Est-ce que je vous ai dit qu'ils n'allaient à Kirkenes que pour passer en Russie ?... Ils parlent le russe tous les deux, car leur mère est de Petrograd... La frontière, là-haut, est moins sévèrement gardée qu'ailleurs... L'extradition n'existe pas avec les Soviets...

Il n'y avait plus besoin de le questionner. C'était lui, maintenant, qui éprouvait le besoin de parler.

— A cet instant encore, je ne sais pas ce que je voudrais faire... Je vous jure, capitaine, que vous ne pouvez pas me comprendre... Il y a eu des moments où je crois que j'aurais été capable de vous tuer, parce que je sentais que vous finiriez par deviner...

— Elle ne vous a jamais dit qui était son frère ?

— Non ! Mais ce n'était pas par méfiance !... C'était plutôt de la délicatesse de sa part... Je me suis mis à épier tout le monde... Evjen, Schuttringer, surtout Peter Krull, que je voyais souvent rôder sur le pont... Je savais qu'ils n'avaient plus d'argent l'un et l'autre... Quand le vol a eu lieu, j'ai compris...

» Je prévoyais que cela n'irait pas jusqu'à Kirkenes... Ils ont eu la même idée... Katia m'a avoué que son frère, tout seul, essayerait de s'enfuir à Svolvaer ou à Tromsö...

» Pour cela, on devait soupçonner quelqu'un d'autre... Moi...

Il se leva, plus nerveux.

— Il faut que j'aille la voir, capitaine ! Je vous jure, sur la mémoire de ma mère, qu'elle est innocente, elle !... Elle tentait de sauver son frère, n'est-ce pas ?... Tenez ! quand elle a parlé de son anniversaire... Ce n'était pas vrai... Elle était inquiète, parce qu'elle venait d'apprendre qu'on ne croyait plus au suicide d'Ericksen, ni peut-être à son existence... Elle voulait créer une diversion... Et tout le monde restait froid !... C'était affreux...

— Votre mère est morte, Vriens ?

— Oui... A Java...

— Et vous êtes enfant unique ! Votre père n'a

plus que vous... J'ai vu sa photographie dans vos bagages...

Il ne conclut pas, entraîna son compagnon vers la porte.

— Peut-être est-il préférable que vous alliez dormir pendant que nous en finissons.

— Non ! Je ne veux pas...

— Alors, promettez-moi d'être un homme ! Vous portez un uniforme. Cette nuit...

— Cette nuit ?...

— Eh bien ! j'ai été content de vous... Vous avez fait honneur à votre école...

Vriens esquissa malgré lui un pâle sourire qu'il essaya de cacher en détournant la tête.

— Il faut maintenant que cela continue... Venez !

Un instant, Petersen avait eu l'impression qu'on écoutait à la porte. Mais, quand il l'ouvrit, il ne vit que Schuttringer, qui faisait les cent pas à l'autre bout du couloir, ne put distinguer que son dos, car il regardait obstinément de l'autre côté. Comme le capitaine et Vriens arrivaient sur le pont, une voix criait :

— Le canot... Là... Il y est !...

Et le premier officier passait en courant. On le suivit des yeux. On le vit grimper sur la passerelle, contourner la cheminée.

Il ne restait que trois canots de sauvetage sur quatre. Au moment où l'officier s'arrêtait, le taud de l'un d'eux se souleva et le soutier se dressa.

— C'est bon !... dit-il.

Petersen regarda Vriens, dont les narines s'étaient pincées. L'officier, un peu troublé, commandait :

— Descendez !... Sortez vos mains de vos poches...

Et, d'en bas, on avait l'impression que Krull riait d'un petit rire silencieux.

— Pas encore à Hammerfest ? questionna-t-il.

Personne ne lui répondit. Le steward, timidement, passait la tête par une porte.

— L'inspecteur n'est pas levé ?

— Il vient de sortir de sa cabine. Il m'a demandé à boire...

En effet, on voyait bientôt surgir Jennings, dont la première parole fut lancée sur un ton de triomphe :

— J'ai vomi, capitaine !...

Il rayonnait, encore un peu faiblard, pourtant. Il aperçut Krull qui descendait l'échelle, suivi du second et d'un matelot.

— On l'a retrouvé ?... Qu'est-ce qu'on va...

Il n'osa pas dire :

— Qu'est-ce qu'on va en faire ?...

Mais il regarda Petersen avec un certain embarras.

Il n'y avait que le soutier à sourire. L'impression dominante, chez tous ceux qui étaient présents, était la fatigue poussée à un degré douloureux.

172

Les paupières étaient rouges, les lèvres décolorées. Personne ne s'était rasé.

Au moment où Krull passait devant la porte du fumoir, celle-ci s'ouvrit et on vit paraître la silhouette fripée de Katia.

L'éclairage venait, non du ciel, mais de la réverbération d'une montagne neigeuse que l'on frôlait. Et c'était un jour livide, désespérant.

Katia regarda Krull avec hébétude, puis chercha Vriens des yeux, l'aperçut, détourna la tête.

— Dans le fumoir ! murmura Petersen après une courte hésitation.

Et le soutier y entra de lui-même, sans qu'on l'y poussât, passa la main dans sa chevelure en désordre, tâta sa barbe qui avait quatre centimètres.

— Voulez-vous prendre le quart ?

Le premier officier fit un signe de tête, disparut dans la direction de la passerelle, tandis que le capitaine entraînait Vriens et l'inspecteur dans le fumoir, dont il referma la porte.

Il y eut un moment de flottement. Petersen et Jennings se regardèrent. Lequel des deux allait prendre la parole ?

Katia avait reculé jusqu'au fond de la pièce. Puis, tout à coup, elle avait collé son visage à un des hublots.

— Rudolph Silberman, je vous arrête... prononça le policier dont la voix manquait d'autant plus de fermeté que le sourire ne disparaissait pas des lèvres du prisonnier.

Au même instant la jeune femme poussa un cri étouffé. Vriens se précipita vers un autre hublot, appela :

— Capitaine !...

On entendait les pas d'un matelot qui courait sur le pont-promenade.

Petersen ne vit presque rien. Il devina plutôt qu'il ne distingua nettement une forme humaine qui enjambait le bastingage et qui disparaissait.

Il ouvrit la porte, se pencha, entrevit par trois fois un crâne rasé qui émergeait de l'écume et qui, la troisième fois, était déjà tout à l'arrière du navire.

— Stop !... cria-t-il dans la direction de la passerelle. Arrière !...

Mais le second ne comprit pas, fit signe de répéter, mit les mains en cornet.

Quelque part, la voix de Peter Krull conseilla :

— Laissez-le donc !...

— Stop !...

Ce fut si brutal que le vapeur se cabra. Mais quand on fouilla des jumelles le sillage du *Polarlys* on n'aperçut plus rien que des remous crémeux.

Tout cela s'était passé avec une telle rapidité que chacun n'avait pu assister qu'à une toute petite partie des événements.

Et maintenant on se regardait avec une stupeur pénible. Evjen arrivait, rasé de frais, lui, avec un pli correct à son pantalon gris et des chaussures bien cirées.

— Que se passe-t-il ?... Pourquoi s'arrête-t-on ?...

174

Penché sur la main courante de la passerelle, l'officier de quart attendait un ordre.

— *Avant !...* finit par lui crier Petersen. *Avant toute !...*

Katia ne s'était pas évanouie, mais c'était un regard insensé qu'elle fixait sur la mer clapotante qui recommençait à glisser le long des flancs du bateau.

— Emmenez-la, Vriens... Mais pas de bêtises, n'est-ce pas ?

Petersen accompagna ces mots d'un tel regard que le jeune homme chercha des paroles de remerciement, n'en trouva pas, se contenta, lui aussi, de mettre tout ce qu'il pouvait de reconnaissance dans ses yeux.

Et le capitaine retira, arracha plutôt, sa peau de bique. Malgré les dix-sept degrés sous zéro, il était en nage.

— Entrez, Evjen... Fermez la porte...

Ils n'étaient plus que quatre dans le fumoir, où la lampe brûlait toujours. Le premier qui parla fut Krull.

— Vous avez compris ? questionna-t-il avec des intonations hargneuses dans la voix.

— Silberman ?... questionna naïvement Jennings.

— Vous ne l'avez pas vu sauter à l'eau ?... J'en avais assez ! Voilà la vérité...

— Silence ! interrompit Petersen.

Et d'une voix nette, l'air décidé :

— Vous m'avez dit que vous étiez avocat...

— Jadis, oui ! Au surplus, vous n'aurez qu'à consulter mon casier judiciaire... J'ai fait des bêtises... Avouez que je n'ai pas essayé de me donner pour un petit saint... Une histoire d'escroquerie et de cocaïne... Puis la dégringolade, terminée en plongeon... De la prison à Cologne et à Mannheim... Quand on arrive à une certaine profondeur, ce n'est pas la peine d'essayer de remonter... Comme ce n'est pas la peine que vous essayiez de comprendre...

» En deux mots, je ne suis pas Silberman, mais Krull... Je me suis embauché à bord du *Polarlys* parce que je n'avais plus un pfennig...

» Aucun mystère là-dedans... Ce n'est qu'une fois à bord, et même après le meurtre du conseiller, que j'ai compris qu'il se passait quelque chose d'intéressant...

» J'ai lu un journal français qui traînait et qui parlait d'une affaire de stupéfiants...

» Tandis que vous vous enferriez, j'ai compris tout de suite, parce que, quand on en use soi-même, il n'y a pas d'erreur possible...

» Vous n'avez donc jamais regardé en face la tête de Schuttringer ?... Rien que la petite crispation, ici, tenez... Il avait eu beau se raser, se faire une tête, mettre des lunettes avec lesquelles il ne voyait pas...

Et il montrait sa mâchoire, l'animait d'un mouvement saccadé.

— Ce petit frémissement-là, impossible de s'y tromper ! Comme il y a bien trois semaines que je n'avais pas vu la couleur de la cocaïne, je me suis présenté gentiment et je lui ai mis la puce à l'oreille...

» Il ne lui restait que douze paquets d'un gramme... Je lui en ai laissé deux...

» Vous n'avez pas encore l'air de comprendre ! De même que vous ne savez pas questionner les gens ! Il faut leur parler leur langue, parbleu...

» A un intoxiqué, on parle de la drogue... Et je vous jure que quand je lui ai dit deux mots de Marie Baron, il a saisi...

» Vous avez assisté à ses exercices de gymnastique, et tout... Eh bien ! rien que ça aurait suffi à me prouver que le garçon se cachait... Parce qu'un type qui prend de la « neige » n'a pas une allure pareille... Il se forçait...

» Il se donnait l'air du contraire de ce qu'il était, ce que tout le monde fait quand il se camoufle...

» J'ai tout deviné, petit à petit... D'abord qu'il était le frère de la petite dame... Pas aussi intoxiquée que lui... Mais enfin...

» Puis qu'il était affolé d'avoir tué son oncle... Mais là ! Affolé !... Terrorisé !... Capable de n'importe quoi pour s'en tirer...

Personne ne songeait à l'interrompre. On le regardait avec une certaine gêne. Evjen surtout, dont la silhouette raffinée contrastait étrangement avec celle du déchu.

— Ils se servaient du jeune officier pour détourner les soupçons... Comme pour le coup du sac...

» Car ce Silberman était un garçon intelligent, je vous prie de le croire... Un seul défaut : il tenait encore trop à sa situation sociale... Il se serait embarqué pour l'Amérique du Sud en qualité de chauffeur ou d'émigrant que tout était dit...

» Mais pour ça, il faut un apprentissage, une lente glissade... Rien que pour s'habituer à aller dans la rue sans faux col, tenez !...

» L'histoire de l'ami qui est venu prendre un billet et qui a disparu aussitôt... Une trouvaille ! Supposez que l'oncle Sternberg ne se soit douté de rien et ne soit pas monté à bord... Supposez même qu'à Stavanger ou à Bergen on ait appris qu'un certain Silberman se cachait à bord...

» Tout de suite on pensait à Ericksen et on laissait les autres passagers tranquilles...

» Un garçon capable de trouver ça et qui, néanmoins... Les nerfs, sans doute !... Un drôle de mélange de sang-froid et de trac...

» Ainsi, à Paris, quand il a vu mourir la petite il n'a pas laissé une trace derrière lui... Il a calculé qu'il faudrait un certain nombre de jours à la police pour toucher son ami Feinstein...

» Il paraît qu'il s'est arrêté à Bruxelles parce qu'il manquait d'argent... Il en a trouvé pour arriver à Hambourg, où il a dû taper son oncle... Mais tout cela avait pris du temps... Rien que trouver des passeports, par exemple, quand on n'est pas à la coule...

» D'un moment à l'autre, un télégramme pouvait arriver de Paris... Une semaine entière ! Cela a dû le détraquer et, quand il a vu son oncle monter à bord, il a fait l'imbécile... Car, à mon avis, Sternberg, qui venait de lire les journaux et de deviner, était là pour le tirer d'affaire et éviter que l'histoire ne lui fasse du tort à lui-même...

» Les nerfs !... Peut-être aussi la drogue... Dans ces cas-là, on en prend des doses massives.

» Je la lui soutirais gentiment... Je le voyais s'énerver...

» Il a surtout pris peur quand il a su que l'histoire du sac était percée à jour...

» Il lui fallait encore de l'argent... Il en a volé et il a eu l'adresse de se dire volé, lui qui n'avait plus une couronne...

» Son idée était d'arriver à Kirkenes coûte que coûte, en détournant les soupçons jusque-là par tous les moyens... Il comptait surtout sur le gamin, qui s'était toqué de sa sœur...

» A Svolvaer, il a aperçu un télégramme adressé à l'inspecteur... Et alors, sa frousse est devenue de la panique... Il est venu me trouver... Il voulait descendre à Tromsö et laisser Katia se débrouiller ensuite.

» Mais pour cela, il fallait qu'on le laisse aller à terre... Vous n'aviez pas l'air de croire très fort à la culpabilité de l'officier... Il ne restait que Schut-tringer ou moi à pouvoir être Silberman...

» Il m'a offert mille couronnes pour me laisser soupçonner pendant vingt-quatre heures... Les voici...

» Qu'est-ce que je risquais ? Un peu de prison ? J'en ai tiré vingt mois et ce n'est guère plus mauvais que la soute...

» J'ai marché... J'ai glissé les pièces d'or dans ma couchette et je suis allé m'étendre dans un des canots...

» Si le *Polarlys* s'était arrêté à Tromsö, c'était fini ! Vous m'arrêtiez mais vous finissiez bien par vous convaincre que je ne suis pas Silberman... Quant à lui, avec l'argent qu'il a eu soin de garder, il trouvait bien le moyen de gagner le continent, puis quelque petit coin tranquille... Des bateaux partent tous les jours de Narvik...

» Quand j'ai entendu qu'on ne faisait pas escale, j'ai eu envie de me montrer... Puis je lui ai laissé jouer sa chance jusqu'au bout...

— Inouï !... gronda entre ses dents Evjen qui examinait avec une curiosité croissante l'étrange échantillon d'humanité qu'il avait devant lui.

— Il n'y a rien d'inouï du tout... riposta Krull. Ou plutôt ce n'est inouï que pour des gens comme vous, qui ont une femme, des gosses, et pas de vice... Donnez-moi seulement deux mois et je vous fais courir aux quatre cent mille diables pour trouver une pincée de drogue... Il a eu de la malchance... Il a exagéré... La morphine n'est pas faite pour les gamines... Après, ma foi, c'est le trac qui l'a poussé... Et le trac est capable de vous faire faire n'importe quoi...

Il se tourna vers le hublot en haussant les épaules.

— Maintenant, il est tranquille ! conclut-il. Est-ce que je dois aller pelleter du charbon ?...

12

Else Silberman

La journée s'écoula dans une atmosphère oppressante. Le paysage, à lui seul, eût suffi à faire naître la neurasthénie. On suivait des passes étroites, qui s'emboîtaient les unes dans les autres comme les galeries d'un trou de taupe. Et le ciel était si bas qu'on avait l'impression d'un couvercle hermétiquement clos au-dessus des têtes.

Des montagnes blanches. De l'eau grise ou noire, selon les reflets. Parfois, très loin, une maison perdue, plantée sur des pilotis, et un petit bateau de sapin à l'ancre dans une crique.

Peter Krull avait regagné son poste après avoir salué ironiquement son auditoire.

Vers dix heures, trois hommes avaient pris place dans la salle à manger, sous le regard inquiet du steward : Petersen, Jennings et Evjen.

L'inspecteur, par hasard, s'était mis à la place de Schuttringer et à plusieurs reprises les deux autres détournèrent la tête.

— Un fou ! grommela soudain Evjen. Je me demande comment il a résisté à une pareille dose...

Car les cinq ampoules de morphine, volées dans la cabine du Lapon, avaient été retrouvées vides chez Schuttringer.

Avant de sauter par-dessus bord, il avait dû en avaler le contenu, car on n'avait pas revu la seringue.

Et, s'adressant à l'inspecteur :

— Qu'allez-vous faire de sa sœur ?

— Je ne sais pas... Il faut que je télégraphie à mes chefs... En somme, il y a deux crimes : celui de la rue Delambre, qui intéresse la police française, et le meurtre de Sternberg qui, commis à bord d'un navire norvégien dans les eaux internationales, ne regarde que nous... La complicité de Katia, dans l'un et l'autre de ces crimes, n'est guère établie...

Petersen ne disait rien, mangeait avec un appétit qui étonnait le steward.

Le reste de la journée se passa sans incidents. Evjen reprit, au fumoir, sa place habituelle, étala ses dossiers et les annota. Comme il rencontrait le capitaine, il lui dit :

— Bien entendu, à Kirkenes, vous dînez à la

182

maison, comme d'habitude... Ma femme sera enchantée... Vous savez que l'inspecteur est plus habile que je ne l'aurais cru... Il a encore retrouvé quatre mille couronnes dans une chaussure de Krull qui ne nous avait avoué que le cinquième de ce qu'il avait réellement touché...

Il y eut pourtant quelques allées et venues, surtout entre trois heures de l'après-midi et sept heures, alors que Jennings dormait, débarrassé enfin du mal de mer.

A plusieurs reprises, Vriens quitta la cabine de Katia, dont il ne sortait guère, et frappa à la porte du capitaine.

La troisième fois, Petersen lui dit :

— Bien entendu, vous ne maintenez pas votre démission ?...

Et le jeune homme ne répondit que par un signe de tête négatif.

— Dans ce cas, je puis vous remettre une avance sur vos appointements des trois premiers mois... A quatre cents couronnes par mois, cela fait douze cents couronnes...

— Mais... c'est la totalité de...

— Allez !...

A six heures, Petersen appela le steward.

— L'inspecteur ?...

— Il dort toujours... Il m'a demandé de le réveiller quand nous arriverons à Hammerfest... Je crois qu'il est temps que...

— Vous me servirez d'abord à dîner dans ma

cabine... Il n'a quand même rien à faire avant que nous soyons à quai...

On naviguait à nouveau dans la nuit. Mais la mer était à peine houleuse. L'accostage se fit sans un heurt, avec une douceur inhabituelle.

Les amarres étaient à peine lovées aux bittes que Petersen, après un regard au couloir, pénétra dans sa cabine et se mit à manger, non tant avec un féroce appétit qu'avec une application anormale.

Il commanda même du vin, ce qui ne lui arrivait jamais et ce qui obligea le steward à perdre près d'un quart d'heure pour trouver la clef de l'armoire où les spiritueux étaient enfermés.

En fin de compte, d'ailleurs, cette clef se trouva dans la poche même du capitaine qui s'excusa.

— Vous n'avez pas de fruits ?...

Les débardeurs déchargeaient des marchandises, en chargeaient d'autres.

Petersen finit par tirer sa montre de sa poche.

— Est-ce que Jennings ne vous a pas demandé de le réveiller ?

— Oui... Il faut que j'y aille...

De la ville, on ne voyait que quelques maisons de bois enfouies dans la neige jusqu'à mi-hauteur des fenêtres.

Le capitaine mangeait toujours. Par la porte entrouverte il vit passer Vriens qui revenait du dehors et qui ramenait un peu d'air glacé.

Au même instant, Jennings se montrait, encore endormi, la bouche pâteuse.

— Je n'en pouvais plus ! soupira-t-il. Je crois que j'aurais été capable de dormir quarante-huit heures... Où sommes-nous ?...

— Hammerfest...

— Depuis longtemps ?...

— Vingt bonnes minutes...

— Personne n'est descendu ?

— Je l'ignore... J'avais une telle faim que je me suis fait servir à dîner...

L'inspecteur sortit. On l'entendit aller et venir. Il revint quelques instants plus tard.

— Vous savez... Je ne trouve pas la jeune femme... Katia Storm...

— Vraiment ?...

— Je suis inquiet... Elle est capable de s'être jetée par-dessus bord, elle aussi... Je ferais mieux d'envoyer un télégramme à Stavanger...

Dix heures ?... Onze heures ?...

Le temps, quand on est là-haut, sur la passerelle, avec dix-huit et vingt degrés au-dessous de zéro, ne se mesure pas.

Ils étaient trois, adossés à la cloison de la chambre de veille. Petersen était au milieu. A sa droite, il avait le pilote, monstrueusement grossi par ses fourrures. A sa gauche, Vriens se tenait immobile, un peu trop raide.

Fut-ce un hasard ? Toujours est-il que la main du troisième officier, tandis que le *Polarlys* roulait lourdement d'un bord sur l'autre, toucha celle du capitaine, hésita, finit par l'étreindre.

— Partie ?... fit Petersen à travers son cache-nez.

— Elle a trouvé un traîneau... Un Lapon et deux rennes... Mais il y a toutes les montagnes à traverser...

La voix de Vriens était lourde de nostalgie, d'angoisses refoulées.

— Elle n'a pas essayé de... ? commença son compagnon.

— Elle m'a défendu de la suivre...

Puis il y eut un quart d'heure ou une heure de silence. Les yeux cherchaient les feux des balises. Une voix annonça :

— Honningsvaag...

Le premier port de l'océan Glacial...

Tandis que le pilote pénétrait dans la timonerie pour allumer sa pipe à l'abri du vent, Vriens prononça très vite :

— Vous savez... Elle m'a tout dit... Ils n'avaient plus d'argent... Ils n'osaient pas télégraphier à leur père, qui habite Berlin... Ils ont dû s'arrêter à Bruxelles, où ils avaient un ami... A Hambourg, ils ont frappé à dix portes... Puis, en désespoir de cause, Silberman est allé chez son oncle, Sternberg, à qui il a raconté une histoire... C'est ce qui l'a perdu... L'oncle a dû recevoir un peu plus tard les journaux de Paris... Il a une fille de quinze ans que Katia... ou plutôt Else, c'est son prénom, adorait.

Les feux de position les éclairaient de leurs rayons verts et rouges, car les dynamos étaient réparées.

On vit la flamme de l'allumette du pilote, son bonnet de fourrure, son visage penché.

— Else Silberman... répéta Vriens.

Et plus bas :

— Les parents de sa mère habitent près d'Arkhangelsk... Elle va essayer de...

Il tira une cigarette d'un étui d'or que Petersen reconnut.

— Avec neuf cents couronnes... Vous comprenez ?... S'ils vivent encore, ils ignorent son existence... Son père est remarié avec une actrice...

Ils étaient appuyés, épaule contre épaule, contre la cloison lisse et froide. Le pilote revenait à pas lourds en grommelant :

— Et la sirène !...

Ce fut le capitaine qui étendit le bras et qui tira trois fois la poignée pour annoncer l'arrivée du *Polarlys* à Honningsvaag, où l'on poussait déjà vers les pilotis des traîneaux chargés de morue.

Le profil de Vriens se découpait dans la lumière verte. La lèvre inférieure se soulevait.

Alors Petersen réunit en un seul faisceau maintes images : des jambes nerveuses, gainées de soie bien tendue, qu'il avait contemplées certain soir ; une jarretelle sombre tranchant sur la chair laiteuse ; le portrait agrandi de sa femme, au mur de sa cabine, et des gosses en blanc sur une toute petite photo d'amateur... La promotion de Delfzijl, enfin, gantée de clair, avec les plus jeunes élèves perchés dans les vergues... Et M. Vriens, le père, en costume colonial, devant une table Louis XVI...

— Ce n'est pas pour nous, mon vieux !... dit-il.

Mais il chercha en vain à exprimer un autre grouillement d'images : Schuttringer faisant ses exercices sur le pont... L'odieuse boucherie, dans la cabine de Sternberg...

Le même homme volant quelques ampoules, avalant la morphine, les yeux égarés, anxieux du moindre va-et-vient, sautant par-dessus la lisse...

Ou bien Peter Krull, qui avait eu une maison dans la Jacobstrasse et qui, une à une, huit heures durant, lançait dans un trou noir des pelletées de houille noire...

— Allons !... Vous voilà un homme...

Et il ne voulut pas voir le sourire de Vriens, un peu triste, un peu forcé, ni son regard qui errait vers les montagnes d'un blanc de cabanon où un traîneau devait s'acheminer, cahin-caha, kilomètre après kilomètre, vers la Finlande et la Russie.

Composition réalisée par JOUVE

IMPRIMÉ EN ESPAGNE PAR LIBERDUPLEX
Barcelone
Dépôt légal éditeur : 46340 - 06/2004
LIBRAIRIE GÉNÉRALE FRANÇAISE - 43, quai de Grenelle - 75015 Paris.
ISBN : 2 - 253 - 14306 - 5

TENDER NIBBLES . . .

"So. Are you going to see him again?" Sandy asked Tess.

"Who?"

"Cream Puff."

"I don't know. I'm not going to pursue it."

"Why not?"

"He's so young, Sandy. It's like playing."

"What's wrong with that, Tess? Just a little something sweet. Nothing serious."

"Just a little dessert?"

"Right. You deserve a treat now and then."

I popped a tiny cream puff into my mouth, savoring its sweetness. And that's how it was to be with Gregg: a little treat now and then, which never seemed quite real because I didn't understand what a treat I was for him. . . .

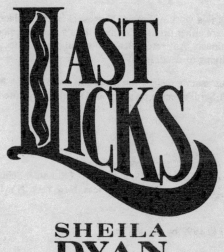

LAST LICKS

SHEILA DYAN

POCKET STAR BOOKS

New York   London   Toronto   Sydney   Tokyo   Singapore

The Commissary's recipes for Killer Cake and Lemon Mirror Cake, and Sardi's recipe for Bocconi Dolce are reprinted with permission.

 A Pocket Star Book published by
POCKET BOOKS, a division of Simon & Schuster Inc.
1230 Avenue of the Americas, New York, NY 10020

ISBN: 0-671-70659-4

First Pocket Books printing January 1992

10 9 8 7 6 5 4 3 2 1

POCKET STAR BOOKS and colophon are registered trademarks of Simon & Schuster Inc.

Cover art by Punz Wolff
Cover design by Irving Freeman

Printed in the U.S.A.

FOR MY CHILDREN
WINIFRED AND BRIAN

"In nature there are neither rewards nor punishments—there are consequences."

—Robert Green Ingersoll
Some Reasons Why, 1896

Acknowledgments

"AS WITH ANY SEEMINGLY SOLITARY ENDEAVOR, THERE ARE THOSE WITHOUT WHOM . . .":

OF COURSE: My parents, family and friends, all of whom have supported me in this consuming project.

CONSULTANTS: Fantes, cooking supply store, Philadelphia; Charles Landow, M.D.; Steve Poses of The Commissary restaurant, Philadelphia; Saverio Principato, Esq.; Victor Sardi of Sardi's restaurant, New York; Allan Schwartz, M.D.

CONSPIRATORS AND CRITICS: Patrick Brett, Doris Chorney, Linda Fields, Harold Gross, Phyllis Gross, Roslyn Kantor, Fred Neulander, Barbara Schwartz, B. Bentley Terrace, Bill Tonelli, Stacey Wolf, and "The Brunch Bunch"—Susan Gorsen, Judy Shapiro, Susan Weiner, and Robin Weinstein.

INSTIGATOR: Helen Kushner, who, one day over corned beef on rye, said to me, "There's a book in all this . . ."

AGENT: Elizabeth Trupin of JET Literary Associates, Inc., a sparkling lady, whose warmth and support are unfailing. Above all, I appreciate her unbounded enthusiasm.

ACKNOWLEDGMENTS

EDITOR: Jane Chelius, a sensitive and talented lady after my own wavelength, who, not surprisingly, always says to me, "It's funny that you called me . . . I was just about to call you." For her insightful and incisive skills, I am most grateful.

WITH LOVE, I THANK YOU ALL

Special thanks for a lifetime of loving, to Sam—friend, mentor, slayer of dragons.

And, to my husband, Bob, for his patience and devotion, a lifetime of love.

CUSTARD CREAM PIE

4 eggs
2/3 cup sugar
1/2 teaspoon salt
1/3 teaspoon nutmeg
1 teaspoon vanilla extract
2 2/3 cups milk
1 9-inch unbaked pie shell

Preheat oven to 425°F.

Beat eggs until completely blended. Add sugar, salt, nutmeg, vanilla, and milk. Stir until smooth. Pour mixture into unbaked pastry shell and bake 15 minutes. Reduce oven temperature to 350°F and bake about 30 minutes, or until a knife inserted about one inch from the edge comes out clean.

Let cool for 10 minutes. Refrigerate uncovered, and decorate with sweetened whipped cream before serving. Serves 8.

CHAPTER 1

Custard Cream Pie

For all its buttery crisp crust, its silky smooth sweetness, its mellow richness, custard cream pie has its downside: It sours. At the moment of the turn, when the nose and tongue can just detect its sharp edge, a custard cream pie is best tossed—at one who deserves not only the injury of the smack, but the insult of the turn.

When we first met in the lobby of the hotel, his height had taken me by surprise. I was used to a smaller man. I noted his thick, curly black hair and the graying, his large, dark-chocolate eyes and the lines radiating from their outer corners. I noted his full mouth—a sexy mouth, I thought, as a candid shot of my mouth meeting his flashed behind my eyes—and his beautifully capped teeth. Beneath his navy blazer, the slight paunch of early success strained the buttons of his blue-and-white-striped silk shirt.

Emerging from the elevator, he had found me with the help of the description I'd given him over the house phone: "I'm in purple."

"Tess? Joe Silvers."

I shook his hand firmly, with excellent eye contact and a demure smile. This man is not your average blind date, I thought, feeling not exactly average myself, catching my reflection in the mirrored wall to the left of the elevator: a vivacious sophisticate in a long, full cotton skirt and blouson top.

"Cindy's right, you are a pretty little thing," he said, smiling broadly, turning me suddenly awkward. My high heels felt too high, and my outfit too baggy—my thin, braless body lost in folds of draining purple.

This was my first date since Stephen and I had separated, and although it had been more than ten years since my last blind date, it all came back to me, including the panic: I shouldn't have had my hair cut; it was too short, accentuating my big ears, my long neck, my large teeth. I'd put on too much blush, and my long lashes, blackened with mascara, looked like spiders. And I was sure that the instant I relaxed my compulsive smile, the lines around my eyes and mouth wouldn't.

All this ran through my mind as Joe guided me by my elbow to Damien's, the cocktail lounge at the rear of the gilt and crystal-chandeliered lobby. This evening was to be a prelude to our tentative dinner date the following evening with our mutual friends Cindy and Richard "The Matchmakers" Castle. *Tentative,* as in *if This Evening goes well.*

"No, I'm not divorced yet. I've only been separated for five months," I answered his question once we were seated and served, nervously running my forefinger around the base of the wineglass before me.

Joe plucked a crimson rose from the small vase next to the tiny brass hurricane lamp lighting our corner booth in the dim, smoke-filled lounge. I nibbled at Jarlsberg and red seedless grapes from a doilied tray and tried to keep the small talk aloft, but my attention was drawn to Joe's hands as he toyed with the rose, caressed it, pulled at the dark velvety petals, and dropped them one by one onto the starched white tablecloth. Such strong, graceful hands, I thought, inventing the sensation of the touch of them on my cheek, my breast. I longed to be touched. I longed to feel the touch of a man's hand on my skin.

"Have you dated much?" he questioned gently as the red petals fell softly from his fingers.

"No. Not really. In fact, you're my first real date," I confided.

He's a big man in oil, a nice man, Cindy had told me. Her husband Richard's old friend from college days. From California. And his trip east was for two weeks. Plenty of time, I mused, envisioning this handsome, experienced man naked, easing me to forgotten passion.

"You must be horny as hell," he leered. . . .

Mute and unflinching, I caught his eyes with mine, searching for motive for his insensitive accusation, hating him for his raw accuracy, his jarring exposé. Pinning him with my gaze, I grabbed the shiny object nearest my right hand . . . swung upward and across . . . viscous red spewed from his throat in great pulsating globs as the silver cheese knife severed his carotid artery. His warm, unbelieving eyes were fixed on mine. His mouth opened to protest, but no words came forth, only blood. Splotches of red fell onto his hands, onto the white cloth. I reached out to touch a warm, wet, crimson pool.

. . . Mute and unflinching, I picked up a soft red petal. Rolling it between my fingers, I sought Joe's eyes with my own, finding not a trace of remorse. But honeyed words dripped from his mouth—condescending babble about women, sublimation, Shirley MacLaine, and mind over sexual matter.

We slipped back into small talk, sipped at wine, picked at the cheese tray. He commented on my apparent sense of togetherness, my stability in the face of trying emotional times. He understood about divorce; he had been through it twice. And the noise in the lounge grew unbearable.

If he had just suggested his room, I would have said no, but what he actually said was, "Do you feel secure enough to come back to my room?" Well, after all, we had just spoken of my inner security, my psychic maturity. Could I now deny it all and say no? Yes. I said yes. We could go to his room.

* * *

I sat in the only unoccupied chair in his elegant room with the high ceilings and ornate crown molding, a low rocker upholstered and skirted in green and gold brocade. A handsome leather briefcase sat on the desk chair at the far end of the room. On the back of the chair, Joe carefully draped his jacket. Unbuttoning his cuffs and turning them up as he walked toward me, he asked if I would care for more wine. No, I answered, having had enough wine already to erode my judgment. He threw himself upon the massive four-poster next to my chair and, toes to heels, nudged off his polished black tasseled loafers. From The Bed, looking as though he was going to fall asleep at any moment with his hands folded behind his head on the overstuffed down pillows, Joe halfheartedly asked me about my newly founded catering business—Just Desserts—my politics, my ambitions, while I rocked, trying to look as comfortable as I pretended to be, wondering when would be the best time to leave.

Suddenly I was aware that he had stopped talking and was staring at me. Sitting up, he swung his legs over the side of The Bed to face me.

"May I kiss you?" he asked.

"No," I replied shyly.

"Why?"

"Because it would make me uncomfortable," said I without a hint of nervousness, without a shift in position, totally in control, although ambivalence was taking root somewhere in the pit of my stomach, threatening to choke off resolve.

He lay back again and switched conversational gears. He told me that my hair was pretty, though a bit short and a little out of fashion, and was I thinking of visiting California sometime?

And as I was on the verge of standing, to put an end to the evening, he slithered from The Bed, knelt in front of my chair, and he was still higher than I because he was so tall and my chair was low and he didn't ask again, he just kissed me.

Swirls of warm, swirls of soft, swirls of sensual pleasure

5

beginning in my mouth and spreading in concentric circles engulfed me, bound me. But I was completely in control. I wasn't doing anything that I didn't want to do . . . except that I had said no, which he interpreted as yes because I hadn't said NO! NO! NO! NO! NO!

"NO!" I said, "NO!" rejecting his seductive tongue and the tender hand that was sliding under my skirt up my thigh. He stood up obediently and lay prone across The Bed, chin in hands.

I dared not leave right after his big play because it would have looked obvious, childish, prudish, and, besides . . . I didn't want to go.

"Were you ever unfaithful to your husband?"

"No."

"You're still a goddamned virgin!" he yelled. He *yelled!* He also told me I was petite, delicate, and feminine, and so very alluring. That I was innocent and naive.

He started to get up, but once on hands and knees he hissed my name—"Tesssss"—challenged me with his eyes, reached over and took my hand. Acquiescing, as if in a dream state, I stepped out of my shoes and joined him. We knelt together on The Bed, facing one another. I started to say something.

"Shhhhh," he whispered, tracing the shadows beneath my deep-set eyes with his finger.

What am I doing here? I wondered, but didn't resist. "I'm vulnerable, and you're trying to seduce me," I said.

"You have a strong will and a strong intellect."

"Intellect has nothing to do with it."

"I am consciously going to stop trying to seduce you."

"It's time for me to go." Finally.

But he leaned to me, loosely circled his arms around me, and kissed me. Once again swirls of warm, swirls of soft, swirls of infinitely sensual pleasure engulfed me. I kissed him back warmly, thoroughly, but I was becoming aware of my hands as they hung impotently over his shoulders. I could not embrace him, I could not touch him. As if they were no longer a part of me, they would not close around him. Instead, like wet gloves they hung over his shoulders even as the rest of my body opened to him, quickened to him.

He pulled me to him and sought the soft elastic band binding panty to thigh. Reaching beyond, he touched and caressed. He pressed himself against me. I could feel his erection against my belly. . . .

NO! screamed in my head, but my knees abandoned me and we fell together into the mass of pillows on the bed. I can't! I thought, grasping at a glint on the nightstand as he rolled over me. His despicable leer once again challenged me, steeled me, allowing my trembling hands to finally embrace him. And with the embrace, the silver letter opener I clutched in my fist sank deep into his back. Shock clouded his eyes; blood welled up in his mouth mixed with saliva and spilled over his soft lower lip in a crimson thread.

. . . "NO!" I said. "I can't," I said, withdrawing my arms from his shoulders and sitting back on my heels, trying to regain my composure. He asked me something, but I don't remember what. I only remember answering as I slipped off the bed, "I'm an ambivalent person."

The elevator descended slowly toward the lobby with little jogs and bumps. Standing close, pushing me into the corner cf the car, Joe asked if we would still have dinner the next evening with Cindy and Richard . . . if I'd stay with him after dinner. I smiled lamely, with my mouth. . . .

My hand found the red STOP button behind my back. The car jolted to a halt. Joe fell backward as the tip of my foot grazed the back of his ankle, hitting his head on the polished marble floor. I fell over him. Stunned, he was unable to speak, though his mouth was agape beneath me and his eyes darted about my face. NO! my eyes screamed, NO! as I crushed his mouth with mine. His wrists were caught in my grasp above his head, his long sprawled legs bowed around me. Bells were ringing as my tongue licked his into submission. I felt his erection amass beneath my thighs. Relinquishing his left wrist, I reached down to free his engorged penis and lift my skirt to a bundle between us. Hoisting up, I hung in midair just long enough to catch his wide-eyed amazement, the unchecked enthusiasm on his face. Pulling silken panty aside, I dropped abruptly, impaling myself on him. Almost immediately the quake began. Visions of barren California acres dotted with drilling rigs played behind my eyes. Up and down and up and down and the tremor that numbed fingers and toes erupted in a gush and a run of grips that closed and opened and closed and opened around him, leaving him on the brink on the edge on the verge of his own orgasm. His hands grabbed my buttocks as he continued to pump. His eyes were tightly closed, his tongue jabbed at air in and out of his dry mouth. In an instant I freed myself from him, caught his hands, and closed them around his rigid organ. Close he was, almost he was, continued he did the business by himself, yanking and stroking, pinching and pulling in a paroxysm of frenetic motion. Watching from the corner, I was in complete control. The bells stopped ringing when I pulled out the STOP and within seconds the doors to The Elevator opened to reveal a gallery that had gathered in answer to the bells, in time for them to witness the writhing hulk on the small marble floor spew forth exultations of ecstasy, spasmodic spurts of opalescent emission.

. . . "NO!" I said, "NO! I can't," just as the elevator doors opened and we stepped out into the opulent, deserted lobby.

Perplexed, he walked me to my car in the parking lot next door, kissed me lightly, and watched me drive off.

I felt I had handled everything just fine, that I had coped well, that I was in complete control—until at a red light halfway home someone in the car next to me yelled, "PUT YOUR LIGHTS ON, LADY!" Then I almost collided with a mini-van after running a stop sign. I was out of control, disoriented by passion. I could imagine the headlines in the paper the next morning: YOUNG WOMAN KILLED IN CRASH. DRIVER UNDER THE INFLUENCE OF LUST.

* * *

Since that night, I've been subject to fits of passion. I'll melt, I'll liquefy, I'll soon go up in a puff of steam, perchance to be carried by clouds to where he is, and I'll rain on him one morning. But I'd rather push a ripe custard cream pie in the bastard's lubricious face.

Smack!

The rude sound of the dollop of sweet whipped cream hitting the cooled surface of the custard jarred me from my reverie. Daydreaming again. Driven inward by the routine of whipping and spreading. So this is the single life. Weird evenings with weird men followed by ambivalent ruminations lasting for days, weeks. Lust followed by rage. I didn't think it would be this hard.

RASPBERRY TORTE

8 eggs
1 cup sugar
1/4 teaspoon salt
1/4 pound shelled filberts, grated
1/4 pound shelled walnuts, grated
3/4 cup raspberry jam
chocolate glaze (below)
powdered sugar
1 pint fresh raspberries

Preheat oven to 350°F. Butter two 9-inch cake pans. Line them with wax paper and butter the wax paper.

Separate the eggs and beat the yolks until thick and pale. Gradually beat in 1/2 cup sugar. In a separate bowl, add the salt to the egg whites and beat until soft peaks form. Gradually beat in 1/2 cup sugar and continue beating until stiff peaks form. Fold the whites into the yolks. Fold in the nuts. Pour into pans and bake for 30 minutes. Turn cakes onto a rack and remove wax paper. Let cool.

Split each layer horizontally and spread layers, except top, with raspberry jam. Put layers together. Ice sides with chocolate glaze. Dust top with powdered sugar and stud with a crown of fresh raspberries.

Chocolate Glaze

6 one-ounce squares bittersweet chocolate
4 tablespoons butter

Melt the chocolate and butter over moderate heat in the top of a double boiler, stirring continuously until smooth.

CHAPTER 2

Raspberry Torte

"Daydreamer," my second-grade teacher had told my mother. "She's always staring out the window. I can't imagine what she's thinking about."

Plotting, probably. But today . . . what was I thinking just before the banging brought me back to reality, standing at the center-island counter of my double-oven-plus-microwave Poggenpohl kitchen that my now-estranged husband had bought so I could make gingerbread children when I wasn't out selling four-bedroom, two-and-a-half-bath (with family room) homes to couples with two-and-a-half children, a dog, and a Volvo station wagon—part-time careers I had established after burning out at the end of nine years as a second-grade teacher? All those kids, and none came home with me.

I had taken well to the business of moving people around. When Stephen left, I was almost making a living with real estate sales commissions. Establishing Just Desserts had been serendipitous. The gingerbread cookies I had lovingly created for years for family and friends became a sought-after commercial product after I had donated a hundred of them to the synagogue brunch and fashion show the year before. Soon I found myself going from gingerbread to tarts, from tarts to tortes, from tortes to pies, lemon rolls, and chocolate logs. The dessert catering business filled an inner need in me as well as the holes in my finances. There's

something satisfying about cooking, especially desserts—
the sweet end, the final taste in your mouth.

"Tess, Tess! Open up, are you there?" Sandy banging at
the back door. Here to pick up the tortes for her dinner
party. Was it that late?

"I'm here, Sandy, come on in," I shouted. But what had I
been thinking about?

She bolted through the door, admitting a gush of crisp fall
air into the pantry where two of her three raspberry tortes
sat on a cast-iron pie rack. The cold air briefly filling my eyes
and nose jogged my memory. I had been thinking of the
smell of frost that had greeted me that morning through my
open bedroom window, and how it had evoked feelings of
solitude. This was to be my first winter alone. It seemed like
only days, not four years, since Stephen and I had moved
into this house, our dream house—my dream house.

Stephen had rushed into the kitchen unexpectedly at
noon, carrying with him the crisp smell of frost. "What's for
dinner tonight?" he teased, eyeing the half-unpacked boxes
of kitchen equipment and canned goods on the floor, and
the piles of china, pots, and pans on the countertops and
table.

I scrambled down the stepladder to greet him, leaving the
roll of Rubbermaid shelf lining on the topmost cabinet shelf.
"Hi! What a nice surprise. You here to take me to a
well-earned lunch?" I asked, embracing him, inhaling the
autumn cold that seemed to emanate not from the surface of
his gray London Fog, but from deep within him. His icy lips
brushed mine as he patted my back with one hand, and then
he headed for the desk in the open family room beyond the
kitchen, dodging boxes of books and files.

"You mean you're not *making* us lunch?" he threw to me.
"I thought you wanted to play house and cook three meals a
day in your shiny new kitchen!"

I hated it when he was sarcastic.

"Tess, did you see the tax file for this year lying around? I
distinctly remember taking it out of a box and putting it on
the desk last night."

"Nope. I haven't been out of the kitchen all morning, and it isn't in here. So. How about lunch?"

After a moment he walked back to the kitchen, the file in his hand. "I thought you'd have lunch on the table for me! What have you been doing all morning?"

"Stephen, I'm serious . . . and I'm hungry, and I thought maybe we could—"

"I'm serious, too," he said, feigning a scowl. "I'm really disappointed. You've been in this big house with the big kitchen for almost twenty-four hours now, and no hot meal!"

"Would you settle for a hot wife?" I tried, seized by a need to be held.

"I would have, but since you mentioned lunch, you've got my stomach growling for food."

"Okay, so take me to lunch."

"When you have so much work to do here? Look at all the shelves you have to line!"

"Bye, Stephen," I said, turning my back to him, climbing up the stepladder, giving up.

"See ya," he said, patting my rear as he left.

"RUB! Don't PAT!" I yelled to him. But the door had shut. He was gone. And I was left to line the shelves and grumble to myself, "You pat a dog . . . you pat a friend's small child . . . you pat your buddy on the football team. You RUB your wife."

This isn't at all the way I had pictured it, I thought, no longer hungry, stepping down the ladder, clearing a space on the counter for a mug of hot coffee—installing the space-saver coffee maker under the cabinet next to the pantry door was the first thing I had done that morning. And why am I lining these shelves, anyway? I wondered, knowing full well that I lined kitchen cabinets because my mother lined kitchen cabinets, even though *she* had lined them when I was a child because the shelves then were painted wood, and she continued to line shelves—even though the cabinet shelves in her present apartment are laminated with plastic—out of habit. I lifted the receiver from the wall phone near the coffee maker, punched in my mother's number, poured the coffee with my free hand, and sat at the counter, stretching the new, white, tightly coiled wire. As the phone rang, I added sugar to my coffee from the yellow box that had been wrapped in newspaper—my mother, too, always wrapped everything in newspaper when she packed.

"Hello."

"Hello, Mom?"

"Hello, dear. How are you?"

"Okay."

"You don't sound good. What's wrong?"

"Nothing. I guess I'm just tired from the move."

"You're not doing too much, are you?"

"Well, I've been unpacking the kitchen stuff this morning, and lining shelves. . . . By the way, Mom, why do you line shelves?"

"I always line my shelves. It protects them. It keeps them clean."

"But our shelves are laminated, Mom."

"Look, I always line shelves. What can I tell you? Everything is different these days. If you don't want to line your shelves, don't line them."

"But I *am* lining them. I only asked—"

"You asked, and I'm telling you. I always line my shelves."

"So how are you feeling, Mother?"

"Fine, dear. Bernice Kaiserman—you know, the lady two doors down the hall—and I are going to lunch soon. Did you have lunch yet?"

"No. I'm not very hungry. I'm having a cup of coffee."

"You have to eat, Tess. That's why you're tired. You don't eat enough. You never ate enough. And I don't know why you decided to move into that big house. It's too much for you to keep up. You don't need all those rooms."

"It's what I want, Mom, and someday the rooms will fill up—"

"From your lips to God's ears. Tess, you're almost thirty. I don't know what you're waiting for. A man wants children, you know."

"I just turned twenty-nine, Mom. So don't worry, children are in my master plan."

"Your problem is you have too many plans. Real estate, a new big house. What was so wrong with your apartment? What was wrong with teaching? Tess, I—"

"Mom, I've got to go."

"All right, dear. Call me later. But don't call until after dinner tonight. I might go visit your Aunt Sarah. Remember, she's moving to Florida next week. Don't forget to call to say good-bye."

"I won't. Gotta go. Bye." I hung up and walked from the kitchen through the family room to the front hall. I walked into and out of the empty-but-for-boxes-and-drapes living room and dining room, and up the stairs. I looked into the fourth bedroom, to the right of the stairs, which was to be my office, and noted my desk, filing cabinet, and boxes of paperback books. Walking around the third bedroom, which was to be a guest bedroom, I pictured twin beds covered by rainbow-striped comforters, and a window seat holding a rainbow of throw pillows. Right now it housed Stephen's weights, rowing machine, and stationary bike. The second bedroom was completely empty, but I could picture, first, a haze of pink ruffles and white lace enveloping a twin four-poster brass bed, and alternately, a splash of primary colors surrounding a race-car bed—I had seen one in the children's furniture store in the new shopping center, where it was matched with a gas-pump chest of drawers. Yes. This would be the nursery. Well, of course—I let my mind wander—first there would be a crib, and then the fancy furniture, and then, when the second baby came, the first would be moved to the guest bedroom. And then—

And then the phone rang. I didn't want to talk with anyone. I let it ring and walked into the master bedroom feeling inconsolably alone, looked down at the unmade bed with the rosy sheets, the orange sherbet and pale blue fine wool blankets, and the creamy eyelet comforter all invitingly atangle, lay down in the middle of it, and pulled the comforter over my head. Tears ran down my nose and dropped onto the king-size down pillow. Closing my eyes, I curled up with my hands between my legs and discreetly rocked back and forth. The overwhelming intellectual anesthesia and emotional analgesia of sexual arousal quickly enveloped me, insulated me, and I rocked faster and faster. Yes. This makes it better ... like when I was little, and alone, and afraid. Yes. The insistence of impending orgasm drew me farther and farther from my thoughts, closer and closer to that special momentary place where all wrongs are righted ... where, for an instant, there are no wrongs. Then, driven from aloneness, I rocketed into the soft black womb of the id—

And the phone rang. Feeling consummately guilty, I answered it, out of breath ... caught. It was the Welcome Wagon.

Yes. A time not unlike this morning—the smell of frost, the sanctuary of my bed, the palliative touch of Onan.

"Don't you ever lock your back door? Someone could break right in," Sandy scolded, startling me back to the moment.

"I don't even think about it," I said, somewhat warm and disoriented from my rememberings.

"God, Tess. You okay? You look flushed."

"I'm fine. I've just been busy. Have a seat, your tortes are almost ready. This is the last one," I said, spooning powdered sugar from the yellow and white box into the aluminum sifter I held over the torte before me.

"They look wooonderful!" she said, perching herself in a high cane-back chair at one end of the counter, propping her small pointed chin in her hands.

She shouldn't be a Sandy, the name is so incongruous with her looks, I thought, noticing not for the first time her delicate, pale skin; the high color of her cheeks, like raspberries in cream; how black her eyes and hair were, not a trace of gray. I was only three years older and ... What was it the salesman had said to me when I took my old raccoon jacket in to be restitched? Something about how refreshing it was to see that, unlike most women *my age,* I wasn't trying to cover the gray frost streaking the front of my hair. This, as he reached out and teased a fallen lock from my eye with his finger. Pig.

"I've got news, Tess."

"News? So do I," I said.

"You first."

"Okay. What do you think about me selling my house?"

"Really, Tess? Why? You looove this house. And where would you go? And this kitchen! Could you cook anywhere else after cooking here?"

"I've been thinking about it for a while. It's too big. It makes me feel too alone now that Stephen's gone."

"But lots of divorced women live in large homes."

"Usually with children, Sandy. That makes a difference."

Sandy pulled a sympathetic face.

"So I was thinking of the new townhouses that are going to go up on the old Karistan Estate. I saw a brochure. They're going to be nice. The model I like has a huge eat-in kitchen and family room combination—with a fireplace—and two large bedrooms. I can use the second bedroom as an office. And the master bedroom has a sitting room that overlooks the living room. It's very open."

"Sounds great, but do you want to rush into this? You're not even divorced yet."

"I've made up my mind. I'm putting my house on the market today. Now. What's your news?"

Sandy looked like she wanted to say more on the subject, but she didn't. "Remember Mark Weiser?" she asked.

"Who?"

"Mark Weiser, Barbara's almost-ex, the judge."

"What about him?"

"He ran his Porsche into a tree. The police are calling it an accident, but Barbara told Bob Cooperman that Mark—you *did* hear that he was caught dealing drugs, didn't you? . . . Well, he was," she continued, not giving me a chance to answer, "and Bob said it was *Barbara* who blew the whistle! She couldn't stand having the kids go with him on weekends because she knew he had stuff in his apartment. Well, anyway, Barbara told Bob that Mark had pleaded with her not to testify at his hearing, that he would kill himself before he would be humiliated in a courtroom."

"My God. Dead?"

"As a doornail."

"So you think he did it on purpose?"

"Absoluuutely."

"Maybe he was strung out."

"More like he was strung up. And, by the way, we're talking a million in insurance."

"For Barbara?"

"For Barbara. Probably a posthumous guilt offering."

I did not miss the narrowing of her eyes, the wisp of a smile on her lips. Yes, I too thought, maybe there is some justice in this world after all. The man was a degenerate. Black-robed, he sat on a bench steeled with arrogance, wielding the scales of justice over petty druggies and corporate thieves, while turning blind eyes to his own depravity.

"I didn't know he was selling drugs, but I knew that he used them," I said, lowering the sifter to the counter without releasing it. "You know, he tried to entice me into the bathroom for a line of coke and God knows what else at Millie's party three years ago," I confessed, adding, to point out that I hadn't taken the pass personally, "And everybody knew that he had been running around for years."

"Oh, yes," she concurred, casting her own stones. "Remember the night Charlie had an emergency at the shore hospital and I went to Barbara's dinner party alone? Remember, I was wearing a black knit sweater? You know the one, with the rhinestone bow on one shoulder and the low V-neck? Well, he followed me to the powder room and right there in the hall he put his hand into my bra!"

"You never told me about that."

"You never told me about the invitation to the bathroom."

I lifted the sifter and poised it over the torte.

"Well, he kept a lot hidden under those black robes," she continued after a short silence, shifting the guilt back to its rightful place. "And I'll tell you something else you might not know. His secretary used his American Express card to buy clothes at Best Suited. And she was always driving his car around—"

"The Porsche!"

"No. Not the Porsche, the Cutlass. He would have *died* before he let anyone touch his Porsche. Hah! He did! Maybe that's why he killed himself in it, so that they'd go together."

"So what did you do?"

"What did I do when?"

"When he put his hand in your bra."

"Well . . . I let him kiss me . . ."

I put the sifter down again and watched Sandy's eyes turn coy, then angry.

". . . just once. I was curious. Besides, I was really pissed at Charlie. I mean, do you know how many parties I've had to go to alone because he refuses to get a partner?"

You could have smacked him, I thought, lifting the sifter once again. You could have laid him out, I thought, setting my lips in a hard line. Not Sandy, I thought, she loved to be lusted after. "Mm. When's the funeral, Sandy?" I asked. "I suppose I should pay my respects—to Barbara, that is. I never had any respect for Mark."

As I gently tapped the sifter, releasing a final dusting of sugar, I felt the tiniest twinge of guilt. I supposed one shouldn't speak ill of the dead. Then again, I supposed there were exceptions. There were so many candidates for exceptions. Sandy's husband, for instance. I wondered if Sandy had heard what I had heard—that he kept a cookie in the "investment" condo they had bought at the shore. Sandy had told me it was rented, that the income would decorate their own home. Sure, it was rented, I figured—by Charlie.

"It's tomorrow at eleven. Charlie and I are going, if he gets home in time. In any case, I'll pick you up if you want to come."

Pondering the invitation, I pictured Mark in his coffin, immaculately groomed. That would be new for Mark. I wondered if it was true, what they say about dead men, that they have permanent erections. That wouldn't be new for Mark, I thought, remembering the rest of the story about the invitation to the bath, what else I hadn't told Sandy. That Mark had kissed me, too—or at least he tried to. That he had exposed himself. That I had pushed him into the bathroom. That he had pulled me in with him and kicked the door shut. . . .

"You're not really such a goody-goody, are you? You're really a lot hotter than you look, aren't you?" he slurred, grabbing me by the shoulders, pushing me to my knees. "Okay, Miss Disneyland. Do you know what time it is? It's Howdy-Doody time," he said, dropping his pants (he wasn't wearing underpants). "Hey, kids, I'm Uncle Bob, this is Howdy-Doody," he said, fondling his erection. I guessed it wasn't true, what they say about drunk men, that they can't get it up. "Let's all sing! *It's Howdy-Doody time, it's Howdy-Doody time,*" he sang, his slightly flagging erection waving before my eyes. "Come on, Tess, Howdy's wilting. Give Howdy a kiss . . . and sing! *It's Howdy-Doody time, it's—*"

"It's sopraaaano time," I warbled, grabbing the dangling scrotum before me and pulling myself to a standing position. Obediently, his voice hit C above high C as his knees cracked on the ceramic tile.

. . . I should have. I really should have. Instead, I had pulled away, totally flustered, completely mortified. "I'm sorry," I had heard myself squeal as I stood up, opened the door, and scurried back to the party.

"I'm sorry?"

"You're sorry about what, Tess? Tess? Hey, space cadet, you're sorry about what?" Sandy's whiny voice delivered me from my internal digressions.

"Sorry, Sandy, um, I'm sorry this is taking so long," I recovered as I finished the torte with a crown of fresh red raspberries. "And I've decided not to go to Mark's funeral. I'll visit Barbara at home. And maybe I'll bring a razzzberry torte, in memoriam. That's a just dessert for the judge."

CREAM PUFFS

1 cup water
8 tablespoons butter
1/4 teaspoon salt
1 cup sifted flour
4 eggs
1 cup heavy cream
2 tablespoons powdered sugar
1 teaspoon vanilla extract
chocolate glaze (use 1/2 recipe from Raspberry Torte)

Preheat oven to 450°F.

Bring water, butter and salt to a boil. Remove from heat and add flour all at once. Stir vigorously until the dough leaves the sides of the pan and a ball forms around the spoon. If necessary, beat the mixture over low heat for a few more seconds. Cool slightly. Add the eggs, one at a time, and beat until the mixture is smooth after each egg.

Drop the mixture by rounded half-teaspoons onto a greased baking sheet, leaving 1 1/2 inches between puffs. Bake for 10 minutes; then reduce temperature to 350°F and bake for about 15 minutes more, until they are golden-brown and no fat bubbles remain on the surface. The sides of the puffs should feel rigid. Cool.

Whip cream until stiff; add sugar and vanilla and continue to beat until very stiff. Cut off tops of puffs, remove excess center, and fill with sweetened whipped cream flavored with vanilla extract. Ice with chocolate glaze. Makes about 20 small puffs.

CHAPTER 3

Cream Puff

"Did I tell you he called me a virgin?"

"Um," Sandy managed through a mouthful of roast beef, coleslaw, and Russian dressing on rye.

Watching her lose the battle with the recalcitrant strand of slaw hanging out of the corner of her mouth, I decided never to order a roast beef special when on a date—if I ever had another date. "Did I tell you I decided that even though he was sexy, he was a real jerk?"

"Um-hum," she mumbled, adding, after swallowing, "I can't believe it took you two months to figure that out, or that you're still obsessing about that dumb date!"

"So, I'm neurotic," I confessed, pushing my spinach salad around on the plate.

"I have to be honest with you, Tess—from what you told me, you're lucky he didn't strangle you."

"Okay, Mom. You're right. But so was he—about my being a technical virgin."

"Don't worry. You haven't had your last orgasm."

"Sandy! Lower your voice, this booth is not soundproof." The Mykonos Diner: purveyor of fine food and superfine flash; an establishment on the cutting edge of gossip and rumor. I had my suspicions that the plush, chandeliered booths were wired.

"Sorry," she squeaked before attacking her sandwich half from a different angle.

The large clock over the counter showed one-fifteen. I was showing a contemporary semicustom home with an in-ground pool at one forty-five. The house was twenty minutes from the diner. If I closed the sale at the asking price of two hundred and fifty thousand dollars, it would mean a seven-thousand-dollar commission. If I sold it for two hundred thousand, it would mean a fifty-five-hundred—

"Tess. Yoo-hoo! Where are you?"

"Counting chickens."

"You should be as confident with your dates as you are with your deals!"

"I remember what it's like to make a sale," I answered sharply.

"Not to change the subject, but do you want to have dinner with me and the kids? Charlie has to be at the shore hospital early tomorrow morning, so he's staying there overnight."

"You forgot already! Tonight is my big night out."

"Aha! The music appreciation class starts tonight, right?"

"Right. It should be thrilling, since I'll probably be the only one in the class who knows a fugue from a fuck. Then again, the difference is growing dim."

"Here we go again. I'm afraid the subject of your stagnating libido is wearing thin. Now, will you get out of here before you're late for your appointment?"

"But you haven't finished yet," I protested.

"Just go. I'm fine. And I'll pay the check on the way out; it's my turn."

"So what will you do tonight?"

"I might go over to Barbara's."

"How's she doing?"

"Amazing. She looks great and seems to have pulled herself together fast."

"I think I could pull myself together pretty fast with a million dollars."

"This is a discussion for another day, Tess. You're late! Go!"

"Okay, okay. Hug the kids for me. Talk to you in the morning."

Settling into the corner of the oversize mauve cotton-velour sectional sofa in my family room the following morning, Sandy tucked her legs under her and wrapped her hands around a mug of coffee. "It's getting cold out," she said, shrugging in an attempt to shake off the morning chill.

I continued dropping tiny globs of thick batter from a teaspoon onto a greased cookie sheet in two even rows. "Puff shells for cream puffs, for Myra Freedman's father-in-law's birthday dinner," I explained from the kitchen counter. After placing the sheet in the oven, I poured a mug of coffee, added sugar from the cork-stopped glass canister on the counter, and joined Sandy in the family room.

"The sale, Tess, did you make the sale?"

I smiled coyly, settling into a nest of pastel throw pillows on the sofa, and sipped my coffee.

"You did! How much?"

"Two thirty-five."

"Fantaaastic!"

"Well, I *have* been working on that deal for four months," I said modestly. "Now I hope the buyers get their mortgage. I'd have to bake a lot of cream puffs to make six thousand dollars."

"You're such a worrywart! It'll be fine. You're sooo good at what you do, Tess. Your client must be ecstatic."

"I hope I can do as well for me."

"Six thousand isn't bad, Tess."

"No, I mean in selling my house. You know it's been on the market almost two months and only one couple has been through."

"It'll sell. I don't have to tell *you* that this is a lousy time of year to try to sell a house. Besides, they haven't even started the townhouses you're interested in."

"True, true. But preconstruction prices are always the best."

"I think you'd be better off waiting to make sure the

development is going to turn out as nice as you think it will."

"Okay, okay, enough of this. It's a moot point. I can't think of buying until I get someone interested in my house."

"You're still intent on selling?"

"I'm still intent on selling."

"So. How was the class?"

"Class?"

"Your music class last night."

"Ah, the class. Elementary, but at least I got out for an evening."

"Anybody there?" Read: Any interesting men?

"Actually, there was this adorable guy, but too young."

"So?"

"So what?"

"So, was he interested?"

"You've got to be kidding. He couldn't have been more than twenty-four."

Sandy's eyes lit up when I dropped that bit of information, and then narrowed.

Gregg Hart had the look and demeanor of a California surfboarder—six-feet-four, lean and laid-back. He had long, straight blond hair, a soft, full mustache, and huge, round blue eyes. Beneath high cheekbones were dimples big enough to sink your tongue into. In his deep, sonorous voice, he'd told me that he had graduated college as a business major, but that he was building houses—literally *building* houses. He wore tight jeans.

I was thirteen when I noticed the tight jeans of Gavin Storms. He was older, maybe sixteen, but still in junior high. He was tall, all legs, as they say; not quite all legs, I noted. He'd swagger through the halls of Hawthorne Junior High School in cowboy boots and tight jeans, the vertex of his slowly striding legs bulging. The mysteries stuffing those jeans occupied my daydreams through two semesters of Spanish I.

Walking home from school one spring afternoon, I spotted Gavin Storms rooted to the sidewalk a block away from me, across the street. His legs slightly apart, arms down at his sides, Gavin gazed up the street. Even at that distance, even at that age, I could distinguish his cocky sneer . . . his bulges. The object of his focus was a girl in a white blouse and short blue and green print skirt who stood wavering directly across the street from me. She stared at him, he stared at her, neither aware of me staring at them. The girl was crying. She kept wiping her eyes with her hands and moving one step ahead and then one step back until she suddenly ran forward, which prompted a somber Gavin Storms to stride toward her with his long, booted legs. When they met, the girl wrapped herself around Gavin—who was a good foot taller than she—pressing herself against his bulges. He smirked. I waited awhile for them to separate, but they stood fast, and I finally walked away.

"Tess, put your ears on, your timer went off. And you didn't answer my question. Was he interested?"

"Well, he was very attentive, and he asked for my number. He said he might need help with the assignment," I said, leaping up and sprinting to the oven to remove the browned and puffed shells that would later be filled with sweet whipped cream and topped with bittersweet chocolate. "And I'm sure that's all he wants, Sandy. He's so young, what would he want with me?" But I smiled; she smiled. I transferred the hot shells to a cooling rack, bagged cooled shells and dropped more globs onto the cookie sheet. Sandy sipped and stayed long enough to warm up before she had to pick up Rebecca from nursery school.

Two days later Gregg called to ask my advice about the theme he was writing. "It's been a while since I wrote a paper for school," he apologized.

"How old *are* you?" I asked.

"Twenty-seven. How old are you?"

"Thirty-three."

"Oh . . ." His voice dropped. "I'm really only twenty-two."

The following week he showed up at class with one of his three roommates (to check me out?). As he left, he invited me to stop in to see his apartment "sometime."

I did, the following week after class. His two-bedroom apartment resembled a college dorm—a mess of laundry and newspapers, dirty dishes and worn furniture, an unmade sofa-bed in the living room. But Gregg's bedroom was in perfect order. His bed was made, magazines were stacked neatly in a corner, clothes were out of sight, vacuum tracks streaked the carpet. Surely his neatness was a sign of maturity beyond his years, I decided. Only later did it dawn on me that he had cleaned up for me. He showed me his Bruce Springsteen album collection—a poster of the Boss filled one wall—his college yearbook, pictures of his parents and two sisters and his four-year-old nephew. I smiled in appreciation through it all, and then I left.

Gregg called several times over the next few weeks to discuss the class and the over-the-holiday theme assignment. It should have been obvious that he was interested in me, but I wouldn't believe it. He was, after all, only twenty-two and incredibly handsome. Then, on New Year's Day, he called to ask if I would help edit his theme. Yes. He came to my home late that evening.

As always, I was struck by his height, by his eyes that seemed always to find me, and by his beautiful face. His youth excited me. We edited. I had suggestions for him. I had fantasies about him—about seducing him. When he asked to see my paper, "It's in my study," said I. "Would you like to see my study? It's upstairs."

"Shur," said he in his laid-back drawl.

As we climbed the stairs, I experienced the oddest sensation—that this wasn't really happening, that I was making it up, watching a movie. I couldn't believe I was going to seduce this young, young man. I didn't believe I *could* seduce him.

Sitting down beside him on the love seat next to my desk, I handed him a rough draft of my paper—paralleling great works of art and music by dates of composition. I watched him read and pictured myself falling into his arms, swooning from his baby-fresh aroma, feeling his firm young flesh beneath my fingertips, my lips, the tip of my tongue. Suddenly, my fantasy became reality as he looked up and placed his long, strong fingers on my thigh. I remained quite cool, quite the sophisticated woman, and placed a hand on his wrist. He leaned over and kissed me hungrily, his mustache brushing the tip of my nose.

"I've wanted to kiss you for a long time," he said when our lips finally parted.

"Yes," said the sophisticated woman, not missing a heartbeat. "You're very attractive."

But he noticed the smoldering lust beneath her cool exterior. "You're warm," he said, running a hand around the back of her neck.

"Yes," she said.

I wondered, as he kissed me again, should I or shouldn't I? I was in complete control, I wouldn't do anything I didn't want to do. In fact, he was probably as scared as I—maybe more so. After all, he was dealing with an experienced older woman. He probably couldn't wait to get back to his apartment to tell his roommates all about it.

"Do you want to stay for a while?" the experienced older woman enticed.

"Shur," drawled the smooth young man. "Do you want to get into bed?"

I hesitated long enough to make him feel like he was skating on thin ice.

"That's okay, you don't have to . . . but *I* want to," he reassured me.

Sweet. The question still was, did *I* want to? It had been eight months since Stephen left, since I'd made love to a man. Maybe I was thinking that I had to prove to myself that I could do it, that my body was still in working order, that I wasn't scared of men or sex or being hurt, that I could do anything I wanted to do and that I wanted to do what everyone else wanted to do, that I was still desirable . . . *that I was real*. Maybe I was thinking about how few people get to live out their fantasies. Maybe I was thinking that he was indeed the most delicious-looking man I had ever seen. If anyone was skating on thin ice, it was I.

Yes, I wanted to.

I led him to my bedroom, left him by the bed—"I'm going to slip into something more comfortable," said I— and retreated to the bathroom, grimacing as that old, old line rattled around in my head like a tire wrench. But I forgot about my trite exit when struck by déjà vu while changing. Pulling a loose-fitting black silk camisole over my head, I remembered.

I was in a hospital, six years ago. I had showered and washed my hair, as per the nurse's orders, and was pulling a green cotton hospital gown over my head—the shroud I would wear the next morning to the operating room where I would undergo plastic surgery on my fallopian tubes, to make them more attractive to my husband's sperm. Anesthesia terrified me: I felt I might die. As I dressed, I thought, How cruel to require one to prepare one's own body for death. But the terror was tempered by an odd excitement, an excitement based in an old memory.

I was in a hospital. I was five years old, standing in a crib, in a long, cold, gray hall, holding on to the cold metal rail, screaming in terror, waiting to be taken into the operating room to have my tonsils removed. I remember being carried to the bright operating room and laid on a table. I screamed, *"NO!"* as my arms and legs were held down, *"NO!"* as someone put what looked like a strainer over my face—like the kind my mother used in the kitchen—and a white towel over the strainer, *"NO!"* as a fog of ether smothered me. There was no air, only the acrid fumes that penetrated my eyes, nose, and mouth, that made my skin tingle, go numb, my ears go deaf even to my own shrieks, that blotted out my reality as the world blackened around me. Although my arms were held fast, I reached out with both hands and grasped at the black, tried to pull holes in it, tried to pull myself from the mounding black that engulfed me, lifted me into the silent abyss.

I can remember this because I came back: It wasn't physically painful—this small death—in fact, it could have been an exciting, pleasurable trip—this going and coming —but for the terror, but for the force, the binding of choice.

As I checked the fit of my new camisole in my bathroom mirror, I felt bewildered by the craziness of my remembrances—at a time like this.

Returning to the bedroom, I found Gregg naked, lying on his side across the bed, his head propped up with his hand, his very long penis draped across his very long leg. His smooth, youthful, almost hairless body was subtly muscular and tanned from the waist up. *Cheesecake* crossed my mind, but it didn't quite fit. I sat on the bed and leaned down to put my lips to his. After that it was all rushing hearts, flushing skin, flailing arms and legs.

"I'm sorry it was so quick," he apologized when he had finished, falling asleep as the words left his mouth.

"Short but sweet," I lied, still feeling the pain of his final thrust.

But that was not the end of it. Sweetly is how we ended it . . . after he woke . . . when we made love again . . . without the confusion of fear and the unfamiliarity of foreign bodies.

"See, I tooold you!" Sandy said with an approving smile, pouring herself a mug of coffee the following morning. "So?"

"So, what?"

"So, how was it?"

"Fun . . . and kind of scary. He's so beautiful— inexperienced, but beautiful," I said, remembering how inexperienced I must have seemed, being as frenetic as he. "He's as yummy as these cream puffs," I added, dribbling melted semisweet chocolate over the tops of Toby

Handleman's four dozen cream-filled miniature puffs on the counter.

We tittered.

"I'm so glad your first time was a nice one, Tess. I've heard sooo many stories!"

"I know," I said, and related my neighbor Millie's story about her friend in Pittsburgh who ran from a date's apartment—leaving her fur coat in his closet—when he started to push her around, telling her that she was a bad girl and had to be punished. *And he'd seemed so normal,* Millie's friend had said.

Aghast, Sandy asked, "Did she get her coat back?!"

"Nope. He hung up when she called him, and she was afraid to confront him alone and embarrassed to call the police. So she reported it lost to her insurance company. They pointed out that the coat was five years old and paid her enough to buy the left sleeve of a new coat. She bought a puppy for her kids."

Sandy shook her head, looking genuinely disturbed, although I wasn't sure what aspect of the story had bothered her the most. Giving her the benefit of the doubt, I said, "There are a lot of scary people out there. Luckily, I've never run into any real wackos. Of course, my experience is rather limited. When I was in college I dated guys in my class, and I didn't lose my virginity until I was a junior."

Sandy got a settled-in-for-the-season look about her as she listened to my rather ordinary tale of my infatuation with and defloration by Stuart Singer, an ordinary-looking, ordinary student in my abnormal psych class who I decided was extraordinarily interesting by virtue of the fact that he was the only guy who showed an interest in me, and how, after a monthlong separation for winter semester break which had turned us both into rabid autoerotics primed to pounce upon one another, it all ended the split second I saw him: He had changed his hairstyle; I changed my mind.

"So what about after college? Didn't you sleep with any guys before you met Stephen?" she asked when I had finished, which was not the question I would have asked.

"Nope. Stuart Singer was the only one. And it wasn't until

years later, when I decided what a nerd he was, that I finally stopped feeling guilty about dropping him because of a change of part."

"Oh, Tess. What a terrible pun!"

"Sorry. I couldn't resist."

"So whatever happened to Stuart Singer? Maybe he turned out to be a really great catch, Tess."

"Are you trying to say I was ahead of his time?"

"That's two!"

"Sorry. Well, as I was saying, I decided he was a nerd when I bumped into him shortly after Stephen and I moved into this house."

"Oh. You were already married. That's funny."

"That's defense. I was trying to make myself feel better about being with Stephen and not Stuart. You're right, you see. He actually was a great catch. He married a pediatrician and had four kids and runs a very successful advertising agency."

"And you weren't happy with Stephen?"

"I guess it was when I moved here that I began to wonder if marrying Stephen might have been a mistake."

"Really? From what you've told me, it sounded like you were *never* sure about Stephen."

"What I mean is, I guess it was the first time I began to think I could live without him, regardless of whether living *with* him was a mistake or not . . . and that maybe I was wondering if he really wasn't who I thought he was . . . and that maybe I didn't like who he was, as opposed to not liking some of the things he did. King of Haim Ginott turned inside out. Understand?"

"I'm not sure." Sandy looked at me and screwed up her face. "Tess, why *did* you marry Stephen?"

Now there was THE question . . . the one to which I had no answer, not even for myself, I thought, remembering when I had first met Stephen.

Contrary to the opinion of many of my single friends, I believed that there was always something positive about a blind date, even if it was only the excitement of anticipation. So when Aunt Sarah told me that Uncle Martin, who was an attorney, was involved in a business deal with a young, single attorney, and that she had told Uncle Martin to give him my number, if it was okay with me, I said sure, even though I couldn't believe that anyone associated with Uncle Martin—who, according to my mother, conducted most of his business on the underside of a rock—could possibly provide anything more than a single evening's diversion with a lower life form. Stephen Fineman—the blind date—was, however, impressive. He dressed impressively, he dined impressively, he talked impressively about his clients and his business, using figures that read like long-distance telephone numbers. He was slim, attractively graying, and aloof enough to hold my interest. He was also almost thirty, which, to me at twenty-two, made him an older man . . . and therefore even more interesting. On our first date he told me a lot about himself, including the fact that he hadn't married yet because he was too selfish, a comment that I chose to ignore, ignoring, too, my belief that a woman should pay heed to what a man tells her on a first date, because he will invariably tell her who he really is.

The *first* first time I made love with a man—that was Stuart Singer—had been on a date that was after too many to count, and until I met Stephen, I hadn't dated anyone since Stuart long enough to decide it was long enough to make love to him. The first time I made love with Stephen was on our third date, which seemed long enough because when I was near him my heart thumped and my mouth was dry, and when he touched my hand I felt the world stop, and when he kissed me the world disappeared. So I guess it's not so surprising that once he made love to me, he became my world. I was very young.

"I was very young, Sandy," I finally replied to her question.

"That's an answer?"

"It's the best I can do."

We slowly nodded at each other.

"So. Are you going to see him again?" she finally asked.

"Who?"

"Cream Puff."

"Oh, I'll see him in class."

"I mean, are you going to *see* him again?"

"I don't know. I'm not going to pursue it."

"Why not?"

"He's so young, Sandy. It's like playing."

"What's wrong with that, Tess? Just a little something sweet. Nothing serious."

"Just a little dessert?"

"Right. You deserve a little treat now and then."

"Right."

"Right," she echoed.

I popped a tiny cream puff into my mouth, savoring its sweetness. And that's how it was to be with Gregg: a little treat now and then, which never seemed quite real because I didn't understand what a treat I was for him.

LEMON MIRROR CAKE

FROM: Commissary Restaurant, Philadelphia

Angel Cake

4 egg whites
6 tablespoons sugar
1/2 teaspoon vanilla extract
1/3 cup flour

Preheat oven to 350°F.

Beat egg whites until frothy. Gradually add 3 tablespoons of the sugar and beat until soft peaks form. Add vanilla; beat until peaks just barely stand (not stiff). Quickly sift 3 more tablespoons of sugar with the flour over the whites. On mixer's lowest setting, beat batter until just combined, scraping sides of bowl (mix thoroughly, but avoid overworking). Pour batter into ungreased 9-inch false-bottomed cake pan. Spread it quickly from the center, making batter flush with the pan's sides. Bake 20 to 25 minutes. Cool cake completely in the pan.

Lemon Mousse

1 cup lemon juice
1 envelope unflavored gelatin
1 tablespoon grated lemon rind
1 cup sugar
2/3 cup heavy cream
5 egg whites

In a saucepan, sprinkle gelatin over the lemon juice; let sit for 5 minutes. Stir gently over medium heat until dissolved (do not boil). Stir in rind and 1/2 cup sugar; stir to dissolve. Pour the mixture into a large bowl. Refrigerate until it is the texture of an unbeaten egg white, stirring every 10 minutes. Meanwhile, whip heavy cream until stiff and refrigerate. Once lemon mixture is ready, work quickly. Beat egg whites and 1/2 cup sugar to soft *peaks; then fold into gelatin mixture. Fold in whipped cream. Pour mousse over the cake in the pan, making the top smooth. Cover pan with plastic wrap and freeze the cake until the top is hard, about 1 to 5 hours.*

Raspberry Glaze

2 tablespoons water
1 1/4 teaspoons unflavored gelatin
1/2 cup raspberry puree (5 ounces frozen, sweetened, whole raspberries, pureed)
fresh raspberries

Sprinkle gelatin over cold water in a small saucepan; heat just to dissolve. Whisk in the puree; pour immediately over frozen cake, tilting back and forth for even coating. Refrigerate cake for 1/2 hour to set glaze. Transfer to serving dish. Decorate with fresh raspberries. Serves 10.

CHAPTER 4

Lemon Mirror Cake

Sunday morning brunch conversation at Mykonos with Sandy and Janet was predictable: sex and money—usually the lack thereof. Listening to each other's tales of deprivation, we were hyper-empathic; that is, no matter how bitterly one of us might complain, the others understood only *too* well, each secretly feeling at least *as* deprived, if not *more* deprived.

This morning was no exception. Janet was relating an episode of her continuing financial battles with her ex-husband (Leonard Meyer, M.D., an obstetrician/gynecologist who, if you were to believe his depositions to the family court, was so impoverished he was forced to live in a HUD-subsidized apartment house—complete with roaches, he told their son, Sean, who told Janet, who, in an unfortunate fit of frustration and rage, told Sean that his father was an asshole). Sandy greeted this debasement of the medical profession with defensive incredulity, citing Charlie's long hours with his patients, resulting in disappointing (although she seemed not to be wanting for any necessity in life apart from a sable coat and a Jaguar) recompense. Truth be told, Leonard, too, was not wanting for any necessity in life, including a forty-some-foot sailboat that he'd "sold" to his brother Albert—a man who got seasick eating in a waterfront restaurant—for one dollar shortly before he left Janet and "borrowed" from his brother almost every weekend when the weather was nice, and a fifty-some-thousand-dollar Mercedes Benz, which Leonard told the court was not his personal property but was leased by the corporation for which he worked, failing to mention that "the" corporation was "his" corporation.

Thirty-two years old, five-foot-five and not thin, Sandy's cousin Janet had moved to the area from upstate New York five years ago with Sean—now age nine—looking forward to the closeness of family, and a part-time job as a dental hygienist in Sandy's dentist's office—that's Terrance Applebaum, D.D.S.—following her divorce, an event, Janet had related, precipitated by "Leonard's sleazy affair with the little twit from his office who would give him all the love and attention he deserved and none of the aggravation." Read: Leonard left Janet to marry his very young—twenty, to be exact—very impressionable, nonigravida receptionist. "Would you believe an obstetrician who hates women and kids!" she had said, further explaining that he'd made The Twit sign an agreement that they wouldn't have children. "I don't need any more children. I need a wife who'll take care of *me*," he had cried to Janet, who had cried to Sandy, who later told me, who couldn't understand why anyone would want to leave this warm, funny woman with wildly wavy auburn hair streaked with silver, hazel green eyes made greener by tinted contact lenses, and a perfect set of never-braced, big white teeth. Perhaps it was because Dr. Leonard Meyer couldn't handle the fact that his son was handicapped, a victim of cerebral palsy. I had first met Janet and Sean the morning of Sean's fifth birthday.

Sandy and I went over to Janet's to help with Sean's party for sixteen five- and six-year-olds. I had been in my new house about two months and was already fast friends with Sandy, whom I had met at the supermarket when I oohed and ahed over Rebecca in her infant carrier while waiting in the express line. So one day, when Sandy told me she was going to help at her cousin's son's birthday party and asked if I knew how to make a birthday cake, I said I'd make the cake for her if I could help at the party, too. I never could resist a roomful of kids.

Sean was a charmer, and a typical five-year-old—on wheels—which, I came to understand after knowing them awhile, was surely as much a tribute to Janet's strength as it was to his. The party was a success, i.e., the kids went home happy and the three of us were done in. So. After the party, after dinner, after bath and bed for Sean, and after Sandy nursed Rebecca and put her down on Janet's bed between two king-size pillows, the three of us shared a bottle of wine and three dozen of my chocolate chip cookies in Janet's living room while Janet told the story of Sean's catastrophic birth. It was a story Sandy had heard before, and one that Janet would tell over and over throughout her life—a kind of litany of acceptance. "Lenny was devastated when it happened," she started. She always started obliquely—with her husband's pain. She told us that it was months before Lenny could admit that Sean wasn't going to get better. "Actually, he never said that," she clarified, "he just stopped talking about it. You know, it's so incredibly ironic—I was married to an obstetrician, and I had this major, MAJOR problem at Sean's birth." Abruptio placentae, one of obstetrics' most dangerous complications, she explained, had robbed Sean of his potential to walk and many other motor skills, and Janet of her uterus. "Sometimes I think doctors have a harder time with this kind of thing than other fathers, just because they *are* doctors and they can't do anything to make it all right," she said with greater compassion for Leonard than she would ever express for herself. "We were really lucky," we would hear Janet say many times over the years. To Janet, *lucky* meant that she hadn't bled to death, that Sean hadn't died of oxygen deprivation, that Sean wasn't mentally retarded as well as physically handicapped, that Leonard could afford to provide the special care that Sean needed—even if she had to take him to court to compel him to provide it. Watching Sean and Janet in their individual struggles—he with his uncooperative muscles, she with her uncooperative ex-husband—I never had the feeling that she and Sean were at all lucky, just very, very brave.

Today the struggle was about a special-needs summer camp Janet had found for Sean, where a wheelchair was neither out of place nor an impediment to an enriching camping experience. It sounded good, Leonard had agreed, but it was expensive.

"Sooo," Sandy piped up.

"Sooo," Janet mimicked, "Fuckface told Sean that he can't afford to send him to overnight camp this summer."

"Jaaanet."

"Saaandy. Grow up. I'm being kind. Do you know what he had the gall to tell his son? 'Don't worry, your *mother* can send you to camp.' Now, why can't Fu—why can't F.F. afford it? you may ask. Well, because he and The Twit—unencumbered as they are—are going to Italy for three weeks in May," Janet started.

"They're probably going to a medical meeting, so it's all deductible. Doctors don't make as much as you think," Sandy lectured. "You know how decrepit my car is? Well, we can't afford a new one until Charlie's Mercedes is paid off. I, too, used to think that doctors' wives were able to have whatever they wanted," she sighed, changing the subject.

"You were only half right: doctors' *second* wives get everything they want!" Janet said with possible malice aforethought, sending Sandy into a pout.

Sandy is such a baby, I judged . . . and Janet sounds so bitter. But the fact is that Janet is what is called "painfully honest" by those who know, and "bitter" by those who have no idea. I knew she wasn't the only ex-wife of a professional to fall from homemaking and motherhood, triyearly vacations, charge accounts at Saks and Bloomie's, a new car every two years, and fine restaurants and theater on Saturday nights . . . to an entry-level job, a week's vacation at home with the kids in December, bills from Marshall's and Filene's Basement, a new muffler or brakes for the old car every year, and pizza and a videotaped movie on Saturday nights with the kids—thank God for the children! And despite it all, from what I could see, Janet had remained the warm, caring mother, the interested, generous friend that Sandy had said she was before her divorce—if sometimes a little too honest.

It was Janet who interrupted my star-skipping with, "So how was your blind date last night?"

"Not bad, but nothing special. He's just a salesman," I answered—understanding that, for Janet, the subject of Leonard Meyer, M.D., in any form, was over for now—and I shared with them the hours I had shared with Marv Kravitz (a man who had gotten my number from Phyllis Becker, a woman who carpooled with Sandy for Rebecca's ballet class and whom I hardly knew, but who'd known Marv since high school) at Le Petit Champignon, including a description of our dinner: I had sweetbreads in Madeira; he had escargot in burgundy; we shared a rack of lamb in mustard, with baby veggies; a small mixed salad vinaigrette followed the entrée; with pots of tea—Earl Grey for him and chamomile for me—we relished a small plate of white chocolate mousse in raspberry sauce garnished with fresh raspberries and slices of kiwi, and a lemon mirror cake for two. This elegant layering of angel cake and lemon mousse is frozen, and then topped with a hot raspberry glaze that's cooled in the refrigerator to a shiny clear mirror finish. "Oooh, look at that pretty lady in the mirror! She looks almost good enough to eat," Marv had crooned with a sly smile as we peered at our reflections in the top of the cake.

"Nothing special, she says! Actually, we *all* eat like that *all* the time!" Janet teased.

"I mean *he* wasn't special."

"So, are you going to see him again?"

"Next Saturday."

"Special enough."

"Better than being alone."

"Alone? So where's Cream Puff?"

"I see the name's sticking," I answered, not answering,

silently savoring the memory of Gregg's second visit two weeks ago.

"So, have you seen him?"

"Not in two weeks."

"Why not?"

"Janet, this is not an ordinary relationship. It's an ephemeral kind of thing," I said, sounding as pretentious as I felt.

"You mean he calls you when he's horny?"

Leave it to Janet to cut to the bone, I thought. "Well, I get horny too," I said.

"So why don't you call him?"

"Because I don't want to make more of this than it really is." How it *really* was, I realized as I said it, I *really* didn't know.

"You know, Tess, I don't think you *really* know how it *really* is," Janet said, understanding how I really am.

"God, Janet, don't play shrink."

"Maybe you *need* a shrink."

Sandy, who had been sitting sucking at her coffee, chimed in, "I think you *both* could use a good shrink. At least you get a little excitement in your lives. All Charlie does is work."

"So, how's Harvey?" I asked Janet, ignoring Sandy, but wondering if the vague rumor about Charlie's mistress in their shore apartment was, in fact, true.

"Harvey's Harvey," she answered, ignoring Sandy.

"Who's Harvey," Sandy asked.

"I've told you about him . . . haven't I?" Janet said, drawing Sandy back into the fold.

"If you did, I don't remember."

"Well. Harvey Cohen is a financial planner who does work for Terry, and ever since I cleaned his teeth about five months ago, he's been coming on to me."

"Oh, Janet, you think eeevery guy who smiles at you is coming on to you!" snipped Sandy.

She should talk! I thought.

"Then, about three months ago," Janet continued, "Harvey was in to see Terry about some business, and on the way out he pulled me aside and asked me to have lunch with him the next day, which I did. And then he asked me to spend the following Saturday with him."

"Oh? So how was it?" Sandy asked.

"All I can say is that he pushes all the right buttons for me."

"See that! And you keep saying that all the good men are married."

"They are. He is."

"Jaaanet! No wonder you didn't tell me about him before."

"Well, if I didn't, Sandy, it was probably because I didn't want to hear 'Jaaanet!' "

"It's just that I don't understand—"

"The only thing to understand is that I didn't go after him, he came after me. And if I hadn't accepted, someone else would have—he was looking. And, besides, there's no one else around, so why should I be celibate?"

"You mean you only see him because you're horny?" I sniped, missing the mark a bit.

"I'm glad I'm married. I couldn't deal with the single life," said Sandy.

Neither could I, I thought, mentally trying to sort out the difference between sleeping with a married man who plays around and sleeping with a single man who plays around. There was, of course, the issue of marital infidelity. There was also AIDS. Married men could get it and give it to their unsuspecting wives. Married men were definitely losing points. As to what all this said about the "other" women who consorted with them . . . well, that needed further sorting out.

It was David I called as soon as I got home from brunch.

David Ross, Stephen's officemate, occasional business partner, and closest—make that *only*—friend, was one of the nicest people I had ever known, and with his honey blond hair and brown eyes lighted by specks of gold, one of the most attractive, almost pretty beneath his carefully trimmed beard. David was also warm and caring, a svelte six-foot-one of sensitivity carefully honed by years of soul-searching through encounter groups and several modes of psychotherapy. He did not, however, stitch himself into any of the disciplines that he tried on, but gleaned the softest, most giving traits from each. So, despite his years of training, he was not commercialized, not molded into a smooth, slick, glowing social machine; he was sort of fuzzy around the edges. And when you listened to him, you felt that he was listening to you. Stephen once commented that in David's practice of law, he was smart enough, but in a dumb sort of way: He had some great ideas, but he didn't know how to carry them out. David was smart in a dumb way when it came to women, too. Women loved him, but he didn't seem to know what to do with them. He dated a lot, but at thirty-one he had no wife, no steady girl. In fact, in the five years Stephen and I had known David, he had never had a significant relationship with any woman. But for the strong sexual vibrations I felt when I was near him, I might have thought him gay.

"I need the name of a good shrink," I cried over the phone.

"A shrink? What for, Tess? You're a rock, one of the few women in the world I can count on for rational behavior," he praised.

"I don't think I'm coping well with single life," I confessed.

"Are any of us?"

"You seem to do okay."

Silence.

"So, who's the shrink?" I asked again, not knowing what else to say and beginning to feel uneasy.

He gave me the phone number of Dr. Michael Lerner, and then said, "Tess, I want you to know that I'm here for you. This has nothing to do with Stephen. I care about you, and I want to help you in any way I can."

"Thanks, David. I know you're there."

"Okay," he teased, forcing the softness from his voice, "call Lerner, but don't let him mess with your terrific neuroses. You know I love you just the way you are! Understand?"

Understand? What? That he loved me? Could he love me? Maybe he's been waiting for *me*, I thought, remembering our years of friendship, the times he'd joined Stephen and me at dinner or a movie, with or without a date, the many times he'd stopped over for a drink, a cup of coffee, unannounced . . . always warm, always caring, never out of line.

"Tess! You home? Knock, knock!"

"I thought I heard a rapping at my door," I had greeted David in the pantry that afternoon with a smile, panting slightly from the dash from my office. I kissed him lightly on the side of his mouth and he gave my arm a rub. David never pats, I noted.

"How ya doin', kiddo? Bake anything irresistible today?" he asked, heading straight for my cookie jar—a mammoth ceramic creation shaped like a house, complete with two children holding cookies, standing under a tree.

"Only chocolate chips," I warned before he lifted the lid, referring to the Toll House cookies I make all the time, for myself, from the original recipe on the back of the chocolate chip package—the ones my mother made for me when I was a child.

"*Only* chocolate chips, she says," he said, diving in and coming up with a handful, and then heading for the refrigerator, a cookie already in his mouth. "Milk?"

"I'll get you a glass . . . and a plate."

Once settled at the kitchen table with his milk and cookies, David told me what a lucky guy Stephen was to have found someone who was not only beautiful and smart, but who could cook. He was always telling me that. He was always telling Stephen that. Neither of us believed him.

"Honestly, David, I can't understand why some lovely lady hasn't swept you off your feet long ago."

"You did. But you were already married to Stephen."

"Right. With that attitude, you'll never get married. Don't you ever get serious?"

"I am serious. You just won't believe me." And he laughed, devoured a cookie in one bite, and washed it down with a gulp of milk.

"So, how is my husband?" I asked, wondering if he'd be home on time tonight . . . for a change.

"Oh, right. I told him I was stopping here on the way home, and he asked me to tell you that he'll probably be a few minutes late. The man is so disorganized."

"Tell me about it!"

"Don't worry. I keep my eye on him for you. I told him that I was going to join you two for dinner and that *I* didn't want to be kept waiting." He hesitated for a moment, then added, "That okay with you, Tess? Mind a tagalong?"

"What? No date tonight?"

"It's a slow season."

"You know you're always welcome, David."

Watching him in my kitchen, munching on cookies like a little kid, being as pleasant and supportive as I could imagine a man could be, I tried to imagine what it would be like to be married to David instead of Stephen. He was so attractive . . . and when he got up to leave—"I have to stop at home for a minute. I'll see you at Antonio's at six-thirty," he said—and gave me a hug, I kept the feeling of his arms around me after he had gone. *"You swept me off my feet. You shouldn't be married to Stephen,"* I imagined him saying to me while he buried his soft beard in my neck. And I grew warm imagining his hands on my back, on my backside, his mouth on my neck, on my mouth, his long white fingers slipping between my . . . An image of David and Katrina plastered itself over my fantasy. Katrina, the long-legged, long-haired dancer from the Pennsylvania Ballet Company who spoke in whispers—when she spoke at all—was the last lady I had seen David with. We were celebrating David's birthday at the Fountain Room in the Four Seasons Hotel. She couldn't keep her hands off him, in her own quiet way, and they didn't come back to our house after dinner— Katrina had said she had a present for David at her apartment. I pictured David making love to Katrina . . . her long slim legs entwined with his . . . her long, straight,

46

golden hair swirled around the two of them. . . . And I cringed at the thought of my short legs, my short boyish hair, and . . . Katrina. She probably made that name up for the theater, I decided. And why was Stephen always late? I wondered, now totally annoyed. And as much as I enjoyed having David around, why did Stephen not mind that David was always around? It was as if he used David as a buffer, so he didn't have to get too close to me. Yes. Stephen had trouble being close, I thought, believing that Stephen loved me very deeply . . . so deeply that it scared him. Yes. It felt nice to be loved so deeply. And I continued my fantasy, but replaced David with Stephen . . . Stephen telling me that he loved me so much that it scared him.

Yes. *I'm* never out of line. But David. Do I understand David—who he is? how he feels? what he's saying? I always believed it was Stephen that David wanted to be close to, a strong male bond to stave off the loneliness of singleness. Then again, David and I had remained friends even after Stephen and I separated. But David was like that, able to divide his loyalties successfully. Of course, I fought with myself, it *could* be me. No. I'm not his type. Not at all like those young, leggy, blond creatures who ran through his life leaving no fingerprints on his soul, barely lifting the dust from his id. Surely he was just being his usual caring, sharing, nurturing, warm, sensitive—

"Tess? Are you still there?" I heard David question over the phone, over the buzz of my inner monologue. "Tess, I want to be sure you understand what I'm saying."

"Of course I understand," I finally answered, not understanding at all.

I wanted to make something special for Jacqui Berkman's Friday evening dinner party, something that would reflect the pretensions of one who spelled Jackie *Jacqui*. So I called Le Petit Champignon and got the recipe for their lemon mirror cake. I was picturing Jacqui admiring the finished cake, admiring herself in its shiny glaze, when I was struck by an odd thought seemingly from nowhere: What would Jacqui see? Tall, extraordinarily thin (she always had five pounds to lose, but no one could figure out where), with blunt-cut, short, straight brown hair to her earlobes, parted in the middle, accentuating her sunken cheeks and sharp nose, her thin lips: One of Tom Wolfe's social X-rays, the way I see her; chic, exotic, the way she sees herself. "Don't you think I look exotic with my hair this way?" she had asked me at a cocktail party, stealing a glance at herself in a large oval mirror on the wall behind me. I remember thinking at the time how her high-fashion taupe dress hung on her bones, drained the color from her gaunt cheeks, how there was no possible way her thighs could touch. Exotic? No. "Yes," I said, "it gives you a really different look." Different from what you see in the mirror, I thought.

Setting out the ingredients for the cake, I considered that even in mirrors we probably don't see ourselves as we really are. This idea crystallized the nebulous mental meanderings that had plagued me since my first meeting with Dr. Lerner—Michael—almost a month ago, on a Tuesday, at eleven.

Remembering my first visit with Michael made me want to hide in a closet. I had tried to impress him with my intelligence, generosity of spirit, charm, sense of style, my youth (surely I was younger than he)—my image of myself as a totally desirable woman in complete control of her being. Right. That's why I was sitting in a shrink's office. Surely he saw right through me, understood that I was a total fraud.

By our third appointment, this past Tuesday, I was a little more comfortable—a little less comfortable than I am in a dentist's chair—comfortable enough to notice that Michael was actually younger than I by three or four years. Then again, perhaps he looked younger than he was. Average in height and build, Michael was above average in looks. The waves in his black hair hid early strands of silver. His dark eyes were alive behind clear-framed glasses. I liked the way he sat in a black leather Eames chair, in *front* of the desk rather than *behind* it, so that he sat facing me, close to me, as

I crossed and uncrossed my legs on the sofa across from his desk. Behind the desk, against the back wall, a trough of tropical trees and plants—some nearly six feet tall—were warmed by a row of track lights in the ceiling. Light from a row of tall casement windows on the right covered with old-style wooden venetian blinds formed glowing stripes across the floor behind Michael's chair.

"So, how do you see yourself?" he asked after I had shared a few vignettes from my growing-up years.

Yes, I look pretty. Yes, I'm having a good time, I remember thinking as I checked the hall mirror of my girlfriend's home. I was nine, maybe ten, and I was dressed up as a Dutch girl for a Halloween party. And my mother had put bright red lipstick on my mouth and circles of red rouge on my cheeks and shiny black mascara on my long eyelashes. But I had to keep looking in the mirror to know that I was.

Attractive, I remember thinking as I walked by the wall of mirrors at one end of the girls' gym, stealing a look at myself wearing a fluffy blue and silver strapless prom gown. But the boys, whose attention I begged as I walked daintily to and from the girls' room, appeared oblivious to me.

Yes, an eye-catcher, I remember thinking, glancing at my image in a tall, ornate pier mirror in a hotel lobby, perceiving a lovely young lady in black taffeta at a college dance. But it seemed that the young men whose attention I was trying to will were totally unaware of my presence.

"Oh, yes, we've met before," said the middle-aged lawyer's middle-aged wife when we were introduced at some professional function I was attending with Stephen several years ago. "You're noticeable." Was that a compliment? Does "noticeable" mean "attractive"? The men in the room didn't seem to notice me at all.

"I don't know, Michael. Isn't that why I'm here? Do you want to hear something weird? I'm not even sure if I know what I really look like."

"That's right," he said, leaving me wondering what he meant by that.

"Several people have told me that I don't photograph the way I actually look . . . and someone—the first husband of an old friend—once told me I was many women in one, always changing. I don't see myself as that complicated. He also told me he loved me," I babbled on. "And another friend, Alan Garfield, my friend Millie's husband, once said, 'You have a thousand faces in you.' . . . Does that mean he loves me? And he told me I was memorable. Is that anything like noticeable? And how does one remember someone who's always changing?"

"Perhaps that's why one remembers," Michael offered gently.

I looked at him blankly and did not respond, but something somewhere inside me clicked and I felt the back of my throat tighten, my eyes become myopic behind a film of moisture, my ears fill with soft static as I pulled myself in.

The buzz of the oven timer roused me from memory to the warm, sweet aroma of baked cake and the drone of the mixer. I turned the mixer off, retrieved the golden sponge cakes from the oven and set them on a rack to cool, and put the bowl of whipped cream in the refrigerator. Sandy walked in—on her way home from dropping Rebecca off at nursery school—as I was sitting down at the counter for a coffee break.

"Hiii! I see coffee's on," she said.

"Morning. My! Don't we look glowing! What's up?"

"Oh, nothing much. It's just that the nicest thing happened," she said, pouring herself a mug of coffee and opening the refrigerator to look for milk. "Anyway," she continued after sitting at the counter, pushing the mixer to the side, "I was coming out of Rebecca's school and I bumped into Danny Foster—remember him? Ruth's husband? You know . . . Ruth, the potter? I've got one of her pots in my living room by the fireplace. Well, Danny was dropping Matthew off at school—Matthew's the youngest of, would you believe, five! Can you imagine! Five! I can't find time enough for two. . . ."

No, I couldn't imagine all those warm little bodies, those sticky sweet hands, those loving little arms.

Catching the shadow that crossed my face, Sandy caught herself. ". . . I mean, you know I'm thankful for two healthy kids, it's only that I find it hard to imagine *five*—"

"I know," I said, offering a helping hand. "It's always hard to place yourself in someone else's shoes."

"Right. Anyway, we almost literally bumped, and he made a big fuss about how nice it was to see me, how wooonderful I looked. . . . Tess, I think he was coming on to me. I mean, the way he grabbed my arms when we bumped, like he didn't want to let go, and he made such a fuss—"

You probably had your lashes going double time, I thought to myself. "You do look bright today, Sandy," I said honestly, noting her canary yellow cashmere sweater-blouse—opened to the third button.

"Yes, I think so. His wife doesn't do a whole lot with herself. She wears those long skirts and heavy sweaters . . . she neeever wears any makeup, and her hands are so rough from throwing pots. I'll bet her nails never saw a coat of polish—what nails she has!"

"Sandy," I groaned, watching her slender hands flutter around like birds with scarlet-tipped white feathers.

"Oh, Tess, I'm not trying to be mean, but Danny actually said something about how put-together I always look."

"My, my!"

"Oh, it wasn't really anything . . . but I'll bet he would like it to be something."

"You may be right," I said, softening my attitude, feeling a sting of jealousy. "You know, men don't make passes at me. I always hear women talking about all the married men who make passes at them. Not me."

"Tess, I can't believe that."

"No, it's true. Maybe I give off the wrong vibrations."

"You mean you want married men to come on to you? You'd have an affair with one?"

"No. I'm only saying that it would be nice to believe that I'm desirable."

"Oh, come on, Tess. You're so attractive. You just don't know what a pass is!"

"Do you think so?"

"Absoluuutely. Guys look at you all the time when I'm with you."

"Never. They're always busy looking at you."

"Are you kidding? You turn heads, Tess. I've been green with envy lots of times. And I marvel at how you stay so cool and unaffected."

"That's because I'm unaware." I got up to turn the cakes out. Running a knife around the edges of the pans, I recalled one incident: "Well, there was one guy, when Stephen and I were still together—"

"Who? When? Where?"

"Didn't I ever tell you about the French doctor? At the Legal Aid Society dinner dance . . . oh, it had to be two, three years ago."

I related the story to Sandy while making the lemon mousse, which was as silky as the soft yellow satin dress I had worn that night.

Clingy, backless—a no-underwear dress. Stephen hated it. I loved it. It made me feel alluring, although I was sure no one ever took notice of me.

Stephen and I walked slowly among the crowd, stopping before familiar faces, reacting automatically to automatic conversation. Soon bored, I toyed abstractly with my inner switches. The right stance, a measure of inner tension . . . I turned on, flashing a smile toward Stephen.

"What's the matter?" he responded predictably, disappointingly. I faded, turning my attention to the crowd herding toward the tables for dinner.

Although I had planned to maintain my usual low profile, I changed my mind when seated. Above the haze of legal jargon, a treatise on the color and clarity of fine wine was being delivered by the man to my immediate right, René Breton, a plastic surgeon from France and the brother-in-law of a local judge, whom I had met briefly about a year before. Although he had been in this country for more than ten years, he had retained a heart-melting accent. Switching on, I felt my eyes light up, my heart pump a blush to my cheeks.

The slight, middle-aged doctor turned his inquiring blue eyes to me. "Some wine?" he offered.

"Thank you, yes," I said, smiling.

After filling my glass, he stood up and proposed a devastating toast in the spirit of his profession: "Here's to flapping thighs, sagging breasts, and falling faces."

Immediately I became aware of my tiny breasts, gelatinous thighs, and the faint smile lines on my thirtyish face, but managed to maintain a measure of inner tension as the Frenchman sat down and touched his glass to mine. When he asked me to dance, I was startled and confused for a moment, not knowing if I should ask Stephen for permission, or just say yes . . . or no. With the finesse only a totally nonplussed woman can summon, I cast a dazzling smile upon René, turned to Stephen, and, placing a hand on his, asked, "Do you mind?" Without waiting for an answer, I offered my hand to René.

He took me in his arms, grasping me closer than I thought possible while still dressed, and I suddenly realized that I hadn't danced with a man other than Stephen in years. When I first heard the compliment, it whizzed by my ear like a snatch of someone else's conversation. I thought I heard it, then wasn't sure, then was sure but didn't want to be, then was not sure and wanted to hear it again.

"I'm sorry, what was that?" I queried obtusely.

He said it again—slowly, deliberately: "You are a very beautiful woman."

I pulled away slightly to search his eyes. Surely he sensed my surprise, I thought. Surely he loved my surprise, I later thought. Managing a quiet "thank you," I allowed him to gather me in his arms once again and whirl me about. The compliment was beating in my ears. He'd called me beautiful, a beautiful woman. Then it was fluttering inside me, tickling a giddy smile to my lips. The compliment, a small bird with large wings, beat under my heart as I became aware of the Frenchman speaking.

"You are beautiful, stunning."

Oh, the deliciousness of it! Don't stop, don't ever stop, I thought to myself as the bird thrashed around wildly inside me.

"Of course," he added decorously, "I mean it sincerely, and without any improper intent."

"Of course," I echoed, embarrassed and flustered, not quite sure if he meant it or not, not quite sure if I wanted him to mean it.

Dancing with René through a second musical set, I slowly became aware of Stephen standing just a few feet away, his eyes following me and my admirer as we laced through and around the other couples on the dance floor. In a moment he was beside us, a hand on René's shoulder.

"Pardon me, this is our dance," Stephen said coolly, reclaiming me from the arms of my surprised partner.

I fell into comfortably familiar steps, and preened mentally.

"I know tomorrow is Sunday, but the accountants have arranged a tax meeting, so I'll be gone most of the day," Stephen announced.

"Oh, that's all right, I have plans for tomorrow," I parried with sangfroid as I pictured myself and the French doctor doing incredibly lewd and lascivious things in one of those motels with the water beds, video cameras, and hourly rates.

"What a greaaat story, Tess. So, did he call?"

"You are incredible." I laughed at Sandy, putting the now completed cakes in the freezer. "I never considered that I would ever bump into him again, and I certainly didn't think he'd actually call me. But, guess what."

"He called."

"He called. One afternoon after Stephen and I had separated, ostensibly to find Stephen. At first I thought he really wanted to find Stephen. Then I thought, A business call? In the afternoon? At home?"

"So did you see him?"

"You've got to be kidding. I gave him Stephen's office number."

"It could have been fun."

"I doubt it. But the point is, I fell for his line. I didn't even know it was a pass! I really thought he had meant what he said." I began cleaning up, putting the pans and bowls, beaters and spoons into the dishwasher. "Then he called and I realized . . . I felt so dumb!"

"Tess. How do I explain this to you? Why do you think he complimented you?"

"Because he heard I was newly separated and figured I'd be easy."

"But you weren't separated at the dance. And he didn't call until after you were separated."

"But *he* was still married!"

"So, what did you want him to do—divorce his wife so he could say something nice to a pretty lady who caught his eye at a dance?"

I noted exasperation in her voice. Was I exasperating?

"God! Tess, you're exasperating."

"But am I attractive?!"

"Look in the mirror!"

"Mirrors don't work."

"They work for some things," Sandy said, then broke up in a howl of laughter. I threw my arms around her and we laughed until tears ran down our faces, remembering what I had related to her the previous Sunday.

"So how did your date go last night?" Sandy had questioned at Sunday brunch (Sandy and I were alone; Sean was being treated by a school friend's family to a day in Philadelphia, including a show at the Fels Planetarium in the Franklin Institute, so Janet had treated herself to a day in New York City with Harvey, who had told his wife he had to attend an investment seminar). Sandy was referring to my third date with Marv Kravitz.

In my head I quickly reviewed the developing gestalt.

Marv was a nice man, terribly hurt by a wicked wife who ran off with the director of her little theater group at her synagogue. Well, she didn't exactly run off with him. My dentist's hygienist's husband ran off with her brother's wife. They ran off to Australia. Marv's wife moved into The Director's center-city apartment—about twenty minutes from Marv. Marv's fourteen-year-old son, Zachery, visited his mom every other weekend and Wednesday nights for dinner.

A manufacturers' rep for boudoir mirrors, Marv was every inch the salesman—the inches that he had. When he had pulled up to the house for our first date a month ago in a very long navy blue Lincoln Town Car, I watched from my kitchen window as he descended from the plush velour front seat to the driveway. About five-foot-four and slight of build, Marv looked like a little boy. We reached the front door at the same time, but I waited for half a minute after he rang the bell before I opened it, taking time to check myself out in the art deco mirror above the chocolate-marble-topped credenza in the foyer. Hair okay. Makeup okay, although the dark shadows under my eyes attested to a lack of sleep the night before. And I did look awfully thin. So I smiled vigorously to appear more alive as I opened the door. "Tess?" "Hi, Marv," I greeted him, extending my hand as he walked through the door. His small hand gripped mine overly hard. We both smiled a lot, made our way through the formalities of how lovely my home was, how lovely I was, what a lovely evening it was. He held my coat for me with an exaggerated flourish—"Your coat, madam!" The car door was opened for me with the same flourish. Watching him walk briskly around the car to the driver's side, with his head held a little too high, his arms swinging a little too wide, I was reminded of Spanky of the Little Rascals, and I wondered if tucked away in a closet in Marv's home was a beanie. He was sweet, though, and it was nice talking to a man who wasn't overtly weird, so at evening's end, when he walked me to the door, kissed my hand—with a flourish— and asked me for another date, I accepted.

And after a second date—we saw the latest Woody Allen movie and ate dinner at a local Italian restaurant, and he gave me a peck on the cheek at my door and rubbed my hand as he told me that he had found it hard to concentrate on his work since our first date—I accepted a third date.

"It was bizarre," I finally answered Sandy, and shared with her the hours I had shared with Marv on our third date.

After an intimate dinner and a bottle of wine at Charades, a nouvelle cuisine restaurant in the area ("We should eat light," he had said cryptically), Marv asked me back to his home—to show me his line.

"Is that anything like etchings?" I teased him.

"Do you mean, is my line just *a line?*" he retorted.

I laughed nervously and wondered if I should go, because, after all, wouldn't that mean that I was willing to . . . and was I willing to . . . ? No, I wasn't ready to . . . but no, I didn't want to appear the prude, and no, it wasn't very late, and no, I wasn't ready to go back to my big, empty house, so, yes, I would go, have a cup of tea, see his line of mirrors, and then it would be late enough to call it a night.

So there we were in the early American country kitchen of his three-bedroom, two-bath ranch home, with the plate rail above the dark wooden cabinets and the Pennsylvania Dutch hex signs on the wallpaper. Marv was fixing me a cup of Earl Grey tea, which I love but don't drink at night because it's loaded with caffeine, but which I said was fine because it was all he had and I wanted to be agreeable. And I was leaning against the built-in phone center—a kind of raised desk in an alcove with a wall telephone—when he set the tea on the table, came over to me, put his arms around me, kissed me lightly, and pressed his body to mine. He was just about my size, which felt nice, and he smelled good, and when he kissed me again, seriously, his mouth was warm and soft. I felt my blood stir.

"Oooph! What you're doing to me!" he said, slowly grinding his pelvis against mine, pushing me against the desk behind me. "Oooh! Feel that? Feel what you're doing to me?" he said, pushing harder, his eyes closed, his face puckered up in ecstasy. But the only hard thing I felt was the knob of the desk drawer poking me in the ass. He kissed me again, passionately, running his little hands up and down my back. "Oooh, yes, yes," he whispered in my ear. "Feel it, feel it," he rasped, pushing into me. But the harder he pressed, the harder the knob bit into me, until, in pain, I pushed away from the desk—into him. "Oh, yes, that's good!" he responded, misinterpreting my movement as passion. "Come with me, *mon cherie,* I want to show you my line," he said, suddenly pulling away, holding my hand, leading me toward the bedroom wing off the front hall. What was intended to be the third bedroom, between his son's room and the master bedroom, was Marv's showroom. The walls were hung with mirrors in brass frames, wooden frames, carved frames, mirrored frames. There were full-length mirrors for walls and doors, and wide mirrors to go over bureaus and dressing tables. Marv showed me around the room, guiding me by my shoulders from behind, stopping before particular mirrors to point out favorite designs —"Look at the detail on the French baroque piece"—and to nuzzle my neck. Did he, in fact, roll his eyes upward to look into the mirror as he kissed my neck? I wasn't sure the first time, but he did it again. Yes, he definitely looked at us posed in front of the mirror, his face in my neck, his hands running down my arms—and he closed his eyes quickly when he saw me looking at him looking.

"Very nice," I finally said, pulling away from him. "It's a lovely line, Marv."

"But you haven't seen the best ones yet—my private collection," he said, taking me by the hand again, leading me to the master bedroom.

A king-size mahogany four-poster bed with a mahogany canopy stood against the back wall. On the wall, between the low headboard and the canopy, a large mirror in an unusual bronze and brass frame—"Isn't it fabulous?" said Marv. "I got it at an estate auction in New York"—appeared to be improperly hung so that the top tilted slightly away from the wall. In front of the windows on the right was a love seat covered in a floral fabric matching the drapes on the windows. Next to the love seat stood a small round antique table, and on it was a tiny crystal lamp and a six-inch oval mirror in a hand-cut glass frame—"I found that in an antique shop in Connecticut," Marv said. In the corner across from the foot of the bed, to the right of the love seat, was a handmade brass brazier from India, the top of which had been electrified and hung from the ceiling on a long brass chain. Its shapely dome, hanging low over the footed bowl planted with ivy, was punched out in an intricate design, throwing an eerie light over the room and snowflake patterns on the soft-rose walls. This was the only light on in the room. Next to a mahogany triple dresser on the left wall was a matching highboy. Above the triple dresser hung a huge mirror in a gilt wooden frame—"From my grandmother's home. It was her mother's," he explained. Along the wall in front of the bed, next to the brazier, were three antique cheval mirrors—"My prizes," he said proudly as he paraded me before them, touching each one, causing them to tilt slightly in their freestanding frames. Two were rectangular: One, in a heavy brass and iron frame, had been imported from Italy; the other, elegant in a simple cherry frame, was English.

"This is my favorite," he said, stopping in front of the last glass. The large beveled oval mirror was framed in heavily carved ebony and mounted on solid brass swivels in an ebony stand that was taller than the glass itself, its sides terminating in thick, eight-inch finials. Here and there on the glass were small patches of gray where the silvering was eroding. "This is a very old piece, from the eighteenth century. The wood feels wonderful. It's so smooth and hard," Marv said, reaching up to stroke one of the finials slowly with his left hand. Grinning lasciviously in the mirror, still stroking the finial, he took my hand with his right hand and pressed it into his groin. My heart skipped a beat and then began to race. I saw everything at once in the mirror—his eyes, my eyes, my hand in his hand in his mushy crotch—and before I could move, his arms were around me and he was kissing me tenderly, smelling wonderfully of something musky, and then he was behind me unbuttoning my cream silk blouse, kissing my neck. And I just stood there letting him, watching him undress me in the mirror in the dim, eerie light. It was all quite strange. We were disembodied from He and She in the mirror, but the feelings of those bodies remained with us.

I watched Her standing naked and flushed. He took Her hands and ran them along the sides of Her body. I felt Her hardened nipples as He steered Her hands across Her breasts, which appeared larger than I had remembered them to be, but the touch of Her hands sent a familiar charge through me. "You are beautiful . . ." He said, ". . . look how beautiful . . . so smooth . . . so tight . . ." drawing Her right hand toward the dark triangle, pressing closer behind Her. I felt the soft, the wet, as He guided Her fingers . . . I felt the waves of pleasure, the tension as He slipped Her fingers to and fro, as He rocked behind Her. My knees gave way and I found myself on the floor, on the soft gray carpet, looking up at Marv, who was suddenly out of His clothes, moving the cheval glasses on their casters out from the wall, forming an alcove of mirrors, tipping them slightly downward on their swivels so that I could see Her looking down at me. And He spread Her legs gently so I could see Her soft hidden parts. . . . I watched as He knelt, His small penis hanging limply, and touched Her swollen pink flesh . . . and I quivered and moaned softly . . . and He lay down between Her legs and put His mouth to Her flesh and I felt the unbearable velvet of His tongue, the tiny spasms in the muscles of Her tense legs and arms—and I did not miss the small bald spot on the back of His head reflecting the tiny flakes of light from the brazier—and just when I was lost in pleasure, when I thought I would explode with pleasure, he suddenly stood up.

"Don't stop!" I heard myself cry out.

"Wait, it's not over," he said, pulling me up, kissing me, coaxing me to my knees, pushing the mirrors upright. We watched as He moved close to Her. "Touch me," He said . . . and She reached out to touch Him, to stroke Him until I felt His member slowly swell, filling Her hand, growing hard and smooth, growing and growing much beyond what one would have expected of a thing so small

. . . or so it appeared in the looking glass. I watched as He moved back and forth, forcing the great burning cock up and back in Her small fist. "I love a woman with small hands," He said. "Look how big it looks in that small hand. . . . Look how big and hard it is. . . . Feel how hot it is. . . . Oooh, what you do to me," He said, rocking up and back. But suddenly He stopped, pulled me to my feet, took me to the bed. And when I lay crosswise on the bed and looked up, I saw the secret mirrors of the canopy reflect Her smooth, shapely, outstretched body. He took Her hand and placed it between Her legs. . . . "Oooh, doesn't that feel good, isn't that hot," He said. And I was watching Her caress herself . . . yes, She knew how, She knew where, how fast, how hard, when to stop so it wouldn't end . . . when a soft sound drew part of me to another dimension coming toward me—the reflection in the great ebony cheval mirror that Marv wheeled to the edge of the bed. And shortly I was surrounded by reflections so that when he lay next to me, we two had become twelve. He watched, I watched, They watched, as He stroked himself to mythic proportions . . . as bodies touched and turned and played and burned . . . as the headless woman in the mirror lowered herself onto Him. I felt the filling the stroking the exquisite pleasure and I closed my eyes and flattened my body full of him against him and he watched as She moved creating wondrous friction inside and outside and he began to move and he came in a long loud cry and I watched as She stroked His body with Hers until my fingers and toes went numb and my inner eyes went black and I was swallowed into the abyss.

"Wow," I whispered in his ear.

"Oooh, what you do to me," he said to . . . to me? . . . to Her in the mirror?

And it did not end there. The night went on for eons as the mirrors multiplied the seconds the minutes the hours as they multiplied our bodies over and over and over . . .

When I said good night to Marv at my front door, he asked us out for the following Saturday night, and we accepted.

* * *

And last Sunday Sandy had listened intently to my adventure and said only, "Wooow," when I had finished.

And now Sandy and I were practically choking with laughter. "Have a good time tomorrow night!" she managed through her cackles as she was leaving to pick up Rebecca. "And to think you said he's nothing special, just a salesman."

"That's right," I said, "he's just a salesman. A damn good one. He does it all with mirrors."

FLOATING ISLAND

The Islands

2 cups milk
1 teaspoon vanilla extract
5 egg whites
2/3 cup sugar

Over low heat, warm milk and vanilla in a deep skillet to a simmer. While milk is heating, beat egg whites until foamy. Slowly add sugar, continuing to beat until whites form stiff peaks. Off the heat, drop egg whites by large, rounded spoonfuls into the milk. Return skillet to very low heat and poach islands for 2 more minutes, until firm to the touch. With a slotted spoon, remove the islands and drain on a towel. Refrigerate on a platter.

The Custard

2 cups milk (from the islands plus fresh)
1 teaspoon vanilla extract
5 egg yolks
1/2 cup sugar
1 tablespoon apricot brandy

Strain milk into 2-cup measure and add fresh milk to fill. Heat milk and vanilla in top of a double boiler to a simmer. Blend egg yolks and sugar. Stirring constantly, slowly add hot milk. Return mixture to top of double boiler, add brandy, and cook, stirring constantly, until mixture thickens. Plunge the top of the boiler into ice water, and stir occasionally until the mixture is cool. Strain custard and refrigerate.

The Caramel

1 cup sugar
1/2 cup water

Cook sugar in a heavy saucepan over low heat until it melts and turns golden brown. Off the heat, stir in water. Return pan to heat and simmer for about 10 minutes, until the caramel is smooth and slightly thickened. Cool at room temperature.

The Assembly

Float islands in custard in a crystal bowl. Drizzle caramel sauce over each island when serving. Serves 8–10.

CHAPTER 5

Floating Island

On a blustery Friday in March, I pretended I was engrossed in whipping egg whites into meringue and poaching them into tiny islands that would float on sunny vanilla custard in a crystal bowl at Paula Reuben's dinner party that evening. The snowy archipelago on the cooling rack reminded me of the chains of islands illustrated on maps. It's not true that no man is an island, I mused. We're all islands, and the water around us is deep, and cold, and treacherous. I was really waiting for Stephen.

I had said *NO!* the night before when he called, waking me at eleven-thirty. *NO! I won't take you back!* But I knew he wouldn't accept no. Sure enough, at a little after four, just as I had set the finished sea of custard in the refrigerator to chill, the doorbell rang. Reaching for the doorknob, I saw Stephen through the glass panes, and the wisp of a smile that had crossed my lips dissipated. My heart began to race, my skin to tingle and go numb as I pulled within myself, away from him, remembering, in an instant, all at once, all the times before when he had come and gone . . . the promises . . . the betrayals.

"Stephen, where are you?" I had questioned him one night in bed as he lay on his side beside—not around—me. "You're not with me."

"Oh, I don't know," he answered, gazing at a spot between my chin and my shoulder.

"Something's come between us," I said. The small clues were there—the little things that appear unimportant when listed, but are, in fact, the very things that define the ebbs and flows of a relationship. Sentimental songs on the radio, such as "You Don't Send Me Flowers Anymore," prickled me. Like pop psychology or pop art, pop songs often hold essential truths in their clichés. Stephen had stopped holding my hand in the car. We were making love quickly— fucking; there were no lingering Sunday mornings in bed with brunch at four, no predawn, dreamlike conjoinings. It was more than the bloom off the rose, the honeymoon being over; it was deeper than that. We had been married only three years. Surely, I hoped, he wasn't bored with me yet. Surely, I felt, he was bored with me. "Are you bored with me?" I asked.

When we first met, I had believed him when he told me how much he wanted a home—his own home, with his own lawn, not a rented *unit* or a condo with a *collectively owned* lawn. And I had believed him when he told me he loved children. We talked a lot about children—I guess *I* talked a lot about children. But I also believed him when he told me that he was an island, floating from one woman to the next, that he never let anyone into himself, that he got bored easily. So why did he keep calling? So why did I continue to see him? Our bodies loved, melded when we made love, when we slept, when we held fast to the warmth of each other, that's why. We felt safe with each other when it was only skin between us, because his skin my skin became our skin. So I believed him when he went away on business trips and called me every evening to say he missed me, intimating that he was dining, and sleeping, alone. I believed him when he went on mini-vacations to this island and that mountain, not to be away from me, he said, but to be by himself—a fine line that I chose to believe in.

And I believed him when he promised me he spoke to

Dorothy Oberman—his former bookkeeper and former lover—"occasionally . . . on the phone, not in person, and only because she needs to talk to me. . . . I told her I'd always be there for her, as a friend." Even when he came to me reeking of perfume one evening—the personification of a cliché—I believed him when he swore he had seen Dorothy "just this once, to give her some money to help her out of a jam" . . . that he hadn't made love to her. I remembered a character in a Doris Lessing novel telling how she'd smelled another woman on her man when he came home to her one night. She *knew* he had been unfaithful. Forget the temporal scent of *another woman* on the hair ends, the pore rims of a man; confronted with Opium pressed into a white-on-white cotton shirt, all *I* knew was that I wasn't going to believe anything I didn't want to believe. So I allowed Stephen to "prove" his fidelity to me: He made love to *me* that night—passionately. A cliché that should have proved something, but it wasn't fidelity.

I suppose I knew it; I know I felt it. I simply chose not to believe what I felt: that there was a lot he didn't tell me, that he was breaking promises to me. Until even when we were skin to skin I felt apart from him—then I chose to be away from him. And it was painful. Like a burn victim, living without skin, all nerve ends exposed, nowhere could I find comfort. This must be love, I thought, never having experienced anything like it before. So I believed him and forgave him for his unconfessed sins when he cried to me that he, too, was in great pain and begged for another chance.

And so we married, to provide skin for each other's charred souls. But the soul is merely the spindle around which the rest of us winds: the day-to-day, the experiences of a lifetime—that thread from which we each weave our private beliefs, our public tales. And skin provides no armor against our deceptions.

"Of course I'm not bored with you," he had answered after a while, but added, "Maybe I'm just not the kind of man who can be married."

I was silent.

"I love you," he said, trying to hold back the crashing void. "I want to be with you, but maybe I can't be married."

"What are you trying to tell me, Stephen?" I asked, ignoring the fact that he'd already told me.

"Nothing. Nothing. Only that I'm trying to adjust, and it's not easy. But it'll be okay. I'll adjust."

"You'll adjust to what? Is it that we're alone? That we don't have children? We've tried so hard, Stephen. I feel a void, too," I said, assuming that he felt a void. "But at least I have you. I'm grateful for that. At least we have each other. I thought you felt that way, too."

"I do, Tess. I do. In fact, maybe it's better that we don't have children. I want to be with you, but I don't want to be in a place where I have to be every day because I *should* be or I *have to* be."

"You want me but you don't want responsibilities? You mean you don't want to be responsible to *me*," I answered in anger, aware that I was dragging him into deep waters and we were going to drown. "Please try to be honest with me," I pleaded over his silence. "You have to let me know where I stand with you. That's only fair," I ended, ignoring the fact that he had already been honest.

But soon after there was that Wednesday morning phone call from Carley "Wonder Woman" Statten's husband, who was even more honest with me. I suppose I wasn't surprised to learn that Carley, who had been Stephen's secretary for almost two years, was having an affair with him, not really surprised, that is. Stephen readily confessed to his yearlong "dalliance" with Carley, but begged for forgiveness on the grounds of "stupidity," "male ego-gratification," and "vulnerability"—to her big tits, I reckoned. He'd fire her, he'd never see her again, he said. He couldn't bear the thought of losing me. "You've already lost me," I lied to us both, and told him he'd have to move out. He did, into one of the sleazy investment apartments that he and David owned on the fringe of respectable society. But I missed him desperately, and I consoled myself by believing that he needed to leave in order to stay. And when he called every morning to plead for time and understanding, and every night to tell me that he loved me, I finally consented to go to a marriage counselor with him.

Marty Steinheiser, M.S.W., was a small man, about fifty, with pale blue rheumy eyes, livery lips that collected bits of white foam at the corners when he talked, and a balding head. I spent considerable moments contemplating the stripes of long hair that spanned the top of his head, ear to ear, wondering if they reached his shoulders in the shower, whether they stayed put when he made love to his wife, *if* he made love to his wife. He came highly recommended.

In our initial, joint session in Marty's dim office, sitting in heavy mahogany and leather armchairs across from his heavy mahogany desk that held the single light in the room—a brass apothecary lamp with a green glass shade—I yelled about Stephen's dishonesties, his infidelities. Stephen listened, staring at his fingers meshing and unmeshing around his crossed knees. I interpreted his silent listening as agreement, contrition. Sitting behind his desk, Marty listened, bobbing his head now and then, lowering his seemingly lashless lids, thumping his receding chin with a stubby forefinger. I interpreted *his* silent listening as agreement, sympathy. When alone with Marty, I cried about Stephen's infidelity and my infertility, and Marty soothed, "I understand how you feel. . . . This must be very hard for you. . . ." and excused, "Consider the fragile male ego. . . ." and judged, "Perhaps the greater sin is to be unforgiving." When alone with Marty, Stephen listened as Marty told him about his own marital difficulties with an unforgiving wife. When Marty separated from his wife, Stephen and I separated from Marty.

We dated. We went on weekend trips to New York City to see the ballet and to Vermont to ski. Still angry, I drew a line behind which I was determined to stand, and wait, and watch. Until I felt sure of him, I wouldn't let him come home. But I needed his skin. So we lived apart and we slept together. I had the illusion of control. It was probably what he'd wanted all along.

Then one Thursday night when, after eight staunch

months, I was inexplicably feeling flutters of trust and the
need to relax, to fall against the man who continually
expressed a desire to be there for me, Stephen called from
Chicago, where he'd been on business since Monday.
"Come to me from the airport tomorrow," I appealed, "I
miss you."

We hugged when he arrived Friday evening, but we didn't
really kiss. He didn't seem hungry to see me. He made
himself a drink, told me quickly of the business of his trip,
and asked about my week. I was quiet, content in having
him beside me, having the comfort of his presence, trying to
ignore the ghost of a wall that I sensed around him. "I just
needed you near me," I explained.

"I had an interesting flight home," he said abruptly as we
sat on the sofa, his hand resting on my knee. A red flag
waved in my head. "Sitting next to me was this woman . . ."
NO! wailed in my head. ". . . thirty years old, divorced,
blond . . ." Red flares shot off. *NO!* I don't want to hear this.
". . . a paralegal for Leiber, Armstrong, Block, and Cohn—
you know, Bart Armstrong's firm—the guy who wanted to
involve me in that crazy bond deal last year. Small world."

I felt all the blood in my body race to my hands and the
cavities behind my eyes. "Oh?" I said, trying to control the
quiver, the quake, the red rushing up my neck, the pounding
in my ears. "And I suppose you took her card?"

"Yep." *BASTARD!*

"And you gave her yours?"

"Sure. . . ." *SADIST!* ". . . She said maybe she could be
of some help to me with—" But I didn't let him finish.
Falling on him, I pummeled his shoulders and arms with my
fists. His arms flew up protectively, and I retreated, more
shocked than he by the incredible anger that had been
summoned from somewhere inside me. He looked at me,
half smiling. "It was only business!" he defended himself.

"Bullshit!" I yelled. But feelings of guilt for my lack of
reason, my hostile and uncharacteristic assault, dampened
my rage. And the paralysis of ambivalence set in: *He* wasn't
responsible for his seat assignment; or was he? People *do*

talk on planes; but most people don't exchange business cards. Or do they? Isn't that what business cards are *for,* for *business?* Isn't that how *business* is carried out, deals are created, fortunes made? But Stephen had more connections with that law firm than *she* could possibly have. And I noted that she had given him *two* cards—a corporate business card designating her a paralegal for the firm, and a personal business card, emblazoned with her home telephone number, designating her a "consultant," a clearly ambiguous term advocated for use on such cards by magazine advice columns on "the single life." Better than writing your name on the wall of a telephone booth, I reasoned.

We went to bed early. We didn't make love. I felt betrayed, but I wasn't sure how.

Stephen said he was trying to be honest with me when he told me, a week later, about the lunch he'd had the day before with Elayne Darby, the blonde from the plane, who, he said, had called *him* because she wanted to share some information with him about the bond deal, information that only *she* was privy to because she was on *intimate terms* with one of the law partners. Read: She was sleeping with him. Then, in an effort to coax her into sharing more of this information with him, which, it turned out, was nothing he didn't already know—which was nothing *I* didn't already know—he took her to dinner one evening, and then to lunch again. And then—small world—a few weeks later they met again on a plane, this time on a trip *to* Chicago. So he had dinner with her one night in Chicago at this excellent little Thai restaurant she knew of, and maybe lunch one afternoon—he couldn't remember for sure. Of course, it was all business.

All of this he told me one night when I was in enough psychic pain to question him about the distance once again growing between us. And, as he is wont to do when I ask the right questions, he told me part of the truth. But *she* told me the *whole* truth when she called to tell me that she was having an affair with Stephen and that I shouldn't try to hold on to him because she intended to fight for him. What is this? I wondered, falling down my own private rabbit hole. Am I living in a grade-B movie, an afternoon soap opera? I, who groaned at such clichés in television sitcoms I refused to watch and best-selling novels I refused to read, was living in one. Maybe *this* is real life. Maybe *I'm* not fighting hard enough for my man, I concluded desperately.

So I yelled at Stephen and told him that I wasn't going to let go that easily—easily?—that I was determined to put our marriage back together because I believed we needed each other. After two weeks of passionate browbeating—by me—and penitent chest-beating—by him—I listened on the other phone when he called Elayne from my apartment to tell her that he loved me and that he wasn't going to see her anymore, that it was (I shuddered at the triteness) just one of those things. I listened as she called him a fucking pig and told him that he'd never have any further dealings with Leiber, Armstrong, Block, and Cohn, that she wouldn't miss him at all, and that, by the way, he was devious, withholding, and untrustworthy. I would have bowed out more gracefully, I thought, victorious. And, although I felt he *was* devious, withholding, and untrustworthy, we started dating again. And, after a while, when I was beginning to believe that we could never be together because he could never be honest with me, I decided that we should be together because as long as we were apart he had no reason to be honest with me. So he moved home. So we moved to a new house. And I believed him when he said that *this* time it would be different, *this* time he would be honest with me, *this* time he knew what he wanted.

Until the next time, which was three and a half years later, when, after a particularly edgy week, Stephen came home late with a curious story concerning a traffic jam, a traffic ticket for speeding, an old friend from college days, his friend's girlfriend, and a few drinks in a hotel lounge, although not necessarily in that order. These facts were clear: Stephen was upset; he had been drinking; he reeked of perfume. Again! Remembering Doris Lessing, I accused him of being with another woman. "I danced with my friend's girlfriend," he insisted. I told him to leave. He spilled: He had seen Dorothy. . . . She had called him; she needed money again. . . . She was hysterical. . . . He agreed to see her, once, in a public place. So they met in a bar and had a few drinks, and he gave her some money . . . and of course he hugged her when he left, because she was so upset . . . and he got a ticket on the way home for speeding because *he* was upset that he had broken his promise to me not to see her again. "She looked so old," he said. I don't know what Lessing's character would have done, but I put my arms around my man and held him. I felt so sorry that he had to face that disgusting remnant of his degenerate past. I felt so good that he had been honest with me.

But he had been more honest with Dorothy—when he told her that he would always be there for her, but he would never marry her, even if he left me . . . which he was thinking of doing. This *she* told me when she called me the next day—Why do they all call me? Why can't I figure these things out myself?—to tell me that David had found out that Stephen was sleeping with her in the same sleazy apartment Stephen had occupied three years earlier, where, unbeknownst to me, she had taken up residence when he moved back home. And in a seizure of guilt under David's condemning eye, Stephen had met with Dorothy to tell her that she'd have to move. "So," she said to me, "I thought you should know *all* about it." *All* included a quick synopsis of her former husband's infidelity and the bitch who took him from her and the bitches who kept taking Stephen from her.

I quietly placed the receiver in its cradle—I couldn't believe I had listened for as long as I had—even as she continued to cry to me—to *me!*—about Stephen's unfaithfulness. Her point was an interesting one: Stephen had not been unfaithful to *me,* he had been unfaithful to *her.* And that made all the difference. So *this* time when he begged for forgiveness, *this* time when he told me he loved me, that he couldn't live without me, I didn't believe him. *This* time, even though I still loved him, even though I could have forgiven him again, I told him no, because *this* time I could not forgive myself.

"Stephen." I closed the door behind him and turned to face him in the foyer, frozen with resentment.

"I want to come home. I'll do anything you say. I need to be here. It's all I ever wanted," he stumbled.

His pathetic demeanor stoked my anger to the point of release. "It's not what you *ever* wanted!" I raged. He cringed, cowered as I overwhelmed him with abhorrence, with hateful accusations, venomous imputations: "You're treacherous! You disgust me! You can stand there and tell me that while you were fucking *her,* all you wanted was to be with *me?* Liar! Cheat! Perfidious prick!" Yes. I liked that one. But the eruption left a void inside me into which my outside began to sink, and I felt his arms go round me— structure for my collapsing being. His sobs were in my ear, his tears on my cheek, tears that primed my own, and my tears arrested his. But he held me still, tighter than ever before, tighter than I have ever been held, and I clung to him, though it seemed that I could never be held long enough, or hard enough.

Not hard enough to dispel the encroaching ogre, the unnameable terror that had visited me in the night in my fever in my mother's arms . . . never long enough, always a hunger for more, just a moment more, to make it real.

But he held me that hard, that long, long enough for me to feel finished and that I could let go first.

I noticed that it had darkened outside as we sank to the stairs where he sat one step below me, his arms wrapped around my legs, his head in my lap. And I bent over him, cradled his head in my arms, laid my cheek on his hair, the soft touch of which always surprised me—prematurely gray, it looked like steel wool, a metallic quality that matched his wiry body, his steel gray eyes, his cold, hard edge. I wept again, easily, quietly, for a long time, long enough to wash away the fantasy, to say good-bye to the man I had wanted him to be, pretended he was. "You have to go now," I said gently, but with a conviction that moved him to his feet and out the door without so much as a whisper. He was gone. We both knew he'd be back. I knew it would be different.

"Let me understand this," said Michael Tuesday morning, "he put his head in your lap and you cried on him?"

I nodded.

"That's wonderful."

Why? I wondered, but didn't ask because I was overwhelmed with sadness. Why? I didn't ask. "I think I was saying good-bye," I said.

Michael saw my face contort, my shoulders hunch over as if I had taken a blow to the gut. He left his seat, sat down beside me, and put his arm around me. Was this to be it: the opening up; the letting go? Was I going to allow myself to allow him to comfort me? No. I was too aware of him next to me, of the awkwardness of our juxtaposition—what to do with my crossed legs, what to do with my shoulders, what to do with my arms, my hands, my limp hands that couldn't just hold on to this small island of peace. Although frustrated now, as well as in pain, I fought the tears that choked me. Michael stood up to remove his jacket—this was to be a production, my breaking down—then returned to sit beside me, and this time I turned to him and put my head against his shoulder. He removed his glasses and gently held me. Then it struck me: Michael had removed his jacket, he had removed his glasses—he was undressing! No, of course he wasn't. What a strange association. I was in pain, Michael was trying to comfort me, but I was distracted by motions. My emotions were stifled by motions. I was discomfited, but I was no longer moved to the threat of tears, no longer moved. Frozen with inhibition, I felt graceless, ungrateful, ugly. I . . . I . . . I! What about him? What about Michael? Now I felt guilty as well as frustrated and in pain. I hadn't given a thought to how Michael was feeling. I had assumed: He didn't feel; he was just trying to do his job—building bridges from island to island.

ROCKY ROAD ICE CREAM CAKE ROLL

5 eggs
1 teaspoon vanilla extract
1/2 teaspoon salt
1/3 cup sugar
1/3 cup cornstarch
1/3 cup flour
chocolate marshmallow ice cream
4 one-ounce squares semisweet chocolate
1 1/2 tablespoons solid vegetable shortening
1/2 cup chopped almonds

Preheat oven to 375°F. Line a 10 1/2 x 15 1/2-inch jelly-roll pan
with wax paper.

Separate the eggs and beat the yolks with the vanilla. In another
bowl, beat the whites until foamy. Add the salt to whites and
beat until soft peaks form. Slowly add the sugar and beat until
stiff peaks form.

Spoon the whites over the yolks and sift the cornstarch and flour
on top. Fold the mixture to blend, and spread it over the wax
paper in the pan. Bake for 12 minutes, or until a toothpick comes
out clean.

Turn the cake out onto a towel and remove the wax paper. Trim
crumbs away and roll the cake up lengthwise with the towel. Let
it sit for a minute, then unroll. Roll it again with the towel in it
and let cool. Unroll it and spread a half-inch of softened
chocolate marshmallow ice cream on the cake to the edges. Cut it
in half and roll up the two halves. Wrap in wax paper and
freeze.

Melt semisweet chocolate squares in the top of a double boiler
with the shortening. Mix in chopped almonds. Lay the frozen
rolls in the middle of a sheet of wax paper. Glaze each roll with
melted chocolate mixture. Return the rolls to the freezer until
ready to serve. Serves 12.

CHAPTER 6

Rocky Road Ice Cream Cake Roll

"Big News . . ." Sandy had promised me when she called at ten o'clock Friday morning to ask me to meet her at the diner for lunch. News meant a juicy piece of gossip about someone we knew well, or something perfectly horrible about someone we barely knew at all. Occasionally a single item encompassed both criteria. This constituted Big News.

". . . But first we've got to find Janet," she had said. I had no idea where Janet was—she was off on Friday when she worked Thursday evening, which was the case this week. Sandy said she'd explain all at lunch.

I finished baking two sheets of sponge cake for the Rocky Road ice cream cake rolls Charlene Platt had ordered for her seven-thirty dinner party, showered and dressed, met a real estate client—Vincent Salvatore, business broker, bodybuilder, gourmet cook . . . and single—at his two-bedroom, two-bath, condominium townhouse that he wanted to sell for two hundred and twenty-five thousand dollars, and made it to the diner by one o'clock. Sandy was waiting.

"You won't belieeeve what's happening," she started even as the hostess was leading us to our booth. We ordered quickly—two small Greek salads, coffee—without looking at the menu, and then Sandy continued. "Do you remember a woman I mentioned to you months ago? I met her at Rebecca's nursery school? Eileen?"

I shook my head, totally unfamiliar with the name, somewhat distracted, considering the desserts I had to put together after lunch, and the new listing I'd just got, and the very attractive man who'd given it to me.

Sandy ignored my lack of enthusiasm and began to relate the most bizarre tale: It seemed that she had become friendly with Eileen, who was the mother of one of Rebecca's nursery school friends, Karen. After a time, Eileen began confiding in Sandy about her husband's inattentions, inconsiderations, inabilities—the latter of which he blamed on her being six months pregnant and "gross." Now, Sandy (she tells me this for the first time) had had experience along these lines in that Charlie had handled her pregnancies with the sensitivity of a yak—"He said he got the creeps when the baby moved . . . and that my breasts were too big."

"Charlie said that? But he's a doctor," I said, sounding really dumb.

"He's shy, though, I guess," she stammered quietly, coming to the defense of . . . her husband? her choice of husband? I contemplated the difference as Sandy continued her story. Eileen hadn't bought Sandy's attempts at assurances that "he'll be okay after the baby is born. . . ." Neither had Sandy. "I was trying to make her feel better, Tess, but I was sure her husband was playing around."

"Why?" I asked.

"Well, he made a pass at me!" Sandy answered.

Hah! I knew it! This is going to be another banal tale of suggestive conversation and eyeball fucking, I thought, shoveling anchovies and feta cheese into my mouth to keep from saying something I'd regret.

"It was a couple of weeks ago—it was the only time I met him—at the spring celebration at school," she said. The Pass was a bit of flirting by the snack table when Sandy had dropped that "Charlie is sooo busy we're like two ships passing in the night"—I couldn't believe she actually said that—and he had replied that she better be careful that she didn't "dry up."

"Sandy! I can't believe he said something so disgusting!"

"He didn't mean it that way. He was just trying to be friendly."

I closed my eyes momentarily and shuddered. "Okay. So go on with the story."

"Well. Eileen was sure her husband was seeing another woman, so she lifted his paging beeper from his briefcase before he left the house yesterday, and picked up his calls as if she were the answering service, then forwarded the messages to the real answering service. And this morning Eileen was very upset because, of the nine calls she picked up yesterday, three were from a woman who wouldn't leave her name, but on the third call left a message: 'Reservations at the Wayfarer are all set. Dinner is at seven tomorrow night.' That's tonight, Tess," Sandy explained. "But Eileen's husband had told her at the beginning of the week that he was flying to Pittsburgh tonight for a weekend investment seminar, and the Wayfarer is a small restaurant and bed-and-breakfast place in Cape May. So guess where Eileen will be at seven o'clock tonight."

"The Wayfarer."

"Right."

"Gutsy lady," I cheered.

"Not so fast, Tess. You haven't heard the other side of the story," Sandy warned, pausing to catch up on her salad. And then, "I called Janet to chat last night—I forgot she was working—and Sean told me he was going to visit his grandparents for the weekend because Janet was going to be away, but he didn't know where . . ."

"Oh shit," I said, catching on.

". . . and then this morning, when Eileen tells me about her husband—did I tell you his name is Harvey?—going away for the weekend—"

"Say no more. Harvey is Janet's Harvey Cohen and Eileen is Mrs. Cohen. Right?"

"Right."

"So much for Janet's rationalization that *this* married man is okay to date because he hasn't slept with his wife for over a year . . . that his wife is cold, unaffectionate, and hates sex . . . that she's a weak, incapable woman and that as soon as he finds a way to break the news to her without driving her to suicide, he's going to leave her. Did I leave anything out?" I asked in a rising voice.

"Well, Janet said that when you date a married man, at least you know he isn't fooling around with anyone else. And you know the way things are nowadays, Tess."

"Oh, yes. Well, I guess Janet doesn't count the wife as 'someone else,'" I spewed with considerable bile, understanding more than ever that I didn't understand the way things were nowadays. "So, where's Janet?! I suppose we do have to find her to warn her," I allowed.

"That's the big question," Sandy said. "I've been calling all morning, but there's no answer."

"Why doesn't that woman get an answering machine?!" I asked the chandelier. Why is everyone so hurtful? I asked myself, picturing poor Eileen (whom I've never seen in my life) crying into her hands above her belly big with child. I felt angry not only with Harvey (whom I've never met), but also with Janet for embracing the contemporary credo that *(a)* it is justifiable to do something hurtful if it will be done by someone else anyway if you don't do it, and *(b)* the justification of a hurtful act is increased proportionately by the number of people practicing said act. I felt angry, too, with Sandy for buying into Janet's rationalization . . . and with myself for feeling so damn self-righteous.

I left Sandy to finish her salad and tried to call Janet from the pay phone near the rest rooms. The telephone rang and rang and . . .

"Hello."

"Janet! Am I glad I caught you! Are you planning to drive to Cape May this evening?"

"How did you know, Tess?"

"Don't go!"

"What?"

80

"Don't go. Harvey's wife found out and she's going to be there!"

"Oh, Tess, thank you! I'll never do married again . . . I promise."

. . . and rang. Defeated, I went back to the booth and joined Sandy for one more cup of coffee before I had to return to my kitchen.

"You seeing Mirrors tomorrow night?" she asked.

"No. Marv has to be in Chicago to see a client. But I have a date."

"Ohhh. Who?"

"David. We're going to the movies."

"Oh, he's not a date."

"I know. But he called last night to tell me that his Saturday night date canceled and he was dying to see this movie—"

"So good old Tess will baby-sit," Sandy sneered.

"Actually, the way I look at it, he's baby-sitting me," I retorted, feeling hurt. "Why so resentful?"

"I'm not! But don't be so coy, Tess; you know you have a crush on him."

"Sandy! He's only a friend. Besides, I'm definitely not his type."

"Don't you wonder what his type is, Tess? Have you considered it might be *male*? I mean, aaall those arm-hangers he dates—"

"Really, Sandy," I said. Bitch! I thought. *You'd* like to have a go at David yourself—and you probably would if you knew about the bimbo Charlie's got shacked up in his shore condo . . . a story known to everyone, *except* to you . . . because you're so involved with your *imagined* intrigues that you can't see the real thing.

"Tess, what are you thinking? You have the oddest look on your face." But she didn't wait for an answer. "I'm going to the bathroom, and then I've got to get to my haircut," she said. "George gets furious when I'm late."

"Right. I'll pay the bill; it's my turn. And then I'm going

home, so I'll try calling Janet," I said, already feeling guilty for my unstated anger, my unfair mental indictment of Janet, Sandy, and Charlie, who, for all I *really* knew, was a good, hardworking, faithful husband—even if he was a nerd.

Back home I tried Janet's line again, to no avail, and then set about rolling chocolate marshmallow ice cream in sheets of sponge cake, coating them with bittersweet chocolate glaze and chopped almonds, wrapping them in wax paper before freezing, and trying to reach Janet between steps. When I tried Janet's line at about five o'clock, I got a busy signal. Thank goodness, I thought, redialing immediately. Still busy. I tried every four or five minutes for about a half hour until, finally, it rang . . . and rang . . . and rang. . . . I couldn't believe I had missed her.

Driving over to Charlene Platt's to deliver her cake rolls, I thought I saw Janet's car headed toward the expressway. I followed it for a block until I could see for sure . . .

And then I stepped on it, following her onto the expressway. I drove close behind her and sounded my horn. I saw her look into her rearview mirror, but she speeded up. I pulled up next to her in the left lane and sounded my horn again. Alarmed, she looked over, and I motioned for her to pull off at the next exit. Half a mile up the road she exited and I followed her to a gas station just off the ramp. We both jumped out of our cars.

"What's going on?" she asked.

"Janet! Am I glad I caught you! Are you on your way to Cape May?"

"How did you know, Tess?"

"Don't go!"

"What?"

"Don't go. Harvey's wife found out and she's going to be there!"

"Oh, Tess, thank you! I'll never do married again . . . I promise."

* * *

. . . but it wasn't her. Defeated, I turned right at Charlene's corner, dropped the desserts off, and returned home.

I was dozing in front of the television in the family room that night when the phone rang. At first I thought the ringing was coming from the television—an old Barbara Stanwyck movie, *Sorry, Wrong Number*—but it persisted beyond Barbara's answering the telephone in black and white, so I fumbled for my telephone, noting that it was eleven-forty.

It was Sandy. She was quite beside herself. "You won't belieeeve what I've been through tonight. Tess, I had to call you. I hope it's not too late."

It was. "No, of course not. What happened?" I asked, coming to as I remembered this afternoon's conversation . . . and Janet. "Did you find Janet?"

"No. Just listen, Tess." She related a bedtime story even more bizarre than the lunchtime tale: Eileen had called Sandy hysterically about nine-thirty to ask if Karen could spend the weekend at Sandy's house. A terrible thing had happened: Harvey had been killed in an accident . . . she didn't know whom else to call . . . her parents were flying up from Florida late that night, Harvey's parents were flying in from Ohio in the morning . . . she had no family in the area. So Sandy went to Eileen's to comfort her and bring Karen home with her as soon as Sandy's mother arrived to stay with Sandy's children. "Where was Charlie?" I asked. Charlie had an emergency at the shore hospital and was staying overnight.

As Sandy was driving to Eileen's she remembered Cape May, the Wayfarer, and Janet, and realized that she had no idea how any of it fit together, so by the time she reached Eileen's, Sandy was in quite a state herself. And when she walked into the house, Eileen collapsed into Sandy's arms, sobbing out her incredible story: Eileen had gone to the Wayfarer at seven o'clock after walking on the rocky beach and wandering around the Victorian town for a good three hours in an attempt to compose herself. She inquired about the Cohen reservation and was taken to a table where, already seated, was a woman who, because of her diminutive size, short, curly chestnut hair, triangular face, and almond-shaped hazel eyes, could have been taken for Eileen's younger sister—if she had had one, which she didn't. The woman took no notice of Eileen walking toward the table, but when Eileen sat down, recognition and then alarm registered on her face—

"It wasn't Janet!" I interjected.

"It wasn't Janet."

"So where's Janet?"

"I don't know, but is she going to be pissed when she hears this story!"

"So go on," I said, fully awake now, picturing the scene as if it were an old movie on television: a quaint little restaurant, pink roses and baby's breath in a crystal vase and a tall white candle on the table for two . . . the pregnant wife, the other woman.

"I'm Eileen Cohen. I believe we're waiting for my husband," Eileen said.

The other woman froze, white-faced.

"I hope you don't mind my intruding, but I thought we should meet," Eileen said.

The other woman opened her mouth but said nothing.

"You're the only one I can learn the truth from . . . and I'm the only one who can be truthful with you," Eileen said.

The other woman's pallor gave way to flush. Her eyes filled with tears as if the infusion of color were a physically painful process. "I didn't know you were . . . Harvey didn't tell me . . . I didn't want anyone to be hurt—"

"I understand," Eileen said, completely controlled, resting her arms across her obvious belly. "How long have you been seeing my husband?" she asked, a question that evoked a lengthy life history from the other woman, the salient points of which were as follows: Penny Jamison, divorced mother of five-year-old twin boys, an accountant for an insurance firm in Philadelphia, had been seeing Harvey for about two years. She had met him two years after her own husband, an attorney, had left her for his office manager.

"I would never date a married man before I met Harvey. I never wanted to hurt another woman the way I'd been hurt. But Harvey was so persistent, and I felt so sorry for him . . ." Penny stopped momentarily and stared at Eileen. "I don't understand. . . . You're so pretty . . . and you're expecting a baby! Harvey told me that you and he hadn't slept together for years, that you weren't well—mentally, that is. I can't tell you how sorry . . . but I honestly believed that he was going to leave you," she said, desperation crowding her voice. "I thought my prince had come. You don't know what's out there, Mrs. Cohen."

"I'm beginning to find out . . ." was all Eileen said before the police arrived.

"The police?" I questioned.

"Oh, Tess. Be still and let me finish the story. I haven't told you the worst of it!"

"Mrs. Cohen?" the short, dark state policeman asked, to which Eileen nodded. "Ma'am, I'm afraid there's been an accident . . ." Now both women blanched. When the officer told Eileen that Harvey's Saab had gone out of control in the southbound lanes of the Garden State Parkway and had plowed into the back of a flatbed trailer hauling a mobile home, that he had been thrown through the windshield and had died instantly, that the authorities had tried to phone her at home and finally reached the baby-sitter—who had taken Karen to the playground after dinner—who told them where she could be found, that he had felt it best to come personally to tell her, that he would drive her to the hospital, if she wished, or home, she stared at him in disbelief. The officer put a hand on her arm to steady her as she stood up, facing him, but she pulled her arm away, swinging around toward Penny, who sat unsure of her role—after all, what does one say to the widow of one's dead lover, especially when one is in at least as much pain as the widow herself?

"SLUT! It's your fault that my husband is dead. He was coming to see you!" Eileen roared, shocking the officer and the diners in the intimate little restaurant, and helping Penny to find her voice.

"Don't call me a slut, you—you BITCH!" she said, rising from her chair. "If you knew how to hold a man, he wouldn't be dead. He wasn't running *to me* . . . he was running *from you.*"

"Stop! Hold it, Sandy. I don't think I can take any more of this. The whole world is a goddamned cliché!" I yelled into the phone. "Just tell me the bottom line here: Was there a fight to the death? Or did the officer arrest them both for disturbing the peace . . . or for unjustifiable stupidity?"

"Bottom line: The officer took Eileen home after a terrible shouting match—"

"No blood?"

"No blood. Just guts."

"How's Karen?" I asked, suddenly remembering the littlest victim.

"She's sleeping. She has no idea what's happening."

Nobody has, I thought. A man lies to his wife, lies to his mistress, and in the light of truth, does their loving image of him wither like a vampire in the light of day? No. The women blame each other for their pain. He alone is absolved, bleached white like a stained sheet in the light of the sun. "Sandy, I'll talk to you later. *I've* got to go to sleep," I said, hanging up, falling quickly into a fitful slumber. . . .

In the diner at Sunday morning brunch, Janet listened to Sandy relate Friday's events while I fought with a blinding sunbeam intruding into our window booth. As the story unfolded, Janet grew more and more distressed until, in a rage, she yelled as loud as she could, "That two-timing BASTARD . . ."

"Three-timing," I muttered to myself, squinting against the offending sliver of light.

". . . It's a good thing he died, because if he hadn't I would have killed him myself—AFTER I castrated him!" Janet finished in tears.

Incredibly, everyone in the diner stood up and cheered

and then began tapping their water glasses with their spoons. I wanted to join the crystal ensemble, but the sun was in my eyes and I couldn't find my spoon . . . and the ringing glasses continued to get louder and louder . . . and the sunbeam kept finding my eyes no matter where I turned.

. . . And the ringing telephone finally awakened me to the glaring rays of the morning sun from the skylight above my bed, burning through my closed lids. Groping for the phone, I remembered the weird dream I had just had and noted that it was no weirder than the events of the day before. "Hello?" I said, thick-tongued.

"Tess, it's me. I hope it isn't too early. Did I wake you?"

Yes! Of course! "No, it's okay," I mumbled to Sandy. "What time is it, anyway?"

"I did wake you. I'm sorry, but I had to call. Janet just called me. She heard about Harvey on the radio last night on her way to New York—"

"To where?"

"She was on her way to White Plains, New York. Harvey had told her he was going there for a weekend seminar, and she decided to surprise him. Today is—was—his birthday."

"It looks like the surprise was on Janet."

"You're sick, Tess. Look. Janet's really strung out. She couldn't sleep once she got home, but waited until a decent hour to call me."

"What time is it?"

"Six-fifteen."

That's a decent hour? I thought. "So go on," I said.

"I told her I'd come right over, but she said she wanted to take a shower and be alone for a while. She's coming here at nine."

Janet and Sandy were already drinking coffee at the kitchen table, and Sandy's mother, who had slept over, had taken the three children to the playground by the time I got to Sandy's house at nine-thirty. My mother had called to tell me that after seeing a news special about AIDS on television last night, she couldn't sleep a wink . . . and that I should go back with Stephen. "A wife has to learn to close her eyes to certain things," she'd lectured. A long, rambling defense of my position served only to increase my mother's conviction that I was a failure as a woman, to decrease my sense of self-esteem, and to increase the profits of the telephone company, that powerful entity that makes it possible for someone in Florida to reach out and smack someone around in Pennsylvania. So I was not only late but distracted when I sat down next to Sandy. "Sorry I'm late," I muttered.

Janet, who had obviously been crying before I arrived, started anew, holding her napkin to her face. Sandy started to catch me up: Janet was twenty minutes from White Plains when she had heard the news broadcast about the accident. She almost ran amok on the Tappan Zee Bridge when the words "Harvey Cohen, dead from injuries" bored into her ears, when the words "southbound lanes at five-thirty this afternoon" threw her into a state of confusion. But she made it to the hotel where Harvey was supposed to be staying—of course he wasn't—and she sat dazed in the lounge long enough to down a brandy and two cups of black coffee before driving home. Now she blamed herself for the accident and—

"Whoaaa! Back up. You lost me," I said.

By this time, Janet had stopped sobbing, and she told me the rest of it herself: At about five o'clock yesterday afternoon, Harvey was wheeling south on the Garden State Parkway toward Cape May, New Jersey—although Janet thought he was wheeling north toward White Plains, New York, and his wife was supposed to think he was flying northwest to Pittsburgh, Pennsylvania—when he called Janet on his new car phone. "Hi! Baby! No more long lonely road trips!" he said, explaining that this newest toy—a birthday present to himself—had been installed the day before, and she was his first call. Janet had walked in from a long day of vanities only seconds before her phone rang. She'd gotten a haircut and manicure, then bought a sexy black lace teddy with a snap crotch at the Perfumed Garden.

She had stopped at Castlemeyer's to pick up the small chocolate chip birthday cake she'd ordered earlier, with traditional sugary white icing, blue and yellow flowers, and blue HAPPY BIRTHDAY HARVEY. She bought blue birthday candles at Gifts and Greetings and spent three-quarters of an hour poring over their birthday cards filed under "Love" until she found the perfect one, more than an hour picking out a pigskin ticket and passport folder at Travels, and another half hour agonizing over the style of the monogram that the saleswoman then embossed in gold on the folder's lower right corner. All this for a man who, if you listened to Janet tell it, was only a good fuck. "It's nothing. I'm in charge of this relationship," she had assured Sandy and me on more than one occasion.

So. The phone had rung and it was Harvey calling from his car phone, and Janet, who was all excited about her plans to surprise him later that night at his hotel in White Plains, decided to tease him a bit, to get him primed, aroused for her arrival.

"Haaarvey," she whispered over the phone, setting down her packages, settling into a comfy chair, "do you know what I'm doing right now?"

"Tell me, honey."

"I'm thinking of you, sweetheart. Do you know why?"

"Tell me, doll," he answered, being sucked into the mood by the sex in her voice as he sped south in the fast lane of the Garden State Parkway at just under seventy miles an hour.

"Because I just got out of a hot, hot bath . . . and I'm lying on my bed all warm and tingly . . ."

Harvey fumbled to turn down the radio and turn on the cruise control so that he could pay close attention to the sweet sounds coming over his phone.

". . . and I thought how nice it would be if you were here beside me . . . how good your skin would feel on mine . . . how good it would be to have you touch me like only you can . . ."

Harvey grunted small sounds into the phone as he listened intently, lost in the fantasy.

". . . I'm on top of my satin comforter . . . and I've got all my pillows piled up around me . . . and the shades are drawn . . . oh, Harvey, it's like being in a warm, soft nest. And my skin, Harvey, it's so soft from the hot bath oil. I'm rubbing some of the oil on my tummy right now. It feels sooo good, Harvey, so slippery smooth, and warm and wet—"

"Your tits, doll, rub it on your beautiful tits. Tell me what it feels like."

"Oh, Harvey. It feels wonderful . . . my nipples are getting so hard . . . they're standing right up . . . I'm running my fingers around and around my nipples, Harvey—"

"I'd love to be there to rub them for you, gorgeous."

"You are, Harvey. You're right here with me, touching me . . . and, Harvey, you're getting so hard . . . Oooh, I want to suck it, Harvey . . ."

By now Harvey had his fly open and his wang was sticking out acutely, just below his seat belt. He told Janet to hold on a sec while he cradled the phone between his left ear and shoulder so he could grasp the steering wheel in his left hand and his considerable erection in his right. Yesiree! He had the world by the balls: a hot rod in each hand and a hot bitch in his ear.

"Christ, sweetheart! I feel like I'm eighteen again. Did I ever tell you about the White Shadow," he asked Janet, gripping his dick, flirting with memories of his first car—a pre-owned, white Austin-Healey with a soft, red leather interior that his parents had bought for him when he graduated from high school.

"Sure, honey. She was your best girl, wasn't she?" Janet said, feeding his fantasy.

"You know, I can still remember the silky feel of that six-hour compound and wax job I gave the old girl. God, I was a cocky bastard stretched out in her low-slung seat, one hand on the steering wheel, the other on the gearshift, peeling out at lights, downshifting around corners. . . . What a turn-on!" And as he pictured the White Shadow speeding through the old neighborhood in the wee hours of the morning, his right hand shifted his dick up and back . . . until he found a rhythm . . . and he was drawn back to the voice in his ear . . .

". . . Yes, lover, you're getting me so excited. I can't keep from touching myself. . . . I know I shouldn't touch myself, but, oooh, it feels sooo good . . . and the oil is running down my belly, Harvey, and, ooooh, Harvey, it's running into my honey pot. Oh, Harvey, I can't help it . . . I have to touch myself . . . Yes . . . It's so hot, Harvey, it's so soft and wet . . . and my fingers are in it . . . and I'm imagining it's you, Harvey, rubbing up and back . . . Can you feel it, Harvey?"

Now Harvey was really going at it . . . up and back and up and down . . . he was having one helluva time. But he kept his eye on the road, his left hand on the wheel as he approached his supreme moment.

". . . Harvey . . . lover . . . I can see how big and hard you are. . . . I'm slipping my fingers into me and it's you, honey . . . I can feel you in me, Harvey . . . in and out . . . faster, honey . . . oooh, Harvey . . . oooh, lover . . . oooooh . . ."

And with this momentous moan of pulse-pounding passion, Harvey stretched his legs out as far as he could and started to jerk in his seat, trying to get enough body English into the act to finish himself off, but his seat belt wouldn't give him the necessary leeway. . . . "I'm comin', doll . . . I'm comin'," he rasped through the phone, while fumbling with the seat-belt latch, trying to free himself. "I'm comin', doll!" as the latch finally gave way and his pelvis thrust forward and his dick hit the steering wheel so his left hand jerked in a kind of reflex action, which pushed the wheel sharply to the right, steering the Saab into the right lane, which at the time was, unfortunately, occupied a short distance up by a mobile home on a flatbed trailer, and what with Harvey's cruise control set at seventy . . . well, the last thing Harvey saw was the back door—and the bumper sticker JESUS LOVES YOU.

"JESUS!" was the last thing Janet heard over the phone.

"Oooh, Harvey, was it as good for you as it was for me? . . . Harvey? Harvey? Are you there, honey?" The line had gone dead. "Those fucking car phones!" was all she said before slamming her phone down, scooping up her packages, and running to the bedroom to shower and dress for the evening.

"I guess I left the house about eight-thirty so I'd get to Harvey's hotel by ten-thirty," Janet continued. "He had said he'd be back in his room by ten and he was going to call me to say good night. I had it all planned . . . how he'd be so excited from the phone call . . . and how he'd be so pissed that I wasn't home when he called at ten . . . and how I'd knock on his door . . . and . . . but I killed him, Tess!" she sobbed, grabbing my hands across the table.

Yep! You blew the bastard right off the road, I thought. "You didn't kill him, Janet," I said, squeezing her hands tightly. "It wasn't your fault. Do you know where he was going? Didn't Sandy tell you where he was going?"

"White Plains," Janet cried.

Obviously Sandy had not told her.

"No, Janet. He wasn't going to White Plains, and he wasn't going to Pittsburgh like he told his wife, either. He was on his way to Cape May," I said, throwing a piercing glare at Sandy, who leaned back in her seat, rolled her eyes upward, and pressed her lips together.

"What are you talking about, Tess? That's not possible."

"He was on his way to Cape May to meet someone else, another woman, for his birthday celebration."

"How do you know?"

"His wife told Sandy."

Sandy found her courage about there and she finished the story, which finished Janet.

"That BITCH!" Janet choked out.

"Which bitch?" I asked, not without a touch of sarcasm.

"Both of them!"

"Oh! A brace of bitches!" I informed Sandy, who squinted

contemptuously at me. "And I suppose Harvey was their innocent victim?"

"You don't understand, Tess."

"From what I could see, it wasn't I who didn't understand," I whined to Michael on Tuesday, pouting in a corner of his leather couch, my shoeless feet tucked under me, my arms folded. "Maybe it is me. Am I nuts? Or is the whole world nuts?"

"You're not nuts," was all he offered.

"So everyone else is nuts, right?"

"I love it when you're black and white," he said, laughing.

"What's that supposed to mean?"

"It means that for some reason you must have it one way or the other. There's no in-between, no gray."

"Why?"

"I don't know why."

"Yes, you do. You're supposed to help me when I get stuck."

"Why do you think Janet, and others, get involved in no-win relationships?"

"Because she, they, don't think very much of themselves."

"And why do they make excuses for their lovers who treat them poorly?"

"Because they have to . . . so they don't see what ugly people they've allowed themselves to get involved with . . . so they don't see how ugly they've become."

"You think Janet's ugly?"

"No," I said. *Yes,* I thought, and then suddenly felt ugly myself. "Not ugly; sad. She's so smart and she's acting so dumb, like she doesn't understand how demeaning that relationship was to her. I don't understand it, I don't understand any of it . . . what goes on out there!"

"Out where?"

"There! In the world."

"Out *there?* Where are you?"

"I feel like I'm on another planet."

"And the men on your planet are so wonderful? Like your husband, for instance?"

That cut deep. Tears welled up, but I put my head back so they wouldn't spill over, so they'd drain back behind my eyes and run down my throat in a hot stream of contempt. I wanted to answer him, but I was afraid that I'd choke on my pain, so I just glared at him until the feeling was pushed back down.

"That hurt, didn't it?"

"Not really," I lied. "I know you're right." What I meant was it hurt like hell *because* I knew he was right.

"So, men are a pretty scummy lot."

"That's a trick question," I said, understanding that it was, in fact, a question, not a statement, and that if I said yes, which I was inclined to do, Michael could infer that I thought he was scummy, too. I didn't think Michael was scummy. Of course, I didn't know Michael that well. For all I knew he might be wonderful to his clients, but scummy to his wife. After all, he didn't get personal with his clients. Of course, if I said that to Michael, it would hurt his feelings because that would be denying the extremely personal relationship that's supposed to develop between therapist and client. Then again, it probably develops on the side of the client but not on the side of the therapist. I mean, after all, a client only has one therapist, but a therapist has many clients, and one could not expect one's therapist to be personally involved with every client. Talk about burnout! And surely it would be conceit for me to think that I would be one of a chosen few whom he felt personally involved with. On the other hand, I wasn't feeling extraordinarily personally involved with Michael . . . so why was I going through these mental machinations when the man asked me a simple question . . . that wasn't really a question?

"Oh? How's that a trick question?" he asked.

"Well, you want me to say either yes or no. That men—all men—are scummy, or are not scummy. It's not as simple as that."

"I see. You mean it's not all black and white."

"Right. Now. In my experience, I've come across a lot of scummy men."

"That sounds like a fair statement. Have you met any men who aren't scummy?"

"One or two."

"One or two?"

"Well, one besides you."

"I'm not scummy?"

"I don't think so."

"Thank you. And who's the other?"

"David. David Ross. Stephen's friend. You know David —he gave me your number."

"Yes. I know David."

I waited to see if he had any further comment. After all, he had been David's therapist for two or three years. He was, in fact, David's last therapist. But Michael wasn't talking— professional confidence, of course. He waited for me to continue. "Well, I don't think David is scummy," I said. "In fact, he's got to be one of the sweetest people I know. I consider him a close friend. I feel I can trust him. Sort of."

"What do you mean, sort of?"

"I mean, as far as I can see I can trust him. I haven't had any really personal dealings with him, so I'm not sure I can really trust him."

"Personal dealings. You mean you haven't slept with him?" Michael was leaning forward in his seat now. He was into this conversation. He had an opinion. I could tell. He wanted me to know something. Oh, God. Maybe he knows David is gay! I thought. If anyone would know, Michael would know.

"No. That's not what I mean."

"Oh. You *have* slept with him?"

"No! What's going on here? Why are you pushing this?"

"I'm not pushing anything. You said you haven't had any personal dealings with David. But you also said he's a close friend, that you can *sort of* trust him. So I was trying to understand what you mean by 'personal dealings.'"

I sat there and glared while caterpillars and ants crawled

around in my stomach making me teary-eyed, uncomfortable. Cotton filled my ears. I wanted to scream, "YOU DON'T UNDERSTAND." But I knew he understood far better than I, so I decided to trust him because it was too painful not to. "Okay. Personal dealings, as in sex," I said quietly.

"So, men get scummy when you have sex with them."

"It does seem to bring out the worst in them," I said, growing more uncomfortable, wondering where this was going to lead. Afraid of where this was going to lead? Afraid of what?

"And David? Where does he fit into this?"

"I'm not sure. He's kind of an enigma. We're friends. I find him attractive. Sometimes I think he finds me attractive. But I'm not at all his type."

"What's his type?"

"You should know that better than I."

"I know what he's told me."

"Has he told you he's gay?" I dared to ask.

"No. Why do you ask that?"

"Well, it's just that his social behavior with women is so superficial."

"You mean your friendship with him?"

"No. I mean his dating habits. He dates these . . ." I didn't want to say "bimbos," because that's such a demeaning term to women, and I'm a woman, and I didn't think I should join the scummy men who use it. ". . . these superficial women. He has superficial relationships with them and then goes on to others. It's almost as if he doesn't want to be involved with them at all. Like he's only doing it for appearances. Like maybe he's really a closet gay?"

"It's possible."

Aha! "And he's so sweet and nurturing. Men just aren't like that!"

"I see. Women are sweet and nurturing. So if a man is sweet and nurturing, he must be gay. Well. That's black and white!" He laughed again.

"You're laughing at me again! That's twice today. You're going to give me an inferiority complex!"

"I'm going to give you a complex!" He doubled over in laughter. "Hah! That's rich! I'm going to give this model of self-esteem an inferiority complex!"

An attempt to suppress the smile pulling at my face was in vain, and the effort made me blush hot and crimson.

So there I sat burning red with this stupid grin distorting my heretofore indignant demeanor, and he sat on the edge of his chair, and taking my hand in both of his he looked directly in my eyes, smiled, and said, in the most gentle, nurturing, loving way, "You're a neat lady, Tess." A soft, warm glow enfolded me, and for a moment, for just an instant, I felt like a little girl . . . and very, very special. "I don't think David is gay, Tess," Michael continued seamlessly, letting go of my hand, sitting back in his seat, getting back to my question. "I found David to be an extremely sensitive man who, in fact, likes women very much."

"But all those women he sees? If he likes women so much, why doesn't he stick with one?" I asked, feeling like Michael and I were comrades in an intrigue, in a secret hideaway, talking secret things, things we'd never tell anyone but each other.

"Maybe the women he dates aren't his type."

At home that night, I unplugged the telephone in my bedroom, curled up in bed with a large dish of chocolate marshmallow ice cream that I topped with a scoop of chopped almonds left over from the Rocky Road ice cream cake rolls, and started to watch a videotape of a vintage Sherlock Holmes movie, *The Woman in Green*. As the familiarity of the old movie wrapped around me like the comforting arms of a gentle, trusted grandfather, I slowly lapped at the smooth, sweet ice cream. And I tried to remember the comforting aura at Michael's office, to recapture the sweet taste of being special, but I bit into a chunk of almond, filling my head with an unbearable crunch, breaking the mood. I felt cranky. I didn't want the almonds in my ice cream disrupting my peace. I felt annoyed at myself for dumping them into my dish. And as I tried to pick them out, to push them aside, I understood: Life starts out okay—smooth and sweet—but we manage to mess things up . . . we put hard things in our way. And growing more perturbed at the offending almonds pervading my ice cream, I realized something else: Once you crap up your life, it's not easy to smooth it out. Descending to the kitchen, I dumped the whole bowl of homemade Rocky Road into the sink and started over with a fresh dip. Elementary, my dear Watson.

Life should be so easy.

CHECKERBOARD CAKE

3 ounces semisweet chocolate
4 cups sifted cake flour
2 cups sugar
2 tablespoons baking powder
1 1/2 teaspoons salt
1 cup unsalted butter (softened)
1 1/3 cups milk (room temperature)
1 tablespoon vanilla extract
4 eggs

Preheat oven to 350°F.

Melt chocolate in top of double boiler and set aside.

In large mixing bowl, combine flour, sugar, baking powder, and salt. Mix on low speed for one minute, until well blended. Add butter and 1 cup of milk and beat at medium-high for 1 1/2 minutes, scraping sides of bowl.

In another bowl, combine vanilla, eggs, and 1/3 cup milk and beat lightly. Add to batter in three parts, beating at medium-high for 20 seconds after each addition. Scrape sides of bowl after each part.

Divide batter in half. Stir melted chocolate into one half of the batter.

Grease and flour the bottoms and sides of the special cake pans from the "Bake King Checkerboard Cake Set" (#1200) (manufactured by C. M. Products, Inc., Subsidiary of Chicago Metallic Products, Inc.). Place the divider into one prepared pan and pour in the two batters (dark and light) as described in the instruction booklet "How to Use Your Checkerboard Cake Set" that is included in the set. Repeat procedure for each pan.

Bake pans in the center of the oven for 25 minutes, revolving the pans once after 12 minutes.

Allow cakes to cool in pans, sitting on racks, for 10 minutes before removing. Assemble the cake according to directions in the instruction booklet. Serves 10.

CHAPTER 7

Checkerboard Cake

I was having a terrible day. It had been a terrible weekend, and before that a terrible week . . . when I stopped to think of it, I couldn't think of when it hadn't been terrible. Of course, that wasn't how it was, but that's how it felt the Monday afternoon in May I struggled with the checkerboard cake I was trying to perfect for my new clients, the Chessmen, a group of men and women who met at the library the first Thursday of each month to play chess. I hadn't been aware of their existence until one of the members, Gus Kolodner, got my name from Linda Bliss, the special events director at the library, who had mentioned to Gus that Coffee, Cake, and Criticism had its refreshments catered by Just Desserts on the third Thursday of each month.

The idea of featuring a checkerboard cake on the dessert table for the Chessmen made me feel extremely clever, but after a morning of preparation and concoction, I stood in front of a counter covered with dirty dishes and a lot of crumbs. Something had gone wrong.

I had borrowed the special round pans with the circular metal insert and the recipe for the cake batter from Sandy's mother, who had inherited them from an aunt. She said she had never made the cake herself, but she remembered that her aunt's cakes were in three layers, each consisting of three concentric circles of alternating chocolate and vanilla, looking very much like a bull's-eye. Supposedly, once the layers were baked and stacked together, cemented by chocolate icing, slices of the finished cake would have a checkerboard design. Personally, I couldn't picture the whole thing, but, on faith, I made the cake batter. Then, finding only one insert—consisting of two concentric circles on an odd frame—for the three pans, I assumed the other two inserts had been lost, and figured I'd make one layer at a time. After removing the first layer from the pan, I was faced with the bizarre metal contraption embedded in the cake. An attempt to extricate it neatly failed. Stubbornly, I tried a second layer . . . and a third. Finally, I was left with three large chocolate cupcakes—the centers of the bull's-eyes— and a pile of crumbs. I no longer felt clever. And the failure added to my already agitated mood, which had been precipitated by the events surrounding the death of Harvey Cohen almost three weeks ago, and further exacerbated by several lovesick phone calls from Stephen—I refused to see him— and a disastrous Sunday night date.

"Disastrous, Tess? How bad could it have been?" Sandy had questioned over coffee and a bagel earlier in the day when I had just started to make the batter for the checkerboard cakes.

"Trust me."

"From what Cindy told me, this guy sounded like a winner."

"Alan Persky, another blind date from the folks who brought you Joe Silvers, the California Kid."

"Oh, Oil Wells!"

"Yep. Alan is another of Richard's old college friends, also nice-looking, also lots of money—"

"But?"

"Booooooring!" I trilled. "He took me to Atlantic City to have dinner at one of the gourmet restaurants in Caesars Palace, but once we got there he spent hours at the craps table, totally ignoring me."

"Did you finally eat?"

"Oh, sure—at ten o'clock! And all he talked about was himself—all the way to Atlantic City, all through dinner, and all the way home. You know, he never asked me one question about myself. 'Richard tells me you bake cookies and sell houses,' he said early in the evening, and then made some sexist remark about how that probably gives me lots of time to play tennis with the girls."

"Yuck!"

"And you can't imagine how hard those stools at the blackjack tables can be, when you can find one to sit on, which I finally did after standing for an hour and a half watching Alan crap out."

"You played blackjack?"

"No. I found a stool at an empty table and watched the crowd."

"Anyone interesting?"

"Actually, yes. I saw George Cantelli."

"THE George Cantelli?"

"Uh-huh."

It really was him, I remembered, turning the mixer on medium and watching the spinning beaters blend the raw ingredients into a smooth batter. George Cantelli, a comedian of international and transgenerational renown . . . and I was no more than fifty feet from him! That I could see him at all was surprising because there were so many people hovering around his table on the cocktail platform, and there was so much smoke in the casino that my eyes were tearing. But it was George Cantelli all right. I had heard he was performing in Atlantic City, and there he was, a lot smaller than he looked on television, but a lot better-looking. And it certainly appeared that he was staring back at me. Then again, he was probably looking at someone behind me, I thought. But it did seem that whenever I looked over to him, he caught my eyes with his. No. Unless he walked over and knelt before me, I wouldn't believe he was actually looking at *me*. Not that I looked bad. It was a mild night and I was chicly romantic in a bone linen midiskirt and a matching, long, silk sailor blouse. When I looked over again, he wasn't talking to anyone . . . and his eyes did seem to stop on mine. This is crazy, I thought, a mixture of hypoglycemic hallucination and boredom. What was really crazy was that I didn't grab a cab and go home instead of sitting on that high chair like a dunce, waiting for an inconsiderate blind date to lose his money. I only hoped there'd be enough left for dinner. Well, Georgie, I thought, it's just you and me. So, where's your wife? I was sure I'd read that he was married. Of course, what would that mean to a Hollywood type? Then again, what would *I* mean to a Hollywood type? Moot question, but there was nothing better to think about. So. There. It happened again. Eye to eye. I wonder if he thinks I'm someone he knows. I have been told that I look like a million different people. What would I do if he actually came over to me? Another moot question. But I played with it as I straightened my back, suddenly aware of my tendency to slump when I sit. Head up, shoulders back . . .

"George Cantelli, I presume."

"I'm afraid you have the advantage."

"Tess. Tess Fineman."

"I've been noticing you, Tess Fineman. You're a noticeable person. Perhaps you were aware that I've been watching you from across the room."

"Oh? No, actually not. I thought I was watching you."

"I'm flattered. You're alone. Are you waiting for someone? You shouldn't have to wait for *anyone.*"

"Just my blind date. But I've grown quite weary of him."

"Perhaps we could have a drink?"

"I'd like that enormously."

"Won't you step this way," he said, taking my hand, leading me toward a small private booth in the bar area, straining to keep his hands, but not his eyes, off my incredibly delicate unpadded shoulder.

"Thank you. I . . ."

. . . Oh, oh. He's getting up. There goes my entertainment, I thought, as George Cantelli walked away from his table and down from the bar platform. Losing sight of him in the crowd, I turned my attention to the nearby blackjack table. I had watched the dealer draw twenty-one three times in a row, to the disgruntlement of the four men at the table, when I became aware of someone standing just behind me, a little to my left. I turned my head to find George Cantelli standing there smiling and waving toward the table to my right, but before I could turn away he looked at me and smiled anew. I smiled back and then turned my eyes, if not my attention, back to the blackjack table. This was it, my chance to be really cool, really sophisticated. I could hear myself telling Sandy about my big adventure in the casino with—are you ready?—GEORGE CANTELLI. As I sat coolly watching the men at the table win then lose then win then lose, I could feel George's eyes burning the back of my long, alabaster neck, velvety with blond fuzz. "Love fuzz," Marv called the fine, fuzzy little hairs at the nape of my neck that George Cantelli watched glisten golden in the bright light of the casino. I could feel the hairs stand up to meet his lustful gaze as a blush crept by them, tinting that svelte, graceful curve. *Perhaps we could have a drink,* he'll say, touching me lightly on the back of my neck, barely ruffling the fuzz. *I'd like that enormously . . . very much. . . . I'd like that. . . . Certainly. Thank you, that would be delightful. . . . Of course. That would be very nice. . . . How kind of you. . . . How . . .* Should I just leave my date at the table, I wondered, or should I tell him I was going? Nonsense. George wasn't going to talk to me. Then again . . . Perhaps if I turned and smiled again. There. He responded with a smile of his own and stepped forward, placing himself—I couldn't believe it!—beside me. *Nice day, isn't it? . . . Nice casino, isn't it? . . . Are you staying here?*—no, that's his line. *Are you enjoying your stay? . . . You are a marvelously inventive entertainer, a creative genius. . . . A drink? I thought you'd never ask! . . . Of course. I'd like that enormously. . . . It would be my pleasure*—no, that's his line . . . As I turned once again toward the blackjack table, I could see George out of the corner of my eye staring at my profile, my left profile with its sharp, sophisticated edge. Now's my chance, I thought—head up, shoulders back—as I shifted my eyes to the left, catching his, then turned my head slowly, sensually, till we were face to face.

"Mr. Cantelli"—I extended my hand—"Tess Fineman. I . . . I'd very much like to have your autograph." My God! I'd asked for his autograph! Clod! Jerk! I couldn't believe I'd said that!

"Certainly, if you have a pen, I don't seem to have one on me," he said, letting go of my hand, patting his pockets in search of the mundane object.

"I don't either, but I'll find one. I enjoy your performances very much."

"Thank you," he said politely, the fire in his eyes extinguished by my insipid request for his autograph instead of his body.

Utterly embarrassed by my gauche, star-struck behavior, I hopped off my stool and hurried away to find a pen. When I returned, he was still standing there, held by the inertia of disappointment, no doubt. He took the pen from me and mechanically signed his name, *George Cantelli, with best wishes to Tess*—he did remember my name—on a cocktail napkin. Still smiling, he walked off, leaving me to hop upon my stool once again, clutching my booby prize.

"Tess. Tess! You're lost somewhere."

"Sorry," I said, turning off the mixer.

"So? Did you get his autograph?" Sandy asked.

"Whose?"

"George Cantelli! Didn't you just say you saw George Cantelli at the casino?"

"Oh. Yes. Of course," I said, digging the crumpled cocktail napkin out of the pocketbook I had left on the kitchen table the night before.

"That's exciting!" she said, smoothing the napkin on the table, impressed. "Did you get to talk to him?"

"Just briefly. I told him I liked his act. He shook my hand."

"Well! That had to make your evening."

"It helped," I said. To make it a disaster, I thought.

I dumped the crumby mess in the trash, setting aside the giant cupcakes for Sandy's kids, washed the pans, and then sat in the family room with a cup of coffee and a tranquilizer: the crossword puzzle in the Sunday *New York Times Magazine*. I find peace in the knowledge that the puzzle has a black and white solution. There's no gray in a crossword puzzle. It helps to focus me, draws me together when my thoughts pull me in myriad directions. Control. As I work toward a solution, I feel in control. I must remember to tell Michael about my puzzles, I thought, penciling "AMAH" in 27-Down, for "Japanese nurse." Sitting quietly filling in squares, I relaxed. The checkerboard cake conundrum would wait till tomorrow. Yes, tomorrow is another day.

"She's left home and is having an affair now," said one therapist to another on his way out of the conference room in Michael's office suite. I heard this over the *swishhh* of the white-noise machine in the waiting room Tuesday morning.

"Was she having an affair while she was still at home?" questioned the other therapist.

"No," he answered. "I wouldn't let her."

I wouldn't let her. That's control. It's not the kind of control that I have guarded so furiously, the kind of control that makes motion transcend emotion in a kind of bastardization of Marshall McLuhan. They're talking control where it counts, over others' emotions.

I thought about the conversation I had overheard as I settled into my favorite spot on Michael's sofa, drew my legs up, and tucked my feet under me. But all I said was, "It's starting to rain pretty hard out there." And then I proceeded to bitch about my life, my inability to seize the moment, my failed cake. He listened silently. Then, finding nothing else to say, I decided to try to take the wheel, exhibit a little control in our relationship. I asked him about his life.

"I'm at a good time in my life right now," Michael

answered openly. "I'm happy. I'm doing work that I love, I have love in my life."

I have love in my life. He was referring to his wife, a woman who equaled him in impressive credentials—an award-winning artist who held a chair at the university—and good looks. And I'd bet her cakes didn't fall apart.

I have love in my life. He could do anything. Control.

Envy. I felt envious of Michael. He had love in his life. He had it all. I wanted it.

"I can teach and do research. I'm at a point where I only have to see the clients I want to see," he continued his musing.

"I feel privileged," I said obediently, letting him know that I caught the mirrored compliment, and that I would hold it to me because I, too, thought he was outrageously bright and talented.

"You *are* privileged," he said, reinforcing his point. No mere musing, this was control. He was in control. "Yes," he was saying as he lolled back in his easy chair, cradling the back of his head in his hands. "I'm doing what I want. I'm where I want to be."

God, he looked open, inviting. Smug. It struck me that he wasn't wearing a tie, which he usually did, just a yellow shirt open at the neck and a camel sport jacket. He was casual. Actually, he was a little mussed up. It was becoming. The gray in his wavy black hair showed in its slightly tousled state. He looked comfortable. He was comfortable with his life. Maybe too comfortable. Yes. There it was. The chink in the perfectly crafted being. Complacency. A toehold into the control center of the inner man. Bravo! for arrogance. Here! Here! for egocentrism. But beware complacency. The bogeyman will get you if you don't watch out!

Driving home, I had an epiphany: Take the rings out of the pan *before* baking the cake. Thank you, God.

Back in my kitchen, I readied my ingredients and equipment for Checkerboard Cake II, and set about my task with newfound fervor. Totally in control, I scooped and measured, mixed and poured—one layer at a time—and then slowly, carefully, I removed the metal rings from the pan and watched the three circles of thick chocolate and vanilla batter wed, but, lo and behold, they did not blend! Perfect bull's-eyes met my proud gaze as I set the three pans in the oven.

As the kitchen filled with the sweet smell of baking cake, I wiped the countertops and put the bowls, spoons, and other utensils into the dishwasher, turned it on, and sat down with my as-yet-uncompleted crossword puzzle. There was 16-Down: a seven-letter word for "dominate" that ended in "OL." The answer had been eluding me. Then, 16-Across: a three-letter word for "food fish." Of course! "COD." And the c in "COD" gave me "CONTROL." And the drone of the dishwasher in the background reminded me of the drone of the noise machine in Michael's waiting room . . . and the conversation between the two therapists about control . . . and my conversation with Michael, also about control. Funny coincidence. Cod. Funny word. Cod . . . as in codpiece, a kind of sixteenth-century fly for men's tight breeches, I thought, picturing Shakespearean players in their tight breeches and exaggerated codpieces. And the thought of codpieces, tight pants, men's bulges, made me flush. And I thought of Michael and wondered about his complacency, his possible lack of control.

"I love my work, too, Michael," I had said. "My business is growing, slowly but surely. It's the rest of my life that I can't handle," I had complained, referring to the lack of love in my life.

"Of course, I'd rather be a success than have some meaningless affair," I had said, meaning, of course, give me a good fuck and I'll be a success if you want me to . . . I'll be anything you want me to be.

He knew what I really meant. He always knows what I really mean even if I don't say it.

"I understand," is what he had said. . . .

* * *

"I always understand you," he said, moving from his chair to the sofa, taking my hand in his, pressing it to his lips. I knew his lips would be soft. "I've understood you since the first day we talked," he said, brushing my tousled hair from my eyes with his fingers. I knew his touch would be tender. "You do have love in your life," he said, moving closer, close enough for me to see the tears behind his glasses. I knew he would be vulnerable. "You see, Tess, I love you. I want to make love to you," he said, taking me in his arms, kissing me fervently. I knew he would be passionate. And the waves crashed on the rocks.

. . . The splash of water on my bare feet pulled me from my daydream. Water, sudsy water everywhere. The dishwasher. Something with the dishwasher. The dishwasher was out of control. I was out of control.

By the time I cleaned up the floor, called the repair service, unloaded the dishwasher, and rinsed its contents in the sink, my cake layers were baked and cooled. They plopped out of their pans neatly. All's well, I thought, stirring the smooth, bittersweet chocolate icing. I assembled the layers, scored the top of the iced cake with a crisscross design, placed the finished cake on a pedestal plate lined with a paper doily, and set it aside. Then I iced the three cupcakes from the day before, planning to take them all to Sandy's house after dinner for a taste test. As I cleaned up the bowl and utensils from the icing, my mind kept drifting back to the tender tears of vulnerability I had imagined in Michael's eyes. Horny. I was definitely horny. Out of control . . . hostage of hormones . . . victim of viscera.

Vincent Salvatore called about five-thirty. He had gotten a telephone call from Lorraine Farber, a divorced attorney I had brought to see his townhouse Monday evening. She told him she wanted to work out a deal to buy the townhouse directly from him for less money. He was appalled, he said. "I think she was trying to screw you out of your commission," he said. "But I wouldn't have any part of it. Maybe you should come over and we can review the figures and see if we can't put together a deal the lady can't refuse."

Interesting, I thought, as I remembered the two of them flirting with each other at his house.

"Sexy bedroom. Yes? Decorated for the romantically inclined," he had teased, smiling broadly, revealing straight white teeth amidst his heavy black beard. He was referring to the Pablo Picasso erotica hanging on the midnight blue walls, the midnight blue satin sheets on the low platform bed, the small stereo speakers secured in all four corners of the ceiling. Lorraine wet her lips and smiled. "This is the master bedroom," was all he had said to me when I first saw the house. "And you'll love the bath," he said to Lorraine, taking her by the elbow, leading her into the master bath, which featured a large, clear-glass-enclosed steam-shower with four shower heads and a long marble bench built into the back wall. "Big enough for two . . . or three," he said, holding her arm, his black eyes watching me watch him and her in the mirror. Not a chance, I thought, inferring an invitation to a *ménage à trois.* Then again, he was only flirting with Lorraine, I thought, trying to show her what a macho guy he was. I was just a prop. I did not miss that she moved almost imperceptibly closer to him, tilting her head slightly toward him. Did she blush? I wasn't sure. But she took her glasses off and fluttered her eyelashes. "Veeery nice," was all she said.

"How about seven-thirty, Vincent? That should give you time to have dinner."

"You don't eat dinner?"

"Well, it will give me time to grab something, too," I answered.

"Tell you what. Why don't you come over at six-thirty and we can eat dinner together. I hate to eat alone. And you'll find I'm a very good cook."

"That's very nice, Vincent," I said, taken aback, not sure

whether I should say yes . . . or no . . . or . . . "I'll bring dessert!" I said, eyeing the checkerboard cake on the counter, knowing that Sandy would understand. Anything for a sale, I thought. But what I was feeling was unsettled . . . and the soft warmth of Vincent Salvatore's hand in mine when we had shaken on the listing of his home.

". . . and so I hope you don't mind if I don't bring the cake tonight," I told Sandy over the telephone while putting a fresh coat of polish on my nails.

"Of course not. Is he cute?"

"Sandy! This is business."

"Right. Is he cute?"

"In a rough sort of way. He's dark and solid-looking. He lifts weights. Oh, and he's got a beard."

"Sounds interesting. Call me when you get home tonight."

"Sandy, this is business."

"Right. Call me. Bye!"

As soon as I put the phone down, it rang.

"Hello? Just Desserts? I want to order a pineapple cheesecake." It was Marv.

"Sorry. We're out of cheesecake."

"Okay, then I'll have a cherry cheesecake."

"Sorry, we're out of cheesecake."

"Okay, then I'll have a blueberry cheesecake."

"Sorry, we're out of cheesecake."

"So then I'll just have a plain cheesecake!" he finished our ritualistic telephone conversation, a holdover from our brushes with *Sesame Street*—he with his son, and me with Rebecca and Jonathan on Saturday mornings at Sandy's house.

"How about a fuck?" I said, surprising both of us.

"Oooh, what you do to me, sweetheart! You know what's best about our relationship? Regular sex. . . ."

Surely he jests! Sex with Marv is not exactly what one would call regular, I thought with relish for a split second, until I realized that what he meant was regular as in *steady*, not regular as in *standard*. And I suddenly felt used.

". . . It sure makes life less complicated. Cuts out all the games," he continued.

"Right," I said. Wrong, I thought, becoming aware that I didn't like his game anymore. I wanted to be wanted for my flesh and blood, not my illusive image, which is a reflection of not only the beheld, but also the beholder. Go fuck yourself, Marv! I yelled in my head. That's what you've been doing all along, anyway.

"So, when will I see you this weekend, Tess? I thought we could spend Saturday together and go to the zoo. Spring is here! The animals are starting to mate. It's a great show!"

"Oh, Marv. I'm so sorry, but I'm going to be out of town this weekend. I'm going to . . . a seminar. Yes, a real estate seminar in . . . White Plains. I won't be back until late Sunday night."

"Oooh, am I disappointed. Well, that's the way the mirror cracks! I'll call you next week. Okay?"

"I'm going to be pretty busy next week, Marv. How about if I call you when I see a break."

"All right," he said softly after a long pause. "I understand. Hope to hear from you soon."

"Sure, Marv. Thanks for calling. Bye."

So much for that, I thought, putting the telephone down gingerly.

Cake in hand, I arrived at Vincent's townhouse at exactly six-thirty. Up to that point, my interactions with Vincent had been all business, and even as I stood at his front door, I insisted to myself that this was a business call. But when he opened the door, I was seduced by the sight of his Reeboks, blue jeans, and sweatshirt depicting Mozart, the strains of a Bach Brandenburg concerto, the bouquet of sautéed garlic. I left my pretense on the patio and allowed myself to drift into this business of sensuality.

Vincent greeted me with a glass of wine, relieved me of my cake, and led me to a barstool at the counter in the small kitchen with the butcher-block countertops and white ceramic tile backsplashes. "The chef is at work," he declared, picking up his own glass from the counter and draining it as he turned to the stove. He pushed up his sleeves, revealing sizable forearms, and with a long-handled, flat wooden spoon proceeded to orchestrate our dinner amazingly in time to the very, very quick concerto in G major that surrounded us. He manipulated the implement in his right hand while deftly maneuvering the pots and pans with his left. White clam sauce simmered, angel-hair pasta churned in boiling water, plump capers rolled about in white wine and lemon juice thickened by a lump of sweet butter, and the music played on. I watched with admiration as Vincent drained the pasta, sauced the veal, and tossed the salad, thinking, A man in control of his kitchen is a man in control of his life.

"Dinner is served," he announced, carrying the dishes to the small, square, glass and stainless steel dining table. Once I was seated, Vincent lit the candles on the table, dimmed the hi-tech steel and enamel light overhead, and placed a basket of hot garlic and cheese bread before me . . . leaning close to me . . . telling me that the recipe for the bread came from his grandmother who lives in Sicily. And I could have fainted from the exquisite aroma of the bread . . . of the after-shave? cologne? soap? that emanated from Vincent.

I tasted everything. "It's wonderful, Vincent. I'm impressed."

"Then I've succeeded," he said, smiling a very quiet smile, giving the electricity between us room to build. "I wanted to impress you."

"Oh?"

"You attracted me the first time we met. I tried to flirt with you when you brought the lady lawyer over, but you were tough. Ve-ry pro-fes-sion-al. So I figured I had to get you out of your business suit . . . so to speak."

That did it. As good as dinner was, it was over for me. I remembered all at once all of those scenes in movies where the man rubs the woman's foot with his under the table, rubs his leg against hers under the table, puts his hand on her knee under the table, touches her hand as he passes the pasta, touches her face as he dusts a crumb from her chin, and I felt Vincent all at once all over me. And he hadn't even touched me.

"You're not eating!"

I flushed. "I'm not as hungry as I thought I was."

"Yes. Appetites tend to supplant one another. I feel it, too."

That's saying it like it is, I thought, flushing deeper.

Bach filled my ears. Vincent filled my wineglass. "To a sensual evening," he said, touching his glass to mine.

I drank the wine quickly in an effort to hydrate the desert that had taken over my mouth.

"You have a fine body, Tess."

That's direct, I thought—a pass even I can't miss. "Oh, it's fine, all right," I said, laughing nervously, "for a teenage boy."

"And I'll bet you're going to complain that your thighs are too chubby, too. Most Jewish girls say that."

Very direct. No games played here. "Well. My legs aren't my best feature." I couldn't believe I was discussing my body as if it were a piece of equipment with this . . . this stranger!

"I personally don't like a woman with chicken legs. Soft thighs make soft cushions."

I couldn't respond. Tumbleweeds were blowing around my tongue.

"I'm looking forward to this evening, Tess."

Dinner wasn't This Evening? Of course not. *Dessert* was This Evening. I guessed *I* was Dessert. No. I changed my mind. *He's* Dessert.

"It's going to be fun," I heard myself say.

"Fun?" He sounded hurt. Maybe *fun* was too frivolous an adjective for this Macho Guy, this Latin Lover.

"Yes. Fun," I repeated, feeling my spinning wheels click into gear. "It's always best when it's fun."

"You're okay, Tess." He laughed, putting his napkin on the table. Dinner was over. Vincent stood up, took my hands, and pulled me to my feet. He put his extremely muscled arms around my waist and kissed me. It was nice, relaxed.

Okay. So far I was okay. I was also dizzy—from the wine, the Bach, the garlic, Vincent. "Oooh, Vincent, what you're doing to me," I said, totally in control of my loss of control.

"This looks serious," he said, his arms around me, walking me backward, toward the stairs.

Serious? Could he possibly mean *serious* as in *I could really get serious about you?* No, no. He means *serious* as in *We're going to do It.* Kicking off my flats, I put my stockinged feet on his Reeboks, letting him carry me to . . . whatever, accepting with abandon that walking backward on his feet was about as serious as this was going to get.

Upstairs, he gently placed me on the bed and pulled my bulky cotton sweater over my head. Lying beside me, his mouth latched onto my right breast, he somehow dealt with my slacks and panties, and the next thing I knew Vincent was between my legs doing something so incredible with his tongue that I came in a flash with a yelp, and then again . . . and again . . . and again. . . . The man was impressive—and he didn't even have his pants off. It didn't occur to me to wonder if I was impressing him. Then we were both naked, and I found out just *how* impressive he was. And then it was morning and I awoke with Vincent plastered to my back, his black beard nestled between my neck and my shoulder. I smiled. He stirred. He was on top of me, kissing me, and all I could think of was my morning mouth . . . *garlic* morning mouth. He felt my reticence, wiped *his* mouth on the midnight blue satin sheet, and kissed me again. And then he was behind me, his hands all over the front of me. It felt like Sunday morning.

Sunday mornings with Stephen were warm and wet. I'd wake slowly, encased in Stephen, and we'd made love before I even opened my eyes. Behind me, his arms around me, his morning erection rooting between my thighs for acceptance, he'd kiss my neck, rub my breasts in a spiral of circles starting wider than they deserved. The first fuck of the morning was slow and hot. Then we would doze . . . tease and play . . . doze . . . tease and sometimes play again . . . and sometimes we wouldn't get up until two or three in the afternoon.

"You do okay for a teenage boy," Vincent teased, after.

When he left the bed to open the aluminum mini-blinds, there, in the wash of sunlight, I finally saw the full splendor of his beautiful body. From my reclined position, he looked like a marble statue, larger than life, every muscle, every feature chiseled to silky definition. Imagine! Michelangelo's David . . . in bed with me, Tess Fineman.

"Brunch?" he asked.

"Of course."

"Mykonos okay?"

"Sure." And I thought of Sunday brunch at the diner with Sandy and Janet, watching the singles come in with their Saturday night dates. Well, at least this was the middle of the week. No one would know.

At brunch, I couldn't eat very much, again. And again, he noticed. "It's exciting, isn't it? Being with someone new."

"Actually, I find it uncomfortable," I said honestly.

The rest of the meal was quiet, until the waitress asked, "How about dessert?" Vincent immediately replied, "We're having it at home."

I looked at him and he winked at me, and that wink undid me, again.

"Your cake, Tess. We didn't eat your cake last night."

"Yes."

But as soon as we walked in the door of his house, his arms were around me again, and there I was on his feet again as he walked me backward to the stairs again and he carried me up to the bedroom again and this time I didn't wait for him to undress me, I pulled off my sweater and pants and panties, and before I could see that he, too, was undressed his head was between my legs and his impressive organ straining its latex jacket was in front of my eyes and all I could do while he did whatever it was that he did so well was to hold on to his staff for dear life as I came over . . . and over . . . and over . . . and over . . . until, exhausted, I cried, "UNCLE!"

"Wha?"

"Uncle!" I said, then gave him his due until he spilled in a gush. And then—yes, and then—and then he turned and we thrashed and heaved until, hooting and laughing, we were both spent . . . again.

"You were right," he said, lying back in exhaustion.

"About what?"

"It was fun."

We did finally get to my cake . . . after we rested, after we showered and dressed . . . after we made a pot of coffee.

"You do the honors," he said, handing me a knife and a plate.

Faced with my experimental creation, I was pulled back to the real world where I felt a little unstable, a little unsure. I approached the checkerboard cake with trepidation, wondering if, this time, I had gotten it right. The knife cut a wedge in the three layers. Slowly I inched the wedge out of the cake. . . . "STRIPES!" I cried.

Preparations for Checkerboard Cake III included pencil and paper. But as I sketched cake layers and three-dimensional bull's-eyes at my kitchen table later that afternoon, I found I couldn't concentrate. I went to the phone and dialed. "Sandy?"

"Tess! Where have you been? I've been trying you all day. Didn't you get my messages on your machine?"

"Sorry. I forgot to look at the machine when I came in."

"I waited for your call last night, and then tried you this morning, early . . ."

"You want company for dinner? I'll bring dessert."

"Sure. Charlie's working late. So where were you?"

"Playing chess."

"Chess?"

"See you in an hour. Bye."

I played the tape on my answering machine. There were eight messages:

BEEP. "Tess! Where are you? You were supposed to call me back last night."

BEEP. "Good morning, sunshine! It's Marv! What an early start! Just wanted to tell you that I'm going to miss you this weekend. So, if you'd like to have dinner tonight, tomorrow, or Friday, I'm at your service. If not, have a productive weekend in White Plains. Ciao!"

BEEP. "It's me again. Thought maybe you were in the shower earlier. Where are you? Do you want to have lunch? Call me when you get in."

BEEP. "Tess? It's David. It's one-forty. Just checking in. I'm okay. You okay? Peace."

BEEP. "Just Desserts? This is Gus Kolodner from the Chessmen. I wanted to tell you that we're looking forward to your goodies Thursday night, and on behalf of our membership I'd like to extend an invitation for you to join us for the evening. You don't have to call me back. See you Thursday, either way."

BEEP. "Tess, it's three-thirty. Now I'm worried. Call me!"

BEEP. "It's Stephen. I want to see you. Please, Tess. Unless you call me, I'll be over at seven. It'll be okay. Really. I love you."

BEEP. "It's Mother, dear. Why aren't you home? There never seems to be a right time to call you. Call me when you come in. I'll be at home."

What she meant was, *I'll be home, where I belong, unlike you, who are off to God knows where! doing God knows what!* You're right, Mother, there never is a right time for you to call me, I thought.

I dialed Stephen's office number, but hung up when his secretary answered. I just won't be here, I thought, remembering that I'd be at Sandy's. That's better. That way I won't even have to talk to him. What to do about Marv? Nothing. And I'll call David when I get home tonight, before I go to bed. Gus. The cake. Tomorrow. I can't think about that now. Maybe I'll just make the fudge bars and honeyed granola . . . and I have two sour-cream coffee cakes in the freezer. That should do it. Right.

At five thirty-five I embedded a cherry candy heart in the iced top of each of the three oversize chocolate cupcakes, boxed them, and left for Sandy's.

After dinner, after story time—when I read Rebecca and Jonathan *my* favorite book, *Put Me in the Zoo*—after bath time washed chocolate icing off grateful faces and chocolate crumbs down the drain, after bedtime quieted the house, Sandy and I sat down to mugs of tea and the third chocolate bull's-eye.

"Well?" Sandy said, picking the cherry heart off the cake and popping it into her mouth.

"Well what?" I teased.

"Well, so where were you, what happened?"

"Well . . ." I started slowly, "I was at Vincent's town-house for dinner . . . and I stayed for brunch."

Sandy couldn't contain herself. "So, so, so?" she begged, on the edge of her seat.

"So. He had invited me to dinner to talk about the sale of the house—you remember I told you about the lady lawyer I took to see the house? Well . . ." and I related the whole story, leaving out not one juicy morsel. And Sandy giggled and tittered, laughed and clapped her hands like a little girl hearing a favorite fairy tale where the beautiful princess has her cake and eats it, too.

"Tess, you're incredible! So when are you going to see him again?"

"I'm not."

"What! You've got to be kidding. You knooow he's going to call you again."

"It doesn't matter. I don't want to see him again."

"Why not? He sounds faaabulous!"

"So was Gregg . . . and Marv."

"Was? What's this *was?* Did they appear in the obit column this morning?"

119

"I pretty much told Marv yesterday that I didn't want to see him anymore. And Gregg . . . well, he called last week and I told him I was *involved*. I felt weird with the idea of sleeping with Gregg while I was still seeing Marv. So I said I'd call him when I was free."

"That was monogamous of you."

"Well, that's what made me comfortable."

"So now you're not seeing Mirrors or Cream Puff, why can't you see the Italian Stallion?"

"The Italian Stallion? You do come up with them!"

"It's my most major talent. But, actually, it's you who comes up with them, I only name them. So how come?"

"How come what?"

"How come you won't see him again?"

"Because it was just sex. That's all. We have absolutely nothing in common, nothing to talk about."

"How do you know? You didn't talk!"

"I know. Trust me."

"Okay. So what's the matter with pure sex?" she demanded.

"I don't know. It was fine for what it was, but there was so much missing. It was like Chinese food. Three hours later you're hungry again—deep down."

"So?"

"I guess what I'm trying to say is that it happened because of the right chemistry, the right circumstances, the right tensions. . . . It was totally spontaneous. I went over because I thought it was business, and I certainly couldn't do that again. . . . I mean, if he called and I went out with him again, it would be tantamount to saying, 'Okay, I want to fuck, too. Do we eat dinner first, or do we just get naked and do It?' Look, it was great fun, but it wasn't a performance that would hold up in a rerun. . . . What I'm trying to say is that I don't think I'm a casual person, Sandy. I don't want *just* sex . . . I want *the rest.*"

"I'm not saying you should *marry* him! You know, Tess, I think you're scared."

"Of Vincent? Not a chance!"

"Not Vincent. Someone much more formidable: YOUR-

SELF! Of admitting that you get horny like everybody else and that good sex now and then is good for you."

"Not so. How about Gregg? Remember? Just a little dessert?"

"That's different. Cream Puff stood for something else. You thought he wanted you for your intellect, your maturity, your life experiences. You felt like the Romantic Older Woman. The sex wasn't even that good. You were his mentor, so you had a rationalization other than libido to sleep with him."

"God, Sandy. You're beginning to sound like Janet. You make me sound so neurotic."

"Hey. We all have something."

By then the mugs were drained. I felt drained. I picked up the last crumb of cake on the end of my finger and licked it off. "I think I'm depressed. I'm going to go home and sleep for a year."

"You know what your trouble is? Too much sex. You've been overorgasmed, orgasmed out. You're too mellow! Go home and sleep and have some nightmares . . . tense up again and you'll feel great in the morning."

Very early Thursday morning I pulled the coffee cakes out of the freezer for the chess club meeting that night—just in case. But after I made the fudge bars and the granola, I decided to take one more shot at the checkerboard cake. It was such a good idea; I couldn't let it go.

The phone was ringing when I walked into my kitchen after gathering ingredients from the market for Checkerboard Cake III.

"Hello," I answered, putting the grocery bag on the counter.

"There you are! I thought maybe you moved and didn't tell me." It was David.

"Uh-oh! I forgot to call you back last night. I did get your message. Sorry. Anything special?"

"Only that I was thinking about you. The last time we talked, you were pretty upset about Janet and her boyfriend.

You going to be home for a while? I met a client at the diner, and thought I'd stop over for a last cup of coffee before I go back to the office."

"You look okay," David said, giving me a brotherly kiss and an awkward hug about ten minutes after we hung up.

"I'm fine." I poured us each a mug of coffee and sat at the kitchen table with David. The yellow legal pad full of bull's-eye drawings was still there from the day before.

"What are these?" he asked.

"A puzzle. I'm trying to make a checkerboard cake," I said as David picked up the pad, turning it this way and that, trying to understand.

"Explain."

"Okay. Men are supposed to have a good sense of spatial relationships. See if you can figure this out. . . ." And I explained the pans to him, and the three layers, and the chocolate and vanilla batters, and the bull's-eyes. ". . . but I ended up with STRIPES!"

It didn't take him thirty seconds after I had finished my spiel. "You have to alternate the colors, Tess," he said.

"But I did. That's how I got the bull's-eyes."

"No. I mean you have to alternate the order of the colors in the layers. The top and bottom should be the same, but the middle has to be different. Black, white, black . . . white, black, white . . . black, white, black," he explained, drawing more bull's-eyes on the yellow pad.

"I can't believe it's that simple."

"It is. Here, I'll show you," he said, drawing a three-dimensional diagram of a cake with a slice cut out of it.

"Checkerboards! Amazing! Why couldn't I think of that?"

"Perspective, my dear girl. You got stuck on those chocolate-centered bull's-eyes. You needed a new perspective."

"You're a genius!" I raved, giving his hand a squeeze.

"I'm just a fresh pair of eyes. You've been staring at the problem too long."

I smiled at the drawing for a while, and then at David, and then at the drawing again, and then my smile faded.

"Speaking of staring at problems too long. . . . Do you think I'm terribly neurotic?" I asked, turning serious.

"Time out. What's going on here? I thought you said you're okay."

"I lied."

"So what's the matter?"

"Everything."

"Everything is very big."

"Well, almost everything."

"I'm here. I'm all ears," he said, leaning toward me, elbows on the table, holding his mug in one hand, his beard in the other.

"I don't know. It's just that . . . why do things have to be so complicated? Why can't I go out and have a good time, come home, and forget it? Why can men be that way and not women? Why is there always more to it for a woman?"

"I'm not sure what you're talking about."

"Sex. I'm talking about sex!" I blurted out, suddenly sorry that I'd started the conversation, suddenly blushing and uncomfortable.

"Can you give me a few more clues as to what, specifically, this is about?"

Unable to turn back, eat my words, start over, I stumbled out a quick explanation about a date with a guy who meant nothing to me, but I slept with him anyway because . . . "I don't know why," I lied.

"And now you feel guilty about satisfying a few animal urges."

"That's what Sandy said."

"Perspective. It's all perspective. I guess men don't feel guilty because we've been brought up to believe that we're *supposed* to have animal urges detached from human feelings. But all people have the same needs, Tess. And, shocking though it may be, the truth is that women have a need for fucking, and men have a need for loving. Life isn't as black and white as a checkerboard," he said, picking up the pad and dropping it on the table with a smack. "And people aren't as black and white as chessmen." He said this with an edge of . . . anger? pain?

"You're right," was all I could think of to say. Although what I wanted to do was stand up and come around behind him, and hug him, and tell him that I didn't mean to hurt him, that I knew he was different— No, no. That's not what he wanted to hear. He's *not* different, is what he said. Men are not what we think they are. They're not what a lot of men think men are. And I guess the same goes for women.

"Got to go," he said, standing abruptly. "Got a lot of work to finish. Chin up, everything will work out okay. Just don't be so hard on yourself. Talk to you next week. Got a hot date this weekend," he said as he walked out the door. "She's going to take care of all my male animal needs. Owwooooo!" he howled to the sun and then laughed and then was gone.

Checkerboard Cake III was a success. I cut it into thin wedges that I arranged on a thick cardboard plate stapled with white doilies. Checkerboard slices! They were beautiful. And Gus was delighted. Just Desserts had another regular customer. I wouldn't stay at the meeting, however.

"Oh, I can't blame you, it gets pretty tense here," Gus said. "Chess is a game of power, you know. The people who play it are into control."

I wanted to say, "Is that anything like being into leather?" but, instead, I smiled sweetly and went home.

HONEYED GRANOLA

3 cups rolled oats
1 cup wheat flakes
1/2 cup wheat germ
1/2 cup bran
1/2 cup sesame seeds
1/2 cup cashews
1/2 cup sunflower seeds
1/2 cup shredded coconut
1/4 cup peanut oil
1/4 cup honey
1 teaspoon salt
1/2 cup raisins
1/2 cup chopped dried apricots

Preheat oven to 225°F.

Mix all of the ingredients except the raisins and apricots in a
bowl and spread thinly on a cookie sheet. Bake for about one
hour, until golden brown, turning once. When cool, add the
raisins and apricots. Serves 20–25.

CHAPTER 8

Honeyed Granola

Michael always had his own agenda. I could tell by the way he would cut me short when I started on something he didn't consider relevant that day, how he steered toward something he had a mind to and fought me when I tried to override him. I let him win, aware that I usually covered my agenda as well as we sidestepped and bowed, advanced and retreated, turned this way and that in a dance that drew us ever forward, ever closer to The Truth . . . and to each other. That glorious Tuesday in May, it was my attraction to him—the inevitable attraction a client develops toward a successful therapist: that is, a therapist who is succeeding with the client. It is what must happen to a client—being attracted to one's therapist—to prove the therapist's skill and the client's cooperation, the failure of which to occur proving . . . what? failure of the client? or failure of the therapist? Moot question. I was attracted.

I had said something that held him, and he stared at me, smiling.

"Why are you looking at me like that?"

"Like what? I don't understand," he said, leaning back casually in his chair, his hands on his thighs.

"Of course you understand. What's going on?" We were both smiling, but I was squirming because he kept gazing at me, waiting for me to catch on? or to crawl into a corner and hide? or to demand that he stop? What?

"No, I don't understand. What do you think is going on?"

I tried to cooperate: "You're staring at me."

"Staring?"

"You're staring and smiling at me."

"So?"

"So why are you staring and smiling at me?"

"Oh, I don't know. What do you think?"

Truth. Tell the truth. Cooperate. "You're flirting with me."

"I'm flirting with you?" His smile broadened to a grin.

Tortured, I burned in a blush. "You're appreciating me."

"Yes. I'm appreciating you, and you think I'm flirting with you. That's interesting."

Stay honest. "You *are* flirting with me, aren't you? Trying to get me to like you." Wipe that silly grin off your face or I'll hate you forever, I thought. "You know I like you," I tried to appease him.

His grin melted into a grimace of feigned puzzlement. "Are you flirting with *me?*" he asked. "Do you think something's happening between us?"

That's it! He asked for it. Honesty, right in the face: "Are you asking me if I want to have sex with you?" I asked bluntly, leaning forward in my seat. "If I want us to get naked and do It, right here on the sofa, on the floor, with the door unlocked, with your colleagues just steps away? If that's what you're asking, the answer is no. No, not here, not now. But in some other world in some other time? Of course." I hesitated and searched his being for a response. Whatever it was, it didn't show. He is good. I continued: "I'm supposed to be attracted to you, aren't I? It's part of the therapy, right? So don't flatter yourself, I'm not trying to seduce you. I don't do married. Remember?"

Of course he remembered. Still no response. Control. Maybe too much control. Maybe that was the response.

"Besides, it's a lot easier to find a good lover than a good therapist," I finished.

Just then I thought I detected a glint of excitement in him. Maybe it was the way the light hit his eyes as they flitted away from my face to fall momentarily upon my naked shoulder, bared accidentally by the shifting wide boat-neck of my cream cotton sweater when I folded my arms in front of me. An almost involuntary shrug of my shoulder boosted the sweater back to its proper place, and his eyes back to mine. He might have love in his life, but perhaps he also had a need for flight from the ennui of complacency.

"So you think I'd be a good lover?" he asked.

What about the good therapist part? I wondered.

"Well, maybe it is easy to find good lovers," he mused to the ceiling, leaning farther back in his chair, linking his hands on top of his head. "After all, you found Stephen, and he was a good lover. Right?"

Hoist with my own petard! I didn't want to do this conversation. Not now. Not when I had an edge. Of course, that's why he'd started it. "Stephen wasn't an especially good lover," I said. "We've been over that before."

"Have we? It must have slipped my mind. So tell me, Stephen wasn't a good lover?"

"Nothing slips your mind."

"Why would you choose a lousy lover if good lovers are easy to find?"

"I never said Stephen was a *lousy* lover."

"Oh. I must have gotten it wrong. What was it you did say? He was inattentive, permitting but not participating, squeamish—"

"I was really responsive to him, and he never failed me," I parried sheepishly.

"Right." He nodded, suddenly shifting forward, elbows on knees. "Like an inflatable plastic doll. Yes, I understand. That's really what a good lover is all about, being available for service. The rest isn't important, right?"

"What rest?" I asked, not really needing to ask.

"What rest? The *rest!* Caring, appreciating you, appreciating your body . . ."

He thinks he would like my body. He's imagining the rest of my body.

". . . wanting to please you, showing *his* need for *you* . . ."

He needs me, he wants to please me. He thinks Stephen

must be a schmuck. He wants me to know that he wouldn't be such a schmuck. He wants to show me that he's a good lover.

"Forgive me. I got carried away for a minute. You don't need to be cared for, appreciated. You're independent."

Sarcastic bastard. I glowered.

He glowered back. His glower was darker than mine. He rolled his chair farther toward me so his knees touched mine. His glower enveloped me. "You were fucking, not making love. You don't make love alone. You were alone! Got that?!"

That's assuming that he is a good lover, I continued my thoughts, fighting off the truths he shot at me, the possibility of his passion for me momentarily supplanting the fact of Stephen's lack of it. Yes, he must be a good lover. He's so sensitive, intuitive. Then again, maybe not. Maybe he's not like that when he's really close, personally, not professionally. After all, he's only human, only a man.

"Alone, Tess," he continued quietly, gently tapping my knee with a forefinger, letting me know that I wasn't alone in there, when I was with him.

I felt tears well up and spill over, carrying satin-black mascara down my cheeks. I supposed swimmer's mascara was de rigueur for women in therapy, and my refusal to use it was my arrogance. Since my first visit to Michael's office, when he'd dropped a box of tissues next to me on the sofa, I'd refused to cry. I would wince and grimace, choke and sigh, but I wouldn't cry. I'd think, *Ya can't make me cry! So there!* So there I was crying, for my aloneness, for my fear of a really good lover . . . a really good love-er.

Driving home with all my windows open, the sun sparking on every shiny surface filling my eyes with blinding gold, the birds chirping unmercifully in my ears, the smells of wet earth, cut grass, and growing things bloating my head, I was in pain . . . painfully aware of my unattachment in the world, my unattachment to the world. The angst of spring, a yearly occurrence, was worse than usual this year. My neighbor, Millie Garfield, had told me her allergies were especially bad this year, too. I wondered if the two were related. Maybe I was allergic to life.

Spring proved to be as short as it was furious, exploding into the heat of summer by the third week in May. June and July all but melted by, leaving disjointed, surrealistic recollections, like mirages in the heat waves of the desert.

I sold three homes, including Vincent's townhouse, although I was careful to be ve-ry pro-fes-sion-al whenever I saw him or spoke with him. He was clearly confounded by my attitude. He asked me out on an actual date once (after he had asked me to dinner at his house again and I had refused). I said I was busy. But he telephoned on business more than was necessary, and he stopped by my house one evening to drop off some papers that could have been mailed. I began to understand the flattery-cum-annoyance a man must feel after having enjoyed a one-nighter with a woman, receiving cutesy studio cards and flirty phone calls. And Vincent must have felt like the woman who wasn't respected in the morning.

I didn't sell my home, although a terrific family—Stan Leibowitz, his wife Michelle, and their three small children —came to see it in June. I was awestruck by their beauty— as individuals and as a family. Stan was the quintessential tall-dark-and-handsome stranger, and Michelle the quintessential natural beauty, with rich, curly brown hair to her shoulders, big brown eyes framed by naturally dark brows and lashes, a glowing complexion, and a terrific figure— despite the fact that she had given birth only six weeks before. She held baby Max, who had a head full of black hair; her husband carried two-year-old Tiffany, a child as delicately lovely as her name; and five-year-old Pamela, reminiscent of a Degas dancer, held fast to Michelle's free hand as I guided them through a tour of my home: "This is the kitchen and breakfast area, and the fireplace in the family room over here works great . . ." et cetera. When we got to the second floor, Michelle took over: "The master bedroom is so roomy! Look, Stan," she directed, walking through the french doors to the sitting area, "we can put a bassinet in here for Max, and there's room for my rocking chair. . . . Pamela, honey, wouldn't you love this room? Look at the window seat," she said when she came to the second bedroom, which, except for the closets, had remained empty since Stephen and I had moved in. The third bedroom, my guest bedroom, she decided would be for Tiffany, and the fourth bedroom, my office, would be for Max, when he outgrew the bassinet. I guess she won't need an office, I thought, watching her with envy as remnants of my dreams of white lace canopies and red and blue race cars swept around me. "She's really something, isn't she," Stan whispered, leaning close to me. Such pride. How nice, I thought. But I did not miss that while *she* was giving my *house* the once-over, *he* was giving *me* the once-over. And after they left I thought about them all, especially Stan, with his dark good looks, his family pride—the way he winked at me in the master bedroom. My God, I thought, now I'm sounding like Sandy! This man with the model family is a MODEL HUSBAND, for goodness sake—a model with a tic in his eye. Are there no faithful men in this world? I cried inwardly, disillusioned.

But when he called three weeks later asking to see the house again, I must say I looked forward to seeing him—the beautiful man with the beautiful family and the tic in his eye. When I caught a glimpse of him through the living room window as he approached my front door, my heart jumped, I blushed; and when I opened the door I was sorry that he hadn't brought the children, and sorrier that he *had* brought his wife. Then, walking quickly through the rooms, I soon realized that *she* no longer seemed interested in the house . . . and *he* no longer seemed interested in me. He was cool, businesslike, asking questions about the neighborhood, schools, shopping. She was impatient, tense, cutting off my answers with her own: "There'll be plenty of time to find that out once we decide on the right house." *No Sale* rang up in my head as I shut the front door after them, disappointed by the capriciousness of home buyers, but relieved by the restoration of Stan Leibowitz as Model Husband, concluding that The Flirtation had been only in my head after all . . . possibly the result of some misdirected longing to belong . . . probably overwhelming jealousy of Michelle Leibowitz.

Marv had been easy. He had taken my hint—I never returned the two calls he left on my answering machine—and stopped calling.

I finally answered Stephen's calls and agreed to see him when he told me he wasn't well. His diabetes—kept under control with insulin injections—was giving him trouble. He had protein in his urine and his doctor said it might mean kidney involvement. He was going for tests. He looked scared. Maybe it was his illness, but I could have sworn there was something else. I was surprised by my own lack of compassion for him, my overall lack of feeling when I was with him, although the hours before and after his visit were loaded with confusing tensions. Maybe the torrents of conflicting emotions canceled each other out, I reasoned, leaving me feeling nothing at all. When I saw him a second time, he told me that the kidney tests showed nothing significant, but the doctor said he should be watched. I slept with him the third time I saw him. It wasn't like I had remembered it. Where's the passion? I wondered as his body heated up next to mine. Where's the involuntary gush of bodily fluids, the rush of blood? Why does he smell different, unfamiliar? He seemed unaware of the change . . . in himself? No. It wasn't he who was different, it was I. "I want us to be together, Tess," he said, after. "We belong together." And my heart pounded and my stomach felt like kneaded sourdough. Nauseated. I felt repulsed. I wanted to be away from this man to whom I was married, for whom I'd thought I had a love that was endless, by whom I had been so hurt that sometimes I feared my anger would consume me. I didn't let him stay the night. And three days later he left for two weeks in the Greek islands . . . alone, he said

. . . with Dorothy, I found out from Janet, who had heard from another hygienist in Terry's office whose husband owned the travel agency that arranged Stephen's trip. Was there no end to this man's treachery? I wondered. "I can't believe you slept with him again!" Sandy screeched when I told her . . . *after* I had found out about Dorothy.

Janet healed from her unfortunate liaison with the late Harvey Cohen. To help speed her recovery, she sent Sean to the special camp she had found, and planned to start suit against her ex-husband to pay for it—an expense he had agreed to cover the summer before (although not in writing), extracting a promise from Janet to pay for all the camp clothes and equipment, and then backed out of, pleading a "cash-flow problem," which, she had explained to us back in February, meant that Sean's summer camp had become a trip to Italy, and (Janet found out in April from a fur salon salesman whose heavily plaqued teeth she cleaned every three months) a down payment for a new lynx coat for The Twit.

"Do you really want to go through another legal battle?" we asked her, remembering chilling tales of her past experiences, from her naive acquiescence to Leonard's demands in their divorce settlement, at the urging of her attorney, "to avoid the trauma of court" . . . to a couple of protracted and expensive bouts of showy posturing between his and her attorneys, including letter sending, affidavit writing, and deposition taking, in an attempt to get Leonard to do for Sean what any normal father would be embarrassed *not* to do, but ending up in settlements where Janet caved in, at her attorney's insistence, "to avoid the trauma of court" . . . to Janet picking up the shortfall for Sean's expenses ever since, again "to avoid the trauma of court." But this time was different, she said. Sean, she explained the facts of life to us, was too young to understand that Mommy couldn't afford to send him to the camp, and too young to be told that Daddy didn't care enough about him not to disappoint him, but old enough to be crushed with disappointment and to blame it on she who was nearest to him—Janet. "So I'm going to have to take my chances in court, although I can't really afford to hire an attorney any more than I can afford to pay for camp!" she told us.

I told David about the trauma of divorce attorneys one night after we had kept each other company at a movie . . . and he was incredulous. "The kid's in a WHEELCHAIR, for God's sake! The man's a DOCTOR! That's DESPICABLE!" he yelled. "She shouldn't have to fight this guy. He's Sean's FATHER! The man's got problems, Tess—SEVERE problems! What a SLEAZE! This OFFENDS me PERSONALLY. . . . What's Janet's number?" he demanded, picking up the phone, calling her right then—eleven-thirty at night—and there—in my kitchen. Quite out of character, he told her to "drag the bastard into court," that there wasn't a judge in the country who wouldn't make sure Sean was taken care of in the style to which a doctor's son should have become accustomed. In high dudgeon, he promised, "And it won't cost you a thing, sweetheart, because I'm going to be your lawyer and I'm not going to charge you a penny. My compensation will be seeing that piece of shit lose his balls in court!"

Well! Janet and I were both taken aback by David's vitriolic tirade, his chivalrous proposal, his voluntary involvement . . . and we were very impressed.

David occasionally fed me Thai food, gentle jazz, Chopin nocturnes, and only the best movies at the Ritz Five—the subtitled, the offbeat, with Vivaldi and Bach between features—and then left August 1 (after filing papers for Janet's lawsuit against Leonard) for a month of backpacking in Europe. He sent me one postcard while he was gone, from the music festival in Salzburg: "Having a wonderful time. Wishing you a month of Mozart second movements." He couldn't have wished me anything nicer—sublime beauty, pure joy, peace—or anything less attainable, it seemed.

Michael, my oasis of rationality in a desert of madness, abandoned me in August when he left for a three-and-a-half-week seminar/vacation with his wife and children in California, via the Grand Canyon and other seeable sights.

Sandy struggled to recover her balance—which was a bit off after Janet's ordeal with the late Harvey Cohen, and my blowing away Cream Puff, Mirrors, and the Italian Stallion, while allowing Stephen back in my bed, even for the one night—by chasing her children around the pool at the swim club in a bikini, drawing a great deal of attention from the lifeguard and the tennis instructor. "I'll say it again," she said again and again, "I'm glad I'm married. I wouldn't know where to begin in the singles world. It's all veeery confusing." She got *that* right.

September brought the first gust of cool air, the first hint of fall, a wake-up call. And suddenly sanity prevailed . . . or so it seemed. I was preparing for Millie Garfield's monthly writers' club, which was meeting that night. Cinnamon-raisin coffee cakes were made early in the morning; oatmeal chocolate chip cookies had been made the day before. All that was left to do was the honeyed granola for munching.

A writer of esoterica, Millie Garfield enjoyed local renown. Her column on astrology appeared in the *Daily News* every Saturday, and her offbeat full-length features were published in *The Philadelphia Inquirer*'s Sunday magazine every now and then, her latest being "The New Brand of Professionals," a story about the growing popularity of tattoos among doctors, lawyers, and other professional men and women. Millie's writers' club meetings were one of my growing number of monthly catering contracts, and I particularly looked forward to those Wednesday evenings, usually attending and staying until the end. The dessert table was simple to prepare—Millie's standard order was, "Anything you think would be nice, Tess, as long as you include plenty of your marvelous granola!"—and the people were friendly . . . weird, but friendly. Millie always managed to put together an interesting program, like the one in June when Jerry Swerdlow spoke about dreams and how writers could tap into their unconscious through dreams to create believable fantasy.

Jerry was a writer of sci-fi stories and nonfiction magazine articles, a creative writing teacher at Temple University, and very, very smart. He was also very, very cute. Tall and lanky, with long dark hair and thick straight bangs, eyes like pieces of polished coal, and a smooth, translucent complexion, he was about twenty-eight, looking eighteen.

After his talk—which was carried out in a darkened room to promote the listeners' relaxation and dreamlike state, a technique that worked so well that one of the gathered (a soft-spoken, confusion-bound woman in her early fifties with unruly gray hair carelessly tied in a knot on top of her head, a woman who wrote of cosmetic fads, medical oddities, and such for supermarket tabloids) nodded off, jolting to wakefulness with a high-pitched shriek and a wild look in her pale gray eyes when the lights were turned on—after his talk, I gave Jerry my telephone number when he told me he was looking for someone to cater a monthly meeting of some other writers' organization. He was, he also told me, single-but-living-with-someone.

Now, single-but-living-with-someone was akin to married in my book, but after he called me a couple of times, first to tell me that the group didn't want desserts catered after all, and later to tell me that he was sorry about the disappointment he might have caused me, and, by the way, could he stop over for a cup of coffee some evening on his way home from his office, just to talk, because I was, after all, such an interesting woman, so easy to talk to, I finally consented to a tête-à-tête because, of course, it was going to be absolutely innocent and, after all, he seemed like such an interesting man, and so young, and so eager . . . and I was flattered.

So he came. And we talked. And he loved that I had fruit and cookies and cocoa, and leftover chicken and spaghetti in the refrigerator. He was hungry. And he told me about his parents dying in a plane crash when he was eleven, how his uncle and his uncle's second wife, who was very young and very attractive, took him in, and how at fifteen his adolescent lusting for his uncle's young attractive second wife was satisfied when she came into his room on a day he was home from school with a fever, rubbed his back, and gave him his first blow job. And that he now related fever with sex and that whenever he got sick he got horny.

The fourth time he visited he told me about his live-in girlfriend, a psychologist, who'd been his best friend since he was eight, and how even though she was his best friend he couldn't talk to her the way he could talk to me—as if he'd known me all of his life—and how capable I must be running two careers and a big house all by myself, and how deep I was, and how attractive I was. How hungry he was. How scared. When he kissed me, I thought his heart was going to burst right through his starched white shirt. Curious, I thought, that I could have this effect on him. I'm always surprised when I have an effect on someone. I want to look over my shoulder to see who's standing behind me.

The tall casement windows on both sides of the family room were open to the breezy summer night and the cross currents pulled a warm draft across the plush putty-colored carpet where we squirmed and fumbled in a half-clothed attempt at lovemaking. What a wonderful body he had: long-limbed and almost childlike in its pale, unbuilt-up leanness; how unchildlike its manliness! What a shame he didn't know quite what to do with what he had. But how good to feel hot skin. How good to feel arms around me; how good to feel him filling me.

"I'm going," he said suddenly, opening his eyes, lifting his upper body to arm's length from me.

"You're gonna come?"

"No, I . . ."

"You came?"

"I gotta go."

"You have to pee?"

"No, I'm going."

"You're going?"

"I'm leaving."

"I want to come!"

"You came!"

"I didn't come."

"I'm going."

"I don't understand."

"I gotta go." And he sprang to his feet, pulling his shorts and pants up in one motion. He was still erect.

When I stood up, my hitched skirt fell, and I just left my panties lying on the floor as I ran to the front door after him. He was halfway down the walk, his shirttails hanging out, and he was struggling to get the keys out of his pants pocket. "Jerry!" I called, and he turned but kept on running— backward.

"I gotta go!"

"This is weird!"

"You knocked my goddamned socks off!" he shouted, one hand deep in his pocket, one leg in his white Volkswagen Rabbit.

As I watched him drive off, I became aware of wet running down my leg. He had come . . . and gone.

Then there was Dr. Daniel Daroff, another very smart man. He was a physics professor and an amateur astronomer who spoke to Millie's group about the summer sky and then ran off before I had a chance to meet him. But he was attractive, and Millie told me he was single, so I enrolled in his summer evening lecture series in astronomy held at the high school in August. Not just to meet him, of course; I thought it might be a nice place to meet other single men and learn about black holes and entropy all at once.

It turned out that I was one of seven women in a group of eight. The only man there was with his wife. They were into stargazing and had a telescope on the roof of their beachfront home in Longport. So I flirted with Daniel Daroff, who was handsome in a poetic way. That is, he was, behind his soft bushy mustache, finely featured, pale, and delicate. I carefully watched his dark eyes, beneath a mop of wavy, light brown hair, darting back and forth from student to student as he lectured, how he walked back and forth across the front of the room in long strides, his arms gesticulating this way and that like a stork attempting to take flight. And when he passed by me, my eyes caught his. He sort of lurched, hesitating on the syllable in his mouth, elongating it, holding it, and though he continued to move forward, away from me, my eyes held his, causing his head to swivel around as he walked. When I smiled, ever so faintly, he abruptly turned his head forward and continued the word, and the lecture.

At the door after class, the Longport couple pelted him with questions about supernovas, but his eyes never left mine as I stood back waiting to meet him. ". . . and I hope you'll explain black holes before the end of the semester," I remember finally saying. Two hours later, sitting on the edge of his desk, I could have taught Carl Sagan something about black holes.

Two weeks later, after three dinners, one movie, and two lunches with Daniel, when I found myself in his apartment kissing him on his Danish modern sofa flanked by two leggy dracaena plants in black rubber tubs, the term "entropy" began to take on new meaning.

He had a wonderful mouth, and he smelled nice. He didn't use after-shave or anything, he just smelled nice. But I thought he was going to just kiss me all afternoon. "Well, I guess we're gonna do It," I heard myself blurt out.

His eyes went wide and wild for a moment—surprise? fear? confusion?—but he took his cue and led me to the bedroom. There he gently unbuttoned my blouse and then, while I finished undressing, started undressing himself. Nice, tight, narrow body, I noted, arranging myself on his bed. Long, pretty legs. Not obviously aroused, he lowered himself onto me anyway. For a minute or two he just kissed me—with his eyes open. Then things got kind of frantic . . . his heart was beating a hundred thousand billion times a minute . . . he kept trying to enter me but he couldn't . . . I was really excited and tried to push up against him in a vain attempt to make something happen . . . he made some funny noises and dropped to one side. "Did you come?" I gasped.

"Sort of."

"Sort of?"

"I think we have to talk."

"Talk?"

We dressed self-consciously and met in the living room. Taking my hand, he sat on the sofa and pulled me onto his lap.

"So talk," I said gently.

"Well, here goes," he started, staring across the room, and all of a sudden his heart started beating a hundred thousand billion times a minute again. "I really don't do too well with women. With sex, I mean. I mean, I really get scared. . . ."

No shit, I thought. His eyes grew large and dark as fancy black olives. He was sweating. He looked ten years old.

". . . And, well, what I've done before is just give massages, you know, like back rubs, and . . ." His voice trailed off along with his attention. He seemed to be lost somewhere momentarily. Then, quite abruptly, he smiled broadly at me. "So, do you want a back rub?"

"Okay," I said, trying to be understanding, trying to understand, wondering just how weird he might get.

"Great!" he said, relieved, energized. Easing me off his lap, he led me, once again, to the bedroom. "So, do you want to take your clothes off?" he asked on his way to the bathroom.

I wasn't sure if I wanted to or not, but I did. Maybe I was curious. Maybe I was crazy.

Minutes later he returned, naked, carrying a paper cup. "My secret formula," he explained, sitting on the edge of the bed where I lay prone. "Now, close your eyes."

I can't believe how trusting I was of this possible lunatic. I closed my eyes. The next thing I experienced was his long fingers sliding across my shoulders on a film of something warm and wet, and the heavy aroma of cloves filling my head. Is this kinky? I wondered as the sweet vapors put me a little off-center.

"It's Baby Magic lotion and baby oil and oil of cloves warmed in hot water. Isn't it great?" he chirped.

It was. I luxuriated in the feel, in the smell, wondering what kinky was.

"Want a front rub, too?"

I turned and watched him. He looked intense as he worked, slowly, gently, carefully avoiding nipples and groin.

"Okay. Now you do me," he said after a while.

This, then, was not to be foreplay, to lead up to; this was to be instead of. I couldn't believe I was there. I can't believe I went out with him again.

Yes, indeed, it had been a surreal summer, I thought, spooning granola into white cardboard boxes lined with wax paper, tying the boxes with thin gold ribbon, and sealing the flaps with self-sticking white labels bearing the gold imprint JUST DESSERTS. It was four-forty. I had to drop off Millie's goodies for her meeting that night—the usually Wednesday meeting was a Friday this month, a meeting I couldn't attend because I had tickets for a concert—and the concert was at seven-thirty, so I would have to leave my house about six-thirty to have time to stop at Millie's and get to the concert in time to get a good seat, so I'd have plenty of time to get dressed and grab something to eat if I finished Millie's order by five. No problem, I thought, signing the boxes with a gold pen, "Just for You, by Tess." *Success is all in the packaging,* I remembered from a college marketing class. No problem, I thought, *if* the phone doesn't ring, which it did, and I considered letting my answering machine pick it up . . . but what if it's Millie, about the meeting tonight? or Janet? Maybe she decided to go to the concert with me after all. I really didn't want to go alone. "Hello."

"Tess?" It was Millie. She had bumped into a man she had known for years through the Friends of the Philadelphia Museum of Art . . . a nice man, an energy consultant, thirty-one . . . two small children . . . his wife had died in a car accident ten months ago; he was dating . . . did she know anyone, he had asked her.

A nice, stable widower with two motherless babes—a possibly sane man! "Sure! Give him my number. In fact, maybe he wants to go to a Chamber Players concert tonight," I half teased.

Five minutes later, I was still packaging granola, the phone rang. "Hello."

"Hello. Is this Tess?" It was Elliot Spector, the Sane Man. I laughed.

"Keep laughing," he said, "because I'm really calling to tell you that I'm *not* your date for tonight, I already have plans, but when Millie called to give me your number, I decided to call and introduce myself and see if we could get together another time."

We chatted and bantered—I was getting better at that—he said he was intrigued, and could we meet for brunch in the morning? No, I was meeting some friends for brunch at the diner. Dinner? No, I already had plans—with Janet. It wouldn't be fair to Janet to cancel . . . and besides, I didn't want to appear too available.

"Well, how about tonight after your concert?" he tried.

"I thought you had a date."

"I do, but it's for an early dinner. She's traveling and has to leave early. What time do you think you'll be home?"

She's *traveling?* "I don't know, probably about ten."

"I'll call you when I'm free."

"This is crazy. I'm not going out that late."

"It's not so late," the Sane Man insisted.

Who was I to argue with sanity? And besides, none of my friends would go with me to the concert so I felt angry and disappointed, and knowing I would be coming home to someone—anyone—would make going to the concert alone not so lonely. "Okay. But don't call after eleven."

Three minutes later, I was still packaging granola, the phone rang. "Hello."

"It's me again. . . ." It was Elliot again. ". . . I'm really excited, I feel like I'm back in high school. Two dates in one night! Don't disappoint me! I'll call you when I get in."

"I won't disappoint you if you call before eleven," I warned, mindful of the shred of control I attempted to retain in this scenario.

Finished the packaging, dressed, ate, stopped at Millie's, got a good seat at the concert, home by ten-fifteen. The message the Sane Man had left on my answering machine informed me that he was "running late," that I should "not wait up," that he would "call in the morning." Read: *I got lucky.*

"So, can we have breakfast?" It was Elliot at nine-fifteen—AM

"I told you I was meeting friends."

"Call me when you get home. Maybe we can squeeze a cup of coffee in before your dinner date tonight."

"I'll call you," I promised, flattered that he was being so persistent, but knowing full well that I wouldn't have time to meet him.

"So I promised to call him when I get home," I told Sandy and Janet at brunch. We giggled like teenagers. My, wasn't dating fun? Sandy still thought it must be as she lived vicariously through me and Janet, but Janet and I knew the truth: The population of single men is like a bowl of granola—what ain't fruits and nuts is flakes.

We were deep into whitefish salad, toasted bagels, and the disappointments of the summer when, out of nowhere it seemed, a strange man grabbed Janet's arm. "Tess?"

Shaking her head, Janet smirked at the man and pointed to me.

Releasing her arm, he took my hand. "Tess!"

"Elliot, I presume," I said darkly.

"I hope you don't mind my interrupting."

It's intrusive and rude, I thought. "Not at all," I said, smiling, holding his hand briefly. "Janet, Sandy, this is Elliot. Elliot, Sandy and Janet."

"Well, I was also meeting someone for breakfast, and when I saw you girls I knew that one had to be you, Tess, so I thought I'd say hello. Nice to meet you all. Call me when you get home, okay?"

He wasn't bad-looking, I thought. He'd rather take out Janet.

"Elliot?" I had called him as soon as I walked into the house.

"I'm on the other phone, let me call you back, okay?" he answered, and hung up.

Five minutes later the phone rang. "Hello."

"So how's it going?" It was Elliot.

"Well, considering that last night you called me to tell me that we didn't have a date, and then you called me to break the date that we didn't have, and then you made a pass at my friend at brunch, to which you were not invited in the first place, and then you practically hung up on me when I called, I'd say everything is going about par," I answered with honesty, honestly irritated.

"Uh, well . . . *cough cough* . . . oh, excuse me, but I seem to have picked up something. In fact, when you called I was . . . uh . . . talking to my doctor. I really feel lousy . . . *cough* . . . so I guess I won't be able to make it today after all. I don't know what it is, but I've felt it coming on."

"Mmm. I've felt it coming on, too."

"You mean on me?"

"Look, Elliot, cut the bullshit."

"Hey! Chill out, sweets! You know, you mature women should learn to loosen up."

"FUCK OFF, ELLIOT!"

Slamming down the phone, I burst into tears. "THEY'RE ALL CRAZY!" I screeched aloud. "THEY'RE ALL A BUNCH OF WEIRDOS! THEY SHOULD ALL BE LOCKED UP!" I was screaming as I dialed Sandy's number.

"Hello," she answered unsuspectingly.

"HOW COULD YOU LET ME GO OUT WITH ALL THOSE CREEPS!" I yelled at her.

"Tess? What's going on? Are you okay?"

But all I could do for the longest time was sob, until, finally, "No, I'm not okay—no, that's not right, *I* am okay . . ." and I explained the Elliot phone call. "It's *them*, Sandy. *They're* not okay. I finally figured it out. It's not me. I'm not crazy. It's not that I'm easily confused, it's that they're confusing because they're crazy."

"You're confusing me, Tess."

* * *

"And that's the way it's been going. They're all so crazy. I mean, women aren't that crazy, are they?" I asked David.

Sitting next to me at my kitchen table Wednesday afternoon, he lifted his drink and studied it through a tight-lipped smile. "Well," he said, turning to me after a moment, "it's all in the way you look at it. I've met some crazy ones, but crazy can be interesting . . . for a while."

"Not for long. Trust me. I used to think it was me. These guys would confuse me and I assumed that I was missing something, that they were tuned in to the real world and I wasn't . . . so I'd go along for a while . . . but things wouldn't clear up. But after this absurd little dance with Elliot—Sandy calls him Datus Interruptus—it finally hit me: They're nuts. They don't make sense . . . not my kind of sense."

"I have to tell you, Tess, I was wondering how long it would take you to come to your senses . . . so to speak," David said, smiling.

"So. Where are all the sane men?" I rambled on, embarrassed by his perception. "They're married, of course," I answered my own question. "I've never done married. Maybe I should try married," I said, remembering my attraction to Stan Leibowitz.

"It depends on what you want from the relationship. Now, if it's just sex . . . well, married men are basically safe. They usually don't want to leave their wives, they just want a little something more," said David, playing devil's advocate.

Closing my eyes, sighing, I contemplated his words and wondered bitterly if it were all as insipid as it sounded. Were there no faithful *and* sane men in the world? Were there no real meaningful relationships—the kind that are attached so deep down that they aren't pulled loose by every lusty vibration that prickles the skin? Not according to my mother, I thought, the image of her tearstained face fleeting before me.

"Men!" she railed. "None of them are any good." It seems that good old Mr. Hammerman, our next-door neighbor, had stopped in while I was at school and his wife was at work to help my mother unjam the garbage disposal. And he made a pass at her. "The nerve of him!" she cried to me when I walked in that afternoon and found her busy busy busy cleaning closets. "'I'm hungry,' he said to me. So I offered him some pound cake. But he said, 'You don't understand. I'm hungry for you, Miriam.' *I* understand! I understand that men are animals. They're all the same. And your father was no different," she threw at me.

My God. I was only twelve! Was that any kind of thing to say to a child? But I now understood her anger. I plucked a Wheat Thin from the small tray of cheese and crackers I had laid out for lunch and fiercely pulverized it between my molars, remembering my own recent brush with adultery, with Stan Leibowitz when he had come to see the house, for the third time, one day near the end of August—alone.

"Sure. Come on over," I said when Stan Leibowitz called at one-thirty on a steamy August afternoon to say that he hadn't bought a house yet, that he was still interested in my house, if it was still for sale. And I said that it was. And he asked if it would be all right if he came right over, since he had just left a lunch meeting in town and didn't have to return to his office. And I said, "Sure. Come on over." And then I ran around the house making sure toilets were flushed and closed, my dirty clothes were in the laundry basket, and the counters were neat. I went into my bedroom to make the bed, but I found the colorful slept-in disorder of the bed alluring, so I left it . . . and in a blatant fit of sexism, I threw a black silk nightgown on the foot of the bed and sprayed perfume around the room. What a clever sales ploy, I thought, although I wasn't at all sure what I was intending to sell.

"It's nice to see you again, Tess," he said, taking my hand at the front door. "I brought you these." He pulled a small bouquet of flowers from behind his back.

"For me?" I squealed, hating the sound I made.

"They were on the lunch table at my meeting."

"That's very sweet. Would you like a cup of coffee? Or would you like to see the house first?" I asked, quite aware of the invitation to visit I had offered. Quite aware of how *really* nice it was to see him again. Quite aware of my self-disgust.

"Coffee would be great. The coffee at lunch was terrible."

We sat at the kitchen table, had coffee and chocolate chip cookies, and chatted for at least half an hour, during which time he told me that Michelle was having difficulty making up her mind about a house, but that he was going to take the bull by the horns and choose one he felt was best for them. And I commented that when we first met it had sounded as though she knew exactly what she wanted. And this gave him an opportunity to tell me of the troubles they'd been having, about her unpredictable moods, her unkind words . . . her coldness. "I'm trying to get her to talk to someone, a psychologist or something like that," he said, and then went on to tell of his pain, his loneliness, his frustration— highly sexual man that he is, he explained. My response to all of this was not what I might have expected: not a dash to my phone book to give him Michael's number . . . not empathetic mumblings about postpartum blues, the inevitable difficulties in even the best of marriages, the worthiness of making the effort to hold it together. No. My response was a tilt of my head and a soulful gaze, a fluttering of my eyelashes and a quiet sigh. "It must be so difficult for you," I murmured.

"Yes," he replied with lowered eyes.

But then, with the ball back in my court, I became aware of my inner conflict, my confusion of illusions. Was Stan Leibowitz making a pass at me after all? Was *I* making a pass at *him? Me?* Tess I-Don't-Do-Married Fineman? And I thought of all the unkind thoughts I had for others who indulged in extramarital affairs . . . and I thought about my ideal of the Model Husband—the Faithful Husband. Looking at Stan, I saw the illusion fade, leaving a man, just a man, sitting across from me . . . a very attractive man . . .

an attractive, uncrazy man. And, as I already feared that maybe I attracted crazy men because *I* was crazy, sitting quietly in my kitchen with attractive, uncrazy Stan, I realized my need to know if I could attract a sane man . . . a basically decent family man who, when the going around home got rough, felt a need for a shoulder, a reassuring arm, a tender hand, I rationalized. Sure! I argued with myself, give them a shoulder and they take a hand! No, I retorted, everyone needs a hand now and then. And why shouldn't we help each other? I was convincing, but I still wasn't convinced. "How about if we take a look through the house now," I wimped out, letting my head go numb.

So he followed me up the stairs and I was very aware of him behind me, studying the back of me. And I took him through the three *other* bedrooms first, saving the master bedroom with its unmade bed and perfumed air for last. And he seemed a lot more interested in the movement of my hands as I pointed out windows and closet space than in the windows or closet space. I did all the talking. And when we walked into the master bedroom, even I was taken in by the seductive smell, but it was he who said, "There's something awfully inviting about this room." I noted with pride how his eyes went straight to the tangle of colors on my unmade bed and rested for a time on the nightgown. Without a further word, Stan took me by the elbow and walked me through the french doors to the sitting area where the mirrored closet doors reflected the two of us taking entirely too long to reflect on the love seat, barrel chair, two end tables, and television console. "Great little room," he said, sitting on the love seat. "I'll probably spend most of my evenings here."

"You'll have to wait until the baby moves to his own room."

"Well, he's sleeping through the night now, so by the time we move in, he'll already be in his own room."

"It sounds like you've made up your mind about my house," I said, sinking into the barrel chair, swiveling it suggestively from side to side.

"I've made up my mind," he said, standing, taking two steps toward me, kneeling in front of me, taking my hands in his. "Tess, I've thought about you every day since I met you."

I'm not really going to fall for this, am I? I asked myself, already falling, my head spinning, my blood coursing through me, warming me, dampening every part of me except my mouth. "Stan, this isn't . . ." I tried through that arid orifice.

"Be nice to me, Tess. I promise, you won't be sorry."

I was already sorry, but it was too late. I was overcome by the musky smell of him, by the touch of his lips on my cheek, my chin, my lips.

So even when he uttered the despicable words "I know you, Tess. I could tell the minute I met you that you weren't afraid of married men. You've got that look in your eyes," momentum drove my arms around his neck, my mouth to his. But somewhere in the remnants of my sanity, the word *married* registered, invoking images of *his wife* and *their three babes. . . .*

And as his warm, fluid tongue washed the cobwebs from my mouth, setting off tiny spasms in my lips, my arms, and my fingers, my foot, flanked by his bended knees, swung upward in a solitary jerk. His lips left mine and he fell backward, writhing and breathless, grasping his injured parts with both hands. An image of ripe figs bursting, spewing ten thousand golden seeds, exploded in my head.

. . . That's what I wanted to do . . . for his wife, his children . . . for me . . . for dashing my illusions. But instead I put my hands to his shoulders and gently pushed him away. "Stan, this isn't right. You were wrong. I can't do this. I'm sorry," I said, jumping up and running from the sitting room, from the bedroom, down the stairs, to the kitchen, where I waited for him at the pantry door . . . waited until he caught up to me looking very annoyed, and told him that I'd decided not to sell the house, after all. "So please don't

call me again," I said, feeling very crazy, and very angry—
at us both.

"Have you ever done married?" I asked David.

"Only once. It was a mistake and I felt terrible about it. It
didn't last very long."

"None of your ladies last very long. Don't you ever get
involved?"

"Not really. Well, for a short while, when it's new, when
it's exciting. But it doesn't stay that way, so after a while it
just finishes on its own."

"Don't you ever want anything more?"

"I didn't know you cared, Tess."

"But I do," I answered, feeling my anger fall away like a
molt, leaving a soft, vulnerable part of me exposed. This is
probably the only decent man left in the whole world, I
thought—perhaps overstating his goodness somewhat—
and I do care about him. Yes, I do care, I thought. "I do
care," I said.

"I don't think you want a married man. You'd get hurt.
And you'd feel very guilty," he said, veering from my
confession . . . for a moment.

"You're right." I indulged his obvious discomfort. "So
I'm stuck with the crazies. No guilt, just bewildered and
horny."

He was quiet and still for a long moment, and then:
"Horny can be taken care of."

"Easy for you to say."

"No, Tess. This isn't at all easy for me to say. Do you
know what I'm saying?"

I thought I knew, but I didn't want to . . . or I was afraid
to. Sex. He wants to have sex with me. No. He wants to
make love to me. He loves me! *Does* he love me? Or does he
want to be a Friend Plus Sex? Could I have sex with David?
My God! What about Stephen? Doesn't he care what
Stephen would think? Do I care what Stephen would think?
Warm. I'm getting warm. I'm blushing, I can feel it creeping
up my chest, my neck, he'll see it. Caught.

He caught my hand in his. "We'd be good together, Tess."

I can't believe he's saying this. This is real, it's happening, he's trying to seduce me. What to do? What to do? "I—"

"Really good." He put my hand to his lips and teased a finger with his tongue.

Hot. I felt hot and squirmy. Sex. Love. Yes. I need sex and love. In that order? This isn't happening. "I—"

His arms were around me. When did he stand up? When did I stand up? Was I standing? There was no floor beneath my feet. He's holding me up. He's so tall. Don't I have a say in this? "I—"

He smells so good, his mouth is so soft on mine. How can thin lips be so soft? What a dumb thing to think at a time like this. Do I want a say in this? Oh, this would be a good one on Stephen! The phone! Let it ring, I'm busy. Go away, world, I'm not in, I'm out, I'm gone. "I—"

"I want you, Tess. I've wanted you for so long. I want to take care of you."

Yes, take care of me. Take me. Take me. "I—"

His mouth again, on mine. NO! I can't do this.

"NO! I can't do this!" I said, pulling away.

"But, Tess . . . I thought—"

"You thought wrong," I said. But seeing his crushed expression, all I wanted to do was wrap myself around him and kiss him again. "No, not wrong, but—"

"I don't understand, Tess, but I'm sorry. You have to believe that I'm sorry if I . . . I wasn't trying to take advantage of you. I'm not very good at this."

"I think you're *very* good. I almost—"

"I mean I'm not very good at telling how I really feel. Do you understand what I'm saying, Tess? Do you understand any of this?"

"No, I don't understand," I said, finally telling it like it really was.

"Neither do I," he said, cautiously rubbing my shoulder. "But I do know that I don't want to lose you. Promise me you'll just forget this happened. We'll pretend I wasn't here today. Someone else was . . . my evil twin brother, Lenny the Lech."

"I promise, I promise," I lied, laughing nervously with

David, trying to wade through the bog of awkward desire, back to the familiar shores of friendship.

I hadn't seen Michael since his return the first week in September. A twenty-four-hour stomach virus had kept me close to my bathroom the first Tuesday he was back and I chose to skip the week altogether and come the following Tuesday, a day he was going to be away for some teaching obligation. So I made the appointment for Thursday. After the weekend fiasco with—without—Elliot, I felt an intense need to whine to Michael and was angry that our Tuesday appointment wasn't going to be until Thursday. But then, after Wednesday with David, I was glad the appointment had been put off until Thursday. What was I going to do when I no longer had Michael to dump on? I wondered while driving to his office.

"What am I going to do when I don't have you to dump on anymore?" I asked Michael after I'd politely inquired about his vacation, and then waited for him to ask how I'd gotten along without him, which he didn't, which made me feel he didn't care, which made me feel angry and dependent, which made me ask him what I was going to do when he was no longer around, understanding how abandoned I felt when he wasn't around, not yet understanding that I wasn't always going to feel that way.

"You're planning to quit therapy?" he asked.

"No. Not now," I answered impatiently. "But I won't have you forever."

"How about if we worry about that when the time comes," he said, and then, after a pause, "So what's been happening?"

"Not a lot," I lied as my inner eye scanned the mirages of summer.

"How's the business going? Making anything new?" he fished.

"It's going well. I've been involved with granola lately," I said, not knowing why I said it.

"That's a fruit and nut mixture, isn't it?"

"With grains and honey. I use it a lot for fill-ins. You know. Bowls of honeyed granola instead of pretzels or potato chips."

"Sounds healthy."

Healthy! Hah! I laughed.

"What's so funny? What did I say?"

"Just that granola is healthy. It's an inside joke."

"Can you let me in on it?"

"Well, the summer's been rather strange, and the other day I found myself comparing men to granola. You know. What ain't fruits and nuts is flakes."

Michael laughed. I laughed. I turned red. Michael sat there chuckling at me, shaking his head. "So not a lot happened this summer?" he asked.

I sat squirming, not knowing how to respond to his snare.

"I guess granola is a step up from scum," he challenged.

Oh, God! He remembered our conversation from months ago! He probably writes it all down, I thought. "It can get scummy if it stays around too long," I said cryptically, wanting to leave.

Instinctively he changed the subject. "How's my friend David? What's he been up to?"

I told Michael about David's trip to Europe, about the postcard . . . about the day before, which was what I wanted to tell him all along.

"So not a lot happened this summer," he said again after a time, settling back in his chair. "So what is this? Budding romance?"

"More like blooming insanity!"

"Why's that?"

"He's Stephen's friend, remember!"

"I see."

No, he doesn't see, I thought. "And besides, if this goes any further, I'll probably end up losing a good friend," I illuminated quietly.

"Oh. Now I see. David will get scummy."

"If he hangs around long enough, which he probably won't."

"So he'll just disappear after a fling?"

"Well, maybe not exactly. We *are* friends. But maybe we won't be friends anymore."

"Sex and friendship don't mix?"

"Not from what I've seen."

He sat watching me be contradictory.

"So you don't have to worry," I continued. "I'm not going to seduce you because I need you as a friend." Now, why did I say that? How did we get back to last month's conversation? I'll bet he thinks *I* write it all down.

"Well, I'm glad to see you consider me a friend," he said.

I guess my hour is up, I thought, catching him glancing at his watch. Michael: my friend . . . for an hour a week. I knew I wasn't being fair, but I held on to my thought as I wrote out a check, as I walked out the door, as I drove home, feeling like a flake in a sea of granola.

CHARLOTTE RUSSE

1 envelope unflavored gelatin
1/4 cup water
1/3 cup sugar
1/2 cup milk
1 1/2 teaspoons vanilla extract
1 cup heavy cream
sponge cake (see Rocky Road Ice Cream Cake Roll)
1 pint strawberries
3 tablespoons kirsch (cherry brandy)
1 tablespoon sugar

Sprinkle the gelatin over 1/4 cup cold water and let it stand for 5 minutes. Mix the sugar and milk in a saucepan, add the gelatin, and cook over medium heat until the sugar and gelatin dissolve, stirring constantly. Remove pan from heat and stir in the vanilla. Chill in the refrigerator. When thick and syrupy, beat the mixture until it is fluffy.

Whip the cream to soft peaks and fold into the chilled gelatin mixture.

Line the bottom and sides of a 1 1/2-quart mold with slices of sponge cake. Spoon in the filling and chill for several hours. While it's chilling, slice strawberries and set in kirsch and sugar to marinate. Unmold; garnish with sliced strawberries. Serves 6–8.

CHAPTER 9

Charlotte Russe

It was inevitable. It had been only a matter of time until Charlie blew his cover. The time came, as always in these matters, too soon . . . or too late . . . and the revelation was more like the peeling of an onion—layer by layer—than the lifting of a lid.

Sandy had walked in so quietly I wasn't aware that she was standing in the doorway until I turned off the mixer and looked up from the softly peaking mound of whipped cream in search of vanilla extract. Her skin was paler than usual, her puffy eyes underlined with black smudge. She had been crying. Before I could get a word out, before I could reach her, she folded into the nearest chair and sobbed out the worst of it.

"Charlie's been screwing his operating room nurse in our shore apartment!"

Sitting down beside her, I put a hand on her arm. I knew the pain. "Is that it, then? I thought someone was sick or dying. This can be fixed," I lied.

"No, you don't understand. The apartment is theirs. Charlie's been paying for it, furnishing it. . . ."

I shook my head slowly in disapproval.

". . . And that's not the worst of it."

"So what's worse?"

This naive query triggered a new spate of tears and sobs.

I put my arm around her shoulders and tried a different question. "How did you find out?"

Amidst hiccups and sniffles, Sandy sputtered out a classic small-world tale: Charlie had hired a decorator—who billed Charlie at his office—to put the shore apartment together . . . a black marble table had arrived from Italy and the decorator wanted it delivered before he left for two weeks in the Caribbean . . . his secretary tried to call Charlie at his office, but he was in the operating room . . . Charlie's secretary gave the decorator's secretary Charlie's home phone number, saying, "I'm sure Mrs. Solomon can take care of this for you" . . . and the decorator's secretary called Sandy to tell her that her black marble table had arrived from Italy and was sitting in the warehouse awaiting delivery . . . and Sandy said, "My black marble table is sitting in my living room" . . . and the secretary checked her records and read the delivery address to Sandy . . . and Sandy said, "To where?!" . . . and the secretary repeated the address and Sandy hung up and called the hospital, demanding to speak with Charlie, who was still in the operating room . . . and when he finally got on the phone she demanded that he come home immediately or their marriage was over . . . so he did . . . and, being the weak, repressed, guilt-ridden creature that he is, he spilled . . . but being the dishonest, spoiled, cowardly toad that he is, he spilled slowly—over three days—with all the requisite histrionics, while Sandy listened tearless in disbelief, until this morning when she woke up and understood that it wasn't going to go away.

"Sandy, I'm so sorry," I sympathized.

"But that's not the worst of it."

"What could be worse?"

"Tess, he wants a divorce. He was setting the apartment up for himself and his . . . his—"

"How about 'slut'?" I offered.

"And that's not the worst of it."

"So tell me already, what's the worst of it? Don't tell me she's pregnant!"

"I only wish. You see . . . the fact is that . . . well . . . oh, Tess, *she* is a *he*," Sandy said finally, burying her face in her arms on the kitchen table.

Right. Operating room nurse . . . as in male nurse. How we all do assume. So Charlie was gay. So Charlie was leaving Sandy. I knew some of the pain.

I remembered when I got the call from Jim Statten, Stephen's secretary's husband, early one Wednesday morning: "Did you know that your husband and my wife," et cetera . . . how the words had echoed in my head even after I hung up the phone . . . and how I'd looked in the mirror to see if I was real, if this was really happening . . . how I saw myself crumple, like wet crepe paper . . . diminishing, bleeding, disintegrating. And *I* had only lost out to a pair of great tits.

Days later, Sandy and I sat interminably in a diner booth over turkey clubs and endless cups of coffee, rehashing. I tried to be alternately cheerful, furious, indignant, and nonjudgmental.

Sandy was alternately silent, tearful, baffled, and belligerent, but consistently pale and depressed as she struggled with the triangles of sandwich that grew dry before her. "I had no idea, Tess. . . . I mean, he gave me absolutely no idea. Everything had gone on as it always had. . . ."

How *had* everything gone on before? I wondered. In all the years I had known Sandy, I had never really gotten to know Charlie. He was nice to me, but aloof. Without contradiction from Sandy, I figured that behind closed doors, she and Charlie had something good going, despite the rumors to the contrary, which I chose to believe or disbelieve on any given day. How we all do assume.

". . . How could he do this to me? It's so humiliating. What am I supposed to do? What do I say to people? What do I say to the kids? How am I supposed to feel?"

"How *do* you feel?"

"I don't know. One minute I'm embarrassed, then angry,

then hurt. And I'm scared, Tess . . . you know . . . about AIDS."

"Maybe you should have a blood test, Sandy."

But she continued, not hearing me, "Sometimes I miss him, and sometimes I'm just glad he's gone and I don't have to wonder where he is and what he's doing."

"You used to wonder?"

"Well, yes," she admitted. "I guess I knew something wasn't right for a long time."

"Did you suspect someone else?"

"No. Well . . . I guess I did suspect there was someone because he . . . well, I just figured if he wasn't making love to me, there had to be someone. Of course, that was only after a long time. For a while, I thought he was just overworked or something."

"How long are we talking about here, Sandy? You never indicated anything was wrong."

"A looong time."

"A few weeks, a few months?"

"How about two years." She shrank in her seat.

"TWO YEARS?" I heard myself blurt back at her in amazement as candid shots of Sandy at parties, dinners, and such started clicking off in my head: shots of Sandy batting eyes at others' husbands; of Sandy in low-cut blouses and clingy sweaters brushing up against would-be adulterers; of Sandy in tiny bikinis splashing water on assuming young men. My usually critical attitude was tempered by the picture of Sandy now before me: neglected, humiliated, wronged.

"Ever since Jonathan was born. He never came near me again."

"What did he say?"

"First he said he was depressed, that the responsibility of being a father of two was hard on him, that I should give him time. So I gave him time. Then he said that while I was nursing the baby I didn't turn him on. So I stopped nursing Jonathan after two months. Then he said the night feedings were keeping him up, and he started sleeping downstairs on the sofa-bed in his den. Then Jonathan started sleeping through the night, but Charlie stayed downstairs because he said he was afraid I'd get pregnant again. So I had my tubes tied. Remember how sick I was after that surgery, Tess? Then Charlie stopped making excuses."

"You mean he still sleeps downstairs?"

No answer.

"Did you talk to anyone about this? Your mother? A doctor? Someone?"

"I wanted to see a psychologist, but Charlie wouldn't go with me. He said it was my problem. He was happy."

Charlie was happy. Charlie was gay. Charlie was a prick.

"I don't know how you get over something like that. What a rejection. Another man. Sandy said she feels she can't be much of a woman if *he* married her," I related to David over lunch in my kitchen the following day.

"Maybe she should look at it as a compliment," he tried.

"Maybe she should kill him! And why are you defending him?" I shot back.

"Why are you so angry?"

"I can't stand seeing Sandy so humiliated."

"That's all?"

"It's just that there seems to be no end to it."

"To what?"

"To . . . to . . . SCUM!"

"Scum?"

"SCUM. As in Shallow Callous Unfaithful Men."

"As in Charlie?"

"As in Charlie, Leonard Meyer, Harvey Cohen, Mark Weiser—and let's not forget Stephen!"

"Quite an ignoble fraternity."

"Scum. All of them."

"Stephen, too?"

I didn't answer.

A slight shrug of his shoulders failed to dispel the concern that had clouded his face. "Tess, are you finished with Stephen?" he asked.

"Of course," I lied. "Why?"

He didn't answer.

Taking advantage of his silence, I changed the subject back to Sandy. "Do you think Sandy's sexy?" I asked.

"I think you're sexy."

"David, I'm serious."

"So am I."

"Well, do you?"

"Sandy's very attractive."

"But do you think she's sexy? I mean, do you think she has a sexy body?"

"I think your body's sexy, Tess. Can't you tell? Just looking at you . . . just thinking about you arouses me."

His words aroused me. I felt my heart stop and then practically jump from my chest. I flushed.

"You're flushed, Tess."

I started to tremble as he reached across the table and took my hands in his. "David, I—"

"No. Don't say anything yet. Let me—"

"I—"

"Please." He was quiet for a moment. And then, "Tess, I can't stop thinking about that day last month when my evil twin brother embarrassed you. I can't tell you how sorry I am that it happened. No, not that it happened, but that it happened that way. Tess, I want to make love to you. I want more than anything in the world to hold you and take care of you. I've never felt this way about anyone and I don't know how to do it right, but I have to tell you how I feel. And I'm not insensitive. I'm sure you have some feeling for me, too. Tell me I'm not wrong."

I was dumbstruck. Such honesty . . . such caring. "You're not wrong, David," I said, not quite dumbstruck.

"I haven't been with anyone in a long time, Tess. I can't even remember the last time I had a date."

I smiled, remembering the last time I had made love to a man. Daniel Daroff. Well, *almost* made love to a man. And I blushed, remembering the last time I kissed a man. David. Yes, I thought, we have some unfinished business, David and I. But what about our wonderful friendship? What will happen to our special feelings for each other, feelings not clouded by sex . . . by sex and jealousy . . . by sex and jealousy and dishonesty?

Confused by my silent smile, David cried, "Oh, God, Tess. There isn't someone else, is there? You never said . . ."

"No. No one else. I haven't even had a date since August. I was just thinking of kissing Lenny the Lech in my kitchen . . . how good it felt . . . how I want to kiss you again, but I'm afraid."

"Of what? Of me?"

"Of whatever it is that makes scum."

"I think I'm being insulted."

"No, no. It's just that I don't want to lose our friendship. You're the best friend I've ever had. We care about each other and we go out together and enjoy each other and we're attracted to each other and we're honest with one another and we're not jealous of each other's relationships. I'd say that's just about perfect."

"Not quite, Tess. I *am* jealous when you tell me about a date, about your problems with men."

"Ah . . . so. What do you think we should do about this?"

"I think you should let me carry you upstairs and make mad, passionate love to you."

"But will you respect me at five o'clock?"

"I'll even take you to dinner at six o'clock."

"But . . . will we still be friends?"

"The best of friends."

"Promise?"

"Cross my heart and hope to die in the scum pond."

And he carried me upstairs and we made mad, passionate love . . . Well, we made love, but mostly we giggled and blushed when, being so nervous, neither of us could get it quite right . . . except that when there's so much good feeling, nothing could be really wrong.

"God! You have a beautiful body," he said after this and that, running his hand along my flank, across my buttocks.

"David, you don't have to—"

"You have a great body! Look at yourself," he demanded,

pulling me to my knees, turning me toward the mirror over the dresser across from my bed.

"Okay. So I'm not fat."

"Lots of people are *not fat*. But *you* are sexy," he said, squeezing my thigh. "Look at these gorgeous legs!"

"You *like* my chubby thighs?"

"A great ass, too."

"And my tiny boobs are a real turn-on. Right?"

"Do you think I should get my boobs siliconized?" I had asked Stephen one December evening after the office personnel Christmas dinner party had put me face to face with Carley Statten for the first time since he'd hired her six months before. Actually, face to face is not an accurate description of our meeting, as her height and spike heels set her shoulders about level with my eyebrows, and her very large breasts swelling over the decolletage of her very short red satin sheath directly in my line of vision—or so it seemed at the time. "Nice meeting you," she had said, looking everywhere but at me. "I have this terrible cold," she added quickly, putting a tissue to her face, hiding her eyes from mine. And sitting across from me later at the long, narrow banquet table, she was fidgety. "I really shouldn't be out tonight. I don't feel very well," she informed me, putting her hand to her face, across her bosom, as if suddenly feeling her exposure. "I'm glad we've finally met. I've heard so much about you," I offered with an edge. I had heard Stephen brag to colleagues, "Have you seen my new secretary?" I had heard Stephen repeat his clients' remarks about the new secretary—appellations such as "Amazon," "Woman of Steel," "Playboy bunny." It seemed that the legendary Great Legs of Alex Gordon's secretary were being supplanted as the building's resident-fantasy-object by the Great Tits of Stephen Fineman's secretary. "Wonder Woman" was my choice, I decided, watching her choke down a shrimp cocktail. Her dry-endy hair was nonetheless long and black, her oily uneven skin only a slight detraction from her dark, almond-shaped eyes, well-arched eyebrows, and sharply defined nose and chin. Yes, I could picture Carley in a Wonder Woman costume looking every inch the cartoon character—and just as one-dimensional.

"Silicone? Now I'm really worried about you," Stephen had answered my late-night question. "I think you're becoming psychotic. Maybe you should talk to a shrink."

"You've got great nipples," David soothed, running a finger around the left one, which stood up instantly. I closed my eyes, succumbing to the soft warmth of his tongue and lips, the exquisite nip of his teeth that sent a current of pleasure right through to the end of me. Touching here, there, we delighted again, anew, in the delicious juxtapositions of the hards and softs of our bodies.

"It was absolutely the last thing I would have expected to happen," I swore to Janet and Sandy Sunday morning in the diner, feeling the need to defend my liaison with David, which felt as tentative as it was passionate, leaving skid marks on our psyches.

"Sure," Sandy said, looking very jealous indeed.

"What's with the face?" Janet chided her.

Sandy rolled her eyes.

"I'm sorry, Sandy. I guess it's not too tactful of me to talk about this right now."

"Stop patronizing me, Tess. It has nothing to do with me. I just can't stand to hear you be so . . . so *surprised* about David. After all, you've been flirting with him foreeever. You should hear yourself! 'Can you imagine, girls! David and meee!' Surely the lady doth protest tooo much!"

Look who's quoting Shakespeare! I thought venomously. "Maybe I did want it, but I never thought it would actually happen," I defended myself. "It was a fantasy for me. It still feels like fantasy."

"Well," she concluded, "I guess it settles one point: He's not gay. Then again—"

"Then again, I'm glad somebody's getting something," Janet jumped in. "And, Tess, stop being so defensive! You're allowed to have a feast while all around you are starving. So enjoy it for all of us! And, I have to tell you, he's real pretty. And I *don't* have to tell you what I think of him! He's been a prince dealing with the camp thing."

"So when will it be finished?" I asked, pulling in my spines.

"Well, you know how Leonard's managed to get the hearing put off a few times? The judge finally demanded that the motion be heard right after New Year's. That was *after* David sent a letter to the court explaining that I have to sign Sean up for camp again soon, and they still haven't been paid for last summer. The camp director's been a doll about waiting for his money. Would you believe that David wrote that he'd be personally responsible for the fee if things didn't work out in court? Tess, if things don't work out with you and David, I have dibs on him."

"By the way, Tess," Sandy started again, "how's Stephen taking your affair with David?"

"Stephen's not," I said. "As far as he and the world are concerned, David and I are just the good friends we always were. Actually, I think that's where it's at . . . sort of."

"A Friend Plus Sex. Have I got it right?" Sandy sneered.

"Right," I avowed, not believing it for a minute.

"So, Sandy, what's with your divorce? Is the good doctor being decent?" Janet changed the subject again.

"So far. He said he's going to keep depositing household money in my account each month, and he'll take care of the taxes and everything. But I also know that he's hired an attorney. A big gun. I guess I should get one, too."

"I'd say that's a good idea," Janet agreed. "Save yourself some energy; let the lawyers battle it out. You have nothing to lose, because the only thing you have is the kids . . ."

". . . And you know he won't want the kids!" Janet and I said in unison. We all laughed, including Sandy.

"It's going to work out, Sandy. You'll see. You won't have to live vicariously through Tess and me anymore," Janet teased. "You'll be able to experience firsthand the glamour, the excitement . . . the horniness of single life!" We all laughed again. "We'll show you around. We'll buy you an answering machine—by the way, ladies, the answering machine you got me for my birthday is great. We'll fix you up with all our old blind dates!"

"Aaaagh! I thought you were my friends!" More laughter.

"If you find something good, I'll watch the kids!" I added.

Sandy turned and hugged me. "You *are* good friends."

"Nah! Tess just loves your kids," Janet said.

"Thanks, guys." Sandy sniffed back a tear. "I don't know what I'd do without you. And, Tess, I'm really glad for you . . . about David, I mean. I'm sorry about what I said. I haven't been myself lately."

"Don't worry about it, Sandy," I said, wondering who she'd be next.

"How's it going with David?" Sandy asked over a chef's salad at Mykonos, where they were about to condo our booth. She was looking better now that the word was out, now that the rumor rush had boiled up and subsided, now that her day in court—which had become a necessity when Charlie's lawyer succeeded in convincing Charlie that Sandy was going to clean him out and advised him to cut his voluntary support of his family in half, and Sandy's lawyer succeeded in convincing Sandy that Charlie intended to force her out of her big home and into a full-time job—had provided her and the children with a monthly support check that would do nicely (although Charlie and Sandy each thought they were being taken) until a settlement could be reached.

"Nice. But I keep waiting for him to disappear," I answered.

"Why do you say that?"

"As we've all noted, he never stays with anyone very long."

"But this is different. He's your friend—at least, that's what you keep telling me. 'He's just a friend,' remember?"

"Well, obviously he's not *just* a friend anymore, and I'm sure it's getting in the way. I mean, I can still talk to him and everything, but . . . well . . . it feels different."

"I should hope so."

"What I mean is that, before, when we were just friends, I felt we'd *always* be friends, no matter what. But now that we're lovers, I have the feeling that at any given time he could decide that he's bored . . . or something."

"That you're not so great after all? Now that he's finally conquered you?"

"Something like that."

"You're weird, Tess."

"You noticed."

"You're weird . . . but you're cute . . . and you're not horny. So lighten up. Don't be so hard on yourself."

"You're right. I'm not horny," I said, cracking a smile. "The sex is really good."

"The sex is always good for you," she said, laughing.

"So, how are the kids?"

"Tess, you don't have to change the subject. I know you think I've been deprived all this time, but you don't have to feel sorry for me. Because I haven't been. Deprived, that is."

"Oh?"

"I have a lover."

"Oh?!"

"George."

"George? Not George who cuts your hair! I thought he was—" I stopped myself.

"That's the one, and he's not."

Then again, she hadn't known her husband was gay either, I thought. George. I had difficulty focusing on this new situation. With each new twist, my kaleidoscopic view of Sandy's life changed. "How long's this been going on?"

"Six years."

"SIX?"

"Well, I've known him six years. I've only been sleeping with him for two years." She came into color as she answered my puzzled expression in a spirited duet with her hands: "There was this instant attraction when we first met. I mean, he looked like he couldn't wait to get his hands on me, and he always took a looong time with my hair. He'd been recently divorced, and I felt a little sorry for him, so Charlie and I had him over for dinner one night . . . and then I had lunch with him occasionally . . . and he would stop in during the day for a cup of coffee now and then . . ."

She sucked him right in, I thought.

". . . and after Jonathan was born and Charlie was so cold . . ."

I listened intently, trying to put it—my reaction, not her story—together. I was thinking that maybe I shouldn't be feeling so sorry for her. After all, she and Charlie were each playing their own little games, and who knew which had come first? Sandy was such a flirt, and she always seemed so needy. Now I was wondering who else she . . . My mind flipped through the candid shots again and came to a screeching halt at one of Sandy and Stephen in my kitchen —embracing. Just a friendly hug, he had said when I walked in from the dining room. I wondered then, and I was wondering now. Guilt-stricken, I tried to stop thinking. "I'm glad you haven't been deprived, but I'm surprised you never said anything about it. Does Janet know?"

"She didn't, until last night. I had dinner with her and Sean. It was kind of fun having a little secret."

Little secret? Try *double life,* I thought, wondering what other little secrets she had, feeling hurt that my good friend had been holding out on me. I was always so honest with her.

I bumped into Sandy on a miserable day three weeks later in the parking lot of the shopping center. I was between a settlement and an appointment to show a house—which, this being two days after Christmas, represented an unusual flurry of real estate business for that time of year—and I had stopped to pick up flour, sugar, and eggs at the supermarket for some baking I had to do that night—which was the usual flurry of dessert business for that time of year. She looked tired, disoriented.

"I have to talk to you, Tess."

"Step into my office, Mrs. Solomon," I said, leading her out of the freezing drizzle into my four-year-old maroon Toyota four-door, where, for the next twenty-five minutes, she explained to me how Charlie had come over the night before to beg for her forgiveness, to tell her that he must have been crazy to leave . . . that he really loved her . . . that he wanted to work it out . . . that he wanted to come home . . . while the motor of the Toyota hummed to keep us warm.

"But what about The Guy?" I asked.

It was insanity, he had told her . . . a midlife crisis . . . a remnant of some adolescent homosexual craving . . . that being away from Sandy had made him realize that he really desired her.

"Do you believe him?"

"I want to."

"Maybe you should get some professional help on this."

"It's going to be fine, Tess. Just the way it used to be."

I wondered how it used to be. I wondered if she really knew how it used to be.

"What time are they coming?" David asked, licking the beaters from the mixing bowl of whipped cream.

If dessert is the most satisfying part of a meal, surely the last of the batter on the beaters is the most satisfying part of the dessert, I thought, remembering my mother's kitchen, and how, when I was a good little girl, my reward was licking sweet goodies from the beaters. And I remembered the day my mother discovered the rubber spatula, and how cheated I felt as I watched her manipulate the cruelly efficient implement, leaving nothing at all to lick from the beaters or bowl. Yet I had been so very, very good. Whoever invented the rubber spatula must hate kids, I had thought, promising myself that when I grew up I'd never use one, a promise I hadn't kept, with one exception: When it came to beaters, the good guys always got the last licks.

"Tess?"

"Hmm?"

"What time—"

"Oh, seven-thirty," I answered. This post–New Year's dinner was a command performance. Sandy had asked me to invite Charlie and her for dinner as a show of support for their renewed relationship. "Besides, Charlie and I have some news," she had said, refusing to divulge The News until we were all together.

"What's the big secret?" David asked.

"I can't imagine. You know Sandy. Everything with her has to be dramatic."

"More important, what's for dessert?"

"A yummy custard molded in sponge cake and topped with whipped cream and strawberries marinated in kirsch and sugar. It's a special dessert for Charlie. He loves sweet things," I explained.

"Is that supposed to be a pun?"

"Unintentional, I assure you. But the dessert is quite intentional," I said.

"What's that supposed to mean?"

Smiling my most Mona Lisa smile, I continued stirring the custard over a low flame.

That evening, Charlie was, as usual, aloof but obligingly pleasant. A smile stamped his soft, scrubbed-looking face that was reminiscent of the faces on Campbell's Soup cans. Sandy, as usual, hung on him like a mantle. David and I kept up a steady flow of inane conversation.

As I poured the coffee at the end of dinner, Charlie cleared his throat for attention and pronounced The News. "Tess, thanks for having us here tonight. You've been a real friend to Sandy, so I know you're going to be happy to hear that I'm going to be your neighbor again." Sandy cuddled closer to him, taking hold of his hand, the one playing with the coffee spoon.

I don't know why I felt surprise. What had I expected? Then again, the surprise was not the reconciliation, which was obviously expected, but that Charlie was moving back into the house. Perhaps I thought they would date while each living out their own private fantasies in their own private worlds in a kind of collusion of mutual delusion. "Well! Welcome home, Charlie. We'll celebrate with a dessert I made especially for you," I said, placing the dessert in front of him. "It's a charlotte russe," I added, smiling a wicked little smile.

Charlie's small khaki eyes met mine for an instant that had to be counted as a first. In them, disbelief dismissed comprehension. An almost imperceptible knit in Sandy's eyebrows signaled her vague sense of something gone awry.

David choked on his coffee. "It's nice to hear things have worked out for you two," he finally managed, silencing the unspoken consideration of intent.

"Thanks, David. I think we're going to be okay. Right, Sandy?" Smiling, Charlie gave Sandy a little push with his body—sort of an inverted hug.

Fitting, I thought. "Dessert, Charlie?" I asked, mounding a sizable portion on a plate.

"Yes, ma'am."

"Sandy?"

"Of course! When did you ever know me to pass up something so sinfully good?"

Never. Absolutely never, I thought as the candids started to flash in my head again.

"Tess, I have more news for you. There's going to be a new addition to the family," she said. Did she blush?

"You're not pregnant!"

"No, no. George Davidson. Do you remember George? The guy who does my hair. . . ."

I can't be hearing right, I thought.

". . . Well, I was getting my hair cut last week and he was saying how his lease was coming due and they raised his rent, and I was just saying how I was looking for someone reliable to baby-sit for the kids sometimes so Charlie and I can have more private time together, and he was teasing about how he'd baby-sit if it meant cheap rent, and I was saying how there was an apartment over the garage—"

"You didn't—"

"I most certainly did. George is moving in next week. Isn't that great?"

Was that a sneer on her lips as she leaned back against Charlie's shoulder? "Great," I agreed obediently.

"I thought it was a great idea, too," Charlie chimed in. "We're going to use the rent money to buy Sandy a new car. Hers is a good five years old and takes forever to warm up."

"Sometimes I have to start the engine and then come back to the house for a second cup of coffee before I leave," Sandy added, confirming the need for a new car . . . and therefore the extra income . . . and therefore the new tenant.

"So. George. He's single?" I poked.

"Yes," said Sandy, appearing a bit alarmed at my pursuance.

"And he doesn't live with anyone?"

"No. Actually, he did have a roommate, but it didn't work out. Charlie thinks he's gay, but I don't think so. You've met him, Tess. Do you think he's gay?"

"Not from what I've heard." Bitch.

"How's it all working out?" I asked Sandy when I met her for breakfast at the diner two weeks later. I knew that the moves had gone smoothly. Sandy had kept me abreast of Charlie's moving back . . . and George's moving in. I had to admit, the scenario appealed to my sense of irony, justice, and intensely black humor.

"Weeell . . . everything's going just great! Charlie is positively ecstatic about being home. He just loooves being with me again. He can't keep his hands off me!"

"And George?"

"He can't keep his hands off me, either! I can't believe I pulled this off."

I couldn't either. And I was beginning to wonder who was pulling what off whom.

"It's so exciting. George and I have this signal, you see. If he's home and wants company, he leaves his window shade up. I can see it from my kitchen window."

Company? Read: A Fuck.

"He's a very private person, Tess. He's an artist, you know. And not only with hair. He's a sculptor. And he promised to do a bronze of me."

In the nude, I presumed.

"I know it's risky, but—"

"Sandy, wouldn't it be easier to use the telephone?"

"Not really. He never knows if Charlie is here or not. You

know Charlie walks to the train when he goes to University Hospital."

"I see," I said, trying to make sense out of nonsense. "So why don't you call him?"

"Well, I do, if his shade is up. But I'd neeever bother him if his shade is down. Even if his car's there, he might be sculpting. As I said, he's a veeery private person."

"I guess I don't know a lot about these things, Sandy. But it sounds strange to me. Are you sure you know what you're doing? As your friend, I have to tell you, you really sound off-the-wall."

"Don't worry, Tess. It's like a game. And I have to tell *you*, it's wonderful fun."

"Right." Almost as much fun as Russian roulette.

"What more can I do?" I asked Michael the following Tuesday. "And, remember? She called *me* weird!"

"No. I don't remember. She called you weird? You? Hah!" He leaned far back in his seat, chuckling.

"Oh, wonderful! Just what I need! My therapist thinks I'm weird!"

He didn't respond, but he stopped laughing.

"You didn't say that, did you?" I asked meekly.

"What *did* I say?"

"You laughed at the idea that Sandy called me weird."

"Right."

"But it wasn't because you thought *I* was weird; it was because you thought *she* was so weird. You were agreeing with what I had said to you."

He didn't respond.

"Right?" I begged the question.

"But you thought I was laughing *at* you, not *with* you. Who thinks who is weird here?"

"I think Sandy is weird. I think I'm weird."

"Right."

"Am I weird?"

He made a fist. "Do you want a shot in the arm or in both arms?"

I felt shy, dumb, but most of all, I felt young. And, looking at Michael through the fine mist in my eyes, I felt his loving aura wrap fleetingly around me.

One bitter cold morning that felt more like February than March, I sat at my desk working out income tax figures on my calculator while listening to Sandy rationalize her situation over the phone uncomfortably cradled between my shoulder and ear. Nothing added up, not the figures, not Sandy.

". . . After all, considering what Charlie did to me, there's almost nothing that I could do that would be unjust. Right?"

She had a point.

". . . And all I'm really doing is protecting myself. I mean, suppose Charlie decided to leave again? At least this way I have someone to fall back on. . . ."

Oh, you mean just like before, I thought.

". . . And, besides, what am I supposed to do with this wonderful friendship between George and me? Throw it away? Would that be fair to George? Or me? I mean, forget the sex part . . ."

First she'd have to; hearing about the sex was my favorite part.

". . . we have this reeeally close relationship. He's been my best friend . . ."

I thought I was. Now, why doesn't this column add up?

". . . and I've inspired him to a creative zenith. . . ."

Creative zenith?

". . . He's doing things he's never done before. . . ."

I'll bet. How I hate numbers.

And as she prattled on about how nobody was going to get hurt because George was so clever, and she was so careful, and how she really did love them both, I kept coming up with wrong answers on my adding machine.

After about forty-five minutes, Sandy suddenly exclaimed, "Uh-oh! I got so involved in our conversation I forgot about the car! Tess, let me call you back, I was going to go shopping this morning and I left the car warming up in the garage." Click.

I don't think I had said one word during the entire call. Sandy was wrapped up, but not in conversation.

George died the next morning in the intensive care unit of University Hospital. Charlie had died twenty hours earlier in George's arms, above the garage . . . above Sandy's running car . . . above suspicion. The sweet sleep that overcame them both was not the swoon of posterotic passion, but the coma of carbon monoxide poisoning.

LADYFINGERS

3 eggs
1/2 cup + 1 tablespoon sugar
1 teaspoon vanilla extract
pinch of salt
2/3 cup sifted cake flour
powdered sugar
6 squares bittersweet chocolate

Preheat oven to 300°F.

Separate eggs and slowly beat 1/2 cup sugar and vanilla into egg yolks until they form a ribbon and are thick and pale.

In another bowl, beat egg whites with salt until they form soft peaks. Add 1 tablespoon sugar and beat until they form stiff peaks.

Spoon about a quarter of the whites onto the yolks, sift on about a quarter of the flour, and fold gently. Repeat until whites and flour are all partly blended into yolk mixture.

Use a pastry bag to squeeze lines of the batter onto two buttered and floured baking sheets (about 4 x 1 1/2 inches). Sprinkle with powdered sugar and bake in middle and upper levels of oven for about 20 minutes, until lightly crusty and light brown under the sugar. Remove with spatula and cool on rack. Melt chocolate squares in a fondue pot or the top of a double boiler. Dip the tips of cooled ladyfingers in melted chocolate and set to dry on wax paper. Makes about one dozen.

CHAPTER 10

Ladyfingers

Standing pallid by Charlie's coffin at the graveside funeral service, Sandy was a portrait of pain. Her white face was a scream held in a frame of black hair, her eyes black eddies of pain. I wanted her to be angry, to take satisfaction in her just, if inadvertent, revenge on her two faithless lovers. But guilt enveloped her; loss, like her long black coat, overwhelmed her.

She had called me about eight-thirty two evenings before. She was crying. "Tess! I need you! Come now!" she managed, and then hung up. Spurred by the urgency in her voice, I sped to her home, running a red light and two stop signs. Two police cars, their lights flashing, were in front of her house; an ambulance was pulling out of the driveway. All I could think of was the children. The front door was open. I ran in and found Sandy sitting at the kitchen table, ashen, clutching Rebecca. A police officer was talking on the telephone.

Sandy looked up. "Oh, Tess! He's dead!"

My heart stopped and a knot grew in my throat, choking me, forcing tears from my eyes as I thought of Jonathan. "JONATHAN!" was all I got out.

"He's asleep, Tess; he doesn't know," she answered, allaying my worst fears.

177

"Sandy, what's going on?" I asked, able now to run to her and put my arms around her.

"It's Charlie! He's dead! I killed him!" She began crying anew.

My eyes found those of the officer who was hanging up the phone. "What's happened?" I implored.

"It appears to have been an accident, in the garage apartment, ma'am," he started. "It seems that Dr. Solomon and Mr. Davidson"—*George?!*—"were asleep in the apartment when they were overcome by carbon monoxide coming from a car running in the garage below them. . . ."

Recalling the morning's telephone conversation with Sandy, a wave of nausea washed over me . . . remembering my inattention . . . my silent criticism . . . her quick exit. Her words—*"I left the car warming up in the garage"*—echoed in my head.

". . . They took Mr. Davidson to the hospital," the officer continued, "and the paramedics said he might make it. We didn't reach Dr. Solomon in time."

"OH MY GOD, SANDY!" I exclaimed, hunching over her, burying my face in her hair. We wept. My tears were as much tears of relief for the children's safety as they were tears of sympathy for Sandy's pain.

When the officer left, Sandy asked me to call her parents. "I have to lie down," she whimpered, relinquishing Rebecca to me. I sat with Rebecca cuddled against me on the sofa in the family room until she fell asleep. After carrying her to bed, I called Sandy's parents.

I called Janet when I got home, drained, about eleven-fifteen . . . after Sandy's parents arrived . . . after Sandy was coerced into sleep by a whopping dose of Jonathan's Benadryl, the only thing in the house with a sedative effect. Janet was, of course, shocked, but not too shocked to see the scales of justice swing into balance: "BLASTED IDIOT! He deserved it, Tess. I mean . . . so, he was gay. FINE. But he had no right to treat Sandy that way. So, he chose the life he wanted. FINE. But why couldn't he be honest with Sandy and let her choose hers? Because he wanted it all, THE

BASTARD! They ALL want it ALL! Poor Sandy must be devastated. . . ." And Janet ranted on for quite a while. And we both grew very, very angry. "I hope the CREEP had a lot of insurance!" Janet ended.

Then I called David. He wasn't shocked. I don't think anything shocks David. He was concerned, for Sandy . . . for the children . . . for me. Most of all for me. "Are you sure you're okay? Do you want me to come over?"

"I'm okay," I lied. "I just want to go to sleep."

The next morning I called Sandy. She didn't want company, she didn't want to talk, but she talked . . . and talked. What she told me was that George had died a few hours before . . . that her mother was making funeral arrangements for Charlie, it would be a graveside service the next morning . . . that she had no idea who was taking care of George's arrangements, and she didn't care . . . that she was confused, and scared. . . . "Suppose the police think I did it on purpose!"

"Not a chance," I told her, all the time wondering, What if they do?

"Two people, Tess. I killed two people!"

Déjà vu crept over me. When had I had this conversation before? Janet. Yes, after Harvey died. Why is it that when a man is literally consumed by adulterous passion, the wronged woman is consumed with guilt?

Dinner at Janet's house that night was tense as we waited for Sean to go to sleep so we could Talk. Finally, at nine-thirty, "I can't believe this has happened, Tess," Janet started.

"Neither can I."

"Do you think Charlie and George were seeing each other before George moved in?"

"Who knows? But I'd say, no. Remember, Charlie was involved with the guy from the hospital."

"True. But it's possible he wasn't any more faithful to his boyfriend than he was to Sandy. Remember Harvey?"

We shook our heads. There was little else to say . . .

except, "How do you think they were found?" Janet queried.

"Well, University Hospital called Sandy looking for Charlie, and—"

"No! I mean, how do you think the police found Charlie and George? Do you think they were naked?"

"Janet! Only you would think of something like that!"

"Oh, no, Tess. Only I would *say* it!"

Yes. I had to admit, there is a bit of the voyeur in us all. Even so, I decided to let Janet accept the responsibility for *our* thoughts. "Well, anyway, the officer said they had been sleeping," I said.

"Right. That's what they *said*. What did you expect them to say—'Dr. Solomon and Mr. Davidson were found in a lovers' embrace'? What do *you* think they were doing?"

"I guess what everyone else does—one way or another."

Janet slouched into the sofa and nodded in agreement. Suddenly she giggled and then mugged a serious, brow-knitted face. "Now," she said, "I can understand Charlie being hot for George. He was quite a hunk. But what I can't understand is what George would want with bland, chubby Charlie!"

We both giggled. The wine we were nipping from Waterford crystal goblets—Janet had pulled out the good stuff in a warped gesture of support for Sandy—was doing its job, easing the pain . . . until we thought of Sandy, which was what we had been avoiding all night. And then Janet started to rage against MEN—their insensitivity, infidelity, undeveloped sense of fair play. And then Janet started to cry for Sandy, for herself, for all the pain. And I joined her, until we were both tuckered out, and I went home. David and I would pick her up at ten o'clock for the funeral. It was going to be dreadful, we had agreed.

It was dreadful. The morning was cold and blustery. Almost two hundred people showed up, and most stood because only about forty chairs were set up around the mahogany coffin perched on a sling over the open grave. A worn, green canopy covered the grave site. Janet, David, and I stood at the back of the last row of chairs facing Sandy and the children. David held my left hand; Janet held my right. The whispers in the crowd were deafening, only bits and pieces of which could I hear clearly. "... *Do you think she'll sell the house? ... She's so pretty, she'll do all right. ... Lots of money there. ... Doctors are no better than the rest. ... Of course she knew. A wife knows. ...*" God! People are cruel. I looked around at the faces. Most looked curious, not sad. Necks craned to see the bereaved widow. Only when the rabbi spoke was there quiet, and when he had finished his short service, the whispers roared louder than before. "*... queer ... only an orderly, or was it a nurse ... did Sandy's hair ... justifiable homicide ... next year we'll dance at her wedding. ...*" I hated them all.

At the close of the service, Sandy, holding Jonathan, stood up, as did Rebecca, Charlie's parents, his two brothers and sisters-in-law, his grandmother—on his mother's side—and Sandy's parents, who stood next to Sandy. Filing past the coffin, each picked up a stone or fistful of dirt and placed it on the lid. Sandy remained standing by the coffin, a portrait of pain. Jonathan, a blue-snowsuited fireplug, straddled Sandy's left hip; Rebecca clung to her mother's black-booted leg. A strong unit, they would survive, I thought as I watched them be brave. And then the coffin was lowered. Horrified, Rebecca cried out, "NO! THAT'S MY DADDY!" —an exclamation that tore through the cold, clear day. Sandy's mother pulled the startled Jonathan from Sandy's arms, allowing Sandy to drop to her knees and envelop her screaming daughter. For all my penchant and facility for bizarre and hyperbolic fantasy, nothing I could imagine could come close to the grief and terror I saw in that child.

The scene reminded me of the absence of my own father, who had died in a car accident with my two-year-old brother, Jamie, when I was five, and I started to cry, for Rebecca, for me, a spontaneous outpouring that was quickly squelched by a question: Had I really been better off without my father, as my mother had told me, as I thought Rebecca might be without Charlie? I hoped Sandy would never say anything like that to Rebecca. She would never forgive her mother for that.

Rebecca's macabre cry brought to mind another time, another funeral.

The very first funeral I remember attending was only a few years before, for someone I didn't know—the grandmother of Jack Moskovitz, a longtime business associate of Stephen's. Stephen couldn't be there, he had to be in Atlanta on business . . . would I please go in his stead . . . it would mean a lot to Jack—although I had met Jack and his wife only twice before they'd moved to Arizona several years ago. And of course I said I would go. After signing the book in the foyer of the funeral home, I entered the small, dimly lit chapel. It had a faintly musty smell. The front wall was paneled with redwood; the Eternal Light, hanging above and to the right of the dais in its contemporary brass holder, glowed an eerie red-orange. Most of the seats were already filled when I walked down the center aisle toward the front, toward the first row of seats on the left where Jack sat with his wife, two teenage children, his mother, and three others I couldn't identify. In front, on the right, propped up at an angle in the corner, was the beige coffin. The top half of the lid was open, displaying an elderly woman in a starched blue lace dress with a small spray of blue silk rosebuds pinned at the center of the frilly high neck. Her gray hair was in curls, her lips and cheeks pinked, her eyes closed. Pink spotlights cast a kind of plastic life on the face of the corpse. I imagined it being a scene from a horror movie about a doll shop for the elderly, where life-size, aged dolls were bought by old people for companionship in their second childhood. I stopped halfway down the aisle, waiting for . . . what? . . . the old doll's eyelids to pop open and reveal bright blue glass eyes? her arms to suddenly pop up, reaching out for me? Finally moving forward, I kissed Jack and his wife, reintroducing myself as Stephen's wife, and, with a sympathetic smile, briefly pressed the hands of the other mourners in the front row. And all the while I could hear nothing of what was said to me because my ears were filled with the buzz of flowing blood. I found a seat, close to the front of the chapel on the right. My eyes never left the doll in its lacquered box. I only vaguely remember the service—the rabbi's eulogy, the congregation's whispers and recitation of the Twenty-third Psalm, the mourners' silent weeping. But when attendants closed the lid of the coffin, lifted it from its corner, and placed it on a dolly, and the pallbearers walked it slowly up the center aisle, a single voice pierced the thickness of the moment: "GOOD-BYE, MAMA!" This came not from a child—that is, not from a child young in years—but from Jack's mother, the elderly child of the dead woman, who lunged from her aisle seat to wave a frantic farewell to her mother. My heart stopped. My eyes filled. My body hair stood on end. I felt nauseated. Funerals are barbaric, I thought.

I didn't go to the cemetery. Instead, for no conscious reason, I drove to my mother's apartment—she hadn't yet followed her sister Sarah to Florida. I told her—for the first time, although I had known for a while—that she would have no grandchildren . . . that the surgery I had had was an attempt to correct misshapen fallopian tubes, not a D and C for excessive menstrual bleeding, which is what I had told her at the time of the surgery so she wouldn't know I couldn't do even such a natural thing as conception right . . . but that apparently the surgery was a failure, because here it was two years later and I was still a barren woman. Somewhat distracted, my mother told me that I never did eat right, that I didn't get enough sleep, that a man wants children, which seemed to be an odd thing for her to say since she had so often told me, "Your father—may he rest in peace—never had time for his children." What I wanted was her touch. I seemed to remember it from somewhere in my past . . . when I was feverish . . . when she'd press her long, soft fingers to my forehead, to my cheeks, to check my temperature. Sitting with my mother after Jack's grandmother's funeral, I cried in my head, "Mommy, I'm hurting." But all I felt was her distance. That's when I first noticed the deepening wrinkles around her eyes and mouth, the fine lines developing on her over-rouged cheeks, the kink in her short, gray hair. When did she get old? I thought. I still felt like a little girl—her little girl. I felt that she might die before I grew up . . . that I might never grow up.

All this I recalled about a month after Charlie's funeral as my electric mixer traced deep furrows in the thick batter that would soon be delicate, chocolate-tipped ladyfingers for Gail Shusterman's younger sister's baby shower. Roses of homemade strawberry and lemon ice were already made and boxed, and I'd baked an orange-glazed pound cake the night before. The ladyfingers were the last of the order, and they would be done in plenty of time for the eight-o'clock shower. My mother had called about eleven to remind me that I hadn't called her for over a week. Stephen had called soon after to "check in." Although he was calling every other day or so, he made no effort to see me. I was beginning to feel that maybe we could be friends after all. And then Sandy had called to see if I'd be home about two, and would I like company for a cup of coffee? She was fine. The kids were fine. "Sure," I said. And then I started to think about how surprisingly well Sandy was handling the horror that had taken over her life, which brought to mind Charlie's funeral . . . and so on.

"Friends? You and Stephen? Are you craaazy?" Sandy asked later that afternoon, sitting at my kitchen table over our coffee and the few misshapen ladyfingers that hadn't made the cut.

"Maybe it's spring fever," I answered. "You know. Trees bud, flowers bloom . . . I sprout wings of fancy. I lose my mind."

"I'm serious, Tess. You don't want to be friends with Stephen, you want it to be the way you thought it was . . ."

I wondered how she thought it was, how she thought *I* thought it was.

". . . and if you think *he* just wants to be friends . . . Well. Maybe you have lost your mind." Sandy had toughened up over the last few months.

"I haven't seen him. Not for a while. But he hasn't been feeling great, and I think it helps him to know that he can talk to me."

"It matters to you how he feels?"

"We were . . . *are* married, Sandy. Obviously I still have some feelings for him. But I know it's over. Don't worry. I'm just trying to be civil."

Sandy rolled her eyes. "Not to change the subject," she changed the subject, "how's David these days?"

"Amazingly still around."

"Does Stephen know?"

"If he does, he's not letting on."

"Tess, are you and David in love or something?" she asked after a long pause.

What's with the edge on that question? I wondered. "What's love?" I asked, wondering why I was being evasive.

"I don't know. I thought you'd know. You have more experience than I do."

"Maybe in finding out what *isn't* love," I said.

"Oh. I've had my own experience along those lines," she said, growing pale and teary.

I wondered if it was pain she felt, or just emptiness. She'd seemed happy when Charlie had moved back home. And she'd had something—I didn't know what—with George. Ego, maybe, or revenge. But love? The truth was, only Sandy knew how Sandy felt . . . no matter how *truthful* she was with anyone about her feelings . . . including me, her best friend. Well, usually her best friend.

"Do you want to know how I really feel about everything that's happened, Tess?"

"If you want to tell me," I said, surprised by her sudden need to share her feelings, something she hadn't done at all since the funeral. And the coincidence of our thoughts startled me, as it always did, whenever it did, which was often. Sandy would say I was witchy. I would say that we weren't good friends for no reason.

"Relieved. I feel relieved. Does that sound strange?"

"No."

"I know I was caught up in craziness, and now I'm

relieved that it's over. I mean, I guess I loved Charlie when I married him, but we didn't share very much. You know I told you about how we didn't have sex after Jonathan was born? Well, the truth is it wasn't a whole lot better before Jonathan, or even before Rebecca. You know, like maybe once every few weeks? Even when we were first married. I didn't think it was normal, but he kept telling me everybody's libido is different. How could I argue with that? So I figured I was oversexed. Actually, *he* said that. He even told me to see a psychiatrist because I was a borderline nymphomaniac. And of course I took it to heart, because, after all, he was a doctor. I thought he should know about these things. And all the time it was him! Why couldn't I see how strange our relationship was?"

Why couldn't you? I thought, and then quickly answered my own question when I thought of my own assortment of aberrant relationships. "You're asking *moi?*" I asked.

"Actually, I never could figure out why you put up with Stephen."

"Right. Well, that's sort of different."

"Why?"

"I'm not sure. But it is. Hey! We're not talking about me. We're talking about you."

"It's all part of the same conversation, Tess. I mean, I have to find out what's normal. It's obvious that I didn't know abnormal when I was in it. So . . . what's normal?"

"What do you mean?"

"I mean . . . well . . . sexually. You tell me that sex is good with David, and it was good with Stephen . . . and there were the others. They may have been strange, but the sex was good, wasn't it?"

"Some of it was fun. But it wasn't always so great. Sandy, what are you getting at?"

"I'm confused, Tess. I don't know what I'm supposed to feel."

"What, specifically, is so confusing?"

"Tess . . . I've never had an orgasm with a man."

I was taken aback by this confession, as candids of sexy

Sandy clicked through my head, but I tried to be understanding. "Well, it sounds like you didn't have a whole lot of opportunity," I said. And what about George? I wondered to myself.

"I thought it was going to happen with George. But it didn't turn out that way."

"Yes. What about George?" I asked, now that she had brought it up.

"Mostly George and I talked a lot. I was flattered because he was always telling me how wooonderful I looked, how exciting I was—"

"So?"

"So it was all talk. I mean, we kissed a lot and I kept waiting for him to get into some really great sex—whatever that is—but we only did it a couple of times and it wasn't anything great."

"But the way you talked about him—"

"I know. I guess I was trying to convince myself. So . . . how do you?"

"What?"

"Get off with a guy?"

"You mean have orgasms?"

"Um-hmm."

"It depends."

"On what?"

"The guy, my mood, a lot of things."

"But you can do it."

"Not every time. But I always did with Stephen. . . ." I said wistfully, my mind drifting momentarily away from Sandy's concerns to my own.

"I can do it myself," she filled my pause in a small voice.

"Well, that's a start."

"But it's not normal."

"Why not? What's normal?"

"I don't know. I'm asking you."

"First you have to have a normal guy."

"Like your gallery of freaks was nooormal!"

"Let me restate that," I said, cracking the tension with a

laugh. "First, let's drop the word *normal*. Now. Good sex requires two people who like each other—"

"Like you like Stephen?"

"Okay. Let's say two people who like each other's bodies—"

"Two people as in any two people?"

"What do you mean?"

"I mean as in a man and a woman, or two men, or two women."

That threw me, made me feel dumb. This wasn't going to be as easy as I thought. "Well, yes, but for me it's a man and a woman."

"But it could be two men or two women."

Something's not right with this conversation, I thought. "Sandy, what are you trying to say?"

She flushed. She got up from the table, poured herself another cup of coffee, and hung around the center island, picking up ladyfinger crumbs and eating them one at a time.

"Can I help?" I asked.

"It's just that . . . ." She was close to tears. "Tess, I'm not who you think I am." She turned her back to me as she swept the remaining crumbs into a neat pile. "I think I'm gay . . . and I don't know what to do . . . and . . . ." And the tears came.

"Sandy . . ." I soothed, jumping to her side, putting an arm around her quaking shoulders. She turned to me and hugged me hard.

Sandy gay? I wondered. Well, her men are gay. That doesn't mean anything. Then again . . . And I felt her full breasts against my own flat chest. It startled me. It felt nice. I wondered if men missed that when they hugged me. And then I wondered if it felt *too* nice. They were a lot different from what I had . . . not so different . . . a lot different. Could Sandy be gay? What if she kissed me . . . what if she just took my face in her hands and kissed me. . . . What would I do? . . . Why would I think that? But if she did, would I like her full lips on mine? . . . I like a man with full lips . . . would I like a woman's? . . .

* * *

She took my face in her hands. "I knew you'd understand, Tess, because we understand each other, we're the same, you and I," and she kissed me, her full lips pressing mine.

. . . No. I don't think I'd like that. But her breasts . . . would I like to touch them, press them like I press my own when I feel horny, when there's no man around, when I do it myself? I like the feel of my breasts as I imagine a man would like the feel of them . . . but wouldn't hers feel nicer? They're so much bigger . . . so different from mine. Is that why I'd like to feel them, because they're different? What am I feeling? What is she feeling? Does she want to touch me? What would I do if she tried? Could we ever be friends again? Would I punch her out? Worse yet, would I like it? . . .

And she ran her hand down my side and rubbed my thigh and she took my hand and put it on her breast; it felt soft and alive . . . and she put her hand on my tummy . . . and lower. I felt myself blush . . . flush? "Do you want a back rub?" she asked . . . and I was on a sofa and she rubbed my back. . . . "Do you want a front rub?" she asked . . . and I turned and she touched me the way I would touch myself. . . . "I want to finish you off," she said—I read that in a book once—and she put her mouth to me and as I felt her tongue on my flesh I pictured her flesh and it was my flesh and when I touched her I felt my touch . . . like in a mirror . . . like for myself.

. . . It would be like doing it for myself, I thought, so how bad could it be? A woman knows a woman's body. . . . But what about the rest? Yes, for me there would have to be *the rest,* I thought as Sandy clung to me in my kitchen by the pile of crumbs on the counter. How familiar she felt . . . like my modest mother, whose ample bosom—which I'd never seen unclothed—cushioned me as I hugged her in the airport when she left for Florida . . . like when I was a child. And Sandy's sobs ebbed to sniffles and hiccups, and I held her like a child . . . like my child.

"What should I do, Tess?" she asked, pulling away, wiping her eyes and nose on a kitchen towel.

"About what?"

"About . . . who I am."

"Who do you think you are?"

"I guess I don't know."

"Well, I know you're a sweet, caring, beautiful woman, a wonderful mother, and a dear friend who's been through a lot lately and who needs some time to sort it all out. Sandy, do you think you're gay just because you don't have orgasms with men?"

"That's part of it. But . . . well . . . it's just that I'm so much more comfortable with women."

"But you seem to like men. You're always telling me about this one and that one making passes at you, and how flattered you are."

"I know. But I never said I was comfortable with it, did I? Well, I'm not. I feel like I'm on display, and I have to smile and act flirty because that's what they like."

"So you do it because *they* like it?"

"No. Well, yes. I mean, I like to have their attention, but at the same time it makes me really uncomfortable. What I really like is coming back to Janet or you and telling about it. That has to be considered strange." She looked at me askance, embarrassed. "Tess, do you think I'm gay?"

"I think you're confused. And I'll throw one of your speeches back in your face: I think you're scared of yourself."

"I'm sorry about that, Tess. I guess I must have sounded terribly pompous."

"No. I think you were right. And you probably understood how I felt because you felt the same way. Birds of a feather, they say." I pulled a stool up to the counter. "Sit here," I ordered, uncovering a plate of perfect ladyfingers. "You're going to help me give these a manicure." I removed the white wrappings from several semisweet chocolate squares and placed the chocolate in an electric fondue pot set at low, and we watched the squares melt around the edges, eventually engulfing themselves. Then, one by one,

we dipped the tips of the ladyfingers in the hot chocolate—
like brown nail polish—and placed them on sheets of wax
paper to cool and harden.

"You know, Tess, I really love you," she said, smoothing a
sheet of wax paper on the counter.

"You do, do you?" I said noncommittally.

"You're a good friend, Tess, and I want you to know what
you mean to me."

What do I mean to her? I wondered. What does she want
to mean to me? What if she is gay. What does that mean?
Birds of a feather . . . does that mean I'm—no. And I
wrestled with my feelings of caring for my friend and
worrying about how I cared for my friend, and wondering
why I had to wrestle with any of it at all. Maybe I'm an
unconscious gay. Unconscious, maybe. Latent. That's the
word. Maybe I'm a latent gay. Maybe that's why I choose
poor relationships with men. But then there's David. . . .
But he's just a friend, a friend plus sex . . . and I'm still not
so sure about his gender identification. Maybe he's bi. A
friend plus sex? So couldn't two women have that? Is that
what Sandy wants? Would I want that? Maybe I'm bi. Could
I do that? Maybe . . . on a desert island . . . with no men
. . . after a long, long time. But I'd rather be with David.

"What are you smiling at, Tess?"

"Me. I find myself amusing, Sandy," I said, relieved that I
found myself to be, after all, straight—well, as straight as
anyone really is.

"Sandy, what you have to do is find a man who loves you
and you'll be able to work out the rest." Of course, I
understood that I was talking from my own newly confirmed heterosexual bias, and that if Sandy was, in fact, gay,
I was not being of very much help to her. But I didn't think
Sandy was gay. She couldn't be. Birds of a feather and all.

"I have to tell you, Michael, it was unsettling. There I was
trying to comfort my closest friend—female friend, that
is . . ." I added for Michael's benefit, because I didn't want
him to think that I thought Sandy was a better friend than

he, even though he was a clinical friend. . . . Perhaps that's a bit austere, I corrected myself to myself: even though he was a *professional* friend, as in *paid* friend . . . No, no, Michael is a friend—just a friend, I lied to myself, deciding to debate the inequality of our friendship some other time; there were more pressing issues right now. ". . . and all these lusty thoughts, supposings, fantasies, whipped through my mind. It scared me a little."

He didn't say anything, but he looked very serious.

"And now you're scaring me. Why do you look so serious? Do you think I have any reason to believe those thoughts were to be taken seriously . . . as in maybe I have some latent homosexual feelings?" I asked, my latent insecurities twisting my stomach into a four-in-hand.

"Why are you so concerned about what I believe?" Michael asked.

"You're the expert. You know. You know who I am better than I do."

"Nobody knows you better than you do."

"So if I think something about myself, even for a moment, it could be true?"

"Do you believe that?"

"I don't know what to believe! You're supposed to help me decide what to believe, what's real and what's made up. If I knew what to believe, I wouldn't be here!"

He rolled his chair forward until he was inches from me. Leaning forward, his elbows on his knees, his head tilted up to me, he said nothing for a long moment. "Is that why you're here," he asked finally, "for me to tell you who you are and how to live?"

Yes, I thought, that's what I want. . . . Yes, make it easy for me. . . . Yes, because I don't believe what I tell myself. "No," I answered. He waited for me to finish, even though I thought I had nothing more to say . . . but I finished. "You only know what I tell you . . . one way or another. You're my Captain Marvelous Magic Mirror and Secret Decoder Ring, the one I sent for from the back of a cereal box when I was seven . . . and it never came . . . until now."

His mouth stretched slowly into a smile, and he started to rise, to move toward me.

Oh, God. He's going to hug me. He liked what I said. I learned something important and he's going to hug me for it. My reward. Reward? So why do I hate it so? Why, when I see him stop and think, when his closed-lip smile spreads slowly and he puts his hands on the arms of his chair, pushing himself up and forward, why do I squirm inside and outside and want to put my arms out, my hands up . . . why? *No, don't, don't hug me, don't,* I entreated silently.

"Why won't you let anyone hold you?" he'd once asked, sensing my discomfort. Good question. "That's not true," I had lied. I hug people, I let them hug me, in greeting . . . in farewell . . . in sex . . . in pleasure. But not in pain. A hug is a momentary melding, a sharing of body and soul. I can share my pleasure, I can share others' pain, but I can't share my pain. In pain, I wrap my arms around myself, shield myself from others' arms.

So . . . here he comes. He seeks to compliment, not console. He seeks to share with me this pleasure, not knowing that to me it's pain. So . . . he's going to hug me . . .

"No! Don't do that. Don't touch me!" I implore. Hands up, a shield against his advance, I cower in the corner of the sofa. I push away his challenging hands. I stand and push away the intruding body rising to meet me, push away the demand for reason for calm for obedience. "Go away! Leave me alone!" But he's persistent, he's determined, he'll have his hug, he'll not let me be neurotic about this, he'll make me like it, show me it's okay, it's nice, it's what I really want. Squared off, eye to eye, adrenaline finely focuses attention and I feel the dissociation, the numbing as all energy turns inward, then spews forth in one brilliant line of force, strengthening arm, contracting fingers to fist. I am steeled, I am stone; my arm alone can move and it moves on its own. Such power, such release, relief as stone fist meets flesh.

* * *

. . . So . . . I let him. I let him hug me as I put my head down—in deference? to avoid an imagined kiss? to what?— as I obediently lean forward in my seat and carefully place my limp hands on his shoulders or around him or . . . what to do with them? where to put them? while he hugs me. Why don't I just hug him back? I want to, I really want to. So why would I rather smash him in the mouth?

"Impotent rage," he said, mind-reading again.

Is that anything like entropy? I wondered, fiercely trying to organize the chaos swirling in my head. But the more I thought, the more chaotic my thoughts became. Control. I was losing control, I thought. Michael seemed to be disappearing down a long hole as he sat back down in his chair . . . his voice echoed as he quietly spoke words I didn't hear . . . and I wondered if it was I who was falling into the abyss, not Michael. I felt frustrated, angry, as adrenaline-induced blackness started to close in on me. I leaned forward and reached out to tear at the black, to grasp reality. I grabbed Michael's jacket sleeves, and from somewhere inside me a most awful demon erupted: "YOU'RE TRYING TO DRIVE ME CRAZY! I CAME TO YOU FOR HELP! YOU'RE NOT SUPPOSED TO DRIVE ME CRAZY!" I yelled. "Do you know what I want? What I REALLY want? I want to be FREE! Free to say what I feel and not give a SHIT what anybody thinks! I want to feel what I feel and not feel WRONG about it! You're so DAMN SMUG sitting in your chair, DIRECTING our conversation, CONTROLLING our relationship, PLAYING with my head. WHY am I so concerned about what YOU BELIEVE? Because you DO know more than you say. Because, although you'd like me to believe we're friends, we are, at best, UNEQUAL friends! And why do you insist on hugging me when you know—you MUST know—that it makes me uncomfortable? Are you some kind of SADIST?! If you're so GODDAMNED SMART, why can't you MAKE ME COMFORTABLE . . . so that I can hug you back and not worry about what I'm feeling, what you're feeling? Because that's what I really want to do, Michael. I want to hug you and tell you that you're the only person in the world who has

ever loved me . . . who has ever REALLY loved me. AND I
HATE YOU FOR IT. I HATE you because it's a kind of in
vitro love, not for outside this room. And nobody—DO
YOU HEAR ME?!—NOBODY outside this room knows
how to do it! You're a TEASE, Michael! A FUCKING
TEASE! You're SPOILING me for the REAL world!"

As I bellowed my last words, I realized the black was gone
and I was standing in front of Michael in his chair. And I
thought that I had blown it all, I had finally shown him what
a jerk I was . . . what a spoiled, ungrateful woman—little
girl—I really was. I stood before him wide-eyed, waiting for
retribution . . . for him to be stern with me and tell me that
I was obviously an immature, narcissistic bit of flotsam asea
in a vast universe of more important matters.

"Are you finished?" he asked.

"Yes."

"That was great." And he stood up and applauded,
clapping his hands slowly, nodding his head. And when he
stopped clapping he stood there gazing at me, appreciating
me. And I finally understood. Unequal friend? Of course
not. Michael wasn't an *unequal friend,* because he wasn't a
friend—at least, not as in *friend* who could become *friend
plus sex.* I had had it all wrong. But that was only natural.
After all, doesn't every little girl fall in love with her daddy?
And if he loves her well enough, then she can love, and
trust—which is, after all, the better part of love—another.
She can become a woman . . . and an equal. I stepped
forward and put my arms around him, my surrogate father,
rested my head on his shoulder and held tightly for a
moment, feeling not yet an equal, but very much loved.

"Am I hard to hold?" I asked David Wednesday afternoon.
He had arrived around one o'clock at my request—I'd left a
message on his answering machine the night before. It
didn't seem to me a particularly complicated question.

"That depends," he answered.

"On what?"

"Whether you mean it literally or figuratively."

"Oh?"

"There's a school of psychology that takes after some Eastern thought . . . that to have is not necessarily to hold, but is to enjoy. For example, you see a beautiful flower, but if you pick it to hold as your own, it will die. But if you don't try to own it, you will have it to enjoy."

I must have missed something, I thought. I asked a simple question and I'm knee-deep in something I'm not sure I want to explore. "So I guess I meant literally," I said.

"Well, that's an entirely different matter," David said, smiling, moving closer to me on the sofa, putting his arms around me, holding me close. "See how easy you are?"

Yes, this did seem easy, letting David hold me. He could hold me forever . . . but it won't be forever, I thought, wondering just how long it *would* be, and I held tighter . . . and the more I thought about him letting go, the tighter I clung . . . and I was sorry I had started the conversation.

We made love right there on the sofa. It wasn't in either of our plans for the day—he was going to be late for a deposition, I was going to be late for a meeting with the owner of an expanded Cape Cod who was moving to New Mexico and wanted to sell quickly. I felt more passionate than usual, and after David left I felt more alone.

What was it that David had said about holding, figuratively speaking? Did Sandy really want to hold me, figuratively or literally? Why wouldn't my mother hold me? There were some things about this loving business that weren't going to be easy . . . even for a loving, lovable person, I thought.

"SHIT!! SHIT!! SHIT!! I'M LIVING IN A FUCKING SOAP OPERA!" I screamed aloud in the shower, while the driving hot water numbed me, the billowing steam filled my eyes and nose, puffed my skin. Then I remembered how I felt when I yelled at Michael . . . how I felt he loved it, loved me for it, because it was honest . . . because loving isn't only about sweetness and light. And I remembered feeling that no matter what I chose to say or do, Michael would love me . . . because I deserved to be loved. And anyone who tried to be unlovable to me had better WATCH OUT!

Stepping from the stall I caught my reflection in the mirror above the sink.

Eyes flashing, skin flushed, steam emanating from my enlarged form, I raged from my cubicle: SUPER BITCH! Ready to fight for Truth, Justice, and the Loving Way!

Stephen had called while I was meeting with the Goodmans —owners of the Cape Cod—and had left a message on my machine asking me to call him back, which I did, after I made a few early inquiries regarding a buyer for the Goodman house—Maggie Pritchert had told me weeks ago that a client of hers was looking for a Cape Cod in the area, and I had a client who was looking for a ranch home, and, after all, what is a Cape Cod but a ranch home with guest quarters?—and after I threw a salad together for dinner. It was seven-fifteen. Stephen said he wanted to talk, not on the phone; could he come over . . . for just a few minutes? "Sure," I said, totally in control.

"I just wanted you to know something, Tess," he said, sitting at the kitchen table, after some small talk, after I fixed him a tumbler of bourbon on the rocks and sat across from him with my diet Sprite. "I realize how much I've hurt you in the past," he said. He took a sip of his drink and held the cold glass to his cheek. Something gold sparked between the slightly open ends of his starched white collar, beneath the loosened knot of his navy and green silk tie. "I want you to know that the business with my trip to the Greek islands last summer taught me something. . . ."

The mention of that trip with—with The Pig tensed me, sent flares rocketing through my head. And then, as he shifted his shoulders, I could make out the shapes of tiny naked golden women, hands to feet, encircling his neck. A souvenir from Greece, no doubt, I thought. A trophy chain, I speculated, picturing myself hanging with the rest of them, promising myself I wouldn't ask him about it.

". . . I've been ashamed ever since. And you have to have noticed that I've left you alone, Tess. I've tried not to intrude into your life, because I understand how awful that must have seemed to you . . . *I* must have seemed to you. And you were right. It *was* awful. *I* was awful. . . ."

The rockets fizzled.

". . . I guess I'm just here to say I'm sorry. I know I've said it before, but I wanted to say it again, to your face, with no ulterior motive . . ."

Red flags waved. Stephen did nothing without an ulterior motive, I thought.

". . . other than to let you know that I still care about you. That I want us to have something together. Whatever it is you choose, Tess. I want you to know that I haven't seen Dorothy in months. I ended it. For good this time."

"How'd she take it?" I asked, immediately wishing I could take back my words.

"Not great. But that's not important."

It shouldn't be, but it is, I thought, thinking that he had treated her as badly as he had treated me. Not that I felt sorry for her, except that I did, somewhere deep inside where, when push came to shove, I sided with my species. "Good," I said. "She doesn't deserve anything great."

He didn't respond.

"New necklace?" I asked.

"Just something I picked up in Greece," he said, further loosening his tie and opening his collar so I could have a better look.

"It's you," I sneered.

He didn't answer.

"So how are you feeling?" I changed the subject.

"Much better. The doctor thinks that I probably had a virus or something. My kidneys are in great shape. It had me worried for a while."

"What happened to your thumb?" I then asked, although I had seen the bulky bandage on his left hand when he first walked into the house.

"Nothing much. I jammed it in my desk drawer—the drawer got stuck and I was trying to shut it. I thought it was just bruised, but then it got really sore. The doctor said it's cellulitis—some kind of infection in the skin. You know, because of my diabetes these little injuries can blow up," he said, smiling a crooked, scared little smile. . . .

And as he spoke, holding his hand on the table for me to observe, I saw his thumb begin to swell, straining the white bandage. Dots of red appeared as the tiny square holes of the gauze filled with blood. The dots spread out until they connected and the entire bandage was weeping red . . . and the thumb continued to swell, constricted in the middle by a thin band of adhesive . . . and the gauze grew fat and logy and suddenly Stephen cried out in pain as the thumb BLEW UP, sending blood and bits of flesh and gauze about the table, the floor, the ceiling as he screamed in pain, in agony. . . . "You DESERVED that," I barked sadistically. . . . "That's what you did to my heart!" I shrieked. . . . "Now you know what it feels like," I squealed.

. . . "It's okay, Tess. Really. I'm taking an antibiotic. It'll be fine," he said, trying to assuage the seemingly uncalled-for shock that showed on my face. He put his hand on his lap, out of sight.

I must be mad, I thought, standing and fetching a plate from the counter. But he would deserve no less, I rationalized my madness. "Some ladyfingers?" I offered, removing the plastic wrap from the plate of chocolate-dipped ladyfingers left over from Monday.

"Will they massage my insides like only you can massage my outsides?"

"Don't get cute, Stephen," I said. Very tough, Super Bitch, I complimented myself.

"Okay, okay. I was only joking . . ."

And now he's going to tell me that I can't take a joke, I thought, arming myself for rebuttal.

". . . but, sorry, Tess. I shouldn't have said that."

Disarmed.

"Listen, I really have to go. I said what I wanted to say. I hope you can find a place for me somewhere in your heart, if not your life." And he stood, scooping three ladyfingers from the plate.

"Thanks, Stephen. Take care," I said, watching him leave, feeling the emptiness of my home close in around me as he drove down the driveway, away from the house . . . away from me.

"Whatcha doing, Sandy?" I said into the phone in the family room, setting the plate of ladyfingers on the cocktail table, settling into the sofa, piling the throw pillows around me.

"I just put the kids to bed. What's wrong, Tess, you sound funny."

"I don't know. I feel . . . lonely. I feel all alone and I wanted to hear a friendly voice."

"I'd come over but I can't leave the kids."

"I know."

"Do you want to come here?"

"No."

"Why don't you call David?"

"I don't know. I have some thinking to do before I see him again."

"Sounds heavy. Do you want to talk?"

"I don't know what I want. Listen, I'll talk to you later. Okay?"

"Sure, Tess."

"Okay. Later. Bye." I hung up before she responded, and sat in the family room without turning on the television. Feeling needy, but not sure of what I needed, I picked up the phone and pushed some buttons. "Hello, Mom?"

"Tess? What's wrong, dear?"

"Nothing, Mom. Why should something have to be wrong?"

"Because you rarely call me just to say hello."

She had a point. "Well, nothing's wrong. I just called to say hi. How are you?"

"I can't complain. How are you and Stephen doing?"

Here we go again. "We're not doing. I really don't want to talk about this again!"

"All right. But you don't have to bite my head off. Are you very busy with your baking?"

"Yes. Actually, I'm getting new jobs almost every week now, and a few monthly jobs. I can't believe how this has blossomed."

"That's wonderful, dear. It's just a shame that—"

"What, Mother?"

"Well, that you're alone."

Like a knife in the heart, her words struck me down. That's why I called, Mother, because I'm alone! Because I'm lonely! You're my mother. You're supposed to make me feel better! I thought. "It's not my fault about Stephen! I tried! It didn't work! I did everything I could and it wasn't enough! So stop trying to make me feel guilty!" Super Bitch yelled through the phone, my body hot and trembling.

"But, Tess—"

"And another thing, Mom, how come you never tell me that you love me? All you ever do is criticize me, tell me what I do wrong. You even criticized me when I told you I couldn't have a baby. You never even said you were sorry . . . that you hurt for me. Didn't you know how much I was hurting? You're never there for me, Mom. Where are you? With Jamie and Daddy? They're gone! But I'm still here. I'm still here, and I need you to love me!" My God! Where did all that come from? I thought, waiting with stopped heart for a response.

Silence. There was silence on the other end of the phone. . . .

And after a moment a voice, a strange voice: "Tess? This is Mrs. Levy, your mother's neighbor. I was here watching television when you called, and all of a sudden she fell over! I'm going to call the hospital! She looks terrible, all blue and distorted, I think she had a stroke . . . or a heart attack! What did you say to her? What did you do to your poor mother? I think she's dead!"

. . . "Tess?" my mother finally said. "I'm coming up. I'm coming up on the first plane I can get tomorrow. I'm sorry, dear. I'm sorry if I didn't do things right. It's not always easy—"

"Okay, Mom. Okay. Everything's going to be fine. We'll talk. It'll be fine."

"Are you going to be all right tonight?"

"I'm okay, Mom. I just had to let you know."

"I can't talk now, dear," she said, her voice trembling with bridled emotion. "We'll talk tomorrow, when I see you."

"Okay, Mom."

"Tess . . . I love you."

"Thanks, Mom. I needed to hear that. Bye, Mom."

After I hung up I turned on the television and reached for the plate of ladyfingers. Like puffy fingers, old-lady fingers, they lay on the plate. I picked one up and ate it, savoring the softness, the sweetness mingled with the salt of my tears.

PINEAPPLE UPSIDE-DOWN CAKE

1 very ripe pineapple
1 1/2 sticks butter
1 cup dark brown sugar
1/4 cup juice from the pineapple, or canned red maraschino cherries
1/2 cup milk
1 egg
1 1/2 cups flour
2 teaspoons baking powder
1/2 teaspoon salt
1/2 cup sugar

Preheat oven to 400°F.

Pare, core, and slice the pineapple into 1/2-inch slices. Over low heat, dissolve the brown sugar in 1/2 stick of butter in a 9-inch cake pan. Off the heat, add the pineapple juice. Arrange about five slices of the pineapple in a single layer on the bottom of the pan. Place a cherry in the center of each ring.

Melt one stick of butter in a saucepan. Off the heat, beat in the milk and egg. Add the milk and egg mixture to the flour, baking powder, salt, and granulated sugar in a mixing bowl and beat until smooth. Pour the batter over the pineapple slices and bake for about 35 minutes, until a toothpick comes out clean. Cool in the pan for 10 minutes. Turn the cake out, pineapple slices up, on a serving plate. Serves 8–10.

CHAPTER 11

Pineapple Upside-Down Cake

Mondays I experimented. This Monday it was pineapple upside-down cake. I had sold a colonial condominium townhouse to a middle-aged widow the month before—a sweet Italian lady who loved to bake for her three sons and their wives, and her two grandchildren, children of the middle son, the ophthalmologist. From that deal I walked away with a nice commission and three wonderful-sounding recipes. The secret of her grandmother's pineapple upside-down cake, she had told me, was fresh pineapple. "My grandmother would *never* use *canned* anything . . . unless she had canned it herself!" Mrs. Tassoni had boasted to me.

The phone rang just as I had cut into the hard, prickly skin of the pineapple, piercing my finger on one of its sharp barbs. It was Stephen.

"I have to see you, Tess. Will you be home about four?" he asked.

I sucked at my injured finger, drawing a salty drop of blood into my mouth before I answered. "I don't know, Stephen, I have a lot of errands to run," I lied, trying to decide whether or not I should see him . . . whether or not I wanted to see him.

"Please, Tess. This is very important. I promise I won't stay long. I really have to see you."

"What time did you say?"

"About four. But I could come later if it's better for you."

"No, not later," I said, thinking that if he came later it might turn into dinner, or if he came later yet it could turn into . . . I didn't want to think about it. . . . No. I don't want you here, I thought, feeling uncomfortable and conflicted, wanting to drop the phone and run out of the room, out of the house, to run away. But instead I said, "Four is okay, Stephen," and then I hung up, cutting off whatever he said in response. I returned to the deliciously sweet pineapple covered with perilous barbs.

I was glad my mother had left the morning before. After all, how would I have explained Stephen's visit after I had so painstakingly explained why we weren't seeing each other, why it was over, why it was, in fact, best that way? She had said nothing; but at least this time she didn't disagree, she didn't criticize. As I pared and cored the pineapple, I recalled my mother's weekend visit and felt pleased with myself. She had come. She had cried and told me she loved me, that I was the most important thing in her life. She also told me how hard it had been being a widow . . . how hard it is to lose a child . . . how sorry she was for me that I had no children, that she had no grandchildren. I saw how different she and I were, and that neither of us would ever be what the other wished. But we reached an understanding—that we were very different, but that the love between a mother and daughter transcends differences. And that was enough for now. It had been a good visit.

"Something smells good," Stephen said when he stepped through the front door. "What is it?"

"Pineapple. I tried a pineapple upside-down cake this afternoon. An experiment. I think it's a winner," I answered, leading him through the living room into the kitchen.

"I'm leaving my practice, Tess," Stephen blurted out, before he sat down, before he even took off his jacket. He looked awful. He'd found out about David and me! I thought. A blush of guilt burned my face.

"You're what?" I asked, already formulating excuses and apologies in my head. But I was wrong. It had nothing to do with me. It had nothing to do with David.

"I'm in a lot of trouble, Tess. I'm probably going to be disbarred."

"I don't understand." David never said a word to me! I thought, feeling betrayed.

"Of course you don't. You don't know about any of this. Nobody does."

"Doesn't David know?" I asked selfishly.

"No."

"Stephen, what's it all about? Sit down. I'll get you some coffee . . . or would you rather have a drink? Tell me what's happening."

Stephen took off his light gray suit jacket, hung it on the back of a kitchen chair, loosened his yellow-and-gray-striped tie, and sat at the head of the table. "Coffee would be good," he said, slumping in the chair, staring at his hands tightly clasped on the table in front of him. "I don't know how all this happened, Tess."

"How all what happened?" I asked as I measured coffee into the filter, filled the reservoir of the coffee maker with water, and pulled two mugs from the cupboard . . . trying to stay busy, to avoid having to sit near him, to look into his eyes.

He began to talk, and his story sounded like page one of the *Philadelphia Inquirer:* ATTORNEY INVADES TRUSTS— *Investigation Reveals Multimillion-Dollar Embezzlement— Forty-year-old Charter Acres attorney Stephen Fineman has been indicted for invading clients' trust fund accounts in amounts totaling more than two and a half million dollars, according to Montgomery County district attorney Harold Bradford. If found guilty, Fineman could face disbarment, fines, and up to fifteen years in prison. . . .*

As I listened, I found it difficult to reconcile the illusion of Stephen with the reality of Stephen for two reasons: his need for the illusion . . . and mine. Always immaculately attired in a custom-made suit, silk tie, and shined shoes, in the eyes of his friends and business associates Stephen appeared the epitome of success. Listening to him talk about his maneuvering and manipulating of funds, one could take Stephen Fineman for the Machiavelli of venture capitalism. Successfully building tremendous gross returns, fabulous investment potential, Stephen seemed to enjoy unassailable business acumen. But beneath the panoply of sartorial splendor and slick self-assurance, Stephen Fineman was no more than a gambler, and beneath the solid facade of fancy figures, his investment fortress was no more than a house of cards.

It had started innocently enough, Stephen recounted. He had borrowed a little from one trust to cover the losses of another—and his personal accounts—when things hadn't moved as quickly as he had calculated. And then some deals went sour, and Stephen's *borrowing,* which was really *stealing,* increased to cover new quick-profit deals made under the unrelenting pressure of debt . . . and those deals had also soured. "I had everything planned. It was going so well. And then it all fell apart." With this, his fingers unmeshed and his hands fell to the table palms up, like small dead creatures.

I felt sorry for him. "I guess it's hard to see a bad investment coming," I offered.

But his ego got in the way. "They weren't bad investments! I know a bad investment when I see one," he defended himself.

"Well, they must have been risky."

"Not really. You see, there's liabilities, and there's contingent liabilities," he started. This was to be a lecture of business buzzwords intended to excuse, to obfuscate.

I sat down next to him and listened attentively for a couple of minutes as he explained contingent liabilities, debt service, cash flow. "Okay, Stephen, okay. Now talk to me about the bottom line," I said, growing impatient. "The bottom line is one business term I understand completely. And if I understand anything you're telling me, the bottom line is that you stole a lot of money from your clients and you can't return it. So you might go to jail."

"I could lose everything I have, Tess. Everything."

There was a time when I felt Stephen could figure a way out of any kind of mess, but before me now was a defeated man. I got up and poured coffee into the mugs on the counter. I put two teaspoons of sugar in mine and one teaspoon of sugar in his, the way I had done hundreds of mornings, and then sat at the table again, placing the steaming mugs before us. "Do you want a piece of cake?" I asked, as if I were speaking to a hurt child. And the child in him nodded an assent. I got up again, cut into the still warm cake sitting on the center island counter, and slid a slice onto a plate along with a fork. As I set it before Stephen, I began to wonder what he wanted from me. As always, I made it easy for him. "Stephen, can I help?"

"I don't know, Tess."

Of course you do, I thought.

"I want to get this all settled. I want to start over again. I want another chance," he said forlornly.

With business? With me? "I don't have the kind of money you need, Stephen."

"No, Tess. Honest—I didn't come for money. I know you don't have it. But there may be something you can do . . . for both of us."

For both of us? The only thing I could do for both of us is shoot him, I thought, feeling immediately guilty for the rearing up of such unsympathetic feelings. "For *both* of us, Stephen? I didn't know I was involved in this," I said.

"You're not. Well, not really . . ." Something in his face changed. I could almost hear the *click, click, click* of a calculator, the *whirrr* of a computer emanate from his being. A hard glaze slipped over his eyes as he reached across the kitchen table for my hand. "I want to put my property into your hands for safekeeping. For us."

He got my attention. "What do you mean?"

"When the shit hits the fan, they're going to come after everything I have. Tess, I've managed to put away some cash and bonds over the years, and I need you to keep it safe for me."

"Safe?"

208

"I want you to hold it for me . . . you know . . . until this whole legal mess is over."

Of course I knew. "Do you mean *hide* it for you? Can we really do that?" I questioned with a carefully executed note of naiveté, while my heart picked up tempo and blood coursed through my veins, through my brain, waking the sleeping shrew within.

"Of course. It's no big deal. I had it in my bank box; now I want you to keep it in yours."

"How big a deal is it, Stephen?"

"About a hundred thousand in cash and . . . uh . . . two million in bonds."

I softened to his words, but I didn't miss that although he could be facing disbarment, even jail, what was foremost in his mind was his money. "That's a *very* big deal, Stephen," I said, allowing my eyes to grow wide.

He put his other hand on my hand and tried to let his face go liquid, resulting in an insipid grimace. "I need you to help me, Tess. See me through this and I'll be yours forever. I'll be everything you've ever wanted me to be."

Ah. A hook was baited. The question was, whose hook, whose bait, who would bite?

Carefully I pulled. "I don't know, Stephen."

"Tess, please. Anything. Ask me anything and I'll do it. Whatever you want me to do . . . any way you want me to do it . . . I trust you with my life. Please, just promise you'll think about it."

"I'll think about it."

I didn't miss the barest hint of a smug expression that animated his pasty face. He thought he had won, and he pulled the plate holding the slice of cake toward him, picked up the fork, and cut into the sticky sweet. It looked good. It looked right. Stephen swallowed it in seconds. "Good, Tess. Very good."

Very good indeed.

"I saw Stephen last night."

"Last night? You saw him last night?" Michael prompted.

"He called yesterday morning to ask if he could come over and I said yes. I didn't want to see him, but I couldn't say no."

"You didn't want to see him?"

"Well, I guess I did want to see him or I wouldn't have said yes, but I didn't *want* to want to see him."

"That's perfectly understandable."

"Okay. I did want to see him, but I didn't want him to know that I wanted to see him."

"So you said yes so he'd think you didn't want to see him."

"Stop twisting everything I say!"

"I'm sorry. I'm just trying to get this straight."

"I saw him last night and listened to him complain about his financial problems and his plea for help. I said I'd think about it. And then I slept with him."

"Oh! So you fucked him."

"We made love."

"It was okay?"

"It was okay. I hate Stephen but I love his body. And I told him that."

"You told him what?"

"Well, I kicked him out in the middle of the night. 'So you used my body and now you're tossing me out,' he said. But I told him, without a bit of pretense, that he was right. That I never had a problem with his body. I loved his body; I hated him."

"That's great," Michael stroked, "that's great. So what kind of help did he ask for?"

"Well, it started with business—he wants me to help him save his fortune." And I related the details to Michael.

"Are you going to help him?"

"I don't know. I don't want to help him. I don't want to get involved. But I thought that if I could help myself, then maybe—"

"Great! Turn it around on him! Get his money and send him to jail! Con the con man! How could you do it?"

"Michael! That's horrible!"

"Oh. You didn't think about it that way. I see."

"I didn't say I didn't think about it. In fact, as we sat talking, I had it all figured out in my head . . . just as you said. But I'm not sure I could do anything like that. It's not in me. Besides, he's too smart to let anyone get the best of him. I'm sure he has this all mapped out. And anyway, I don't want his money. I don't want anything from him."

"Nothing at all. That's why you keep seeing him."

I sighed. "Well, that's a little harder to sort out."

"How's that?"

And I told Michael about the rest of the evening—well, I gave him the gist of it while rerunning *all* of it in my head. "After he finished the cake, he came on with the old seduction act," I started.

"I miss you, Tess," he said, his face collapsing into the soft folds of self-pity. "I think about you all the time. I think about how you look, how you feel, how you taste."

How I taste? Stephen's shrink must be writing his material, I thought—*if* he's seeing a shrink. Then again, he probably got it from some pop-psychology book. In any case, I didn't like his newfound sensitivity. It seemed insensitive.

"Don't you miss me at all?" he asked, rising from his chair and stepping behind mine.

Yes, I wanted to say. Yes, I miss fucking you, I miss your body curled around mine at night, I miss your mouth, your tongue, I miss your skin. "No," I railed, "I don't miss your lies, your disrespect, your lack of consideration, of compassion. . . ." My denial grew in intensity, usurping my sense of control, my embarrassment at his ill-fitting words, ending in a scream of pain. ". . . No, I don't miss you! I hate you!"

". . . with the usual pleas for forgiveness . . ."

"Don't say you hate me, Tess. Don't. I want to love you. I want to make it all right again."

"It was never all right."

211

". . . and I folded . . ."

Bending over me, he wrapped his arms around my shoulders and kissed my neck. I felt the rush, the stirring, the quickening of my blood. My head fell back and he kissed me, upside-down. He ran his tongue along my lips until they parted, allowed him in. Tears spilled from my eyes down the sides of my face, little whimpering sounds escaped from my throat as he licked the tears from my cheek.

". . . and we made love . . ."

We hadn't made love in almost a year. And unlike that singular episode last summer—that singularly unsatisfying episode—making love to Stephen this time was wonderfully familiar, exquisitely heated by his absence. I wanted to stuff him inside me and keep him there, where he could be a part of me, where he could only pleasure, not hurt, me. After, we fell into the perfect sleep of sated sexual desire. Waking around three to the heat of Stephen's body, the pressures of his chin in my neck, his leg on my leg, I felt like a cradled babe, unaware of the cold hard world to be met . . . eventually. Holding back reality, I concentrated on pacing my breathing with Stephen's to avoid the warmed sour puffs of night breath emitted by his rhythmic gaspy exhalations. I didn't want to reposition myself; I wanted to stay wrapped in Stephen's body. The heat of it, the weight of it, the presence of it comforted me. How to keep his body there and yet not have to face him in the morning? How to avoid reality? These were the burning issues of the night.

". . . and I woke up about three in the morning. That's when I told him that I didn't want him there anymore."
"So he left?"
"Yes."
"And then?"
"And then I fell asleep. . . ."

I fell asleep quickly after he was gone, but not before I recalled our lovemaking . . . and then our evening's conversation. We had made love, but he wasn't fucked . . . not yet.

"Why are you looking at me so funny?" I asked Michael, whose eyes seemed to be boring through mine as he tapped the index fingers of his folded hands against his bottom lip.

He loosened up and smiled. "Why do I always have the feeling there's a whole lot going on in your head that you choose not to share with me? That's just a feeling I get . . . it may not be true at all. I'm not always very accurate about these things," he said.

Bullshit, I thought. "Bullshit," I said.

"I just thought I'd ask."

I held out for a short time and attempted to stare him down. When he allowed me to win, I decided to be honest. "I guess I do think a lot—little scenarios, mostly rememberings, nothing that would interest you." Well, at least partially honest.

"I'm sure you're right; I wouldn't be interested in what you're thinking."

"Well, maybe some of it would interest you, but I guess I just can't tell you everything. Not yet."

"Not yet. Well, it's probably not very important," he said with a wave of his hand.

We both fell silent. And then a need to understand welled up within me. "Michael, do you actually want me to tell you everything? As in *everything?* As in how we made love, how we slept? That's not really important, is it?"

"Only to you, Tess. What's important to me is how what happens between you and Stephen makes you feel, how you react. What's important to me is that *you* understand what you're feeling when you experience something and when you rerun these scenarios through your head."

"As I said, I love Stephen's body, but I don't like Stephen. Is that strange?"

"Maybe what you have to understand is what it is about Stephen's body that you feel you love, and what needs you have that his body satisfies," he answered, ignoring my question about being strange.

"You certainly know how to ground things, don't you?"

"It's hard to catch a bird on the wing."

"What are you into? Eastern mysticism?"

He took my hand between his own. "Whatever it takes to help you understand whatever it is you have to understand." And then he smiled at me until I smiled.

The week had been a tumultuous one: five showings of a sprawling, five-bedroom, Spanish-style ranch home on Tuesday and Wednesday, which amounted to a lot of admiration but no sale. Then, of course, there was Stephen's Monday visit, and Michael on Tuesday, which had left me thoughtful. But I couldn't be bothered with mind-benders, I had a lot of work to do if I was going to finish filling the order for the evening's meeting of Coffee, Cake, and Criticism, the book club that met the third Thursday of the month at the library. I had already made three dozen chocolate chip cookies early in the morning. Last week I had made and frozen one dozen mini-cheesecakes that had to be filled with fruit. And I had to make a pineapple upside-down cake. I had cut holes in the tops of the cheesecakes and was filling them with blueberry and cherry topping when the phone rang. "Hello."

"Tess? It's me. . . ." It was Janet. ". . . I had to call. I'm in the middle of clients, but I'll be off for lunch in about an hour. You going to be home? I've got something to tell you."

"What?"

"Not now. Wait till I see you. Are you going to be home?"

"All day. What is it?"

"Not now! See you a little after noon."

At twelve-ten Janet came bursting through the door. "I don't have a lot of time. I have to stop at the bank for Terry before I go back to the office. How about some coffee?" she said, heading for the pot.

"Now, what's the important news? You finally got a court date, right?" I asked, setting out a plate of cheese, crackers, and raw veggies I had put together for our lunch after making the batter for the cake.

"Bless you. I'm starved!" she said. "And, yes, David said we're set for the second week in May. Absolutely for sure this time. But that's not my news."

Once we sat at the kitchen table, Janet spilled. "Well, Tess, do you know Angel Santos, from Harold Bradford's office? You know, the district attorney? Well, Angel was in our office this morning, and while we were waiting for her X-rays she told me about the break-in, and I had to call you immediately—"

"What break-in? I don't know what you're talking about. No one broke in here."

"No, no, not at your house—at Stephen's."

"Stephen's? Start over, Janet, I don't know anything about this."

"No. Of course you don't. God, I'm not doing this well at all."

"You're not doing WHAT well?!"

And Janet told me the bare bones of a story . . . about how the police had answered a security alert at Stephen's townhouse Sunday afternoon . . . about an unidentified witness outside the house who told the police of sounds of violence coming from the second floor of the house, and then disappeared . . . about the police breaking in and finding Stephen in the bedroom, not in danger, but in flagrante delicto. "And, Tess, you'll never guess who was with him—that awful Dorothy Oberman!"

DOROTHY! HE WAS WITH DOROTHY! I couldn't believe my ears. I barely heard Janet's editorial comments about Stephen's lack of taste . . . Dorothy's lack of scruples . . . their combined lack of class and overabundance of brass. "Janet," I broke in as I felt myself breaking down, "Stephen was just here on Monday. I . . . we slept together—"

"The man is OUTRAGEOUS, Tess! I can't understand why you continue to be involved with him. Get a divorce

and get it over with! It's not going to get any better," she
finished gently, compassionately.

We fiercely munched our meager repast to the last of it
without further conversation; the loud crunch of celery,
cauliflower, and crackers somehow sufficed. Besides, what
more could be said? The details of the break-in were known
only to those who had been there.

Janet left at twelve thirty-five, never imagining for a
moment the complexity of The Details as they'd actually
happened. But before the day was out, I would learn all The
Details from one who had been there, and that night they
would keep me awake when I played them back like a bad
movie in the theater of my imagination.

MGM PRESENTS

"FATAL DETAILS"

Based on a true story
Color by RealityColor, Inc.
Starring:
Stephen "The Prick" Fineman
Dorothy "The Pig" Oberman
and featuring:
!!Why, The Little Traaamp!!
(and we don't mean Charlie Chaplin)

It was not a dark and stormy night. It was four o'clock on
a cold, damp Sunday that was fading away like a drab
watercolor painting left out in the rain. Stephen turned in
bed onto his left side and curved his body, still heated from
lovemaking, around the back of his lover and cupped his
hand around her right breast. She smiled to herself as he
kissed the nape of her neck, because she knew they would
make love again soon—as soon as his body dozed off the
postcoital fatigue. She waited, half awake, half dreaming,
anticipating the shared benefits of his remarkable recupera-
tive abilities.

Outside, a cream-colored Ford sedan coasted by Stephen's townhouse, stopping for a moment to observe the

forest green Volvo station wagon in the driveway. The Ford disappeared around the corner, and then returned, parking in front of the house. The driver appeared agitated, and sat for a time with the motor off, staring at the house before lighting a cigarette.

A warm puff of air smelling of sex escaped from beneath the light bed covers past Stephen's nose as he shifted his body to relieve the pressure on his left shoulder. Aware of his erection, he pressed into the smooth white buttocks in front of him and massaged the breast in his hand. The lady whimpered soft sounds of acquiescence. She turned to him, and their lips and tongues met in an erotic commingling of tastes and smells. Impassioned, they emitted simultaneous moans of gratitude for each other's presence. Together they felt the electric tingle of nerve ends, the heat of skin . . . they heard the soft lapping of water in the mattress beneath them . . . the sudden explosion of sirens—SIRENS! The security alarm! Footsteps on the stairs . . . running up the stairs. The entangled couple bolted upright, pulling the covers up to their chins, searching each other's startled faces for explanation.

Dorothy Oberman burst through the bedroom door, her bright red mane flaring wildly from its dark roots, her painted eyebrows arching high above blackly outlined eyes that appeared as though they were going to pop out and fall upon the bed for witnessing the treachery of the ever-faithless lover. But it was not Stephen she addressed in a shriek of unimaginable dimension. "BITCH! WHORE! Get out of MY BED!" she hurled at Stephen's guest from the foot of the bed, shaking a small pudgy hand that clutched the house key Stephen had given her—for *his* convenience, not *hers:* he had *not* given her the code for the alarm. With her other hand she snatched down the bed covers, exposing the abashed couple, who now shrank from each other. Stephen turned and fumbled with the alarm panel on the wall behind the bed until the siren was quieted, while the nude woman, tight-lipped and narrow-eyed, slipped from the bed. But she did not try to cover herself, did not attempt to escape her attacker's scrutiny. *Eat your heart out, Pig!* she thought to herself, walking defiantly to the mirrored dressing room beyond Dorothy, displaying, with a slow, careful gait, her admirably perky breasts and enviably cheeky ass.

"WHORE! You goddamned CUNT!" Dorothy called after her. "Don't you ever come here again or I'll RIP your face off! You leave MY man alone or I'll cut your TITS off!" Her words spewed forth with beads of foamy spittle. When she turned again to Stephen flattened against the bed, he saw tears of fury drag a trail of black mascara down her inflamed, trembling jowls. Stephen thought he had never seen a woman as ugly as Dorothy was just then, and yet it was she his eyes were fixed upon, not the mirrored image of the silky, trim figure across the room. He was fascinated by Dorothy's extravagance of emotion, her coarseness of tongue; he was excited by her overabundant form quivering with rage. And as the dressing-room mirrors reflected myriad beauties hastily donning clothes, Stephen only had eyes for the Harpy before him who was slowly, outrageously disrobing, exposing quarterback shoulders turned soft . . . pendulous, blue-veined breasts . . . a pouch of striated abdominal flesh bisected by a deep, brownish scar running from navel to evidential black triangle . . . thick thighs dimpled with cellulite . . . knees like swollen faces. She stood naked in front of the bed until her rival emerged from the maze of mirrors. The clothed figure walked past Dorothy and Stephen, flashing a contemptuous look of incredulity at them both. Stephen watched as she silently left the room; he listened with a sense of relief as she descended the stairs and exited through the front door. He then turned his attention back to the perspiring body approaching him. Saying not a word, Dorothy got into the bed, causing Stephen to bob up and down ridiculously as her weight created great waves in the water mattress. Stephen allowed her to envelop him in an embrace, to stroke his penis to an erection that disappeared into the vast cleft of her sex when she climbed atop him.

After closing Stephen's front door behind her, the *other* other woman paused below the open bedroom window to give her inner chaos and outer composure a chance to equalize. She was having a hard enough time believing the scene her eyes had just witnessed, and hearing the faint sounds of passion escaping from the room above took her yet another step further from how she thought reality should feel. And when the police showed up in answer to the alarm, the woman shamelessly fell upon the two officers with a quick but vivid tale of sounds of violence coming from the upstairs window of Stephen's house. She left them breaking through the front door. This is like being in a Woody Allen movie, she thought, glimpsing the policemen's forceful entry into the house through the rearview mirror of her Volvo just before she turned the corner. And, as with Woody Allen's movies, she wasn't sure if it was comedy or tragedy.

But I hadn't *yet* learned The Details when I burst into tears soon after Janet left my house. What she had told me was enough to keep me in tears as I boxed the cooled cookies, as I wiped the counter, getting ready to put the pineapple cake together. Dorothy again, I thought. What kept him going back to her? What did she have that I— No. I wouldn't let myself think like that. He'll pay for this. He'll pay for my pain. I remembered Monday night . . . first the soft loving, then the hard facts. He'll get his, I thought . . . and I'll get mine. I reached for the ripe pineapple next to the sink, brought it to the counter, and began twisting off its serrated top when I suddenly realized that I hadn't spoken to Sandy all week. Surely Sandy "You Heard It Here First" Solomon must have heard about The Break-in. And she hadn't called me! It wasn't like her to try to spare me the details. So I put the pineapple down, wiped my hands, picked up the receiver, and punched in Sandy's number.

"Hellooo!"

"Sandy. Did you hear about Stephen's little fiasco?" I blurted.

"God, yes, Tess. I was afraid to call you. You going to be home for a while? I'll come over."

Sandy walked in as I finished cutting the pineapple into rings. "Hi, stranger," I said.

"God. I'm sooo sorry, Tess. How did you find out? I should have told you. But there's a little more to this than you've already heard."

"How much more?"

"Well, this is kind of haaard," she said, taking off her forest green parachute-silk bomber jacket, laying it on a kitchen chair.

"Sounds like coffee time," I said, pushing to one end of the counter a bowl of cake batter, the cutting board full of pineapple, and the large, buttered pan. Sandy settled on a stool at the other end of the counter and I joined her with mugs of coffee. She said nothing as I got up to get milk from the refrigerator for her coffee and, while I was at it, retrieved the jar of maraschino cherries I would need for the cake. "Okay, so talk to me," I said, stirring sugar into my coffee.

"I don't really know how to say this. . . . You've been such a great friend and all. . . ."

I couldn't imagine what was about to come out of her mouth, but judging from her reddened face and downcast eyes, it was obviously something she didn't want to say, and probably something I didn't want to hear. So I consciously relaxed my shoulders and back and concentrated on listening to Sandy with my stomach, not my heart or head—a technique for unemotional, nonreactive listening I had read about years ago in some pop-psychology article.

But nothing I could have done would have prepared me for ". . . I've been in touch with Stephen, Tess."

Every organ reacted: My head exploded; my stomach heaved; my heart stopped; my spleen stewed; my gall bladder burned. I pictured myself starring in *The Exorcist*—my head spinning around and green guts spewing from my mouth. "You what?" I queried quietly, feigning calm, looking her straight in her long, black, lowered lashes.

"Oh, I only saw him a couple of times. It wasn't anything, really . . . but—"

"But why? What possessed you? . . . How? . . . I'm really at a loss, Sandy. Maybe you better start from the beginning," I said, bewildered, befuddled, deflated, as the old picture of Stephen and Sandy embracing in my kitchen developed in my head like a Polaroid photo.

She began, "Actually . . . remember one night, a few years ago, Charlie and I were here for dinner? The night Charlie got called to the hospital just as we were sitting down to eat? It was during a teeerrible thunderstorm? Well, you had called us into the dining room, and I walked through the kitchen, where Stephen was picking at something from a dish on the counter. And as I walked by him, we hugged. . . ."

The EMBRACE! So I was right! It was special.

". . . I don't know why, we just turned to each other and hugged. It was like the whole world disappeared, Tess. I don't know how else to explain it to you. Anyway, for years I guess I coveted him a little. And I felt the attraction was mutual . . . you know."

No, I didn't know, I didn't want to know.

". . . But, of course, you're my best friend, Tess . . ."

And how do you treat your enemies, dear Friend!

". . . and I neeever, eeever thought of cheating with Stephen . . . until you two separated. . . ."

And THEN? Bitch!

". . . Even then it was only a fantasy, because, well, I was still married to Charlie, and I was seeing George. . . ."

And God knows who else was turning through your revolving bedroom door!

". . . And then after the accident . . . you know, when Charlie and . . . well, after the accident, Stephen came to see me . . ."

BITCH! You never told me that, I thought as I stood up in a fit of nervous energy, pulled my ingredients before me, and began arranging the pineapple rings and cherries in the bottom of the cake pan.

". . . and he was so kind, and so sensitive," Sandy continued, ignoring—maybe understanding—my sudden frenzy of activity. "Nothing happened, Tess. Honest. He just told me he would be there for me if I needed an ear, a shoulder. . . ."

A PRICK?!

". . . Tess, it's not that I didn't believe you when you told me all those things about Stephen; it's just that I thought, well, I guess I thought maybe he would feel less threatened with me—I mean, you're so strong and all. . . ."

You thought, BITCH, that he lusted after your gorgeous little body.

". . . And then . . . well, you know how I was feeling about myself? And then you told me how good in bed you and Stephen were? So I started to think about how, if he was so good for you, maybe he'd be good for me. . . . After all, you weren't living with him anymore . . . and you had David . . ."

I stared at Sandy, dumbfounded.

". . . so I called him."

"YOU called STEPHEN! What could you possibly have said, Sandy?"

"Don't be so naive, Tess," she said.

I felt the chill of her contempt-born-of-guilt pour over me. BITCH! SLUT! I could have strangled her—twisted her gorgeous little head off, like the top of a pineapple. . . .

Instead, I picked up the bowl of thick batter and dumped it over her head. I watched the yellow mud coat her silky black hair, slowly spread over the grossly padded shoulders of her scarlet cotton-silk-blend sweater, and drip off the tips of her prized boobs. Her hands went up in a startle reflex and her mouth dropped open long enough for me to stuff a maraschino cherry in it. She wiped batter from her eyes.

. . . She wiped tears from her eyes as my tears dripped into the bowl of batter I was mixing furiously with a wire whisk. "How *could* you, Sandy."

"Tess, I didn't mean to hurt you. You have to understand. I didn't think you'd care . . . with David in the picture, and everything. I only did it once, Tess. Hooonest. And you were right about him, and I got what I deserved—I mean, you can't imagine the shock . . . Dorothy just breaking in on us and the alarm blaring away—"

SANDY! HE WAS WITH SANDY! Sandy was the *other* other woman, the police's unidentified witness! I felt the blood drain from my head, my heart—which stopped midbeat—my entrails. I thought if I looked down at my bare feet I'd see all my blood draining out of my toes like little spigots.

"You were there! It was YOU?"

That's when she told me *all* The Details. . . .

I was stunned . . . too stunned to react.

". . . You were sooo right, Tess, the man's an animal, and he's still screwing around with that old bag! I mean I reeeally can't understand it."

I reacted. "YOU can't understand it!" I erupted.

"It was terrible for me, Tess. You just can't imaaagine . . . the man is an absolute aaanimal!"

"And YOU, my dear, are a perfect ASSHOLE! Of course you don't understand. You're a self-centered, conceited little SNOT who doesn't have a whit of understanding or compassion for anyone else!"

Now it was Sandy's turn to blanch. Actually, we both blanched. She couldn't believe I had said what I said—and neither could I. Sandy started to cry and apologize to an embarrassing degree—embarrassing to me, that is, until I began to believe that she was more hurt than I, conceding to myself that, in fact, I was trying to break away from Stephen . . . that I did have David . . . that Sandy was still recovering from a devastating series of events . . . that she was vulnerable, and Stephen was a shit . . . and that they both got what they deserved in the end . . . and that Dorothy The Pig had got a taste of what she deserved into the bargain.

"Okay, okay, Sandy. Stop crying. I want you to know that it hurts a lot to know that my best friend would gamble with our friendship, with my feelings. But I'll forgive you . . . this time," I said, turning back to my cake, stirring the batter with a wooden spoon.

"Oh, Tess. I promise. I'll never, ever do anything to hurt you again."

"So. Tell me . . . did your little scheme work?" I probed coolly, undeniably curious.

"Did it—? OH! Did it *work*. Well . . . yes," she answered in a small voice.

"As they say, every cloud has a silver lining," I said, supporting my friend who was still a friend but not the same friend—or perhaps I was not the same friend.

"Now, it didn't happen right away," she began spilling all in the wake of forgiveness. "I mean, not the first time we did it, but the third time—"

"The THIRD time!"

"Are you sure you want to hear this?"

"Every word."

"Well, by the third time I was so hot . . . and he was so insistent that I be satisfied . . . he tried everything . . . I mean *eeeverything*. And I just did . . . well, not *just*, but with a little concentration I did. It was sooo exciting, Tess. And then when I was waiting for him to start again—"

"AGAIN?"

"Well, then the sirens started—"

"STOP! I don't want to hear that part again. Just tell me how you had the nerve to lie to the police that it sounded like someone was being killed up there? That was brilliant!"

"I don't know, Tess. But I was sooo angry that when the police pulled up, I didn't even stop to think. I just ran up to them and said it!"

"Incredible, Sandy. I didn't think you had it in you," I said, beginning to understand that there was a lot in Sandy that I had missed.

"I didn't think I had it in me, either. I mean—"

"I understand what you mean. Well, maybe some more good will come of this," I said, already rehearsing in my mind what I was going to do as soon as Sandy left.

"I see you've still got tooons of work to do, Tess, so I'll get out of your way. Talk to you later," she said. "Okay?" she added with a touch of uncertainty as she walked toward the back door.

"Sure, Sandy. Talk to you later."

* * *

"Stephen, it's Tess," I murmured sweetly into the phone after Sandy was gone, after my cake was finished, after I had settled into a comfortable corner of my sofa in the family room. "I've thought about what you said and I decided to help you." I turned my eyes upward as I uttered these deceptive words, savoring every syllable that rolled off my splendidly forked tongue. "Why don't you come over tonight and we'll talk about it."

"I'll be there, Tess!" he said, elated, ecstatic, inside-out with delight.

Hanging up the phone, I pictured him rubbing his hands together, thinking that he had won. And then I headed for my shower; it was Super Bitch that Stephen was going to have to deal with tonight. Stephen, I thought as I stepped into the steamy cubicle, *now* you're going to get fucked! Yes. Not only pineapple cake would be upside-down when the steam cleared.

DEVIL'S FOOD CUPCAKES

Cake

1 3/4 cups sifted cake flour
1 1/2 cups sugar
1/3 cup cocoa
1 1/4 teaspoons baking soda
1 teaspoon salt
1/2 cup shortening
1 cup milk
2 eggs
1 teaspoon vanilla extract

Preheat oven to 350°F. Line cupcake pans with paper cups.

Sift flour, sugar, cocoa, baking soda, and salt together into large bowl. Blend in shortening and 2/3 cup of the milk. Beat 2 minutes at medium speed. Add the rest of the milk, the eggs, and vanilla, and beat 2 more minutes. Fill cups about two-thirds full and bake about 20 minutes on lower shelf, until centers rebound to the touch.

Remove cups from pans and cool on a rack. Makes 24 cupcakes.

Frosting

2 one-ounce semisweet chocolate squares
1/2 teaspoon vanilla extract
6 tablespoons unsalted butter

Melt the chocolate with the vanilla in the top of a double boiler. Off the heat, beat in the butter, a little at a time. Then place the top of the double boiler into a pan of cold water and beat the chocolate mixture until it is cool and creamy. Spread on top of cupcakes.

CHAPTER 12

Devil's Food Cupcakes

All the windows in my house were open, as were the sliding glass patio doors in the family room and kitchen, on the first Thursday of May, which was also the first warm day of spring, a season that was slow in coming this year. Trees were still greening; the usual brilliant explosion of spring flowers was, instead, a slow drizzle of color. Well, it's finally warming up, I thought. Sooner or later we late bloomers all warm up and take off. I was blending shortening, milk, flour, cocoa, and sugar in the mixer, which would soon emerge from the oven as devil's food cupcakes for Lisa Gross's seven-year-old daughter, Alison, to take to school for her birthday party on Friday. Lisa had ordered a traditional birthday cake with sugary white icing and pink and blue flowers, but Alison had other ideas. It would be devil cakes—as she called them—or nothing, and they were to be frosted with chocolate fudge, she informed her mother. And she wanted her name on each one . . . just Ali, not Alison . . . in script, in shocking pink with a silver candy dot over the i.

"I'm so sorry, Tess," Lisa had said to me over the phone late Wednesday afternoon when she called to change her order from boring birthday cake to daring devil cakes as per her daughter's instructions.

"No problem, Lisa. You tell Ali that she made a very good

choice, and a birthday girl should always have her choices,"
I said.

All girls should have their choices, and not only on their
birthdays, I thought, watching the batter become thick and
smooth, remembering what my mother had said to me when
I told her Stephen and I were separating . . . that I had
asked him to leave . . . that women these days have options.
"You're a married woman," she had said, "you have obliga-
tions. YOU HAVE NO OPTIONS!"—a dictum that had left
me paralyzed for days. But I had remained steadfast.
Stephen left, and I found out that options beget options,
that life is not the straight road my mother believed it to
be, but a series of forking paths requiring an endless series
of choices. Lulled by the slowly turning bowl, I reviewed
the events of the past week surrounding my most recent
choice. There was Stephen's visit last Thursday evening
to discuss, in strictest confidence, our pact . . . the long
weekend filled with ambivalence about The Pact and
such considerations as my promise to Stephen that I'd
say nothing about it to anyone . . . my Tuesday meeting
with Michael, when I told him, in strictest confidence,
of The Pact, and agreed to run everything by an attorney
to make sure I couldn't get hurt . . . my Wednesday evening visit with Alan Garfield, Millie's attorney husband,
who discussed The Pact with me, off the record, in strictest
confidence.

Later, David stopped in, unexpectedly, in time to sample
a cupcake still warm from the oven. He came to tell me, in
strictest confidence, that Stephen was leaving the office and
his practice, and that he was going to be indicted for
embezzlement. I, in turn, told David that I had known for
over a week but that I felt I couldn't say anything . . .
because Stephen had taken me into his confidence. David,
looking hurt, said something about my skewed sense of
loyalty, and I pouted, feeling guilty, guiltier than if I had
broken my promise to Stephen. So, in strictest confidence, I
spilled, telling him all about The Pact. And when he
expressed concern for my welfare, I told him about my visit
with Alan, and he said that I should have come to him—had

I forgotten that he was a lawyer, too? When I didn't answer, he said, "I'm trying to understand, Tess. You aren't easy."

That was odd. I thought I was very easy.

Stephen had been surprisingly easy, I related to Janet, in strictest confidence, over tea and imperfect devil cakes the following night, explaining The Pact to her. "Stephen has some cash and a fortune in unregistered bearer bonds that he wants me to keep for him in a bank box, in my name," I said.

"You're kidding! Why would he do that?"

"He said he can't trust anyone else."

"But why would he have to involve anyone else? He's a smart man; he could figure out some way to do it himself. This doesn't make sense, Tess."

"Well, I think it's his way of maintaining a connection with me through this awful mess. And my cooperation won't go unrewarded," I added.

"Thank you, Dr. Faust. Did you consider that maybe he's involving you so he can *blackmail* you into taking him back, or—God, Tess, this sounds really awful—maybe he's trying to corrupt you so you'll be as bad as he is, and—"

"And then I'll *want* to take him back. Thank *you*, Dr. Freud. Don't worry, he's not that smart."

"It doesn't take a brilliant mind, it takes an evil mind, Tess. And we all know—"

"I think you're getting carried away, Janet."

"Okay. So maybe I am. But I'm sure this isn't legal, Tess."

"Legal, illegal. Let's not talk so black and white. I explained everything to Alan Garfield—hypothetically speaking, of course—and he said nothing can happen to me . . . as long as I don't know anything about any of this, which, of course, I don't. I mean, I'm just a dumb little housewife whose husband asked her to keep some papers—in sealed envelopes—in her bank box."

"Sealed envelopes? What would that prove?"

"Well, Stephen will mail the cash and bonds to himself and give me the unopened envelopes. That will prove they're his property."

Janet slumped in her chair and rolled her eyes. "Tess, this does not sound kosher."

"Well," I conceded, "Alan did raise an eyebrow at the whole thing, and he said that as an attorney he couldn't advise me to be involved in it, but, strictly as a friend, he told me I shouldn't worry."

"Some friend! Will he be your attorney when they indict you? No, no! Scratch that. If that's the kind of advice he gives, maybe you wouldn't want him for an attorney."

"Don't worry, David will defend me."

"Get serious, Tess."

"Look, Janet, no one can prove I knew what was in the envelopes . . . and that presumes that I'll even get involved and be asked to open my bank box . . . which won't happen because Stephen and I are separated."

"I don't like the whole thing, Tess. Then again, there are possibilities here. Such as, you could run off with everything, and he wouldn't be able to say anything to anyone."

"A key point, my dear."

"As I said. Possibilities."

"No. I mean a *key* point, literally. He keeps both keys."

"Dumb pun, Tess. Of course you know you could tell the bank you lost the keys and have the box drilled."

"I never would have thought of that."

"But I did."

"Well, I'd never be able to do anything like that. However . . . if the keys happened to come my way—"

"Yes?"

"Mmm. . . . Let's just say we never know what we're capable of doing until we're tested."

"That's a little gray for you, isn't it?"

"I'm learning, I'm learning."

"Now, another key point. What was it you said about rewards?"

"If he dies, I'm a very wealthy woman."

"Fat chance. Then again . . ." She paused, catching my eye. ". . . you could kill him!" We both laughed.

"Well, as long as he's alive, I'll have his undying love . . . and twenty-five thousand dollars," I said.

"Right. I notice he sweetened the pot with hard cash. Wasn't taking any chances, was he?"

"I think I did okay."

"I don't know, Tess. It sounds like a devil's pact to me." She paused again before asking, "You didn't sleep with him, did you?"

"No, I didn't sleep with him."

"You turned him down?"

"He didn't ask."

"Oh. How'd that make you feel?"

"Honestly? I guess I felt disappointed. But I think that was strictly ego. I did good, Janet, believe me."

"I don't know. I'm still not sure I understand what *you* believe you're doing."

"I feel like I'm in control for once. You see, if I have control of Stephen's money, I have control of *him*. I like that. I don't know what's going to come of it, but—"

"But who's in control of *you*, Tess? This just doesn't sound like you at all."

"So . . . you could say the devil made me do it."

"*That* I'd believe."

"And even if I never touch it, it feels nice having all that money under my control," I told Sandy the following Friday morning in my kitchen, in strictest confidence.

"I wish I could say the same. You know, Charlie's estate still isn't settled," she said, changing the subject.

"What's the hang-up?"

"Charlie's insurance policy has a double-indemnity clause in case of accidental death, and they're holding off payment because of the unusual nature of the accident . . . or something like that."

"What does the Great Malcolm Westmeyer, Esquire, say?"

"That I shouldn't worry . . . that I'll come out okay. But he didn't say for how long I shouldn't worry! All I know is there are letters going back and forth between Malcolm and the insurance company, which result in letters from Malcolm's accounting department to me advising me of my tab. One thing's for sure, Malcolm Westmeyer is going to come out of this okay."

"I'd say you won't do too badly either, Sandy."

Sandy averted her eyes and nibbled tiny bits of a chocolate chip cookie. "Um. You know, Tess, Charlie had lots of properties, but by the time they're sold, after I deduct the sales commissions, taxes, and legal fees, I'll be left with diddly," she said. "And, um . . . maybe you could sell them for me . . . you know . . . as a frieeend?"

"How's that?" I questioned.

"Weeell. You could charge me a low commission rate, and I could give you cash, and we'd both make out well."

"Sandy! I can't do that. I mean, if we were talking your house . . . well, it could be worked out. But we're talking big numbers in commercial property, maybe hundreds of thousands in gross profits, tens of thousands in commissions. There's no way to hide that kind of money."

"But it won't be a problem hiding Stephen's money in your bank box?"

The nerve! "Hold on, Sandy. I'm not doing anything really wrong," I said, feeling like a criminal . . . feeling very sorry that I had mentioned The Pact to Sandy, who, I was finding of late, was not exactly who I thought she was.

"I'm sorry, Tess, but you can't imagine how aaawful this is. After all I've been through . . . and now I'm going to be left in the poorhouse!"

"Spare me, Sandy. You're going to be fine!"

"That's what Malcolm keeps saying, but I think he's only concerned about how fine *he's* going to be."

I was growing impatient. I had promised myself that I'd never do this, but I couldn't help myself. . . . "If you want to see financial problems, look at Janet," I started.

"But she only has one child."

"Come off it, Sandy! Janet has to manage a job and the house, which, by the way, is mortgaged to the hilt. And she has to take care of Sean. Can you even begin to imagine the emotional energy alone that raising a child like Sean requires? And she's doing it essentially alone. All Leonard does is send checks. She has to be a father and mother to that child. You'll never have to work unless you want to. And your house, which was paid off by mortgage insurance, is kept immaculate by Estelle, your sleep-in housekeeper, who also helps you with your two very normal kids."

"Janet didn't have to buy a new townhouse. She could have rented an apartment."

I couldn't believe she had said that. I didn't know Janet when she had found her single-story townhouse, but I remember her telling me about her search for a ground-level apartment that could be fitted with extra-wide doors for Sean's wheelchair . . . and how it was an impossible mission . . . and how, when she looked at the development she lives in now, which was just being built, she almost kissed the sales agent when he showed her a ranch unit, and she almost kissed the builder when he agreed to customize the doorways for her at no extra cost. I remembered all this, and I wasn't even there at the time. Sandy was. But I let it pass. I did remind her, however, that when Janet finally landed a decent-paying job with Terry, her ex-husband tried to cut back on her support. "She had to pay an attorney to help her hold on to whatever money she had!" I screeched.

"But it didn't go to court. She settled with him."

"And how did she settle? In exchange for his not cutting back on child support, she agreed to give up half of her alimony after three years when he convinced her she'd be remarried by then—and her lawyer agreed! I notice *he* didn't marry her."

"Okay, okay . . . so you're right," Sandy admitted, backing off. "But, Tess, this all gets sooo complicated," she whined.

Things appeared a lot less complicated to Judge Bennett in the Montgomery County courthouse, as Sandy and I heard from Janet and David that evening in Janet's living room: "Tess, it was divine! I almost kissed the judge! And you should have seen Leonard, he was positively *livid*. . . . I was waiting for him to jump up and down in a fury and crash through the floor like Rumpelstiltskin. . . ." Janet went on and on, her green eyes brilliant with glee. ". . . And David was incredible, you should have seen him—like a knight in shining armor. . . . I did kiss *him,* Tess. You *were* incredible David."

David sat smiling until Janet came up for air and a sip of wine, and then, "Disraeli said, 'Justice is truth in action.' All we did was tell the truth," he protested modestly. We applauded, and then David stood up to take the stage. He related the details of the story, playing all the parts himself, a veritable one-man show—quite unlike the reserved David we thought we knew so well, obviously pleased with himself and the result of his efforts. "Picture this," he started. "Kendall, Lenny's attorney, was quoting all kinds of figures, pleading relative abject poverty—relative to other physicians and kings, I suppose—and denying the promises he had made to Janet, calling her a liar and a greedy bloodsucker and casting all manner of aspersions. Then, after letting Kendall go on for a while, the judge leaned forward and cut through all the bullshit with a wave of his hand—which happened to be holding a letter. 'Mr. Kendall,' the judge said, 'I have a letter here from a doctor who states that in his professional opinion, this child—this *handicapped* child— NEEDS to go to camp in the summer . . . NEEDS to go to this particular camp. Now, you've inundated the court with a confusion of figures, Mr. Kendall, can you manage one more, please? Could you tell us how much money Dr. Meyer managed to put in his pension fund last year?' "

With this, Sandy and I squealed and kicked our feet like two-year-olds. We were getting the picture.

". . . And Kendall told the judge that the records showed fifty thousand dollars, but that the real figure was only forty thousand . . . and the judge's very bushy right eyebrow flew up to meet his hairline. 'The camp costs twenty-eight hundred dollars, Mr. Kendall,' he said. He noted Janet's meager income, her scant IRA, and ordered Lenny to pay for last year's camp tuition *and* expenses, and to pay for camp and expenses *this* year!"

"And wait till you hear this!" Janet added. "On the way out of the courthouse Leonard and his attorney were in front of us, and we heard Leonard say—loud enough for us to hear—that he was sure the judge wasn't swayed as much by his big income, as by my big tits . . ."

"You're not serious! What a slimeball!" said Sandy, aghast.

". . . so I caught up with him and told him that he was right, because, considering my financial situation, my breasts were probably my biggest asset!"

"You didn't!" said Sandy, appalled.

"You're one of a kind, Janet!" I cheered. "You've really got balls!"

"I do now—Leonard's! Do you think I should frame them or bronze—"

"JAAANET!" Sandy cried.

"Actually, with your guts, I can't believe you used to let Leonard push you into lopsided settlements," I said.

"I guess it was a power thing. You know. He has the money—I have to take care of Sean. I was always afraid that if I made waves he'd cut us off. In fact, I was almost ready to settle with Leonard again today before the hearing when he offered to pay this year's camp fee if I agreed to pay for last year. You know, half a loaf and all that. But David insisted that the judge hear the case."

"Aren't you glad you did? Next time you won't be so quick to settle. In fact, after this maybe there won't be a next time. Maybe Leonard's learned a lesson," I said.

"Now, there's a great title for an obscene movie— *Leonard Learns a Lesson.*" Janet laughed, shaking her head, and then sobered. "It *was* obscene, you know. I can't imagine how Leonard allowed it to go to court. Wasn't he embarrassed? I mean, he's supposed to be a professional . . . a parent. He's supposed to be a man." She tried to squelch the emotion that seized her, but tears escaped from her eyes. "Anyway," she sniffed, "I hope you're right, Tess, but the man's a bulldog; when he gets his teeth into something he doesn't let go."

"I can be pretty tenacious myself, Janet. Just let him try something again," David jumped in, clearly enjoying his role of protector.

"You really were wonderful, David," Janet said, giving David a hug.

"It's true, David. We're all impressed," Sandy added, clearly impressed.

Make that *admired* protector, I thought in a flash of jealousy that caught me by surprise, shamed me. I pushed the mean little thought away. Yes, what David did best was nurture, protect, I thought, beginning to understand just how important these qualities were in our relationship, finally admitting to myself that what I needed was someone to take care of me. It crossed my mind that if it were up to David, I'd never be out in the rain without an umbrella, I'd always eat a good breakfast, I'd never, ever get lost, and . . . well, yes . . . I'd always get my boo-boos kissed. Okay, so I was older . . . so I made more money . . . so I was the female . . . but *he* was so good at caring, at taking care.

"Oh, Tess! I almost forgot the best part," Janet cried, bringing me back. "The judge asked David for an accounting of his fees—he was going to make Leonard pay them! When David told the judge he wasn't charging me anything, he ordered Leonard to pay for my trip to Maine for visiting day at camp for last year and this year."

"Can he *do* that?" I asked.

"Can he? He did," David replied.

"Well, here's to a happy ending." I raised my glass in a toast.

"And here's to Sean, a brave little guy who has a very brave mom," David added.

"And here's to Judge Bennett, who had the distinct pleasure of giving the devil his due," Janet finished.

PEARS FLAMBÉ

Poached Pears

1/2 cup sugar
1 1/2 cups red wine
1 1/2 cups water
3 cloves
zest of 1/2 orange
zest of 1/2 lemon
1-inch piece of vanilla bean
4 firm, slightly underripe pears
4 tablespoons Grand Marnier

Simmer sugar in wine and water until dissolved. Add cloves, zests, and vanilla bean. Simmer 20 minutes.

Take pan off heat. One at a time, peel the pears and drop into liquid. Barely simmer about 3 minutes, until pears are tender. With a slotted spoon, transfer pears, standing up, to a shallow, flat platter. Warm Grand Marnier. Ignite 1 tablespoon Grand Marnier and pour over warm pear. Repeat for each pear. When flames go out, allow pears to cool and then refrigerate, covered, several hours.

Crème Anglaise

1 cup milk
1 cup heavy cream
vanilla bean from pears
4 egg yolks
6 tablespoons sugar
1 1/2 teaspoons cornstarch

Bring milk, cream, and vanilla bean just to a boil and remove from heat. Let stand 10 minutes. Slowly beat egg yolks into the sugar until mixture is pale and creamy. Beat in cornstarch. Vigorously whisk milk mixture into the egg mixture. Return to very low heat and cook, stirring, about 15 minutes, until the sauce is thickened. Do not boil. Remove from heat and take out the bean. Cover and refrigerate.

The Assembly

Place each pear in a pool of crème anglaise in a dessert bowl. Serves 4.

CHAPTER 13

Pears Flambé

Ken Briskin, a clean-shaven, slim six-footer with dark brown, neatly styled hair, hazel eyes, manicured nails, and polished shoes, was a newly divorced orthodontist when I met him at a singles social at a hotel in Cherry Hill, New Jersey, in the middle of June—a fund-raising event sponsored by the Variety Club. This was not an event I would have chosen to go to on my own. I was, after all, in a relationship with David. Then again, there must have been some reason I agreed to go with Sandy when she asked— begged—some reason other than her insistence—"Oh, Tess, you haaave to come with me! It's only ten minutes from the bridge. I'll drive . . . I'll take you to dinner first!" she had implored. "Janet has another date with what's-his-name, Bones—you know, the chiropractor—and I just cooouldn't go alone. I've never been to one of these things. I'd be teeerrified!" Some reason other than my ego— "You're sooo good with people," she had wooed me, "and men reeeally like you, they'll talk to you." Perhaps I was, in fact, trying to pull away from David, just a bit, as our relationship grew closer; but I wouldn't have admitted it to myself at the time. That would have meant admitting that I was as attached to him as I later realized I was . . . later, as in while being embraced by Ken Briskin in his restored, historical Philadelphia townhouse . . . but that was later.

* * *

Yes, *later,* as in *last night,* I thought the morning of July 7 as I fished eight firm, ruby-fleshed pears from their simmering California red wine bath and set them two by two on a platter to cool. They look like chubby little bodies flushed from a hot tub, I thought, smiling, reaching for the squat bottle of Grand Marnier and the blue box of matches. Flaming the pears with the orange liqueur was my secret step in the otherwise standard recipe for the dessert I was making for Millie's dinner party the following night— chilled poached pears served in crème anglaise. I uncorked the bottle, lit a match, poured an ounce or so of the golden liqueur over a pair of pears, and then touched the lighted match to the top of each, setting them passionately ablaze. After igniting the last pair, I stared at the soft blue flame, remembering the details of the social I had let Sandy drag me to not quite a month ago.

Sandy and I hung around the corners of the room dimly lit by tiny bulbs covering the dark ceiling like a starry sky. We each nursed a single drink for about two hours, trying not to talk to each other. Sandy was perfectly coiffed, perfectly made-up, and attractively costumed in a red linen—linen amazingly never looked rumpled on Sandy—straight skirt, matching V-neck, short-sleeved, collared shirt that showed off her finer points, and matching (I couldn't believe she'd found them) red sling-back high heels. She talked to one or two other women who also were trying not to talk with their own friends. I, demurely attired in a long khaki skirt, long, off-white bulky cotton sweater, and flat sandals, observed the crowd feeling somewhat condescending because I, after all, had a lover . . . someone I'd see the following night. So, while Sandy was briefly involved in a conversation with a permed fifty-plus-year-old brunette in a tight black silk jumpsuit, Ken Briskin walked up to me smiling the smile of one who had found a familiar face in a crowd. "Well, you look like someone my age who's probably read, or at least heard of, *Ulysses.*"

"It's on my bookshelf, waiting. I wink at it at least twice a week," I said, smiling. "But I'd guess you're younger than I am."

"Thirty-one, next month," he offered.

"Thirty-five, in two months," I followed. Out of the corner of my eye, I saw Sandy, who was to my left a little behind Ken, watching us.

"I'll take you out for your birthday," he said.

"I'm already busy," I said, instinctively protecting David's territory.

"I had a feeling you weren't going to be easy," he said. "Just don't tell me you're already taken."

I noted that Sandy had moved next to me and was smiling at Ken. "Oh, no, nothing like that," I sort of lied. "It's just that I always spend my birthday with family," I totally lied, totally ignoring Sandy.

"Well, we'll talk about your birthday when I take you out for my birthday."

"Hiii!" Sandy interjected, extending a hand to Ken. "I'm Sandy Solomon, Tess's friend. We came here together. Actually, I dragged her here because it's the first time I ever attended one of these functions," she rattled on, holding Ken Briskin's hand, sucking his eyes with hers. "Tess wasn't interested in coming because she's pretty much spoken for—"

"Oh! Is that so?" he asked, dropping Sandy's hand, dropping his smile, turning his eyes to me.

"I—"

"It's sooort of true, isn't it, Tess?" she said before I could get two words out.

"Not really," I finally managed.

"I knew you were too good to be true," Ken said to me, while Sandy, now standing close—very close—to Ken, realized she had gone a bit too far. Grabbing Ken's arm, she tried to make it better. "Weeell," she said, "maybe not . . . what did you say your name was?"

"Ken. Ken Briskin."

"Maybe not, Ken Briskin. I guess I'm a little more enthusiastic about Tess's suitors than she is."

"Then I'd like to call you. Could I have your number?" Ken asked, almost turning his back to Sandy . . . who looked devastated.

"Sure," I replied, rummaging through my pocketbook. Not wanting to appear pretentious, I pushed my business cards aside, wrote my name and telephone number on an old supermarket receipt, and handed it to Ken. I was aware that Sandy was watching, and that she was thinking that it was *she* who had come here looking for a date, not me. But I wasn't going to worry about it. After all, it was she who had insisted that I come. And besides, I thought, guilt slowly usurping arrogance, who knew if he would actually call me? And even if he did . . . maybe he had single friends.

"We really have to go, Tess," Sandy said, glancing at her watch.

"It was nice meeting you, Ken," I said, shaking his hand.

"It was my pleasure, Tess. I'll call you. By the way, my birthday is July 6. You're not busy, are you?"

"I am now." I tried not to look at Sandy.

"Great! And maybe you're not busy next Friday?"

"Call me."

"I'm sorry," I said in the car as we crossed the bridge to Philadelphia, although I immediately wondered why I was apologizing.

"For what?" Sandy replied, not convincingly.

"I'm not sure. But I think you're disappointed."

"There wasn't a soooul there that I would have wanted to go out with. That's not your fault. But," she continued, "you didn't have to ignore me when the one nice guy in the room came over to us. . . ."

Us?

". . . You could have introduced him to me before I finally had to introduce myself. . . ."

My heart dropped to my stomach. Mea culpa! Mea culpa! I mentally beat my breast. She was right. I had ignored her. I had ignored her and I knew I had ignored her. I don't know why I had ignored her. I can't believe I had ignored her.

". . . Frankly, Tess, I had the feeling you were trying to

ignore me and keep him all to yourself. I mean, especially after you had told me that you were *only* going along for the ride."

"I didn't do it on purpose, Sandy. I didn't realize you were standing next to me . . . and then, when I did see you, I didn't want to interrupt him to introduce you . . . and you actually didn't give me a chance." But it was no use. How could I ask her to excuse my behavior when *I* couldn't excuse my behavior? I had already forgotten about *her* behavior.

What an evening that had been! A real eye-opener, I thought, wrapping the dish of pears and placing it in the refrigerator to chill overnight. And, speaking about eye-openers, there was last night! I grabbed a sponge, wiped the stovetop and counter, and poured the hot poaching wine with its bits of lemon and orange peel into the sink, mentally making a list of ingredients I had to buy for the custard sauce I planned to make Friday afternoon. Just as I finished cleaning up, the phone rang. It's Sandy, I witched as I picked up the phone. She wants to know how my date with Ken went last night. "Hello, Sandy!"

"Hiii! How'd you know it was me?"

"I took a wild guess."

"Sooo. How was Braces' birthday dinner?"

"We had a nice time."

"God, Tess, you're sooo understated! Where did you go? What did you do?"

"Well, we went to dinner at Le Petit Champignon—"

"Did you have lemon mirror cake for dessert?"

"That would have been disloyal to Marv!"

"And you *are* loyal. By the way, Tess, what did you end up doing about a birthday present?"

"Listen, I can't talk right now. I just finished poaching pears, and I've got to take a shower, get dressed, and be at a settlement by one o'clock—the Spanish ranch. It finally sold, but the buyers are nuts—would you believe they wanted to test the electric can opener before they would sign the agreement?—so I don't want to be even a minute late."

"When can you talk?"

"Breakfast tomorrow. It's Janet's Friday off, give her a call. Tell her I've got an interesting breakfast story."

"Well, okay. Sounds intriguing. Can you give me a hint?"

"Um. If you get a phone call from Ken, don't be surprised."

"Me? From Braces? What's the story? I thought he was mad about you! I mean, *three* dates in two weeks . . . and now he wants to call *me?*" She sounded confused but, judging from the sudden lilt in her voice, victorious.

"I'll tell you tomorrow."

"Now! Tell me now. Did he remember me? Did he ask you for my number?"

"Yes, he remembered you. Listen, I've got to go. I'll see you in the morning, about nine-thirty at Mykonos? And don't forget to call Janet."

"I won't. You've got me so curious!" she bubbled.

A crack of thunder awakened me Friday morning at six-thirty. Lightning flashed above my bed, momentarily brightening the blackened sky beyond the skylight. It was pouring. A wonderful day to stay at home, I thought, and then remembered that I was meeting Sandy and Janet for breakfast. But that wasn't until nine-thirty, so I didn't have to get up until eight-thirty, so I had time for another two hours of sleep, I figured, burrowing farther down in bed, sandwiching my head in my folded king-size pillow to block the rumble and crash of thunder, pulling the sheet and comforter over my face to block the morning light, the flashes of lightning. I felt myself drift. . . .

Sandy and Janet weren't at Mykonos when I arrived, but Stephen was sitting in a booth near the front of the diner. I sat down across from him and he asked the waitress to bring me a cup of coffee. Then he got up and sat down beside me. "So, you've been screwing David. How long has that been going on?" He looked odd, drunk or drugged . . . something.

"It's none of your business, Stephen. Are you all right?"

"I'm sick. You made me sick. You betrayed me . . . you and David. You always loved him, didn't you? He always loved you. I know that. Did you think I was blind?" He put his hand to his temple and I noticed it was bandaged.

Oh, my God! I thought. I can't go through this again! Not his whole hand! So I didn't ask.

"You don't care about me anymore, do you? You didn't even ask what happened to my hand." And he thrust his bandaged hand in front of me. And it started to seep red, to weep, it started to swell.

No! I don't want to see this, I thought, and I tried to get up, but he held me to him, against his feverish body, puffing his hot breath into my face . . . and I struggled to get free . . . and I tried to scream for help, but I was too constricted to make a sound . . . and I heard a siren . . . it was an ambulance coming for Stephen, to take him to the hospital . . . or was it the police? was he going to jail? . . . and the siren got louder and louder as I struggled harder and harder, trying to free myself from his constraint, from his suffocating, sour breath.

. . . My alarm was blaring as I awoke, finding myself entangled in my bed covers, straining against unyielding sheets, suffocating beneath my pillow. A dream. What a terrible dream, I thought, finally freeing myself from the twisted linen, pulling the pillow from my face and breathing fresh air. And I could see through the skylight that the sky was clear and bright. The storm had passed. *That* storm had passed.

"Sooo! What's with Braces?" Sandy asked even before we were seated, while we waited in the foyer at Mykonos for Janet.

"I gave him your number because I decided that I wasn't going to see him again."

"He turned out to be kinky?"

"Oh, there's Janet. Let's go."

Once seated, Sandy pressed on. "Sooo! Was he kinky?"

"Is who kinky?" Janet asked.

"Ken," I answered. "And—"

"Aha!" Janet interrupted. "It was The Third Date with Ken Wednesday night. Details, please!"

"Okay, okay," I said. "But you're going to find this very uninteresting."

"A first sexual encounter with someone new is never uninteresting—to hear about, that is," Janet retorted. We all laughed.

"Why do you assume I slept with him?"

"Well, it *was* your third date. Rule of thumb and all."

"Maybe by *your* thumb."

"Well, didn't you?" Sandy jumped in.

"Do you want me to start from the beginning . . . or the juicy part?" I teased.

"From the beginning," said Janet. "Context, Tess. I need context!"

"Okay. In the beginning was heaven and earth—"

"Tess, PLEASE!" Janet scolded. "Fast forward to the evening of July 6."

"Okay. The evening of July 6 Ken picked me up at seven—looking extremely dapper and smelling wonderful —and took me to Le Petit Champignon, where we enjoyed a delicious feast of—"

"Skip the dinner, Tess, and get to dessert—dessert as in once you left the restaurant."

"Right. So we went back to his beautiful townhouse, where he gave me a gracious tour, and then fixed me a drink in the kitchen—"

"The KITCHEN! Why do you always end up in the kitchen?" Sandy blurted impatiently.

"It wasn't her fault, Sandy," Janet explained. "If you'll note, the man didn't have the right moves. He should have fixed her a drink first, and *then* given her The Tour, which, naturally, would have *ended* in The Bedroom." More laughter.

"Hey! Are you going to let me tell this story or not?"

"Go, go, go," said Janet.

"So he fixed me a drink in the kitchen and we stood by the counter chitchatting, and then there was a lull in the conversation and he sort of looked like he wanted to kiss me—"

"What's *sort of* mean?" Sandy broke in.

"Sort of, as in he stared forlornly at me with watery eyes, and the vein that runs down the middle of his forehead was sort of sticking out and throbbing."

"So then?" they asked in unison.

"So then . . . I kissed him."

"You kissed *him?"* Sandy questioned.

"I kissed him and he dropped his drink on the floor and put his arms around me and kissed me back with great ardor."

"With Great Ardor!" Janet repeated to Sandy. "And?" she questioned me.

"And it was nice."

"Nice! It was *nice?* Is that all you have to say about glasses smashing on floors and GREAT ARDOR? NICE!" Janet exclaimed.

"It was nice. And that was it."

"THAT was IT!" she exclaimed again.

"That was it. I've never experienced anything like it before, but although his mouth was nice—very nice—it was the wrong mouth."

"I think I've heard this in a song somewhere," Janet mumbled.

"What I mean is, well, everything was right, right, right . . . but somehow it was all wrong. Understand?"

"Not in a million years," Janet answered.

"And I was worried about *him* being kinky!" Sandy sighed.

"No, listen. Let me try to explain."

They were all ears.

"I was really looking forward to this date. The guy is young, very attractive, a professional, bright, somewhat intellectual, an interesting conversationalist, he has a quirky sense of humor . . ."

"He likes her puns," Janet explained to Sandy.

". . . he asks lots of questions, doesn't just talk about himself, dresses well, smells good, and he's a really good kisser, which I had learned when he kissed me good-night after our second date . . ."

They sat taking in every word, not knowing where I was going.

". . . so I was looking forward to our third date, and I thought maybe we'd fool around just a bit—get to know each other a little. But when the opportunity presented itself, something inside me turned off. It was like someone flipped a switch, pulled a plug, something. And all I could think of while we kissed was, 'They're the wrong lips . . . they're not David's lips,' and I suddenly missed David terribly and I couldn't wait to get home to call him—"

"I must be going mad," Sandy broke in. "I could have sworn you just said that you were in love with David!"

"I guess I did, didn't I."

"Well! It's about time," said Janet. "We were wondering how long it would take you to figure it out."

"You knew?"

"A friend always knows," said Janet.

"So is that when he asked for my number?" Sandy asked again.

"Well, yes, that's when I gave him your number."

"Ken, we have to talk," I said once his lips had left mine, while he clung to me, rocked me in his arms.

"We have all the time in the world to talk. Right now all I want to do is kiss you."

"That's what we have to talk about," I said, trying to be gentle.

"All right," he said, sobering up, pushing the broken glass with the side of his foot into a pile. He led me by the hand to the study next to the kitchen, where we sat together on a tan leather love seat. "Now. What's so serious?"

"Me, I'm afraid. I just realized that I'm serious about someone I've been seeing."

"And that someone isn't me."

"Right. Ken, you're a very attractive and desirable man, but—"

"But you're in love with someone else."

He's so intelligent . . . so grown-up, I thought. "Right. Honestly, if I had known I wouldn't have led you on, but I wasn't aware of it myself until I became attracted to you. That doesn't make much sense, does it?"

"It does to me. In fact, I take it as a compliment."

After I thought about it, it made perfect sense to me, too.

"He must be the suitor your friend Sandy mentioned."

"Yes." I was mustering a second apology, but Ken beat me to it.

"I'm sorry if I embarrassed you. But I have to tell you that I'm very attracted to you, and if you ever find yourself . . . that is, if you ever find that you'd like to see me, I'd like you to call me."

I was sorely tempted to take his number and hide it away . . . just in case. But I thought of all the women's business cards Stephen had stashed away over the years, and a wave of nausea choked back a positive response. "You're incredible!" I finally said. "Listen. You are just too, too nice to let go completely. Would you be interested in calling a friend of mine?"

"It depends. It wouldn't be Sandy, would it?"

"As a matter of fact, yes."

"She's a pretty lady . . . a little hungry, but pretty."

"Not hungry, just anxious. She's a widow and she doesn't have her sea legs yet. I think you two would enjoy each other."

"So do you think he'll call?"

"I'll bet he does. He said you were very pretty."

"Did you call David when you got home?" Janet asked.

"Better than that. I drove over to his apartment and gave him the birthday present I had planned to give Ken."

"I'm so glad you're home, David," I said when he answered the door in his bathrobe at 12:15 A.M., very surprised.

"So am I . . . now," he responded. And he kissed me and held me.

And I wanted to tell him that I had been to dinner with

249

this guy, Ken, who was one of the nicest men I have ever met, and one of the best-looking, and one of the smartest. *But it was really weird, David,* I wanted to say, *it was weird because being with Ken made me miss being with you. And the more he wanted me, the more I wanted you.* But all I said was, "I have a present for you."

"Oh, right! Ken's birthday present," Sandy squealed. "What did you finally decide to give him?"
"Me."

Ken did call Sandy, about a week later, and after that I saw very little of her. So it turned out to be a passionately paired summer: Sandy and Braces, Janet and Bones, me and David. It was funny that Sandy never came up with a nickname for David. It was also funny that we didn't triple- or even double-date. We all went our separate ways. I know that Janet spent a lot of weekends and days off at her man's shore home, but she'd call me occasionally when he wasn't sleeping at her place. Sandy all but disappeared. During the day it seemed like Jonathan was always with Sandy's mother or the housekeeper, and Rebecca was at camp. Ken's patients must have been at camp, too. At night, Ken didn't leave Sandy's until the wee hours—"Of course I can't let the children find him here in the morning," Sandy told me during a rare phone call. But it was Janet who told me that Charlie's estate was finally settled and that the insurance company had honored the double-indemnity clause. She had heard it from her mother, who had heard it from her sister, Sylvia, who was Sandy's mother.

I was busy with a steady flow of dessert customers, and real estate agreements and settlements that had been spawned in the spring by families who were moving into the area and wanted to be settled in their new homes before the school year started. And I was busy with David, although I still hadn't shared my revelation with him—that I loved him. What if I told him and he said, "Tess, I'm sorry, but I didn't mean for this to get so serious. I just wanted us to be friends—friends plus sex." What would I do? So I said nothing. I enjoyed our summer together and continued to keep a part of me away from him.

"Why do you think I can't tell him?" I asked Michael the last Tuesday of July—the last Tuesday I'd see Michael until he returned from a weeklong meeting of psychologists in Maine, and then a three-week family vacation in Woodstock, Vermont. ("Clay courts! And grass courts, too," Michael—an avid tennis player—had told me the week before.)

"Why do *you* think you can't tell him?" he answered my question with one of his own.

"You know, Michael, I really hate it when you sound so shrinkish."

"I'm sorry. I didn't mean to sound . . . shrinkish," he said, perceptibly shrinking from the word itself. "I only thought you might have a better idea of why you can't tell him than I have."

"The fact is, you already know why I can't tell him, and you're just waiting for me to figure it out."

"Help me!" he pleaded to the ceiling. "Tell me"—he turned back to me—"why are you still trying to do both our parts? Why don't you make it easy on yourself? You do your part and let me do mine. I promise I won't think you're dumb if you answer a question to which I may already know the answer, if you promise that you won't think I'm dumb if I don't know all the answers you think I know."

"You've got a deal."

"Good. Now we're getting somewhere."

"I'm afraid."

"Of what?"

"I'm afraid of rejection."

"I'll buy that. See how easy this is?" And we both laughed.

And I gave him a big hug when I left and told him to have a good August, and that I'd miss him.

David called to tell me about Stephen's indictment the second Wednesday of September. I thought it interesting that Stephen hadn't called to tell me about it himself, although the truth was he hadn't been in touch much since leaving his practice. Maybe it was because he knew about David and me. Neither of us had told Stephen, but once he left David's office we were more relaxed about our affair. And word gets around.

David had learned of the indictment through legal contacts. The newspaper carried a small item about it the following day. It could be a year or two until the matter would be settled—trial, appeals if necessary—until Stephen would have to go to jail—if he had to, which he probably would, according to David. I called Stephen to tell him how sorry I was. He thanked me for calling, for helping him save his pension. He asked how David was.

"He probably knew all along," David said to me Saturday night over pasta primavera at La Diva, our favorite local Italian restaurant.

"Do you think so? He's never said a word."

"I'm not surprised. Stephen's a funny guy. We were friends and office roomies, but he shared very little of his life with me. Obviously, other than a few mutual ventures, he didn't share much of his business with me either, and he rarely said anything about his personal life. It was a real surprise when you two split the first time, and even more of a surprise when you got back together. What surprised me most was that you and Stephen made it as long as you did."

"Why?"

"Wishful thinking, maybe," he confessed.

"Really? You really thought about me when Stephen and I were together?"

"You didn't know? No, of course you didn't. You were so involved with Stephen."

He rubbed his hand over mine on the table. "There's a poem, Tess, written by Emily Dickinson. It reminds me of you." And he reached into his pocket, took out his wallet, and retrieved from a small compartment under his driver's license a folded, worn piece of paper on which a poem had been handwritten. He gave it to me.

Unfolding it, I began to read it to myself; I continued to look at the paper even as David recited the poem to me word for word:

> "The Soul selects her own Society—
> Then—shuts the Door—
> To her divine Majority—
> Present no more—
>
> Unmoved—she notes the Chariots—pausing—
> At her low Gate—
> Unmoved—an Emperor be kneeling
> Upon her Mat—
>
> I've known her—from an ample nation
> Choose One—
> Then—close the Valves of her attention—
> Like Stone—"

My heart was beating so hard I lost my breath. I thought I'd swoon—yes, swoon, like in ye olde days—as his depth of feeling overwhelmed me. "That's so beautiful . . . and so sad," I said after a quiet time. "And it made you think of me?"

"Because you're beautiful. And because it used to make me sad to see you so closed to loving."

I tried to swallow the lump of feeling that rose in my throat, and managed to ask, "How long have you had that in your wallet?"

"Since the day after I first met you . . . when I fell in love with you."

The lump won. I wanted to embrace David right there in the restaurant and tell him that nobody had ever said anything like that to me before. Nobody had ever made me feel the way I felt just then: loved—in love.

"And? But?" Michael questioned on Tuesday.

"But. But I couldn't move, I couldn't say a word. I sat there and cried without making a sound, holding myself. It was as if the whole world had disappeared, including David, and I was alone with my feelings."

"What were your feelings?"

"Pain. I was hurting. And I couldn't understand where the pain was coming from. Certainly not from David. So it had to be coming from inside, from myself." I waited for Michael to say something, to encourage me to go on, because what I had to say was difficult. For a moment, just a moment, I even foolishly wondered if he would understand. But I was on my own. Michael was going to sit quietly, attentively, and wait for me. "Then I remembered sitting here with you, how I felt loved. And I looked up and saw David sitting back in his chair watching me . . . the way you do . . . but different somehow—he needed me. Only I could bridge the distance between us, I realized. At that moment it was David who was in pain, and all I wanted to do was ease his pain."

"I do love you, David," I said, reaching across the table, putting my hand on his. Grasping my hand, he smiled through pressed lips and nodded slowly. Tears ran into his beard. And we sat there for a long time, feeling relieved and grateful for each other.

When I finished relating the story to Michael, I felt a small sense of loss. "I feel sad, Michael. I feel like I've let something go."

"What's that?"

"I feel that I've moved away from you."

"Part of you has . . . with my blessing."

He leaned over and kissed my forehead, and I understood that nothing had been lost, only changed.

"Do you realize this is the first Sunday brunch we've had in months?" Sandy reminded Janet and me as we settled into our booth at Mykonos on a warm Indian summer morning late in September. Although once we were into our first cups of coffee, it felt like we had never missed a Sunday. But we did have some catching up to do. By now we were all aware that Bones, the chiropractor, had moved into Janet's house. Sandy and I had finally met him—and were reminded that his name was Arthur Segal—at Janet's house Friday night. She had invited us to dinner, an event that also gave Janet an opportunity to meet Ken Briskin. It turned out to be a nice evening. Arthur, not yet married at thirty-seven, was a huge man who looked like he could crack your bones quite literally, but he had a gentle, friendly manner that invited ease. He was clearly mad about Janet, who was clearly mad about him, as was Sean. "Tell me again about the time you ran a sixty-yard touchdown at Temple!" he had begged Arthur on his way to bed after Janet kissed him good-night. Ken was clearly delighted to see me—much to Sandy's chagrin—but he was clearly crazy about Sandy. "I owe you, Tess!" he said to me sometime during the evening while standing behind Sandy, wrapping his arms around her as she squealed, loving the public display of affection as much as the affection that inspired it. He was as affable and charming as I had remembered him to be. And David and I were clearly in love and loving every minute of it.

"Thanks again for dinner, Janet," Sandy said once the coffee was poured and orders were taken. "It was a nice night. Ken thought you all were great."

"It was nice. Thanks, Sandy. Arthur enjoyed it, too. We'll have to do it more often," she replied, understanding, as we all did, that we probably wouldn't do it often at all. But whenever we did do it, it would be nice.

"So what's the story with Arthur? Are you going to get married or anything?" Sandy asked.

"For right now, it's 'anything.' We're very happy just the way we are. I think we're going to play house for a while and then go from there. We both want to be sure. But, between you and me—and not a word to anyone, either of you—I think I can safely say that marriage is a definite possibility."

"Oh, Big Secret!" Sandy teased, disappointed that Janet didn't have any real news to spring on us. "Can you do any better than that, Tess? You and David were positively glooowing!"

"You do have a way of putting things, Sandy."

"So?" Sandy pushed.

"So I'm not divorced yet." What I didn't say was that until that very minute, I hadn't thought of Marriage, and neither had David—at least, he hadn't brought it up. Marriage . . . Tess Ross, I mused.

"Tess, what are you nodding about?" Sandy asked, bringing me back to brunch.

"I was just thinking. . . . Well, Sandy, what's up with you and Ken? You looked very cozy the other night."

"Weeell . . . he really is wild about me. And the kids like him a lot. He's very good with them. He said he always wanted children, but his ex-wife—she's a radiologist—didn't. I think that was one of the reasons for the divorce—besides her affair with the hospital administrator."

"Well, he seems like a sweet guy—and cute. And Tess tells me that he's pretty bright."

"And he's got money," Sandy added. "He drives a Mercedes and he has looots of people working for him in his practice, so he has lots of time off. It's been a great summer. He's taken me everywhere. We even took the kids to Disney World for three days when camp was over. It's sooo nice not having to worry about finances!"

"You went to Florida? That's one I didn't hear about," Janet chimed in.

"Don't feel bad, I didn't know about it either," I said. "So what's it going to be with this guy, Sandy?"

"Oh, I don't know. We're taking it one step at a time. I'm just clearing up all of Charlie's estate business."

"I thought that was taken care of over the summer. Janet said that—"

"That's true, but there were loose ends. Like my attorney, for instance. You wouldn't believe the enooormous bill I got from him just last week. I can't imagine what he does to warrant it. I swear they make it up as they go along."

"Now, now, Sandy, let's not disparage the legal profession," Janet defended.

"I guess with your successful day in court and David's

new standing in Tess's life, we'll never be able to tell another lawyer joke," Sandy agreed.

"We'll just have to pick on doctors," Janet offered in compensation, "but we'll have to be careful to spare orthodontists and chiropractors."

We all laughed at the evanescence of our alliances, and I thought of pears flambé—how hot they burned one day . . . how cold they were the next—and I stopped laughing.

ORANGE BOMBE GLACÉE

Bombe

1 quart vanilla ice cream
1 cup water
1 envelope unflavored gelatin
1 cup sugar
4 tablespoons lemon juice
1 cup orange juice
1 tablespoon grated orange rind
3 egg whites
1 cup heavy cream
candied orange peel
fresh mint leaves

Line a 2 1/2-quart mold with about 1/2 inch of softened vanilla ice cream and place in the freezer.

Sprinkle gelatin over 1/4 cup cold water and let stand for 5 minutes. In a saucepan, mix together 3/4 cup water, sugar, lemon and orange juices, and orange rind. Add the gelatin and heat, stirring, until the gelatin and sugar dissolve. Chill the mixture until it thickens and then beat it to a froth. In a separate bowl, beat the egg whites until stiff peaks form. Fold them into the thickened mixture. Whip the cream until soft peaks form, and fold it into the mixture. Spoon the mixture into the ice-cream-lined mold. Cover with wax paper and freeze for several hours. Unmold and decorate with candied orange peel and mint leaves. Serves 8.

Candied Orange Peel

3 oranges
2 cups sugar
3/4 cup water
3 tablespoons light corn syrup

Peel oranges with a vegetable peeler, removing the colored plus a little of the white part, and cut the peel into 1/8 x 1 1/2-inch strips. Simmer in a pan of water for about 15 to 30 minutes, until tender. Drain and cool.

In a saucepan over low heat, melt 1 cup of sugar in 3/4 cup water and the corn syrup. Add the peel and cook over low heat until much of the syrup has been absorbed, about 15 minutes. Remove from heat, cover, and let stand for an hour, and then drain. Lightly toss the peel in a plastic bag with 1 cup of sugar.

CHAPTER 14

Orange Bombe Glacée

When I was a child, my very favorite summer treat was an orange Creamsicle, a vanilla ice cream Popsicle coated with orange ice. Memories of this cool sweet and its context— Atlantic City shore, hot sun, hot sand, salty air—washed over me like a refreshing ocean wave as I prepared orange mousse for an orange bombe glacée. A frozen dessert of molded vanilla ice cream filled with orange mousse, orange bombe glacée is no more than an inverted Creamsicle. The bombe was to be the finale of Carla Herman's Friday-night dinner party for six at seven-thirty.

I noted it was five to one. I'd made delicate chocolate lace cookies, to be served with the bombe, in the morning; the dome-shaped metal bowl lined with an inch of vanilla ice cream was in the freezer. The dessert would be constructed and frozen solid by five—along with a small one in a custard cup I was making to indulge myself. I'd unmold the bombe glacée onto Carla's silver plate, decorate it with mint leaves and candied orange peel, and have it in her freezer before six, I figured, whipping egg whites to a froth.

Janet had called earlier to ask if I could meet her for lunch at the diner. She had the day off. And, by the way, did I know where Sandy was? she had asked. I hadn't spoken to Sandy for three days. And I was too busy to go out to lunch, but I told her she was welcome to lunch in my kitchen.

I was spooning the orange mousse into the center of the molded ice cream when Janet walked through my back door.

"Wait till you see the shoes I bought at Rosie's!" she said, dropping her pocketbook on the kitchen table, pulling a shoe box from a silver plastic bag imprinted with a black rose logo. The shoes were beautiful. Janet pulled off her sneakers and socks and modeled the sleek high-heeled pumps. "Aren't they wonderful, Tess? Lots of toe cleavage," she said, holding her foot out for me to note the deep V-cut front.

"They're gorgeous. What are they for?"

"My black lace dress. I'm wearing it to Arthur's cousin's wedding next week."

"Great choice. You look wonderful in black," I said, picturing her auburn hair piled on top of her head, setting off the elegant black dress. "You'll be smashing."

"You *do* think it's okay to wear black to a wedding, don't you?"

"Are you kidding? I've heard of at least three weddings in the past year where the entire bridal party wore black and white."

"Next thing you know, brides will be wearing black!" she said.

The sudden memory of a dream I'd had years ago, a week before I married Stephen, sent a chill through me: I was a bride dressed in a long black gown with a long black veil. I have to remember to tell Michael about that, I thought.

"Tess, you look like you've seen a ghost. Are you okay?"

"Do I? I've got to get a little sun on my face. I think I have been pale lately." I finished filling Carla's bombe—and my little one—covered them with plastic wrap, and put them back in the freezer. "Done. Now we can eat."

We sat at the counter nibbling at cold leftover stir-fry right out of the serving dish, sipping coffee, then more coffee while I boxed the lace cookies, and more coffee to wash down pieces of broken cookies. Janet told me she and Arthur were off to the shore for the weekend as soon as Leonard picked up Sean for a rare weekend sleep-over.

"What's the occasion?" I asked.

"Beats me. Every couple of months he gets pangs of guilt, so he asks Sean to spend the weekend with him and The Twit."

"Does Sean like her?"

"It's hard to tell. He doesn't dislike her, but he tells me she's dumb."

"Eleven-year-old boys can be very perceptive."

"And many go downhill from there! Actually, she's nice to Sean, but he says she tries too hard. She tries to do too much for him. I think she embarrasses him. I feel a little sorry for her. She's very young, and Sean says his father doesn't pay much attention to either of them."

"So why does he bother at all?"

"As I said. Guilt—the bond of the absent parent, even the *good* ones. Linda Gordon's husband is just the opposite of Leonard. He'd do anything for his kids from his first marriage. Linda complains that what Jeff would like to do is cut himself up into tiny pieces and feed himself to his children—like fish food. Guilt, Tess."

"Some people don't deserve to have children," I said wistfully, my mind embracing an image of David playing with his nephews, thinking what a good father he'd make; I felt suddenly inadequate as I remembered my mother's admonition, "A man wants children."

"There you go again, Tess! You're pale as a ghost. What's wrong? Are you sure you're all right?"

"I'm fine. I'm fine. I was just thinking—"

"About what?"

"I was just feeling sorry for myself because David would make such a good father and I can't have children." I heard my voice crack.

Janet was off her chair and next to me, hugging me in an instant, and much to my surprise, I was crying like a baby in her arms. "Hey, hey, Tess. What's going on here?" When my sobs ebbed, she pulled away to arm's length, her hands on my shoulders. "You two are going to get married, aren't you!"

"I'm not divorced, Janet, did you forget that?" I said,

sounding a bit testy, annoyed at myself for my uncharacteristic emotional outburst.

"But you want to get married. Right?"

"I don't know what I want. I'm not sure I have the right to marry David. He loves children, Janet."

Janet sat back in her seat. "Have you talked to him about it?"

"Not really. We don't talk about marriage. I think he's waiting for me to bring it up, and I'm not ready to discuss it. He knows I can't get pregnant, though. That was a discussion we had when we stopped using condoms."

"So why aren't you ready?"

The unburdening softened me, and I spilled. "First I've got to get divorced, and what with Stephen's legal problems, I don't think this would be a fair time to ask him to have to deal with a divorce, too. He still views me as a major emotional support."

"You're not going to put your life on hold in consideration of a man who never once considered you, are you?"

"I feel I owe him something, if only not to kick him when he's down."

"You owe him NOTHING!"

"Well, we'll see. I have to tell you, Janet, as much as I think I'd like to settle down with David, as much as I love him, I like my privacy, too. I love it when we're here or I'm at his apartment, but I also like it when I'm home alone, doing . . . whatever. Does that sound weird? Do you think I'm getting old and rigid?"

"We're all getting old and rigid. And no, I don't think you sound weird. Everyone likes their own space now and then. I must confess that sometimes I hide in the bathroom; I sit on the pot with the lid closed just so I can be totally alone for a while. The shower is another hideaway, but you can't stay in the shower very long—the hot water runs out."

"Ah, confessions of a water-closet recluse!"

"Oh, well, we all have our little perversions."

"More coffee?"

"No, thanks. I'm already wired for the day. Tess, is David pushing for you to divorce Stephen?"

"David doesn't push. He's the most laid-back man I've ever met. He seems to understand me so well. And what he doesn't understand, he accepts. Sounds a bit unreal, doesn't he?"

"Sounds like a saint. So, even if he won't push, I will. Get it done, Tess!"

"Look who's pushing. Mrs. I'm-Happy-with-a-Live-in. Well, maybe you and I'll have a double wedding."

"Wouldn't that be a hoot!" Janet cried.

"Hey! We'll include Sandy, too. She and Dr. Perrrfect look pretty serious, too."

"Oh, I don't think Sandy's going to wait that long. Last week I caught her trying on engagement rings in Strawbridge's. 'Just to get an idea . . . in case he asks,' she said. She's as happy as a pig in shit with this guy."

"Well, we can't blame her, Janet. After the men she's been involved with, Ken is heaven-sent."

"And loooaded, as Sandy will tell you."

"Yes. Well, hopefully she'll learn that it's not what she needs from him."

"What *I* need is two days on the beach, and it's supposed to be another gorgeous weekend. The way the weather is going, we could miss autumn altogether," said Janet, carrying her mug and fork to the sink.

"Don't worry. By Halloween it'll be cold. Happens every year. Almost overnight."

"Right. So right now I'm off to pack." She picked up her pocketbook and the bag holding her new shoes, and was on her way. I watched from the back door as she walked to her car. "Listen, Tess," she said, turning toward me, "do something fun with David this weekend. You've got to lighten up. If you feel like visiting us at the shore, just give a ring. On second thought, you don't have to call. We'll either be in the house or dead-ass on the beach. Just come."

Janet's kind offer was accepted gratefully. Saturday morning, David and I drove to Beach Haven, where Arthur owned a two-bedroom bungalow on the beach. It had been built by his uncle and aunt—his father's eldest brother and

sister-in-law—thirty-five years ago. When they had died—
he ten years ago, she six years later—the property was left to
their two sons, who had little interest in Beach Haven. So
Arthur, who had fond memories of bare feet on hot tar roads
and the house that used to be the only house on what used to
be a quiet beach in what used to be a sleepy little shore town,
bought it from his cousins. Beach Haven wasn't as quiet as it
had been thirty years ago, but you could still leave your
doors unlocked when you went to the beach, he told Janet.
He really loved the old bungalow built high up on stilts—
now flanked by two large, contemporary homes of cedar and
glass—a staunch survivor of many storms over the years,
with a real masonry fireplace and a huge picture window
overlooking the beach. In the winter Arthur would go there
when the moon was full over the ocean, build a fire, and
watch the white snow cover the silver sand.

We found Janet and Arthur as she had said—dead-ass on
the beach—at about ten in the morning. It was a bit nippy
when we arrived, but the weatherman had predicted clear
skies with a high of seventy-five to eighty, and by eleven we
were able to shed the jeans and sweatshirts we had worn
over our bathing suits. I felt incredibly tired. I couldn't
remember ever feeling so tired, even though my week hadn't
been particularly stressful or busy. So I took advantage of
the soft sand and the warm sun, and dozed in and out as the
sound of the ocean pulled me back to my childhood. And I
half dreamed, half remembered the time when I was playing
near the edge of the water and a huge wave engulfed me, and
I tumbled over and over and over until I didn't know which
way was up, and water was in my mouth and my ears and
my eyes, and I couldn't breathe and I was scared. . . . And
then I half remembered, half dreamed the dream I used to
have when I was a child, where I would be engulfed by a
huge, dark wave at twilight, and I would tumble over and
over and over until I didn't know which way was up, and
water was in my mouth and my ears and my eyes, and I had
to take a breath . . . and I found I could breathe underwater,
like a fish . . . like an unborn babe.

That evening we feasted on hot dogs grilled on a hibachi

on the tiny back deck, and homemade potato salad. After helping to polish off two bottles of wine, David and I graciously accepted Arthur's invitation to stay through Sunday—after offering the obligatory "Oh, we couldn't impose on your hospitality any more," and throwing in the empathetic "You two came here to be alone!"—because after all, we allowed them to convince us, all that wine, and the late hour, and Sunday would be another glorious day. And it was.

Monday was an entirely different story.

"I told you it would get cold by Halloween," I reminded Janet on the phone Monday night, after a gray, drizzly, sixty-degree day, dropping to forty at night, with a five-day forecast of more of the same.

"But there are still two weeks until Halloween."

"And it's still not *cold,* just miserably cool."

"I'm not ready for this, Tess. Neither is Sean. Either it's the weather or he's coming down with something. He's been lethargic since he came home from Leonard's last night. Listen, did you hear from Sandy while we were away? I tried to reach her today and she's still not home. I called Aunt Sylvia, but nobody was home there either."

"Not a word."

Tuesday was an entirely different story.

"Hellooo!" It was Sandy on the phone, awakening me at nine in the morning.

I had overslept. How I hate gray weather, I thought, feeling as gray as the day. "Sandy! Where were you? Janet and I were getting worried."

"Not to worry. What are you doing for lunch? I have neeews! I have something to show you!"

"You're engaged!"

"Nope! Come to lunch and I'll tell all. Janet can make it at twelve-thirty for about half an hour."

I had a settlement scheduled for eleven-thirty that I figured would take about an hour. Leaving room for snags, I told Sandy to meet Janet and that I'd get there as soon as I could.

There were snags. I arrived at Mykonos at one. Sandy and Janet had finished their Greek salads and Janet was half out of the booth when I walked up the aisle. She fell back into her seat when she saw me, folded her arms on her chest, and smiled mysteriously.

"So what's the news?" I questioned as I slipped into the seat next to Sandy, who was suddenly coy.

Janet dropped the bomb: "Sitting next to you, for the first time anywhere, is Mrs. Kenneth Briskin."

I was speechless. "What!" Well, almost speechless.

"See!" was all Sandy said, thrusting her left hand in front of me, the ring finger of which bore a sparkling circlet of chunky round diamonds.

"I'm speechless!" I said. "When did this happen? Where? You didn't tell us? This really *is* news!" Well, almost speechless.

"This is where I came in," said Janet, sliding out of the booth, taking the check with her. "This one's on me, Sandy. Congratulations!" Janet leaned over to kiss Sandy after I had kissed Sandy and moved to Janet's seat.

"Okay," I said, once Janet had gone, "tell me all!"

And Sandy related a story of true love, passion, security —the whole ball of wax—and how she and Ken felt there was no reason to wait, that they both had wasted too many years already, and that if you don't know The Real Thing after three months, you wouldn't know it after three years. Did I detect an oblique reference to me and David in that statement? I wondered. I decided I was being paranoid and that Sandy was only trying to justify her own impulsive behavior.

". . . sooo," she continued, belying my defense of her, "maybe you were wise in not getting a quick divorce to marry David. There must be reasons for your putting it off. I think you would know by now if it was The Real Thing. After all, Tess, you've known David for yeeears."

What I couldn't understand was how we'd got to talking about me and David when she obviously had sooo much to tell me about herself and Ken. I ordered a BLT on toast and some coffee, and then, ignoring Sandy's comments about my relationship, asked her if her elopement had been sudden or planned, if anyone had known about it.

"I guess it was sort of sudden. The only people who knew were my parents and Ken's mother and sister. And we only told them a week before."

"What did your parents say?"

"They were real happy for me. After all I've been through, I think they were glad to see me settled. And they absolutely looove Ken."

"And his mom?"

"She was just happy he was happy. And, being a widow herself, she understood why I didn't want a fancy wedding."

A fancy wedding they didn't have. They had been married Friday morning by Ken's rabbi in Philadelphia. Ken's mother and sister and brother-in-law, Sandy's parents, and Rebecca and Jonathan were the only guests. They all went to dinner afterward at the Four Seasons Hotel, and then Sandy and Ken stayed at Ken's townhouse for the weekend. The real honeymoon—three weeks touring Europe—was to take place next spring, she explained. "You know, those things take time to plan, Tess."

"Well. I'm thrilled for you. You look radiantly happy, and Ken certainly seems like a terrific guy. But I have to admit I'm a little hurt that you never said a word to me. I would have loved to have seen you get married, and I'm sure Janet would have, too. Why the secrecy?"

"I was afraid to say anything. I didn't know how everyone would react. You know"—she lowered her voice—"some people could get jealous."

"Who are 'some people'?"

"Well, I'm sure Janet would love to marry Arthur. And I'm not so sure how you would have taken it. I mean, you'd probably say that it hasn't been very long since Charlie died . . . and that I don't know Ken very well. . . ."

And the further she went, the further behind I followed,

far enough behind to see that the distance that had come between us was not going to be made up easily, maybe never.

". . . You understand what I'm saying, don't you, Tess?"

Better I shouldn't get entangled in what she made out to be interpersonal conflicts, but which were, in fact, self-conflict, I thought. I told her that the only thing that was important was that *she* understand. I meant that. I wished her happiness. I meant that, too.

The following Sunday, we tried Sunday brunch all together—the six of us. After we had greeted each other, and Janet and I had kissed Ken and welcomed him into "the family," and Arthur and David had kissed Sandy and given Ken hearty handshakes, Janet said that she had news—Big News. "Sean's going to be a brother," she announced.

We all looked at her agape, not knowing what to say, not sure if this Big News was good news or bad news.

She quickly helped us. "No, no! Not me! The Twit! The Twit is pregnant! She told Sean over the weekend that he's going to have a baby brother or sister—which is probably why he was acting so funny when he came home, Tess. Sean finally told me yesterday."

"But I thought they had an agreement not to have children," I said.

"They did. What poetic justice! One of life's luscious little ironies! I can't wait to talk to old F.F. and congratulate him."

"F.F.?" Ken questioned.

"Fuckface—her ex-husband," Sandy explained with an affectation of disapproval.

The men were blown away by the appellation, and they listened in awe as Sandy, Janet, and I each tossed our own sentiments regarding Janet's baby-in-law-to-be into the cauldron of ill will.

"Maybe she'll have twins!" Sandy offered. "And I hope she knows enough to ask for a full-time housekeeper."

"Not a chance," Janet answered. "Sean tells me she scrubs the kitchen floor herself—on her knees. But twins. Now, there's a possibility. Twins run in Leonard's family."

"A touch of colic would be nice," said Sandy.

"Oh, for sure!" Janet agreed. "Sean was a colicky baby. It almost drove Leonard out of the house."

"I think they should have a girl," I added my own evil. "That means he'll have to pay for a bat mitzvah *and* a wedding!"

"*If* The Twit sends her to Hebrew school," Janet interjected. "But she'll probably have the baby baptized. Leonard would go mad! And his parents would disinherit him! Oh, what a splendid idea."

The men were rapt. David alone was heard mumbling something.

"What?" We turned to him.

"Eye of newt, and toe of frog, wool of bat, and tongue of dog," he repeated with a wicked smile. "It's an old family recipe."

Although Janet had appeared positively thrilled at brunch, and as things, and people, aren't always as they appear, I wasn't surprised to hear her later express at least a little hurt that Leonard had deserted one family to start another, at least a little anger that Leonard's new child might rob Sean of what little attention he was receiving from his father, as well as his inheritance, and at least a little anxiety that Leonard's financial responsibility to his new child might prompt him to ask the courts to decrease his responsibility to Sean. "You'll cross those bridges when you come to them," I said, trying to ease her fears. "Just tell me why it is that I always have bridges to cross. For once I'd like to feel my feet on solid ground long enough to get my balance," she answered.

But her fears soon took a backseat to her delight with the ensuing events related to the baby-in-law-to-be. More Big News was served at brunch the following Sunday, a meal the men chose to skip. "Guess who called ME?" Janet started, and didn't wait for a response. "Old F.F. himself. The man must be absolutely at his wits' end to call ME." And Janet told of Leonard's plea for help, for friendship in his time of betrayal. "I suppose Sean told you . . ." he had started. "Obviously," Janet interpreted to us, "that's what he had in mind when he invited Sean for the weekend." The Twit, said Janet, had tricked Leonard into getting her pregnant—according to Leonard. We all wondered what, sometime later, a judge would wonder: Shouldn't an obstetrician know about birth control? The fact that he couldn't reasonably oversee his wife's taking her pill every day was a loose end that we, The Jury, chose to brush aside, as would the judge sometime later when Leonard would make a public discussion of his private problems. Janet said that Leonard had threatened to have the marriage annulled unless The Twit submitted to an abortion. She had refused. His attorney told him he didn't have a case. He cried to Janet that she was the only one who could understand. And in an effort to evoke a sympathetic response from his former mate, Leonard had instead delivered the most damning provocation: *"You know how I am."* He had begged Janet to talk with his present wife, to convince her that an abortion would be best. "It would be better for all concerned, including Sean," he had said to Janet. "I'm not going to live forever. Wouldn't you like to see Sean get everything he's entitled to?"

"Can you imagine!" Janet said to us.

"What did you say to him?" Sandy asked.

"I said, 'Thanks for thinking of us, Leonard. Don't worry, I'll talk to her. I *do* know how you are.'"

Tuesday night Janet called to tell me that she had received another phone call—from The Twit!

"So, what did you tell her?"

"I didn't have to tell her a thing. She told me! Leonard told her he was going to divorce her and give her and the baby nothing because she had broken their agreement. Of course, she swore that she hadn't missed a pill. Then she said that—wait until you hear this!—she said that Leonard was always crying about how I had raked him over the coals, took him for everything he had, stripped him bare . . . so she called me to get the name of my lawyer!"

"That's wonderful! Did you give it to her?"

"Of course!"

Later, a judge—with a raised eyebrow—would conclude that "even a man with only a law school degree knows that it takes two to have a baby," and that Leonard would be financially responsible for his offspring. This was after Leonard, embittered and embarrassed among his peers, had left his home, and after The Twit had delivered a healthy baby girl and was well into a romantic relationship with the obstetrical resident who had assisted in the delivery—a young single man who, initially, took pity on the young thing who had been taken advantage of by an older, heartless man, and who, finally, was taken in by her. "All's well that ends well, Tess," Janet would say. Ending well, in this case as in most, having more to do with one man's getting what he deserved than justice for all.

Thursday morning I awoke from a disturbing dream of confusion and nausea—something about trying to find something or somebody . . . running back and forth between two houses . . . growing weary and dizzy—to David's gentle hand on my arm. "You okay?" he asked as I rubbed my eyes, trying to gain balance in a bed that refused to be steady. But it was my extra-firm Sealy Posturepedic, not David's water bed. So why was it moving? What felt like a fist in my stomach gave me the answer that I didn't take time to contemplate, and I bolted from the bed to the bathroom and heaved whatever was left from Wednesday night's linguine and clams into the toilet. David was but a step behind me, holding my head, making calming sounds, sounds I hadn't heard since I was a little girl. When I was through, he gave me a glass of water and helped me back to bed. "I guess you're not okay," he said, trying to sound chipper, but sounding concerned instead.

"Do I feel hot to you?" I asked him.

He put his hand on my neck, his lips to my forehead. "Nope. I don't think you have any fever. Maybe a touch of food poisoning, though." And we reviewed our dinner at La Diva, discovering that we had eaten nothing in common but the salad. "So it wasn't the salad," he concluded, desperate to be helpful.

David made me tea and toast with jelly, and when he saw I was beginning to perk up he showered and dressed and left for his office. He called almost hourly, and I told him I was fine, just very tired. And I promised that I'd call the doctor if I wasn't feeling better by the next morning, and he said he'd stay over again that night, but I told him that I was going to bed early and it would be better if he slept at home.

Friday morning was a repeat of the morning before. I called my gynecologist—the only doctor I had—hoping for some over-the-phone remedy, but he told me I should come in to see him, reminding me that my last checkup had been more than a year ago and that we might as well get everything checked out at once. Just what I'm in the mood for, I thought, a pelvic, a rectal . . . shit. Why hadn't I just called the pharmacist? I thought, poised over the toilet.

David arrived about five-thirty. He had called several times during the day—before and after I'd visited Dr. Ebert—and after I told him that Dr. Ebert said I was going to be fine, he told me that he'd be over as soon as he could leave the office.

"How's my patient?" he asked, walking into the family room, finding me bundled in an afghan on the sofa. "Not too good I see," he said, noting a *Brady Bunch* rerun on the television. "Down to rock bottom. It looks like I arrived just in time!" he said, pulling a quart of his mother's homemade chicken soup (for me), a corned beef sandwich (for him), and two Sherlock Holmes videotapes from the grocery bag he was carrying. Just what the doctor ordered, I thought. And he sat down beside me and kissed me and held me, and told me that he loved me and that he was going to take care of me.

"But who's going to make the coffee cakes for Joanne Freed's Saturday-morning meeting?" I teased.

"Take me to your kitchen. I'm a fast teach."

"Just kidding. Joanne said the coffee cakes I have in the freezer will be fine. She didn't want anything fancy. She's only having some of her neighbors in to discuss putting up a light at the corner of Dogwood and Red Oak," I said, holding him close.

"Yep. That's a bad corner. So. What exactly did Ebert say was wrong? Did he think it was something you ate?"

"Not exactly. But he said I'll be fine," I said, and then picked up the ringing telephone.

"Hello, Tess?" It was Janet. Were we doing anything tonight? Maybe we could go to dinner or a movie, she suggested.

"I'm not feeling great, Janet. A touch of something. David's here with chicken soup and a couple of old movies and . . . yes, he is a sweetheart," I said to her, looking at David. "Listen, we'll all have brunch Sunday. Call Sandy. Okay? . . . Good. See you Sunday."

"You will come Sunday morning, won't you?" I asked David.

"Sure. Anything you'd like. Got to keep up on the really important news!"

"You're horrible!"

"I'm sorry."

"No, you're not."

"Yes, I am. Want me to show how sorry I am?" he said, leering at me.

"Later," I answered, getting warm all over, blushing. Blushing! Oooh, what this man does to me! I thought.

I ate the chicken soup and a quarter of David's sandwich. He ate the rest of the sandwich. We fought for the pickle. He won. "Not with your tender stomach," he insisted.

"Now for dessert," I announced, getting up from the sofa for the first time since David had walked into the house. From the freezer, I took the mini orange bombe glacée that I had made three weeks before and had forgotten about, and then discovered when I was looking for the coffee cakes for Joanne.

"That looks interesting. What is it?" David asked when I brought the unmolded bombe into the family room.

"It's a bombe," I said, setting it on the coffee table before us. "It's one of my favorite desserts."

"It's a very small bombe," he pouted. "Am I going to get any of it?"

"Nope," I answered, suddenly struck by a pun, "it's all for me. I have a rather large *bomb* for you."

"Oh?" He looked appropriately puzzled.

"David," I started, wrapping my arms around him, "a most remarkable thing has happened. . . . We're going to have a baby."

KILLER CAKE
(CHOCOLATE CHIP FUDGE CAKE)

FROM: Commissary Restaurant, Philadelphia

Cake

6 ounces unsalted butter
6 ounces unsweetened chocolate, chopped
6 eggs
3 cups sugar
1/2 teaspoon salt
1 tablespoon vanilla extract
1 1/2 cups flour
1 1/2 cups chocolate chips

Preheat the oven to 350°F. Grease two 9 x 1 1/2-inch cake tins and line bottoms with wax or parchment paper.

MIX CAKE BY HAND. Melt butter and unsweetened chocolate together over simmering water. Cook to lukewarm. In a large bowl whisk together for 1 minute the eggs, sugar, salt, and vanilla. Whisk in the butter-chocolate mixture. Stir in flour and chocolate chips. Pour batter into prepared pans and bake for 30 to 35 minutes. Do not overbake; cake tester should not come out clean. Cool on racks and remove from pans as soon as cooled.

Frosting

1 1/4 cups sugar
2 tablespoons instant coffee
1 cup heavy cream
5 ounces unsweetened chocolate, finely chopped
4 ounces unsalted butter
1 1/2 teaspoons vanilla extract

Combine sugar, coffee, and cream in a small, deep, heavy saucepan. Stirring, bring to a boil. Reduce heat and simmer 6 minutes without stirring. Remove from heat. Add chopped chocolate and stir until it is melted and blended. Add butter and vanilla. Whisk well. Chill until mixture begins to thicken.

Assembly

Put one cake layer bottom-side-up on a cake plate. Spread with one-third of frosting. Top with second layer, also bottom-side-up. Trim the circumference of the cake. Pour all but 1/2 cup of the frosting on top of cake, spreading it over top and sides. Put the reserved icing into a pastry bag fitted with a small star tip and pipe 16 rosettes around top of cake. Refrigerate if not serving immediately, but bring to room temperature before serving. Serve with lightly sweetened whipped cream. Serves 16.

CHAPTER 15

Killer Cake

"I couldn't have conceived of the kind of feelings I've been experiencing, Michael," I said on Tuesday morning, punning unintentionally.

He smiled at me but said nothing, allowing me to bubble unimpeded.

"I mean, I used to say I wanted to be happy, but I didn't really know what *happy* meant. And David! Well, you should see him! He's insane with happiness! He can't do enough for me. I think he'd like to pick me up and carry me around inside himself. Can you picture it? A big, blond mama kangaroo!"

Michael sat nodding, smiling, beaming—a mother hen watching her newly hatched chick, I mused, not missing the influx of maternal metaphors suffusing my thoughts. "And I was so surprised!" I continued. "I know that sounds strange, but with my history of infertility . . . and my periods have always been irregular so when I miss one, I don't think anything of it . . . and I figured I was gaining weight because I was relaxed, and happy with David—not to mention eating a lot of my own desserts!"

Michael chuckled.

"And when I called my mother, she was so excited about being a grandmother she didn't even mention my marital status! She said she'll be up here this weekend . . ."

Michael nodded and threw me a thumbs-up.

". . . and she said she may consider moving up north. I'm not sure how I feel about that, but I think it's interesting that she'd move away from me but she'll come back for my baby. . . . Well, she's not doing it yet, so I'm not going to think about it."

When I was quiet, Michael asked, "And how did your friends react to your wonderful news?"

"We all met at the diner for Sunday brunch—I'm sure that doesn't surprise you. And even though I was feeling queasy and looked like hell, something must have been shining through, because the minute I sat down in our booth, Janet said, 'Tess, what's up? You look positively ethereal!'" And I recounted to Michael how, when I told the gathered that I was pregnant, Janet practically dove across the table to hug me, all pink-faced and squealing, which made me turn pink and squeal along with her . . . and how Arthur, grinning a bigger grin than the one he displays while describing his sixty-yard touchdown, leaned over and hugged me and Janet together . . . and how they relinquished me to Ken, who was sitting to my left . . . while David, who was on my right, sat back thoroughly enjoying the hug-in, gratefully accepting the handshakes and kisses he deserved as the expectant father.

"Sandy wasn't there?" Michael asked.

"Sandy was there."

"Oh. You didn't mention her."

"Aha! You noticed." And I related to Michael how, while five at our booth were pink and squealing, one alone was pale and silent: Sandy. Until, when the gush had subsided, she said, dripping with affectation, "Well! That *is* news, Tess. I can't believe you didn't call me! I mean, here we all are being so excited and . . . well, is this what you two want? I mean, well, we're so pleased for you, I hope *you're* pleased with your news." And how her patronizing posture momentarily damped the exhilaration of the moment. Until Janet saved the day. "Of course it's what she wants!" she defended me. "It's what she's always wanted!" And Sandy sputtered, "I was just trying to be sensitive to Tess's feelings. . . . Tess knows I'm really happy if she is. Right, Tess?"

"Sandy was jealous," Michael said.

"Sandy was jealous," I confirmed.

"I guess that made you pretty angry."

"Not me. You know I don't get angry."

He laughed in my face. "Oh, I forgot with whom I'm conversing—my placid petunia."

"Okay. So maybe I was a little annoyed."

"A little annoyed. HAH! I'll bet you wanted to punch her out!"

"Close," I admitted, giving in, laughing with him. "Now, you have to understand that I figured she might be jealous—not of my pregnancy, but of the attention I'd get. In fact, on the way to the diner I said to David, 'Watch Sandy. She's not going to be so happy.' And he thought I was being unfair."

"You think she's not happy for you?"

"It's not that. Sandy filters everything through her own little world. She sees others' lives only in terms of her role, or her imagined role. And she doesn't have a very big role in this scenario. Am I making sense?"

"I understand. Do you think that means she doesn't care?"

"I don't *care* if she cares."

"Well, I guess it's not really important," Michael said, dismissing the importance of Sandy with a yawn and a shrug.

I was learning that when Michael said something wasn't important, it meant that he thought I might not have considered how important it really might be. I set him straight. "Of course Sandy's important, Michael. She's a friend. But she's not perfect, just like my mother isn't perfect, and David isn't perfect . . . and you're not perfect. Of course," I allowed, "some are less imperfect than others."

Michael smiled.

I continued rather pretentiously, "If I want to be friends with Sandy, I have to accept her imperfections . . . just as she'll have to accept mine. Although I must admit that lately I've found her hard to take, which makes me feel guilty. . . . Anyway, who knows—she could decide she doesn't want to be friends *with me!* Of course, *we* know, in that case, that it would be because *she* doesn't understand what's important."

Michael kept smiling at me.

"I'm rambling, aren't I?"

"You're great. You're just great. And you're going to be a mommy."

"Right," I replied, turning inward for a moment, enjoying the thought. And then, "I'm going to be a mommy, and David's going to be a daddy, and you . . . well, Michael, I've had some interesting thoughts about you since I've become pregnant."

"Is that right?"

"Yes. I have to tell you, one of my first considerations was where you fit into all this . . . where to put you. . . . I mean, if it hadn't been for you, David and I might never have gotten together, and so I feel you played a big part in my having this baby. At first I thought maybe I'd like you to be the baby's godfather—your surrogate-father role notwithstanding, you're not exactly its grandfather. For one thing, you're too young." We both laughed. "And then I wasn't sure if *godfather* was right, either. What I'm trying to say is that when I thought about it all—me and David and the baby and you—I kept wondering, 'What's wrong with this picture?' You see, as much as I know you care, Michael, I don't expect that you're going to come over to our house and take little Bambino to the zoo. And I don't expect you'll want me to call you every time Bambino gets a new tooth or says a new word. Of course, maybe you'll want to see a picture of us all every few years? But I won't expect that you'll send me a picture of *your* family. All of which made me think of some of our earlier discussions . . . about our unequal friendship . . . about you being a *paid* friend. And I decided that there was some validity to my feelings. Michael, you *are* paid, and our relationship *is* unequal. But now I understand that my discomfort was not with the relationship we have, it was with my perception of it and what I thought it should be. I didn't understand the Therapy Thing. I didn't believe that I could get what I needed from you without your falling in love with me . . . without your thinking that I was uniquely unique, truly special—and it goes without saying that I couldn't think of myself as that special. Intellectually I knew that every person is unique, and, in my own inimitably convoluted way of thinking, I felt that if all people are unique or special then there is nothing special about being special, and that if there is nothing special about being special then you'd have no reason to care especially for me, which only reinforced my feeling unworthy of love. . . . Are you following this?"

Michael was sitting forward in his chair, listening intently with his hands enmeshed under his chin. But he said nothing, which made me feel like I was onto something important.

I continued. "You know, I think I'm solving a mystery here."

No reaction. Or did I detect a trace of a smile?

"Well, until now I just couldn't put together what I felt and what you said, and I kept throwing the *paid friend* bit up to you as if it implied insincerity. . . . Did you ever read Frost's poem about 'boughten friendships'?"

He didn't answer.

"Well, anyway," I continued, deciding that Michael was not at this moment interested in my intellect, but my guts. "You *do* care," I continued, "but not in the way that I thought I needed you to care."

He nodded silently.

"Here, in this room, you let me know that you understand who I am, Michael. You introduced me to me, to that part of me that is not unique but is like everyone else—my guts—and also to that part of me that *is* unique—warts and all, as they say. I guess part of my problem was that I couldn't understand how you could love *all* your warty clients, but that you'd have to in order to help them. So I believed that for a fee you effected a model of loving them, like following a recipe from a book, a model that was good enough to fool them into thinking that you really did love them. And that seemed so dishonest. But what I now know is that you connect with them on a level where we're all equals—at the gut. You could call it a *psycho-umbilical cord."* I smiled. He didn't. I continued, "Now I understand that you don't have to *love* them, not in the popular sense of the word. Does this sound at all religious to you, Michael?"

He ignored my question. "Who is *them?"* he asked.

My face reddened, but I pushed on. *"ME,* Michael. I guess I'm talking about *me.* What I'm really trying to say is that I didn't need you to *love* me, Michael, I only needed you to care good enough—to do a good enough job as therapist— so that I know what it feels like to be loved, to show *me* how to love me, so that I could let someone else love me . . . someone like David . . . and so I could love him. You did that for me. And for that I love *you*—in the popular sense of the word . . . in the popular but unromantic sense of the word . . . well, maybe a little romantic, but we've been through all that before, haven't we?"

Michael smiled.

"I know that I'll always consider you my baby's godfather in a sense, but that *you* don't need that, and my baby won't need that. Does all of this make sense to you, Michael?"

"What you're saying is that you didn't understand how it all fit together and worked, and now you do."

I nodded slowly. "Do you know what you are, Michael? You're a catalyst. You make some extraordinary changes occur, and then you simply drop out of the picture un-changed."

"You think I'm unchanged?"

"Well, I suppose I have had some effect on you, if only by further confirming your abilities as a therapist by being a successful client. And I suppose that you could have learned something new by learning about me . . . because I am unique . . . something that could help to make you even better at what you already do so well, or maybe even something that could serve you in your personal life. Because we are all unique, we do all learn from each other, don't we?"

"Yes."

"So I guess I can feel pretty good about being good enough to do something good for you."

He smiled.

I gloated silently at my arrogance, feeling quite equal for just a moment. And then I remembered the rest of my agenda. "Michael, I have to tell Stephen about the baby. I have to ask him for a divorce, a quick divorce." I tried to explain to Michael how loathsome a task this was for me, knowing that I'd be confronting Stephen at a time when it looked like he could lose everything, while I had it all, and I'd be asking him for more . . . for blood. "I'll feel like a vulture picking at his bones!" I cried.

"Some of my best friends are bone-pickers," Michael teased.

I told him he sounded like Janet, who had asked me why I couldn't take pleasure in the deed. Why I couldn't savor the moment. "After all he's done to you! You should tell him in the middle of Veterans Stadium, thumbing your nose for the close-up camera!" she had said to me on the phone Monday evening. "You should take a full-page ad in *The Philadelphia Inquirer:* DEAR STEPHEN, I WANT A DIVORCE SO I CAN MARRY YOUR ONLY FRIEND AND HAVE HIS BABY. LOVE, TESS."

"Sounds like Janet has some great ideas. Did she happen to mention billboards, or skywriting?" Michael asked.

"Very funny. You know, you're being hateful."

"I'm being hateful? Well, maybe you're right. After all, Stephen's been such a nice guy—"

"Now you're being sarcastic."

"Hmm. I can't seem to get it right today, can I? So I'll be quiet. Tell me what you think you should do."

I understood his point—the one he didn't have to verbalize. "I have to ask Stephen for a divorce," I said, adding, for my own justification, "but I have to do it my way—with kindness."

"Just remember to be kind to yourself," Michael said, with kindness.

* * *

On the way home from Michael's office, I tried to think of exactly what I was going to say when I called Stephen. No. I couldn't ask him for a divorce over the phone. It had to be done face to face. So. Location would be the most important factor, I decided. The Location Thing was a spin-off of my real estate training, it seemed; it was a displacement of priorities in an effort to relieve anxiety, in fact. So a silly but functional inner monologue ensued regarding Where To Tell Him. I didn't want to tell him in my house, which used to be *our* house; someplace public would be better. But not a restaurant; too many people. I was going to show a house on Thursday—north of here, near a park with a lake. It was quiet, open, familiar. I'd ask him to meet me in the parking lot at the lookout. Yes. Perfect.

Wanting to *getitoverwith,* I called Stephen as soon as I got home,before starting to prepare a chocolate Killer Cake for Andrea Snelling's husband's birthday dinner that night.

Harold Snelling was a chocolate freak and nothing, absolutely nothing, would do for his birthday except a Killer Cake, Andrea had insisted. A dense, fudgy cake laden with chocolate chips and covered with a rich chocolate fudge frosting, Killer Cake can do in all but the most extraordinary sweet tooth, according to ardent fans of the famous Philadelphia dessert. But Harold was up to it, Andrea had said. I told her I charged extra if my face broke out or I gained more than five pounds within three days of making it. We had laughed again.

My telephone conversation with Stephen was more somber. I told him I had to talk to him, that Thursday would be good, that I would meet him on the hill overlooking the lake at one o'clock. Yes, he knew where I meant, but why couldn't he come to the house? he asked. "Please indulge me," I appealed. "Sure," he said, sounding incapable of putting up a fight.

My mission accomplished, I set a large ceramic bowl next to the ingredients for the cake on the island counter and began the blending process—by hand with a large wire whisk. As I slowly whisked together the eggs, sugar, melted chocolate and butter, vanilla, salt, flour, and chocolate chips, I was taken by the richness of the mixture . . . by the name of the cake. *Killer Cake,* I thought, picturing a diner dying of pleasure while eating a slice . . . a glutton dying of suffocation while trying to stuff the whole thing down . . . diabetic Stephen dying of it, I thought, an unnamed rage whipping through me. . . .

Later that afternoon, Stephen slipped into the kitchen and spied the Killer Cake sitting on a white pedestal plate in the middle of the counter. He ran his finger through the sweet, buttery icing on top of the cake, sucked it off his finger. He picked at the crumbs on the delicate white doily at the base of the cake and licked them from his fingers. He stuck his fingers into the side of the cake, gouged out a frosted chunk riddled with sugary chocolate chips, and pushed it into his mouth, repeating the cranelike motion over and over until he had devoured the whole thing. I watched him turn pale, ashen, sweaty, as the infusion of sugar flooded his bloodstream. And then I watched as a glistening redness, starting at his feet—he wasn't wearing socks—traveled up his body, indicating his rising blood-sugar level. I watched his ankles redden . . . his hands . . . wrists . . . and then his neck extending from his starched white shirt. And then his face turned red and started to bloat. His eyes and mouth formed great O's as his head swelled like a balloon, growing bigger and redder until it exploded with a mighty KABOSH! leaving his limp body to fall on the white tile floor, spattering it with blood.

. . . What an image! Janet would love that one, I thought, tittering ever so slightly at my morbid sense of justice, at my ability to mete it out so excessively in my fantasies. I continued to whisk, watching the thick batter fold over and into itself. Voluptuous, I thought. This is a voluptuous cake. I'm voluptuous, I thought, voluptuously pregnant. Passionate, I thought, breathing in the sweet, heavy perfume of chocolate. This is a cake of passion. And my heart started to pound as I felt passion rush through me, awakening lust.

And I laughed aloud at myself, at my mercurial emotions, wishing that David would walk in just then.

Standing on the edge of the precipice, Stephen looked smaller than I would have described him. He was short, I noted, surprised that I hadn't seen him as *short* before. He was no more than five-foot-six, though he always claimed to be five-foot-eight. And he was slight—slim-shouldered and -hipped, thin-armed and -legged. But his tummy spilled over the waist of his designer jeans, puffed out his yellow knit pullover shirt. Standing round-shouldered, sway-backed, his posture suggested that of a small boy. Is this what happens to us when we are defeated? Do we become children again? Are we really just children blown up into grown-ups by success? Are we deflated by defeat like pricked balloons?

He had arrived before me and was looking down toward the lake. He looked painfully alone. I felt that if I approached him, touched him, instead of easing his aloneness I would become a part of it. We would be two people isolated from others, and no less isolated from each other. "What's in your head?" I asked, standing a few feet from him.

"Nothing," he responded without turning.

"You must be thinking about something."

"No. Not really. Look down there, Tess. Look at the lake and the blond trees."

Blond trees? I stepped closer to him, close enough to see over the edge of the cliff, to see what he saw below. The huge oval lake was as still and reflective as a mirror, the near end edged by willows, their autumn gold-leafed branches tossing in the breeze like hair—yes, like a woman's blond hair being brushed in front of a mirror, I fancied. Every now and then the sun would flash in the giant mirror, momentarily blinding voyeurs. *"Blond* trees?" I queried.

"They look like heads of hair, don't you think? What a sexy bitch that Mother Nature is. A real siren. Now, there's a lady I'd like to do."

"I think with Mother Nature it wouldn't be you who does the doing," I played along.

"Maybe. But what a way to go—sucking on The Big Tit, getting sucked into the center of being."

"You want to be God, don't you? You want to be able to control everything," I said.

He turned on me. "You've been spending too much time with that shrink of yours, Tess," he said. "He's got your head filled with a shitload of psychobabble. Or is it David who's making you so self-righteous?"

I backed away. This wasn't going to be easy, I realized. "Stephen, let's not be angry with each other. We've been doing pretty good for the last few months."

"I'm sorry," he apologized, looking forlorn again. "So tell me, why did you want me to meet you? What's going on?"

"I have something to tell you, Stephen. And something to ask."

"Whatever you want. I've told you that before."

"I want a divorce, Stephen. I was going to wait until—"

"A divorce? You're asking me for a divorce? Now? I thought we had things settled, arranged. I thought we agreed—"

"I agreed to help you, but I never agreed to stay married."

"No. Something's going on here. What is it, Tess?" he asked with growing hostility, stepping toward me as he attacked.

And I retreated, away from the edge of the cliff, until my back was against a large oak.

"Remember, Tess, I *know* you! I want the truth!" he yelled.

"David and I are getting married," I blurted out.

"Yes. Of course, that's it," he said, looking struck. "But I'm surprised, Tess, surprised you couldn't wait until I got my head above water. For God's sake, can't you see I'm drowning!"

"Stephen—"

"Revenge, Tess? Is that what this is all about? It's not like you. David's put you up to this, hasn't he? Sweet, mild-mannered David . . . two-faced prick!"

"It's not like that, Stephen. Really. Let me explain," I begged, trying to appease, to ease the turmoil that gripped him.

"I *need* you, Tess. Don't you understand how much I—"

"I'm pregnant, Stephen."

His body tensed. He looked like a trapped animal, I thought, continuing to talk, hoping to defuse his reaction: "I hope you can be happy for me. . . ."

He flinched.

I'm not doing this right! screamed in my head. ". . . You know it's what I've always wanted, Stephen . . . what I wanted for *us*, but—"

"That's not what you wanted!" he lashed out, taking hold of my forearms, frightening me. "You know what you wanted from me? This!" he yelled, sliding his hands to my wrists, pulling my left hand into his crotch. *"This* is all you really wanted from me!" He pushed the heel of my hand into the softness of his genitals until I could feel the stirrings of an erection. I was aroused by the feel of him, by the hardening of his body, the softening of his eyes. And arousal displaced fear. The slackening of my body, the slight parting of my lips gave me away, strengthened him, set his teeth. His eyes lost the softness that had staved off my fear of him. It seemed a moment frozen, a freeze-frame, our facing each other, raw with feeling. I thought I'd faint from the overwhelming realness of it. What happens now? What do you do when the quake begins, when it's all erupting to the surface, when it can't be pushed back under? I knew even as I felt him release my left wrist, as I watched from outside myself his arm swing back . . . and I couldn't move . . . his lips draw back exposing clenched teeth . . . and I couldn't cry out . . . his eyes squint and his face redden. And my eyes filled with tears even before the blow, just from the thought of it, more from the thought of it than the pain of it. And as I fell to the ground I felt nothing, but heard the crack of skin on skin . . . and as I yelled out I heard nothing, but felt the sting of skin on skin . . . and as my body skidded across the damp leaves I saw nothing, but heard the yelp thwacked from my throat . . . and as I lay, stunned, propped on one scraped and swelling forearm, I saw the red drops, I watched the blood drip into a large, browned leaf—blood from my open, silent mouth.

"Tess!" Stephen gasped. "I didn't mean . . . I'm sorry, I—" and he knelt down to me.

I stood up. And as I brushed my hair back from my face with my fingers I felt the soreness, pictured the shiny blue swelling that would soon be there, and I became aware of the metallic taste of blood. Turning away from him, embarrassed to face him, embarrassed at how I must have looked, I walked back to the edge of the cliff and looked down at the lake, the blond trees. I tried to summon Super Bitch, but old feelings of impotence washed over me. I wanted to close my eyes and be carried to the trees by the wind, be embraced by the trees and rocked to sleep. I swayed to the music in my head: "Rockabye baby on the treetop." I wished Stephen would disappear . . . go away . . . do away with himself . . . shoot himself with the gun he kept in the glove compartment of his car—another *male thing* I didn't understand. A loud crack woke me from my reverie, and I turned to find him standing oppressively behind me, near the big oak, looking up at the darkening sky, as startled as I by the unexpected brilliance of nearby lightning, the disquieting crack of thunder. He's still here, I thought. "You're still here," I said.

"We better go before it pours," he answered.

"It *was* what I wanted, Stephen," I cried. "I wanted our baby. Remember how we tried? Remember my surgery? Maybe if we had succeeded . . . maybe we could have made it work . . . maybe—"

"You mean if *I* had succeeded, don't you!?" he flared anew. "You're the proof! You're pregnant! So it had to be *me,* right? Isn't that what you're really saying? *I* didn't succeed?"

"No, Stephen, I—"

"Well, lady, I've got news for you. The reason you didn't get pregnant with me is because that's the way *I* wanted it. I had a vasectomy, Tess, before I even knew you!"

NO! I thought as his words ricocheted off me, leaving

painful nicks in my consciousness. "No . . ." was all I could say.

"YES!" he yelled.

"I thought it was *me*," I whimpered. "All those years . . . I thought I had let you down . . . I felt so inadequate. And all that time . . ." Stephen stepped toward me, triggering a rush of adrenaline. "How COULD you!" I yelled. "How could you DO such a thing? How could you LIE to me . . . all that time? And you let me go through surgery! What kind of a man are you?"

"I couldn't tell you," he said, looking at his feet, cowed momentarily by my reproach. "I was afraid you'd leave me. And besides, your doctor said you probably couldn't get pregnant without the surgery . . . so maybe you wouldn't be pregnant now if you hadn't had it. So maybe I did you a favor."

The enormity of his selfishness overwhelmed me; but I held onto my sanity, understanding that later, when I was alone, I could allow myself the luxury of letting go, of breaking down. Now I had to be rational. I had to understand, so that later I could believe that what had happened had really happened. I began to remember the facts. "Your sperm count, Stephen. It was normal."

"I knew someone at the lab."

"Who would falsify a sperm count?" I asked naively.

"The technician."

Then I understood. "A woman, you mean. *Another* woman you slept with before me."

"Not *before* you, Tess. I was seeing her at the time."

"No—"

"AT THE TIME! UNDERSTAND! I've always had women in my life. But I loved YOU, Tess. I LOVE you. The rest are just the way it is for me. It's business, it's men's business. I have no fantasies about my life. It's YOU who have the fantasies—about me, about us, about what I wanted. You have no idea what I want. You have no idea who I am!"

"I, I, I! What about ME, Stephen?"

The wind had picked up, blowing dry leaves around our ankles and clouds heavy with rain across the sky above our heads. Anticipating the cooling, cleansing wetness on my throbbing face, my soiled hands, I stood fast watching the lightning, stroke after stroke connecting the clouds, the clouds and the earth, in an evanescent network of light. The accompanying thunder was deafening: God's warning that great powers were at work, I thought. Stephen watched, understanding that there was little he could do to make a mark on the universe, not understanding that the marks he made on people were more important, still not understanding that every relationship *is* a universe. And I started to hurt, from the inside out. My blood ran suddenly hot and fast. I trembled with rage. . . .

"YOU ARE A SMALL MAN!" I erupted, pointing a finger at Stephen from an outstretched arm. He stepped back, toward the great oak. And, as if I had pointed the way for God, for Zeus, for the powers that leave us essentially to our own folly but drop in for an occasional *gotcha!* a thin, bifurcated streak of light bolted from a place in the sky to where Stephen stood—one prong piercing the grounded leaf filled with my coagulated blood, the other striking Stephen's left shoulder, forming, for an instant, a connection of incredibly graphic moral content. For me. That's for *me,* I thought. Stephen did not cry out, he just lit up, froze as he was lifted off the ground and thrown against the tree in a posture reminiscent of cartoons of terrified cats—the ones that look like they have lightning inside them—and then fizzled and slumped, singed and smoking. But he didn't fall to the ground . . . his feet never touched the ground. I walked over to his body and saw that he had been impaled on a broken branch stump . . . that it went into his back and held him under his shoulder blade. The gold choker chain of naked women he wore had branded his neck, and had fallen to the ground before him in molten eighteen-karat lumps. I saw that his fly had been soldered shut. And then I saw the heart carved into the massive tree trunk just to the right of Stephen's slumped head. Inside the heart was carved *S. K. & L. E. 1961.* Stephen would never have done such a thing for me, I thought. I reached out and touched his left shoulder . . . I supposed his heart had stopped . . . closed my hand around his left shoulder and put my ear to his stilled chest . . . I had heard that's what happens when one is electrocuted . . . closed my other hand around his right shoulder and pressed my body to his. "Good-bye, Stephen," I said.

. . . As I stood there I felt my boundaries fall away, and I waited for a gust of wind to carry my essence off . . . but instead I felt Stephen's arms go around me to hold me together. He's still here, I thought. We were still standing by the edge of the cliff overlooking the lake. I started to cry again, and then the rain came and mixed with my tears, washed away the dirt, the blood, the clouds that fogged me in. I saw how easy it would be to push him over the edge of the cliff. I could picture him plummeting into the lake, a floating island suspended on the cracked mirror surface for just an instant before the water took him in, sucked him into its center, and closed over him.

"Good-bye, Stephen," I said, pushing away from him, pushing against him, pushing him back, horrified at the thought of how far he had pushed me. "YOU'RE A SMALL MAN, STEPHEN! And you're going to get SMALLER, and SMALLER, and SMALLER, until there's NOTHING left of you, and then you're going to understand what it means to be FUCKED!" I raged, irrevocably reclaiming the power that I had so easily, so eagerly relinquished to Stephen so many years before. Then, as quickly as my rage had ignited, it dissipated, and I saw Stephen again as I'd seen him when I first arrived—small and childlike. I walked by him, eschewing his outstretched hands. And I left, leaving him atop the hill in a brewing storm to feel his smallness at the center of his universe.

BOCCONE DOLCE
(SWEET MOUTHFUL)

FROM: Sardi's Restaurant, New York

4 egg whites
pinch of salt
1/4 teaspoon cream of tartar
1 1/3 cups sugar
6 ounces semisweet chocolate pieces
3 tablespoons water
3 cups heavy cream
2 pints fresh strawberries

Preheat oven to very slow (250°F).

Beat egg whites, salt, and cream of tartar until stiff. Gradually beat in 1 cup of sugar, and continue to beat until the meringue is stiff and glossy.

Line baking sheets with wax paper, and on the paper trace three circles, each 8 inches in diameter. Spread the meringue evenly over the circles, about 1/2 inch thick, and bake in the very slow oven for 20 to 25 minutes or until meringue is pale gold but still pliable. Remove from oven and carefully peel wax paper from bottom. Put on cake racks and dry.

Melt the chocolate pieces with 3 tablespoons of water in the top of a double boiler. Whip cream until stiff; then gradually add 1/3 cup sugar and beat until very stiff. Slice 1 pint of strawberries.

Place a meringue layer on serving plate and spread with a thin covering of melted chocolate. Then spread a layer about 3/4 inch thick of the whipped cream and top this with a layer of sliced strawberries. Repeat layers of meringue, chocolate, whipped cream, and sliced strawberries, then top with third layer of meringue. Frost sides smoothly with remaining whipped cream. Decorate top in an informal pattern, using remaining melted chocolate squeezed through a pastry cone with a tiny round opening, and dot with whole ripe strawberries. Refrigerate for 2 hours before serving. Serves 8.

CHAPTER 16

Boccone Dolce
(Sweet Mouthful)

It's funny sometimes, the way things turn out. My mother used to say that things always turn out for the best. The question is, the best for whom? Another question is, exactly when do things *turn out?* I've discovered that life isn't exactly a series of independent events, each with a beginning and an end. There is only one beginning—birth—and one end—death. What's in between—the middle—is life. The middle is an evolution of events that never *turn out* definitively. Look at my life, for example: I married Stephen and I couldn't get pregnant. And then my marriage failed. So, according to my mother, it was for The Best that I had never had a baby. Whose best? Mine, the would-be baby's, Stephen's? Probably all concerned. But it had Turned Out, in fact, that I *had* married Stephen. For whom was that The Best? Not me, certainly. Perhaps it was The Best for Stephen and he just didn't know it. But, as things Turned Out, we separated and I fell in love with David and now I'm going to have a baby. My mother would say that it was for The Best that my marriage to Stephen had failed, because I was now able to have a child—something I could never have done with Stephen. Certainly it was for The Best for my mother, who wanted nothing more than to be a grandmother, although, according to her, perhaps it wasn't for The Best for her to have been a mother. And I believe it was for The

Best for me; I have always wanted a child. I'm sure it's for The Best for David, too, but surely not for Stephen. Perhaps The Best all around would have been if I had not married Stephen in the first place. Then again, if our marriage was, in fact, for The Best for Stephen, then things would not have Turned Out for The Best for him if we had *not* married, even though, it later Turned Out, we divorced. Now, who is to say that the way Things have Turned Out, as they now stand, is for The Best, and for whom? I suppose that will depend on how the child Turns Out, and how my impending marriage to David Turns Out. For The Best, I hope.

This was the convolution of thoughts in which I was lost as I swirled whipped, sweetened egg whites onto a cookie sheet with the back of a spoon, forming an eight-inch circle that would be baked into a layer of crunchy meringue for perhaps *the* most delectable of desserts: Boccone Dolce— Sweet Mouthful. This creation from Sardi's of New York consists of layers of meringue, melted chocolate, sweetened whipped cream, and fresh sliced strawberries, frosted on the sides with whipped cream, and decorated on top with whole strawberries and drizzles of melted chocolate. Boccone Dolce, in my opinion, *always* Turns Out for The Best—for everyone. Today it was being turned out for David's birthday dinner. He wouldn't let me make a dinner party for him—far too exhausting, he had said—but he'd agreed to my making his birthday cake. Janet and Arthur and Sandy and Ken were to meet us at La Diva for dinner at seven-thirty, after which we'd have coffee and birthday dessert at my house. It had been snowing all morning, the big-flaked kind of snow that falls slowly from a bright sky through crisp, dry air, fleshing out the skeletal trees, covering the ground like a soft, thick blanket. The oven timer buzzed—indicating two finished meringue layers— and the telephone rang simultaneously. I picked up the phone and cradled it on my shoulder as I pulled from the oven the two cookie sheets bearing the lightly browned circles of meringue.

"Hello, Tess?" It was Alan Garfield. He had good news for

me, he said. My divorce from Stephen should be through by the end of the month . . . first week in February for sure.

What a nice birthday present for David, I thought: a wedding date. "We can have a Valentine's Day wedding!" I said, delighted with the news . . . delighted with the way things were turning out.

I returned to my labor of love, slipping the meringue disks onto a cooling rack, placing the third cookie sheet in the oven, pouring the cream into the mixing bowl, watching it triple in volume, burying the spinning beaters, while the *whirrr* of the mixer lulled me into reminiscence. I recalled the day above the lake two months ago, and the late-night telephone call from Stephen a week later when he told me that he would give me a quick divorce, when he told me that he was filing for bankruptcy, that his trial was to be in mid-February, and that he was planning to go away for three weeks in January, alone, when he told me that he was so sorry for so many things he could never make it up to me even if he had another lifetime, that he wished me well and hoped I'd be happy. I had thanked him for his cooperation, for his good wishes, and then I asked him about the trip he was planning. I don't know why I asked him about that; there were so many more important questions. He said he was going to a quiet island—where he could clear his head. It was important to him that I know he was going alone, he said. I told him it was no longer important to me if he traveled alone or not. But that wasn't true. As much as I didn't want to believe it, as I spoke with him I realized there still remained a remnant of a tie between us, albeit a tenuous one. Perhaps it would break with the divorce, or my remarriage, or the sale of my house—I had finally found a buyer—or the birth of my child. I knew it would break . . . and then I wouldn't ask any more questions.

Sandy startled me—she was practically next to me by the time I noticed she had walked in. "Hiii!" she said.

I turned off the mixer. "Boy, did you scare me! I didn't hear you come in."

"I told you not to leave your back door open. You don't

know who might walk in. I see coffee's on," she said, walking toward the coffee maker.

"Pour us both a cup, Sandy, and grab some crackers from the cabinet. There's egg salad in the fridge. We can have lunch. The meringue in the oven has another fifteen minutes to go," I said, covering the bowl of whipped cream with plastic wrap, placing it in the refrigerator, and retrieving the soup-bowl of egg salad I had made the day before. "So how's it going?" I asked once we were settled at the counter.

"Not bad, Tess," she answered quietly, clearly a new Sandy—more thought, less vowels. She looked thin, but not drawn, not unhappy. And as I watched her carefully spread egg salad on half a piece of Melba toast, I remembered the afternoon, just a month ago, when she had called me.

"Tess, I have to see you! I don't know what to do!" she cried.

"What's wrong, Sandy?"

"It's Ken. He's not . . . nothing's what . . . oh, Tess, it's all so complicated."

"Okay, Sandy. I'm here. Come over." Well, I thought intuitively as I made fresh coffee and finished making the tuna salad I had planned for my lunch, it looks like the honeymoon may be over . . . before it even begins. Within minutes, Sandy's green Volvo—which, she had told me excitedly only a week before, Ken was going to trade in for a BMW as soon as the new models came out—was parked in the drive and Sandy was walking through my back door, red-eyed and sniffling. But my heart didn't stop, or even skip a beat in dread; she didn't appear that upset . . . not like when Charlie had died, not even like when she had found out about Charlie's affair—more like when she'd told me about her affair with Stephen.

"Tess, you're just not going to belieeeve this," she started, pulling a mug from the cabinet and filling it with coffee.

I got the milk from the refrigerator and sat at the table. "I think I'd believe almost anything these days, Sandy. What happened?"

She took off her red fox jacket, dropped it on a chair, and

sat down across from me. "Okay," she said, looking right at me—and broke into tears.

I took her hand across the table. "I'm here, Sandy. Tell me what's going on," I insisted, beginning to get concerned after all.

"He's BROKE, Tess!"

"What?"

"He's broke. He owes the casinos a fortune."

"Ken? A gambler? I—"

"Can you belieeeve it?"

"As I said, I can believe almost anything," I replied, finally understanding how an orthodontist could have so much time off from work. He was seeing fewer and fewer patients because he visited the casinos in Atlantic City several mornings a week. Then he wined and dined Sandy on the weekends, impressing her by paying for everything with new hundred-dollar bills, which were really short-term loans from the casinos—cashed-in chips, obtained on credit. A nasty little cycle, really. Unfortunately, Sandy liked her position in the loop well enough not to ask too many questions, taking his half-truths about his successful practice and complicated real estate investments at the shore as the whole truth. "But what I don't understand is how you didn't know he was at the casinos so often."

She offered no explanation. There was none, save her own penchant to see only what she wanted to see. *That* was something I could understand.

"Tess, tell me what to dooo. I do love him, you know . . ."

I was glad she said that, because I really didn't know.

". . . and I think he . . . well, I think we need help."

"Things going well with Ken?" I probed, watching Sandy swallow a mouthful while spreading egg salad on the other half of the dry brown rectangle.

"We're working on it," she answered. "Michael's been a big help already. I'm so grateful that you recommended him to us, Tess. He's helping me and Ken understand about the gambling, and a lot of other stuff . . . about both of us. But I think we've got a long way to go."

"I think you're doing great, Sandy. How are the kids?"

"They couldn't be happier. They're absolutely mad about Ken. Would you believe that Rebecca asked Ken if she could call him Daddy? He was thrilled. And speaking of children, how's the little mother-to-be?"

"I'm terrific. And I got some good news today. Save February 14," I told her, explaining Alan's call.

"Oooh! I love weddings! I'm so happy for you, Tess."

"Thanks. I am looking forward to feeling settled—if one can ever feel settled."

"Well, I feel settled. And I owe it all to you, Tess. I mean, what if you hadn't gone to that singles party with me? And what if you hadn't gone out with Ken? And suppose *you* had fallen for him? Can you imagine! But, most important, you sent Ken to *me* . . . and then you sent *us* to Michael." She put the canapé down on her plate and looked at me with a kind of rueful smile. "You know, Tess, a couple of years in therapy wasn't exactly what I had in mind when I told you how Ken and I were going to get to know each other during our delayed long honeymoon—remember the three weeks in Europe we were planning? That really would have been a nice trip, but . . . well, isn't it incredible how this all turned out?"

I was tempted to recount to her my earlier thoughts, but I decided to let it slide and suffice with, "It certainly is. For the best, just like my mother used to say," while running through my head was a song by the Rolling Stones, the one that says that we don't always get what we want, but we just might get what we need.

Dinner that night was delicious. First we shared four different pastas, and following entrées of veal and shrimp we shared a large bowl of green salad tossed with olive oil, balsamic vinegar, and freshly ground black pepper. We also shared four bottles of wine—all except me, that is. I was allowed one glass, David informed me before dinner. Sensing an impending pout, he added, "Besides your being pregnant, we need a designated driver! So it all turns out—"

300

"I know. For the best," I finished his sentence, chuckling to myself.

Following dinner we returned to my family room, where I set before the six of us espresso and the Boccone Dolce. It was gorgeous. And the taste . . . well, there were no just words!

"Where did you get fresh strawberries in January?" Janet asked.

"They're in all the supermarkets. Aren't they fabulous?"

"What's the crunchy part?" asked Arthur.

"Meringue—it's made of egg whites and sugar, baked to a crisp."

"I can't believe we're still eating! After that dinner! But it's too good not to eat!" said Ken.

And we ate the whole thing. Janet had pulled the empty cake plate across the coffee table to her, from which she and Arthur were scraping the last crumbs of meringue, the last dabs of cream, with their forks, then with their fingers, when the phone rang. I picked up the receiver next to the sofa.

"Hello," I said. And I must have paled as I listened to the voice on the phone, because David jumped from his easy chair and knelt in front of me, his hands on my knees. After hearing a lot of sputtering and half-asked questions, the gathered heard me say, "I'll be there shortly." But when I put the receiver down, I didn't move.

"Tess, what is it?" David asked. "Who was that?"

"It was a nurse from University Hospital," I answered. "I have to go there . . . right away."

"What is it?" David repeated, alarmed.

"It's Stephen. I have to go—he may be dying. . . ." And I pulled away from David and was off the sofa. "My boots. What did I do with my boots?" I asked the floor . . . and found them in the foyer . . . and by then David had his coat on and mine in his hand.

"Let's go, you'll explain in the car," he said, then turned to the others, telling them to make another pot of coffee and he'd call from the hospital.

On the way to the hospital, I told David what the nurse

301

had told me: Stephen had been brought to the hospital by ambulance in a state of shock; he was suffering from a severe infection; he was accompanied by a friend who had told the doctor that he was married to me.

"But Stephen's supposed to be in St. Kitts."

"I know. He must have picked up something on the island," I said. What I was imagining was tetanus, rabies, typhoid, picturing a tanned, feverish Stephen lying on crisp white sheets with a beautiful nurse at his side. What I found when I reached the hospital was something I could never have imagined.

First of all, what he had picked up he hadn't picked up on St. Kitts. He had brought it—or should I say *her*—with him from Philadelphia: Dorothy. Of course, she was not precisely what made him sick—not to say that finding out he had taken her didn't make *me* sick. Be that as it may, when David and I walked into the emergency ward, the nurse at the desk gave me an envelope containing Stephen's valuables—his wallet, watch, keys—and we were directed to a room. As we walked down the hall, Dorothy came running to us, meeting us halfway.

"Thank goodness you've come, Tess. He's dying and the doctors need your permission to treat him—" she'd started, when a doctor emerged from a room and walked over to us.

"Are you Mrs. Fineman?"

"Yes, I—"

"I'm Dr. Gerstler, and we have a life-threatening situation here, Mrs. Fineman," he said as we walked briskly to Stephen's room. He stopped at the door and turned to David. "Are you a member of the family?" he asked.

"No, not exactly—" David started.

"Then you'll have to wait out here." The doctor took me by the elbow, steering me into the room.

I wonder if Stephen's wife's husband-to-be or Stephen's wife's baby's father would be considered a member of the family? I thought involuntarily as we approached the bed, reproaching myself immediately for the inappropriateness of the thought. As I said, nothing I could have imagined would have prepared me for what I was to see . . . and hear.

Stephen was breathing in short, fast gasps. His skin was sweaty and as gray as his hair; his closed eyes were dark pits, his cheeks sunken. Tubes snaked from every orifice.

"Stephen," I said, touching his arm and recoiling from the clammy feel, from the putrid smell that seemed to emanate from him. "Can he hear me?" I asked the doctor, who shook his head.

And then there was the matter of the huge bulge under the bed sheet, over Stephen's midsection. An enormous erection, was what instantly came to mind, the lewd picture disintegrating beneath a wave of guilt as I realized almost as quickly that the protrusion was some sort of frame designed to keep the sheet from touching him.

"Mr. Fineman has a life-threatening infection," Dr. Gerstler explained coolly. "Fournier's gangrene—a spontaneous fulminating gangrene of the penis."

FULMINATING! GANGRENE! I cringed, and my eyes involuntarily shot to the tent over Stephen's groin. Then the doctor said something about it going untreated for too long, that "the tissues are dying and sloughing away, clear down to and including the *corpus cavernosa,*" that "the patient had become toxic . . ." and then more medico-babble about *Hemolytic streptococcus* or *staphylococcus* being the likely villain.

FULMINATING! GANGRENE! TOXIC! reverberated in my head. I looked quizzically at Dr. Gerstler. "Toxic?" was all I managed to say.

He explained, "Essentially, this means that your husband has become poisoned by the agent that infected his penis."

Oh! You mean *lust!* I thought, not believing that I could think such a thing at a time like this, shocked by my lack of compassion.

The doctor took my incredulous look as lack of understanding. "Mrs. Fineman," he tried again, "your husband could die if we don't take drastic measures very quickly, and we need your permission."

"Drastic measures?"

"Surgery."

"Surgery?"

"Amputation."

"Amputation?"

"Amputation of the penis. We may be able to save the testicles," he said, averting his gaze from mine, resting it on my just-obvious pregnant belly.

A lot of good his balls will be without a bat! I thought, my eyes falling involuntarily to the doctor's groin. Staring at Dr. Gerstler's fly, I felt the situation begin to sink in. Amputation of the penis or Stephen could die, the doctor had said.

"Can I get you a glass of water, Mrs. Fineman? Please, sit down, I'm afraid this has been a shock." And he led me from the room to a seat in the hall. "What more can I tell you? Your husband has an unusually severe infection. We must operate soon or I can't promise—"

"How did this happen? I don't understand."

"We're not sure. We understand from Mrs. Oberman that your husband had been in the Caribbean. She also told me that he's diabetic, and that could certainly have been a big factor here," and he continued on about diabetes and poor circulation and the incidence of infection, and then he excused himself and said he'd be back in a few moments, and he disappeared into Stephen's room. He knew all the proper names, all the medical jargon, but he didn't know The Details.

Dorothy knew The Details, and within seconds of the doctor's departure, she was by my side. "David went to make a phone call. He told me to tell you that he'll be back in a few minutes," she said, wringing her hands. And then she told me The Details:

It seems that Stephen had been having a bit of a problem with impotency of late. Understanding that impotency can be a problem in diabetics, he sought the aid of his physician, who told him that his impotency was more likely the result of psychological problems than physical ones, and that perhaps a therapist was in order. Much vexed, Stephen went to a new doctor, who also told him it didn't appear that his problem was caused by his diabetes or anything else of a physiologic nature, and also suggested a therapist. "But what if it *is* my diabetes?" Stephen pressed. "Well, we have had success with papaverine," he told Stephen, explaining the use of the drug, which, when injected into the penis, causes a pharmacological erection that can last a fairly long time. "Fairly long?" Stephen queried. "Upwards of two hours," the doctor replied. Well, that was all Stephen had to hear. Superman in a bottle! "Can you imagine the fun we could have!" he told Dorothy . . . and, I assume, others. But the doctor wouldn't recommend drug therapy—"Not yet. Let's wait and see," he said. So Stephen, who has always had a bit of a problem dealing with delayed gratification, went to his own source: a cute nurse who worked for a urologist Stephen saw a couple of times a few years ago for some nonspecific infection that made him think he had the clap, but he didn't, and when the infection cleared he saw the cute nurse a couple of times. "Stephen Fineman! What a nice surprise," she exclaimed when he called her recently. "Stephen Fineman! What a nice surprise," she exclaimed when he showed her the best time, the longest time.

"He told you that?" I asked Dorothy, who'd told me that last part on a long sigh of resignation.

"He tells me everything," she replied.

I didn't believe he had told her that.

And she continued, "So he brought this stuff with us to St. Kitts. And we used it a couple of times, and it was incredible. He just went on and on and on . . ." she said, looking me right in the eye. Vicious bitch! "And then one afternoon he asked me to inject it. . . ."

One *afternoon?* I thought to myself, picturing their pasty white bodies sequestered in a dark, stagnant little room fitted with a wall-to-wall bed, humping into a sweat while, outside, the glorious sun warmed the silky sand, the blue-green sea and gentle breezes cooled the bronzing bodies.

". . . He was a little too smashed to fill the syringe . . ."

In the *afternoon?*

". . . and maybe we were out of clean needles . . . maybe I forgot to change the needle . . . I don't know . . . but at any rate, sometime later, during the night, Stephen woke up. He said his prick ached, and it was all red. Well, we figured it was from too much screwing around. . . ."

Maybe she's not so dumb after all.

". . . But by morning it was swollen and the red was spreading and he was in pain. And then he got a fever and we got scared. I wanted him to see a doctor, but he said he didn't want to be treated on a foreign island. Luckily, we were able to get on a flight to New York the next day. But by then he was in terrible shape. His penis was horribly swollen and it was turning black and blue. He could hardly sit in the plane. By the time we got home, he was almost delirious with pain and fever, and his penis—ohh, it was oozing pus and the skin was all black and peeling off . . . and there was this terrible smell. . . ." Here Dorothy turned pale and her eyes watered. "I've never seen anything so awful!" she cried, bowing her head, putting her hands to her face. "And then he collapsed!" Dorothy clutched my arm with both hands and put her face close to mine. "He can't die, Tess. Please, don't let him die. He's all I have!"

Then you ain't gonna have much, lady, I thought, pitying, but not forgiving. Pulling my arm from her grasp, I stood up and walked to the door of Stephen's room. The doctor and a nurse were behind the curtain that was pulled around the bed. I stood there folding and unfolding the top of the manila envelope containing Stephen's things, attempting to digest The Details, and then I looked down at the envelope. The *keys,* I thought, ripping open the envelope, pulling out Stephen's key ring. On one end, the smaller end, were three keys, two of which were keys to safety deposit boxes, one of which was the key to *my* safety deposit box—the one with all the money in it. And I realized that I had Stephen by the balls in more ways than one. It's funny the way things turn out, I thought to myself, considering the many shades of gray, remembering Michael's counsel: *Be kind to yourself.*

The doctor approached me with the consent for surgery. "Mrs. Fineman, we have the operating room ready for your husband," he said. "All we need is your signature on this form and we'll take him right up. He's failing quickly. If we wait much longer, he might not survive the surgery."

I looked at the doctor, then I looked into the room where

the smell of death was suffocating. I thought of how I had loved Stephen and how he had abused me, misused me, how he had been unkind, uncaring, unfaithful, how he was treacherous, deceitful, and base, how he had embarrassed me, humiliated me, degraded me . . . how he had hurt me . . .

How sweet revenge will be, I thought. Stephen will finally get his just deserts. And I won't have to plunge a knife in him, riddle him with bullets, drop poison in his drink—all I'll have to do is not do anything. It is funny sometimes, the way things turn out. "I'm sorry, Dr. Gerstler, I can't sign that. I couldn't possibly allow you to mutilate him in that way," I wailed, dabbing at my dry eyes with a tissue.

"But, Mrs. Fineman—"

"I know he'd rather die than live without his manhood. Surely you can understand. Surely any man can understand!" I emoted to the ceiling, my hand at my brow.

"But he *will* die without the surgery, Mrs. Fineman!"

"I'm sorry, Dr. Gerstler, but I've made my decision."

Before the morning light was bright, Stephen Fineman's light went out.

The funeral was graveside. The casket was closed. No one would have to remember him lying too still, too rigid, an empty form in white satin. No one would have to recognize as essentially Stephen's the made-over face approximated from photographs. No one would have to guess at how he might have looked when an overwhelming population of microbes wrested him from life—not at all himself. More than a hundred people showed up—mostly women. And he quite lucked out with the weather. It was a cold, clear day, there was no wind, and the sun shone so brightly many of the mourners wore sunglasses to protect their eyes from the glare off the snow. A low rumble of commentary continued among the men during the service, snatches of which I heard quite distinctly: "*. . . wife left him . . . never had kids . . . didn't have many friends . . . indicted . . . died before the trial came up . . . helluva way to keep from going to jail . . .*

*liked the ladies . . . wouldn't have had much of a life if they'd
cut off his dick . . . funny the way things turn out . . . for the
best . . ."*

For the best? I wondered, looking to my mother standing
beside me with her classic countenance of concern, remembering her censure when I called to tell her of Stephen's
death by deliberate disregard. "MURDERER!" she had
yelled at me. "But they would have mutilated him, Mom!
Unmanned him!" I had tried to justify my inaction. "Better
you should let him die?" she'd retaliated. "He would have
wanted it that way," I had begged, my self-righteous wall of
rationalization crumbling beneath the realization of my
irresponsibility. "How do you *know* how he would have
wanted it? He was out cold!" she'd impugned. "But—" "No
buts about it. You had NO RIGHT to play God!"

She was right. I had had no right, because, despite what
others might think, allowing Stephen to die possibly wasn't
Best for Stephen . . . although it might have been, had he
said so . . . but he hadn't . . . so we'll never know. And not
knowing makes it Not Right, I reasoned, the sweet taste of
revenge turning bitter with contrition.

The short service concluded, the women were now filing
past the coffin. They were crying, and each had something to
say as she passed, placing a flower or a bit of earth on the
coffin. I couldn't quite make out their words, but I recognized many of them. Of course Dorothy was there, her eyes
black and blue with smeared mascara and eye shadow, and
so was Sandy in her long black coat and black boots. I saw
the blonde from the airplane, and various medical technicians and nurses dressed in white. And Wonder Woman was
there, walking on her toes to keep the spiked heels of her
black patent leather boots from sinking into the soft earth
around the open grave.

Turning to me, my mother asked, "What are they saying,
Tess?"

I left her standing behind the rows of now empty chairs
and walked toward the line of women by the coffin. As I got
closer, I could see their tears, squeezed out of angry red
eyes—tears of rage, not sorrow. I couldn't hear their words,

but their lips were moving, and it looked like they were all whispering the same thing: *"She should've . . ."* *"She should've . . ."* something. I got a little closer and watched their thinned lips: *"She should've cut it off."*

"Well?" my mother asked when I returned to her side.

"They're agreeing with you, Mom. They're saying that it would have been Best to have saved his life," I said, relaying the sum if not the substance of their words.

. . . "We don't have much time, Mrs. Fineman," Dr. Gerstler said, holding a chart with the consent form in front of me.

Overwhelmed by the irony of it all, understanding that there is no revenge as sweet as justice, I reached for the glint of the silver Cross pen in his hand. "Where do I sign?"

David was in the shower when the doorbell rang, and by the time I got to the door the UPS man had gone, leaving a cube-shaped package addressed to me on the porch. I didn't recognize the return address. Settling back into the sofa in the family room, I peeled the brown paper from the package, revealing a layer of gift-wrapping. I carefully removed the pretty opalescent bow and the shiny white paper embossed with blue and yellow hearts, and opened the white cardboard box to find a cuddly soft, light brown Gund bear nestled amidst leaves of pale blue tissue paper. "Golly! Gotta Gund!" I said aloud, laughing to myself, and then put the bear down beside me and opened the slate-blue-lined, ivory envelope that was tucked between the side of the box and the tissue paper. In it was a letter written in blue ink on several sheets of ivory vellum stationery enhanced by an embossed, slate-blue border. It began:

Dear Tess,
    You might think it strange for me to be writing to you like this, but I wanted to wish you the best on the birth of your baby.

Consumed with curiosity, I turned to the last page to discover the author, and was shocked and appalled to find it was from Dorothy Oberman. But the handwriting was so gracefully elegant, so contrary to the coarseness of the writer, that I stayed my disgust and turned back to the first page, where I read further:

I also want to apologize for the pain I may have caused you in the past. I hope you'll believe me when I say that I did what I did because I love Stephen, and that I would never hurt anyone intentionally. I'm not proud of my behavior, but Stephen and I go way back, before you, and although you may find this hard to understand, when he was with you (even when he was married to you), I felt he was "cheating" on me.

Most important, I want to thank you for saving Stephen's life. That terrible night at the hospital you were holding not only Stephen's life in your hands, but mine, too.

You might think that life is not very good for me now that Stephen has lost so much, including his career, and probably, for a time, his freedom. And his physical "loss" is terrible. But, truly, I feel none of that matters as long as we're together. In fact, he needs me now more than he ever did before. God knows, I need him. And don't think badly of me when I say this, but I no longer have to worry about him being unfaithful to me.

Stephen is still very bitter, but, for what it's worth, *I* feel you did the right thing.

I know that you and I will never be "friends," Tess, but I hope you can forgive me. I wish you happiness.

Most sincerely yours,
Dorothy

Oddly moved, already forgiving, I reread the letter until I was startled by my baby's distant cry triggering the warm, tingly sensation of my milk letting down. I slipped the pages back into the envelope and then into the big patch pocket of my wraparound jeans skirt. But before I had a chance to get up, David had scooped Sam (named for my father) from his bassinet in our bedroom and brought him to me—for the second time in the last hour.

"Time for dessert!" he teased, laying Sam in my arms. "Hey, what's going on here?" he asked, seeing my flushed face and my eyes grown teary with mixed emotions. "What's wrong, sweetheart?"

"Nothing's wrong, David," I answered, pressing my lips to the soft blond down on Sam's head. "Everything is just right. I was thinking how lucky we are, and I guess I was kind of overwhelmed." I unbuttoned my blouse and we both watched in awe as Sam rooted around for my breast and, finally latching on, suckled contentedly.

"Hey! Who sent the cute bear?" David asked, spotting the stuffed toy and its wrappings.

"It's from Dorothy, David."

"Dorothy? You mean Dorothy Oberman?"

"Yes."

"Well, that's a surprise."

"Quite. I'll tell you about it later."

"About what?"

"Later, David," I sighed, the corners of my mouth curling to the barest glimmer of a smile. "For now let's just say that it appears things really have turned out just the way my mother always says—for the best."

Kathryn Lynn Davis

SING TO ME OF DREAMS

The *New York Times* bestselling author of *Too Deep For Tears* brings us a rich, sensuous novel filled with the intimate yearnings and passions of a turbulent family, their lovers and friends, and the one extraordinary woman, Saylah, who enters their lives.

There is a future I do not seek, but which will come to be, just the same...

With these words echoing in her heart, Saylah sets off on a journey that will take her through all the mysteries of the human heart—from a tranquil life of simple joys to the world of white settlers in the lush, unspoiled Pacific Northwest.

Available in Paperback from Pocket Books

POCKET
B O O K S

408-01

The author
seller-turne
glittering w
with a stor
against devastating odds.

BIJOUX

WYATT McNEILL: The father of her best friend, he took an interest in Jewel's career . . . and, more dangerously, in Jewel herself.

HADLEY McNEILL: Wyatt's son, he taught Jewel the meaning of love—beyond career, beyond success.

SASCHA ROBINOVSKY: Talented, tempestuous and romantic, the Russian designer swept her off her feet, nurtured her talent, and married her. In return, Jewel gave him her heart . . . until she learned the awful truth . . .

EDWARD RANDOLPH: His sexual preferences allowed no romance between him and Jewel—just the most honest and trusted friendship. And as Jewel's best designer, he was also her greatest weakness.

ALLEN PRESCOTT: With his support, Jewel shaped Bijoux International into a towering empire. But unbridled ambition—and forgotten enemies— threatened to destroy her dream-come-true . . .

"Glitz and glamour . . . with characters who are interesting . . . ENTERTAINING!"

—*Rave Reviews*

BIJOUX

MEREDITH RICH

ST. MARTIN'S PAPERBACKS

All of the characters in this book are fictitious, and any resemblances to actual persons, living or dead, is purely coincidental.

Published by arrangement with Doubleday

BIJOUX

Library of Congress Catalog Card Number: 88-27159

ISBN: 0-312-92339-2

Printed in the United States of America

Doubleday edition/August 1989
St. Martin's Paperbacks edition/November 1990

10 9 8 7 6 5 4 3 2 1

India, my jewel,
this one is for you,
with all my love forever

Acknowledgments

Thanks to Elaine Giovando, Bonnie Knickerbocker, and Eric Shelton for the information they supplied. And thanks to Barbara Lowenstein, Abner Stein, Loretta Barrett at Doubleday, and the people at Collins for waiting so patiently for this one.

Prologue

1988

"Hell, I don't have *time* for this!" Jewel Prescott muttered, although no one was within earshot.

She let her head drop forward over her desk, closed her eyes, and growled out loud. Kneading her knuckles hard into the back of her neck, Jewel tried to unlock the tension in her pressure points. The muscles fought back, refusing to budge. Her long neck stretched out painfully, slowly to the left, backward, to the right, forward. Her brain was signaling for a break; it was time to shut down her mind, her thoughts. But hell, she couldn't give in to the stress.

Jewel found herself back at work on the spring catalog. What had started out to be a simple, classic sales device seemed to become more complicated and annoying every season. Of course, it all came with success. In the beginning she had made all the decisions. It was a snap. Now, heading the jewelry empire that she had founded, Bijoux International, she had a number of department heads who

1

deliberated for weeks on matters that she had once settled in minutes. And, of course, paying her staff the fortune she did, she was obliged to listen to what they had to say. Even take their advice often enough that they wouldn't quit and go to work for the competition. Happy workers didn't scatter secrets in the marketplace. So Jewel listened to their ideas and paid them whopping salaries, in return for their allegiance.

Jewel was aware of her reputation; she *was* difficult to work for. Temperamental, quixotic, aloof, those were descriptions of Jewel Prescott that the press had bandied about over the years. Also: talented, savvy, original. *Oh, for the good old days,* she sighed out loud. And then thought better of it. *No, cancel that . . . cancel.*

Jewel closed her green-contact-lensed eyes. Cupping her hands over them, she opened her eyes again, seeing only darkness. The darkness alleviated the ache in her head and the pressure that pounded behind her eyes, but it produced an anxious panic in some other part of her psyche. A feeling of claustrophobia.

"Jewel? Are you okay?" Meg Higdon, her assistant, stood in the doorway, tall and splendidly leggy in a black chamois skirt cut nine inches above her knees.

"Yeah. Just the usual headache. Get me a couple of Tylenol, would you? Extra strength."

Meg brought the Tylenol and set it, along with the photographs and layout for the February ads in *Vogue* and *Town and Country,* on Jewel's desk. "Check this a.s.a.p. Mike needs to know before five." She shook two tablets out of the bottle and poured a glass of Evian water. "It's been a high-stress week for you."

Jewel shrugged. "No worse than usual. Not enough sleep. This weekend I plan to make up for it."

Meg looked puzzled. "But aren't you flying to Rome Friday?"

Jewel stared at her assistant. "Rome?" Then she

laughed, covering. "Well, that's what I mean. I'll get plenty of rest on the plane."

After Meg had gone, Jewel swallowed the Tylenol and sat for a moment, staring out over St. Patrick's Cathedral and waiting for the pain in her head to recede. The trip to Rome . . . Jewel wondered how it could have slipped her mind so completely.

While Señor and Señora Gomez-Archuleta chatted in rapid Spanish with some friends who had dropped by their table at Odeon, a perennial late-night hot spot in downtown Manhattan, Allen Prescott, Jewel's husband, turned to her, his smile fading.

"Christ, Jewel, what's going on? You haven't said two words all evening. I was counting on you to chat up Olga while Giulio and I talk around a price on the Monet."

Jewel looked at her husband. Her attractive husband. Her attractive, once-wealthy husband who was now art poor. His vast fortune hung on the walls of their Fifth Avenue apartment and the house in Connecticut. There was also a storage loft somewhere in lower Manhattan for which Jewel paid an astronomical annual rent.

Allen Prescott acquired. He never disposed of his acquisitions. And so, having swept through a vast inheritance—Oklahoma oil money—he now relied on Jewel to write the checks. Jewel admitted, in rare moments of charity, that it was probably fair; she owed Allen a great deal. Once she had even been proud of his art collection. His gee-whiz enthusiasm was what had impressed her most about him in the beginning. But art had become his obsession. Buying from private collectors, buying at auction, buying from the artists themselves; that was how he spent his days, and most of his evenings.

"I don't have anything to talk to Olga about," Jewel said sotto voce. "Do you see what she's wearing? That Cathalene Columbier necklace is obscene. Emeralds and aquamarines, with gold *and* stainless steel panels? I didn't think even Cathalene could turn out something that atrocious. Anyway, I have a headache. I just want to get this over and go to bed."

"For a change," Allen said. "Why can't you just make an effort and try to help me?"

"Help you! When have I not?" she hissed indignantly. "You owe me a hell of a lot."

Allen gave Jewel's foot a swift nudge under the table as the other couple breathily said their farewells, full of hugs and "lunch soon," to the Gomez-Archuletas.

Jewel flashed Señora Gomez-Archuleta a dazzling smile. "I was just chatting with Allen about your necklace, Olga. It's one of Cathalene's pieces, isn't it?"

"Oh, yes. She is so *very* talented," Olga Gomez-Archuleta gushed, fully aware of what she was saying; it was no secret that Jewel Prescott and Cathalene Columbier were bitter rivals. "It is beautiful, isn't it? Giulio gave it to me as a little gift for having my appendix out."

"How sweet," Jewel smiled. "And how appropriate! Tell me . . ."

The suite at the Hassler, overlooking the Piazza di Spagna in Rome, was one of the few that the hotel had not redecorated in the past few years. The rooms were an anachronism, from a time that Jewel had never experienced except in books—an era when young American heiresses were escorted to Europe on the Grand Tour, prior to engagement, marriage, and a lifetime of devotion to children, charity, large staffs, and palatial homes.

Her lover, Mike Marshall, thought the rooms somber and depressing, not romantic enough. He wanted to switch to a smaller suite on the fifth floor that was bright white with a balcony overlooking the Spanish Steps and Bernini's fountain. Mike's style was clean-cut and contemporary. He liked the Rome that translated into the clothes of Giorgio Armani, the textile patterns of the Missonis, the Italy of twentieth-century fashion.

The designer in Jewel agreed. But the part of her that had grown up poor craved the splendor of days past, the elegance that her own heritage lacked. Grand hotels such as the Hassler made up in some small part for Jewel's poverty-ridden childhood. Of course, most people did not know about that childhood. She told Mike that this particular suite brought back memories of her seventh birthday.

"Jewel, darling," Mike said as his hand gave up on caressing her breast, "sex takes two people, unless one of them is a corpse."

Jewel smiled apologetically. "I'm no corpse. My back hurts too much. Unless it's rigor mortis. Would you be a love and rub it, darling?"

Mike was Bijoux's art director as well as her lover. She had hired him because of his impressive background with Saatchi. But it did not hurt that he was young and tall and called to mind the youthful Clint Eastwood.

"All right," he sighed. "Turn over. I'll rub your back. Then you can rub some part of me. Your choice."

Jewel stretched out her naked body and turned over. Mike dug strong fingers into her shoulders. "Hmmmm . . . that's . . . good," she moaned.

"At last we're getting somewhere. You've got to snap out of this depression, Jewel," Mike said as he worked up and down her neck. "You haven't lost it. And anyway, even if you coasted for years on what you've already designed, no one would notice. Rich women will keep buying Jewel's bijoux until their husbands divorce them for somebody younger. And then the new wives will head straight for Bijoux. It's kind of like the food chain."

"Hmmmm," Jewel mumbled, her face buried comfortably in the soft down pillow.

"I'm hooked on you, Jewel," Mike whispered. "Why don't you leave Allen? We make a great pair."

"Let's not talk about it now," she forced herself to say. "Darling, could you move down to my lower back?"

Mike worked his way down to Jewel's buttocks. She was the only woman he had ever known who could turn him on by being passive. He pressed his erection against her thighs as he leaned his face down into her short blond-streaked hair and kissed behind her ears. "I love you," he whispered. "Tonight I'm your Roman lover. *Carissima . . .*"

Then he became aware of her even, rhythmic breathing. "Jewel . . . *amore mio?*"

But Jewel was asleep.

Jewel sat in a maroon leather wing chair in the parlor of the Sheldon Arms School. The chair emanated the stuffy, stifling atmosphere of generations of proper girls being educated for matronhood. Jewel could not have imagined herself lasting a semester there. But it was the Right Sort of Place, and Jewel was determined that her daughters would have the advantages that Sheldon Arms could provide. And it was less than an hour's drive from her house in Washington, Connecticut. At one time that had seemed like a marvelous convenience; now she spent so little time there that it hardly mattered.

Jewel waited impatiently, sipping Constant Comment tea as she checked out the other parents gathered in the well-worn room for parents' weekend. They were, by and large, a conservative, cashmere-and-tweed group. Most of them, Jewel was sure, had attended Sheldon Arms when they were young. They seemed content and secure to be back in the hallowed halls.

Content and secure, that is, until their gaze met Jewel Prescott's. When old money meets new money that blatantly flaunts it, old money generally feels threatened. Under Jewel's unsmiling inspection they began to look ill at ease. Jewel—wearing an outrageous Christian Lacroix suit, with blood-red lipstick, and her own gold-and-ruby earrings and necklace—looked as if she could devour any of them. Her hair, now auburn, was very short, and slicked down behind her ears with Tenax. Today's contact lenses were tinted violet.

"Mummie!" Beryl Prescott called out as she burst into the room, flinging her arms around Jewel. "You look wonderful! Oh, I'm so glad to see you! Amber said you wouldn't make it, but I told her you would. You promised to come."

Jewel smiled. "I wouldn't miss it for anything. Where *is* Amber?" she asked her youngest daughter, who was now fourteen and a freshman. "I sent Miss Foulke to find both of you."

"Oh . . . well, she must still be getting dressed," Beryl smiled. "Her skin is really clearing up . . . you'll be so pleased. And she's making much more of an effort this year than she did at Dalton. She's a writer on the yearbook staff."

"I'm glad to hear it," Jewel said. "She needs to become more enthusiastic about things. Boredom is an indulgence." She looked at her watch. "But if she doesn't hurry up, we'll miss our dinner reservation at the Yardley Inn. It was completely booked. Meg had to beg and cajole them for a table. The only time they had open was six-thirty. Uncivilized, I'm afraid, but it's the only decent place for miles."

"But didn't they know who you were?" Beryl asked.

"Well, apparently not. Or at least not the person who takes reservations. This part of Connecticut is very comme il faut. They still wear their ancestral diamonds. I'm not in vogue up here."

Beryl laughed. "That's silly. There was that huge spread in last month's *New York* magazine."

"Ah, but this is Connecticut, darling," Jewel said with a smile. "Well, let's think of where else we'll eat if your sister doesn't show up soon."

"I'm here, Mother."

Jewel turned to see her fifteen-year-old daughter, Amber, looking pretty much the same as when she had left for school two months before: a mess. Her shirt was tucked carelessly into an unflattering pleated skirt and partially hanging out at the back. Beryl had been kind to say that Amber's acne was improving. Her face was a mine field of erupting spots, and her oily hair looked as if it had not been washed for days.

Jewel, however, took a deep breath and smiled, reminding herself that she must bite her tongue rather than criticize. Amber's therapist in New York had put all the blame on Jewel for her daughter's problems. "God," Jewel had told Allen, "one would think shrinks would have the good sense to realize who pays the bills." Nevertheless, Jewel was not one to be intimidated into feeling guilt.

"Amber, darling!" Jewel said, embracing her daughter while trying not to let her cheek brush against the small, greasy hills on Amber's face. "You look wonderful. I thought we'd go and have lobster at the Yardley Inn."

"Shellfish is bad for my skin," Amber said.

"Oh, well, whatever. But we'd better hurry or they'll turn us away at the door."

"When were you ever turned away?" Amber said. She was tall, with good bone structure, but at present all possibilities for attractiveness had gone awry, out of willful neglect. "Where's Daddy? Didn't he come?"

"He's off at an auction in London," Beryl said enthusiastically. "I told you, remember? And there's going to be a big one at Sotheby's over Christmas. Some duchess's entire collection of art and antiques. He promised he'd take me. Maybe we could all go! It's really interesting. Daddy knows so much."

"Yes," Jewel said, "he knows a great deal about art."

At the Yardley Inn, Jewel was recognized after all, and they were seated immediately. After ordering a martini and two ginger ales, Jewel dutifully began quizzing the girls about their classes and teachers and extracurricular activities, exuding as much maternal enthusiasm as she could muster under the circumstances.

It had been a hell of a day. Things at Bijoux International were starting to unhinge because Jewel was having trouble handling the stress. The deal to open a store in Atlanta had dissolved because she had lost her temper with Travis Peterson, her would-be partner on the project. Peterson thought Jewel was a brilliant designer but did not want her to have control over every business aspect of the Atlanta store. Jewel, of course, could not let go a minutia of control over *any* of her stores. She *was* Bijoux. So, in a fit of temper, Jewel had told Travis Peterson to take his money, roll it into a fat wad, and shove it up his wife Antonia's ass.

Well, not having a store in Atlanta wasn't the end of the world. But allowing herself to lose her temper that way, that was something to come to terms with.

And, of course, there had been the quarrel with Anna McNeill Ferguson, a head-on collision after all these years. That had really ripped Jewel open, to discover that Anna still hated her so much for what she had done.

The past. You couldn't get rid of it, no matter how hard you tried. But what was the lesson?

"Mummie!" Beryl was saying, indicating the waitress standing by their table. "She wants to know if you want another martini."

"What? Oh, no thanks. Why don't you bring me a club soda?" She had work to do later, at home. "I'm sorry, darlings, I'm just a little preoccupied."

"For a change," Amber said, glaring at her mother with the petulant sulkiness that Jewel had come to expect from her.

"Let's talk about what you two want to do tomorrow," Jewel said, trying to sound perky. "I thought we might go shopping and see a movie."

"Oh, let's talk about what *you* want to do tomorrow," Amber whined.

"Oh, Amber! Mummie's just making a suggestion,"
Beryl said quickly. Even though she was a year younger
than her sister, she had assumed the role of family peace-
maker; she did not want this evening to turn into a scene
between her mother and Amber. "I think it'd be fun to go
shopping, Mummie. And there's a movie with River Phoe-
nix playing in Danbury. Come on, Amber, what do you
say?"

"I have to stay at school and work on my history term
paper," Jewel's elder daughter said. "I don't need any
clothes, and I heard it wasn't a very good movie anyway."

Back at her house later that evening, Jewel headed upstairs to try to get some work done.

"Oh, Miss Jewel, I thought I heard you come in,"
Nushka Krupa, the housekeeper, said, emerging from the
kitchen. "How was your evening with the girls?"

"Oh, fine," Jewel said. "Beryl seems to be doing wonderfully. Amber's just scraping by, as usual. They'll be
spending tomorrow night here, by the way, after the parents' dinner."

Nushka nodded. "Is there anything I can get you, Miss
Jewel? You look tired. A cup of tea?"

"Sure, Nushka, that sounds great. And maybe a few
crackers. I'm working late tonight."

Up in her room, Jewel got a sketch pad out of her briefcase and optimistically propped up the pillows on her bed.
She turned on the television, flipped around the dial, and
stopped at an Errol Flynn swashbuckler. Then she slipped
on her nightgown and snuggled into bed with the sketch
pad on her lap. Closing her eyes, Jewel conjured up images of faceted pink tourmalines. But all she could picture
were loose stones glistening against a background of dark
green velvet. Loose stones were not what she needed to
think about. The cut gems had to transform themselves
into jewelry so sparklingly unique that each piece would
fit the image of Bijoux.

Her creativity had vanished months ago; it had seemed to disappear overnight. She was faking it now, coasting on variations of her old designs. No one had noticed so far. At least, nobody had had the guts to mention it, except Mike. But they would, if she could not regain the magic soon.

Jewel opened her eyes and tried to let her imagination enter the world of the pirates in the film on television. Seventeenth-century Spain, it looked to be. She thought of the Spanish Queen, whichever one it was, and what her vast collection of jewels would have been like. She began sketching, concentrating on the old-fashioned look of ornately scrolled gold, paired with more modern tourmalines, and perhaps peridots or tsavorites.

But it was no good. There was no inspiration behind the drawings. Jewel tossed aside her pencil with a sigh. Her head hurt again. *What's taking Nushka so long with the tea?* she wondered.

Closing her eyes with a sigh, she tried to sort through things. How sweet her daughters had been as babies, yet how difficult Amber was now. How gallant Allen had been when they were first together; how desperately she had needed him then. What a great friend her partner Edward Randolph was, and how snappish she was with him these days.

Her mind flickered to her old friend Anna McNeill, who now hated her enough to want to see her dead. And Hadley McNeill, Anna's brother, the great love who had disappeared from her life. There was, of course, Cathalene Columbier, who would love nothing better than to dance on the grave of Bijoux International. And Sascha Robinovsky, the romantic, impossible father of her daughters, who was threatening to upset her equilibrium again. What had happened in her relationships with all these people? Where had all the feeling gone? She thought about what a sexy lover Mike Marshall had been, how bored she was with him now, and the tireless loyalty of Meg, her assistant.

And what a total bitch she herself had become.

Now, with her fortieth birthday looming around the corner, Jewel wondered what was she going to do about herself and her life. Something had to give, if for no other reason than to keep Bijoux International from sinking under the weight of her enormous ego. There had to be an exciting new world to conquer, to stave off boredom. And, Jewel realized, she had to reconcile herself with the world she inhabited now. She had everything, but she *enjoyed* nothing.

If only someone could open up her head and pour in some emotion, some warmth. Her soul was as dead as her creativity. Jewel wanted to be able to care again, about herself and the others with whom she shared her life. No, that was another aspect of the problem: she didn't share her life. She *controlled*—her own self as well as others.

All of a sudden, a wave of nausea swept through Jewel. She dashed for the bathroom. Her first thought was that she must have eaten a bad cherrystone clam at dinner. Food poisoning.

As she reached the bathroom, a strong attack of dizziness overtook her, and a grayish cloud passed before her eyes. She grabbed the sink and, heaving, willed her way toward the toilet. Before she made it, her knees buckled underneath her and she crumbled onto the white-tiled floor. Helpless, she could feel her consciousness falling down something dark and bottomless, sinking deeper and deeper. Then the nausea and dizziness went away, and a strange, disoriented euphoria took their place. In the darkness, she could feel warm, golden light bathing the inside of her head.

She could hear someone calling her name: Maddie . . . Maddie . . .

Then she blacked out completely.

Book One

1960–1978

1

1960

"Maddie . . . Maddie? I'm afraid you have to run along home now."

Madeleine Kathleen Dragoumis looked up from the book she was reading. "Oh? Is it late, Miss Lathem? I guess I lost track."

Jane Lathem smiled at her small, thin fifth-grade pupil. Maddie was an enigma. She was a quiet, reclusive child whose academic skills were more suited for a grade or so lower. But she was obviously so determined to improve that the teacher had resisted sending her back. Maddie read voraciously, anything she could get her hands on, yet, when it was time to write a story, her spelling was appalling and her grammar awkward and inadequate. But she was good at math and seemed to enjoy numbers, especially when Jane Lathem had the class perform exercises where they were given a certain sum of pretend money, to learn how to budget. Maddie always figured out how she

15

would spend her money, to the penny, before anyone else in class.

More than anything, Maddie enjoyed reading books and magazine stories about rich and successful people. She loved the idea of money. It was obvious to Jane Lathem from the way Maddie dressed that the child had not seen a great deal of it in her life. Not that many of the kids at the Green Mountain School had, but Maddie seemed worse off than the others. There had never been a high level of income in that corner of Pennsylvania. Now that the only factory in town had shut down, nearly everyone was desperate. Many families were moving away to search for employment. Jane Lathem herself had spent the past few weeks sending off letters applying for teaching jobs in more affluent parts of the state.

"Well, it's four-thirty, dear. I'm afraid we have to close up shop now. Come on, I'll drop you off. You can take that book with you, if you've finished the rest of your work."

"Oh, thank you, Miss Lathem. But I think I'll walk."

"You'll do no such thing. It'll be getting dark soon, and you live clear across town, don't you? Come on, get your things." Jane paused. "Actually, I'd like to have a talk with your mother."

"Oh, well, er . . . she won't be home yet. She got a job waitressing over in Thomasville."

Jane Lathem locked the classroom door behind her. It was almost Thanksgiving and Maddie was wearing no coat, only a dingy-white nylon sweater over her cotton dress. "What time will your mother be home?"

"Oh, soon. By dinnertime," Maddie said quickly.

The teacher shrugged. "All right . . . I'll meet her another day. You tell her to call me and make an appointment. But I *will* drop you off. It's far too cold out for you to walk, dressed like that."

Maddie did not want her teacher to know where she lived. But it *was* cold, and she didn't relish the walk. To solve the dilemma, she accepted the ride with gratitude but asked Miss Lathem to drop her at Johnny's Cash Store, a couple of blocks from where she lived. Maddie told her teacher that she had to buy groceries for dinner.

As soon as Miss Lathem's car was out of sight, Maddie skittered home the back way, through shadowy alleys, to her house. "House" was a more than generous term, although that's what it had once been. Currently, it was one of a row of condemned structures, the best of the row, and Maddie shared it with a stray cat she had found and named Scrappy. Occasionally, a bum would wander in for the night, and she and Scrappy would hide quietly in their secret room in the basement until daylight came and she could sneak off to school. Nowadays, with the town so poor, she usually had the house to herself. Bums traveling east or west on the train did not bother to get off at Green Mountain; they knew there were no handouts there.

Maddie knew it too. Of course, there were a few shop-keepers who always gave her some nearly perished food at the end of the day—Maddie told them she needed it for her family's dogs and chickens—but she was careful never to go to any of them more than once a week, for fear of overstepping her welcome. The lady at the Salvation Army had known Maddie's mother, and she always set aside the best clothes she got in Maddie's size. But in a poor, mostly Catholic town where the citizens had large families, the pickings were slim. The Salvation Army was fixing to close down too.

No one, however, not one person in town, knew that the ten-year-old girl had been living alone, with Scrappy, for over four months.

Maddie got by. Children at school made fun of her clothes, which never fit because she was so bony. They also had caught her between periods stealing parts of lunches—an orange here, a cracker or half of sandwich there—and had threatened to report her to the principal. But when her eyes had welled up with terrified, heartfelt tears, even the least charitable child had felt sorry for her. Maddie continued to steal food from lunch boxes, but the children pretended not to notice. She was quiet, and there was a sweet sadness about her that kept the biggest bullies from teasing her. For the most part, Maddie kept to herself and the kids ignored her.

Nobody could understand how Maddie happened to appear so poor when she was always telling Miss Lathem about her mother waitressing, and her father working in a "big, important job" in New York City. Eventually the kids figured out she was lying about her father, which she was. They weren't sure what the truth was about her mother. Neither was Maddie.

Maddie's father—there really had been a legitimate father—had taken off only weeks after her birth. Maddie's mother carried around a small photograph of him in her wallet. Maddie loved to look at it: he was a large, handsome man with dark wavy hair and intense Greek eyes. Maddie had seen his name, Nick Dragoumis, typed on her birth certificate. She never knew what happened to Nick. Her mother refused to talk about him.

Maddie believed, with no evidence at all to go on, that he went to New York and became rich and famous. One of her favorite fantasies—one of her *many* fantasies—had it as only a matter of time before Nick Dragoumis would long to see his beloved daughter whom he had deserted at birth. Then he would send for her. After their loving reunion, Nick would take her to live in an elegant town house in some beautiful neighborhood, and she would be the best-dressed girl at her private school.

Maddie's mother, Lulu Fleishman, had grown up in another hamlet in the area, poor and from a large family. She was plain, but made up for it with the opposite sex by having large breasts and a slim, supple body. At sixteen she left home and went to Pittsburgh, where she struggled for two years to make ends meet. When she met and mar-

ried Nick Dragoumis, a bartender at the rough neighborhood bar where she worked, she thought her life had
changed for good. But she got pregnant right away, and
although Nick stuck around for her nine months, he
didn't hold an image of himself as a father. So he left.

Lulu was a waitress, that part was true. She supple-
mented her income by becoming a hooker, although Maddie didn't know that was the name for what her mother
did. After Nick deserted her and the baby, Lulu left Pittsburgh, for reasons known only to herself, and began drifting around western Pennsylvania. There were relatively
few clients in any small factory town, and they were
mostly married with not much extra money to throw her
way. Still, Lulu never went back to live with her family,
nor did she return to Pittsburgh.

Lulu took care of Maddie reasonably well until the
child was nine. It was then that they wandered into Green
Mountain and began living for free in one of the condemned row houses. At that point the dismal quality of
her life began to overwhelm Lulu. She slipped into a deep
depression and spent most of her time looking out the
window, crying. Occasionally, she would get herself together enough to go out at night and return the next
morning with some money.

Maddie found the local elementary school and, after
several months, managed to drag Lulu over to enroll her.
Maddie got a Saturday job sweeping up for Mr. Vlasic,
who owned a small grocery store that specialized in his
homemade sausages. On Saturday evenings, Maddie and
Lulu would dine on bratwurst and sauerkraut, compliments of Mr. Vlasic. They would eat in the boarded-up
back room, indulging in candlelight instead of going to
bed just after dark. On those Saturdays Maddie could almost trick herself into believing that she and her mother
were a normal, happy family.

One day, while Maddie was at school, Lulu took off,
simply up and left town. She wrote a note to her daughter,

telling Maddie that she had gone to visit relatives and
would return soon. She cautioned Maddie to stay put and
not tell anybody that she was alone, on the threat of severe
punishment when Lulu returned. Pinned to the note were
two ten-dollar bills.

During the day, surrounded by her classmates and
made brave by her secret hardship, Maddie was pragmatic
about her life. Nights were horrible, though. She did not
feel the least bit brave, alone in the dark, surrounded by
spiders and mice and strange creaking noises. Maddie
cried often, confused and scared, totally bewildered by her
mother's sudden departure. She told herself that something important must have happened, that Lulu would
probably return with enough money for them to live in a
real house. Better yet, Maddie liked to fantasize that Lulu
would return with Nick Dragoumis. These thoughts carried Maddie through the first night and many subsequent
ones, although she often cried herself to sleep, clutching
her cat tightly for comfort and courage.

Maddie accepted the day-to-day scramble for food (the
days she didn't ask for handouts, she stole, but only from
the one supermarket in town that was part of a big chain).
She and Scrappy became content enough with their living
arrangements, at least until Lulu returned and they could
move. The basement of the house was dry and warm
enough. She had dragged old mattresses from upstairs to
insulate the little basement room (and taken several cans
of Lysol from the janitor's closet at school to make them
smell decent). Every week or so, Maddie stole clean sheets
from clotheslines around town, and returned them dirty a
week later. She did that with socks and underwear too. At
school, after all the children had gone home for the day
and she had the bathroom to herself, she washed herself
and brushed her teeth. Maddie often borrowed Miss
Lathem's scissors, when she wasn't looking, and kept her
hair cut very short because it was easier to keep clean and
dried faster in the chillier weather.

Once or twice, Maddie made plans to go search for her mother. But when it was time to turn the plans into action, the child realized that she had no idea where to begin looking. Except for telling Maddie that she had been born in Pittsburgh, Lulu had never divulged even the tiniest snippet of information about her own past. Every so often Maddie had asked Lulu if she had grandparents and where they lived. Lulu had only answered, "As far as you're concerned, you don't."

Scared as Maddie was, as much terror as she felt when she woke up in the middle of the night and realized that the worst nightmare imaginable—that her mother was gone—was *real,* she was determined that no one discover her situation. That kept her from trying to make friends with whom she might have gone home occasionally to have dinner or spend the night. Friends' parents would pry, and Maddie knew she could not risk that. They would send her off somewhere, to an orphanage. And how would her mother—or her father—ever find her then?

"Maddie . . . your mother never called me for an appointment. Did you give her the message?"

Maddie looked up at Miss Lathem. "Er, well . . . I guess I forgot."

Jane Lathem smiled. She was a strong-featured woman, in her midthirties. A nose that was too long and thin kept her face from being pretty, but her skin was rosy and flawless and her hair was always shiny-clean and curled into a neat pageboy. She wore matching skirts and sweaters, always accessorized with a scarf around her neck or a belt. To Maddie, Jane Lathem was beautiful and the most stylish woman in town.

"It's not that I have anything bad to say about you, Maddie," Jane assured her. "You're working hard. Your spelling and grammar are improving. I enjoy meeting the parents of my pupils, getting to know them a bit. Maybe I'll stop by this weekend."

"Oh, gosh, we're going to Harrisburg," Maddie said quickly. "To visit my grandparents."

"Well, that's nice, Maddie. I'm sure you'll have a wonderful time."

"Yes ma'am, I will. My grandfather owns a movie theater, and we're going to the movies . . . and *out* to dinner in restaurants every night."

Jane Lathem nodded distractedly, searching for a mislaid spiral notebook. She had been frantically busy the past month. Her class was too large for one person. The ten-year-old boys were a rowdy handful, and she was still trying to find another job for next year. Putting her hands on the notebook, it occurred to her suddenly that she had let her initial concern for Maddie slip away with the weeks; Maddie was there, waiting, when she arrived at school in the mornings and the child was always the last to leave. Maddie never complained, but it was as if she dreaded going home.

"I'll drop you off today," she said. "Perhaps your mother will be there."

"Oh, no . . . I don't think so," Maddie hedged, "Thursdays she works late."

"You mean she won't be home to fix your supper?"

"Well, she always leaves something for me. Cold chicken or beef stew or something."

Jane Lathem nodded. "Well, I think maybe I'll buy a sandwich and eat with you. A child your age shouldn't be all alone after dark."

Maddie swallowed, her throat dry. A terrible panic wedged itself into the pit of her stomach. "I just remembered. She *is* coming home tonight."

"Then I'll stop in and say hello."

"No! I mean, the reason she's coming home early is 'cause she's having a party. It's a surprise birthday party for one of her friends. I have to help her get ready."

"Maddie," Jane Lathem said firmly. "I am taking you

home. If your mother isn't there yet, I'll wait for her. If she's busy I'll merely say a quick hello."

As Jane Lathem's emerald green Dodge crossed town, Maddie searched her brain for a solution. She could jump out of the car at the next red light and take off down the street, but Miss Lathem would never give up after that. Maddie would have to stop going to school to avoid Miss Lathem's persistent probing. On the other hand, her teacher was so intent on learning the truth that Maddie considered coming clean about the situation. But what would happen then? Miss Lathem would undoubtedly be required to report Maddie's predicament to someone. Then everyone would know. The whole town. The humiliation accompanying that thought was unbearable. Even worse, she would be carted off to some foster home where they probably would not want Scrappy.

As the car neared Johnny's Cash Store, Maddie felt more and more panic-stricken. Suddenly, she knew what she had to do. The car slowed down, then stopped at the small intersection across the street from the grocery store.

"Which way now?" Jane asked.

"Oh . . . could you wait here a minute? I have to run into the store and buy some Coca-Cola. I'll be right back."

"Do you have money?"

"Oh, yeah. Mama gave me five dollars this morning."

Maddie walked slowly across the street and into the store. She looked back at Miss Lathem and waved. She said hello to Johnny, the middle-aged owner, and headed quickly through the store to the back exit that led to an alley. She ran all the way home, her heart beating wildly. When she got there, she slipped into the dark house through a back window and grabbed Scrappy, holding him close up against her face until her breathing returned to normal. This was it. This was the end. Miss Lathem would not be able to find her tonight, but Maddie knew she could never show her face in school again without facing a barrage of questions that she would be forced to answer.

"We've got to move, Scrappy. I know Mama's not coming back. She would have been here by now if she planned on coming. So what we've got to do is pack up our things and sneak onto the ten o'clock train. You know, it's funny, Scrappy," she said, tears trickling down her face into the cat's fur, "hearing those trains all the time. I don't even know where the ten o'clock goes to." She squeezed the cat so tightly it meowed and tried to pry itself loose from her grasp. "Well, it'll be a surprise, won't it? An adventure."

She put the gray cat down before it scratched her. "Okay, you stay here while I go over to Mr. Vlasic's and see what kind of food we can get. I'll get a jar of water too."

As she headed for Vlasic's store she peeked around the corner to see if Miss Lathem's car was still waiting in front of Johnny's. It was, but Miss Lathem wasn't in it. Probably she'd gone in to find out what was taking so long. Maddie scurried away in the other direction, trying to invent a story to convince Mr. Vlasic to part with more food than usual.

Maddie was so preoccupied as she crossed the street that she did not notice the maroon car speeding up the street toward her until it had screeched to an ear-piercing halt to try to avoid hitting her. The front bumper knocked her off balance and jolted her back to reality. She fell to the ground in front of the tires, stunned but, as far as she could tell, unhurt.

"Oh my God . . . my God!" the man who was driving the car wailed as he leapt out of his Plymouth. "Little girl . . . I didn't see you. You darted out in front of me. Help! *Help!* Somebody! Help . . . call an ambulance. The child is hurt!" he screamed into the darkness of the empty street.

Maddie scrambled to her feet, more scared by the fuss he was making than by her own near-death. "I'm okay

. . . really. You didn't hit me. I lost my balance *after* you stopped the car," she stammered. "Really, I'm fine. I don't need an ambulance."

But people had begun swarming out into the street from nearby houses. The ambulance had been called, she heard someone say, and the police. Someone else threw a coat over her shoulders and sat her on the hood of the car. The crowd huddled around her as the man tried to explain what had happened. Maddie's leg hurt a bit, but she knew it didn't hurt enough to be broken. She kept insisting to everyone that she was fine. All she knew was that she had to get out of there, over to Mr. Vlasic's before he closed up for the night. But how could she get away now? Some woman was insisting that she be taken to the hospital for observation. Someone else was asking whether her parents had been called.

And then, horror of horrors, Maddie looked up to see Jane Lathem's emerald green Dodge turn the corner and head down the street toward the commotion.

This is the end, Maddie thought, trapped. *It's too late to escape.*

2

1968

"And graduating with highest honors, with a scholarship to the University of Colorado, it is my great pleasure to award this diploma to the class valedictorian, Madeleine Kathleen Lathem."

Ernest Johnson, the robust principal of the Pine Ridge High School in Pine Ridge, Colorado, twisted his mouth into a broad smile. "We're proud of you, Maddie," he continued over the loud applause that bounced off the walls of the school auditorium on the stifling, early June day.

Jane Lathem, sitting in the third row, bit her lip hard and tried to fight off the tears that were gathering behind her eyes. She might as well have tried to stop the rain that was falling outside.

Dammit, she thought, *I swore I wouldn't do this.* And then she thought, *What the hell, why shouldn't I? Maddie's my child as much as if I had given birth to her myself.*

26

And she let them run down her cheeks, tears from a heart bursting with love and pride.

Jane reached for a tissue, and blew her nose discreetly. She was not the only parent in the room who was crying. A burst of pleasure engulfed her. She was indeed a parent. Maddie was her daughter, as far as anyone in Pine Ridge knew.

Later, while Maddie dressed for the prom, Jane Lathem tried to focus and store away every moment of this special day. It was hard to believe that she and Maddie had been together for seven years. And now it was almost over. Maddie would be leaving for college.

If Doctor Evans was right, Jane would be leaving too.

But this was not the day to think about that. This was Maddie's day. Maddie didn't know anything about Doctor Evans's diagnosis. There was no reason for her to know, not for a while yet. Maybe not at all. Maybe the doctor was wrong. Maybe she'd live to see Maddie's college graduation, see her married, grandchildren . . .

Seven years. The time had sped by in what now seemed like an instant. In the very beginning the going had been rough financially. Jane's salary was low, and Maddie— after years of near starvation—was an eager mouth to feed. But Jane did not deny the child anything. She tried hard to make up for the hideousness of Maddie's life before she came to live with Jane, that night after the car had nearly killed her, so long ago.

Jane knew about emotional pain and physical hardship firsthand, having been orphaned herself in her teens, when her parents and brother were killed in a boating accident. Her parents had been in debt, overextended in the small laundry they owned. In the months after their deaths, Jane saw everything she thought she had inherited slip away to settle their estate. She was left with nothing except for her personal belongings and a few mementos.

Fortunately, being an excellent student, she had been

awarded a full scholarship to the University of Pennsylvania. Unfortunately, her luck did not improve beyond that. Jane fell in love, but her boyfriend got her pregnant the first and only time she slept with him. Gerald was on scholarship too, and planning to become a lawyer, which meant six more years of school. He and Jane could not afford to settle down and have a child.

Jane had been raised a Catholic. But there was no choice. If she had the child alone she would be forced to give up her scholarship and dreams of having a good education. Even if she had the child and gave it up for adoption she would miss school and perhaps lose her scholarship. So Gerald raised the money and drove Jane to the squalid two-story house where she submitted to the moral and physical horrors of an illegal abortion, performed by a "doctor" who smoked a cigar while he tormented her uterus.

Afterward Jane felt unbearably guilty. She told Gerald that she could never see him again. And then God punished her for her sin. Like some other unlucky young women of the time who were forced to have abortions under unsanitary conditions, Jane developed an infection that eventually led to her sterility.

After that, it seemed that every young man Jane dated seriously wanted to get married and have a family. Knowing that she could never provide the family, she always broke up with them, on one pretext or another, never admitting the truth. Then she accepted a teaching job in Green Mountain, where there seemed to be no eligible young men at all. At thirty-four, Jane forsook all hope of ever finding a husband who would accept a barren wife.

Then, miraculously, God had a change of heart and forgave her: Maddie appeared in her life, needing her desperately. Soon after the child moved in with her, which was the very night of the accident, Jane landed a teaching job in another part of the state. Still, she hired a private detective to track down Maddie's mother. It was an expense Jane could barely afford, but she felt that was her obligation. If she had brought in the police they would have taken Maddie away from her, and the courts would have awarded the child to a foster family. Jane was sure they would never have given Maddie to her, a single woman living alone.

After months went by with no trace, Lulu Dragoumis began to fade from Maddie's memory. Finally Jane told the detective to call off the search; she had done her duty and by then could not bear the thought of giving Maddie up. But she lived in terror that one day Lulu Dragoumis would reappear and demand her daughter back. Jane decided that she and Maddie had to leave Pennsylvania for good and go to another part of the country.

On the enthusiastic advice of a friend who had gone to Denver, Jane decided to move to Colorado. It was a healthy place to bring up a child, and the chances of Lulu Dragoumis showing up there were next to none. Jane took night courses to get her Colorado teacher's certificate and got a job in Pine Ridge, a small town north of Pueblo. They rented a stone house by a lake, surrounded by aspen trees and unlimited sky, and at last felt a deep peace settle over their lives.

When they moved from the East, Maddie took the name Lathem and posed as Jane's real daughter. It was easier that way, and no one questioned the relationship. Maddie and Jane were both slim, with brown hair and blue eyes. They *looked* like mother and daughter.

Seven years. Beyond compare, they had been the best seven years of Jane Lathem's life. And if Doctor Evans was right, and they turned out to be the last ones as well, at least she could be grateful to God for the timing. He had kept her together with Maddie while the girl had needed her most.

Now that Maddie was graduating and heading off to college, well . . . if God was ready to call Jane, she would greet Him with a prayer of thanks on her lips.

"Mother? Are you all right? You're staring into the onions."

Jane glanced up, startled, from the chili she was preparing.

Maddie was in the kitchen doorway. Her hair was ironed straight and hung almost to her waist. She was wearing a shocking-pink strapless taffeta gown that she had found in a resale shop in Denver. It had been ankle length, but Maddie had cut it off and refashioned it so that now it billowed out from midthigh. It was the sort of outfit that *Vogue* showed models wearing in New York. Miniskirts for evening were a style that had not heretofore made their debut in Pine Ridge. But Maddie had always been independent of mind and fashion. That's how she made up for not being able to afford the classic clothes that everyone else wore. She simply created her own style, on the limited budget she could afford.

"My goodness, look at you! The dress turned out great. You're beautiful, darling."

Maddie smiled, pleased. "Do you think Tommy will like it?"

"If he doesn't he's either blind or brain dead," Jane snorted. With the corner of her apron she brushed at her eyes. "Onions," she muttered. Then suddenly she gasped. "Oh . . . I almost forgot. Wait right here. I have a present for you."

She ran upstairs and was back in a moment with a small box wrapped in pink tissue paper with a white bow.

"Happy graduation," she said, handing it to Maddie. Her eyes glistened. "I'm so proud of you!"

Maddie kissed Jane, then accepted the box. They had always lived on a tight budget. Maddie knew that Jane could not afford anything expensive. But when she opened the box, she gasped.

"An opal pin!" It was in the shape of a heart. "It's beautiful! I'll wear it tonight. Right here." She pinned it to the waist of her dress. "Oh, it's perfect!"

Jane smiled. "I'm glad you like it. I was really lucky. I unearthed it at the church rummage sale. I took it to the jeweler in town and he cleaned it up for me. The opals are absolutely real, he told me. I know girls don't wear pins very often nowadays. You might want to make it into a pendant sometime."

"Don't start apologizing. I love it just as it is. You know, this is the first real piece of jewelry I've ever owned." Maddie gave her a big hug. "This is the best day of my life . . . next to the day I moved in with you."

By the time summer had ended and Jane had driven Maddie to Boulder to get her settled, Jane knew that she had inoperable cancer. But Maddie was so happy—on the brink of college and dating Tommy Morgan, the local bank president's son—that Jane could never seem to find the right moment to break the news to her. Not telling Maddie seemed to make Jane stronger, and Doctor Evans marveled at her determination.

Maddie had no idea of Jane's condition, except she noticed that Jane had lost weight and seemed to go to church more often than usual. But Maddie thought nothing of it . . . until later.

It happened around Thanksgiving. Doctor Evans called Maddie the day Jane was admitted to the hospital. Maddie was distraught. The doctor was surprised that Maddie still had been told nothing of Jane's condition.

Tommy Morgan drove Maddie to Pine Ridge at once. There she stayed, by Jane's side at the hospital, for fifteen days.

During that time, Jane was sedated and in terrible pain, but she made great effort, in her lucid moments, to help Maddie prepare for the future.

"Work hard at the university," Jane counseled. "No matter what, get your degree. I know you want to be an artist, but a degree's still important. Artists have to eat . . ." Jane closed her eyes from the effort of speaking.

"I'll be fine," Maddie tried to assure her. "Just rest now, and don't worry about me. I mean, I can always marry Tommy. He's going to be a banker like his father."

Jane squeezed Maddie's hand. "Don't marry him . . . unless you're sure it's the right thing to do. Don't give up your dreams."

"Oh, don't worry. I'm going to be famous! You wait and see . . ." Tears welled up in Maddie's eyes. She wanted so badly for Jane to be around to see her become famous. Jane was her family, and her best friend. It didn't seem fair that she had to die now, when there should have been so much time left.

"Oh, Jane . . . how can I thank you for all you've done?"

"Thank me?" Jane whispered. "You don't . . ." she trailed off.

"You know," Maddie swallowed, afraid of the silence, "sometimes I try to imagine what would have happened to me if you hadn't come along when you did that night. Where I would have ended up."

"Do you," Jane struggled to get out the words, "ever think about . . . your real mother?"

Maddie shook her head. "Not really. Except to wonder what happened to her. And out of curiosity, what sort of traits I've inherited from her. A long time ago I used to think about what I'd do if she suddenly appeared and wanted me back." She squeezed Jane's hand. "But I knew the answer, even then. I would've stayed with you. You're my mother now. There's a connection between us as strong as blood." Tears came to her eyes and she sniffed and swallowed quickly so that Jane would not see her cry. But Jane's eyes were closed. She was breathing evenly, asleep.

"A few years ago . . ." Jane said sometime later, after she had dozed a bit, "I took out a life insurance policy. It's in the drawer by my bed at home. You . . . are the beneficiary . . ." She closed her eyes for a few moments, then opened them again. "Promise me, Maddie . . . that you . . . will never spend the money unless you . . . have no other choice. Save it for an emergency. Invest it . . . save it . . ."

"I promise, Mother," Maddie whispered. "I promise."

Jane's eyes drifted shut again, and her light grip on Maddie's hand fell away. She lived several more days, but it was her last conversation with Maddie.

Maddie stayed by Jane's bedside until the end.

The week after Jane Lathem's funeral was spent in a blur of financial legalities, all the inevitable things involved with closing out a life. The hospital bill, fortunately, had been covered by Jane's teachers' group-insurance policy. The life insurance money came to fifteen thousand dollars, and Maddie put it into a savings account at the bank until she could figure out the best way to invest it. Then she slowly, painfully, went through Jane's clothes and belongings. Except for the furniture, some photographs and books, Jane's Timex and some costume jewelry, Maddie donated everything to the Salvation Army. She could not afford to pay storage on the furniture, an ill-matched assortment at best, so she sold the lot of it to an auction house for two hundred dollars.

Once all that had been taken care of, Maddie had to decide what was to happen to Scrappy, her beloved cat, the remainder of her family. Maddie couldn't bear to part with her old friend. On the other hand, she wasn't allowed to keep a pet in the dormitory at school. She thought about sneaking Scrappy in, but the cat loved to roam the outdoors. He would be miserable, confined to a small room with a litter box. One of Jane's friends, an English teacher at the high school, had been taking care of Scrappy during Jane's illness. And so, in the end, Maddie arranged for Ellen Peterson to keep the cat.

"Don't you worry, Scrappy. I'll be back," she promised, hugging him before she left. "I'll come first chance I get."

But even as she was saying it, Maddie knew in her heart that she would never return to Pine Ridge. And perhaps Scrappy knew too, for the cat squirmed in her embrace, jumped down, and walked stiffly away.

Before taking the bus back to Boulder, Maddie walked over to the empty house by the lake and sat on the floor of the vacant living room, quietly trying to assess the impact all this had on her life. If anyone had a reason to cry, she did, abandoned *and* orphaned, but her well of emotions had dried up.

The house had been rented, and a new family would be moving in before Christmas. So fast. It was amazing that someone's entire life could be disposed of so quickly. In scarcely more than three weeks, Jane had gone into the hospital, died, and now there was nothing left of her at all. Except a few photographs and Maddie's memories.

Maddie had been unbelievably strong, all of Jane's friends and associates at school had said so at the funeral. And she had remained strong while she dispassionately handled the details surrounding Jane's death. One thought, though, nagged at her consciousness and would not leave her alone. Not actually a thought: an emotion. And that emotion was not grief, but anger.

Maddie was furious that Jane had not told her she was ill. Everything that Maddie had done at college that autumn mocked her with its triviality as she replayed it against the backdrop of Jane's suffering and slowly dying . . . alone.

"You could've told me, Mother," she said aloud, softly. "You *should* have told me. I could have missed school. I could've missed one lousy semester, to be with you!" The words came louder and faster, tumbling out in anger and frustration. "You always told me to tell the truth. Why couldn't *you* tell the truth? *Why?* Don't you see *you* were important to me? Not school, not— I shared your life, Mother, why couldn't you have let me share your illness?"

Her words seemed loud in the bare room, and she stopped suddenly, feeling guilty and terribly confused.

Maddie got up and walked from room to room in the empty house, almost in a trance. She tried to imagine the new family moving in, what they would be like. In a couple of weeks the house would be full again, decorated for Christmas. New voices would fill the rooms.

The tears came, at first slowly, then in a downpour. Maddie leaned against the kitchen counter and cried and screamed hysterically for over an hour. In her misery, Maddie cried for Jane, for Scrappy, for the empty house.

And for herself, for being left alone again.

3

For the rest of the year at the university, Maddie never seemed to catch hold of the momentum. On the surface things seemed fine. She attended classes, turned in papers on time, maintained an honors average, and continued to go out with Tommy Morgan, the boy she had dated since sophomore year of high school. Inside, however, she felt undefined and dull, as if she were gliding through her life, not living it.

Just before the end of the school year, Maddie broke up with Tommy. It had been coming for months. At Pine Ridge High, the two of them had shared many interests. But at Boulder, Tommy had become totally engrossed in the party scene. Maddie had found, over the long winter, that they had had little to talk about anymore. Their friends were his friends, and she considered them immature. Finally, she realized that she was happier during her time apart from Tommy than with him, and decided to

call it quits. When she suggested that they begin seeing
other people, Tommy took the news well, so well in fact
that Maddie realized that she was no longer what he
wanted either. She had changed too. Since Jane's death,
she had lost the ability and desire to enjoy herself.

When summer came, the summer of '69, Maddie decided to remain in Boulder to take several business
courses, as a practical counterbalance to her major in art.
She looked for a part-time job and finally found one that
appealed to her: working in a jewelry shop.

It was better than a waitressing job; Maddie had morning classes most days and the shop's hours were from
noon to seven. Even though she would make less money
than waitressing, she would have more time to study.
And, in lieu of higher wages, the shop's owner had agreed
to teach her about jewelry design, the area of art that had
begun to capture her fancy.

Maddie had loved jewelry since she was a small girl and
used to pore over magazines to see how rich people lived.
Over the years, for holidays and birthdays, she had almost
always made some sort of trinket for Jane to wear. Their
first year together, when they had been so poor, Maddie
had given Jane a bracelet made of dyed string, masking
tape, and feathers plucked from the school janitor's
feather duster. Another year she gave Jane a necklace of
acrylic-painted safety pins. Maddie loved to collect old
beads and rhinestone buttons and string them with unusual things, such as plastic hearts or soldiers out of
Cracker Jack boxes. The idea of working in a jewelry store
excited her enormously.

The shop's owner and chief designer was a young man
named Brady Gardner. Actually, Maddie was not crazy
about his designs, although he was a skilled craftsman.
His work was too elaborate, she thought, bordering on the
tacky. But it was popular, both with the tourists and with
a regular local clientele. The shop had a continuous flow
of activity.

Brady Gardner's studio was directly behind the shop, connected by a glassed-in walkway filled with English ferns and bougainvillea. Often Maddie would come to the shop early and wander out back to watch Brady work before it was time to open up. By the end of her second week, however, Maddie realized that this was not going to be much of an apprenticeship. Brady Gardner jealously guarded his work. He was too busy to take time to show her even the simplest techniques.

Gardner had an enormous ego about his work. A bachelor at twenty-eight, he also held a high opinion of his looks and sex appeal. Hidden away in the back of a drawer, he kept a secret notebook with the names of all the women he had slept with, beginning at the age of fourteen. It gave him great pleasure to get out the book after each new conquest and enter the name. The last name he had entered was number three hundred, even. He hired Maddie because she was pretty and unattached. Mentally he was already penciling her in as number three hundred and one.

"What are you going to do with this turquoise?" Maddie asked. She had just locked up the shop and had ventured back into Brady's workroom to collect her paycheck.

"Turquoise?" he said with disgust. "Here, *look* at it. It isn't at all like turquoise. It's malachite and azurite, put in a tumbler for two weeks to get that sheen."

"It's pretty," Maddie said, ignoring the insult. "What are you going to do with it?"

"Haven't decided. Mo just brought it to me today, along with some Mexican opals. I have to sit with the stones and see what they say to me. Hey! Don't touch."

"I was only looking."

Brady scooped up the tray of stones and put them into his safe. When he had finished, he looked at Maddie and smiled. "Oh, it's Friday. I guess you want some money."

Maddie nodded.

"Doing anything tonight?" He undid the rubber band of the ponytail that kept his hair out of his way while he worked, and shook his head briskly. His sand-colored mane fell loosely beyond his shoulders.

"Studying. I have a test in accounting in the morning."

"Jesus, don't you ever have fun?"

"Of course. But I have this test." In truth, Maddie couldn't remember the last time she'd enjoyed herself. One's college days were supposed to be a kick, but thus far Maddie had felt the kick only in her backside. The pressure to maintain her grades and her scholarship was always with her.

"You know," Brady said, turning off the light over his worktable, "you're too serious."

Maddie shrugged. "Maybe."

He grabbed his denim jacket from a hook next to the door. "I'm knocking off early tonight. Why don't you let me buy you some dinner. You have to eat."

"No, I don't . . ."

Brady fixed his eyes on her, cajolingly. Maddie had known that it was only a matter of time before he made his move. His friend and gem supplier, Mo Steiner, had warned her about his reputation as a womanizer, but she didn't find him tempting. Brady, with his perfect features and long-lashed blue eyes, was far too good-looking. Maddie did not like men who were prettier than she was. Not that she was bad-looking, with her thick, shiny brown hair that hung below her shoulder blades, and her clear blue eyes, full mouth, straight nose, and high cheekbones. But she wore no makeup, convinced her features were too exaggerated to accentuate them more. Jane, and others, had told her she had the basic potential to be a model. And she did, although she did not believe it.

"I won't take no for an answer," he said.

Well, Maddie thought, *what the hell.* She was hungry. Having a decent meal with Brady Gardner was better than her usual Pepsi and Hershey bar out of the dorm's vending machines. "All right, why not?"

"I love your enthusiasm," he said. "Maybe you should take etiquette instead of accounting."

"Look," Maddie snapped. "I'm tired. I don't need this."

"Need what?"

"Your fucking condescending attitude. You talk to me like that all the time. Like I'm some . . . dumb bimbo! Like you're doing me a favor to even let me work here." She walked past him, out the door and down the pathway that led to the street.

"Hey, wait! I'm sorry." Brady caught up with her. "I was going to take you for pizza. But to apologize, how about a steak and some wine?"

"Let's get one thing straight," Maddie said. "It's just dinner. That's all."

"Hey . . . it's fine with me," Brady said offhandedly. "Dinner is all I want."

Brady took her to a new French restaurant near the university, and insisted she order the chateaubriand, the most expensive item on the menu. He selected a bottle of Nuits-St.-Georges.

"This is very good," Maddie said simply. The wine was far better than any she had ever tasted, but she was afraid of overpraising. She lived in fear of betraying her unworldliness.

Brady glanced around the intimate room, waving to several friends. He was pleased that his pretty employee seemed impressed by the restaurant, and hoped a couple of glasses of wine would loosen her up a bit. He had seldom seen a more uptight nineteen-year-old in his life. There was a real air of self-preservation about her—a guarded resistance to divulging anything of a personal nature.

"Tell me about yourself. The only thing I know is that you want to be an artist. Or maybe a jewelry designer?"

"Maybe. I haven't decided yet."

"Well, tell me your life story. Like, where you come from. What your favorite hobby is. Who you like better—the Beatles or the Stones. Anything you want to lay on me, I'll listen to."

"I don't like to talk about myself," she said truthfully, an old habit that years with Jane had not erased.

"I've noticed." Brady decided to stop trying to make conversation. If she wanted to talk, fine. If not, they'd sit and eat in silence. Maybe he could smoke her out that way. Maddie was an enigma to him; she was intriguing. It made the game more fun.

They sipped their wine in silence. Finally, it occurred to Maddie that Brady really was not going to talk anymore unless she opened up. He wasn't happy merely discussing movies or books or even talking about himself, the way most men seemed to be; he appeared to want to get to know *her*. Of course she knew Brady could not possibly be interested. It was just his form of seduction.

The steak arrived, with pommes frites, and haricots verts sautéed in garlic. Maddie dug in hungrily. She had never been to such an expensive restaurant before, and she knew this meal would cost Brady a lot of money. In spite of what she thought of him, he was making an effort. There was no point in acting shitty because he had a reputation as a ladykiller.

All Brady had asked her to do was talk about herself. An innocent enough request. Except she couldn't do it. Telling about her past seemed more intimate and embarrassing to Maddie than stripping off her clothes in a public place.

Suddenly, she had an inspiration.

"Well, I guess I have to tell you sometime. It might as well be now," Maddie said, after she had bolted half of her steak. "My father died in prison. For being a spy. He was a scientist at Los Alamos, and I don't know what happened, really. He wrote me a letter from prison one time, swearing he was innocent, that he was framed."

She ate a few pommes frites and took another sip of her wine. The waiter came over and refilled her glass. "My mother was humiliated. We moved to Los Angeles and changed our name. We started a new life. She married a movie producer and had four more children. I'm kind of an embarrassment. When she sees me, it reminds her of my father."

Maddie looked into Brady's eyes. It was going well. She could tell that he believed every word. It was so easy. And so much fun, to make Brady think she was baring her soul to him. But he was being nice to her, and lying like this, easy as it was, made her as uncomfortable as telling the truth. Of course, if he found out she was lying, what difference did it make? He probably lied to women all the time.

Except it made a difference to her.

"No . . . I just made all that up. I'm an orphan . . . that's the truth. And I really don't like talking about it," Maddie smiled, self-consciously. "My favorite hobby is reading. And I like the Stones."

Brady put his hand over hers. "I like you, Maddie. You really are different."

Maddie did not, true to her word, go home and sleep with Brady Gardner that night after dinner. But after that evening, Brady's attitude toward her began to change. He became kinder at work. He was no longer abrupt when he was busy. He took her out to eat fairly often, after work. He even began to instruct her in the lost-wax method of jewelry making. Finally—three weeks after their first date—Maddie decided it was time to let him seduce her.

Maddie was not a virgin. She had slept with Tommy Morgan for the first time when she was a junior in high school. By the time they had broken up, it was as if they were an old married couple. Most of the nights they had spent together during the last semester had been merely to sleep.

The truth was, Maddie did not like sex. She didn't hate it. She wasn't repulsed. She just did not think it was all it was cracked up to be.

That was why she had not been anxious to go to bed with Brady, even after she began to find him more attractive. Finally, though, she knew she had to deliver. She could not expect to dine out with him forever without eventually picking up what was clearly expected to be her share of the tab. Besides, and more important, she was getting valuable instruction from him in jewelry design.

And so Maddie felt it was time to give him her body.

"Here . . ." Brady said, handing her the joint. "Want another toke?" It was a hot evening, and they were lying on a mattress on the screened-in porch of his house.

Maddie shook her head. "If I mellow out any more, I'm afraid I'll fall asleep."

Brady tossed the joint in the ashtray and leaned over and kissed her. "We certainly don't want that to happen. At least not now."

"You know, Brady, you've turned into a pretty decent guy."

"Jesus, listen to the way she hands out compliments. I meant it about etiquette school." He reached out and smoothed her straight, long brown hair with his hand. "I really do like you just the way you are. I never know what to expect. I think I'm falling in love."

"Oh, Brady . . . please. I'll sleep with you. But not if you tell me you love me. I know your reputation. I've heard about that little notebook with all the names."

Brady sat up, annoyed. "What? How? Have you been snooping?"

"Mo Steiner told me. One day he was in the shop and things were quiet. We started talking. He warned me about getting involved with you."

"Mo? That fucker. Jesus! I thought he was a friend."

"Don't tell him I said anything! He was just trying to be brotherly with me."

"He was just trying to put the make on you," Brady said. "Jesus, you can't trust anyone these days."

"Least of all you," Maddie smiled, unbuttoning her blouse. She could no longer remember much about her real mother, but her large breasts were Lulu's greatest gift to her. Maddie's face was prettier, but her body was identical to Lulu's . . . thin everywhere except for her breasts. Maddie, embarrassed when she developed so quickly in the eighth grade, had always tended to wear loose clothing to conceal her body.

"Hey . . . I'm as nice a guy as you're ever likely to find," he said. Then Maddie, without fanfare, took off her loose-fitting blouse and skirt. "Oh my God, your body is outta sight."

Brady quickly undressed, and when Maddie got her first look at him, she whistled. "You're not so bad yourself. I mean . . . you're so big. It's funny, I wouldn't have guessed. You're kind of skinny, and short . . ."

"God, who *did* teach you to deliver compliments?" He reached out for her. "Come here, Maddie, I've wanted to do this since I first saw you."

They made love intensely the first time; and then again more slowly, until daybreak. Brady took his time with her, coaxing her to relax and let go of her inhibitions. He found pleasure points in her body that she had never known existed. She came for the first time in her life and discovered that sex *was* what it was cracked up to be.

Poor Tommy Morgan. After being with him, in and out was what Maddie had thought it was all about.

Anna McNeill had red hair, an acerbic wit, and white skin dotted with freckles. Even with freckles she managed to look glamorous and not cute. She was from New York City and had more clothes, more *expensive* clothes, than anyone else in the class of '72 at the University of Colorado. She had been very popular in the dorm the previous year, but Maddie had never liked her—possibly because Anna and her clique did not pay any attention to Maddie, who kept to herself studying most of the time.

And so Maddie was surprised, when she looked up from her desk one evening, to see Anna McNeill standing in the doorway.

"Hello, Maddie," she said. Her accent was Eastern preppie. "It seems we're in the same boat."

"Hmmm?"

"Both our roommates got knocked up over the summer. So I was wondering if you want to share my room with me. It's a corner one . . . bigger and brighter than this."

"I don't think so," Maddie said. "I'm all settled in . . . and I don't even know you. We might not like each other."

Anna broke into a smile and seemed instantly easier to like. "The girls told me you were blunt. But I like that. I mean, people should always say what they really think. Most people don't." She pulled a pack of Marlboros out of the breast pocket of the Brooks Brothers shirt that belonged to her boyfriend. "Mind if I smoke?"

"No."

"Want one?"

"I don't smoke. My mother died of cancer."

"Oh . . ." Anna said, blowing out the match before she lit her cigarette. "Golly . . . I didn't know. I'm sorry."

"You can smoke, if you want," Maddie said. "It wasn't lung cancer."

Anna started laughing. "You're amazing. You don't say anything expected. I think I'm going to like you. What about it? My room? They're going to make me share it with somebody; it's too big for one. I mean, Harriet Jackson's dying to move in, but she's such a cow." She put her hand over her mouth. "Oh God, that's not nice." She went over and sat on Maddie's bed. "You see? Being around you is going to be good for me. I was brought up to always say the perfect thing . . . no matter what you're thinking. It's so hypocritical."

"So you figure I might be better than Harriet, even though you don't know me?"

"Well, all last year I'd look at you and think, she's so attractive. Or at least she could be . . . with some makeup and maybe a few blond streaks in her hair."

"I don't think you need blunt lessons. You're doing fine," Maddie said straight-faced. And then she laughed, in spite of herself. "Okay, I'll go look at your room. But I have to warn you . . . I might move out before the end of the semester. My boyfriend wants me to live with him."

"Well, I spend a lot of weekends with *my* boyfriend. Long weekends. He's a senior at Princeton."

"Princeton? That's kind of a long drive, isn't it?"

"Well, Daddy has a business jet that I use. Maybe you'd like to come to Princeton sometime. Randy can fix you up. Unless you're madly in love."

Maddie shook her head. "I don't know. I can't decide." She told Anna briefly about Brady. "All right," she said finally, "let's go check out your room. It might work. I've always wanted one of those corner rooms. One thing though, I'm here on a full scholarship . . . I study a lot."

Anna laughed. "Well, I suppose I can live with that. *My* grades are awful. But you can leave the light on all night, if you want. I can sleep through anything."

"Don't you care about getting a good education?"

Anna seemed taken aback. "Well, yes, but college is to have fun. I mean, I don't want to come off as really spoiled, but I'm not really going to have to work afterward. Randy and I'll probably get married and . . . Oh God, I sound like a total nerd."

Maddie smiled. "Well, I guess there's nothing wrong with not having to work for a living. It's just not in the cards for me."

"It's not as if I won't have a career," Anna said defensively, "but what I want to do doesn't pay much. I'm going to work with retarded kids. I'm majoring in Abnormal Psych. My youngest brother, David, was born severely brain-damaged. He's in an institution."

"Oh. I'm sorry."

"Yeah, it really devastated Mummie," Anna said. "I don't think she's ever recovered. She wanted to keep David at home . . . but there was no way. He'd require constant attention. Daddy convinced her that she'd be taking away from the rest of us if she tried to do it. But sometimes I think Mummie regrets her decision."

"Do you regret it?" Madeleine asked.

"Heavens no," Anna replied. "David's in terrible shape. I want to work with children who have . . . *hope.* You don't think that's callous of me, do you? I mean, you have to start somewhere."

Maddie nodded in agreement.

"So . . . what about it?" Anna asked. "Sharing my room?"

"Well, I guess so . . . if you're sure you want me."

"Yes, I'm quite sure," Anna said. "I think we might even become friends. And we're about the same size. You're welcome to borrow any of my clothes. Mummie sends me new shipments every month."

Maddie smiled. "A bigger room and a new wardrobe. I'll go get my stuff."

Maddie was happy that fall and felt special. She and Anna McNeill not only became friends, they were inseparable, except when Maddie was with Brady and Anna was off for her long weekends at Princeton.

Anna was the kind of girl that Maddie had fantasized about as a child—sophisticated, beautiful, intelligent. Of course, Maddie was already intelligent. After Anna finished playing Pygmalion, teaching her new makeup tricks, Maddie was also beautiful. Maddie figured the sophistication would come eventually, if she hung around her new best friend long enough.

As she got to know Anna better, Maddie learned that a great deal of Anna's outer sophistication was merely a protective shell. She was tremendously close to her family and idolized her handsome father, Wyatt McNeill. Anna kept a photograph of the two of them in a silver art deco frame on her desk, and she had long conversations with him on the phone several times a week.

Maddie was evasive when it came to talking about herself. Around Anna she knew she could hold her own in terms of wit and intelligence, but her background was not up to snuff. Anna was always talking about who people were, their breeding. Maddie was forced to face up to the fact that she lacked the sort of breeding Anna and her friends had. If Jane Lathem hadn't stepped into her life, there'd be no telling *where* she'd be now. Certainly not sharing a room at the University of Colorado with the wealthy Anna McNeill. And so she said as little as possible to Anna about her past.

Maddie's relationship with Brady Gardner continued smoothly that fall. As far as she could tell, the great womanizer was being faithful to her. After moving past their initial impressions of one another they had become friends, as well as lovers.

Everything remained perfect with Brady until Anna invited Maddie to spend Christmas in New York with her family. Maddie was ecstatic. She had never been to New York, even though she knew it was where she wanted to live when she finished school. But she felt a bit torn. Earlier in the fall she had vaguely agreed to spend the holidays with Brady.

Ultimately the idea of turning down Anna's invitation —and the chance to fly to New York in Mr. McNeill's private Gulfstream jet—was unthinkable. When Maddie broke the news to Brady he was predictably furious. Assuming that they were spending the holidays together, he had arranged to rent a deluxe condominium in Aspen.

"Brady," Maddie sheepishly tried to explain, "you've just got to understand. I'm *really* sorry. But this is such a great opportunity for me."

"Understand?" he shouted, losing his temper with her for the first time. "Fuck you! I thought we were going to spend Christmas together. I had the whole trip planned. Doesn't that mean anything to you?"

"Yes, I told you I'm sorry." She went over and put her arms around him, but he turned away sulkily. "I really am. But, I mean, we never made *definite* plans. You sort of assumed I'd spend Christmas with you when I said I didn't have any plans . . . Look . . . let's go to Aspen for semester break. Oh, Brady, *please* don't be angry. You told me your family wanted you to visit them. Now you can. You're lucky to have a family that cares about you."

Brady, his feelings hurt, wheeled around to face her. "You really are something else. What, I'm not sure, although a few names come to mind." He stared at her. "You know, Maddie, I really loved you. I was even going to ask you to marry me."

"Oh, Brady, I *care* about you a lot. But you're turning this all into such a big issue. It's *only* Christmas."

"Fuck you, Maddie. You're one fucked-up person."

"Shit, Brady. I'm not fucked up because I want to spend Christmas in New York. It's the first time in my life I've gotten a chance to go there. I mean . . . *New York!*"

"You don't even hear what you're saying, do you? How could you love me and act like this? I've spent all these months patiently teaching you about jewelry making, and you've never once thanked me. You *take*, Maddie, but you don't give," he said quietly. "This is it. I don't want to see you when you come back. There's no point."

"Oh, Brady . . ."

"Get the hell out of here, will you? I've got work to do."

Brady turned away and began setting an amethyst cabo-chon into a silver ring setting. There was nothing else she could say to him now. Brady was angry, but he'd get over it. She would bring him a nice present from New York. In a few weeks, after he had cooled off, everything would be back to normal, she was sure of it.

On the walk back to her dormitory, Maddie replayed their argument in her mind, allowing herself her turn to get angry. Brady was wrong about her. How could he say she took but never gave? How dare he, a man who had slept with hundreds of women?

Then she thought about the past months with Brady. He had shown her jewelry-making techniques and pa-tiently explained gemstones to her. He had lent her books to read. He had taken her out to dinner two or three times a week, or cooked for her at home. He quizzed her before tests. In fact, Brady Gardner had not acted at all like the man she had been warned about. On the contrary, he had shared every aspect of himself with her.

Could Brady actually have been right? Did she take more than she gave? Had she, since Jane's death, without realizing it, become afraid of loving again? Somewhere Maddie had read that in every relationship one person loves more than the other. Certainly Brady loved her more.

Would Maddie ever release her guard enough to give herself completely to anyone?

She was sure she would eventually. But at this point she was not ready to worry about that. Maddie was going to see New York City for the first time in her life.

And that was all she cared about.

4

The dining room of the Wyatt McNeills' rambling duplex on Park Avenue in the seventies was painted buttercup yellow. The color had been chosen by Elizabeth O'Hara McNeill's decorator—an Englishman who also dabbled in color therapy—for its reputed ability to stimulate conversation. A perfect choice, since the McNeills were lavish and frequent hosts to a coterie of friends from business to society to the arts, who had scaled the heights of Manhattan's summits. Twenty-four Sheraton-style Regency chairs—covered in a Chinese floral brocade—flanked three round mahogany dining tables. Over each hung a Russian rock-crystal chandelier that bathed the room with romantic, simulated candlelight. An eight-paneled Ming Dynasty folding screen covered the wall at the far end of the room. The china, which changed according to the guests and mood of the evening, was always

Tiffany, the crystal and silver, heirloom Irish, from Elizabeth McNeill's family.

Maddie could not believe that she was there, sitting with the McNeills at the centermost table, looking at Anna across an arrangement of flowers so exotic she had never even seen pictures of them before, much less heard their names. An air of unreality surrounded it all. After the first day of being nervous and on guard, however, she had begun to relax under the family's unpretentiousness. She was Anna's new best friend, and they treated her accordingly.

Through the windows that overlooked the avenue, Maddie kept stealing glances at the blizzard that raged outside in the glow of the city's street lamps. Perfection. Everything was more ideal than Maddie had imagined it would be.

"See . . ." Anna gloated as if she herself had arranged for the snow, "I told you we'd have a white Christmas. In honor of Maddie."

"Then let's drink a toast to Anna." Hadley McNeill, Anna's younger brother, raised his glass. "To the McNeill family's chief meteorologist."

"We're having a special treat tonight, Maddie. Roast pheasant," Anna said, pointedly ignoring her brother. "Daddy shot it upstate somewhere."

"I've never had pheasant," Maddie said.

"It's okay," Hadley said. "Tastes like chicken."

"Isn't that what they say about everything? Rattlesnake and all that?"

Hadley nodded. "The only thing that doesn't taste like chicken these days is chicken. They pump it so full of chemicals."

"Oh, please, darling, let's not get into all that," Elizabeth McNeill said. "At least not while we're eating."

"But Mother, this is the perfect time to talk about it!" Hadley argued. "What better opportunity to discuss how we're being slowly murdered by what we put in our bodies? Nader eats only cantaloupe. It's the only thing with skin thick enough that chemicals can't seep through."

Hadley was a freshman at Yale. Over the previous summer he had done volunteer work for Ralph Nader. Although he had not actually been one of "Nader's Raiders," and indeed had never met the man, the summer had convinced Hadley to devote his life to saving the environment.

"Yes, yes, Hadley . . . we know all about it. And we agree. But," Wyatt McNeill said, anxious to avoid one of his son's inevitable diatribes on the rape of the land by big business, "I want to talk to our houseguest."

McNeill turned to Maddie. It was hard for her to realize that someone's father could be so attractive and youthful. The fathers she knew back in Pine Ridge were thick around the middle and looked older than they probably were. Was it living in Manhattan or being so rich that made Anna's father different, Maddie wondered.

"Elizabeth tells me you want to be a jewelry designer, Madeleine," he said. The McNeills, with the exception of Anna, had insisted on addressing her as Madeleine ever since she arrived. "Such a beautiful name," Anna's mother had said. "Let's *use* it!"

"Yes. Going around Tiffany's and Cartier and Harry Winston . . . it was like being hit by lightning," Maddie exclaimed. "Suddenly, I had no more doubts. I *am* going to be a jewelry designer."

"Hear! Hear!" Elizabeth McNeill said. She was a beautiful woman, also incredibly young-looking, with the same red hair as Anna, cut very short by Vidal Sassoon. Her skin was porcelain clear; there was no sign of makeup, except for mascara and lipstick. "I'm all for that. And of course when you're famous you'll give us all discounts."

"Of course," Maddie laughed. "And thank you again for showing me all the stores. This was one of the most exciting days of my whole life. Fifth Avenue is even more elegant than I imagined. And the Christmas tree at

Rockefeller Center, with the ice skaters dancing below! I've seen postcards of it, but I never dreamed it would be so dazzling."

"I loved taking you around," Elizabeth said. "Anna's bored with all that, has been for years. I guess it comes from growing up in the city." She lit a cigarette. "I was born and raised in Shaker Heights, Ohio. And I think Manhattan will send a thrill through me till my dying day."

"Yes . . . that's exactly what I felt! *Thrills.* The energy —the *glamour*—of Manhattan is unbelievable."

"Well, it's good to hear you're not disappointed," Wyatt McNeill said as the butler cleared away the soup course, "New York gets so much bad press these days."

"Oh no, I love it here."

"I'm glad." Wyatt McNeill paused. "Madeleine . . . Anna hasn't told us much about you. You grew up in Colorado?"

Maddie felt a sudden panic. She had invented a bit of a story for Anna. Nothing elaborate . . . but Anna's impeccable credentials had made her feel like such a hick. And, after all, she was an orphan; there was no one to dispute anything she made up.

"Well . . . my father was a ski instructor . . . a fantastic skier. He would have been a medalist in the Olympics . . . but he broke his leg . . ." She trailed off. Her head felt light. She reached slowly for her water glass, raised it to her lips, and took several swallows.

"Madeleine," Elizabeth said with concern. "Are you all right?"

"It's just . . . I'm sorry, I feel a bit dizzy." Her cheeks burned, and her stomach was doing little flips. She had come clean with Brady, but somehow the idea of telling the McNeills the truth was unthinkable.

And yet, Anna's family had treated her with such warmth and generosity. How could she lie to them? Some instinct in Maddie told her that *this* was where her real life would lie—in the polished wood and marble of Manhattan with people like the McNeills, not with Brady in a little Colorado shop with a studio in back. A tissue of lies here was something serious that she would have to live and deal with for a long time to come. She could not bear to tell them the truth, but she was terrified to go on lying. Maddie opened her mouth, and even she did not know what was going to come out.

But it was Elizabeth McNeill's voice that she heard, not her own.

"You poor thing, you're shaking." Anna's mother came and put an arm around Maddie and helped her from the table. "I do hope it's not the flu. I'll bet you're just exhausted. Hadley, dear, go ask Lucille to send up a cup of tea. Come along now, let's get you to bed, Madeleine." Gratefully, Maddie let herself be mothered. She felt deeply ashamed to be counterfeiting for these people who had shown her nothing but kindness. At the same time, she felt a tremendous strength-robbing sense of relief. It was as if she had received an eleventh-hour pardon on death row from the governor. She was safe this time.

She might not always be so lucky.

As it turned out, Maddie spent the next week, including Christmas Day, in bed with the recurring fever and chills of an honest-to-goodness flu. The McNeills showered her with attention, coming in to chat or read to her, bringing her books, nursing her first with tea and toast and later, as her strength returned, with tempting goodies from the kitchen. Madeleine loved being treated as part of the family; she felt a real sense of belonging.

By New Year's Eve, Maddie was herself again. To bring in the year 1970, Anna and her boyfriend, Randy Ferguson, fixed Maddie up with Randy's Princeton roommate. His name was Win Burgess. Win had a girlfriend, Anna explained, but she was spending the holidays in Gstaad.

Maddie did not care. She was so in love with New York that she did not yearn for additional romance.

The four of them—Anna and Randy, Maddie and Win —started out the evening at a dance at the Plaza, given by one of Anna's childhood friends. After the New Year was ushered in, they became bored and headed downtown to hear some jazz at the Village Vanguard. By that time, they had gone through four bottles of champagne.

The others seemed accustomed to drinking so much, but Maddie was not. Her light-headedness turned into fuzzy-headedness, and she wished she could go home to bed. But it was not very late, and Win Burgess was putting the make on her. At midnight, when they were still at the Plaza, he had kissed her passionately. He had continued to try to kiss her during the long cab ride downtown. Now his hand was trying to snake up her thigh, under the table at the jam-packed, smoky Vanguard. She kept pushing Win's hand away and he kept putting it back. But, other than physically, Win made absolutely no effort to relate to her.

Maddie did not like anything about Win. In fact, she would have much preferred spending New Year's Eve alone with a good book. But here she was, trying to sneak glances at her watch to see how much longer she had to endure.

"Win," Maddie said, removing his hand once again, "when are you going to start taking the hint?"

"It's New Year's . . . come on." He put his arm around her shoulders. "Get in the spirit. I thought Western girls were wide open," he chuckled. "I really like you . . ."

"No, you don't. We haven't anything in common. You've hardly bothered to say three sentences all evening."

"How can we have a conversation over this noise? We'll talk later, baby . . . when we're alone. But now we have to party. Hey . . . waiter!" he called out. "Hit us with another bottle of the good stuff."

Over the holidays, Maddie had begun to discover that, while she loved Anna and the McNeills, she was not taken with Randy or any of Anna's other friends. They were sophisticated in that they dressed expensively and went to all the right restaurants and discos, but they seemed so inbred. Maddie was made to feel—and she knew it was not her imagination—like the outsider she was. Anna's New York friends had all known each other forever, it seemed. They were always referring to past shared escapades, and to prep schools Maddie had never heard of, such as Kent, Madeira, Choate, Exeter, and St. Paul's. Anna, to her credit, tried valiantly to keep bringing Maddie into conversations, but Randy wanted to monopolize Anna. And they all drank so much.

After another glass of champagne, Maddie's tongue felt swollen and she had trouble getting out even the simplest sentence. She felt dizzy and knew that she could not last much longer. How could the others drink like this and not feel it, she wondered? They certainly acted fine. Anna and Randy were holding hands and gazing lovingly into each other's eyes. Win's hand continued to wander up under Maddie's short sequined skirt. Maddie kept her own hand poised to fend off attack.

Maddie looked around at the other tables. Everyone was having a wonderful time. She was spending New Year's Eve with a drip who treated her like a piece of meat. She thought longingly of Brady and wished she were with him tonight, the two of them alone together in Aspen. It was two hours earlier in Colorado. If she got home soon there would still be time to call and wish him a happy New Year.

"Listen," she told Win, speaking with an effort to sound normal. "I really don't want to spoil anyone's fun, but I don't feel well. I think I'm going to head back to Anna's."

"But I want to stay and hear the next set," Win said.

"Here." He grabbed the bottle of champagne out of the cooler and poured some into her glass. "Have some more."

"No, really . . . I've got to get out of here! *You* don't have to leave. I'm perfectly capable of making it home by myself."

"No," Win blinked. "I'll take you." He pushed his chair back and threw a hundred-dollar bill on the table. "This'll cover me," he told Randy. "Maddie and I are going."

"Oh . . . is everything okay?" Anna asked.

"Sure. I'm just tired. I'll see you later," Maddie said.

Out on the Avenue of the Americas an icy wind blew into their faces.

"Really," Maddie said, "you go back inside. I'll be fine. I just want to go to bed."

"Sounds good to me," Win leered, putting an arm around her and waving in vain at a passing off-duty taxi.

"No, Win. Just me." But if he heard, he did not seem to pay much attention.

All the cabs that headed uptown, however, were packed with merrymakers. Maddie and Win waited for fifteen or twenty minutes and then began walking uptown. Around Fourteenth Street a cab pulled up to the curb to let somebody off and they grabbed it.

By that time, from the walk and the bracing cold air, Maddie's head had begun to feel clearer. Her mind raced to think of ways to get rid of Win when they got to Anna's. She knew that, having brought her uptown, he would insist on being invited in. He was already warming up in the cab, nuzzling and groping and burrowing with hands that, like sharks, seemed obliged to keep moving or die.

"Boy, what a great pair of tits," he murmured in champagne-induced rapture. Irritably she pushed his hands away, for the hundredth time that evening.

"Win, dammit, I said *stop!*" she hissed. But Win feinted low, a hand sneaking suddenly up to the dry coolness of her panties; and then, when she went to defend this position, he pawed triumphantly again at her bosom.

She parried as best she could, embarrassed to scream at him as she would have liked to, because of the driver. Finally, the cab turned the corner onto Park Avenue and slowed to a stop in front of Anna's building. Maddie opened the door quickly and jumped out.

"You keep the cab and go back downtown. I can see myself in from here. Good night, Win," she said briskly, slamming the cab door in his face and rushing inside, past the doorman who could not move fast enough for her.

When she had walked through the lobby to the elevator, she looked back outside through the glass doors. The cab was still sitting there. Win was obviously trying to decide whether to let her get away with the brush-off. Finally, leaning forward, he said something to the driver and the cab pulled away.

Maddie knew that Win was furious, but she could not care less. There was no chemistry between them, no spark of basic friendship. Why go through all the motions when they meant nothing to each other? In the stuffy elevator, the claustrophobic sick feeling returned. By the time the elevator man opened the door to the McNeills' hall, Maddie could barely keep from retching.

The key. She didn't have it; Anna did. She'd have to ring the bell and wake someone. Ordinarily, rather than do that she would have sat in the chair in the vestibule and waited for Anna. But now she was desperate to get to the bathroom. She pushed the buzzer and waited. No one answered. After another minute, she rang the bell again, more insistently.

Wyatt McNeill finally opened the door, looking sleepy, in a silk paisley robe. "Why, Madeleine! Where's Anna? Is everything all right?" He stood aside to let her enter.

"Yes. It's just that I felt bad and left early . . ."

Maddie dashed across the hall toward the stairs. Wyatt

McNeill was in her wake, to help her. Before she could reach the first step, nausea overtook her.

She threw up on the marble floor, in front of him. It was the most embarrassing moment of her life.

By then Elizabeth McNeill was heading barefooted down the stairs.

"Oh dear. Too much champagne, I imagine . . . on top of the flu. Let me get you upstairs and into a bath, Madeleine. Wyatt dear, wake Emory and have him mop the hall."

"No, I'll handle it. You look after Madeleine."

"Oh, I'm so sorry," Maddie managed to say.

"Don't try to talk. Let's get you into a hot tub," Elizabeth McNeill said. "Now, take hold of the banister . . ."

Later, after she had thrown up again, soaked in a hot bath, and Elizabeth McNeill had tucked her into bed— between cool linen sheets—Maddie began to feel better.

"Thank you. I'm so sorry," she kept saying to Mrs. McNeill.

"Don't worry. It happens to everybody, at least once in their life. Those kids drink far too much. It bothers me about Anna, but she gets mad when I say something to her. You just aren't used to the pace, thank God. You're lucky," she said. "Now, close your eyes and get some sleep. You'll feel fine tomorrow."

Maddie nodded. How could she face Wyatt McNeill in the morning? She wished she could talk to Brady. But it was too late to call him now.

A little later, Maddie came out of her heavy sleep long enough to notice that the room was bright. She opened her eyes, shielding them with her hand. The light was on. Anna was standing naked in front of her dresser, looking through her drawers.

"Hi," Maddie said huskily. "You're home."

Anna turned around, startled. "Oh! Yeah, I'm having

trouble finding my nightgown. The black lace one." Her words sounded slurred.

"It's on the hook behind the bathroom door. I saw it earlier."

"Oh, yeah," she hiccuped and stumbled into the bathroom, to get ready for bed. Maddie forced herself to stay awake while her friend brushed her teeth and removed her makeup. Finally, Anna weaved back into the room.

"Did you have fun? I'm sorry about leaving like that," Maddie said.

"Win was furious," Anna giggled. "But that's okay. He's just used to women falling all over him. He'll live." She came over and stood by Maddie's four-poster bed. "Are you ready to see something?" she asked with vinous drama.

"Sure . . . what?"

Anna stuck out her left hand and wiggled her ring finger. "Look!"

On her finger was a three- or four-carat, marquise-cut emerald, flanked by small diamonds. "Randy just gave it to me," Anna said breathlessly, sinking onto the bed beside Maddie. "We're engaged!"

"Oh, Anna!" Maddie gave her friend a big hug. "I can't believe it!" As Anna gushed on about Randy's proposal—in the hansom cab he had hired to bring them uptown from the Village—a feeling of apprehension settled in the pit of Maddie's stomach.

"When do you think you'll get married?" she asked, trying to muster enthusiasm.

"Oh, we've figured it all out. Summer. Probably August. It'll take that long to get everything arranged." She threw her arms around Maddie. "Oh, isn't it *too* exciting!"

"Yes, it's . . . fabulous," Maddie smiled. "I'm so happy for you."

Of course Maddie was not happy for Anna. This meant that after the next semester Maddie would be losing her roommate and best friend. And she hated the idea that

Anna was actually marrying Randy Ferguson. Anna was too good for him, Maddie thought, and too intelligent. She had the money, and the ability, to do something far more worthwhile with her life than organize charity balls.

But, for once, Maddie kept her mouth shut.

The next morning, New Year's Day, Maddie woke around nine with an overpowering headache. She brushed her teeth, took an aspirin, and then settled back woozily in her bed with a copy of *War and Peace*. Anna was still sound asleep. Maddie did not want to go downstairs and have to face Wyatt and Elizabeth McNeill, after having woken them up and puked right in front of them.

The aspirin began to work its miracle, and she read and dozed for several hours. Anna did not stir. Finally, around noon, there was a light tap on the bedroom door. Maddie went and opened it.

"Oh, you're up! Good," Elizabeth McNeill said. "Are you feeling better?"

"Yes," Maddie whispered, "but Anna's still asleep."

Elizabeth swept by Maddie. "Well, she has to get up. We have brunch at the Madisons'. We're due there at one. Darling," she shook Anna. "It's time." She turned back to Maddie. "Well, have you heard the news? Anna woke us when she came in."

Maddie forced herself to smile. "Yes! Isn't it wonderful!"

"Oh God, Mother," Anna groaned. "I don't want to go to Aunt Franny's today. I'm too exhausted."

"You have to. As your godmother, Franny'll be devastated if you don't tell her about the engagement yourself. Come on now, shake a leg."

The brunch they were heading off to was to be given by Peter and Frances Madison. Frances Madison, besides being Elizabeth McNeill's best friend and Anna's godmother, was the famous Broadway actress, Frances Barry. Maddie had been looking forward to the party, to meeting the famous actress in her own home. Now, however, after last night, she did not feel as if she could face anyone at all.

"Er, Mrs. McNeill? I still don't feel well and I . . . I wondered if I could stay here while you go to the brunch. Would that be all right?"

"Of course, dear," Elizabeth said. "You must be sick to death of meeting all these new people. I'm afraid if you get hungry you'll have to fend for yourself. Everyone has the day off."

"Oh, that's okay. You don't mind, do you, Anna?"

Anna had roused herself and was now rummaging through her closet. "I'm only going for a few minutes myself. Just long enough to show Franny my ring. Then I have to meet Randy at the Carlyle for drinks with his father and stepmother, to tell them the news." She smiled at Maddie. Her skin was pale but otherwise she showed no aftereffect from all the champagne she consumed the night before. "You know, I think getting married is going to be the most exhausting thing I've ever done."

After everyone left for the party, Maddie stayed upstairs to read another chapter of her book. Then, feeling better and hungry, she decided to go and fix herself a sandwich. It was fun having the elegant, fifteen-room apartment to herself for a few hours, being able to pretend that it belonged to her.

Heading downstairs to the kitchen, she was startled for a moment to hear voices, then realized that they were merely coming from the television. She turned and headed for the library to turn off the set. As she entered, she jumped back with a surprised, "Oh!"

Wyatt McNeill was stretched out on the beige suede sofa, drinking a beer and watching a football game.

"Oh! I thought you went to the party!" Maddie exclaimed. "You scared me."

"I backed out at the last minute. Peter loathes football,

so I knew I wouldn't get to see the game there. My alma mater's playing in the Rose Bowl." He indicated the vacant wing chair next to the sofa. "Care to join me?"

Maddie shook her head. "I . . . if it's all right . . . I was going to make myself a sandwich."

"Good idea. Make me one too, would you? Anything with plenty of mayonnaise, and lettuce." He held up his empty beer bottle. "And I could use another one of these."

Maddie went to the kitchen, feeling very uncomfortable. She had hoped to avoid a solo confrontation with Wyatt McNeill, not merely because of last night. She always felt ill at ease around him. She wasn't sure whether it was something to do with Wyatt himself, or fathers in general, never having had one herself.

And there was always the fear, whenever she found herself one-on-one with any of the McNeills, that the intimacy would encourage more questions about her background.

Maddie had already gotten in deeper than she liked. They knew her parents were dead. She had buried the ski instructor father in an avalanche in Switzerland late one night in a conversation with Anna. About her mother, Jane, she had been more factual, telling Anna that she had died of cancer, but managing to convey the impression that it had happened in a special sanitarium for musicians.

She knew Anna had passed this information along, and she hoped it would get her through the holidays. She did not have any more details ready.

After a thorough search of the kitchen, Maddie located a loaf of rye bread in the pantry and made sandwiches out of leftover roast beef. She found a jar of dill pickles in the refrigerator, and a bag of potato chips hidden away in a cabinet. Piling it all onto a tray, along with two imported beers, she headed back to the library.

"I hope roast beef's okay."

"Terrific. Great, you brought pickles. I love pickles,"

Wyatt said. "Here, have a seat." He swung his legs off the sofa and sat up.

Maddie took a seat, piled potato chips onto her plate, and pretended to take an interest in the game. "So who's playing?"

"Southern Cal and Michigan . . . my team. We're not doing well. Nearly halftime. Yep, there's the buzzer." He pushed a button on the remote control and muted the set. "This hits the spot, Madeleine. Thanks."

"Look, I'm really embarrassed about last night. I've never drunk so much that I've gotten sick before. I don't drink much at all, actually. Please forgive me."

"There's nothing to forgive. It's part of growing up," Wyatt laughed. "We're all human."

Maddie was starting to relax. Wyatt McNeill acted more like a person than a father. Maddie liked him, in spite of the initial awkwardness she had felt. "I guess you're happy about Anna," she said.

Wyatt shrugged. "Randy's a good enough kid. Good family. But Anna's twenty. I had hoped she'd finish school before she got married."

"Well, she told me this morning that they have it all worked out. She's going to transfer to Barnard while Randy goes to graduate business school at Columbia."

"Good. I'd hate for her to quit school."

They ate in silence for a few moments. Then Maddie said, "Do you mind if I ask you a personal question?"

"Of course not," Wyatt said. "Shoot."

"What is it exactly that you do . . . for a living? I mean, Anna's always so vague about it."

Wyatt McNeill laughed. "I used to have a full-time law practice. Now I'm a deal maker. I put people together, and if it works out, I take a percentage of the business. I travel a lot, all over the world."

"Well," Maddie said, "it sounds interesting." She smiled. "Not that I really understand any more than I did before I asked the question."

Wyatt broke into an amused grin. "Oh, you want to know facts. Anna's always been satisfied with the five-second explanation."

"Well, it's just that, I mean, I know you're successful. But I don't quite understand, and I want to. I don't mean to be rude," she said, thoroughly flustered.

Wyatt stared at her, his brown eyes still crinkled in amusement. "I wish Anna had more friends like you, Madeleine. You've got a good head on your shoulders. I enjoy talking to you." He helped himself to another pickle from the jar. "There are a lot of companies that could be a hell of a lot more profitable. I find the companies, and then I find the management or new ownership to help turn them around. My last deal was Flowers Chocolate Company. We took their candy bar image and turned it into a worldwide gourmet chocolate power. Now I'm working on a new deal . . . a boating company." He paused. "It *sounds* a bit boring. The *doing* is more fun. Putting together the pieces of a puzzle."

Maddie shook her head. "It doesn't sound boring at all."

There was something about Wyatt McNeill that made her like him more and more. What it was, she decided, was that he treated her like an adult, an equal. Jane had done that; they had been friends, above all else. But with Jane it had been different. As much as Maddie would have liked to view Wyatt as a friend, and not Anna's father, it was difficult. Wyatt *was* Anna's father.

Maddie, aware that Wyatt was studying her, began to feel nervous under the scrutiny. Glancing over at the television, she saw the teams lined up for the second-half kickoff.

"Oh, look," she said with relief, "the game's starting."

Wyatt turned up the sound, but looked at her instead of the television.

"I want to ask *you* something personal, Madeleine. Did your parents leave you any money when they died?"

"My mother did. Some insurance. Fifteen thousand dollars."

"And what have you done with it?"

"It's in the Pine Ridge National Bank. I thought about investing it. But I'm not quite sure how."

"Look, my stockbroker's son has just gone into the business. Graduated from Harvard, then graduate school at Wharton. He's a whiz kid, from what I hear . . . and the market's up. My broker doesn't handle such small portfolios, but his son'll do a great job with it. When you get back to school, send me the money and I'll take care of it." Wyatt paused, then broke into a hearty laugh. "From the expression on your face, Madeleine, you look as if you think I'm going to steal your life's savings. But Gary Pollock can quadruple your money in no time at all. Trust me."

"My mother told me you should never trust people who say 'trust me.' "

"Madeleine, you keep me on my toes," Wyatt grinned. "I like that. And I promise you won't lose your money. I just want to help you."

"But why? I mean, why should you be so nice to me?" Maddie asked.

Wyatt smiled at her. "You're Anna's friend. And you're all alone. Someone has to take an interest." He shook his head sympathetically. "Hasn't anyone ever done anything for you just to be nice?"

Maddie swallowed, thinking of Jane. "Yes," she said. "Thanks."

So Wyatt McNeill felt sorry for her. Well, there was nothing wrong with that. She needed all the help she could get.

5

Back in Boulder, after the electric atmosphere of New York City, things seemed to run at half speed. It was winter and very cold, but that wasn't the reason. The energy surrounding Boulder was diffused, unfocused. Madeleine, as she insisted her friends call her now, could feel the difference. She tried to hold on to the vigorous charge that had zapped her in Manhattan, but as the days passed, it became harder. The feeling of happy anticipation that she felt in New York slipped away, fading day by day, until it was only a memory.

Madeleine had hurried to see Brady at the shop as soon as she got back. He was waiting on a customer. His eyes flicked over her and then away, scarcely acknowledging her. Madeleine felt her stomach sink.

As soon as the door closed behind the woman, Madeleine threw her arms around him. Brady shrugged her off.

"Oh, Brady, please don't still be mad at me," she pleaded. "I missed you."

"Really?" he said coldly.

"Yes, really!" She squeezed his arm. "Brady, let's be together again. How about tonight? I want us to make up . . ."

"I'm busy tonight," Brady said shortly.

"Oh, please." Madeleine stared at him, hurt. She held out a gift-wrapped box to him. "I brought you a present," she said. "From Bloomingdale's. Merry late-Christmas. I love you."

"That," Brady said, "is your misfortune." He did not take the present.

Madeleine recognized the line. It was Rhett Butler's, from *Gone With the Wind.*

"Oh hell. Fuck you," she said, turning and huffing out of the shop.

She cried a little, off and on for the rest of the day. But she was not going to beg or humble herself to Brady Gardner. If that was what he expected, he would have a long wait. She decided to keep the shirt she'd bought for him and wear it herself.

After having spent time in New York, Madeleine was more fashion conscious than before. If she was going to achieve a "look" on her budget, she decided, it would have to be a personal, eccentric one. Always one to shop at thrift stores and rummage sales, she found that since Jane's death her mood had caused her to gravitate toward conservative clothes, skirts and sweaters and scarves. Now, her eye sought the outrageous—a clash of colors, a contrast of fabrics, the "found" accessory. She developed a taste for vintage clothing, silks and crepe de chine prints from the thirties and forties being her favorites.

As a Christmas gift from the McNeills, Madeleine's hair had been streaked with blond highlights at Kenneth's. With her jazzy hair color and eclectic way of dressing, she blossomed with new confidence in her attractiveness.

"You know, Maddie. I'm sorry, *Madeleine,*" Anna said one night when they had come back from the library, "you really could be a model if you wanted. You're so thin, but you can eat everything in sight. Your cheekbones are to die for."

Madeleine laughed. "Me? A model? You've got to be kidding. I'm not beautiful."

"You're crazy. I mean, you're not pretty in the Miss America way," Anna admitted, "but you have real style. Your features are strong, and you're very direct. When you talk to people, you look them in the eye. I think that's why older men like Brady fall for you. Boys your own age," she laughed, *"our* own age, are a bit intimidated by you, I think."

Madeleine shook her head in amazement. "Intimidated? I'm the least intimidating person I know."

"Well . . . to you, and me, because I know you so well. But Randy's a bit afraid of you. That's why he . . . kind of ignores you. Because he's not comfortable."

Madeleine longed to launch into a candid discussion of what *she* thought of Randy. But she had sense enough to know it would come to no good. There was no point in giving Anna, now or ever, her opinion of Randy Ferguson. Still, to remain quiet while her best friend threw away her life. . . . Maybe it was worth testing the waters.

"You know, Anna," Madeleine said, handing her half of a Mounds bar, "I've been wanting to ask you if you're having cold feet at all . . . I mean, about getting married."

"Cold feet? Well, sure, sometimes. I mean, it's a lifetime commitment. But Randy's so sure I'm what he wants. He's got confidence for both of us."

Madeleine, the candy eaten, opened her drawer and pulled out a box of saltines. "Want one?"

"You know I can't stand boring crackers. Besides I promised Randy I'd lose five pounds before the wedding. He likes me lean . . . close to the bone."

"You don't need to lose an ounce! Honestly. Sometimes I think you give too much of yourself to Randy. *He's* graduating, so you're getting married. Why doesn't he wait until *you* graduate? Your degree is as important as his."

Anna had gotten her tweezers out and was plucking stray hairs from her eyebrows. "God, Madeleine . . . that's the most ridiculous thing I've ever heard. Of course it will be nice to get my degree—and I *will* get it—but it's not nearly as important as Randy's. I mean, he's got to support me."

"But don't you want to be a person in your own right?"

"I *am* a person in my own right!" Anna flared. "God, Maddie, I'll make worthwhile contributions to society . . . as Mrs. Randall Ferguson. I'll do the right things."

"But you have so much going for you. You're smart, you're beautiful. How can you want to live your life in someone else's shadow?"

"I'm not going to be Randy's appendage, you know," Anna snapped. "I'm going to be his other half. He *needs* me, Maddie. You don't realize how *much* he depends on me."

"I'm sure he does," Madeleine said, "but you don't *have* to need him. I'm not saying you shouldn't love him, or even marry him, if that's what you want. But put it in perspective. Think of yourself! What you want should come first."

"It does. I want Randy." She looked at her watch. "Oh, it's time to call him." Her eyebrows back in a perfect arch, she put away the tweezers and headed for the door. "You know, Maddie," she said, pausing in the doorway, "you're very jealous of Randy. You think he's going to block our friendship. But he won't. You don't give him enough credit . . . you don't give *me* enough credit. Nothing will

ever come between us. You just have to adjust to the idea
that many women feel fulfilled by being with men. You
want to do everything on your own. But someday you'll
fall in love too, and you'll understand what I'm talking
about."

Anna rushed out to the bank of pay phones down the
hall, leaving Madeleine without the last word. After conversations like this, Madeleine wondered what it was she
saw in Anna McNeill. They were so different from one
another. What *was* their friendship based on? Still, after
all was said and done, they were friends, and friends put
up with each other's annoying traits. Madeleine put up
with Anna, and loved her in spite of everything. Anna
probably did the same, although, in truth, Madeleine was
positive that she was much easier to put up with.

At the university in 1970 it was a free and open time, a
time of experimentation, a time of vocalization. People
were banding together to protest the war in Vietnam and
the United States government's escalation of it. And, in
between demonstrations, peace marches, sit-ins, and ral-
lies, all of Madeleine's other friends and acquaintances
were falling in and out of bed with each other with aston-
ishing regularity. Three to a bed, in varying combinations,
and experimental orgies were as common as drugs. Mari-
juana, old hat by now, had given way to LSD, mescaline,
and magic mushrooms. Boulder had become a pop-culture
center during the psychedelic sixties; it was the hip place
to be.

Madeleine, in the past, had protested the war. When she
was with Brady, they smoked grass occasionally. But,
other than getting high and the fact that he wore his hair
long, Brady had little to do with the hippie scene. He was
in his late twenties, had a heart murmur, and wasn't even
worried about being drafted. So Madeleine stayed apart
from most of what was going on. She was concerned with
keeping her scholarship and didn't dare risk losing it.

Having always been a loner, Madeleine never felt the peer pressure to do anything she didn't want to do simply because everyone else was doing it. But, by spring, with Anna seldom around and Brady out of the picture, Madeleine began to gravitate toward the center of the scene.

It was time to experiment.

High-decibel Led Zeppelin was blasting from the record player. Red and green bulbs were screwed into all the lamps and ceiling sockets, giving an otherworldly appearance to the rooms of the old, rambling house near the university that several of Madeleine's friends from the art department had rented. Madeleine was there, sipping Gallo Hearty Burgundy with a guy named Peter Lane, who had been trying to get into her pants since the beginning of the year. Anna, back in Boulder to study for exams, had come along too; Madeleine had talked her into it.

"Hey, what are you doing this summer? Why don't we go someplace in the Caribbean . . . the three of us . . . and do weird things to each other with mangoes and suntan oil," Peter grinned, rolling a joint of Maui Wowie. He was a short, chipmunkish-looking guy whom Madeleine liked as a friend. There was no romantic interest on her part.

"We're going to New York," Anna sniffed. "I'm getting married."

"Married? You're kidding. Nobody gets *married* anymore. It's just a bourgeois trap, man." Peter took a long drag and passed the joint to Madeleine.

"If you only knew how *sick* I am of hearing that!" Anna snapped. She shook her head when Madeleine handed her the joint, and poured herself another glass of wine from the gallon jug that sat on the floor. "Marriage is never out when two people love each other. It's the ultimate commitment. And besides . . . if we're married Randy doesn't stand as much chance of being drafted."

"Hey, I hear you," Peter nodded. "But still . . . don't you want to sample from the menu of life before you make your order?"

Madeleine spoke up for Anna. "Anna's lived more than you, I bet. She's from New York. She *knows* what she wants. Not very many people do nowadays."

"That's right," Anna nodded in agreement.

"Okay, okay," Peter raised his hand in defense. "Two against one." He reached into his pocket. "Look what I scored today. Some psilocybin. It's organic. Really hard to come by, *very* precious." He looked at Anna and Madeleine, hopeful. "Wanna do it?"

"No," Anna said.

"Well, maybe another time. I've heard psilocybin is great," Madeleine added.

"It is. The absolute best. A totally different high from anything else. It's almost spiritual. I mean, people get into sex on mescaline, but this stuff arouses your soul. Not that sex isn't great too."

"How long does it last?" Madeleine asked. She was interested in trying it, but she knew Anna would never go along with the idea.

"Oh, five or six hours, I guess," Peter estimated.

"Haven't you taken it before?" Anna asked.

"Yeah, it's just that you kinda lose track of time. You go into a different dimension where time doesn't matter." He held up a small plastic bag that contained four capsules filled with a yellowish-colored powder. "Look, I'm gonna do it. You're welcome to join me. Or you can leave. I'm not into forcing anyone to do anything they don't wanna do."

Madeleine looked at Anna. "Why don't we? You have to try everything once. And before you know it you'll be married and totally away from this scene."

Anna refilled her wine glass. She clearly wasn't enthusiastic, but she couldn't think of a reason not to try it. She had never experimented with mind-expanding drugs: she supposed she ought to before she got married. After all, Randy had taken LSD at Princeton and said it was super.

"All right," Anna relented. "But you have to *promise* to take me immediately to a hospital if I have a bad reaction."

Peter nodded. "I promise. But you won't. This drug is the mildest of them all. Really far out. You'll love it."

He pulled two capsules out of the Baggie, opened them up, and sprinkled the powder into a glass of water, stirring it with his finger. The powder wouldn't dissolve completely. Tiny mounds, resembling powdered mustard, floated on top. "Here. We each drink about a third."

Madeleine drank first, then Anna.

"Ugh!" Anna said, chasing it down with wine. "It tastes horrible."

Peter drank the last third and went into the kitchen. He came back with a container of lemon yogurt. "Here," he handed it to Anna. "Both of you eat some of this. Shouldn't take drugs on an empty stomach."

Peter's German shepherd, Lady Soul, came into the room and perched by his chair expectantly. "Hey," Peter said, "let's take my friend here for a walk so I don't have to do it later. It'll take about forty-five minutes for this stuff to start working anyway."

They put on their coats and walked out into the cool, fragrant, early May night. Madeleine felt a rush of anticipatory excitement, but by the end of the walk, when nothing had happened, she began to forget that she had taken the drug.

Back at the house, Peter rolled another joint, and this time even Anna joined in. Slowly, Madeleine became aware of something happening. No major rush, more of a secure feeling of well-being.

"This hitting you yet?" Peter asked.

Anna nodded. "I *think* so. I mean, everything in the room looks a little different. All the colors are so vibrant.

But it's very gentle. This isn't at all what I thought it would be."

"There's no jolt . . . no zings," Madeleine said, relieved and disappointed at the same time. "I don't have a feeling of 'Wow, this is it.' "

"That's what I told you. That's what it's all about," Peter reiterated. "What you feel now is about as strong as it gets."

"You're a good drug guru," Anna purred approvingly. She kicked off her high-heeled black boots and snuggled up in her chair. "I feel fabulous."

"Yeah," Peter said, "this is dynamite stuff." He stood and held out his arms toward Anna and Madeleine. "Come with me. Upstairs. I want to show you something."

"We're *not* going to fool around," Madeleine said.

"Who said anything about that? Just come up to my room where we can relax. My housemates'll be coming back from the movies any time now. Things'll get noisy. Come on. I have this far-out Chinese lute tape I want you to hear."

Upstairs, they lay around on Peter's bed and listened to the music. The airy Chinese lutes conjured up nightingales, cherry blossoms, pagodas.

"I'm in a Buddhist temple," Anna said dreamily. "You're right about this being spiritual. It's a major experience. I'm a Buddhist monk . . . I'm at one with the universe . . ." She raised her arms and moved them with the music. "I am all there is," she whispered.

A while later, Peter put on a new tape, Tchaikovsky's *1812 Overture*. While Anna and Madeleine listened, he disappeared downstairs, returning with cups of Red Zinger herbal tea and a bowl of sunflower and pumpkin seeds.

"Hmmm, this music changes my mood completely," Madeleine noted. "I'm not floating anymore. I'm very focused."

Picking up a handful of seeds, she began moving them around on the sheets, as if they were little armies. Anna and Peter grabbed seeds and joined combat. That led them into a discussion of the war in Vietnam.

"This is too heavy," Anna said after a while. "I'm too afraid of war. Please, Peter, please change the music."

He obliged. They listened to the Beatles and smoked another joint. Later still, the sexy whine of Paul Desmond's saxophone playing "Like Someone in Love" permeated the room. Peter nonchalantly removed his clothes and got back on the bed. Reaching out slowly, he ran his hand up and down Madeleine's arm, barely touching her.

"Why don't you get comfortable?" he suggested.

"I am," Madeleine replied. "Like this."

"But bodies are a lot more tactile when you're on this stuff. Sex takes on a whole new dimension. Not only sex. Just touching your own body . . . try it," he urged.

"Well, I suppose I've gone this far. Come on, Anna," Madeleine said.

"Okay . . . but one thing has to be understood. I'm in love and I'm engaged. Absolutely *no* fucking."

Peter rolled over onto his stomach. "No fucking. Just give me a back rub."

Madeleine and Anna took off their clothes, except for their underpants, and slowly gave Peter a deep back rub while he moaned his approval.

After a while he turned over. Anna became upset when she saw his erect penis.

"I said, *no* fucking!"

"Hey, okay. I can't help this, you know. Being in bed with two beautiful women with out-of-sight bodies does this to me." He sat up and readjusted the pillows behind his head. "Hell, I'll jerk myself off if you two'll hug each other for me. The idea of that turns me on a lot."

"No . . ." Madeleine started to protest.

"All right," Anna said unexpectedly.

"Far out!" Peter exclaimed, and grabbed hold of his

erection. "Hey . . . I just had this great idea for a movie. Captain Ecstasy. He's a reporter for an underground newspaper, see? Then he becomes Captain Ecstasy by jerking off. Something in the magical self-contained circuit of his hand, his mind, and his cock working together for orgasm turns him into the greatest fighter against crime and injustice and sexual frustration the world has ever known . . ."

While Peter rambled off into fantasy and masturbation, Madeleine glanced uncomfortably at Anna. She had been surprised by her friend's reaction. Anna was not a touchy-feely sort of person. Even when they greeted one another, Anna never left her cheek in place long enough for Madeleine's lips to make contact. But the drug, or the mood of the saxophone music, seemed to have taken hold of her. Anna reached out her slim, freckled arms to Madeleine and pulled Madeleine toward her until their breasts touched.

Madeleine responded, tentatively wrapping her own arms around Anna's delicate, bony back. It was not that she was turned on exactly, but there was something so exotically different about feeling a woman's soft arms around her, about touching a woman's body. The ethereal quality, the fragility, of Anna's body touched Madeleine on a deep level. She comprehended, for the first time, the totality of the difference between men and women. It was profound.

Madeleine's and Anna's lips brushed together lightly, danced away and then back again. Slowly their mouths opened to each other. As their tongues embraced, Madeleine became aware of a sexual stirring in her groin, both exhilarating and frightening to her. It had never occurred to Madeleine that another woman could turn her on. She had never been excited by the idea of women as lovers.

It was the psilocybin, of course, that had opened them up to the experience. When the drug wore off, so would this feeling that they shared, Madeleine rationalized as her lips caressed those of her best friend.

Then Anna grabbed Madeleine tightly, kissing her more insistently. Madeleine let her hand trail down Anna's body, gently placing it on Anna's thigh. Outside of themselves, seeming very far away, Madeleine was aware that the mattress was bouncing up and down to the rhythm of Peter's hand, moving faster and faster. She heard him moaning, "Far out . . ."

The tape player clicked off. Paul Desmond was replaced by loud sounds of laughter wafting up from downstairs. The three of them seemed frozen in their positions.

The music was gone. So was the mood.

Anna pulled away quickly from Madeleine, suddenly self-conscious. "Hmmm, well, that was . . ." she trailed off, somewhat absently.

They looked at Peter, who was in the process of coming. Dispassionately, they witnessed the event, as if they had both seen men jerk off many times before.

"I'm freezing, all of a sudden," Madeleine said, reaching for her blouse. "Look, my teeth are actually chattering."

"So are mine," Anna realized. "It's cold . . . and I'm starving. What time is it anyway?"

Peter, still lying on his back with his eyes closed, slowly raised his arm and looked at his watch. "Around three."

"Wow, I can't believe it," Madeleine said. "You were right about time on this stuff. I thought it was about midnight. I had no idea it was so late."

"I think we should head back to the dorm," Anna said. "I feel like raiding the candy machines."

The girls finished dressing while Peter watched them from bed. Then they leaned over and each kissed him good-bye, on the cheek. He remained propped up against the pillows, smiling happily.

"Thanks," Madeleine said. "It was really interesting."

Peter nodded. "Yeah, it always is. It always is. Life's a trip, man."

Madeleine gave Lady Soul a hearty pat and headed out with Anna into the night. During the walk home, they tried very hard to appear casual and sober.

The next day Madeleine and Anna both overslept, missing all of their morning classes. Over a shared Pepsi and some saltines, which Anna deigned to eat because she was so hungry, they talked about the psychedelic experience of the night before—and the mind-expanding insights they had felt they had. Each was careful to avoid mention of the sexual part of the evening. Madeleine, in retrospect, had enjoyed it, but was confused by her feelings. She supposed that Anna felt much the same way. It was experimentation, after all.

And a subject best left undiscussed.

The next few weeks passed quickly in a race to complete term papers and cram for finals. Anna left school immediately after her last exam, in order to attend Randy's Princeton graduation and get ready for the wedding.

Madeleine was lonely, left in the room by herself, knowing that Anna would never be back again. Their friendship would never be exactly the same after Anna was married. No more staying up all night together, laughing and talking and eating Hershey bars. She knew that she and Anna would remain chums. But it would be different. For one thing, Randy would be around. For another, Anna would be in New York and Madeleine would still be in Boulder.

Before school ended, Madeleine tried LSD one night with another boy from the art department. He had insisted that he was experienced with drugs, but when the acid took effect, he freaked out and nearly killed himself by trying to fly out of a second-story window. Fortunately, he landed in some bushes, and Madeleine summoned one of his friends in time to administer vast quantities of water and niacin to help race the drug through his system without having to take him to the hospital. The incident scared Madeleine fiercely. It was a night she never wanted to repeat.

She had had it with the drug scene. It was expensive, not to mention illegal. And, at least as far as she was concerned, it wasn't enough fun to counterbalance the terrifying risks involved.

Madeleine remained in Boulder through July, working as a waitress until it was time to fly east to Anna's wedding. One night Brady Gardner came into the restaurant, his arm around a stunning Swedish woman whom Madeleine recognized as the ex-wife of one of her professors. Brady stared right at Madeleine, then turned away without bothering to speak. It hurt her that Brady still hated her so much he wouldn't even talk to her. She hadn't meant it to turn out that way; she had *liked* him.

That night, Madeleine cried herself to sleep, something she had not allowed herself to do very often since her early childhood. Her life in Boulder had turned hollow; she had botched things up. There was nothing, and no one, there for her anymore.

But she had promised Jane that she would finish school. How was she going to keep her promise?

6

The wedding of Anna Chipley McNeill and Randall Porter Ferguson III was a major event in the Manhattan summer social calendar.

Madeleine arrived in New York two weeks early (Wyatt McNeill had sent his Gulfstream jet for her) to join in the final round of prenuptial parties that had been flourishing since June. She had dreaded the inevitable first meeting with Win Burgess, Randy's roommate and best man, after the abyssmal New Year's Eve. But, to his credit, Win behaved politely, or more specifically, as if he had never laid eyes on Madeleine before, which suited her fine.

For the most part, the parties bored Madeleine, much as they had when she had visited over Christmas. Still, she was glad to be included in the wedding festivities. They gave her time to spend with Anna before she rounded the corner into matrimonial togetherness with Randy. And they kept her from having to think about the future.

Madeleine's main escort for the parties was Hadley Mc-Neill, Anna's brother. He was quite full of himself after his year at Yale, but he made up for it by being caustically witty about the events they were forced to attend. He seemed to find them as tedious as Madeleine did, so they developed a common bond. After several evenings with him, Madeleine began to relish his black humor and sense of the ridiculous.

The weekend prior to the wedding, the party moved to the McNeills' summer place in Southampton for another round of fêtes. On Saturday night, after a brunch, a sailing party, a cocktail bash, and a sit-down dinner for sixty, Hadley and Madeleine slipped away from the crowd at the Somebody Mellon's house. Like children, they ran giggling through a maze of landscaped gardens, into an oriental-style gazebo. Under the clear, starry sky, their party chatter lapsed into silence, and they gazed out at the ocean, each lost in thought.

"I'm champagned out. I'm talked out. I'm smiled out," Hadley said finally, wearily. "Want to take a walk along the beach and get even farther away from the madding crowd?"

Madeleine nodded. "You know, it's really exhausting, making endless small talk to people I've never seen before. *And* will never see again."

"Consider yourself lucky. I, you see, *will* see them again. And again. And again. These are people I knew in kindergarten. And after we've finished going to school with one another, we'll all work together, and have affairs with each other's wives. We'll get divorced, remarry, and wind up back here, drinking martinis, when we're eighty."

"You make society seem like so much fun."

"Hmmm. I always wondered why there are social climbers. I guess they're people who don't know any better," Hadley observed.

"Ah," said Madeleine wryly, "if us simple poor folk only realized how happy we really are."

"Now you've hit it," Hadley approved. "We could start a whole new direction in social climbing. Down."

"It's been done. It's called slumming."

"Damn! I always come up with these ideas a season too late."

"It didn't catch on. The thing is, nobody much seems to want to live there."

"You've got a point," Hadley admitted, seriously. He sighed. "Last summer the Pendletons gave a skid row party. Cost thousands. Everyone had a marvelous time. I found it totally disgusting. It turned my stomach." He was silent for a while. "Say you had tons of money, Madeleine. All you wanted. What would you do with it?"

"Well, all this has certainly opened my eyes. If I had the kind of money the people around here have I'd sure spend it on other things besides parties."

"Oh? Like what? Say you just inherited ten gushing oil wells. All your creature comforts are covered, expensively. What would you do?"

"Well, I'd . . . God, this is really hard!" Madeleine laughed, pausing to think. "Of course, I'd try to do worthwhile things: contribute to cancer research and do whatever I could to help people who were worse off. And then, well, I wouldn't sit around on my buns waiting for the cork to fly off the next bottle of champagne. I'd work even if I didn't need the money, because you have to produce, to create, to get a sense of your own self-esteem."

"That's important to you?"

"Yes, of course. It's *everything*. I want to be appreciated for myself, not for how big my bank balance is." She burst into giggles. "My bank balance, however, puts this entire conversation into the realm of high comedy. Let the rich worry about how they're going to spend their money with good conscience. I have to worry about making enough to keep me in SpaghettiOs."

Hadley looked at her, as if scrutinizing her from the vantage point of vast wisdom. "You'll do just fine, Made-

leine. You'll get everything you want. You're focused . . .
you're ambitious. I think whatever you set your sights on,
you'll get."

"You make me sound very cutthroat. I'd like to think I
come across nicer than that."

"You come across very nice," he said quickly. "What I
mean is, you haven't grown up having it all, like Anna and
all of us. So you both want things and despise yourself for
wanting them. I saw you looking at Anna's wedding gifts.
The expression on your face was a mixture of lust and
horror."

"That's not true!" Madeleine shrieked. "God, Hadley,
Anna's absolutely right about you! You make fun of everything and everyone. Can I help it if I grew up poor? I'm
trying not to be dazzled by all this because it's all so unreal. But on the other hand it *is* dazzling."

"Hey." Hadley came over and gave her a hug, then
brushed the top of her head lightly with a kiss. "I'm not
putting you down, really. I'd take you over every one of
those debs in there," he pointed back toward the beach
mansion where the party was still in full swing. "You're
real. That's all I'm saying. You're not contrived or artificial. I like that. I admire it. There's a lot more to you than
meets the eye."

Madeleine smiled wearily. "All right. I'll say thanks,
but let's just not talk for a while."

They took off their shoes and walked along the water's
edge, letting the cold Atlantic waves roll over their feet.
Madeleine considered what they had been talking about.
In truth, she was in the midst of a great conflict, scorning
all these people for their huge fortunes, yet coveting what
they had at the same time. How she was going to come to
terms with that, she wasn't sure. But the first step was to
design fabulous jewelry and become famous and rich.
Then she'd deal with the morality of the situation.

"You know what?" Hadley said after a bit. "You're the
only one I can say this to, but I think Anna's a real ass to

get married now. She has plenty of time. And Randy's so predictable. What possible excitement could there be in a lifetime with him?"

Madeleine nodded in agreement. "To put it bluntly, Anna's terrific and Randy's a bore."

Hadley laughed. "Right on. You know, my sister could take off if she wanted to. She has some money our grandmother left her. She should travel. People don't get married anymore—they live together. If she lived with Randy for a while, she'd get sick of him."

"I agree. I certainly don't plan to get married anytime soon. There's too much to experience."

"Exactly! Look, why don't we find Anna and talk to her?" Hadley said excitedly. "It's not too late! She *has* to call off the wedding. She can spend a year abroad. Hell, we'll go with her."

"Great idea!" Madeleine exclaimed. "Randy'll find somebody else."

"Unfortunately. Women drool over him, although I can't imagine why," Hadley said. He grabbed Madeleine's hand and took off across the sand. "Come on! Let's go steal Anna off into the night."

By the time they finally found Anna she was back at home, sitting on some cushions on the floor of the living room, hugging a bottle of champagne and crying.

"Anna!" Madeleine ran over to her. "What's wrong?"

"Everything!" she sobbed, looking up at them miserably.

"But you're home so early. Did you and Randy have a fight?" Madeleine asked, concerned.

"How could we fight? He hasn't said one word to me all day . . . except in front of other people."

"Well, it doesn't matter. Even when he does talk he doesn't say anything." Hadley sat down on the floor beside Anna, who glared at him with petulant hatred. He detached the champagne bottle from her grasp, took a swig, then passed the bottle to Madeleine, who set it on the coffee table without taking any. "Look," he said, "we came to convince you to elope with us to Europe. Don't do this ridiculous thing and get married."

"I *have* to get married!" Anna screamed. "I have to!"

"Hey, calm down . . . calm down," Hadley said, changing his tone to a more soothing one, "you don't have to at all. Just because Mother's made all the arrangements? It can all be canceled"—he snapped his fingers—"just like that!"

"No, it can't." Anna started sniffing again. Her face was red and splotchy and her nose was running. Madeleine grabbed a box of tissues from behind the television and sat close to Anna, on the other side from Hadley, gently dabbing her friend's face.

"You don't have to go through with it," Madeleine said quietly. "It's much better to call it off now than to get a divorce later."

"No, you don't begin to understand. I'm fucking knocked up!" Anna said through her tears. "It's just impossible, but it's true. I saw a doctor. I only messed up on the Pill once or twice."

"Hey, Sis, it's okay. This *is* the twentieth century, after all," Hadley said. "You can have an abortion. No big deal."

"That's what Randy said. That's what Randy wants."

"But you don't want to have a baby yet? So soon? *Do* you?" Madeleine asked.

"Yes! That's the thing. It *is* a big deal," Anna sobbed. "I've got this wonderful feeling inside of me. I *want* to give birth. I want to have dozens of children."

"Dozens of children? Anna, the peasant of Park Avenue? Really. I don't believe I'm hearing this from my sophisticated sister," Hadley said.

"Well, you are hearing it. And you'd better find Randy first thing tomorrow and talk to him. As my brother, it's your duty to . . ."

"Hey, wait a minute! *My* duty? I don't even *want* you to marry the creep."

"Creep? So *that's* what you think of the man I love!" Anna shouted. She made a fist and hit Hadley hard on his upper arm. He stared at her in disbelief but did not attempt to move away. "Get out of here! Just get the hell out of here, Hadley! I never want to speak to you again! I mean it!"

Hadley stood and took another swig of champagne. He looked at Madeleine. "Okay, she's all yours. This is totally unreasonable. I'm going to bed."

Madeleine sighed and hugged Anna, left in the impossible position of having to calm her down as well as reassure her that nobody thought Randy was a creep. Well, what were friends for if not for times like this? Anna was definitely in a crisis situation, one that had to be dealt with.

"Everything will be all right," Madeleine said as she held Anna and soothed her. She repeated the phrase many times, as it was about all she could think of to say. At last, nearly an hour later, after Anna had gone through both the bottle of champagne and the box of Kleenex, Madeleine convinced her to go to bed; they would deal with it fresh in the morning. "Tomorrow's another day," she heard herself utter wearily, and knew it was time for both of them to get some sleep.

After Madeleine had steered Anna upstairs, and her friend had finally dozed off, Madeleine thought about Anna's predicament and tried to put herself in the same position. How would *she* handle it? Pregnant by a man who did not want her child. She really did not know what she would do. It was horrible. By next week at this time Anna was supposed to be married. What would happen between now and then was anybody's guess.

For the next few days, after returning to the city, Anna ate very little and kept to herself. She had never seemed more fragile or delicate to Madeleine. But she was so tense

and snappish that Madeleine had trouble making even
light conversation with her.

Wyatt and Elizabeth McNeill had no inkling of the
drama that was being played out under their roof. They
put down Anna's lack of appetite to nerves about the impending wedding. Hadley had a job during the day, working for a conservation group, so he was not around much.
Madeleine, to give Anna time by herself, spent most of her
time holed up in the library, reading.

On Wednesday morning Anna came into the library
where Madeleine lounged with the morning's *Times* and a
cup of coffee. Madeleine noticed that Anna's eyes were
dark rimmed and haggard. But there was a bright glint in
them.

"You look tired, Anna. Didn't you sleep?"

"No. Of course not!"

"I'm sorry." Madeleine had grown used to Anna's
shortness. But there was a slightly different tone to her
friend's voice that made her put down the newspaper and
sit up. "What is it?"

Anna smiled tightly. Her face was very pale, so that her
fatigue-bruised eyes and her lips stood out despite the absence of makeup. "I've decided what to do," she said in a
hushed voice that made Madeleine's skin cold.

"About the . . . ?"

"Yeah, the baby."

Madeleine waited.

"I'm going to do what Randy wants. He's the man. He
ought to make the decisions." Anna paused, and the same
chill, humorless smile played at her lips for a moment.
"And he should be ready to accept the consequences for
them."

"What do you mean?" Madeleine asked uneasily.

Anna told her what she had planned.

The Bellavista was a tired and dispirited hotel in the
Eighties, just west of Broadway. It was difficult to tell

what the view claimed in its name might once have been. Now its entrance faced a small Spanish grocery, a Chinese laundry, and a Greek delicatessen, above which were abandoned apartments with broken and boarded windows.

The room, for which Madeleine had paid thirty dollars in advance to a desk clerk too bored even to smirk at the two pretty young women with one small overnight bag, looked out across tenements to a school yard on the next block. The chain-link fence had been rent with bolt cutters, probably long ago, and a dozen preteen boys were playing a noisy game of basketball on the blacktop.

The room itself was small, with a double bed, a bedside table, a bureau, a wastebasket, a suitcase stand with a broken strap, and a print of an Alpine scene bolted to the wall above the bed. There was a bathroom with a small stained tub, a toilet, a sink, and a cracked mirror.

"Oh, Anna—" Madeleine began, but Anna cut her off.

"What time is it?"

"Quarter of two."

"All right."

Anna set the overnight bag on the bedside table. She opened it and took out a white nightgown. She undressed quickly, tossing her clothes haphazardly toward the bureau. Before she put on the nightgown, she pressed her palms against the smooth white of her belly and moved her lips, murmuring something that Madeleine could not hear. Then she pulled the nightgown on over her head and turned down the bed.

"At least the sheets look clean," she said. She lay down and stared at the ceiling.

They waited.

At four minutes of two, there was a knock on the door.

"Who is it?" Anna said.

"Me. Randy. What the hell is this, for God's sake?"

Anna nodded at Madeleine. Madeleine opened the door.

"Jesus Christ," Randy swore as the door swung back, "what kind of a dump is—"

He saw Madeleine and stopped. "What are you doing here?" he asked.

Then he saw Anna lying on the bed.

"Hello, Randy," she said. He took a step into the room, and Madeleine closed the door behind him.

"I'm sorry, Anna, I don't get it." Anna did not answer. Randy looked at Madeleine for help. "You said on the phone she'd decided I was right."

"I said she'd decided to do what you want, Randy," Madeleine corrected.

"Well, whatever. But why do we have to talk about it in this shit hole?"

"You're not here to talk about it," Anna said solemnly.

"What then? What are you two up to?"

Anna reached over to the bedside table and opened the overnight bag. Inside was a jumble of what looked like surgical instruments.

"You're here to do it," Anna said.

Randy turned pale. *"What?"* he croaked.

Anna took hold of the nightgown and pulled it up above her waist. "You put it here," she said, keeping her bright eyes on Randy's. "If you don't want it, darling, you can take it away."

Randy shook his head incredulously. "No," he said. *"No!* Anna, you're crazy." He wheeled on Madeleine. "You put her up to this, didn't you?" he snarled.

Madeleine started to answer, but Anna's voice cut through sharply. "She had nothing to do with it, Randy. It was my idea. You find that so hard to believe? *My* idea. Madeleine tried to talk me out of it. But this is it. We have the baby, or you do the abortion. It's your decision, Randy. You're going to be my husband. I'll do whatever you want."

"Anna, baby." He sat on the edge of the bed and held her hand. His voice was coaxing. There was perspiration on his forehead and in spreading crescents under the arms of his seersucker suit. "I know a very good doctor. He's got a clean office on Park . . . he knows what to do. And he's very discreet, if that's what you're worried about."

Anna kept shaking her head, slowly, back and forth.

"You're mad!" Randy protested, his voice rising to a panicky falsetto. "Honey, I'd butcher you. I don't know what to do. You could die!"

Anna reached out and touched his cheek. "Our baby could die too. If that's what's got to happen, I don't want anybody else but you to do it. Madeleine will assist you. She doesn't want to, but she will because I asked her to. To be able to get help, in case . . . anything goes wrong." She stroked the sweat-soaked hair off his forehead. "It's not a pretty thing, Randy. I don't want it done in a pretty place. But if it's what you want, we're in your hands, darling."

Randy got up suddenly and backed away. "No!" he said. "I won't do it!"

Anna's voice rang out like a slap as his hand touched the doorknob. "If you go out that door, I'm having the baby! I'm not afraid to have it alone. The wedding's off. I couldn't marry a man who was so uncaring, who was so callous. I couldn't marry someone who wasn't man enough to take responsibility for the consequences of his own actions. If you go out that door, it's over, Randy."

Randy stood frozen with his hand on the knob. His shoulders began to shake, and a sob broke from his throat.

"All right." He crumbled. He threw himself down on the bed and hugged her, crying. "All right. You're right. We'll have the baby."

Over his shoulder Anna's eyes met Madeleine's.

"Take the bag," she mouthed.

Madeleine picked up the bag of surgical instruments from the nightstand and went out the door, closing it carefully behind her so that the latch barely made a sound.

* * *

The wedding service was held at St. Bartholomew's
Episcopal Church at Fiftieth and Park. Besides Madeleine, who was maid of honor, there were nine other
bridesmaids. They all wore apricot chiffon garden-party
dresses, with crowns of cornflowers in their hair—Anna's
only salute to the Bohemianism of the period. Anna herself wore a gown of the palest apricot satin and lace from
Henri Bendel and carried jasmine, baby's breath, and
cornflowers. With her red hair and pale skin, she was
breathtaking. Everyone remarked that she and Randy
were the handsomest couple they had seen in years.

The reception afterward at the Metropolitan Club was
lavishly de rigueur. Madeleine thought she had grown
used to excessive entertaining over the past weeks, but the
McNeills outdid themselves. A thousand near-and-dear
friends crushed into the ballroom, transformed for the occasion into an enormous tent of pale apricot silk, with
hundreds of thousands of flowers—jasmine and apricot
tea roses. They dined on rack of lamb, lobster, and an
endless buffet of gustatory delights, wines, and nonstop
Louis Roederer Cristal champagne. They danced to the
music of Peter Duchin until early Sunday morning.

Randy and Anna were forced to leave at midnight.
They wanted to stay—they could sleep together anytime,
why leave a good party early?—but Elizabeth McNeill insisted, for convention's sake. In a flurry of tears and rose
petals, the couple took off into the night in a limousine
bound for the bridal suite at the Pierre. The next evening
they would fly to Italy for a three-week honeymoon.

Back at the McNeills' apartment, a little after three,
Hadley and Madeleine relaxed in the kitchen, leaning
back with their feet propped up on the kitchen table, wolf-
ing down milk and cookies.

"Well, that's that," Hadley said. "A month I'd never
care to repeat."

"Until *you* get married," Madeleine teased.

"Me? Not on your life. I'll live with women but I'll never marry one."

"Why? Aren't we good enough for you?"

Hadley laughed. "Sure. But I don't want to get tied down. Besides, it sounds like Anna's going to have my ration of children. I'm an advocate of Zero Population Growth. The planet's getting too crowded. How are we going to grow enough food to feed everybody? And what food we do grow is contaminated by pollution and chemicals."

Madeleine yawned, got up, and set her glass in the sink. "On that cheery note I think I'll go to bed."

"I'll join you," Hadley said.

By that, Madeleine assumed that he meant he was going up to bed as well. But when she climbed the stairs to Anna's room, he followed her in and flopped his tuxedoed body down on one of the twin beds.

"I've wanted to make wild, passionate love to you since the moment I first laid eyes on you," Hadley said. "Thank God Anna's finally out of the way."

"What?" Madeleine said, grinning, puzzled. "You?"

"Of course me. I'm only a year younger than you. Surely you've noticed how smitten I am?"

"No, I didn't. I mean, I don't know what to say," Madeleine replied. Hadley had a great sense of humor. Was he joking, or not? She couldn't tell.

"Don't say anything. Just get out of that ridiculous dress and come over here."

Madeleine had not slept with anyone for months. She was totally exhausted, but she longed to have a man's arms around her, to feel a man inside her. It had never occurred to her to think sexually about Hadley. He was Anna's younger brother. That's all she had ever regarded him as.

But now she took time to study him from across the room. Anna looked like her mother, but Hadley took after Wyatt—over six feet tall, with the same dark brown hair and large, intense brown-black eyes. His nose was strong, but not beakish. He was thinner than Wyatt, and his cheekbones were extraordinarily well-defined for a man. He smiled at her, waiting expectantly. Nice teeth.

Hadley?

Hadley?

Hadley. Now that she was looking at him, really seeing him for the first time, she realized that it was because of him that she had been able to get through the past few weeks. Hadley had been there for her, at her side, getting drinks, rescuing her from endless conversations with tipsy dowagers, making her laugh, offering himself as a replacement for the loss of Anna to Randy. She just hadn't paid any attention.

"Hadley, forgive me. It never occurred to me that you . . ."

"If only you had looked you would have seen all the signals," he said. "I'm mad about you."

"Well, I guess there is sort of an inevitability about this," Madeleine said, confused about what it was she felt for Hadley. He had been conveniently filed away in her mind as Anna's brother, nothing more, as if that made him a nonentity. But here he was now, emerging as a person, a man who wanted her. She was flattered, but she felt something else: an attraction to Hadley. She realized suddenly that it had been there all along. Except, as Anna's brother, she had automatically put him off limits, as if being attracted to him was incestuous. But the fact that he was Anna's brother was merely that, a fact, not a factor in how she should feel about him.

"I'm beginning to see," she said.

Madeleine walked over to the bed and knelt down for him to unzip her dress. That done, she reached over and switched off the light before she began to undress.

Hadley turned it back on again. He stood in front of her and slipped her arms out of the apricot bridesmaid's dress and let the chiffon slide to the floor in a heap.

"Oh, Madeleine. I've wanted to do this for so long." He leaned over and kissed her bare shoulder. And then he undressed her the rest of the way, slowly and skillfully.

During the hours that followed, Madeleine discovered, to her delighted surprise, that Anna's younger brother certainly knew his way around women.

And she discovered something else. The passion she felt was accompanied by something that intensified the sex and totally engulfed her. It was so different from what she had felt with Brady or anyone else. With Hadley, there was an intense coming together of their souls as well as their bodies. There was a feeling of coming home that she had never experienced before. It was as if she had been waiting for him all along, without knowing it.

And then she realized what it must be: love.

Madeleine was falling, at last.

On Sunday, Madeleine slept until noon. Hadley was not there beside her when she awoke, and she missed him. She showered quickly, threw on jeans and a T-shirt, and found him downstairs at the buffet brunch that had been laid out in the dining room.

He came over, put his arms around her, and kissed her. "You looked so exhausted I tiptoed out so I wouldn't wake you. Good morning, my love."

"Hmmm, yes, it is. I feel like I'm in a daze. Did it really happen? Or was it all a dream?"

"It really happened. Oh God, Madeleine, I didn't know it was going to be like this."

"Like what?" she asked, afraid that he was regretting the night before.

He held her face in his hands. "I mean, all these weeks I've been lusting after you, waiting till the right time to make my move. I thought after the wedding would be safe. We'd get it on, and then you'd take off back to Colorado."

"Oh, thanks very much," Madeleine said, bristling. "God, if I'd known . . ."

"Shhh," he said, "hear me out. I had no idea that this was going to happen, but I'm in love with you, Madeleine. I may have been all along and just not realized it. But now I know, for sure."

Madeleine smiled, relieved. "Oh, Hadley, I'm as surprised as you."

"But how do you feel? I mean, do you love me too?"

"Yes," she nodded, "I do. And I feel wonderful."

After bacon and eggs for Hadley—Madeleine was too euphoric to eat—the two of them walked over to Central Park, holding hands the entire way. It was a hot summer day, and the park was full of sunbathers, Hare Krishnas, mimes, picnickers, musicians, children, dogs, and joggers. And other lovers, although Hadley and Madeleine were too absorbed with one another to notice. They walked slowly, their arms around each other. Every so often Hadley bent over and kissed her hair or her face.

Madeleine was completely happy. She had never before basked in a feeling this delicious. Love. It far surpassed lust.

Hadley, for all his wry, man-of-the-world wit, was totally taken with her. Madeleine had the feeling that he really liked women, more than any of the men she had gone out with. He wanted to know her opinion on everything; he seemed to want to get inside her head and see what made her Madeleine.

"You're so different from my sister," he said later as they headed back across town to Park Avenue, still holding hands. "I mean, you're very opinionated and frank. You get on the defensive sometimes. But deep down, you're a nicer person than Anna. I can't explain why, but I feel it."

"Oh, Hadley, I'm not! It's just that you and Anna are brother and sister. Brothers and sisters never see each other the way other people do."

"How do you see Anna, then?"

"She's funny and kind and giving. She's been so generous to me. She's my best friend for a lot of reasons."

"I'm glad you feel that way," Hadley replied. "I happen to think she's incredibly self-centered. But—I know—my opinion is prejudiced." He stopped and turned so that he could look at her directly. "How do you see *me?*"

Madeleine laughed. "If you'd asked me that yesterday my answer would've been very different from today."

"How so?"

"Well, today I'm in love with you."

"No, don't hedge the question. Love aside, how do you see me?"

"Well, I told you, before I never looked at you as a man, just Anna's brother. A sophisticated guy with a jaded sense of humor."

"Thanks."

"Oh, darling, you know my opinion's changed since last night. You're much warmer, much more open than I ever thought. You always seemed in some kind of protective shell—when I first met you, I think I found you a bit intimidating. I mean, you do tend to have a know-it-all side." She grinned and leaned up and kissed him. "But I've changed my mind. All that is just your form of self-protection. You're the most lovable man I've ever met."

He tightened his grip around her. "God, I wonder how Anna will react when she hears about us."

"I've thought about that. I don't know."

"Well, in the past she's been very jealous of my coming on to her friends. We had a big fight about it once. When I was fifteen, her friend Darcy developed a crush on me and Anna was furious. On the other hand, I've known Anna long enough to know that you can never count on her reacting the way you expect to any situation. Who knows what she'll think?" He shrugged. "I, for one, don't care."

"Well, I do. But then I care about you too. Besides, it'll all be fine," Madeleine dismissed it.

"Don't bet on it. I know my sister."

"Well, so do I!"

Hadley squeezed her again. "Let's not get into our first fight over whether or not Anna will approve of our relationship. Subject closed."

Madeleine nodded. "Subject closed."

"Let's hurry. My parents are going out for drinks. We'll have some time alone." He looked at his watch. "God, it's been nearly six hours."

By Sunday evening, everyone was exhausted. Elizabeth McNeill went up to bed after dinner. Hadley, who had to be at work early the next morning, followed soon after, with instructions for Madeleine to slip into his bed when the coast was clear.

Madeleine took her cup of coffee into the library, to read for a bit before heading up.

A little while later, the double doors to the library creaked open. She looked up to see Wyatt McNeill standing there with a snifter of cognac in his hand and a lost, rueful smile on his face.

"I can't get used to it," he said.

"To Anna being married? I know. I can't either."

"Mind talking?"

"No," she said, closing her book. "Of course not."

Wyatt moved through the room aimlessly. "Things are going to be pretty quiet around here from now on," he said. "I didn't think it would affect me so much. But tonight at dinner it finally dawned on me. Anna's gone." He settled himself in a leather chair by the fireplace. "Seems like yesterday," he reminisced, "that I was looking at her through the window of the hospital nursery. And now . . . she's completely grown up." He smiled apologetically. "An awful cliché . . ."

Wyatt stared down into his snifter, lost in thought. Madeleine quietly sipped her coffee. Then he looked at her almost sheepishly. "I'm sorry, Madeleine. Didn't mean to get maudlin."

"Oh, that's okay," she said. "I'll miss Anna too. Not that we won't still be friends, but it'll be different."

Wyatt nodded. "I know. I hope she's not making a mistake. And I certainly hope she's got sense enough to wait a few years before having children. To give herself time alone with Randy."

Madeleine swallowed. Of course Mr. McNeill would find out soon enough. It was not her place to tell him.

"Well," Wyatt continued, sighing, "life goes on. What about you, Madeleine? When does school start again? You'll stay with us until then, won't you?"

"Thanks, Mr. McNeill, I'd really like to." She wanted to stay more than anything, to be near Hadley before he went back to Yale.

But what was *she* going to do then?

Madeleine bit her lip. "Oh, Mr. McNeill, I don't know what to do. I don't want to go back to Boulder. Now Anna's gone, there doesn't seem to be anything there for me anymore. But I promised my mother I'd get my degree."

"Well, there are other schools. Why not transfer to New York? Barnard or N.Y.U. or whatever? You could even live here. I'm sure Elizabeth would love it—the place wouldn't seem so empty. And you'd be able to see as much of Anna as you like."

"That sounds wonderful," Madeleine said. "But the only places in New York I'd like to go are the Fashion Institute or Pratt. I called them last week. It's too late to apply for this semester. Besides, I'd have to get a full scholarship. And I don't know where else besides Colorado I could do that, at this late date."

Wyatt sat forward in his chair. "If you had your choice —of anywhere you wanted to go—where would it be?"

"*Anywhere?*" Madeleine thought for a moment. Of course, she'd like to go to Yale with Hadley. But she knew her grades, good as they were, were not good enough for the Ivy League. And there was a dream, one she had barely allowed herself to consider. "Well, I guess I'd have to pick Zurich . . . or Germany. The greatest jewelry-design schools in the world are there. My professor at Colorado says if you're really serious about becoming a jewelry designer then you have to go to Europe," Madeleine said. "But, of course, that's totally out of the question unless I dip into my savings. Well, I suppose I could do that."

Madeleine paused long enough to allow the possibility to become real to her. She had never considered it before. She had entrusted Jane's life insurance money to Gary Pollock, the ambitious son of Wyatt's own stockbroker. But she could get it back. "I *could,* couldn't I? I'll have Gary sell some of my stock."

"You could. But I'd rather you kept that money invested. I'll lend you the money you need," Wyatt said, "against your future success."

Madeleine was astonished. "Oh no! I couldn't."

"You've become very dear to us, Madeleine. We care about you, and your future." He put down his glass and leaned forward. "I'll have my secretary get on the phone tomorrow. We'll see what we can do."

"You mean it?" Madeleine shook her head and looked deep into Wyatt's eyes to determine whether he was joking. The look he returned was very serious indeed. "I don't believe this is happening."

"Believe," he said, pouring himself another cognac.

7

God, did she miss Hadley. What was she doing here anyway? Why on earth had she told Wyatt McNeill that she wanted to study jewelry design in Europe? Why hadn't she just stayed in New York so she could visit Hadley on weekends? Now, they were separated by thousands of miles, and God, did she miss him.

The town of Pforzheim, West Germany, had been bombed by the Americans shortly before the end of the Second World War, and much of it had been destroyed. Nestled in the beautiful Baden region on the northern edge of the Black Forest, the town itself was gray and ugly. Reconstructed under the Marshall Plan after the war, the new Pforzheim lacked all trace of its former character. Nondescript, hastily constructed houses and public buildings replaced the distinguished medieval stone architecture that had been blown to bits.

Before the war, as now, the city had been a major jewelry center. In fact, the only museum in the world devoted exclusively to jewelry, the Schmuckmuseum, was located there. But, during the war, the Nazis had enlisted the skills of the Pforzheim jewelers to make small mechanisms for bombs. That was why the jewelry center had been eventually targeted for bombing.

Now, behind the town, there loomed a giant artificial mountain—all the rubble of the bombing's devastation that had been later covered with dirt. The mountain, constructed out of man's destruction, was rumored to contain a fortune in precious metals and jewels. There was probably no truth to the rumor; no one spoke seriously of demolishing the hideous hill to recover the only treasures left in Pforzheim.

The war had been over for a quarter of a century but Madeleine felt awkward about being an American there. It was her country that had bombed this once-beautiful town, and she picked up confusing signals from the Germans she encountered. She noticed that some seemed to overreact to her being American: they appeared almost too impressed. Others, she could feel, still harbored resentment.

"Ich hätte gern einen schwarzen Kaffee, bitte," Madeleine said to the waiter in halting German. She took a seat at an empty table at the Schwarzwalder Konditorei—a plain, rather bleak café near school. It was *das Mittagessen,* the midday break that everyone at the institute took between eleven and two. Rather than choosing one of the more popular cafés where the students hung out, she liked the isolation of this working-class coffee and pastry shop. Sitting alone here was preferable to sitting alone surrounded by tables of students who already knew and liked each other.

Before leaving New York, after Hadley had gone back to Yale, Madeleine had taken an intensive crash course in German at Berlitz. Now she was being tutored at night by one of the associate professors at the trade school. But with the classes all in German, by midday Madeleine's brain was too tired to try to make conversation in German with her fellow classmates. She needed to get away.

The owner of the shop, a tall, careworn woman, brought her coffee. Madeleine ordered a pastry—a thin cake with chocolate and almond flakes—by resorting to sign language. After nearly a month in West Germany there were days when the language seemed to flow through her head easily. Then there were days like today, when her mouth and brain were not in sync and she felt as if she were the sputtering village idiot.

On such days she wondered whatever had possessed her to leave the University of Colorado. What on earth had made her think that she could take such an intensive course, taught in German at a German school? Until she enrolled at Berlitz she had never heard the language spoken, except in a couple of Rainer Werner Fassbinder films in a seminar she had taken. Everyone had told her it would be an easy language to pick up, what with the similarities to English and all. Easy for them to say.

"Excuse me, er, you are American, are you not?"

Madeleine looked up to see a tall, blond young man she recognized from several of her classes. "Yes, I am," she smiled. "I guess it's pretty obvious."

"But your accent is charming. You have a good quality when it comes to learning to speak a new language. You, er, jump right in, I think is the phrase. You are not afraid to make mistakes. That means that you will be speaking with fluency in not very long. Do you mind if I join you?"

"Please do," Madeleine said, grateful to be speaking English.

The young man signaled for the waitress and ordered a beer. "My name is Christof Von Berlichingen."

"Madeleine Lathem," she said, extending her hand. It impressed her that Europeans, even young ones, always shook hands when they greeted friends. "You speak good English. Did you learn it in school here?"

Christof nodded. "Partly. And I have traveled. I have a cousin who is English."

"Have you studied at the institute for long?" she asked.

"This is my second term. The work is difficult, is it not?"

Madeleine grinned. "That's an understatement. You know, it seems to me—when I'm in class—that I'm back somewhere in the Middle Ages. All those long tables, everyone measuring and cutting and sawing in silence next to one another. I really feel that an apprentice in 1500 probably had it pretty much the same."

"Ah," Christof nodded, "you are right. Germans respect tradition. Methods that we are learning have been handed down from generation to generation for many hundreds of years. But it is essential to know the old before we dare to seek the new. When we emerge from the institute, only then will we even begin to explore our creativity in a valid way."

Madeleine finished her coffee and began gathering up her books. "You're right, I guess, but it's overwhelming. There's so much to learn."

"Well, if you need any help with the work please come to me. I will be happy to assist. I felt the same as you in the beginning. But now every day becomes a little less difficult."

"Thank you, Christof, for the encouragement . . . and the offer. And for speaking English with me. I feel a lot better than I did half an hour ago."

Christof stood and shook her hand again. "It has been my pleasure, Madeleine. *Auf Wiedersehen.*"

"*Auf Wiedersehen,* Christof," she said.

Madeleine stopped off at a market and bought some apples before heading back to her boarding house. It wasn't actually a boarding house, but a rambling, Black Forest-style cottage belonging to a family named Fischer, who rented out two bedrooms, one to Madeleine and the other to a shy Danish girl who was a year ahead of Madeleine at the institute.

Herr Fischer taught advanced stone faceting at the institute. He was a small man with a forbidding manner who seldom spoke, even during meals. In contrast, his wife, Lisa, was an enormous, friendly woman, a wonderful cook. The Fischers had three children, ranging in age from seven to thirteen. Madeleine had never lived around young children before and she found them delightful. They were very patient with her German and were always willing to help her with vocabulary. At night, after supper, they loved to congregate in Madeleine's room, when she didn't have a German lesson, and play cards.

Madeleine opened the front gate. Frau Fischer was in the garden raking leaves. Madeleine greeted her as she headed to the front door.

"*Sind Briefe für mich da?*" she asked, hoping the day's mail had been delivered.

"*Ja. Aus den Vereinigten Staaten . . .* Con-nec-ti-cut!"

"*Danke,* Frau Fischer."

Lisa Fischer nodded excitedly and went back to her leaf raking. Madeleine had told Frau Fischer that her boyfriend went to a university in the state of Connecticut. Frau Fischer always seemed conspiratorially happy when Madeleine heard from Hadley.

Madeleine snatched the letter off the hall table and went up to her room to read it. She curled up on her lumpy single bed and gazed at the familiar handwriting. Hadley had been writing to her two or three times a week, and she looked forward to his letters more than she could ever convey to him. The past month had been the loneliest time she had spent since she was a child. Everything was so foreign to her—the language, the people, the teaching methods at the institute. Sometimes she went for days without talking to anyone except Frau Fischer and her children. She missed Hadley terribly. There were many days when she wished she had stayed in the States, to be near him.

Madeleine carefully opened Hadley's letter and pictured him writing it in his room in Saybrook College at Yale. His letters always cheered her up. Yale had gone coed the year before and was still adjusting. He wrote hilarious accounts of his encounters around campus with the opposite sex. Yale's superwomen, he wrote, were superintimidating. It was still hard for him, after a lifetime of all-male schools, to adjust to the idea of screwing a classmate. Of course, he assured her, he was merely joking. Yale's women did not interest him this year any more than last. He was being faithful to her.

Madeleine was not entirely convinced. Taking into account the distance that separated them, they had agreed that they would have an open relationship. It was unrealistic to expect that, out of loneliness, one or the other of them might not occasionally take solace in the company of another person. Thus far, Madeleine had not been tempted to date anyone else, although she did long for friendship. And while she was getting her footing at the institute it was a godsend to have wonderful, tender memories of Hadley—as well as his letters—to fall back on.

Hadley had not reacted well, in the beginning, to her announcement that she was going to school in Germany. But Wyatt McNeill had made him realize that it was a great opportunity for Madeleine. Hadley had not sulked for long. He was too enamored with Madeleine to spoil their last weeks together.

Anna, on the other hand, had been tremendously enthusiastic about Madeleine's school decision. Having just returned from her European honeymoon, she went on and on about what a tremendous growing experience it would be for Madeleine. Underneath that, Madeleine suspected, was relief that Madeleine and Hadley would be separated for the school year.

Hadley had been right about Anna's reaction to his and

Madeleine's affair. Anna did not throw a tantrum or anything dramatic like that, but the news had been met by a definite coolness on her part. She could not believe it happened and kept insisting that Madeleine couldn't possibly be *in love* with her brother.

Yes, Anna seemed a bit jealous, but Madeleine pretended to ignore it. She assumed that Anna would adjust eventually to her best friend's relationship with Hadley. It was merely a matter of time.

"Madeleine! *Das Telephon!*" Frau Fischer called upstairs.

It was the last Thursday in November, and Madeleine suddenly remembered that, in the States, today was Thanksgiving.

Madeleine sprinted downstairs and took the phone into the hall closet, not so much for privacy as to be able to speak loudly. The connection, whenever Hadley called her, was usually terrible.

"Hello, love," Hadley said. "I'm home and the whole family's here to say hi. I'll get back on after."

"Hi, Madeleine! Happy Thanksgiving!" Anna's cheery voice came through. "Oh, I can't tell you how much I wish you were here with us. You should see how big I'm getting . . . five months. Mother had to have Lucille bake a separate turkey just for me," she giggled. She loved being pregnant. She had written in one of her letters to Madeleine, "For the first time since I was twelve I can eat whatever I want and it doesn't matter. This eating for two is fabulous!"

"Send me a picture of you and your belly. It kills me to think that you're going through your whole nine months without me. I really wanted to be your midwife," Madeleine joked.

"Next time, darling. Anyway, the time will fly by. We'll see each other this summer. Oh, hold on. Daddy wants to say something."

"Madeleine," Wyatt McNeill said, "I have to be in your neighborhood—Stuttgart—on business in a few weeks. Are you free to let me buy you a decent meal if I drop over to Pforzheim?"

"Free? I'm *never* booked. I'd love it! Especially being able to speak English for a whole evening."

"Wonderful. My secretary will let you know when my itinerary gets worked out. Then I'll give you a ring when I arrive and we'll make plans."

"Thank you. I'll really look forward to it."

"I'm back," Hadley said. "Upstairs, in privacy. Jeez, you should see Anna. She's gained about fifty pounds already. Puffed up like a gigantic hot-air balloon."

"Oh, you're exaggerating, Had. I'll bet she's absolutely glowing."

"Growing," he corrected. "In all directions."

"You're terrible. What is it with you and Anna?"

"Sibling rivalry. She got all the best toys," he quipped. "Anyway, look, Madeleine, there's something I have to tell you. We agreed to be up front with each other, right?"

Madeleine felt a sinking feeling hit her gut. She knew what was coming. "Absolutely," she said, forcing perkiness.

"Well," Hadley began, "I've had a couple of dates with someone, a girl named Lydia. So far it's platonic. But, Madeleine, the scene at school is so wild. Everybody's sleeping with everybody else. I was wondering if you'd mind terribly if I . . . I mean, this isn't love or anything. It's horniness."

What could she say? She supposed she could say no, but he'd probably sleep with Lydia anyway. "Sure, Had. Do whatever you want. We're not committed or anything."

"Yes, we are committed. I love you. I merely want to fuck her."

"Well, it's okay with me."

How could he ask her this? How could he be so stupid as to think that she'd give him her blessing? How could she be so stupid as to *give* him her blessing? She loved Hadley. She hated the idea of his being with another woman. But she couldn't *make* him be faithful to her; it was her fault that they were thousands of miles apart.

"Maddie, you're the best woman in the world. I love you. There's no one else. There never will be."

Madeleine was getting angry, but she didn't want it to show. "What, Had? Can't hear you . . . the reception's shitty. We'd better sign off. Love you."

She hung up the phone and fumed out of the closet and back upstairs. "Men!" she grumbled out loud as she slammed the door to her room. "Damn Hadley! Damn Germany!"

Perhaps she should pack it in. Quit the institute and take the next plane home. Wasn't Hadley more important to her than becoming a jewelry designer? Or was he? Was he worth blowing her opportunity to study with the best technicians in the world?

No, she was here. And here she was going to stay. If she was going to be the best, she had to study with the best. And if Hadley really loved her their relationship would survive.

Then she burst out crying. She had the feeling she was losing him, and there wasn't a damned thing she could do about it.

Three weeks later, there was a call from Wyatt McNeill.

"I've just wrapped up two days of meetings," he said. "I'm free until Monday morning. If you can spare the time I thought you might let me take you sightseeing around the Black Forest."

"That would be wonderful. I'd love it. I haven't been anywhere since I arrived here."

"Then we're on. Pick you up around six."

The chauffeured limousine arrived on time. Wyatt McNeill was dressed in conservative business clothes that somehow did not match his deeply tanned face. The tan, it seemed, had been acquired during a recent trip to Morocco. The suit was not like his elegant Italian-cut ones. He had bought it in Germany, he told her, to fit in with the people with whom he was doing business.

Madeleine was once again struck by what an attractive man he was. Of course, there was a strong resemblance between him and Hadley. As things now stood, she did not particularly want to be reminded of Hadley. Still, it was so good to see a familiar, friendly face again that she almost cried.

"We're going to stay tonight in Rastatt," Wyatt McNeill said, as the long Mercedes drove out of Pforzheim and along winding country roads. "It's only about twenty-five miles as the crow flies. Unfortunately the crows didn't plan the roads around here."

Madeleine, before Mr. McNeill's arrival, had been afraid that she might feel uncomfortable around him, but that wasn't the case at all. She felt easier with him here than she had on Park Avenue.

"I've booked rooms at the Adler," he told her. "Do you know it? It's a beautiful eighteenth-century inn."

"That sounds lovely, but any place would be fine. It's just so nice of you. To take time out of your meetings and all."

"I couldn't miss the opportunity of seeing you, Madeleine," he said smiling, patting her lightly on the knee. Then he leaned over to the bar. "Want a drink? I'm afraid after the negotiations this afternoon I need a stiff scotch."

"Nothing for me now, thanks." She watched him pour a neat shot. He raised his glass to her, and downed it in one belt.

"That does the trick," he said.

"Is anything wrong?" Madeleine asked. "I mean, did the meeting go badly?"

"Oh, you wouldn't want to hear about it. It would bore you."

"No, not at all. I'm interested . . . really."

"All right, but stop me if you want." He poured himself another shot of scotch. "There's a wealthy German named Karl-Heinz Pschorn. Made his fortune in hotels. Now he wants to buy an American motel chain—the Happy Travelers' Wayside Inns."

Madeleine giggled. "In Boulder everyone referred to them as the Wayward Inns. They were cheap, and popular for weekend rendezvous."

Mr. McNeill nodded. "Exactly. But Pschorn wants to revamp them into high-quality lodges. Figures it's cheaper to do that than start from scratch. Anyway . . . I'm representing Pschorn in his negotiations with the Brown family, who own the Wayside chain." He refilled his glass with scotch and took a sip. "The Browns are quite a clan. Family-owned business. The old man died five years ago and they still haven't sorted out who's doing what. Brother against brother sort of thing, *except* now that they're dealing with Pschorn they've banded together in greed. Our meeting today ended with Laird Brown getting so red in the face I thought he was going to have a heart attack. He's a huge man, extremely overweight . . ." With his hands he indicated Laird Brown's excessive girth.

"How could you think I'd be bored?" Madeleine laughed. "This is fascinating stuff. Real-life drama. It must be exhilarating, dealing like that. Getting into the dynamics of people, trying to read them. Trying to be fair, yet getting the best deal at the same time."

Wyatt McNeill gazed at her earnestly. "Very perceptive, Madeleine. Maybe you ought to go into business."

"I am. I'm not just going to design jewelry. I'm going to open a store. Lots of them."

Wyatt smiled. "So you have it all planned."

"All except how I'm going to finance it. But I'm not worried. I'll figure it out."

"I'm sure you will." He finished his drink and set the glass back in the bar.

They talked about Anna for the rest of the drive. She

had decided to name the baby Randall IV, if it was a boy, and Olivia, if it was a girl. Mr. McNeill, too, expressed some concern over the amount of weight she was putting on. He was still upset that she would not be finishing school—at least in the foreseeable future—but he was glad that she seemed content with the prospects of motherhood.

As they arrived on the outskirts of Rastatt, Mr. McNeill launched into the patter of a tour guide, reading from a green Michelin guide on the area. "The city was once a residence for the rulers of Baden. There are two huge palaces here—baroque and rococo . . . built sometime in the late seventeenth century. One is supposed to be bigger and grander than Versailles."

The driver turned off into a narrow street leading to the Rhine and pulled up in front of the Adler. By the time Anna's father had checked them in, it was nearly eight. They went quickly to their rooms, at opposite ends of the same hall. After they had changed—Madeleine into something more formal, Wyatt McNeill into something less—they met downstairs, to have dinner.

One of the great chefs of the area, Rudolf Katzenberger, owned the inn and presided over the kitchen. By the entrance to the main dining room was a display of old cookbooks. A fire burned in the hearth. There were chintz curtains at the windows, and paintings and wreaths of flowers and herbs on the walls. Old, rustic lamps hung from the wooden ceiling. The tables were covered with linen cloths and adorned with vases of fresh flowers, antique silver, and fine porcelain.

After they had pored over the menu, Madeleine ordered for them both, in German, and translated Mr. McNeill's questions about the wine list.

"I'm impressed," he said. "You sound like a native."

Madeleine smiled, pleased by the compliment. "It's been hard work. Of course, you pick it up fast when you hear nothing but German being spoken all day."

"Tell me, how's school?"

"Incredibly disciplined," Madeleine sighed. "Some of my classes go till seven at night. Before I came, I thought I knew a fair amount about jewelry design. But I didn't know anything . . . not anything classic, at least. And hardly any of the technical stuff. I didn't know flat-metal work at all. There's such a difference between that and the lost-wax method I learned in the States." She laughed. "Don't worry, Mr. McNeill. I'm not going to bore you with the differences. But at the institute I'm required to take an intensive technical course before I'm even allowed to *begin* design. Then there are two years of design, including sculpture, painting, technical drawing . . . and silversmithing, stone cutting and setting . . . electroplating . . . engraving. It's endless! Can you believe what I've gotten myself into?"

"You're not having second thoughts, are you?"

"No, never!" Madeleine said emphatically. "As hard as it is, this is what I want to do for a living. I'm learning my craft. I'm going to be the best . . . and that's exhilarating."

"I'm glad to hear it. Tell me, have you made friends?"

"A few. It's a very international group. There're two other Americans, but we're not in the same classes so I don't really know them. There are several Dutch girls I like. And a German named Christof helps me translate some of the difficult technical manuals."

"Aha! Does Hadley know about this?"

"Oh yes. I wrote Had all about Christof." Madeleine sipped the local red wine that the waiter had just poured in her glass. She did not want to talk about Hadley. "Anyway, Christof is just a friend. He's not my type, but he's very popular. He's absolutely the most fastidious person I've ever met. You can practically see him shudder whenever he comes over to my room to study. I'm a reasonably neat person, but he's obsessive. In fact, Christof told me, in all seriousness"—Madeleine sat up rigidly in her chair and took on a German accent "—whenever the affair is over, and the girl will go on to someone else, I feel good . . . that I am passing that girl on a little more organized . . . and a little more disciplined."

Wyatt laughed heartily. "Well, it doesn't sound as if Hadley has to worry about Christof."

And now the moment she had been dreading. "No, I doubt if Hadley gives it much of a thought." She raised her wine glass slowly to her lips and took a large swallow. "I thought you might have heard, but I guess you haven't. Had and I have broken up."

"Oh." He looked at her with sympathy. "Why?"

"I got a letter ten days ago. He's fallen in love with a Yalie named Lydia. Can you imagine?" she said, forcing a smile. "A Yalie named Lydia? Of course, he insists it's only temporary. But meanwhile, I'm over here, being faithful to him. And he's not coming over for Christmas like he planned." She had more wine. "Oh hell, it's impossible to keep up a relationship from this distance. I can't really blame him. The same thing could have happened to me."

"I'm sorry, Madeleine." But Wyatt McNeill's expression was a curious mixture of concern and relief. "Hadley *is* a bit younger than you. It's a fickle age. And you, I think, are remarkably mature for your age." He smiled. "Well, I'll do what I can to try to cheer you up."

"Just your being here cheers me up, Mr. McNeill. And speaking English."

Wyatt McNeill smiled. "I'm glad, Madeleine."

Dining on specialties of the Baden region—escargot soup, pheasant and roe deer pâté, pike in Riesling-and-cream sauce with noodles, honey mousse—the conversation between them drifted easily from one subject to another. Madeleine noticed how relaxed he seemed. It dawned on her that if he weren't Anna and Hadley's father, she might be attracted to him. But, of course, that was out of the question.

After dinner, along with espresso, Mr. McNeill ordered them each a glass of a one-hundred-proof eau-de-vie made from the Zibärtle, a wild plum of the region. Madeleine could not drink hers. It was far too strong and sweet for her taste. Mr. McNeill knocked his back in one gulp.

"I'm absolutely stuffed," Madeleine said as they finished their coffee. "I think I need some air."

"Good idea," he said. "I'll join you."

Madeleine stumbled on a step as they were leaving the inn, and Mr. McNeill caught her and put his arm around her.

They walked for several minutes, talking about the town, before Madeleine realized that his arm was still around her. Almost as if Wyatt McNeill realized at the same time, he removed it. They continued to talk nonchalantly as they strolled, and when they got back to the inn, he saw Madeleine to the door of her room.

"It's been a fun evening. Very relaxing after being with Pschorn and the Browns," he said, leaning his mouth down to brush hers, very casually. "Call me when you're up and we'll decide what to do."

"Okay. Thank you for dinner, Mr. McNeill. See you in the . . ."

"Madeleine, I wish you'd call me Wyatt."

"Oh, all right . . . Wyatt."

"That's better," he said, his eyes lingering on her before he turned and headed for his own room.

Something had happened between them that night, Madeleine realized. They had evolved from being father and daughter's friend, to friend and friend. Or something else.

She began not to feel as relaxed as she had earlier. There were two more days to spend alone with Mr. McNeill . . . Wyatt.

Anything could happen.

8

 As it turned out, Madeleine's weekend
with Wyatt was innocent. Nothing happened, although
Madeleine detected subtle sexual undercurrents. Wyatt
even mentioned that his marriage to Elizabeth was not as
it appeared on the surface, but Madeleine had been careful
not to pursue the subject.

Wyatt McNeill was an attractive and engaging man,
and she enjoyed his company. That was as far as it went,
or would ever go, she told herself. And to be safe, to avoid
any further awkwardness on her part, she decided not to
accept any more overnight invitations from him.

In truth, she still missed Hadley. He continued his affair
with the femme fatale Lydia, although occasionally he
dashed off impersonal jottings to Madeleine, determined that they would "remain friends." In turn, she sent
him back funny clippings from German magazines, or
sketched anecdotes about her professors and classmates.

She was careful to keep it light because, deep down, she knew she had lost him for good.

Madeleine was devastated, having found love only to have it snatched away after a few short months. One minute she hated Hadley, the bastard, the next she yearned for him. So she threw herself intensely into her studies to avoid moping around or daydreaming that they would get back together.

For Christmas break, at the invitation of her new Dutch friends at the institute, Madeleine joined them in Holland, at a pacifist commune. There she was surrounded by a group of gentle people, about twenty of whom lived full time on the communal farm. Madeleine and her friends added another eight people, but no one seemed to mind. Many of them spoke English and insisted on practicing it with Madeleine.

Madeleine was relaxed with the friendly Dutch people, feeling completely at ease for the first time since her arrival in Europe. The days were full of activity. In the large rustic kitchen of the two-hundred-year-old stone farmhouse, Madeleine even helped make the cheeses and breads that they sold in Rotterdam to keep the commune going. One of the boys, Leo, taught her how to milk a cow, amazed that she had never learned in Colorado. On Christmas Day, Madeleine baked apple pies as her American contribution to the feast.

But in the evenings, tucked into her cot in the drafty barn where everyone slept dormitory style, it was a struggle to force thoughts of Hadley out of her mind. Some nights, no matter how tired she was from the farm chores, she couldn't sleep at all. Finally, determined to banish Hadley from her mind forever, she learned to will herself to sleep by keeping her mind blank and concentrating only on her breathing. If she breathed in and out evenly, not letting any stray thoughts take residence in her brain, eventually she drifted off. The more she practiced it, the faster she was able to fall asleep.

Back in Pforzheim after the holidays, Madeleine was proud that she had made such a strong effort to get over Hadley. It had worked. Although still a bit resentful, she felt as if she had come to terms with what had happened between them. He was out of her life forever.

She never wrote to him again.

Wyatt McNeill returned to West Germany several times during January and February. Although rushed, he always took time to come to Pforzheim to take Madeleine out to dinner. During those evenings, the mood remained casual. Madeleine discussed school, and Wyatt talked about the irritating negotiations that dragged on between Pschorn and the Brown brothers. The deal had taken much longer to put together than originally anticipated.

"The only saving grace," he told her, "is that it gives me a chance to check up on you and report back to Anna."

"I wish I could see her. The baby's due the end of next month. It'll be practically grown before I get to see it."

"I promise you," Wyatt laughed, "by summer it will still look and act like a baby."

Madeleine put down her fork. "I don't think I'll be back for summer. I'm doing well here, and if I work straight through, I'll be able to start design classes next year." She lapsed into silence for a few moments. "And quite frankly, there's nothing for me now in New York. I can't stay with you because of Hadley. And Anna's in the midst of redecorating and having a baby. I'd just be in the way."

Wyatt nodded. "Put like that, I see what you mean. But, Hadley or not, you're always welcome in our house. Perhaps I should talk to him."

"No, don't!" Madeleine snapped. "It's *completely* over between us. Over and done with."

Wyatt McNeill squeezed her hand. "I understand. Let me know how much money you'll need for your summer courses and I'll take care of it."

"Thank you," Madeleine smiled, grateful. "I'll pay back
every cent."

"I know," he said. "But not until you're famous."

"You're so wonderful. What would I do without you?"

"Well, you needn't worry about that. I'm here whenever
you need me."

The winter term at the institute proved easier, particularly since Madeleine was now more fluent in German.
And she had adjusted to the strict discipline. Every assignment had to be executed exactly. "Almost" was not
allowed. This often produced great frustration, but Madeleine thrived on challenge. Learning to measure and cut to
the degree of an eighth of a millimeter had seemed impossible in the beginning. Now, she was starting to get it.
There was an exhilaration in achieving the perfection that
the students strived for and the professors expected. And
in knowing that when she left Pforzheim she would be
among the best-trained in her field.

The teachers at the institute were taskmasters. They
were the best of the best: aloof, but kind and supportive.
They had no time to become personally involved with any
student. There was much work to be done, and they were
rigidly demanding.

Madeleine's technical course focused on teaching her to
saw and solder metals with absolute precision. One had to
learn how to measure and cut exactly, how to join pieces
together. Every line had to be perfectly straight, every
piece perfect in height, thickness, and depth. If Madeleine
missed by the slightest fraction of a millimeter she had to
repeat an assignment.

Her main teacher—a thin, bald, middle-aged man
named Herr Pfeiffer—would not let his students get away
with anything.

For months the class worked only on sawing and soldering metals into exact degrees of thickness. As time went
by, they were allowed to make small models of rings,

square as well as round. Toward the end of the year they would graduate to bracelets and gold chains. At this stage of mastering technical precision, design played a very small part.

One day Madeleine worked painstakingly for seven hours on a model of a simple silver ring, measuring precisely, sawing the metal, then soldering it. When she had finished, she knew it was the most flawless piece she had ever crafted, and her cheeks flushed with satisfaction. As she was putting on her clear glasses to protect her eyes during the polishing process, Herr Pfeiffer came over to the table. Smiling courteously, he asked to see her piece.

Madeleine set it in his hand, nervously. She was filled with expectation of the praise he would lavish on her. She had worked hard; the ring was perfect.

"Ah, Fräulein Lathem," he examined the ring carefully with the jeweler's loupe he kept on a silver chain around his neck, then handed it back to her. *"Nicht schlecht, aber mach es noch einmal, bitte."* Not bad, but do it again, please.

How many times she heard those words come from his lips that year she could not begin to count. *Not bad, Fräulein, but do it again, please.* Still, reflected in his eyes and tone of voice, there was encouragement. Herr Pfeiffer never, even at the beginning of the year, made Madeleine feel incompetent.

Every assignment found Madeleine doing it again at least three or four times before she was allowed to go on to something new. The same held true for her technical drawing class. Over the months, she drew sprigs of flowers until she thought that, come spring, she could not bear to see buds blossom on the trees.

But, despite the frustration, she was learning. Enormous pleasure came from the simple approval of Herr Pfeiffer. Madeleine derived a solid sense of accomplishment as she mastered skill after skill. She was doing what

she wanted to do. She was on her way to becoming a
jewelry designer.

Still, Madeleine longed to be able to toss her technical
drawings into the trash and start designing. Whenever
there was an exhibit of the work done by the older design
students, it depressed her. The "older" students were all
younger than she. Nearly all came from European families
who had been in some aspect of the jewelry business for
generations.

Madeleine's best Dutch friend Katrina's family owned a
jewelry store in Amsterdam. Cristof's father and grandfather were stone cutters in Idar-Oberstein. Brigitte, the
Danish girl who also roomed at the Fischers', would be
the first stone setter in her family, but they owned an
enormous foundry outside of Copenhagen. None of them
had gone to college; instead they had started designing
jewelry, sometimes in their early teens. Had they not
opted for the institute, their alternative would have been
an apprenticeship under the supervision of a master craftsman.

One thing bothered Madeleine. Her friends at the institute were not there only because they wanted to be, but
because they were expected to be. At the end of their two-
to-four years in Pforzheim (depending upon their degree
of proficiency when they arrived) they would return home
and go to work for their fathers, uncles, or cousins, in
family businesses.

Madeleine was at the institute of her own free will. She
had chosen jewelry-making because it attracted her. It was
hard for her to accept that her friends were simply doing
as they were told. She held her tongue for months, but one
evening, over a sandwich and beer with Katrina, she decided to speak up.

"Katrina, I don't understand why you're here. You're
beautiful. You told me you modeled in Amsterdam."

Katrina gave a wide, open smile. "But if I model for five
years, then what? My beauty will not last forever. I think

it is hard for you to understand, as an American. In Europe, there is great tradition . . . and great respect for one's family. That is the way it is. The way one grows up. And the jewelry business is very family oriented, as are many businesses in Europe. I have a friend in Holland who is the seventh generation of her family to run an inn. It would never occur to her to do anything different."

"Yes, but that's what I mean," Madeleine protested. "What about what *you* want? Where's your freedom of choice?"

"I am free to do many things with my life," Katrina said, spreading a dollop of mustard on her bratwurst. "But for my work I am to go into my family's business, and that's that."

"Of course," Madeleine said impatiently. "But why not model now and appease the family later?"

Katrina smiled, an expression of sympathy on her face. "Americans have a different point of view from Europeans. I am not unhappy with my life or with the plan for my future. I like the certainty of *knowing*. There is no indecision, no doubts."

"No doubts about what?" Christof and another German boy, Pieter, joined them, beer glasses in hand.

"Madeleine is acting like an American," Katrina laughed. "She thinks we are wrong to do what is expected of us, and not what we want to do."

"But my dear Madeleine," Christof said, "did Katrina not explain that we *want* to do what is expected of us?"

"It's beginning to sink in," Madeleine said, "but I don't know if I'll ever completely understand."

"You will one day," Christof said. "Now let's have another beer. Tomorrow's Sunday . . . no school. We could make a picnic if the day is sunny."

Another thing about the students at the institute, Madeleine had observed over the months, was how easy it was for them to enjoy themselves. Subjects weren't talked to death. Beer and laughter were what it was all about, the simplicity of having a good time. In other parts of Germany, and all over Europe, there was a great deal of political agitation going on, especially at the university level. But here the students were focused in their own world. Global problems were of little consequence to them.

Madeleine paid for the next round of beer and sat watching her friends. Pieter was telling a joke in German. Madeleine gave her mind a rest and tuned out. Although they were unsophisticated, they were balanced people. And, Madeleine thought, there was nothing wrong in the pride they took in knowing what they wanted to do.

Yes, Anna had been right: this year was definitely a growing experience for Madeleine.

One evening in early March Frau Fischer summoned Madeleine to the phone. It was Wyatt McNeill, calling from London.

"I'm meeting on Monday with Pschorn. I have time to kill in between. How about skiing the French Alps for the weekend?"

Madeleine considered it for a moment. In spite of her previous resolve, she longed to get away from the grayness of wintertime Pforzheim. But it was wiser not to. "Oh . . . no. I, er, we have exams and I have to study," she lied.

"Well, can I take you to dinner?" Wyatt's voice cooled. "Or shall we skip it completely?"

Madeleine did not want to hurt his feelings. "I'd like to see you for dinner. It's just that the whole weekend . . ."

"No problem. I understand."

When Wyatt's limousine, a tan Bentley this time, arrived to pick up Madeleine, she was surprised to see him in new jeans and a pale yellow crew neck sweater. He looked younger than ever.

"My, my . . ." She smiled, getting in. "I live in jeans, but I put on a dress in your honor."

"We'll get it coordinated one of these days," he said lightly. "Where would you like to go?"

"Anyplace, it doesn't matter," Madeleine said, relieved. She had been afraid that he might have checked and found out that she had lied about the exams.

"Then let's head for Baden-Baden. There's a wonderful restaurant just outside town. It has a bunch of stars from somebody or other."

"Sounds great. You'll turn me into a gourmet yet." Madeleine opened her handbag and pulled out a paperback book on wines of the region. "You see, I'm trying to take it all in."

"Oh, let me see it." He reached for the book and their hands touched briefly. The touch sparked a static-electric shock, reviving Madeleine's memory of the apprehension she had experienced during their weekend together before Christmas.

The town of Baden-Baden was world famous for its curative mineral waters, which people had been sipping and soaking in since the Roman emperor Caracalla popularized the spa in the third century A.D. By 1500 there were twelve spas in the town. Later, European society moved in, to holiday lavishly while taking the cure. Besides royalty, Turgenev had had a villa there. Brahms composed there. Victor Hugo wrote. Dostoyevski gambled at the casino. But not everyone loved Baden-Baden. Back in the summer of 1878, Mark Twain wrote a humorous send-up of the town, which he later published in *A Tramp Abroad:* "It is an inane town, filled with sham, and petty fraud, and snobbery, but the baths are good . . . I fully believe I left my rheumatism in Baden-Baden. Baden-Baden is welcome to it . . . I would have preferred to leave something that was catching . . ."

The rich and powerful still frequented the spa for restorative holidays. Besides the waters, they came for the roulette and baccarat tables at the casino, built in 1821 and considered by many to be the most elegant in Europe. In high season, there were also concerts, horse races, and theater.

But on this March evening Baden-Baden seemed cold and drab as Wyatt McNeill's limousine pulled up in front of the Bocksbeutel, three miles out of town. The restaurant was located in an old ten-room inn that was nestled among vineyard-covered slopes. With cloudy skies threatening rain, it was too dark for Madeleine to see the vineyards or the view.

In the restaurant, adjoining a wine-cellar tavern, Wyatt requested a table near the fireplace, to take the chill from their bones. The waiter brought a bottle of Affenthaler, a light local red wine. Within minutes they were cozy and warm. Madeleine was starving, having missed lunch, and could not make up her mind what to have for an appetizer. Wyatt solved the dilemma by requesting that the chef prepare small portions of every appetizer on the menu for them to sample. After that, they launched into a pasta with white truffles, and grilled wild boar with juniper-berry sauce.

The dinner conversation was as general and relaxed as during their other few evenings together. Wyatt seemed in an especially good mood, glad that Madeleine was obviously relishing the meal. Over espresso, however, he slipped into silence. Madeleine told herself that it was a comfortable silence, but she knew better. She waited, almost outside of herself, watching the scene. She was afraid that the moment she had hoped would never present itself was now about to.

"Well, that was really delicious," Madeleine said, trying to sound casual. "But I'm afraid I'm going to have to eat and run. It's time to . . ."

"This *is* an attractive place," Wyatt McNeill interrupted. "Can't I lure you to change your mind and spend the night? Franz can drive you back to Pforzheim early in the morning so you'll have plenty of time to study."

"Oh no—I didn't bring anything with me. Besides, I really have to . . ." . . . *get out of this,* Madeleine thought nervously.

"I have an extra shirt you can sleep in. And you don't need makeup. Come on, you've been working as hard as I have. A change of scene clears the head."

A voice told Madeleine: *No, don't do it!*

"No, thank you," she said out loud. "Really, I can't."

"Relax, Madeleine. You have to learn to enjoy yourself. You're too tense. Come on . . . it's a long drive back. Say yes."

No! the voice shrieked inside her head. *No!*

But different words slipped from her throat. "Well . . . okay," she mumbled.

"Good. You're so serious most of the time, Madeleine. You need to unwind." He signaled the waiter. "I'm having a cognac. Will you join me?"

"All right." Madeleine fumbled through her handbag, pretending to look for a tissue, having second thoughts. "No, Wyatt," she said finally, looking up and taking a deep breath. "I can't stay."

He slipped his hand over hers. "I want you to, Madeleine."

Madeleine sighed again, not knowing what to do. The trouble was, she *liked* Wyatt. But he was Anna and Hadley's father. And he was married, even if there were problems at home, as he had insinuated. This was too heavy a scene for her.

The waiter brought two snifters of cognac and set them on the table. "I want you, Madeleine," Wyatt continued. "It's time. And don't worry. It's right for both of us."

"No, Wyatt. I can't get into this. Don't you see? I like you, but . . ."

"You can't see being with me because of . . . who I am," he said. "Of course I understand. But I'd hoped that over the past few months you'd begun to see me for myself. As the man, separate from the family. And what I told you about my marriage wasn't a line. It was over long ago. Elizabeth and I are husband and wife in name only. At first we stayed together for the kids. But now they're grown. There's no point in keeping up the charade."

Madeleine sighed. This was becoming so complex. "Oh, Wyatt, I've enjoyed our evenings together. I've looked forward to them. But anything more . . . for this to go further, it would be *wrong.*"

He squeezed her hand. "Madeleine dear, what I feel for you is real," he said softly. "I care about you deeply. But I'm not going to force you into anything. I want you to stay. If you don't want to, I'll have Franz drive you back tonight. It'll never come up again."

The intensity of his stare made Madeleine's body tingle. Had she been standing, her knees would have buckled under her. She should get up, walk out the door, get into the car, and go back to the Fischers'.

But she could not muster the courage to do it. Hadley was past history, and Wyatt was a dynamic man, rich and sexy, and he wanted *her.* She was attracted to him too. The attraction had been building over the last months, but she hadn't wanted to admit it to herself. She had blocked it out.

But now they were here. Wyatt was right. It had nothing to do with anything else. They were consenting adults, after all.

Tears welled up in her eyes. "I want to stay. I just wish it weren't so complicated."

"It's not complicated," Wyatt said, wiping a tear away from her cheek. "I want to be with you. To take care of you. This is between *us,* no one else."

"All right," she said so softly it was almost a whisper. She desperately wanted someone to take care of her. How soothing his words were.

He summoned the proprietor and inquired if there was a vacant room. There was, the proprietor assured him; there had been a cancellation.

Madeleine nursed her cognac as long as possible, nervous. By the time Wyatt had settled up the dinner bill and they headed upstairs, there were a multitude of butterflies in her belly. It was a dangerous situation, yet here she was, racing toward it with abandon; as if there were an inevitability about it all. Well, perhaps there was.

The bellboy arrived with Wyatt's luggage from the car. A maid was summoned to light a fire in the hearth and turn down the bed covers. Madeleine, trying to seem nonchalant, wandered over to the fireplace to warm her hands.

Wyatt waited patiently until the activity subsided. When the maid finally left, he hung the Do Not Disturb sign on the outside knob and closed and latched the door.

He came over and stood beside her. The back of his hand brushed her hair lightly, and she responded with an inadvertent shiver. "Are you having second thoughts? It *is* over with Hadley, isn't it?"

"Yes, completely over. But I am having second thoughts. I want this, but I'm scared . . . of the situation. Aren't you?"

"No. It's going to be easy to handle." He kissed her forehead. "I've looked forward to this moment for a long time."

"You mean, you *knew* that I'd . . ."

He took her in his arms. "I hoped that we'd be together sooner or later. I'm falling in love with you. And I know how to get what I want," he added, matter-of-factly.

"But, what about . . ." Madeleine's words were cut off by Wyatt's lips pressing hard into hers.

The next thing she knew she was being swept off her feet, literally, and carried over to the white-lace-canopied double bed.

Wyatt lowered her gently. "We'll talk later. Now I'm going to show you how *much* I care for you, my darling," Wyatt said, kissing her neck.

Madeleine extended her arms and pulled Wyatt to her.

A sigh escaped from her throat as the weight of his clothed body pressed against hers. It was good to be wanted again, cared about. So good that it had to make everything all right. This handsome, rich man wanted *her*. Nothing else mattered except the two of them.

And no one would ever know. This would be their secret.

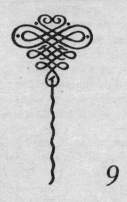

9

True to his word, Wyatt kept Madeleine up all night, making love with the stamina of a college boy. Since he jogged and played racquetball, he was lean and strong. And except for the gray scattered through his black hair, Madeleine didn't think he looked at all his age, which was forty-three.

Wyatt McNeill, her mentor, now her lover. As well as Madeleine thought she knew him, after their first night together he became a different person. This person wanted her for *herself.* All previous connections between them were dispelled. Anna, Hadley, and Park Avenue were light-years away and had nothing to do with the two of them. She and Wyatt were operating within their own universe now.

Was *love* conceived in the dark hours before dawn? Madeleine did not know. Wyatt *said* he loved her. Certainly they both felt tenderness and mutual attraction. But

131

Madeleine was so emotionally confused she wasn't sure how to sort out her feelings.

They slept late, then had coffee and sweet rolls in the room. Madeleine confessed that she had been lying about the exams; Wyatt was delighted that they would have two more days to spend together. He made a reservation for that evening at Brenner's Park Hotel in Baden-Baden, one of Europe's great old-fashioned luxury hotels. Franz was dispatched to move Wyatt's luggage to the new hostelry, then dismissed until Sunday evening.

The afternoon was spent walking around town, gazing at the splendid Edwardian villas, visiting the Friedrichs-bad—the elegant nineteenth-century Renaissance-style spa—and having *Schlag* and Black Forest Cherry Torte at the Café König. The threat of rain had passed, and although there was a chill in the air, it was sunny. Early spring daffodils and crocuses bloomed in abundance in the magnificent Lichtentaler Allee park that stretched along the little river Oos. Madeleine and Wyatt chatted and behaved like two old friends as they walked around town. Once, Madeleine slipped her arm into his, but he subtly extricated it within moments. That was the way it would always have to be in public, she supposed. No physical contact, in case they might unexpectedly bump into a friend or business associate of Wyatt's.

Before heading back to the hotel, Wyatt took Madeleine into the elegant shops along the Kurhaus-Kolonnaden and the Lichtentalerstrasse. He insisted on outfitting her from head (two pearl-encrusted combs to pull her long brown hair away from her face, the way he preferred it) to toe (a simple pair of ridiculously expensive black suede Ferragamo pumps that could be worn day or evening).

In a lingerie shop, Madeleine was embarrassed because Wyatt selected extravagant lace-and-satin Christian Dior underthings, including a garter belt, excluding panties. At Étienne Aigner, he picked out a leather handbag that he insisted she have. Madeleine caught a look at the price tag and did some quick mental arithmetic; did the deutsche marks really exchange into over two hundred American dollars?

Exorbitant price tags did not faze Wyatt. At one of the haute-couture dress shops he chose Saint Laurent and Pierre Cardin day outfits, and a black Valentino cocktail dress with a miniskirt, décolletage neckline, and puffy sleeves to be worn off the shoulders.

Every few minutes Madeleine protested and tried to stop him. But Wyatt was determined to dress her. He hated her vintage clothes, he told her, and if she ever wore anything hippie or tie-dyed around him again he would rip it off her and throw it into the gutter.

By the time they arrived back at the hotel, arms laden with shopping bags, Madeleine had calculated that Wyatt must have spent about five thousand dollars on her in less than two hours. Overwhelming, especially since she knew she would never wear these clothes except with him. The idea of her showing up in Herr Pfeiffer's class in a Pierre Cardin day suit nearly made her laugh out loud.

Before dinner Wyatt ran a bath for them in the enormous marble tub of their suite. While they soaked, they sipped Dom Pérignon from a single crystal-fluted glass. When the water began to cool, they raced with bubbly, untoweled bodies and threw themselves, giggling, on top of the brocade bedspread. For an hour or so they made unhurried love while a thrilling Mozart symphony played on the radio, full volume. Afterward, they dressed and went out for fettuccine Alfredo at the ornate Stahlbad restaurant. Then Wyatt insisted they try their luck at roulette.

"You must be kidding. I'm not the sort of person who could ever gamble. It's the same as throwing money away," Madeleine said. Having been poor for so long, the idea of losing money at whim disgusted her.

Wyatt shrugged. "True. But there's nothing more exciting than *winning*. And I feel lucky tonight." Even though

they were walking in public through the colonnade near
the casino, he bent down and kissed her cheek. "Don't
worry, darling. You don't have to risk a pfennig. Just
watch me."

The famous, white-columned casino was packed with
big-league gamblers, an international crowd costumed by
all the top fashion designers. The gaming rooms—Versailles inspired, created in the nineteenth century by a Pa-
risian stage designer—glittered as much with gemstones as
with gold and chandeliers. Madeleine had never seen so
much jewelry, outside Tiffany's, in her life. She stared so
long at one dowager's emerald-and-diamond necklace that
the lady spoke to her companion, and Madeleine was
afraid they would have her thrown out on the suspicion of
contemplated jewel theft.

Wyatt selected a roulette table and confidently began
throwing down thousand-mark notes. At first he asked
Madeleine which numbers to bet on. She suggested several, and he lost each time.

"The numbers are sensing your disapproval," he
laughed. "From now on I'm going with my own
hunches." He put five thousand marks down on number
thirteen, and won.

While Wyatt played the wheel, Madeleine wandered
around the rococo casino, discreetly trying to check out
the bejeweled ladies. It amazed her that people could be so
rich. She overheard one woman (in sapphires) telling another woman (alexandrite and pearls) that a third woman
(canary diamonds) had lost a hundred thousand dollars
that night, but refused to admit defeat. Beautiful as these
people were, Madeleine disapproved of them completely.

Then suddenly it occurred to her that if she was going
to be a famous jewelry designer she *needed* these women.
Once in business she would be forced to be nice to them.
She would have to try to like them.

An orange-haired French woman, wearing a Plexiglas
choker studded with ball bearings, looked up from a bac-

carat table and glanced at Madeleine. Madeleine smiled at
her. The woman looked away, dismissing her. Madeleine
felt that these people could see through her fancy veneer
and know that she was not one of them. In truth, she was
very young and attractive, a threat to every woman in the
room.

Madeleine decided then and there that part of her education—almost as important as what she was learning at
the institute—was going to have to be the study of the rich
and famous. She would start by asking Wyatt to send her
subscriptions to *Town and Country* and *Women's Wear
Daily*.

From time to time Madeleine caught sight of Wyatt,
who changed tables at regular intervals, part of his grand
scheme. Every so often she returned to his side, but his
betting so much money—even though he was winning—
made her stomach turn. Nevertheless, standing beside him
she noted that they were as attractive as any couple in the
room. The difference in their ages went unnoticed. Rich
men doted on younger women. Madeleine realized that
the only person who objected to the difference in their ages
was *her*. But that was because of Anna.

And Hadley. The hurt Madeleine had felt when he
dropped her still pricked. Every so often Wyatt made a
gesture or did something that reminded her of his son. It
was a difficult situation. Being with Wyatt all day, as
much as she pretended it was not so, made her realize
uneasily that she was not completely over Hadley, even
though she had thought she was. Of course, now she had
to put Hadley out of her mind forever.

After an hour at the casino, Wyatt had recouped his
losses on the shopping spree with Madeleine. Forty-five
minutes after that he had covered the cost of the suite at
Brenner's, as well as dinner at that night's starred restaurant.

At two in the morning, winnings in pocket, they walked
back to the hotel and went to bed. Wyatt was too ex-

hausted from gambling to make love, but at dawn he woke Madeleine, pressing a vigorous hard-on into her belly.

The next day was spent quietly: reading the Sunday *International Herald Tribune,* making love, sipping tea and munching pastries brought by room service, making love, and watching a production of *Aïda* on television *while* making love. At five they decided to pack their things and go for an early dinner before Franz drove Madeleine back to Pforzheim and Wyatt to Stuttgart, where he was to meet with Karl-Heinz Pschorn.

"This has been the best weekend I've spent in . . . I can't tell you how long. You make me feel twenty again," Wyatt said, putting his arm around Madeleine as they looked out their window at the view for one last time.

"It's been wonderful," Madeleine agreed, intoxicated by the high living, "but I wish you hadn't been so extravagant. The clothes are so expensive."

"It's the way I want you to dress all the time. With your bone structure and features, you have an aristocratic beauty. Why disguise it by wearing secondhand clothes and jeans?"

"But I'm not beautiful," Madeleine insisted.

"You're fishing," he grinned. "You're the loveliest woman I've ever known."

Madeleine pulled herself away from him. "Oh, Wyatt, I'm still confused. This *has* been a wonderful weekend. But—you and I—it's not going to work out."

"Of course it is. You're in Europe. The rest of my life is in New York. When the Pschorn deal is settled, I'll find some other excuse to get over here."

"Excuse? You don't mean that Pschorn . . . ?"

Wyatt smiled patiently. "If you hadn't been at the institute I probably never would have bothered. The Brown brothers are notorious for their slimy business tactics. But it was a challenge. Pschorn wanted me, and I wanted you."

Madeleine went over and sat down on the unmade bed. Was it true? That Wyatt had *planned* this, months ago? Back when she had first gone out with him, it had all seemed so innocuous. She had still been in love with Hadley then. This was *much* more complicated than Madeleine had thought. Did Wyatt McNeill *always* get what he wanted? And if he did, what exactly did he want from her?

"You know, Wyatt," Madeleine said, angry at herself and him, "I really feel cheap. This never should have happened. It's *wrong!* You're married. Anna's my best friend. Elizabeth was so nice to me. I feel like a fucking slut!" Tears welled up in her eyes. "I can't see you anymore . . . I'm sorry."

Wyatt was across the room and beside her on the bed in seconds. "Now . . . now. Don't feel that way. What we have is not like that at all." He wiped her tears away with his fingers. "I've told you—for years Elizabeth and I have gone our separate ways. We're good friends, nothing more. Hell, we've been together since college. But we haven't made love for over five years. It's *not* a marriage!" He wrapped her in his arms.

"Anna has probably told you about our youngest child, David," Wyatt went on, holding Madeleine tightly. "He was born when Anna was fifteen. He's severely brain damaged. I'm not sure whether it was because Elizabeth was thirty-seven, or whether it happened during delivery. She was in labor for twenty-one hours." Wyatt took a deep breath and expelled it slowly. "It doesn't matter really. The upshot was that Elizabeth was devastated. David had to be institutionalized . . . there was no way we could take care of him. Anyway, after that Elizabeth never slept with me again. She told me to do whatever I pleased as long as we stayed married until the children were grown."

When he finished, they sat quietly for a while, Madeleine still in his arms. Finally she decided to ask the inevitable question. "Wyatt, have there been a lot of other women . . . since then?"

"No," Wyatt said. "But I won't lie to you. You're the second."

"What happened to the . . . ?" she asked.

"It wasn't serious. We had fun. That's all it was. She got married." Wyatt cupped his hand under Madeleine's chin and centered her face in front of his. His eyes were haunting, sincere. "It was completely different. You see, I *am* serious about you, Madeleine. I love you. I want to take care of you. Don't you see I'm at a crossroads? The children are grown now. My marriage is over. I can't go on like this. I want to start again—with you. It'll take a while, but as soon as I can get it worked out . . . I want to marry you."

"Marriage? But what about Anna and Hadley? We could never . . ."

"Goddamnit," Wyatt flared, "we have to live our own lives, darling! Life is too short to sidestep our own happiness for the sake of others . . . for the sake of propriety," he said adamantly.

"But Wyatt . . ."

"I know what you're thinking," he interrupted. "But I'm not being callous. Elizabeth is an attractive woman. She'll find somebody else. Anna will come around when she gets over the shock. So will Hadley."

The finality of this conversation filled Madeleine with panic. Wyatt may have worked it all out while he bided his time, waiting for the right moment to seduce her. But Madeleine had not adjusted completely to the idea of being with him, much less marriage.

"Wyatt, I'm really confused. This is all happening too fast." She sighed with frustration.

"Don't say anything. I'll put on the brakes. We'll go easy for a while, be discreet until the timing is right." He ran the back of his hand along the line of her cheekbone. "Oh God, Madeleine, I adore you. Every time I look at you I want you." He glanced at his Rolex. "Franz can wait," he said. "Just one last time before we leave? You don't have to undress."

Unzipping his fly, he pulled up her skirt, exposing the pink lace garter belt sans undies.

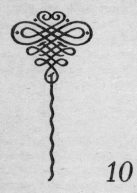

10

"Let's drink a toast to baby Olivia—exasperatingly late, but cute as hell." Wyatt clinked his wine glass to Madeleine's. A dozen snapshots of the infant, only days old, were spread out on the table at Wyatt's favorite Munich beer garden. Anna had given birth to her nine-pound-twelve-ounce daughter three weeks later than the obstetrician's original calculation.

"To Olivia!" Madeleine smiled wistfully. She was sorry not to be able to share the experience with Anna firsthand; now she wasn't sure she'd ever be able to be friends with Anna again.

Wyatt did not seem to feel the real world closing in, but Madeleine did. Sometimes at night, in bed at the Fischers', she wished things were the way they had been. Part of her thought she should end the affair with Wyatt. The other part depended on Wyatt and the fun they had together, traveling and staying at the most deluxe places, shopping, going to the ballet and opera. It was a glamorous world with Wyatt McNeill; she was no longer looking through the window from the outside.

"God, Wyatt," she said, suddenly feeling the difference in their ages, "you're a grandfather now."

"Hey . . . take it easy. I'm a very *young* grandfather. And you're only as old as you feel, my darling. When I'm with you I don't feel any difference in our ages." He grinned, squeezing her thigh under the table. "Do you think of me as an old man?"

"Yes, you're an old lech!" she joked, then softened, aware of the fragility of his ego when it came to his age. "I'm only teasing. No one in this restaurant would *believe* you're a grandfather if you told them. I'll bet you on that." Madeleine smiled at the relief on Wyatt's face and picked up one of the photographs. "Anna says Olivia looks like Randy. But I'm afraid she simply looks like a baby to me."

"Me too," Wyatt chuckled. "Anyway, I'm happy it's all turned out so well. Anna's taken to motherhood like a pro. She's upset you won't be coming to the christening."

"I'd love to, you know that. But under the circumstances . . ."

Wyatt squeezed her thigh again, this time tenderly. "I know, darling. But a year from now it'll be all worked out. Everything will be fine."

Madeleine felt the panic set in. Everything was fine with Wyatt until he brought up the future. She was having trouble enough dealing with the ambiguities of the present to allow herself to think ahead. "We aren't going to talk about that. You promised."

"I know. But I'm tired of hiding out in hotels . . . of having you for a few days every few weeks. I want you with me *all* the time," he pleaded.

"I told you, I have to finish school." Madeleine squirmed. "Please, be patient."

"Yes, yes, I'm being patient. I'll keep on being patient,"

he said, miffed. He picked up the menu and began studying it.

"Did I tell you?" Madeleine said, nervously changing
the subject. "Herr Lippmann, one of the professors at the
institute, is in the hospital with lung cancer. And he
doesn't even smoke. I'm positive it's because of the asbes-
tos pads we use for polishing. And possibly the cadmium
and lead we work with in the gold solder. Anyway, Katrina and I are putting together a petition. To get them to
stop using it. You know, they've been working with those
carcinogens in the jewelry industry for hundreds of years.
It's time somebody did something, and . . ."

"Why don't you have the grilled venison?" Wyatt interrupted, still annoyed. "It's one of the house specialties."

"I want a sandwich." She hated the way Wyatt over-
rode anything she tried to say unless it had to do with
him. It annoyed her to play the role of the adorable
nymphette. Wyatt claimed he loved her for her intelligence, then seemed uninterested whenever she tried to display it.

True to his word, when the Pschorn deal had been successfully completed, Wyatt became involved with another
venture that brought him regularly to West Germany, this
time, Berlin. That way, they logged about two weekends
together a month. Sometimes Madeleine went to Berlin;
sometimes they traveled to the various music, opera, or
ballet festivals that were held around the country.

Wyatt continued to be frustrated that they could not be
together all the time. Madeleine was relieved. Not that she
wasn't fond of Wyatt; not that she didn't thrive on the
attention he lavished upon her.

Most of her energy and concentration, however, were
expended on her studies at the institute, not the affair.

Herr Pfeiffer had become increasingly encouraging with
Madeleine, and her days were wrapped around her craving for praise from the austere German professor. She

longed to be the very best student he had ever had. Like a dog waiting for a treat, she would sit expectantly as she handed him her latest assignment. "Not bad" turned into "Pretty good. Do it again." And now she was often made to do it again only once. At the end of the spring term, Madeleine was honored to be one of four students whom he invited to his home to have coffee and cake with him and Frau Pfeiffer.

When Madeleine was with Wyatt she wanted to talk about the institute, but he made it obvious that he was not interested. Oh, he seemed pleased that she was working hard and enjoying herself, but deep down, Madeleine sensed that Wyatt didn't take her ambition seriously. Although for the most part he kept his word about not discussing the future, Madeleine was sure that Wyatt assumed she would be too busy fulfilling her duties as his wife to have time for a career.

There were definite problems with their relationship. For one, Wyatt wanted to take care of her. That was nice, in part, but Madeleine told him that she was not a flower, that she wanted to make her *own* living. She didn't believe that Wyatt thought she would actually open her own jewelry shop.

Another problem was Wyatt's bossiness. They visited the sights *he* wanted to see, saw the operas *he* liked, ate at the restaurants *he* chose. Madeleine dressed for *him*. He bought her gifts he wanted her to have, regardless of whether she liked them or not.

Madeleine was anything but spineless, but Wyatt wore her down. Often it was easier to give in to him than to fight. And even after a quarrel, they usually wound up doing things his way. Once, Madeleine accused Wyatt of being selfish, and he slapped her hard across the face. Hurt and furious, she told him she never wanted to see him again. To apologize, he showed up at the Fischers' house with an expensive gold chain bracelet with diamonds in it. The bracelet he *knew* she coveted was a contemporary design made of blue Czechoslovakian glass and silver; it was far less expensive.

In bed, however, Madeleine reigned. Wyatt was an accomplished lover and gave her enormous pleasure. Still, she figured out that her youth gave *her* the upper hand. Wyatt wanted her all the time. Madeleine found that she derived great satisfaction from holding back. When she finally let Wyatt have her, he was wild with lust. It was her way of keeping him from calling the shots completely.

But was it love?

On Wyatt's part, it appeared to be. He wanted to start over, have a second family, enjoy himself this time around, now that his fortune was made. But Madeleine slowly admitted to herself that her fondness for Wyatt, her delight in their affair, was not ripening into anything deeper.

It had a lot to do with the guilt she felt. She maintained a sharp definition between her life with Wyatt and her long-distance friendship with Anna. When Madeleine wrote to Anna, she simply did not allow herself to think about Wyatt being her friend's father. She almost convinced herself that Wyatt *was* someone else. In letters, Wyatt turned into Christof, Madeleine's blond German friend. Everywhere she went and everything she did with Wyatt she ascribed to Christof Von Berlichingen.

Anna wrote that she could not wait to meet the handsome Christof: he sounded like a dream.

Then out of the blue, in early June, Hadley McNeill called her. It was a Sunday night, and she had just returned from spending the weekend with Wyatt at the International Music Festival beside Lake Constance.

"Hi, Madeleine," he said. "Surprise."

"Well, it . . . it certainly is. Er, where are you?" she stammered, afraid that he was somewhere nearby.

"New York. Just got out for summer break. I'm on my

way to D.C. next week to spend the summer lobbying against the pharmaceutical companies."

Madeleine smiled in spite of herself. "Good for you, Had. You don't ever give up, do you?"

"Not until they dump me in the ground and cover me up," he quipped. "Look, I, er, I'm sorry about what went down between us. I mean, Lydia and everything. It was just something that got out of hand. You weren't around and . . ." He trailed off. "But it's over. Completely. And I wanted to apologize . . . for acting like such an ass."

Oh God, Madeleine thought, *why is this happening now? Just when I thought I had you out of my mind.*

"Well," she managed to say, "things happen sometimes . . . for the best."

"Oh, Madeleine, I know you're angry, and that's cool. I don't blame you. But I've been thinking lately, about us and what we had. Actually, I've been thinking about you a lot." He hesitated, and Madeleine could hear fragments of someone else's conversation intruding through the crowded wires. "Anyway, I want to see you again, Madeleine. I was wondering, what if I come over this week before I start work? We could talk and . . . Oh hell, Madeleine, I miss you. Lydia and I broke up two months ago, but it's taken until now for me to get up enough courage to call you."

Madeleine sat listening, unable to respond. Why *was* this happening now? Months ago she had fantasized that Hadley would come back. Now, and for all time, it was too late.

But it was so good to hear his voice.

"Madeleine, are you there? Say something."

She sighed. "Hadley, I'm afraid you're too late. I'm involved with someone else."

"Yeah, I know. That German guy from your school. Anna told me. But can't we just spend some time together? Won't you give me a second chance?" he pleaded.

"I want to make it up to you. At least *see* me again. Listen to what I have to say."

All the old feelings came rushing back. "No," she forced herself to say. "It's too late. It's over between us, and there's nothing to talk about." She swallowed to dissolve the lump in her throat. "I'm sorry, Had, but you have to understand. Life goes on."

"Yeah, I can dig it," he sighed, "it does, doesn't it? Well, sorry to bother you."

"No, Had, you didn't *bother* me . . ."

But he clicked off, unable to tolerate more embarrassment.

"Shit!" Madeleine said into the dead connection. "Why did you have to do this to me?" She hung up slowly and wiped the tears from her eyes before heading upstairs.

In her room, she flopped down on her bed, clutching a pillow to her chest. Hadley wanting her back was the last thing she had ever expected to happen. It threw a wrench into the confusion she already felt about her relationship with Wyatt.

Had Wyatt been a substitute for Hadley all along? She had thought that he wasn't. But now, hearing Hadley's voice, she was no longer sure.

Madeleine forced herself to get up and retrieve a small photo album out of her desk drawer, then sat back on the bed to look through it. It was filled with snapshots of her and Wyatt on their various trips together over the past months. She turned to a close-up of Wyatt to scrutinize the handsome, confident man who had everything, yet wanted her. He was wealthy, intelligent, caring . . . everything any woman would want.

She walked back over to the desk and fished out, from the very back of the top drawer, a picture of Hadley that she had been unable to throw away. She hadn't looked at it for months. Now, seeing his handsome face, together with the fresh memory of his voice, made her heart break.

No! It was Wyatt with whom she had cast her lot. There

was no turning back. He offered her more than Hadley
ever could.

Madeleine looked at Hadley's picture one more time,
then slowly ripped it into confetti. Never in her life would
she be able to love him again. She was so upset she
couldn't even cry.

Well, she had been right about one thing she said to
Hadley: life goes on.

If Hadley only knew how messed up it could get.

Despite her feelings, the fact that she loved the son
more than the father, Madeleine continued the affair with
Wyatt on into the summer. She knew that it would have to
wind down eventually. But it seemed to have a life of its
own; she let herself be carried up in the momentum. It was
the path of least resistance, and Wyatt entertained her roy-
ally; he kept her from being lonely. So she forced all
thoughts of Hadley from her mind, as she had done in the
past. And all thoughts of tomorrow.

For her birthday, in late July, Wyatt flew Madeleine to
Venice, to a suite at the Cipriani on Giudecca Island, four
minutes across the lagoon from piazza San Marco. At dinner the first night—in the Cipriani's intimate main dining
room, bedecked with Murano glass chandeliers and floor-
to-ceiling windows flanked by Fortuny draperies—Wyatt
presented Madeleine with a small Chinese lacquered box.

"A birthday gift?" Madeleine asked, surprised. "On top
of all this? You spoil me, Wyatt."

"That's the idea," he said. "I love you, darling. Happy
twenty-first birthday."

From the look of the box, Madeleine suspected jewelry.
Secretly, she hoped that it would not be too expensive or
too conservative. Wyatt's taste was so different from hers.

"Well, aren't you going to open it?"

"Yes. I'm trying to guess what it is."

"You'll never guess."

"A bracelet?" He shook his head. "A necklace? Ring?

A watch? Hair clip? Earrings? An anklet?" Wyatt kept shaking his head and smiling.

"Just open the box," he said, enjoying her.

"All right . . . here goes." Madeleine geared up her smile for an appropriate reaction; she was sure, whatever it was, she'd have to *pretend* to like it. Instead, as she lifted the top of the box, her jaw dropped. "Oh my God! This is unbelievable! I mean, thank you . . . *thank* you!"

Inside, shimmering out from little black velvet niches, was an entire handful of semiprecious gemstones, cut in varying sizes up to a carat: purple amethysts, pink kunzites, ruby red spinels, white zircons, olive peridots, emerald green diopsides, burgundy garnets, blue topazes, yellow citrines.

"I'm overwhelmed!" she exclaimed. "This is fabulous! Think of all the jewelry I can make!"

Wyatt was pleased by her obvious delight. "That's the idea. This is to get you started."

"I know I'm not allowed to display affection in public, but by mental telepathy I'm giving you a big kiss."

"Hmmm, not bad," Wyatt said. "But I think I opt for the real thing. After dinner we'll go back to the room. You'll take off your clothes and let me cover your naked body with these jewels."

"Oh, Wyatt, you're insatiable." She rubbed her knee seductively against his. "Thank you. This is a really wonderful present."

"You're a really wonderful person," he said. "I want you to select your favorites and make an engagement ring out of them." Wyatt's dark eyes gleamed with happiness. "A year from tonight you're going to be Mrs. Wyatt McNeill. That's a promise."

Madeleine's excitement evaporated. Of course, she knew that married men often say they will leave their wives and seldom do. Wyatt might be saying it too, wishing it, without ever intending to leave Elizabeth. But he had talked so earnestly about starting over that she believed he *might* leave Elizabeth. And she couldn't let him do that, not for her. Eventually she was going to have to end things, and she dreaded it. She did not know how Wyatt would react; but she guessed he would hate her. No matter what, she would lose either Wyatt's friendship, or his children's. It was a no-win situation, and she had walked into it with her eyes open.

Madeleine gazed back down into the box of glittering gemstones. The rich certainly knew how to exploit one's weaknesses. But that wasn't fair. Wasn't Wyatt operating out of love for her? Perhaps it was *she* who was using *him*.

Why had she allowed her life to become so complicated? And how was she going to get out from under all this without everybody hating her?

Every problem had a solution. That's what Herr Pfeiffer always said at the institute. And there *was* a solution.

If only Madeleine could figure it out before things got completely out of hand.

Back in Pforzheim, after the weekend in Venice, Madeleine decided that the first thing she would create with the gems Wyatt had given her was a bracelet for her godchild, Olivia, with one of each of the stones in it, in a rainbow of colors.

After painstakingly making a cardboard prototype of her design, she crafted the bracelet at school, during the midday break, for several weeks. Finally, when she was satisfied, Madeleine showed it to Herr Pfeiffer.

"Ah, Fräulein Lathem . . . very nice. This is perfect," he said in German, kissing both her cheeks.

Perfect! Madeleine walked on air for the rest of the day. When it was time to take the bracelet to the post office, she almost couldn't bear to send it off. She hoped that it would please Anna, and that it would be something that Olivia would save for her children and grandchildren—an early piece by the famous jewelry designer, Madeleine Lathem.

* * *

One Thursday afternoon in mid-August Anna McNeill
Ferguson was left alone in Manhattan with baby Olivia;
Nanny Williams had gone to visit relatives in Kew Gardens. Ordinarily Anna enjoyed the afternoons when
Nanny was off. It was peaceful to have the apartment to
herself and Olivia. Today, however, Anna was regretting
her decision to put off going to the Island until Friday.
The heat in Manhattan was oppressive. Air conditioners
whirred in every room of the apartment, but still the air
remained stale and warm. But here she was: some friends
of Randy's were in from out of town, and she had promised to save Thursday evening for them.

Still paying for overindulgences during her pregnancy,
involving chocolate ice cream, Godiva truffles, and jelly
doughnuts, Anna fixed herself a salad with lemon juice
dressing. There were forty pounds to go before she could
fit into any of the clothes she had worn last summer.

After forcing down the salad—she hated dieting—she
took her glass of iced tea to the library, and settled in to
read *The Sensuous Woman,* by J.

Just as Anna had become absorbed in her reading, little
Olivia began crying from the nursery. Anna looked at her
watch.

"Shit, you're a half an hour early," she said to herself.
Why did this always happen? Nanny Williams had Olivia
eating and sleeping on a schedule that was precise to the
minute. But Olivia always seemed to sense when Nanny
was gone and Mummie was in charge. With Mummie running things, they never ran like clockwork.

Anna put down her book and went into the nursery.
The baby broke into a big, gummy grin when she saw her
mother. Her legs began to kick excitedly.

"Well, well, look at you!" Anna said, smiling. "Oh no!
Your bed's soaking wet . . . so is your shirt. No wonder
you woke up early."

Anna picked up Olivia, careful not to get her own dress wet, and carried her over to the changing table.

"It's such a miserable day, why don't we skip our walk in the park and go shopping? Don't you think that would make us feel better?"

The baby gurgled as Anna performed the diaperary functions.

"Good. I knew you'd go for that idea. Maybe we'll find something fabulous for you to wear to Lily Henderson's christening this weekend."

Anna powdered Olivia and changed her into a strawberry-appliquéd cotton sundress with booties and sunbonnet to match. She got the baby's jewelry box down from the shelf.

"Here, let's show off the bracelet Auntie Madeleine made for you," she said, slipping it on the baby's chubby wrist. "Isn't it pretty? It has all the colors of the rainbow." The baby raised her wrist to her mouth and tried to gnaw the gold. "No! It's not to eat . . . it's for decoration. I want to take a picture of you wearing it to send Madeleine."

Anna took Olivia into the kitchen and fed her a bottle of formula that Nanny had prepared. Then she took a couple of snapshots of Olivia and filled another bottle with apple juice for their outing.

Heading down Madison from Eighty-sixth Street, they stopped off at Eightieth and bought Olivia some little French T-shirts and a baby bikini, on sale, and a pink lace tea dress for the christening party. On Seventy-eighth, they picked out a sterling silver picture frame and had it sent, as a christening present. Then they headed for the grown-up shops that were Anna's reward for being such a good, organized mother.

Mother and daughter had barely gotten their bearings at Metamorphosis—a new boutique that Anna had been dying to check out—when Anna began to detect an all-too-familiar baby odor.

"Oh no, Olivia. This is the *third* time today! Okay, kid," Anna said, pulling Olivia out of the stroller. "It's time to hit the powder room." She reached into the pocket of the stroller for a diaper. Except for the apple juice, the pocket was empty.

"Oh damn," she said under her breath. She had forgotten to grab the diaper bag before she left the apartment.

Anna was in the mood to buy clothes; she did *not* relish taking the baby all the way home to change her diaper. The solution, she suddenly realized, was her parents' apartment, a few blocks away. Her mother had laid in a complete supply of baby paraphernalia.

No one would be there, but Anna had the key. Her mother spent summers in Southampton, and her father commuted back and forth for long weekends. He was probably on his way to the Island at this very minute.

Pushing the stroller through the steamy streets, Anna decided she needed to take a cool shower before heading back to the Madison Avenue boutiques. The elevator man in her parents' building was someone new, probably a summer fill-in. He kept the elevator door open, and Anna under a watchful eye, until she produced her key and unlocked the door. She carefully unstrapped Olivia, who had dozed off, and left the stroller in the hall.

"Pugh!" she whispered to the baby as they went up the carpeted stairs to Anna's old bedroom.

From down the hall she was temporarily startled to hear her father's voice, on the telephone, talking loud. She was surprised he hadn't already left for Southampton. Well, she'd talk to him after she'd taken care of Olivia.

Anna headed for her room, placed the baby on the middle of her bed, and cleaned and changed her. Olivia slept through it all.

Deciding she had better let her father know she was there before taking her shower, Anna headed down the hall to her parents' room. Her father was still on the phone. As she got closer, she began to make out his words.

"But darling, it's all set," Wyatt was saying. "We'll meet in Florence. We'll spend a few days there, then fly to Barcelona for my meetings . . ."

Anna stopped dead in her tracks. Her mother had not mentioned a trip to Europe. In fact, Anna distinctly remembered Elizabeth telling her that she was devoting the summer to growing orchids. But if not her mother, then who was *darling?*

"All right," she heard her father continue, "here's an alternate plan. I'll go to Barcelona first, then fly to Paris. You can meet me there. August isn't the best month, but it's still beautiful. I'll book a suite at the Ritz. All right, darling . . . I'll talk to you after the weekend. Yes, I'll call Monday evening . . . I love you."

Anna stood paralyzed. Her father? With a lover? She backed away, down the hall, feeling dizzy and nauseated.

And then she heard him say, "Wait! Are you still on? Madeleine? Yes, one last thing . . ."

Madeleine!

Anna turned and hurried back to her room. Yanking Olivia off the bed, she cradled the baby in her arms and raced down the stairs as fast as her legs could carry her. As she quietly closed the front door, she could still hear her father talking on the phone.

Out on the street, Anna frantically waved down a taxi, threw the folded stroller into the trunk, and headed uptown, home, the sleeping baby in her lap.

11

"I want to go on holiday with you. But it's impossible," Madeleine declared, finishing her Pepsi. She and her friends Christof and Katrina were enjoying their midday break in a beer garden near the institute. The summer term was nearly over, and there were two weeks of holiday coming up before the fall session began.

"But, Madeleine," Christof said, "you must come with us to the seashore. Summer will be over and you will never have gotten a tan."

"Yes, please. We will be lonely without you," Katrina added. The small Dutch girl put her hand over Christof's. They had fallen in love during the summer term at school and were talking of marriage. "We'll have such a fun time. Brigitte is coming, and Anton . . . perhaps Pieter."

"Believe me," Madeleine raised her hands in surrender, "I'd love to. But I can't get out of the trip to Paris."

"Oh, Madeleine," Katrina said, "when are you going to end this affair? This man Wyatt runs your life."

"No he doesn't!" Madeleine said defensively. "He's showing me Europe, first-class. He's terribly generous."

"But you don't love him," Katrina pointed out. "You can't spend your life with a man you don't love."

Madeleine shook her head. "I'm not going to spend my life. But for now, it's working out."

"Madeleine! Madeleine!" A woman's voice interrupted, calling out from down the street.

Madeleine turned to see Frau Fischer hurrying toward them. "I hoped I would find you here." The stout, middle-aged woman paused for breath. "You have a visitor . . . at the house. Come quickly!"

"Who is it?" Madeleine asked in German.

Frau Fischer shrugged. "A young lady. Rather stern. She would not give her name."

"Well . . . I'd better go see what this is all about," Madeleine said, puzzled, hastily giving Christof money to pay for her drink. "See you later, in class." She headed quickly down the street with Frau Fischer. At the corner, they parted company, and the older woman went into a market to shop for the evening's meal.

An odd premonition came over Madeleine as she let herself through the gate to the Fischers' house. Across the street, a black Mercedes with a driver was parked, waiting. She had no idea who her visitor could be, but her hunch told her that something was wrong.

The front door was wide open. Madeleine let the screen door slam shut as she rushed to the parlor where Frau Fischer had left the guest.

A plump young woman with curly red hair stood, her back to the door, looking at the books on the shelf by the mantel. She was wearing a loose-fitting silk chemise and high heels to accentuate her still-shapely legs. Hearing Madeleine enter, she wheeled around.

"Anna!" Madeleine said, breaking into a grin. She rushed across the room to hug her friend. It *was* a shock to see her so overweight. In recent photographs, Anna had been flatteringly arranged into more slimming poses. "Oh, what a wonderful surprise! I can't believe it! Why didn't you tell me you were coming? Did you bring Olivia?"

Anna McNeill Ferguson sidestepped Madeleine's outstretched arms, to avoid physical contact. "I came alone. And I'm leaving just as soon as I've said what I have to say."

Something was very wrong. All sorts of possibilities raced through Madeleine's head, but she had a very nasty suspicion just why Anna had come. Anna's expression, however, was impenetrable.

"Won't you sit down?" Madeleine nervously indicated the sofa. "Can I get you something cool to drink?"

"No. This won't take long."

"What's wrong, Anna? I've never seen you like this. What's happened?"

"You know damned well what's wrong." Anna's voice was flat, controlled. "And I've come all this way to tell you that never in my life have I known anyone as totally amoral as you. I'd like to slap your face. I'd like to do *more* than that. But I wouldn't lower myself," she sneered.

The words struck Madeleine's body as if they were blows. She staggered back and stumbled against a chair. *Wyatt.* It finally hit her. *Anna must have found out.* Madeleine felt as if she were going to faint.

"I don't expect you to say anything in your defense," Anna went on. "You probably think you've done nothing wrong." She paused and dug into her handbag for a cigarette and her lighter.

"Anna," Madeleine began softly. "Please understand. It's very complicated. You can't begin to . . ."

"Oh shut up!" Anna lit the cigarette and exhaled a lungful of smoke impatiently. "Don't say a fucking word. I'm here to talk, and you're here to listen. I know about you and Daddy. *He* doesn't know I know, and I don't want him to. I've told Hadley, of course, and he agrees with me one hundred percent. Neither of us ever wants to see you again. *Ever!*"

"Please, Anna, let me try to explain . . ."

Anna strode across the room, her gray eyes full of loathing, and stood a foot in front of Madeleine. The excess flesh of her postpartum body twitched with emotion. "There's nothing you can say, you bitch! We took you into our family. We gave you everything. And *you,*" she sucked on her cigarette, *"you* fucked us all. Literally. Me, that night in Boulder. Then you fucked my brother. And now you're fucking my father! I hate you more than I thought it was possible to hate another person!"

Anna thrust out her arms and pushed Madeleine so hard she reeled back, losing her balance, sprawling to the floor.

"I'd like to kill you!" Anna shouted. "But since I can't do that, then, somehow, someday I'll make your life as miserable as you've made mine."

Madeleine sat, dazed, on the floor, watching Anna's puffy face distort with repulsion. Anna ranted on, barely pausing for breath. Madeleine could not absorb everything that was being said. Certain words and fragments of sentences penetrated her brain. Slowly it began to sink in.

". . . *never see him again,* do you hear me? You have to break it off *without* telling him that Hadley and I know. We have to protect Mother. Poor Mummie. She cared for you as a daughter. And *you . . .*"

It was what she had dreaded all along. Madeleine's head felt woozy. As she closed her eyes and struggled to catch her breath, Anna's vitriolic words faded into the distance.

Of course, Anna was right, up to a point. But Anna idolized her father: he could do no wrong as far as she was concerned. Of course Madeleine knew she shouldn't have become involved with him, but after all, Wyatt had instigated it. She had been lonely and he had been there, arms outstretched to her, offering *love.* Anna could never understand. She had never been abandoned as a child, forced to survive alone, hungry and cold. Anna had always had everything she ever wanted.

". . . the most thoroughly corrupt, *evil* person," Anna continued, her voice penetrating Madeleine's stupor. "If you ever come near me or my family again I'll see that you regret it, you scum!" Anna snapped open her handbag again. This time she pulled out some tissue paper and unwrapped the bracelet that Madeleine had made for Olivia, hurled it onto the floor.

"I hope I've made myself perfectly clear. If you break off with my father right away, then that's it. You'll never hear from me again. But if you *dare* continue the affair, I'll find a way to have you put behind bars for the rest of your life."

"Anna . . . please. Won't you even listen to my side?" Madeleine pleaded. "You don't understand. You're going too far."

"Too far! Look who's talking. You do what I say. And *think* about us. Think about what you've done. Poor Hadley broke down and *cried* when I told him . . ." Anna stuck out her foot and jabbed Madeleine in the ribs with a pointy toe of her designer shoes. "Get out of my way, you slut," she said with disgust. "You goddamned *slut!* I hope someday you get what you deserve."

With that, Anna left. Madeleine heard the screen door slam shut and Anna's angry footsteps retreating down the walkway. She heard the sound of the door of the Mercedes being opened and closed, the motor starting up, the car driving away. Then there were more footsteps on the walkway, and the screen door slammed again.

"Madeleine! What's wrong?" Frau Fischer asked, alarmed to see Madeleine sprawled on the floor.

"Everything," Madeleine said. She picked up the tiny, glittering bracelet she had made for Olivia.

Yes, everything was as wrong as it could ever be.

* * *

Less than an hour after Anna's dramatic visit, Madeleine heard the phone ring. Up in her room, curled in a ball on her lumpy bed with the curtains drawn shut, she calculated the time in New York. Before Frau Fischer even summoned her, she knew it would be Wyatt. It was Monday; he was due to call.

Madeleine took an aspirin for her aching head before she went downstairs. If only it would all go away. Well, of course, it would. In a few minutes it would all be over.

"Madeleine, darling," Wyatt said after she picked up. "How was your weekend?"

"Oh, it was . . . all right," Madeleine answered, trying to figure out how to tell him what she had to.

"That's good. I want to give you my flight number. Air France, number 534. Turns out I won't make it to Paris until an hour after you. So I thought you might as well wait at Orly . . . then we'll take a cab to the Ritz together."

"Wyatt, I won't be able to come to Paris," Madeleine said softly, trying to gather courage.

"What? What do you mean?"

"What I mean, Wyatt, is I can't come to Paris. I, er, can't see you anymore."

There was a momentary silence on Wyatt's end. "What? What do you mean, darling? What's this all about?"

"Us. Everything." She cleared her throat, stalling. "I've been thinking a lot about us. And it's just not working out. I feel too guilty . . ." Madeleine paused for breath, suffocating. "Oh, Wyatt, you know how much I care about you. But I can't come to Paris . . . I can't marry you. Besides, you know Anna and Hadley would never forgive us if we got married. You'd be estranged from them forever. I couldn't let that happen."

"It won't, darling. Trust me. It'll all be fine after the initial shock is over. They're adults, after all. And we have to think of ourselves."

"I am," Madeleine said sadly. She longed to tell him about Anna. That would make him understand. But she couldn't. "It's just not working. I can never marry you. We can't see each other anymore."

"Oh, Madeleine. Come to Paris. We'll talk about it. We can't break it off this way. We can't break it off. I love you."

"Wyatt, if I came to Paris it would be even harder than it is now. This isn't easy for me, you know. Please, try to understand."

"Understand? What? After all this time you've decided you feel too guilty about my children to go on? Madeleine, we've talked about this." He paused. "Look, just come to Paris. We have to discuss it in person."

"No. I told you, I can't."

"Okay, okay," Wyatt said angrily. "The bottom line is you don't love me. That's it. Isn't it?"

Madeleine paused, hating herself, hating him, most of all hating the moment. "Yes. I thought that I might . . ."

"Darling," he said, pleading now, "please. This is too important to end over the phone . . . I won't let you. I have to see you again."

"No. We can't see each other anymore," Madeleine said, picturing the hatred in Anna's face to gather strength. "My mind is made up. I'm going to the Italian Riviera instead. With friends."

"Oh? Then there's someone else. That's it, isn't it?" Resentment seeped into his voice. "Someone from the institute, your own age? Tell me the truth!"

"No, there's no one else. Oh, Wyatt, I'm so sorry. I'm so grateful to you for everything. You've been wonderful."

"Please, spare me the crap."

"I can't help it, but I don't love you." God, the words kept coming out wrong. If only there had been more time to prepare for this, to rehearse what she was going to say.

"But someone twice your age doesn't quite cut it, eh?" Wyatt sneered.

"You know that's not it! Age has *nothing* to do with it. It's your *family.* I should never have let myself get involved in the first place."

"As it turns out, neither should I, Madeleine," he said. "I'm sorry you feel this way. I've been happier the past six months than I have in years. I thought you were too."

"I was happy . . . Oh, I'm *really* sorry, Wyatt. But there's no future to this."

"There was a future. Didn't you believe that I'd divorce Elizabeth? Is *that* what's bugging you?"

Madeleine sighed. "No. Oh, Wyatt, I don't want to hurt you. You've been so kind. Can't we be friends?"

"No," Wyatt said simply. "We can't. Under the circumstances, you'll understand if I don't continue to finance your education."

"But that was a loan!" Madeleine protested. "I'm going to pay back every cent."

"I doubt it. You enjoyed being kept too much for me to think that you'll ever settle down to a career," Wyatt pronounced coldly. "Or at least a career as a jewelry designer."

"That's a lie! That's a horrible thing to say."

"I don't think so. I've been a damned fool. Good-bye, Madeleine." Wyatt hung up. The sound of his voice was replaced by static.

Madeleine slowly set the phone on its cradle and drifted, trancelike, back to her room. The littlest Fischer child bounced into the hall.

"Madeleine!" she said. "Come see my new game."

Madeleine shook her head. "No, Ursula, I can't play now. I need to rest. I don't feel well." She spoke in English, not even realizing.

The little girl watched Madeleine as she went into her room and shut the door. Ursula didn't understand what Madeleine had said, but she could tell that something was very wrong with the pretty American.

12

The row of buildings on the north side of West Ninety-ninth Street between Broadway and West End Avenue was adorned with window boxes full of petunias and English ferns. Skinny, newly planted maple trees —staked with chicken wire to prevent dogs from taking advantage—gasped out of holes in the pavement, struggling to survive. Gentrification was starting to move into the neighborhood. What had, until recently, been dilapidated tenements were now being remodeled into spacious, one-family brownstones.

The south side of the street, in contrast, was still awaiting the fairy godmother's wand, remaining the *before* to the other side of the street's *after*. Madeleine checked the rentals section she had torn out of the New York *Times,* to see what number she was looking for. Three eighty . . . just as she had feared: even numbers were on the south side.

Walking past a group of Haitians sitting on the front steps of their building, listening to full-volume Island music, Madeleine still could not believe she was back in New York. Although she had liked New York in the past, choosing to return here to live had been mostly an economic decision. She did not want to spend what money she had left on the additional plane fare to California, her second choice. The idea of returning to Colorado was unthinkable.

Of course, Madeleine had considered staying in Europe, but after the confrontations with Anna and Wyatt she had been in a state of confusion. She had not been able to think clearly, especially after she had called her stockbroker, Gary Pollock—the whiz-kid son of Wyatt's broker—who was supposed to parlay her fifteen-thousand-dollar inheritance into a fertile nest egg.

"Well, babe," Gary had drawled on the overseas telephone line, "I knew you were hungry to see that little portfolio grow. So I've put you into two real jazzy stocks, Voisin Motors and Datatrax. You'll be rolling in clover in a few years."

"That's great," Madeleine had said, "but I need money now. To pay for school."

There had been a pause long enough for Madeleine to think they had been disconnected. Then Gary explained that he couldn't sell the stocks *now*. They were highly speculative. They wouldn't be worth anything until the companies really got their footing.

"What?" Madeleine had asked. "Are you telling me that you can't give me my money?"

"Babe, hey, don't get riled. It's cool. It's just that, er, you're in on the ground floor of Datatrax. I got you ten thousand shares, but that's to finance their expansion. Down the road a few years it'll be worth five hundred times what we paid. Right now, we can't sell."

"Well, what about the other one? Voisin Motors?"

"A little problem came up at Voisin. They're reorganiz-

ing. Just filed a Chapter Eleven. Nothing serious . . .
they'll get it all together. But for *now* there's—"

"Are you trying to tell me that out of my fifteen thousand there's *nothing* you can sell for me to be able to stay
in school?" Madeleine screamed, astonished.

"No, no. Let's see . . . there're a few shares of IBM
here that Wyatt insisted I buy you." He paused. "According to today's market, they're worth about fifteen hundred. I can sell that. The others are going to have to wait a
couple of years."

"Okay," Madeleine stammered, "sell the IBM and send
me the fucking fifteen hundred." She hung up in tears.
Wyatt and his damned financial advice. Fifteen hundred
would not cover her tuition at the institute plus room and
board for a year.

She had trusted Wyatt McNeill; he was so wealthy and
successful. Wyatt had said, long before the affair, that he
wanted to help her, hadn't he? A loan was always what
she had considered the money he had given her. She
planned to pay it back, and still would, damn him.

Back in her room at the Fischers', packing to leave, she
had pondered the latest lesson learned: never trust *anyone*.

"Excuse me?" she said to a black man dressed in an
Hawaiian-print shirt. "Number three eighty. Do you
know . . . ?"

"Next block, miss," he said politely, pointing toward
West End Avenue. " 'Tween West End an' Riverside."

It was a culture shock for Madeleine, coming to the
Upper West Side. When she had spent time in New York
before it had always been on the landscaped, well-
groomed East Side, where the McNeills lived. This part of
town, above Eighty-sixth Street, throbbed with the idio-
syncrasies that made New York so eclectic. Soloists from
the Philharmonic lived side by side with cabdrivers from
the Dominican Republic. Koreans manned fruit stores

and East Indians ran stationery shops. A renovated art deco movie house that showed reruns of foreign films sat between a head shop and a thrift store that sold old, dirty shoes. Cuban and Szechuan restaurants sprang up next to odd little establishments that were rumored to be fronts for numbers racketeers. Jewish delicatessens, Irish bars, Mexican take-out places, Latin music stores—they all co-existed, in indifference if not harmony.

Coming from immaculate, rebuilt Pforzheim, Madeleine was not accustomed to the garbage that blew around in the breeze off the Hudson. Or the smell of it, emanating from huge plastic rubbish bags stacked by the hundreds in front of the service entrances of large apartment buildings.

She crossed West End and walked downhill toward Riverside Drive. This block was considerably worse than the previous one. The room she was going to look at was the cheapest she had seen advertised. A musician owned a floor through with three bedrooms and rented out two of them. Besides the bedroom, one was allowed one shelf of space in the refrigerator, and cooking and bathing facilities according to a prearranged schedule. One would not be allowed to use the living room, or entertain in the bedroom.

Stopping in front of 580, Madeleine debated whether to go in. Part of the building was being renovated and looked bombed out.

Oh well, what the hell, she decided. This was no time to get squeamish. She couldn't afford to keep her dingy room in the Chelsea Hotel for much longer.

In the foyer, Madeleine searched the mailboxes for the name of the man who had advertised. There it was . . . number 3B—Sandberg. Several names were jotted above his, in pencil. She pressed the doorbell and, a few moments later, was buzzed in. The dark lobby contained a threadbare sofa. A *Daily News* had been flung down in disarray on the dirty cushions. Next to the sofa was a fake-wood end table with a large plaster lamp with real seashells glued onto the base.

Madeleine walked to the rear and rang for the self-service elevator. At that instant, the door swung open, and she jumped back, startled. A young man balancing a stack of boxes, a blender, and a shopping bag stepped out.

"Sorry. Hold it, would you, love?" he said in a Southern accent. "I've got to get my suitcase and the palm tree." He was slight, with curly blond hair that frizzed around his shoulders.

Madeleine held the door. "Er, are you moving out of 3B, by any chance?"

"I sure am, honey. Couldn't take it any longer." He pulled his suitcase out of the elevator. "Is that why you're here? To look at it?"

Madeleine nodded. "Yes. Is it an okay place?"

"Well, let's just say you have to be *desperate* to live here. The landlord plays electronic music all night long. And then there're the bugs . . . roaches check in but they don't check out. They stay forever. It's like livin' in an Asian kitchen."

Madeleine's heart sank. "I am desperate . . . I've been looking all over town for two weeks."

"You don't want to live here; take my word for it. Okay, you look like a nice girl," he drawled, pausing to scrutinize her for a moment. "Come with me. I've got something better for you. Here, take the blender and the shopping bag."

"Well, I don't . . ."

"Do whatever you want. But you just hit the right place at the right time. I'm lookin' for a roommate. My new apartment has two bedrooms, and I haven't had time to put an ad in the *Voice.*" He smiled. In the process, his blue eyes crinkled up and disappeared behind heavy lids. His clothes were London trendy; he didn't *look* like a weirdo. Madeleine had an instant to make up her mind. She had to trust her intuition.

"Okay," she said. "I'd like to look at it. But I can't promise until . . ."

"Fair enough," he said. "Let's go find a taxi."

Once they were packed inside a cab and he had given the address to the driver—some place near Avenue A in downtown Manhattan—the young man extended his hand. "I'm Edward Randolph . . . pleased to meet you."

"I'm Madel— I mean, Jewel Dragoumis." It was the first time she had actually used the new name she had invented for herself. It seemed odd, calling herself something different. But she would get used to it. And the McNeills would never find her.

"Oh come off it, honey. We're goin' to be roommates. Let's get the name straight . . . the *real* name."

"I'm not sure we're going to be roommates. I haven't committed," Madeleine protested. "I mean, you're a complete stranger."

"I won't be by the time we get to the Lower East Side," he joked. "Come on . . . fess up."

"Well, er, I recently changed my name . . . for my career. I'm not quite used to it yet."

"Then you're an actress?"

"No . . ."

"You're not dealin' drugs, are you?" Edward interrupted. "Or hidin' from the cops? Tell me if you are. I don't need any more hassles in my life."

"No, it's nothing like that. It's very complicated. I just moved back here from Europe," Madeleine said, wiping her sweaty palms on the Zabar's bag in her lap. The cab was not air-conditioned, and New York was in the midst of a humid Indian summer. "There are some people here that I want to avoid. I don't want them to find me."

"Oh goody," Edward grinned with delight. He was smaller than Madeleine and had fresh-faced, boyish looks. "I love intrigue. So, what do you do . . . for a livin'?"

"I'm a jewelry designer." Madeleine held out her arm to

exhibit several bracelets and a ring she had made at the institute.

"Oh, I get it. *Jewel.* Perfect."

"But I don't have a job. It's a long story . . . I suppose if we end up rooming together I'll tell you all about it."

"I have no doubts that we'll room together," Edward said simply. "We're already roommates. Maybe soul mates. I feel like I've known you forever, Miss Jewel with secrets."

Madeleine cocked her head. "Soul mates? But I thought soul mates were lovers."

"Not necessarily. I mean, we might have been in another lifetime. I can guarantee we won't be this time around. I'm gay," he announced without fanfare.

"Oh?" Madeleine said, not exactly surprised. "That's fine with me. I've had it with men anyway." She hesitated. "Anyway, what's this about another lifetime? You believe in reincarnation?"

"Doesn't everybody?" Edward studied her expression and realized that she didn't. "No, I suppose not. I think we've all lived before and we'll live again. My current lover's very big on metaphysics. He's very big, period," Edward giggled. "A bodybuilder named Demetrius. Don't you love it? It's his *real* name, I swear to God."

The cab pulled up in front of a seedy building on Sixth Street between Avenues A and B. Madeleine had gotten her hopes up, but this place looked no better than the last. Edward paid the driver, and Madeleine helped him unload and carry his belongings up three steep flights of stairs. On the fourth floor, they paused in front of a graffiti-covered door, one of two on the hall.

"This is it. Home sweet home." Edward took four keys out of his pocket and unlocked the door from top to bottom.

Madeleine held her breath. The halls had an ammonia stench. Whether it was caused by urine or cleaning solvent she couldn't tell.

The door to the apartment swung open. "Voilà!" Edward stood aside for Madeleine to enter. The large room was a blast of white—even the floor had been painted. It was filled with high-tech furniture that could have come straight from a designer's workshop. Sunlight bathed the room from three windows and a skylight. Floor-to-ceiling steel bookshelves partitioned off the dining and cooking areas from the living room. The sectional, oversized sofa was covered with a fifties red-and-black floral pattern. It provided the only color in the room, except for a large canvas on the far wall that picked up the red and black in a free-form abstract.

Madeleine couldn't believe her eyes. "This is fabulous."

"I knew you'd love it. There are two teensy rooms off this one, so we can each have our privacy. They're big enough to hold a single bed and a dresser, or a double bed and no dresser. I measured. I'm optin' for a high double bed, with drawers built underneath."

"This is a great place," Madeleine said. "But I'm afraid I'm not going to be able to afford it."

"Don't forget we're talkin' Lower East Side. You still have to brave the streets to get here. I'll charge you one hundred until you get a job. Then one fifty. And we share the phone and utilities." Edward paused. "So . . . are you in?"

Madeleine grinned and shook his hand. "Absolutely. This is the first good thing that's happened to me since I came back to the States."

Edward Randolph, it turned out, was a designer too. After graduating from Parsons he had started out as a stock boy at Bloomingdale's and had worked his way up to assistant buyer before quitting to go to work on Seventh Avenue, as an apprentice to an Italian leather designer of belts and handbags. The job paid well but, at twenty-six, Edward was anxious to move up again. He was on the constant lookout for new opportunities.

Madeleine, who was now used to calling herself Jewel full time, enjoyed Edward. He was witty, with a soft-spoken Southern manner, very easy to live with. The evening he helped Jewel move her worldly possessions from the Chelsea Hotel, they stayed up over a bottle of Chianti, and Jewel, getting a little drunk, told Edward her life's story— the truthful, unabridged version—leading up to the unfolding events of the past month in Pforzheim.

"Why, you poor baby," Edward crooned sympathetically when Jewel finished, sobbing into a tissue. "You were caught up in something you merely lost control of. So you've learned a lesson. Now it's time to pick up the pieces and go forward."

Jewel blew her nose. "I'm only twenty-one . . . but already a handful of people would like to see me dead. Oh, Edward, I never set out to hurt *anyone*. Even Brady, in Boulder. I ended up hurting him because I was so dazzled by Anna, but that seems like an eternity ago. I feel like I'm twenty-one going on fifty."

"You've packed quite a few experiences into that small frame of yours," Edward agreed, "but that's what life's all about: livin' and learnin', and above all, havin' fun."

"What about you? I've been monopolizing the conversation for hours. I don't know much about you at all."

Edward smiled. "I was raised to be a real nice boy. And I am. That's all there is to tell."

"Oh no. You're not getting off that easy after I've told you everything. Let's have it. The behind-the-scenes, unexpurgated epic."

"You may regret this . . . or I may," Edward said, opening another bottle of wine. "I grew up on a farm in Gordonsville, Virginia. My daddy's reasonably well-to-do, raises Angus cattle. I went to a boy's prep school nearby. I have four sisters. I was the only boy. My mother adored me. My sisters would always be gettin' into hot water, but not me. In spite of it all, I'm still close to them. I had a girlfriend all through school, Mary Page Scott. Typical normal boyhood."

Jewel nodded. "How come I have the feeling you're leaving out something?"

"You're wonderin' how I ended up gay," he said. "I don't know, really. I sure didn't set out to be. But the guys used to go on about their girlfriends . . . how fabulous sex was. And, here I was, screwin' Mary Page during vacations and I wasn't *feelin'* anything. I mean, I liked her. But she kind of did everything. I didn't have to work very hard." He took off his sneakers and twisted his legs into a lotus position. "I always wanted to be a designer, much to everyone's disapproval. I was supposed to go to Princeton, like Daddy. But Mama pleaded my case, and I got to go to Parsons. It was there that I . . . there was a boy in one of my classes. He was great lookin' and he seemed to be real nice. One night we went out and it happened for the first time. It was like being hit by lightnin'."

He bit his lip with embarrassment. "But it scared the hell out of me. Where I come from, this was something you did not do. So I stayed away from this guy, Mark, and I went home and proposed to Mary Page. We got married that summer. One of those big Southern weddings at the country club . . . off to Bermuda for the honeymoon. Then Mary Page moved to New York with me. She went to NYU while I finished at Parsons. We got along fine, although we were both real busy studyin'. I thought everything was perfect until one day Mary Page comes home and tells me she's fallen in love with her psychology professor and they're havin' an affair. She also told me, rather gently, actually, that I wasn't really cuttin' the mustard in bed. Hell, I thought I was doin' fine. She *seemed* to like it.

"So we got a divorce. Real amicable. Mary Page and I still have lunch together every so often. She wound up marryin' an actor. Then, after all this, I ran into Mark again. And, well, this time around I decided you have to live your life for yourself, not other people. I came out of the closet, as far as my sisters were concerned. But they won't let me tell my parents . . . they think it'll break their hearts. I took Demetrius home for Christmas, and everybody was cool about it. You know, he was introduced as a friend . . . we had separate rooms, that sort of thing. But I'm still not used to it. I was raised to be a mainstream person. And now I find that I'm not. Sometimes it really hurts, deep down. Acceptability is very ingrained in me."

"Well, I find you totally acceptable the way you are," Madeleine said, squeezing his hand.

Edward smiled. "That's only 'cause you're currently fed up with men." But his eyes were glistening, and he reached over and pulled Madeleine to him and hugged her tightly. "We *are* soul mates," he said. "Regardless of whether you believe it or not. We found each other for a reason."

13

　　　　　　To celebrate getting a new job—as a salesperson at the Golden Buddha, a jewelry shop on Bleecker Street—Jewel invited Edward and Demetrius for dinner, her treat, at a Japanese restaurant on University Place. It had been two months since she had moved in with Edward, and they all had become great pals. They went to movies together in the evenings, and museums and galleries on the weekends.

For his part, Edward liked having Jewel accompany him and Demetrius when they went out. Having grown up with four sisters, he was used to having women around. He felt comfortable with them, as long as sex was not involved. Jewel, in turn, enjoyed the fun-loving companionship of Edward and Demetrius. They kept her from sitting alone in the apartment, feeling sorry for herself.

To pay the rent when she first moved in with Edward, Jewel had taken a waitressing job at Borscht, a dairy res-

taurant on Second Avenue. She worked the breakfast and
lunch shifts, having to be there by six in the morning and
not getting off until after three. Then she would come
home and, fighting exhaustion, try to sketch designs for
jewelry.

It was an exercise in frustration. Jewel did not yet have
the equipment or raw materials—save the semiprecious
stones from Wyatt that she had not used to make her
godchild's bracelet—to create the jewelry she designed.
But she was bursting with ideas for pieces that she would
craft when she could afford to. On her days off from the
restaurant, she combed the city to see what jewelry was
out there and selling. She was confident she could hold her
own against the top designers, that it was merely a matter
of time. But biding it was hard.

Finding the job at the Golden Buddha had been a lucky
fluke. Edward happened to be walking by the shop at the
precise moment the owner had put a Help Wanted sign in
the window. He rushed inside and told the owner—a
thirtyish, blond Englishwoman named Betty Blessing—
about Jewel, sweet-talking her into not hiring anyone until
she had interviewed the fabulous Jewel Dragoumis.

At the interview, the next day, Betty had taken to Jewel
at once, and vice versa. They had a great deal in common;
Betty had studied at a different West German academy, in
Hanau, but their experiences had been similar. After two
cups of tea, Jewel not only had a job, she felt as if she had
made a new friend as well.

To celebrate, Jewel put on the Saint Laurent gypsy dress
that Wyatt had bought her in Baden-Baden. It was the
first time she had worn any of those clothes since the affair
ended. Enough time had passed, she thought, but wearing
the dress brought it all back in a flood of sick-making
memories. She was about to take it off when Edward
knocked on her bedroom door.

"Are you decent? I want to show you my new jacket,"

he said, entering. "Oh my God, Jewel, you look super. A Saint Laurent? You've been holdin' out on me."

"Oh, this is something Wyatt bought me. I haven't wanted to wear any of the things. . . ." she trailed off.

"Well, it *is* time to start livin' again. And I forgot to tell you . . . we're all invited to a party after dinner. A friend from my Bloomie's days is celebratin' her anniversary. There'll be tons of interestin' people there. And Bambi asked me to bring you when she heard you were a jewelry designer. Lookin' like that, I just know you'll meet somebody tonight."

"I'm not ready to meet anybody," she sniffed. "But I guess if it looks that good I won't change."

"You look *that* good," Edward said.

After indulging themselves for several hours on sashimi, tempura, and sake, Jewel, Edward, and Demetrius left the restaurant and hailed a cab for the Upper East Side.

"Now, let me give you some background," Edward said once they were underway. "Bambi's a buyer in the Young East Sider shop. Her husband Leonard's a lawyer. Really loaded. Twenty years older than she is, and she's gaga over him. You know, it's really quite sweet . . ."

As the car sped up Park Avenue, Jewel could barely concentrate on Edward's convivial chatter. They were in McNeill territory. Ever since her return from Pforzheim it had made her uneasy to be in that part of town, and she avoided it. She lived in terror of running into any one of them.

Some days Jewel wished she had stayed in West Germany. Katrina and Christof had both offered to loan her money so she could continue studying at the institute. But she already owed Wyatt; she did not want to go further into debt.

It had been a sad parting, leaving Pforzheim, but, true to their word, all her friends at the institute had written, filling her in on gossip and news. Jewel wrote back to them faithfully, determined never to lose touch.

The cab stopped in front of a sterile high rise.

"Isn't this adorable?" Demetrius said. "A building without a wino sleeping in the doorway. They really know how to live up here."

"Admit it," Edward said, paying the taxi fare. "You'd die to have an apartment in a place like this."

"No, I grew up downtown. I *like* litter. It's part of my aesthetic sensibility."

"Well, your aesthetic sensibility is *garbage,*" Edward laughed. "Come on, my dears. Time to party."

Edward's friends were celebrating their first anniversary. This was Leonard's third marriage, Bambi's second, Edward reported on the way up in the elevator to their penthouse apartment.

"Oh, Edward . . . and Demetrius!" Bambi gushed when she saw them. "I'm so glad you could make it. And" —she turned to Jewel—"you must be Edward's roommate," she said, kissing everyone's cheeks. "My heavens, Edward, living with such a beautiful woman, I'll bet you wind up going straight. Oh, don't worry, Demetrius, I'm only kidding," she added quickly.

Bambi grabbed Jewel's hand. "Come with me. There's someone you *must* meet. He's very shy . . . sitting by himself ever since the party started." Bambi and Jewel wove around the mass of bodies. The apartment, large as it was, was not meant to accommodate the number of people Bambi had invited.

On their way across the living room, Bambi stopped by the bar and stuck out her champagne glass for a refill. "Have some champagne, Jewel," she said. "I hope you don't mind helping me out. Sascha seems so sweet. He defected from the Soviet Union about six months ago. I'm afraid he doesn't speak much English." She put her hand on her throat to touch her necklace, a silver-and-topaz choker, of very contemporary design. "Lenny gave this to me on my birthday. Sascha designed it. That's how we met him. Now Bloomingdale's is handling some of his pieces."

They reached a sofa in the corner of the room by the fireplace. A large bearded man with wild, curly, black hair and blue eyes as pale as Paul Newman's sat, empty glass in hand, watching the party. His eyes lit up when he saw Bambi and Jewel coming toward him.

"Alexander—Sascha—Robinovsky . . ." Bambi said, speaking loudly and slowly, above the din of the party. "This is Jewel . . . er?"

"Jewel Dragoumis," Jewel said.

"I wanted you to meet her. She designs jewelry too."

Sascha stared, uncomprehending, then smiled as Jewel stuck out her hand to be shaken. He stood, awkwardly extending the hand that contained the empty glass. He switched it to his left hand.

"Good to meet you," he said, with a thick accent. "You sit."

Jewel smiled and complied. Bambi disappeared off into the maze of guests. "The necklace you designed, Bambi's necklace, it's really beautiful."

"Necklace? Yes . . . necklace," he nodded and smiled.

Jewel was struck by the sadness in the man's eyes. She considered how difficult it must be to defect to a new country, leaving friends and family behind forever. Adjusting to Pforzheim when she had first arrived, barely knowing the language, had been the loneliest time since her childhood.

"Er, instead of English, *sprechen Sie Deutsch?*" she asked, hoping that German would hurl them over the linguistic barrier.

He shook his head. "No German . . . *peut-être vous parlez français?*"

Jewel smiled ruefully. "No, I never learned any French at all."

There was something about Sascha, in ill-fitting clothes

that were too snug in the shoulders, that touched Jewel
deeply. It was an immediate reaction: she knew she liked
this man. He was so out of place among the champagne-
drinking, perfectly accessorized East Siders. In this setting, this Russian bear looked as if he had been caged in a
zoo.

Jewel set her glass of champagne down on the coffee
table. "Let's go someplace quieter and talk," she said, il-
lustrating her words with pantomime. He seemed not to
understand. She pointed toward the door. "Go."

"Ah, go. Yes." He stood and held out his hand to help
her up. His eyes expressed gratitude. "We go."

Before they left, Jewel caught Edward's eye across the
room, and waved good-bye, indicating Sascha with a
quick nod of her head. Edward waved back, mouthing
"Good work."

As they moved through the crush to the door, Sascha
kept his hand firmly locked on Jewel's shoulder. The grasp
of his large hand was so vigorous it almost hurt her. But
his solidity also made her feel secure, grounded.

By the time they had reached the pavement in front of
the building, Jewel suspected she could fall for Sascha
Robinovsky.

"I live in Bronx," he said. "We go."

"No, no," Jewel said quickly. "I thought we'd go to a
bar . . . for a drink." She pretended to hold a glass to
her lips.

"Ah, I have vodka in Bronx."

"No . . . that's not what I want to do. Oh God, you
think I'm picking you up, but really I'm not. I just wanted
to talk." Jewel pointed to a bar across Third Avenue.
"Let's go there and have a drink."

Sascha frowned. "No money. You come to my home.
For vodka."

"Er, no. Not tonight." Jewel steered him uptown instead of crossing the street. "Look . . . I'll walk you to

the subway," she said, frustrated. "How can you get work in this city if you don't speak English?"

"I speak."

"Oh God, Sascha, if you're going to live here you've got to take English lessons," she muttered.

"You teach? I want to learn." He nodded. "You teach."

She rummaged through her handbag for a pen and a piece of paper. Finding a sales slip for some toothpaste she had bought earlier, she turned it over and handed it to him.

"Write down your address . . . where you live," she said distinctly. "And the telephone."

"No telephone," he said, writing the address.

"Oh, great."

"You come home with me."

"No, Sascha. I told you, not tonight. We'll walk to the subway together. Then I'm going home. This is too difficult," she said impatiently. She jotted down her name and number on the inside of a book of matches from the Japanese restaurant where she had eaten dinner that evening.

"I have good vodka. We drink together."

"Maybe some other time," Jewel sighed.

"Time is good now," he said.

"I don't *want* to go to the Bronx. Thank you, but no."

By the time Jewel had walked Sascha to the Eighty-sixth Street subway station and explained that she was going home, downtown, *not* home with him, uptown, she had decided that he was too much trouble to bother with. Sascha Robinovsky would have to be one of the ones who got away.

14

"Jewel, get your ass over here right away," Edward Randolph insisted over the phone. "Sandro's decided to clean out his storeroom. Some of his most outrageous belts and handbags are going for way below wholesale. *Such* a deal," he laughed. "Bring Betty too."

"Sounds great." Jewel turned to Betty in the back of the Golden Buddha. "Betty . . . fabulous sale at Sandro's. Edward says we have to come right over."

Betty Blessing shook her head. "I'm too frantic. I'll have to check it out tomorrow. Some designer called me. He's coming round with his baubles for me to have a look."

"Well, do you mind if I run over there for half an hour?"

"Heavens, no. It's practically lunch hour anyway. Take your time," Betty said.

Jewel spoke again into the receiver. "Okay, Edward, I'm jumping in a cab. Want to have lunch after?"

"Sorry, darlin', can't do." He lowered his voice so as not to be overheard. "I'm breakin' bread with a guy who works for Anne Klein. He's thinkin' of goin' out on his own. There may be a job in it for me."

"Terrific. Okay, see you in a few minutes." Jewel put down the phone and grabbed her coat. "I'll bring a sandwich back here, Betty. You want something?"

"Yes . . . but no," Betty said. "I'm starving myself this week so I can fit into my red slinky for the opera gala Roland's taking me to."

"Okay . . . see you." Jewel was out the door.

"Wait! Jewel!" Betty called out. "I've changed my mind. Bring me some lean roast beef, a dill pickle, and maybe the tiniest bag of chips. Oh, and a Diet Pepsi."

Jewel laughed. "Okay, Betty. How about a teensy bag of Oreos, too?"

"Very funny, Jewel. Skip the chips."

They went through this nearly every day. Betty Blessing dieted and broke diets constantly, to keep her figure a consistent ten pounds over the proper weight for her height. She was always threatening to fire Jewel for eating everything in sight and staying rail thin.

It had been six months since Jewel had moved to New York, and now her life had settled into a comfortable routine, revolving around Edward and Betty, her two closest friends. Edward, of course, knew all the details of her past life, but although she adored him, Jewel regretted having spilled the unexpurgated contents of her twenty-one years to him. When someone knew everything about you, it left you extremely vulnerable, and Jewel hated feeling exposed. Edward had seen all her scars; now, as dear as he was to her, she wished desperately that he hadn't. But what was done was done. No more repeating one's mistakes. It was time to learn from them.

For that reason, when she and Betty Blessing became friends she made Edward swear to absolute secrecy.

"But why?" Edward had asked. "I don't understand."

"Because that's the way I want it," she said curtly. "I'll tell Betty what I want Betty to know. Nothing more, nothing less."

"God, what a mood you're in today, honey. Are you gettin' your period?"

"No, Edward!" she said, exasperated. "And even if I were, my life's my own business. Just because I broke down and told *you* everything in a particularly vulnerable moment doesn't mean I want anyone else to know. I have an intense need for privacy. What people know about you can be used *against* you. I don't want to leave myself open."

"But you and Betty are friends. If you can't trust your friends, who can you trust?"

"No one. I don't trust anyone!" she snapped.

"Well, excuse me! I'm sorry I know so much, since you don't have any faith that our friendship *means* something to me," he said, hurt. "Honesty's real important to me, you know, and I *don't* gossip about my friends. I thought you knew me well enough . . ."

"You have to see my side of it!" Jewel pleaded; she did not want to quarrel with Edward. "There are so many things I'm ashamed of. I don't want to go airing them every time I meet somebody new. It leaves you so open. Please try to understand. I'm not sorry I told you, but you're the *only* one. Please promise me you'll *never* breathe a word of what you know to another living soul."

Edward came over and gave her a hug. "Of course I'll promise. You have my word as a Southern gentleman and a soul mate," he smiled. "Actually, I'm kind of honored to be your only confidant. It makes me feel important."

"You *are* important to me, Edward. You're my closest friend in the whole world. And . . . I guess I do trust you. You've been nothing but wonderful to me." She hugged him back tightly.

"I love you, Jewel. I really do." The corners of his mouth crinkled up into a smile. "As long as we don't sleep together."

"You're safe, darling," she smiled back, teasing. "I've decided to go in for women from now on."

When time came to let down her hair with Betty, Jewel gave a very abbreviated version of her life story, mixing truth and fiction. Betty sensed that Jewel was holding back, and it hurt her feelings. But she had her steady male companion, Roland Axelrod, to keep her from worrying very deeply over Jewel's reserve. And on a day-to-day basis, she and Jewel were really quite chummy.

There was still no man in Jewel's life. Betty often fixed her up with friends of Roland's. Roland was an ex-investment banker who had become a professional poker player. His friends were an odd assortment of mainstream and beyond-the-fringe types. Usually, they were fun for an evening or two, but Jewel had not taken to any of them enough to carry it further. Wyatt had been her latest sexual partner. Edward teased her that she was turning into an old maid. Sometimes Jewel was afraid that she actually was.

Every so often she thought about Sascha, the mad Russian, as Edward referred to him. He had not called her since the evening she had given him her number. And she hadn't been able to bring herself to visit him at his apartment in the Bronx. That was too much of a commitment for anyone who lived in Manhattan. For a few weeks after the party, she had hoped she would run into him somewhere, and she even contemplated taking a course in conversational Russian at Berlitz. But time passed and she neither ran into Sascha nor signed on at Berlitz. Thoughts of him gradually faded from her mind: he was not in the cards for her.

* * *

Jewel returned to the Golden Buddha barely able to carry the bags of bargains she'd picked up at Sandro's sale and lunch for her and Betty. Betty was at the front counter with a man who was showing her his work. Jewel staggered through with her packages and dumped them in the back room. After she had taken off her coat and opened up her container of coffee, she sauntered back out front. Betty was leaning intently over the man's shoulder, oohing and aahing.

"Come here, Jewel. You *must* see these pieces. They're absolutely super."

Betty moved to one side, and Jewel caught a glimpse of the designer. His eyes caught hers at the same moment.

"Jewel?" Sascha Robinovsky said, pronouncing her name *Jew-welll.* "Hello. I am Sascha. You remember?"

"You two *know* each other?" Betty said, astounded. "I don't believe it."

"Of course . . . Sascha." She extended her hand. "I remember I gave you my phone number . . . but you never called."

"Phone number?" He looked blank. "Oh, oh yes. I lose it. Give matches to someone. I want to meet you again. But you never come see me."

"Oh, er, no. The Bronx is a long way."

"I move," he said. "To Spring Street . . . only few blocks from here."

The doorbell rang and Betty buzzed in two women whom Jewel had waited on several days before. Jewel went over to help them. By the time she had sold them matching gold rings, Sascha had packed up his case and was preparing to leave. Betty had accepted several rings and bracelets on consignment. They were contemporary, bold pieces for women, fashioned out of beaten gold, with faceted yellow citrine quartz.

"I'd love to take more, but your prices are too high for

my clientele, Sascha," Betty said. "You should be selling uptown."

"I am," Sascha said. "I sell everywhere I can. Need to make money." He put on his gray tweed overcoat, vintage Good Will, and gathered his portfolio and leather sample case. "Jew-welll?" He came over to the cash register and waited for Jewel to give the women their change. Then: "You come and I fix dinner for you tonight."

Jewel hesitated, considering whether she should be unavailable on such short notice. But she *was* available, so why pretend?

"All right," she smiled. "Where?"

Sascha picked up her hand and pretended to write into her palm. "One Sixteen Spring Street. Third floor." He closed her fingers around her palm, raised her hand to his lips, and kissed her fingers gently. "Eight o'clock," he said as he went out the door.

"My God, Jewel . . . he's to die for!" Betty exclaimed after he left. "Is he not the most dynamic man you've ever met? And so talented! Aren't Russians divine? Where on earth did you meet him? Tell me every last thing!" she ran on without stopping for breath.

"I'll fill you in later," Jewel said, putting on her coat. "Right now I'm going to dash over to the Strand and pick up a Russian phrase book."

On the walk over to Sascha's that evening, Jewel stopped by a liquor store, to buy something to contribute toward dinner. She debated whether to bring a bottle of wine or vodka and settled finally on vodka. Then she could not decide whether to buy Russian vodka: she wasn't sure what his feelings were toward his native country. Finally, to be safe, she bought one from Sweden.

When she reached Sascha's building, she pressed the buzzer, stood on the street and waited, nervously telling herself not to be. Finally she heard his voice calling down from an open window. "Jewel! Here are keys." He tossed

them out the window, and she let herself into the rundown
building, an old plumbing-fixtures factory, she noticed
from a faded sign in the entryway. Walking up the three
steep flights of stairs Jewel breathed in a variety of aro-
matic cooking smells drifting down from Sascha's apartment.

"Welcome." He greeted her at the door, kissing both
cheeks.

Jewel handed him the vodka. "For you," she smiled. "I
hope it isn't too much of a cliché." It had been so long
since she had had a date with someone she found attractive. And the way Sascha had of looking at her, as if he
could penetrate her most intimate thoughts, totally un-
nerved her. It was silly, feeling like this, after all she had
been through. Pretending to cough in order to take a deep
breath, she looked toward the kitchen.

"Whatever you're cooking smells fabulous," she said
casually, following Sascha into the loft. He did not offer to
take her coat so she tossed it onto a lumpy, faded chair
that looked like a thrift-store reject.

"I am great cook," he declared simply, shoving the
vodka into the small, frosted-up freezer. The open kitchen,
dining, and living areas filled one gigantic dingy-white
room. There was a vast expanse of space, with very little
furniture to fill it. The walls were hung with a few abstract
paintings and some posters of the New York City Ballet.
Several photographs of Sascha with another man were attached to the refrigerator door with masking tape.

An enormous gray cat with a tan diamond-shaped
patch on its forehead appeared out of nowhere and began
rubbing its back against Jewel's leg.

"Oh, hello," she said. "Who're you?"

"That is Lisa . . . cat of roommate, Zhenya. He find
her before we move here. In Russia, is good luck for cat to
be first to enter new home. Bad luck if any cat crosses
your path, not only black."

"Really? Do you believe that?"

Sascha smiled. "Yes, I am superstitious about some things. Cat cross my path in Bronx. Next day my apartment was robbed. Lucky I had appointment with my jewelry. They steal only cheap radio and toaster. But they leave big mess."

"Burglars trash places when there isn't anything good to take," Jewel said. "But I wouldn't blame a New York robbery on a cat crossing your path. It was a coincidence." Jewel picked up the heavy cat. "God, she's big. Eating a lot of good Russian food, are you?" she said to the purring animal. "I love cats. I had one as a child. It was my best friend." She paused, thinking of Scrappy. "I think they're good luck."

"Me, I like dogs," Sascha said. "But too much trouble in city. Someday I live in country . . . with big family and big dogs." He laughed. "I dream American dream, no?"

Jewel laughed too. "Then you like it here? You don't regret . . ."

"There are regrets, of course. But now I have found you . . ." he trailed off. "I hope you have big appetite," he said, going over to the stove. "I make pirozhki, and cabbage stuffed with lamb, and good black Russian bread with caviar made from eggplant. I am sad I cannot buy real caviar. But someday soon."

"No problem," Jewel smiled. "I don't like caviar."

"What? How come? We fix that . . . when I can afford."

"No rush. I really can't eat the stuff," Jewel insisted.

"You cannot be lover of Russian man and not like caviar," Sascha said.

Jewel started to object. She was *not* his lover. But she decided to say nothing and let the subject drop. Most likely, he did not mean to use the word. Sascha's English was considerably better than it had been, but she was aware of his struggle to find the right words to express himself.

"Can I do anything to help?" she offered, still feeling uneasy.

He pointed to a chair. "Sit. You drink vodka."

She wasn't sure whether it was a question or a statement. "Well, I never have actually."

"What? You are strange girl," he said, pouring vodka halfway up in two liqueur glasses. He handed her a glass and raised his to her. *"Na zdorovie!* To your health!" He tossed his back with one gulp, then popped a slice of pickled cucumber, from a small bowl on the kitchen counter, into his mouth.

Jewel took a dainty sip. In truth, she did not like the taste of spirits. Wine, she enjoyed, when it was part of a good meal, or beer, with pizza or Chinese food. Anything stronger went straight to her head.

"Drink!" Sascha ordered. "Do not sip. All of it . . . at once."

"No . . . I can't do that," Jewel balked.

He went to the oven and brought out a plate of little meat-filled pastries. "Here are pirozhki. Now, first you drink vodka. Breathe out . . . get rid of breath. Then you drink." He stood over Jewel and watched her. She exhaled, then brought the glass to her lips and let the clear liquid enter her mouth.

"Ugh!" she swallowed quickly, downing the vodka in one gulp. Then she launched into a spasm of coughing.

"Good," Sascha said, ignoring the coughing fit. "Now, follow with pirozhki." He picked one up and shoved it in her mouth the moment the coughing stopped. She took a bite, chewed and swallowed it, obeying. After the jolt of vodka the warm pastry was comforting, delicious.

"Good. Now you know Russian secret. Always breathe out before you drink vodka. Always eat after. Drink . . . eat. That is Russian way."

"That still doesn't keep you from getting drunk, does it?" Jewel asked, smiling. After the initial jolt, she felt a congenial warmth invade her body.

"No. But food and drink, they go together. Always remember. Never drink without food." Sascha refilled their glasses and handed her another pastry. "Never eat without vodka."

"You have to be patient with me," Jewel said, setting the second vodka on the kitchen counter. "If I drink too much it'll make me sick."

"You not used to vodka. You will get used."

"No . . . I don't think so." Jewel remembered that her friend Christof told her that Russians were rumored to coat their stomachs with olive oil so they could drink their comrades under the table. Perhaps she would try it before she saw Sascha again, if she saw him again. It was still too soon to tell what was going to happen, although she knew what *Sascha* thought was going to happen.

"Er, I brought some sketches of my work . . . my jewelry designs," she said. "I thought maybe you'd like to look at them."

Sascha set down his vodka and stared at her with interest. "You design jewelry?"

"Well, yes, of course." The night Jewel had met him, Bambi had introduced her as a fellow jewelry designer. But his English wasn't very good then. He probably hadn't understood. "I make gold rings for Betty's shop. Simple stuff, but there's a market for it."

"Well, where are they? The sketches," Sascha demanded. "Dinner ready soon."

"Oh, well, we don't have to look at them now."

"Yes. I want to see," Sascha said.

Jewel regretted having broached the subject. She had brought the sketches along as an icebreaker. Now too much importance had been attached to them. Sascha waited in silence while she went to get her portfolio.

"There really isn't much here. I only brought a few . . ."

"No apologize. Let me see." He took the portfolio from her and set it on the kitchen counter. Without comment he turned the pages, studying each drawing carefully before going on to the next one. When he reached the end, he closed the book and handed it back to her.

"You show promise," he said finally. "Good, clean ideas. Perhaps when you study you will carry these ideas further."

"But I have studied!" Jewel flared. "At one of the best technical schools in West Germany. And at the University of Colorado. And with the top jewelry designer in Boulder."

Sascha shrugged. "Would be better if I saw actual pieces. Then I could advise . . ."

"Well, I haven't been able to make them. I haven't had time and I don't have the right equipment. I can't afford the materials yet."

"Then you cannot be serious about being designer," he said.

"I am! But it takes time. You know that."

He poured himself another vodka and downed it in one swallow, following it with another pirozhki. "Jewel, please understand. When I arrive in this country I have nothing. Forty dollars and address of Russian family who help other Russians. I come here and take job cleaning vegetables in kitchen of Chinese restaurant in Bronx. I walk around to stores and pawn shops. I walk and look and walk and look. I buy cheap . . . opals, amethyst, pearls, topaz, silver knives and forks. All real stuff nobody knows is real. I take home and melt down. I *make* my own tools and find cheap ones on Canal Street. Sleep only two, three hours a day. In four months I have small collection to show stores. I am good designer. I work hard. Every day I go to stores. Finally get appointments with buyers. They like. They buy. After six months in States, I quit vegetable job and work full time on what I love." He paused and looked into Jewel's eyes. "I do not mean to criticize. But you need to work. The *will* is everything. The will to suc-

ceed. You need more will, my Jewel. And more study. You
have talent, that I can see. But you need to develop."

Jewel sighed and looked away. There was no way she
could top Sascha on the subject of hardship.

And he was right. Ever since she had arrived back in
New York she had made up excuses as to why she couldn't
do what she wanted to do. She thought about her childhood, after her mother deserted her, when she had *really*
been hungry. Life, on the whole, had been good to her
since then. But all she had done the past six months was
whine to herself, in secret, about how she had been mistreated by the McNeills.

"You're right, Sascha. I've been avoiding work. The
rings I do for Betty I can make with my eyes closed. I
guess when it comes down to it, I'm scared. Scared that I
won't be good enough."

"But you will never know if you do not try. Stop taking
vacation," he said.

Something about that made Jewel laugh. Here she had
been grinding away, day after day, making ends meet in
this expensive city. A vacation indeed! Still, she knew
what Sascha meant. And he was right.

"Okay, I'll get off my ass," she said. "I promise."

"Good, Jewel. That I like to hear." He was back over
by the stove, stirring something in a large kettle.

"It must have been very hard, leaving your country and
coming here."

"Hard. Yes. But right choice for me as artist."

"Did you leave a lot behind? Family, I mean."

"Yes, of course. But I wait to leave until after my
mother and father are dead. Now . . . no talk of past.
No looking back, as they say."

"But how did you get out of the country?"

"Everybody think I go on holiday to seashore. I pack
little. Leave everything in Moscow . . . tools, jewelry,
sketches, photographs, books. No one suspicious. I have
connections. Underground. I get to Turkey. Then work on

freighter to States. After three months, I am here. Now, Jewel, no more questions. Past is past."

Jewel nodded, respecting Sascha's privacy, despite her curiosity. After all, she expected people to respect hers. He would tell her more when he wanted to, if he wanted to. That was the way it should be.

"Okay . . . is ready," Sascha said abruptly, scooping stuffed cabbages onto a serving plate. "We eat."

The dining table was a door propped up on two sawhorses. The chairs were stacked orange crates, painted purple. Sascha lit candles that had been stuck into Chianti bottles and prepared a plate for Jewel.

She sat in the chair he designated for her and placed her napkin in her lap. "After dinner, will you show me your work? I'm dying to see more," she said, searching for something new to talk about.

"Of course . . . but you must eat first. I cook a lot of food for you," Sascha said. "To give some fat for your bones."

Jewel laughed. "You think I'm too skinny? Haven't you heard, you can't be too rich or too thin?"

"I don't agree," he said. "You can be . . . both."

There was great seriousness in his eyes, and Jewel didn't pursue the subject. She felt off balance enough as it was.

"The cabbage is delicious. So is everything," she said to cover her embarrassment. "You must have spent all afternoon cooking."

"When I cook for you, Jewel, there is no time . . . only happiness. I will cook for you often," he said without fanfare.

Jewel decided to let the remark pass. "This is a nice loft. Where's your roommate?"

"Zhenya? He is dancer. On tour a lot. Is convenient."

"Hmmm," Jewel nodded. *I'll bet it is,* she thought. "Your English has certainly improved since I met you. You've been working hard."

"I meet Russian girl. She has lived in America five years. We spend much time together. She teach me."

"Oh. Are you . . . do you see her . . . a lot?" Jewel asked, immediately regretting it.

"We are friends," he grinned. "That is all."

Jewel swallowed. "I didn't mean to pry. Anyway, all I really meant is that your English is so much better."

God, why did this man make her feel so uncomfortable? Of course, she knew why. As tense as she was, the physical attraction was undeniable. Jewel wanted to have an affair with Sascha, except the negative angel sitting on her shoulder reminded her that she shouldn't take up with a struggling immigrant. She had her own career to think of. That hinged on good connections with the right people. What she needed was a well-heeled society boyfriend. Not Sascha. But, oh, those pale blue eyes. She could imagine making love to him, being swallowed up, engulfed by the largeness of him.

Suddenly, Jewel realized that Sascha was staring at her, as if reading her thoughts. She felt so embarrassed she almost blushed. He smiled at her, and she managed to grin back. There was no doubt that he wanted her too.

What the hell, she had not slept with a man in many months.

"You are very special woman, Jewel," Sascha said, giving her a look that took her appetite away completely.

She felt nervous anticipation in her stomach.

"I knew I would find you again," he said softly. He walked around the table and held his hand out to her. "This time I will not lose you. Come, my darling Jewel," he whispered. "Food will wait. We eat later . . . when we are more hungry."

Well, okay. She would sleep with him. But that didn't mean she had to become *involved*.

15

A taxi containing Jewel's worldly possessions waited patiently on the corner of Sixth Street and
Avenue B. Edward helped Jewel rearrange suitcases and
shopping bags so the trunk would close. "Where *is*
Potemkin, anyway?" Edward asked. "I thought he was
goin' to help you move."

"Saks called and he had to rush uptown. They're interested in his work for next Christmas's catalog. It'd be
really fantastic," Jewel said. "His pieces would be in all
their stores, all across the country."

"Good for him," Edward said unenthusiastically, but
Jewel didn't notice.

"Here, be a love and take this back upstairs, would you?
It's not going to make it." Jewel handed Edward her col-
lapsible worktable. "I'll pick it up tomorrow."

Edward propped the table against a mailbox. "Well
. . . I'm goin' to miss you, old girl. If things don't work

out you come straight home, promise?" Edward held out his arms to her.

"Oh, Edward, what am I doing?" Jewel giggled happily, hugging her friend. "This is crazy. But Sascha's absolutely overwhelming. He's the most romantic man. Still, I know it's going against everything I've planned . . ."

"Excuse me, lady," the cabdriver interrupted, "but this is no time to have second thoughts. The meter's running."

"I know," Jewel said. "Just hold on a minute."

"Well, nobody said love was supposed to go accordin' to plan," Edward drawled. "And when all is said and done, love *is* everything . . . almost. Sex alone has its moments." He grinned.

"Oh, Edward, you're terrible!"

He opened the cab door for Jewel. "Look, I mean it, if it doesn't work out, don't be too proud to move back here. I'm not rentin' out your room."

Edward's new job had come through, designing belts and handbags for Adrian Kelsy, one of Seventh Avenue's newest darlings. Edward was now going places and clearing three times what he had been making at Sandro's.

"I know how you feel about Sascha. I agree. There are a lot of differences. But it'll work. We're mad about each other. And you'll get to like him." Jewel kissed Edward's cheek and stepped into the cab. "You'll come for dinner soon, for a relaxing evening. Sascha's very sweet and caring. You'll see. It's just that he's had such a hard life."

"I guess so. Defectin' and all." Edward sighed. "Look, for your sake, I'll try to like him . . . I really will." He felt Jewel was making a big mistake, but he knew better than to say anything. God knew he had made a fool of himself over love often enough. He just hoped she wouldn't be hurt.

"That's the spirit. I'll call tomorrow and check in," Jewel said. "And thanks. You're a real friend."

"God, darlin', get the hell out of here before I burst into

tears." Edward turned away, picked up Jewel's worktable, and rushed back into his building.

"Hey, lady, where are we going?" the driver said, putting down his *News*.

"One Sixteen Spring Street," Jewel said, heading off to begin her new life.

It *was* crazy, she knew, moving in with Sascha Robinovsky after only being with him for a couple of weeks. But Sascha was irresistible, and she was madly in love with him. He took up all of her and had been able to banish the ghosts of Hadley and Wyatt McNeill. With Sascha, there was no room for anyone else. And so, Jewel knew, her plans would have to be revised accordingly.

She was unpacking her clothes, trying to find space to put them in Sascha's disorderly closet, when the door to the Spring Street loft was flung open and Sascha appeared. When he burst into a room it was always with great energy.

"Oh, my darling. You are here!" Sascha said, throwing his arms around her. "We celebrate tonight. You are living with me as my woman. And Saks is buying my jewelry!" He burst into a wide grin. "I think you bring me luck. No, I *know* it. My life will change with you."

"Oh, Sascha, with you my life has *already* changed. I'm happy. And it's so wonderful to feel happy again." She looked up into his shining eyes. "I love you so much. This is the real thing."

"Real thing for me too," he said. He took off his overcoat and opened his briefcase. "I make present for you. Here. To celebrate our being together."

He handed her a delicate, eighteen-karat-gold bracelet, engraved with flowers and set with pavé diamonds, sapphires, and aquamarines.

"Oh, Sascha. This is absolutely beautiful." She slipped it onto her wrist and held it up so the gemstones would catch the light.

"I pick blue stones in many different shades—to match your eyes. Color of your eyes changes often . . . many shades of blue."

"Oh, darling, thank you," Jewel said, glowing. "This is the most beautiful bracelet I've ever seen, much less owned."

"Saks want to buy it. I tell them, 'No . . . it is sold.' They want me to copy it. I tell them, 'No . . . it is one of a kind.' " He leaned down and kissed her tenderly. "Only for you, my Jewel."

He kissed her again, more passionately and she responded, ecstatic to be in love again after having been afraid she never would be.

"We make love now," he said. "And then go out to dinner for celebration."

He chased Jewel over to the bed and pulled off her clothes with lustful exuberance. Giggling, she undressed him, then she tried her new bracelet on his erection.

"Oh God, it won't fit," she exclaimed. "You're bigger than my arm!"

"I am big Russian bear," he laughed, letting his massive body engulf her tiny one.

"Yes, you are," she whispered. "And you're mine."

"I love you, my Jewel."

As it turned out, they celebrated by staying in bed for the entire weekend, ordering in Chinese food and pizza rather than dressing and going out. And when it was finally time for Sascha to get back to work, Jewel could barely walk.

But she was deliriously happy.

Early summer sun was deflected through the dirty windows of Sascha's loft. Although Jewel had not yet gotten around to cleaning the old, loose, glass panes, signs of her presence over the past months were in full evidence. Sascha cared nothing about decorating; he considered it woman's work. Jewel could do anything she wanted.

There was now a smattering of furniture, real pieces
acquired from the Salvation Army and re-covered by
Jewel with a bright Swedish fabric obtained below cost
from a friend of Edward's. On the wall above the kitchen
counter was a colorful display of inexpensive Chinese fans
from Chinatown. Jewel's lifetime collection of costume
jewelry from garage sales and thrift shops glittered from
nails bored into the wall alongside the bed. There were
some Indian dhurrie scatter rugs that Betty had lent her.
Old movie posters, cut from a book and staple-gunned
into place, papered the bathroom walls.

The dancer roommate, Zhenya, had moved out after the
first month, much to Jewel's relief. Fortunately, he had
not been around much. The loft was large, but divided in
such a way that it really only suited two people if they
were a couple, and no more than two.

So Jewel was unprepared, this beautiful summer day,
for Sascha's announcement.

"Jewel, my darling?" Sascha said, looking up from his
worktable where he was soldering stainless steel links into
an intricate, geometric design for a bracelet and choker
set. "My old friend Yuri comes to New York tomorrow
from Paris. He will stay here. Go buy inflatable mattress
from sports store. We put in corner."

Jewel stared at him through her dark glasses. She was
standing in the doorway on her way to work, but stopped
dead in her tracks. "Come again?"

"What? I do not understand, 'come again.' "

"You invited your friend Yuri to *stay* here without asking me? And now you expect *me* to go buy him a mattress
and lug it back here myself? You must be out of your
mind," she said indignantly.

"But I am busy. I promise this piece to Saks by end of
week. And you will like Yuri. He is artist. With good
humor."

"Maybe I will. But you could have at least *told* me."

"I did tell you," Sascha said. "Just now."

"But when did you hear from him? There were no letters in today's mail."

"I hear through network. Nikolai called."

"Well, why doesn't Yuri stay with Nikolai? He and Marfa have more room than we do."

"Yuri is old friend. Have not seen him in five years. Much to catch up on. He stays here," Sascha said, matter-of-factly.

"For how long?"

Sascha shrugged. Jewel knew by that shrug that Yuri would be there for anywhere from two days to two months, perhaps longer. "He arrives tomorrow afternoon. We fix big feast to celebrate. I will call Nikolai, Boris, Grigory, Sofia . . ."

"Wait a minute! Tomorrow's Friday. Betty's going away for the weekend. I have to work from noon till eight and all day Saturday. We can't have a party."

"Tell Betty you can't work."

"I *promised!* After all she's done for me, I can't very well flake out on her. Look, we'll have a party Sunday, my day off."

"Yuri comes tomorrow. We must welcome him."

"We can take him out to dinner, for Christ's sake. He'll probably be tired anyway, from jet lag."

"No, Jewel. We have friends over tomorrow night." Sascha got up from his workbench and came over to the door where Jewel stood. He closed it, leading her back into the room.

She knew that he was going to try to change her mood by making love to her. It had often worked in the past. But not this time.

Sascha gazed lovingly into her eyes, smiling. He leaned down and began brushing her face, all over, with tiny kisses. His giant bear paw of a hand strayed down her back and squeezed her buttocks. When he pulled her to him tightly, she could feel his hardness, and she shuddered with uncontrollable excitement. His lips found her mouth, and his tongue dug deeply down the tunnel of her throat.

Jewel was weakening. She knew Sascha could feel her arousal. "I have to get to work," she whispered hoarsely.

"Work can wait. Love comes first." He picked her up and carried her over to the bed, pulling her skirt up and her panties down, roughly. He unzipped his fly and entered her quickly, without further foreplay.

Jewel's anger melted into an emotion more urgent as she rocked and swayed, in a time warp—it could have been minutes or hours—until she screamed out, coming in waves, seconds before Sascha.

Afterward, he held her in his large arms, still kissing her face. Finally, she came back to reality, looked at her watch, and began to disengage herself. He whispered in her ear, "You buy food and vodka. I will cook. Party will start at nine."

Jewel sighed. "You know, sometimes you're fucking impossible."

"But you love me, my Jewel. Don't you love me?" He rubbed his soft, bearded cheek against hers.

"Yes, Sascha, I do. In spite of myself." And of course she did, passionately.

In spite of Jewel's love for Sascha, their relationship ran a bumpy course. She knew she was not the docile creature that he expected in a woman. She was always challenging him, endlessly provoking him into deep discussions on subjects ranging from Dostoyevski (whose complete works she had devoured since she met Sascha, in the hope of understanding the Russian temperament better) to Andy Warhol. Sascha was adamant when he argued. He maintained always that his point of view, whatever it happened to be, was the right one. If Jewel agreed with him about something, then she too was right. If she disagreed, she was wrong.

Jewel hated losing arguments. She liked to have the last

word. But so did Sascha. Often they would come to an impasse. Then they would both fume silently until the phone rang or someone arrived to break the mood, or until Jewel stormed out to go to a movie with Edward. (Sascha, after working his twelve-hour days, was always too restless to sit through movies or plays, which irked Jewel no end.)

There was another area of discord. Sascha was extremely jealous of Jewel's friends. He hated Edward, but wouldn't say why. Jewel assumed it was because of their closeness, although she suspected it might also be because Edward was homosexual. Sascha found Betty Blessing rather brash and could not be in the same room with Roland, her gambler boyfriend, without sinking into a self-indulgent gloom that embarrassed Jewel while the others pretended not to notice. After several awkward attempts at entertaining, Jewel decided it best to see her friends on her own and not include Sascha. Everyone, it turned out, preferred it that way.

On the other hand, Jewel put up with Sascha's friends without complaining. Every Saturday night they would come over and drink and eat and scream over each other in Russian until they were too bleary to gesticulate and shout anymore. But they were a colorful, passionate bunch, and Jewel was intrigued by them. She studied them to find clues to Sascha's behavior. She was curious as to whether Sascha's assertiveness was a Russian trait, or merely Sascha's.

One of the women who came over, a Czech named Marfa who lived with Sascha's best friend, Nikolai, often took time to talk with Jewel while the two of them prepared zakuska, "small bites" or hors d'oeuvre, in the kitchen. Marfa was in her early forties, an actress, and dramatically beautiful, with high cheekbones and wide-set gray eyes. Jewel liked her.

"Well, my darling," Marfa said at their first meeting.

"How are you handling living with a Russian? It's different, no?"

"It's wonderful," Jewel had replied.

"Yes? Well, you are still very much in love. When you have problems, you come and talk to me."

"Why should I have problems?" Jewel's differences with Sascha were just that to her, differences, not problems.

"Why should you not?" Marfa had said. "You are living with a Russian—the most passionate, and exasperating, men of all."

Since Sascha's friends drank and smoked to excess, Jewel generally excused herself after dinner and went to bed, curled up with a pillow over her head to block the light. Except for Marfa and Nikolai, she felt the others regarded her merely as Sascha's woman. She wondered if they arrived one Saturday and some other girl was there whether they would even notice.

But interacting with each other's friends was not what life with Sascha was all about. Life with Sascha meant being with him, encompassed by him, adored by him, lectured by him, and loved by him. He gave all of himself to Jewel, except for the Saturday nights with his friends from his homeland. He was devoted to her and loved her without reserve.

He still cooked for her, both because he wanted to fatten her up and because Jewel was not a good enough cook to suit him. Sascha did, however, consider it his duty to educate her in the kitchen. Jewel, always up to a challenge, proved to be an able student, which pleased him. He taught her how to make a proper borscht. ("There are as many recipes for borscht as there are grandmothers in Russia," he would say.) And he talked her through the proper making of dozens of recipes, including flattened chicken tabaka, and varenyky—dessert dumplings filled with cheese—the way his Ukrainian babushka, grandmother, had made them.

"In Ukraine," Sascha liked to tell her, "a baby girl must learn to sift flour before she can walk and knead bread before she can talk."

"Then how come *you* learned to cook, a man who grew up in Moscow?"

"My mother was ill for long time before she die. It was up to me to cook for her. She tell me her recipes, just like I am telling you."

"Well, one good thing about all this," Jewel joked, "if I don't make it as a jewelry designer I can always get a job at the Russian Tea Room."

They made love every night and often during the day. In bed, their compatibility astounded Jewel. She had only to think something and Sascha would do it. "Sexual telepathy," was how she once described the experience to Betty.

Not unlike Wyatt McNeill, Sascha had opinions on everything having to do with Jewel, from how he liked her to wear her hair (long and flowing) to how he wanted her to dress (jeans *only* when she was working at home, skirts when they went out). He made her eat three meals a day and take vitamins. If she put up a fuss over something he wanted her to do, he'd slump into a silent sulk.

Most of the time, though, Jewel did not complain. At this point in her life she didn't have strong feelings about how she wore her hair, and everyone said vitamins were good for you. Sometimes it was easier to give in than fight, since they still found plenty to argue over.

Most of all, with Sascha, Jewel felt utterly alive. Everything was magnified. Food tasted better when she ate with him, because he enjoyed it with such uninhibited gusto. The city, through his eyes when they went on daily walks together, was more beautiful than she had ever noticed before. Sascha took in everything and shared every insight with her.

Life, according to Sascha, was to be embraced with total exuberance. Even his sudden fits of depression, which

struck sometimes without warning, seemed exaggerated.
He lived in the moment, *for* the moment.

Sascha was the most mercurial man Jewel had ever encountered. One minute he would be open and expansive,
sharing everything with her. The next, something would
set him off and he would close up like an oyster. Sometimes the mood passed quickly. Sometimes he seemed to
bask in self-indulgence. During those times, Jewel would
go visit Edward or Betty. It was more fun than sitting
around, feeling his chilliness cool the loft like a Siberian
winter.

Inevitably, if she did go out, Sascha would be in a rage
when she got home, furious that she had deserted him.
They'd shout it out and then fall into each other's arms, in
bed. When Sascha's moods had passed, they were totally
forgotten by him, and he expected Jewel to follow suit.

On a day-to-day basis, life with Sascha was never dull.
Jewel was endlessly entertained by this incredible, impossible, lovable man.

On the day of Yuri's arrival, Sascha, as was his custom,
rose at six and was already at work—making a wide silver
bracelet inlaid with jade and lapis lazuli—by the time
Jewel had brewed strong black tea, gone out to buy rolls
for their mid-morning break, and settled in to work herself.

Jewel was going through a period of great insecurity
over her designing. Sascha tried to help, but his enormous
professional ego annoyed her. There was room only for
one great designer in the family, *him,* as he let her know
often.

She had cut down her hours at Betty Blessing's shop in
order to get back seriously into making jewelry. Betty had
suggested Jewel try working on a line of inexpensive copies of Victorian pieces they had discovered in an old book
of Betty's from England. Betty felt there was a market for
inexpensive elegant jewelry. Jewel had to come up with a

way to make them look elegant while keeping the price down. Materials were not the problem; she used fake pearls, glass doublets, copper, and German silver—white metal that resembled the real thing. The problem was labor. Each piece took Jewel far too long for the price Betty wanted to pay, since there would be the usual triple keystone markup.

As she worked across the loft from Sascha, she muttered to herself with frustration. "This was really a rotten idea. There's no way I can put all the work that needs to go into these pieces and keep them inexpensive. I need better equipment. I need more space. I'm just so fucking out of practice! Everything I try to do is like starting out all over again. Shit, maybe I'll give up on trying to design," Jewel ranted on. "Maybe I should go back to working at the shop full time."

"No, no, my darling," Sascha said. "You are merely in a sour mood. Your fingers will behave. But you must direct them with your will. Perhaps you are beginning with designs that are too complicated. Start simple, then work up. Perfect your craft. Do it well . . . or not at all. Betty is *wrong,*" Sascha accused. "You should not be doing cheap copies. You should be working to find your own voice as designer. Then, only then, will I see if you have talent or not."

"What do you mean by that?" Jewel snapped. "I've shown you my work from the institute. You said it was good!"

"I said you have promise. And you do. But we will have to wait to see. In my family are jewelry-makers for three generations. It is bred in us. We work for nothing else all our life. It is all I was trained to do." Sascha's eyes glazed over, and Jewel saw a familiar melancholy expression take over his face before he shook his head to clear the memories. "You have American attitude that you can do anything"—he snapped his fingers—"fast . . . fast. You are all impatient. You want fantastic results without work.

But, my dear, there are no shortcuts if you want to design good jewelry. *If* you want to—"

Jewel threw down her pliers, knocking a tray of imitation emeralds onto the floor. "I'm really not up for this lecture. And if you don't like the way Americans do things then why the hell did you come here? There were lots of other countries to choose from."

"Please . . . let us not go into that. I am fortunate to be here. I *had* to leave Soviet Union. There was no place for real creativity anymore." Sascha put down the soldering torch. "Jewel, my darling, you must learn to take criticism. I think you will be good. But you have not worked as long as I have. You must allow time." He got up, went across the room to Jewel's worktable and picked up the glass emerald necklace she was working on. He turned it over and over, examining it carefully. Jewel stood nearby, fuming.

"I see you are *attacking* the problem, Jewel. Is wrong. You must *caress* it first. Live with it. Don't—how is it you say?—don't lock horns. It will come."

"God, Sascha, I've been working on this for three days! Nothing is coming." She blew a piece of hair away from her eye. "I can't stand it!"

"You act like spoiled American debutante."

"Dilettante . . . I think that's the word you want."

Sascha shrugged. "Word not important. Attitude is. Your attitude is shit."

"Thank you very much for your constructive criticism. And now, if you don't mind, I'm going to work. Then I'm having dinner with Edward. I'll be home late. Start the party for Yuri without me."

Sascha turned abruptly to her and flung the back of his large hand across her cheek. "You are one hell of a difficult woman."

"You hit me!" Jewel shrieked. "That may be the way you do it in the Soviet Union, but you hit me again and I'm out of here forever!"

Furious, he slapped her again, same hand, same cheek. Jewel went berserk. She burrowed into him like a linebacker onto a quarterback, except with the bodies reversed. For one-hundred-pound Jewel it was like going up against one of the Caucasus. She stared at Sascha with hatred and began pounding his massive chest. "You are a barbarian, like your ancestors. You don't have the foggiest idea how to treat a woman. Fuck her . . . that's all you know how to do."

He grabbed her hands and held them still. "That is not so! You have never had complaints about the way I make love to you. You are mad because I criticize you."

"I'm mad because you *hit* me! Now, let go of my hands, I'm late for work. And I'm getting out of here for good! You and Yuri will have plenty of room. I'll get my stuff later. I'll call before . . . then I'd appreciate your not being here when I come to pick it up."

"Jewel, darling, this is not end of us."

"Oh, isn't it?"

"It is very deep . . . what we feel for each other. Will not go away so easy." He let go of Jewel's hands.

She strode across the room and grabbed her handbag and denim jacket. "That's what you think. Four months is enough. I've had it! You don't like my work . . . you put down my friends . . . what's the point?"

"The point is us," Sascha said. "You don't love my friends either. The point is us," he said again. "We love each other."

"Well, I don't think so. Not anymore! It's over. Goodbye, Sascha." And with that she slammed the door and headed out to work.

Jewel half-wanted him to open a window and call down an apology to her when she got down to the street. But she knew he'd never do that.

By the time she arrived at the Golden Buddha, Jewel did not know whether to be sad or relieved. Mostly she was still angry from replaying the scene in her head during the seven-block walk to work. Her relationship with Sascha was impossible. Marfa had known what she was talking about: there were *problems,* not differences. Sascha brought out the worst in her. So many things were not working out. But he was right about the sex.

And he was right that it was not over between them.

16

"Well, here we go again," Jewel said, across a table from Edward at Emilio's on Sixth Avenue. Her mussels marinara sat on her plate, untouched, but she was on her third glass of white wine.

"I don't believe you're goin' to leave him," Edward said. "It's a lovers' quarrel. You've had them before."

"Yeah," Jewel agreed, "I storm out and I go back. This time it's different. He fucking *hit* me! I'll tell you, he's got to come *begging*. Oh please, can I stay at your place?"

Edward grinned. "I put clean sheets on your bed after you called. Just in case."

"You know me so well, Edward," Jewel laughed. "What *would* I do without you?"

"Get a room at the Y, I suppose," Edward smiled. "Anyway, stay with me until you've calmed down. Then reevaluate. But don't ask me to help. You know I think you're better off without him." The waiter poured the rest of the wine from the bottle into their glasses, and Edward ordered zabaglione for himself for dessert.

Jewel nodded. "I know . . . and you're probably right. But Sascha's so totally *consuming*. I've never known anyone like him. Oh, I don't know what to do."

"Don't do anything right away. Relax. Come to the ballet with Demetrius and me tomorrow night. Just have fun."

"You're right. A break is what I need. Then I can think clearly."

Two weeks later Jewel was still living at Edward's, her thinking completely clear. Sascha had not called, nor had he stopped by the Golden Buddha. It was over. He did not care about her. That was that.

Then she noticed that her period, which had always been so irregular that she had stopped bothering with birth control, had not come for two months. She began to feel nauseated every morning and could not seem to drink wine any longer without feeling ill after a few sips.

A visit to Betty's gynecologist confirmed the suspicion. Jewel was pregnant. As if she wasn't upset enough by the fight and estrangement with Sascha, now there was this to contend with.

Jewel longed to talk with Marfa—she definitely had problems *now*—but her friend was acting in a repertory company in Wisconsin for the summer. She thought about Anna and what she went through with Randy, and that made her sadder. She missed Anna. It hurt to have a whole chunk of your life that was out-of-bounds, a best friend to whom you could no longer speak.

The McNeills had crept into Jewel's mind often over the past year; she had even come upon Wyatt's picture in the business section of *Newsweek* once. He looked handsome, successful, unchanged. She wondered what was happening in their lives now. Once she thought she saw Hadley getting onto a bus on Fifth Avenue and Fifty-sixth

Street. She had raced to catch the same bus and squeezed through the crowd to the back, only to discover that it wasn't Hadley at all, only a vague look-alike.

Anna was her only friend who had had a baby, and Jewel needed knowledgeable advice. Would she be making a lifelong mistake if she had an abortion? Would she be making a lifelong mistake if she had the baby? And how would Sascha feel, if they ever did get back together, if she told him about the abortion?

"Do me a favor and stop mopin'," Edward said, looking down from a rickety, wooden ladder. He was in the process of painting the kitchen a glossy black. "You haven't left the apartment all weekend. Something's gotta give. Either have the abortion . . . or go tell Sascha and get his input. And I hate to say it, but I think that's the only fair thing to do."

"No! If he can stay away from me, I can stay away from him. He knows where to find me. He obviously doesn't care."

"And you're obviously miserable. God, the two of you both have so much pride. I think *you* were Russian in a former life."

"I can't believe you, of all people, are counseling me to get back together with Sascha," Jewel said, carefully edging around the ladder to get a yogurt from the refrigerator.

"I'm merely saying you should *talk* to him. You're in limbo, kid. You're stuck. The only way you're going to be able to get on with your life is to discuss this with the man involved. I wouldn't say this if I thought you didn't still love him. But he'll listen. He's sure not goin' to throw you out the door and down the stairs. Look, I'll even call him, if you want."

"No!"

"Well then, get your act together. Get on with your life," Edward urged.

* * *

At work the next day Betty told her basically the same thing. And so that evening Jewel swallowed her pride, realizing she was too miserable to do anything else. She washed and blew dry her hair, put on her favorite skirt and sexiest blouse, and took a cab to Spring Street. She still had her keys, and she let herself in the street entrance. After the two straight flights up to Sascha's, she stopped to catch her breath before knocking.

She tapped on the door, then prayed that Sascha wouldn't be home, so she could leave a note for him to call her, but no such luck. She heard footsteps, and the door opened.

There, standing before her, was a tall, gaunt man whom she had never seen before.

"Er, is Sascha here?"

"No . . . he come back soon. You wait?"

"Oh, no. Just tell him Jewel was here."

"Jewel!" The man smiled and opened the door wider. "I am Yuri. You come in. Wait, please. Sascha, he want to see you. He very sad that you leave him."

And then the downstairs door was flung open and Sascha's voice boomed up the stairs. "Jewel? My darling, is it you?" He came racing up the steps, two at a time, until he was in front of her. His arms went around her, and his mouth found hers without hesitation or further words.

"I think I go out for a walk," Yuri said, skirting around the embracing couple and down the stairs.

Later, after they had made very passionate love, Jewel confronted Sascha on his silence of the past weeks.

"You're obviously happy to see me again . . . why didn't you call? Is it because you can't ever bring yourself to apologize?" she demanded to know.

"Nothing to apologize for. You get mad, you leave. Is out of my hands," he explained, not to her satisfaction. "You must do what you must do. I cannot change. I must suffer consequences, but suffering is part of life. To suffer is good for soul, good for art. Creativity comes out of suffering. I work very hard while you were gone."

"But you didn't *have* to suffer," Jewel said. "You could have called me. We could have talked it over."

Sascha shrugged. "I hate you for leaving. I did not want to call you."

"But now I'm back you say you *love* me . . ."

"Yes, my darling, I do," he interrupted. "Is possible to love and hate same person at different times. You must understand. We are capable of anything at any time. When we are together I am faithful to you. I love you. But when you leave, I sleep with another woman."

"What?" Jewel asked, shocked. "Hold on a second. *What* other woman?"

"Her name is Rachel. I will not see her again now that you are back. It was not important."

"It's important to me! We have a fight and the next thing you do is find someone else? Poof! Jewel is gone," she said in a fake Russian accent. "Must find replacement . . . need new woman. Jesus, you're impossible. You know, I really hate you for that. *How could you?*"

"You see," Sascha said, pleased, "it *is* possible to hate someone and love them at same time."

"Ahhhhhh!" Jewel screamed in exasperation.

"My darling, Jewel," Sascha said, grabbing her and pulling her to him. "Come here. I will show you again how much I love you. I miss you so much. We will not hate each other anymore."

"Oh, Sascha . . . I do love you. But you're difficult. I mean, the reason I walked out is that you *hit* me. If I move back in with you, I'm not going to put up with that. You hit me again, and I leave. Forever. Amen."

Sascha made a circle of tiny kisses on her cheek. "I understand. And I promise, no matter how angry you make me, I promise never again. You have my word. I never hit a woman before. It make me feel bad."

Jewel smiled. "All right. And I promise never to hit you."

In early August 1972, with Edward, Betty, Yuri, and Nikolai standing by, Jewel and Sascha were married quietly by the priest at the Ukrainian Orthodox Church on East Eleventh Street. Jewel had never been particularly aware that Sascha was religious, but he insisted that a priest marry them instead of some clerk at city hall. It made no difference to her. She was still in shock from the speed at which the events had taken place.

Sascha, his suffering over, was euphoric to have Jewel back. He would not hear of her getting rid of the baby.

"Abortion is for unwanted child," he told her. "Not for us. We love each other. You are my woman. You have my babies."

He adored children, he assured her, and promised that he'd make a wonderful father. Marriage was important to him, and he insisted that they make it legal as soon as possible.

"But Jewel Dragoumis Robinovsky?" she shook her head, and patted her belly. "How the hell am I going to get through life with a name like that?"

"You will be happy with my name," Sascha said. "You will be happy with me, my darling."

Jewel looked at him and smiled. "Yes . . . I will be. I adore you, Sascha. Even if you are the most impossible person in the world."

"No, no, you got it wrong. *You* are most impossible. I am merely second," he grinned. "And we will not argue about it."

"Just this once, we won't argue about it," she replied.

And so Jewel and Sascha embarked on the adventure of married life together. Sascha made Jewel a wedding band, a thick braided ring of red, yellow, and white gold. To match it, he wove her a delicate choker.

"A fine necklace . . . for a fine neck," he said, tenderly clasping it around her throat.

"And for you," Jewel said, presenting him with an ornate antique brass samovar that she had found in a Ukrainian shop on East Seventh Street, "a fine samovar for a fine Russian."

As wedding gifts, Edward gave them a week's car rental, and Betty obtained a friend's cabin in the Adirondacks for them. Nikolai sent them off with champagne and caviar from Balducci's, and Yuri offered to take care of Lisa, the cat that Zhenya had left behind when he moved out. Yuri also promised—his greatest gift to them —to find another place to live as soon as they returned to the city.

The week of their honeymoon was perhaps the most carefree that Jewel had ever spent. It had been a long time since either of them had communed with nature, and the cabin was set at the edge of a large woods. A long expanse of lawn, filled with field grasses, daisies, dandelions, and black-eyed Susans, wound down to a small, private lake.

The cabin itself was rustically charming, filled with functional antiques and copper pots in the kitchen. There was an herb garden outside the back door, and a large screened-in sitting and eating porch overlooked the lake, where Sascha fished for the trout they grilled for dinner every night.

During the day, while Sascha read or fished, Jewel lay out in the sun or went on foraging walks, returning with blackberries and raspberries that she made into tarts and jam, or fresh corn and tomatoes that she bought from a roadside stand about half a mile away. She felt alive, carrying the baby within her, and healthy. The morning sickness had stopped, and she began having an appetite again. The reality that she would be giving birth in six months began to sink in. She began to sort through names.

"What do you think about Jasmine?" she said in bed one night, after they had made love.

"Is good, strong fragrance. I like," Sascha replied.

"No, no, I mean for a name. For the baby, if it's a girl."

Sascha shook his head. "Is bad luck to name baby before it comes. Same as I told you . . . is bad luck to say *when* baby will come."

"Yeah, but what am I supposed to answer when someone asks me when the baby's due? I can't look blank and say, 'I don't know.' God, you and your superstitions!"

"Many people believe what I do. Is best when someone asks, you say, 'sometime during winter.' "

Jewel sighed. "And now we can't even talk about names until after the baby is born? This is ridiculous."

"You can think about names in your head. But don't discuss with me out loud."

"What exactly do you think is going to happen if we talk about it out loud?" Jewel wanted to know.

"Baby can be born dead . . . or sick. Is best not to take chances, you understand, my darling?" He leaned over and kissed her.

"Not really," she said. "But it's not worth fighting about."

"You know, this is first time I relax since I was teenager," Sascha said. "I forget what it feels like for your mind to take a holiday. No working, no deadlines. Ideas can flow. I am having great ideas for new jewelry. Very romantic jewelry. Contemporary, but fitting as if it should be part of the body . . ." He grabbed a pad from the table beside the bed and began sketching with quick, sure lines. "You see, something like this. Perhaps I use amber, with silver. Before I leave Moscow, I do many beautiful pieces in Russian amber. You like?"

"Yes!" Jewel said, before she even looked at the sketches. "Amber! I love it."

It would be a perfect name for a girl.

* * *

Summer ended, and autumn flew by. Sascha had more work than he had time for, doing pieces now exclusively for Saks Fifth Avenue. With mixed feelings, Jewel quit her job with Betty so she could stay home and help Sascha.

Working for him was not always easy. Jewel had to do Sascha's pieces *his* way, and she was not allowed to finish anything, only to work on them up to a certain point. Sascha made it clear that he wasn't interested in her suggestions or ideas.

Jewel put up with it. She was learning advanced techniques, finishing her schooling at home while apprenticing under a master craftsman. What more could she want? Besides, since she had become pregnant she felt all her creativity went to her belly.

Jewel's days began and ended at the loft on Spring Street, and most evenings were spent there as well. Except to buy groceries, Jewel seldom went out. She glowed with health, but thought she looked fat and unattractive. Her ankles were bloated, and she felt like a gigantic marshmallow in the white down jacket that Sascha gave her for Christmas.

Every so often, she lunched with Edward or Betty, but she began to feel, as the months of her marriage accumulated, that she had less and less in common with her old friends. She was too busy to dwell on it though. Working for Sascha, cooking for him, entertaining his friends who had become almost a family to her now—that took up all of her time.

Since she considered herself back in the apprentice phase of her life, Jewel decided one day that it would aid her future career as a jewelry designer if she understood more about gemstones. She wanted to know what to look for, how to recognize good stones versus flawed ones without having to rely on experts to tell her, when she was finally in business for herself. So she enrolled in an intensive home-study course that the Gemological Institute of

America offered on the identification and evaluation of diamonds and colored gemstones.

Her energy returned, in spite of the large belly and nearly forty pounds of extra weight she was carrying. In the eighth month of her pregnancy, Jewel trudged through snow-slushy streets, rushing here and there, taking out books on precious and semiprecious stones from the library, and going on expeditions to the Museum of Natural History to study their gem and mineral collection. She bought herself a ten-power jeweler's magnifying loupe and began haunting pawn shops and thrift stores, as Sascha had in the old days, for real gems that might not have been recognized.

One day, at a store on Second Avenue, her sleuthing finally scored her a prize. It was a ruby, she was positive, over a carat in size, set into a ring with pearls. It had been tossed into a bargain bin in the back of an old, dusty shop that had been around for decades. Casually, she bargained with the elderly shop owner, getting the price cut in half, from a dollar to fifty cents. Then, feeling smug as hell, she flagged down a cab, just as snowflakes were beginning to fall, and raced across town to show off her treasure to Sascha.

"You won't believe it!" she gushed as she came into the loft, panting from running up the stairs. "I found a ruby!"

"You are right," Sascha said. "I don't believe. Bring it here."

"I looked through my loupe. I thought I saw silky lines. Isn't that what you're supposed to see in Burmese rubies? Silklike inclusions? Oh, Sascha, I know it's absolutely, definitely not glass. Here." She handed it to him, anxious as a schoolgirl to impress her teacher.

"Is very dirty . . . hard to tell anything."

He soaked the ring quickly in cleaning solution, then looked at it through his magnifying loupe. "Hmmm," he said. "Interesting."

"Yes?" Jewel said excitedly. "It's real, isn't it?"

"I clean again," he said. "Need better look."

"Oh, you're driving me crazy! Tell me it's real."

Sascha dried the ring with a piece of soft leather and peered again through his glass. "Yes, just as I thought," he looked up. "It is balas ruby . . . a spinel."

"Shit!" Jewel cursed. "A spinel? Are you sure?"

"Am positive. But it is *real* spinel . . . not synthetic. How much you pay for this?"

"Fifty cents."

"You do good, my Jewel," Sascha smiled. "You know story of Black Prince's Ruby?"

"No," Jewel said, still disappointed.

"It is huge stone, two inches across. Was given to Black Prince of England in fourteenth century, by Spanish king. Later part of Crown Jewels, worn by many kings. Finally it was set into crown for Queen Victoria. Then in this century they discover that famous ruby is not ruby at all. It is magnesium aluminate—spinel. So you see, my darling, spinel fool kings for centuries. And you find good spinel. Worth few hundred dollars. I will make it into special ring for you."

By then Jewel was no longer concentrating on what Sascha was saying. A pain that had begun knifing up between her legs was peaking to a crescendo. She felt weak and dizzy—and scared, if this meant the beginning of labor. Her pregnancy was supposed to have three weeks to go.

"Sascha! I think it's happening . . . call Dr. Abrams," she said.

The next morning, the third of February 1973, after fifteen hours of labor that ended in a cesarian, Jewel woke to find Sascha sitting by her, stroking her hand. Outside, large flakes of snow were tumbling down, the end of a snowfall that had dumped over a foot of snow on the city.

"The baby?" she whispered with a dry mouth.

"Good morning, my darling," he said quickly. "You

now have wonderful baby girl, weighing eight pounds. She is healthy. Big like me." He slipped a ring onto her finger.

Jewel shakily held up her hand to look at it. "It's my spinel," she smiled. The stone had been set into a wide gold band that had been engraved with a delicate leaf design. "It's beautiful. But when did you . . . ?"

"I come home from hospital and stay up all night. Working with great energy . . . joyful energy. Oh, my Jewel, we have a baby. Are you happy, my darling?"

At that moment, a nurse rolled a crib into the room, and Jewel saw her daughter for the first time.

"Oh," she said, as the smiling nurse handed her the baby. "She's beautiful." She counted the fingers and toes, ten of each. "I don't believe it. Me—us—with a baby. It's really happened."

"Yes, and now we can think of name."

"I have a name," Jewel smiled. "Amber."

Sascha thought for a moment, then nodded. "Is good. I like. Baby will be named Amber Anna Robinovsky."

"Anna?" Jewel asked.

"After my *mamitchka,* my mother," Sascha said.

It occurred to Jewel at that moment that she had never before heard the name of Sascha's mother, or father. In fact, he had never talked about his life in Russia, except to impart offhand information, such as how he used to love to hunt wild mushrooms in the country every fall. Whenever she asked direct questions, he always managed to evade them by changing the subject.

But Jewel had never told Sascha anything about her past either.

In fact, he had never asked.

17

"Sascha," Jewel said, polishing to a final luster the engraved silver baby bracelet she had made for Amber, "I'm going out for groceries now. Marfa and Nikolai are coming for dinner, remember?"

Jewel put on her raincoat, tied a scarf over her hair, and braced herself for the cold, wet, early May afternoon. It had been an unusually rainy spring. She had not even been able to take Amber to Washington Square Park, her favorite place to show off the baby, more than twice a week because of the weather.

The dreariness had had its effect on Jewel's mood as well. The obstetrician called it postpartum depression, but what was there to be depressed about, Jewel quizzed him, except the incessant rain? It was true that the baby was a bit colicky. It was true that Jewel was lucky to get two uninterrupted hours of sleep a night. And she did have a cold that had hung on for weeks. But depression because one has given birth to a miraculous creature? Jewel would hear none of it.

"If Amber wakes up," Jewel continued, "please change her diaper and give her a little bottle of juice. I'll nurse her when I get back."

"No, no, no, my darling," Sascha said from his work-table. "I mean it when I tell you I never change baby's diapers. I will give her bottle."

"God, Sascha," Jewel snapped. "Can't you do it just this once? She'll be soaking when she wakes up, and I've got to go to the drugstore, the bakery, the greengrocer's, the butcher's, and the supermarket. Jesus, I do *everything* around here. You've turned me into a fucking slave."

"No!" Sascha said adamantly. "Not true. I *make* you do nothing except change diapers. You do because you want to. You want to learn to cook. You want to become apprentice to me, to know proper jewelry skill. You are happy to be wife with me taking care of you. If you are slave—if that is what you choose to call it—it is because you want to be."

"Oh, spare me," Jewel sneezed. And then sneezed again.

"Darling Jewel, you know we are happy," Sascha said. "You are in bad mood because of your cold. Look, I will call Nikolai and tell them not to come. Then I will ask Yuri to watch Amber. I will take you out for dinner, to the new French restaurant on Prince Street." He smiled, and blew her a kiss. "Okay?"

Jewel nodded, melting. "Okay."

Whenever she convinced herself that things were terrible, they turned out not to be. Marfa had told her once, "To understand a Russian, you must be Russian," and Jewel supposed it was true. She would never understand Sascha completely. He was full of surprises, but life was never dull.

* * *

One day, mostly for fun, Jewel began making whimsical paste-and-plaster figures that she baked in the oven, painted and glazed, and turned into earrings and pins. Street People, she called them, and when Betty Blessing saw Jewel wearing a pair of the earrings, she immediately ordered some for the shop. After two days, they had sold out, and Betty wanted more. Several weeks after that, the owner of a shop on Madison Avenue called Jewel and placed an order, having seen Street People in Betty's window. Soon other stores around town were calling, and Jewel was in full production, selling the pieces as fast as she could make them.

It was a great morale booster for her. The small brightly-colored figures were easy to produce in the midst of tending to Amber. And she could take Amber with her around town when she made her deliveries. Although the jewelry was inexpensive and Jewel wasn't hauling in a tremendous profit, she enjoyed getting out, meeting new people, and having them ooh and ah over both her baby and her designs.

Sascha, however, was critical and condescending. "It is not really jewelry," he told her. "It is fad. It will not last."

"That's fine with me," Jewel said. "I don't want to make Street People for the rest of my life. It's something fun to do now. And I like meeting new people. I've been in such a rut."

"Oh? So sorry," he said coldly.

"No, it doesn't have anything to do with you. It's me. I realize that I've been in a self-imposed isolation. I mean, when was the last time I had lunch with Edward? It was months ago. He's upset with me, and I can't blame him."

Sascha shrugged. "So call him. Have lunch. I am sorry you feel so isolated with me."

"No! Look, I don't want to turn this into a fight. But you have to understand that I need my life with you, *and* apart from you. I feel good about the success of my Street

People. It's been so long since I've done anything on my own, except those rings for Betty that I can do with my eyes closed."

"Okay. Do what you like. I am not jealous."

Of course, Sascha *was* jealous, she was sure. But, as much as she loved him, she had to think of herself too.

In mid-July however, Jewel discovered that there was going to be another person to think of besides her and Sascha and Amber. She began to experience the familiar queasiness of morning sickness, except this time it lasted all day. At first she thought it was flu, but soon realized that flu was wishful thinking.

"This is impossible," she told the doctor when the pregnancy test came back positive.

"What do you mean? Have you been abstaining from sex?" Dr. Abrams joked.

"I didn't think you could get pregnant again so fast."

"You can if you don't use birth control, Jewel. Diaphragms don't work sitting in the medicine cabinet."

"I use my diaphragm!"

"Obviously you don't use it regularly. Let's see, according to the calendar we're talking sometime around February fifteenth. *If* you want to have the baby."

Jewel sighed. "My husband wouldn't think of my *not* having it."

"What about you? It's your body."

"Oh, I'd like Amber to have a brother or sister. It's a little sooner than I'd planned, but what the hell."

As Jewel anticipated, Sascha was delighted with the news. But, as she had not anticipated, this was a far different pregnancy than the first.

"Your blood pressure is abnormally high," Dr. Abrams told her when she went for her fifth-month checkup. "And your edema—the swelling—is worse than last time. To make a long story short, you have a condition called pre-eclampsia. It's a form of toxemia. I don't want to get you upset, but from now on you're going to have to alter your life-style, as they say."

"What do you mean? Am I in danger of losing the baby?" Jewel asked, alarmed.

"Not if you do what I say." The doctor smiled heartily. "But you *have* to do it . . . otherwise there are risks for both the fetus . . . and you."

"What do I have to do?" Jewel was beginning to be scared.

"Basically you're going to have to take to your bed and stay there. I'll give you a prescription for diuretics. And no salt, absolutely none. Have lots of milk and milk products. But the main thing is rest. We have to keep your blood pressure down."

"Oh boy," Jewel said, thinking about how she was going to take care of Amber from bed, and how Sascha was going to react to the news.

"Have your husband call me," Dr. Abrams said before Jewel left the office. "I want to make sure he understands the seriousness of your condition. I don't want you attempting to do anything strenuous. I don't even want you to cook. And absolutely no sex."

Jewel went home and climbed into bed, more depressed than she had ever been in her life. Sascha could see that she was terrified and called the doctor right away, to get the firsthand report.

When he hung up, he went over to the bed and held her in his arms, crying. "I will take care of you, my darling. You will be fine. You will not lose baby. You will not die."

Die? Was her condition that serious? Or was Sascha merely overreacting in his usual passionate way?

"Look, darlin'," Edward said over the phone, after she had told him the news. "I was going to give you a nanny for a few months after the baby was born, as my baby present. Now I'll just give you one sooner."

"But, Edward, I can't accept a gift like that. You know

what nannies cost? I know you're making a lot of money, but I don't want you to spend it on me."

"I insist, darlin'. Look, it doesn't have to cost a fortune. You need someone to come in, do a little housework and cookin', take Amber out for walks. Maybe Sascha can find a Russian grandmother type who'll work part time. But, listen, it's a gift. I don't ever want to be reimbursed."

"God, Edward, you take better care of me than my husband."

"Don't ever let *him* hear that! He hates me enough as it is," Edward laughed. "But put Sascha on the case, to try to find someone. I'll stop by after work to see you."

"Wonderful. Sascha's having dinner with the buyers from Saks."

"Okay . . . I'll cook. Vegetables and brown rice. A nice, healthy, nonsodium, macrobiotic meal."

"Ugh!" Jewel laughed. "How the hell am I going to make it through the next four months? Do you realize without salt I can't even eat Chinese food . . . or french fries . . . or street pretzels . . . or . . . ?"

"It'll do you good to lose some weight, darlin'," Edward teased. "You were gettin' thick around the middle anyway."

"Very funny, Edward! See you later."

That was how Nushka Krupa came to be part of the family. She was Polish, not Russian, and Marfa found her, not Sascha. Nushka was not a grandmother. She was in her forties, widowed, with children old enough to be gone from the house all day. Nushka had an imposing girth that was full of muscle, stringy grayish-brown hair and moles all over her face. She smelled of garlic and cloves and could have been a Slavic witch, but one who practiced white magic. Even Sascha took to her, after having sworn that he didn't want another person hanging around the loft during the day. Nine-month-old Amber adored her and loved cuddling up in her immense lap. For Jewel, it was like having a mother again.

Nushka kept a pot of unsalted soup going on the stove at all times. She made her own yogurt. She baked custards and concocted fruit milk shakes, fussing over Jewel in broken English liberally laced with malapropisms. The lady of boundless energy ran errands for Sascha, without complaining as Jewel had. When she went home at night, she made clothes for Amber, and she never failed to drop by on Sundays, her day off, to see if Jewel needed anything, or to bring a freshly baked pie or loaf of bread. In short, the woman was perfect.

Jewel spent her bedridden days still helping Sascha, working on her home-study gemology course, or listening to language tapes, trying to learn French. Her friends Katrina and Christof had married each other and had left their families' businesses to start their own, somewhere on the Left Bank in Paris. As soon as the children were old enough, Jewel wanted to go there and visit her friends. Sascha was agreeable, since Yuri had recently returned to Paris to live, and there was a large Russian community there.

The months passed. Jewel's condition stabilized, and the doctor was pleased that she was following his advice so conscientiously. Not to have done so would have been even more dangerous than he had let either Jewel or Sascha know. Had the preeclampsia become severe, the fetus would certainly have been lost, and Jewel herself might not have pulled through.

In early January, however, Jewel began suffering headaches, and her edema worsened. Her hands and face swelled up, and the doctor decided immediately upon seeing her, during a regular office visit, that he had better induce premature labor.

Nushka rushed home from the doctor's office, where she had accompanied Jewel.

"Mister Sascha!" she called out with alarm, as she opened the front door. "Miss Jewel need suitcase. Doctor take her to hospital now, in ambulance. Deliver baby now!"

Sascha stopped soldering the bracelet he was working on. "Oh no. And I have deadline for this order . . . no matter. This is very bad?"

Nushka shrugged. "Miss Jewel—she look very worried when she tell me to prepare to spend night with Amber." She located Jewel's already packed suitcase, and added Jewel's toothbrush, hairbrush, and makeup from the bathroom.

She handed the suitcase to Sascha. "Here, you take. You go now. Don't worry, I take care of things here." She picked up Amber, who had begun crying in her playpen. "Not to worry, baby. Everything fine. We change diaper, then we go for walk and buy flour to make cookies. Everything fine, baby." She hugged Amber tightly, and it dawned on Sascha how scared Nushka was.

His own fear began to set in as he got into his overcoat, put the suitcase under his arm, and headed over to St. Vincent's Hospital. For what seemed like an eternity, he paced up and down the hall outside the delivery room. The cesarian was difficult because Jewel's condition had to be monitored carefully. There was danger of convulsions or coma.

When the doctor emerged, finally, from the delivery room, Sascha could not tell from his exhausted face whether everything was all right or not.

"Mr. Robinovsky, your wife has given birth to a girl, but the baby weighs only five pounds. There's reduced circulation that we're working to combat. The next twenty-four hours will be crucial."

Sascha's face went white. "And Jewel?"

"She's weak, but stable. We'll want to keep her here for a while. But since she wasn't suffering from hypertension before the pregnancy there's no indication that the condition will continue. She's been through a lot, though. I would seriously advise against her having more children. In fact, I'm going to recommend sterilization, tying the tubes. Another pregnancy could kill her."

Sascha nodded, the words barely sinking in. "When can I see her?"

"She's still under sedation. You can go in, if you like. But she won't be fully conscious for some time."

Sascha spent the next hours sitting by Jewel's bed, stroking her hand over and over again. She appeared more frail than ever before, thinner, more childlike. When Jewel awoke, around six, Sascha told her what had happened and prepared her for the fact that the baby might not survive.

"Oh no," Jewel cried. "No . . . I have to see her!"

"You can't, my darling. Not now. For now, I get nurse. You rest."

"But we have to decide on a name! She has to have a name," Jewel insisted.

Sascha sighed and smiled. "Yes, if you wish."

"Well, I've been thinking," Jewel said. "I made lists and lists but . . . continuing our gem theme . . . what do you think about Beryl?"

"Yes, it is fine name," he said, not really wanting to think about it until he knew whether or not the child would live. "I go get nurse now."

Jewel knew from Sascha's tone that he did *not* expect Beryl to live. But he was wrong. She had had a dream, two weeks before, that she hadn't told anyone about. In it, Amber was about five and she was playing with a slightly smaller girl named Beryl. Jewel was there too, laughing. They were in the country, having a picnic by a lake. They were all fine and healthy. The only odd thing about the dream was that there was a man there too. And the man was not Sascha.

* * *

Five weeks later, three weeks after Jewel herself was
released, tiny baby Beryl was allowed to leave the hospital.
By then she had gained over a pound and was pronounced
completely healthy. Amber, now over a year old, was very
excited to have a sister, and Nushka might as well have
been their biological grandmother, the way she loved them
both.

"I am so proud to have such beautiful babies to take
care of," she told Jewel. "I am full of luck."

"Me too," Jewel agreed. "Even if I can't have more, I
think I've done damned well."

Jewel had heeded Dr. Abrams's advice and had had her
tubes tied. She didn't want to have any more children with
the risks involved. She had done it, spent four months in
bed, but she could never do it again. Besides, she had two
beautiful daughters. What more could she want?

As she still had to take it easy, Jewel put all her energy
into finishing her gemology course. On Beryl's third-
month birthday, Jewel passed her final exams and graduated as a certified gemologist. She was full of ideas for
jewelry she wanted to make. For the time being, though,
she went back to helping Sascha fill his orders. With the
hefty hospital bills to pay, he was working longer hours
than ever, cramped into the loft with a wife, two babies,
and a housekeeper.

"Tonight I go out to meet Boris," Sascha said one evening, stretching as he quit work for the day.

"But I made jellied veal and potato pudding," Jewel
said. "You'll eat first, won't you?"

Sascha shook his head. "No . . . I tell Boris I meet
him at eight. Is nearly that now."

"Oh well," Jewel sighed. "I'll save it till tomorrow. I
think I'll make a sandwich and get in bed. Beryl will be
awake again at eleven."

"Okay," Sascha said, kissing her on the cheek. "I see
you later." Within seconds he was out the door.

"But, no, I don't think I can join you tonight," Jewel said out loud, as the sound of his footsteps disappeared down the stairs. "Thank you for asking though."

Jewel, for the most part, did not complain when Sascha announced he was going out with his friends, which was more frequent than in the past. She was still too tired to join him. Besides, watching Sascha and his friends enjoy their orgy of eating and drinking wasn't much fun for her. Whenever a bottle of vodka was opened, she had noticed over the years, it was always finished before the evening was over. The Russians loved their drink, but Jewel still could not tolerate spirits.

On the nights when Sascha went out drinking, he came home and woke her up, to make love before falling asleep. On a day-to-day basis, however, Jewel was aware that Sascha was no longer as passionate as he had been.

Of course, she was always tired; that was part of the problem. She had cut back on Nushka's hours, to economize. When Beryl was three months old, Jewel had insisted to Edward that his gift had expired. She could not expect him to subsidize Nushka forever, although it was tempting, since Edward enjoyed being her and the girls' fairy godfather, as he jokingly called himself.

And so she was back to cooking full time, carting laundry out to the laundromat, and doing most of the shopping, in between taking care of the babies and working for Sascha. Her life was hectic, but she knew this phase of it wouldn't last forever. She worried a bit about Sascha's drinking, but mostly she was too exhausted to dwell on anything very long. Winter melted into spring, into summer, into fall.

She realized one day just after Thanksgiving that, although she talked to Edward and Betty often, it had been months since she had actually seen them. They would have dropped by the loft, but Sascha always made them feel unwelcome, and that made Jewel ill at ease. So she

called them and arranged a Saturday lunch, while Nushka
took the children to the park.

"Well, here's to us," Jewel giggled, toasting Edward and
Betty with her first glass of wine in months. They were
having an uptown splurge, lunch at the Four Seasons, by
the pool. "And to our debts that are no more. We finally
got the hospital paid off. Just as well we're not going to
have any more children. We couldn't afford it."

"This is just like old times," Betty said, sipping her kir.
This was her first drink in months too, because she had
joined Weight Watchers. Fifteen pounds thinner, she
looked dazzling in a slinky Betsey Johnson dress. "Except
now you're the most married lady I know."

"Well, *you* might as well be. You and Roland have been
together for five years now."

"*Eight* years," Betty corrected. "Not five. Time
marches on. But I've given him an ultimatum. Either we
get married . . . or it's over."

"What did he say?" Jewel asked.

Betty laughed. "He said he'd marry me if I'd move to
Lake Tahoe with him. Really shrewd of him. He knows I
can't leave New York. But I'm thinking about calling his
bluff. I mean, I could sell the shop; I could *try* Tahoe for a
while." She signaled the waiter for another kir. "I really
want to get married. Perhaps have a baby."

"Why doesn't Jewel take over the shop?" Edward suggested. "You know, seriously, it'd be a great idea. You
could get out on your own, Jewel, and make enough
money to hire Nushka full time again. I think it's hard on
all of you, livin' in basically one room day in and day out.
No wonder Sascha's out carousin'."

"He's not carousing! He's merely seeing friends. Anyway, I can't go out on my own yet. I mean, Sascha needs
me to help him. He's so busy."

"That I know. After that piece in *Vogue,* he's on his

way to the Really Big Time," Edward said, referring to a short article the magazine had done the month before. In the text, the writer had mentioned Jewel merely as Sascha's "appropriately nicknamed wife."

"Actually, Jewel," Betty said, beginning to pick up on the idea, "I think Edward's suggestion is splendid. You've got to get out from under a bit more. Fight for your own identity as an artist. It's wonderful that you're helping Sascha, but you do have to consider *yourself.* If you took over the shop, it would be a nice income. You'd be independent as an artist. And I could marry Roland and try Tahoe. It'd be perfect!"

"All well and good," Jewel said. "But Sascha's and my relationship isn't based on my being independent. I've gotten myself into this position, and I must admit it hasn't been bad. Working for Sascha keeps me from facing my own insecurities."

"Workin' for Sascha has *given* you insecurities. You've lost your balls, darlin'," Edward said firmly. "I know I sound like a broken record, but you're talented. It's just that you've changed, you've become complacent. Too goody-goody and long-suffering. I mean, when was the last time you *laughed?*" Edward paused, realizing he was letting her hear everything he'd been thinking for the past couple of years. "I'm sorry, but you can't spend your whole life in Sascha's shadow. *You* wanted to be famous, didn't you? And you were goin' to pay back that McNeill guy the money you borrowed. What have you done about it lately?"

Jewel blinked her eyes. "God, what is this? Pick on Jewel day? I thought I was very happy."

Betty patted her hand. "Don't get upset, dear. We're merely kicking this around. No one's *forcing* you into anything."

"I know," Jewel sighed. "You're both friends who care about me. All right. I'll think about the shop."

"Good. I mean, I haven't made up my mind yet either," Betty said. "Maybe I'd hate Tahoe."

"Well, girls," Edward said, picking up his menu, "now that nothing's settled, why don't we order lunch? I'm starved."

"Good idea," Betty said. "You know I always am." She looked at Jewel. "I shouldn't say this, but quite frankly, you're looking far too thin. Now you may think it's sour grapes, coming from me, but there's no meat on you anywhere." She turned to Edward. "Don't you think she's too thin?"

Edward nodded. "I'm afraid I agree. I won't make the obvious analogy, but you'd be fabulous in about twenty pounds. And your hair—why did you cut it all off?"

Jewel shrugged. "It's been coming out ever since I had Beryl. It's getting really thin. Cutting it is supposed to thicken it up, so I went over to that barbershop on Astor Place and had them chop it all off. Only cost me three bucks."

"What a bargain," Edward said, rolling his eyes. "Look, after lunch, we're hittin' a health food store and gettin' you some vitamins." He paused. "I thought you took vitamins."

"I haven't bothered for months. There's too much else to do."

The waiter appeared. After Betty ordered her salad, Edward said, "I'll have the lamb chops, and this lady here . . ." he indicated Jewel, "will start with the pasta primavera, a large portion, then she'll go on to the roast prime ribs, the squab stuffed with apricots, a cheeseburger, some grilled fish with beurre blanc, the Caesar's salad . . ."

"Edward!" Jewel laughed. "You're insane." She looked up at the waiter, still giggling. "Just the pasta primavera, please. A half portion."

Edward turned to Betty. "What are we going to do with her?"

* * *

After lunch and a shopping spree to buy vitamins, Edward dropped Jewel off at Nushka's apartment on East Fourth Street, to pick up the children. Walking home, with Amber in her stroller and Beryl tucked into the Snuggli, Jewel felt happier than she had in months. Perhaps it was the wine—she was still a bit tipsy—or perhaps it was the carefree afternoon with Edward and Betty.

Over the past hours, Jewel had become more than a little excited about the suggestion of taking over Betty's shop. As she strolled across town, her mind raced with thoughts of how she would change things around and redecorate. Of course, it would all take money, a commodity of which she was very short these days.

Then a thought popped out of nowhere, one that had been buried for years. Although she hadn't heard from him, she suddenly remembered Gary Pollock, her stockbroker. Hadn't he said that those stocks would be worth something if she waited? Well, time had certainly passed. She would call him on Monday and find out if she had any money at all. Funny, after that last conversation with him, she had put him completely out of her mind.

She unlocked the street door and took Amber out of her stroller.

"Okay, sweetie . . . time for you to walk. That's right. That's a good girl. Up the stairs."

There had been talk among the tenants of fixing the building's dilapidated elevator. It had been broken for years. Jewel smiled to herself as she contemplated the luxury of an elevator, something that most New Yorkers took for granted.

As they slowly made their way up the two flights, Jewel suddenly remembered that she had meant to pick up milk and bread. Well, she would park the kids with Sascha and let him deal with naptime.

Unlocking the door, she let Amber into the loft and headed directly to put the sleeping Beryl into her crib.

"Sascha," she called out, "I'm nipping right out again. I forgot the . . ."

Jewel stopped in midsentence. There, on the sofa, was Sascha, with his arms around another woman. Sitting on the floor were three dark-haired children, two boys and a girl. They looked to be between seven and twelve.

"Come in, my Jewel," he said. "You better sit down. We got to talk."

Jewel took off her coat and hung it on the rack by the door. It fell to the floor, but she didn't bother picking it up.

The other woman, large like Sascha, but with a sensual, dark-eyed beauty, stared at her. With fear? Or hostility? Jewel could not tell.

Sascha leaned forward and filled his glass from an open bottle of Stolichnaya that sat on the coffee table. "You want a drink?" he asked Jewel.

"I have a feeling I'd better say 'yes,' " she said. He handed her a glass, and she sat down in a chair, across from them.

"This woman here is Aïna. She has come from Soviet Union, after many months of travel. She does not speak English."

Jewel did not say a word, but waited.

Sascha took a drink and avoided her eyes. "Aïna is . . . my wife, Jewel. From Moscow," he said, after a while.

"And these here are my children . . . Yuri, Alexei, Tanya."

Jewel was silent. Amber toddled over and climbed onto her lap. She hugged her curly-haired daughter tightly, as a numbness began to invade her body. Was this really happening?

Sascha continued talking, sadly, quietly, but Jewel seemed unable to decipher the words. Perhaps he was speaking in Russian. She wasn't sure.

He talked for a long time. Some of it finally sunk in. Jewel began to realize that she and Sascha weren't really married at all. That it was over, although he didn't want it to be. Somehow he wanted to keep both of them, her and Aïna. He was sure he could make it work.

Jewel glanced at Aïna from time to time. The woman did not understand what was happening. It was obvious that she had not known about Jewel and the babies. She seemed to be as much in shock as Jewel.

"I love you, my darling. I never think this would happen. When Aïna and I say good-bye, it is with understanding that she will stay in Russia. She do not want to leave there, and I do. We part for good, I think. But a part of me has always missed her and children. I am happy they come here. We will work it out. I do not want to lose you, my Jewel. Say something," he pleaded. "Say you do not hate me."

Jewel took a sip of vodka. "I don't know whether I hate you or not, Sascha. But it's over."

"No, Jewel. We work it out," he insisted.

Jewel shook her head. "No, Sascha. No way. The girls and I are moving out."

"Please, my darling . . . we *will* work it out."

"No," Jewel said again. "No." And she took the children and left.

In a dramatically rash gesture that would have been appreciated by Sascha, had he known about it, Jewel walked thirteen blocks over to the Hudson River, and hurled the gold wedding band that he had made for her into the cold, choppy water.

After three years and two babies, Jewel knew everything about Sascha . . . and nothing.

One thing she did know: it was over.

Jewel was in shock. Three years with a stranger. She had cooked for him, knowing nothing of the man who ate her food. She had lain beside him and worked beside him —lain under him and worked under him was perhaps more accurate. She had learned a great deal about his craft, but very little, she reflected bitterly, about his heart. And nothing about his past.

She had loved a man who wasn't there. Now she hated the man who was.

These were phrases, she knew. As she stood above the Hudson and watched its gray shiny surface slide sluggishly beneath her, she made these phrases in her head to test their power to hurt, and knew that they were short on substance. They were not the whole truth, not yet.

Jewel still loved Sascha; or rather, she could not completely believe that she did not. But it was like the shock at the death of a loved one, like losing her mother, Jane. One knew the person was gone but did not believe it. One kept waiting for the loved face to appear at the next corner, to come through the doorway, to call on the telephone, to smile again from the end of the kitchen table.

Love itself was like that too. But the fact that Jewel could not yet fully believe it was gone did not make it any the less dead.

And if every death is a birth somewhere else, the birth of her hatred for Sascha Robinovsky would not be far behind.

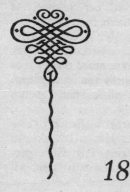

18

Edward popped the cork off a bottle of Veuve Clicquot, and poured champagne into Jewel's waiting glass.

"To us," he said. "Together again. Honestly, darlin', if I were *that way* I'd marry you in a second."

"Well, it seems to be your lot in life to take care of me nevertheless," Jewel said, helping herself to some pâté that Nushka had made.

"At least you had the good sense to change your life around *after* I found a bigger apartment."

The new place was a three-bedroom duplex, half of a brownstone in Chelsea, that Edward had bought. He had moved up again, changing jobs to work for Harry Harper, a hot designer of women's wear who had recently licensed his name for everything from men's sweaters to sheets and chocolates.

"This place is great. It's a real house . . . I feel like a

239

grown-up!" Jewel giggled. "And I promise not to be the woman who came to dinner . . . with her children. As soon as I get it together, I'll be out of here."

"Don't rush," Edward said seriously. "I enjoy havin' my little family. It makes me feel . . . well, let's just say it's fun playin' Daddy. You should have heard the tongues wag when you and the girls stopped by the office today. Nobody knows *what* my story is anymore, and I'm not tellin'."

Jewel laughed. "What's Harry Harper really like? I saw him on TV. They were interviewing him at his farm in upstate New York. He's good looking. His wife's gorgeous. The kids were galloping around on horseback. All too perfect."

Edward shrugged. "That's how he likes to come across. Yeah, he's a nice guy . . . straight *most* of the time. I hear every once in a while he likes to splurge. A cock in the ass to him's the equivalent of whipped cream and nuts on a chocolate sundae to an overweight, middle-aged woman. He strays occasionally, then goes back to his wife."

"You know," Jewel said, helping herself to more champagne, "I read somewhere that some psychiatrists now say there's no such thing as a bisexual person. You're either one thing or the other."

"I wouldn't know," Edward said. "I mean, when I was straight it was just 'cause I was afraid to be anything else. Look . . ."—he leaned forward—"we're talkin' around the real subject that's on both our minds."

"Sascha?"

"Who else? How *are* you? What are you feeling?"

"I'm numb, mostly," Jewel said. "How can you live with someone for so long and know so little about them? Oh shit!" Jewel started crying. "I don't want to do this. He isn't worth it. I *hate* the bastard!" she sobbed. "And I don't want anything from him. No money, nothing. I just want him out of my life forever. Boy, do I have shitty luck with men! Next time, I'm walking into it with my eyes open . . . and they're going to *stay* open."

"Well, at least you're lucid enough to admit that there'll be a next time."

"Yeah," Jewel laughed bitterly, holding out her glass for more champagne. "Men! Can't live with 'em, can't live without 'em. Except for you, Edward. You're the exception."

Edward nodded. "Yes, well, you can live here as long as you want. And we're goin' to get you famous. I've got some ideas."

"Yeah? Well, I want to be *really* famous . . . not just sort of. I haven't been subscribing to *Town and Country* and memorizing all those names for nothing," Jewel said. "Besides, before Jane came on the scene, I had a lousy childhood. I *know* what it's like not to know where your next meal is coming from. Now I'm on my own again . . . but my kids will never have a life like that. I'm going to work my ass off. Amber and Beryl are never going to want for *anything.*"

"I'll help you," Edward said, "in any way I can. And don't worry. Everything's goin' to be all right."

They stayed up talking for hours. By bedtime it seemed that Jewel's entire future had been mapped out for her. It was wonderful to have a friend like Edward, a man who wanted absolutely nothing from her, except companionship.

"Good lord," Gary Pollock said over the phone, "Madeleine Lathem? I thought you'd been abducted by a spaceship. You disappeared totally. I didn't know how to get in touch with you."

"Have you wanted to get in touch with me?"

"Sure . . . things are looking up. Datatrax was bought by GE, and Voisin Motors reorganized under new management. Let's see . . . I'll just punch it up on my computer here. Yeah, you're doing okay, babe."

Jewel couldn't believe it. "I am? How okay? If I were to sell . . ."

"Don't sell! The market's going up."

"Gary, I need money. That's why I called you."

"Okay . . . right now they're worth something in the neighborhood of thirty-five grand."

"*What?*" Jewel laughed, stunned. "Thirty-five thousand dollars?"

"You heard me, babe."

"Oh my God, I don't believe it. Wyatt McNeill was right. You *are* a whiz kid."

"No longer, babe. I turned thirty last week. You seen McNeill lately?" Pollock asked.

"Oh no. Not for years," she said quietly.

"Well, I ran into him a while back. He asked me about you, matter of fact. Wanted to know if I'd heard from you."

"Listen, Gary, I want you to do me a favor. I owe him some money. I figure it comes to about eight thousand dollars, including interest. Could you send him a check for that, out of the money from the stocks? And don't give him my address. Just write a note telling him that I appreciated his financial support when I needed it and that, as promised, I'm paying him back."

"You sure you don't want to give it to him yourself? I got the feeling he wanted to see you again."

"Sell all the stocks," Jewel said, ignoring what Gary had said, "and after you've taken out Wyatt's money and your commission, send me a check for the balance. To P.O. Box 2337, zip code 10011. And thanks. When I get rich, I'll look you up and open a new account."

"You're on, babe," Pollock said. "Good luck."

Edward took Jewel and her daughters to spend Christmas with his family in Virginia. His parents and sisters were exuberant to see Edward with a woman. They treated Jewel as family, hoping that Edward was about to

finally settle down. Amber and Beryl were showered with
toys from Santa, and Christmas morning under the thirty-
foot tree made Jewel wonder whether she and Edward
really should get married. She couldn't imagine winding
up with anyone nicer, but sex was the problem.

Sex was always the problem. With Sascha she had
tossed all her plans in the air because he was so good in
bed. With Wyatt she had lost her best friend because she
was so flattered that he wanted her. Jewel decided it was
time to stop thinking with her vagina and give her brain a
shot.

"You know, I've finally figured it out," Jewel told Edward, after they had returned to New York. "A good sexual relationship has to be an affair. A good marriage has to
be a financial arrangement. If I ever fall in love again, I'm
not going to marry the guy! What I want for a husband is
a rich, straight, best friend."

"Which leaves me out," Edward said.

"I've thought a lot about us," Jewel said, pouring herself a glass of milk to go with the bag of chocolate chip
cookies she was devouring. "But if we were married I'd be
jealous of your lovers. I might not know who they were,
but I'd know they existed."

"But you could have lovers too," Edward said. "Maybe
we *should* get married. There are worse ideas."

"No, Edward. I love you too much to marry you,"
Jewel said. "You're on to all my flaws. We know each
other too well."

Edward wiped away the milk mustache from Jewel's
upper lip. "Yes, that we do."

"You know," Jewel went on, "talking to my stockbroker about Wyatt McNeill made me think of Hadley. We
were really happy together, except it didn't last very
long."

"What do you suppose happened to him?"

"Hadley? Probably married a preppie and works on
Wall Street." Jewel shrugged. "I have no way of finding

out. Can you imagine if I called the McNeills and said, 'Hi, this is Madeleine Lathem . . .' "

"Good God," Edward interrupted. "Madeleine Lathem! Do you realize that this is the first time I've heard your real name?"

"Well, Dragoumis is my real name. Jane Lathem was my adopted mother."

"I can call."

"What?"

"I can call the McNeills," Edward said. "Say I'm an old college buddy. Where'd he go?"

"Yale."

"It figures. What's the number?"

"KL5-1332, unless it's changed."

Edward dialed. "Is this the McNeill residence? Yes, this is Edward . . . Bentley. I'm a friend of Hadley's from Yale. I'm in town from L.A. and I wanted to look him up. Oh? Really? My goodness . . . yes, well, I'm not surprised. Is there an address?" Edward signaled Jewel to hand him a pencil and he jotted down an address on the pad by the phone. "Oh yes . . . Bentley . . . Edward. Well, thank you. Take care."

"What?" Jewel asked, excited. "Where is he?"

"Kashmir. Working for CARE."

"Is he married?"

Edward shrugged. "Don't know. I didn't want to be too quizzy."

Jewel smiled. "So he really did it after all. Broke away from his background to go out and help the world. Good for you, Hadley. Good for you."

She wondered if she would ever see him again. Then dismissed the thought. Even if she did run into Hadley McNeill somewhere, he probably wouldn't bother to speak to her.

Betty Blessing's lease on the Golden Buddha was about to expire: the rent was going to double. She and Jewel spent weeks looking and finally found a tiny shop on West Broadway, in Soho, for a fraction of the rent the old place commanded.

"It *is* tiny," Betty said.

"But it's a great location. And if I cover the walls with mirrors, it'll look bigger."

"Hmmm . . . yes, and with marvelous lighting . . . I think it'd make it."

Jewel threw her arms around Betty. "Is this really happening? I'm so excited."

"You bet it is, baby. We're really doing it!"

Betty had agreed to sell her business—inventory and suppliers—to Jewel, on a time arrangement. Jewel would pay installments for two years. If Betty hated Lake Tahoe and wanted to return to New York within that time, Jewel would take her back in as a partner.

"Only one thing," Jewel said over coffee, after signing the lease. "And I don't want to hurt your feelings. But I was thinking I might change the name of the store."

Betty laughed. "God, I don't blame you. The Golden Buddha's a name whose time has come and gone. What do you have in mind?"

"I was thinking of Glitter, or Sparkles, or Bijoux . . ."

"*Bijoux,*" Betty repeated. "I like that. It's marvelous, actually." She looked at her watch. "God, I've got to go pack. Can you believe after all these years Roland's taking me to meet his mother in Florida? I'm beginning to feel so legitimate. I think marriage is going to be tons of fun."

"It can be," Jewel said, hugging her friend good-bye. "As long as you don't pick a bigamist."

"I think you should send the bastard to jail," Betty said, "instead of getting an annulment."

"Much as I hate Sascha, I wouldn't want to be responsible for putting him behind bars. I owe him something. Without him I wouldn't have Amber and Beryl. They're my life now . . . I'm so happy to have them."

"Well, entre nous," Betty said. "I think I may be pregnant."

"That's great!" Jewel bubbled. "You know, I think you'll go to Tahoe and it'll be the last we'll ever see of you. You'll really be happy there."

"I think so too. Things are picking up for all of us," Betty said, hailing a cab. "Talk to you soon. I know Bijoux is going to be an enormous success."

Jewel spent the next two weeks working nonstop, moving Betty's stock from Bleecker Street and making the most of the space in her hole-in-the-wall shop. Edward helped her build shelves, and Demetrius, no longer Edward's lover but still a friend, came by and consulted on the lighting. It was his suggestion to illuminate the wall niches and glass cases with tiny, white Christmas tree lights that they found, off season, at a factory in Chinatown. Demetrius did up an alarm system for Jewel for half what her other estimates had been.

Finally, on Valentine's Day 1975—just after Beryl's first birthday and Amber's second—Jewel opened Bijoux. To celebrate the day, she displayed the jewelry among little chocolate hearts and red tea roses.

"What a year this has been," Jewel said, ringing up a sale, after a remarkably active first day. "Do you think my life's going to settle down now?" she asked Edward, who had taken off from work early to come by the shop.

"I wouldn't bet on it," he said. "Now you're goin' to have to work your little tush off."

"Thank heavens for Nushka. I've been so busy I think the kids are beginning to think she's their mother."

"I have an openin'-day present for you," Edward said when the shop had emptied out and they were alone. "I called a friend at *New York* magazine and told him about the shop. He's interested . . . and promised to stop by. If he likes it, there's a good chance of gettin' it into Best

Bets. I also called *Glamour, Vogue, Cosmo, Harper's Bazaar, Mademoiselle* . . ."

"That's fabulous!" Jewel cried. "Thank you! Oh, Edward, I can't believe it's happening."

She had read somewhere that when you're ready for a big opportunity you always attract an obstacle first, and that you must get over the obstacle before you can move ahead. Jewel coldly viewed her years with Sascha as having been her obstacle. And now she was over him. She did not give him credit for having helped her finish her jewelry education and perfect her craft. She only allowed him an offhand role in the creation of Amber and Beryl, and now, as time went on, his importance in that feat began to diminish in her mind. *She* was the one who had suffered their births, after all; Sascha had only participated in the fun part.

But some nights she dreamed of him, dreamed they were back together as a happy, loving family. On those nights she would wake up from the dream and cry. When she wasn't busy hating him, she still missed him.

Before closing up for the day, Jewel slipped her arm through Edward's and paused to study her glittering, precious shop. It was perfect, as she had imagined it would be. Success was around the corner, and Bijoux in Soho was merely the beginning.

"But you have to start somewhere," she told Edward. "And of all the places in the world, West Broadway in Soho in New York City ain't bad. It ain't bad at all," she laughed giddily.

Jewel was finally on her way.

19

Wedged into a minuscule space on West Broadway, hardly
bigger than a refrigerator, we unearthed Bijoux beyond our
wildest dreams. There are stunning displays of delicious
mostly costume trinkets, gleaming among tiny Christmas
lights. Jewel Dragoumis, the shop's owner and chief designer, had us salivating over her nonpareils—enamel rings
inlaid in motifs patterned after Oriental rugs ($175–$450,
depending on width of the band). Mark our words, Jewel—
she swears it's her real name—has created a gem of a shop.
Bijoux, 435½ West Broadway. Hours: 12:00–8:00, Tuesday–Sunday.

Jewel smiled as she reread the piece in *New York*, slipping
it into an art deco frame to hang in the shop. Ever since
the article appeared, three weeks earlier, dedicated shoppers had been flocking downtown to check her out. It was
madness. In less than six months, she was a success,

mostly thanks to Edward's tireless propagandizing to People Who Matter at the magazines.

But success had its price. Jewel hadn't seen a movie or play since the shop opened, and the idea of a summer weekend in the Hamptons with Edward was as farfetched as a trip to Mars. Every night, after she put the girls to bed, she made the enameled, Oriental-rug-patterned rings that were the current rage. She worked mornings before the shop opened and on Mondays, her day off.

It was exhilarating, and frustrating. There weren't enough hours in the day to make jewelry, tend the shop, and be a decent mother. Nushka, of course, kept Amber and Beryl happy and occupied. And although part of Jewel knew she was missing out on precious hours of their childhood, she rationalized her absence. Her ambition and struggle for success, she told Edward, was every bit as much for Amber and Beryl as it was for herself. They would have the best childhood possible. Once she had it made, she would have plenty of time for her daughters.

Jewel was already contemplating expansion, which, of course, to do right would take time and a lot more money than she could put her hands on. So expansion could wait. For now, there were only two things missing from her life: a man to do things with and the time to do them.

Edward's new boyfriend, Peter, who had recently graduated from a course of Silva Mind Control, told Jewel that the powers of positive thinking and creative imagery were the key to getting what you wanted in life. If you concentrated, meditated, and were *very* specific about what you wanted, it would come. Peter said he got cabs in rush hour all the time that way. He had also landed a great new job. So Jewel visualized and created images every night as she drifted off to sleep. What the hell, it didn't cost anything.

And, within a week, along came Cathalene Columbier, tiny with large doe eyes and a short, boyish haircut. She looked no more than twelve, but swore she was twenty-one. She was French but spoke practically accent-free English.

"Hello? Are you Jewel? I am Cathalene . . . from Paris," she said, walking into the shop one day. She was wearing an oversized Grand Canyon T-shirt, khaki shorts, and sneakers without socks. "I'm a friend of Katrina . . ."

"And Christof! They wrote me ages ago that you were in the States and might show up," Jewel smiled. "But I'd forgotten. You design jewelry for their shop."

"Yes, I do wire work. Very delicate. I have samples with me. Would you like to see them?"

"Of course. Here." She set an empty black velvet tray on top of a glass case.

"These I did in Santa Fe—silver wire with turquoise chunks stuck in," Cathalene said, taking a leather box out of her large canvas handbag. "They'll go over well in Paris, perhaps not in New York."

"Hmmm, you're right. Indian jewelry's had a big revival here, and now it's pretty much done. But your workmanship's excellent. I adore the ring you're wearing."

Cathalene held out her finger to display a ring fashioned out of intricately-woven gold and silver wire, with a one-carat chunk of amethyst crystal in the middle. "Yes . . . it's one of my favorites. I had a bracelet to match that I traded to a friend in L.A. for room and board."

"If you want to make some of those for me, I'd be interested. In fact," she said, reaching under the counter and bringing out a leather pouch, "I bought some Brazilian topaz crystals from a guy who stopped by here the other day. See . . . orange, gold, yellow, pink, blue. I hadn't figured out what to do with them. But if you want to use them we could work out a deal. And I'll buy your pieces outright, rather than do consignment."

Cathalene picked up the small crystal chunks and looked at them. "Yes, they'd do very well. The only problem is, I'm living with a guy in a studio apartment, and he works at home. He's a writer. Do you have a place I could work?"

Jewel laughed. "I use my bedroom. I turned it into a workshop and sleep on a pull-out sofa that I usually don't bother pulling out." She paused. "Here, well . . . what you see is what you see. There's no back room."

"This is okay. If I sat behind the counter I could work there," Cathalene suggested. "I don't need much space. I could even handle sales when you want to go out. I'm good at talking to people."

Jewel couldn't believe her luck. If Cathalene worked in the shop it would free up Jewel's time considerably. And Cathalene's wire work was technically flawless; Jewel knew it would sell.

"Okay." Jewel shook hands with the small French girl. "We're on. When do you want to start?"

"How about tomorrow?" Cathalene said.

Cathalene was the perfect solution to Jewel's problems. She was happy to weave her rings while tending the shop, and the arrangement gave Jewel more time to stay home with the children and make her own pieces. It was a profitable arrangement too. Cathalene's rings and bracelets began to sell as fast as she could make them.

As for her own work, Jewel was flying high. Edward introduced her to his boss, Harry Harper, and he liked the new pieces she was working on. They were influenced by art deco, employing elements of stainless steel with faceted smoky quartz and cubic zirconium. Harper commissioned her to do the jewelry for his next spring's womenswear show.

"Edward's been raving about you for some time now," Harry said. Traces of a New Jersey accent outlined his words. "I'm glad we could finally get together, Jewel. You don't mind if I call you by your first name? Women are so uptight about that these days."

Jewel shook her head. "I don't mind. As long as I can call you Harry."

Harper laughed, displaying the whitest teeth Jewel had ever seen in her life. "Look, my wife and I are having a party on Saturday, just a cocktail thing, for Genevieve Davis, who's in town for a few days. Edward's coming . . . why don't you drop by too? Bring a date, if you want. There'll be people there you should meet. And . . ." he quickly picked through her jewelry samples on his desk, "wear this . . . and this, and this. With a black dress. You're thin enough to wear one of the models' samples. Ask Emma, my secretary, to find you one before you leave."

"Well, thank you but . . ."

"You suspect I'm putting the make on you?" Harry asked bluntly. "Believe me, as attractive as you are, I'm not. You have a lot of talent. It's time you started working the main rooms. And I'm going to help you." With that, he stood abruptly. "I have a lunch date." He headed for the door, then paused. "Be there Saturday."

Jewel did not know what to make of Harry Harper. All his money and power, yet he seemed genuine in his praise of her work. Maybe he liked her too, and this was the way he operated, but she knew she could deal with that. After gathering up her jewelry, she headed down the hall to Edward's office, to report on the meeting.

"Fantastic, darlin'," he responded. "You never can tell with Harry. I thought he'd like your work, but everything depends on the mood of the day. He got praised in *WWD* this mornin', so this was good timin'."

"And he asked me to his party Saturday. Some shindig for Genevieve Davis, whoever she is."

"She's London society. Owns a club there. Mistress of one of the world's financial leaders, Sir Charles Harding, who happens to be one of Harry's backers for the new menswear division. Harry's out to give Pierre Cardin a run for his money." Edward glanced at his watch. "Oh, late for lunch. Sorry I can't take you, but it's business."

"That's okay," Jewel said. "I'm going to wander around the Museum of Modern Art for a little inspiration. Cathalene's minding the store till four."

"Jewel," Edward said before he left, "it's terrific that Harry likes you. He's a powerful man these days. But as a word of friendly advice, I'd try not to . . ."

"Step on his balls?" Jewel said. "And act like a good little girl? I liked him. He wasn't what I was expecting."

"Good. Just remember, he's mercurial. You have to watch yourself, but he can take you places."

"Okay, Daddy." Jewel smiled, as they walked to the elevator together. "I'll be nice to the boss. At this point, I'm willing to do anything to get ahead."

"You don't have to go *that* far. Just be reasonable." The elevator appeared, and Edward stepped on. Jewel stayed back. "Aren't you comin'?"

"No, I have to pick out a dress for Saturday night."

Edward smiled and made a victory sign with his fingers as the elevator door swung shut.

After about forty-five minutes of wandering around the Museum of Modern Art, jotting down notes, feeling totally exhilarated from the morning's meeting with Harry Harper, Jewel stopped in front of one of her favorite objets, a box made by Joseph Cornell in 1940, titled Taglioni's Jewel Casket. The brown hinged case contained a necklace of glass stones, jewelry fragments of red, blue, and clear glass chips, and twelve ice cubes made of clear glass. The interior of the lid was covered with brown velvet, framing Cornell's inscription.

Jewel turned the page in her notebook, and began jotting down the story: "On a moonlight night in the winter of 1835 the carriage of Marie TAGLIONI was halted by a Russian highwayman, and that enchanting creature commanded to dance for this audience of one upon a panther's skin spread over the snow beneath the stars. From this actuality arose the legend that to keep alive the memory of this adventure so precious to her, TAGLIONI . . ."

Jewel was suddenly aware of a man standing next to her, watching her write. She glanced up, and he smiled.

"I'll dictate, if you like," he said, and started reading slowly from the file card. ". . . 'TAGLIONI formed the habit of placing a piece of artificial ice in her jewelry casket or dressing table, where, melting among the sparkling stones, there was evoked a hint of the atmosphere of the starlit heavens over the ice-covered landscape.' That's it," the stranger said. "A very romantic legend."

Jewel slipped her pad and pen back into her handbag. "Yes, isn't it? Thanks for dictating." She took a good look at the man and made a quick appraisal: not bad. Attractive in a young bankerish sort of way, wearing a conservative gray suit, with well-shaped light brown hair. His eyes were light brown too, behind round wire-rimmed glasses. He was about six feet tall, and his body was slim and long waisted.

"I've been following you," he said. "Watching you write secret thoughts in your little notebook."

"Oh you have, have you?" Jewel smiled. "I'm casing the place, getting ready for the big heist."

He nodded. "I won't tell, but I think that guard who just passed behind you pricked up his ears. They may not let you leave without intense questioning."

"Why were you watching me?" Jewel asked.

"I like to pick up women in museums."

"Oh? Well, you're direct. I like that."

He shook his head. "Actually, I don't. Pick up women in museums. I've never done it before . . . but I was struck with you. Extremely curious about what you were writing."

"Well, I'm sorry to disappoint you, but it's just random thoughts. Ideas, catch phrases, anything that might inspire me later."

"Then you're a painter?" he said.

Jewel shook her head. "I design jewelry." She looked at her watch. "And I have to go."

"Don't," he said, following her out of the gallery. "Come downstairs and have some coffee with me. Or lunch. You look as if you could stand a meal."

Jewel hesitated for an instant, and he picked up on it. "Aha!" he smiled. "You don't want to . . . but you can't think of a good excuse."

"I have to get downtown."

"Right this minute?"

"Okay," Jewel relented. A cup of coffee. A little flirtation. MOMA was a safe enough place to talk to strangers. And this stranger seemed rather nice.

"I'm Allen Prescott," he said as they walked downstairs.

"Jewel Dragoumis."

"What a great name," he said. "Is Dragoumis Greek?"

Jewel shrugged. "I guess. Actually, I don't really know."

"Oh? Most people have some idea of what their heritage is."

"Most of the people *you* know, maybe. But Dragoumis took off when I was a couple of weeks old. We haven't kept in touch."

That silenced him. But after they had sat down with coffee and pie, Jewel decided to make an effort. Allen Prescott was nice-looking, well dressed, perhaps someone she would like. "So, here we are."

"Having coffee and apple pie." Allen smiled. "And trying to decide whether this is a pickup that's going to lead somewhere. Or whether we'll shake hands in fifteen minutes and head back off to our lives . . . never knowing what might have happened if we'd given it a chance."

"Are you a writer? You have a great imagination."

"I'm working on a play. But then I've been working on it ever since I graduated from college."

"Where was that?"

"Brown. I majored in art history and minored in creative writing."

"Then you must be well off," Jewel said.

"What makes you think that? I could have gotten a scholarship."

"Your major. People who have to make money usually wind up with something more . . . business oriented. I don't mean to be nosy. It's just something I've observed."

Allen laughed. "Well, I work. I have an office downtown."

"Where you write your play?"

"My play's recreation, actually. Day to day, I manage money."

"Oh?" Jewel smiled. A financier. A wonderful contact for when she was ready to expand Bijoux. "Then why aren't you downtown managing money now? Instead of wandering around the museum."

Allen shrugged, grinning. "You think I'm lying. That I'm some ne'er-do-well who hangs around this place picking up women. Actually, I wanted to see the Matisse show again before it closes."

"Yeah," Jewel nodded, "it's a great show. Someday I want to be rich enough to collect art. Just think about it. Back then, some of those paintings were bought for next to nothing. I mean, can you imagine owning a Matisse?"

"I do some collecting," Allen said.

"You do? That's fantastic." She was impressed, if he was telling the truth.

"Well, at one point I wanted to be a painter," Allen said. "But fortunately I discovered early on that I have no talent."

"Why do you say fortunately?" Jewel asked.

"Because if you don't have talent and you *know* it, you save yourself years of frustration and rejection. Then I discovered I do have *one* aptitude when it comes to art. I recognize talent. I have a sixth sense for it. Every painting

I've bought has at least doubled in value," he said casually.

"That's great. But it's an expensive hobby." She still didn't believe him, this stranger telling her he collected art, insinuating that he was rich as Croesus.

"Oh, I had a little family money . . . a bit of an inheritance that I decided to gamble on the art market," he said.

Jewel nodded, not wanting to pry, but wanting very much to believe him.

"I grew up in Oklahoma. A very normal boyhood. Except I had this one aunt . . . my father's oldest sister. The renegade of the family. She used to take me antique hunting with her, and to furniture auctions. She loved furniture. I got interested in the paintings. She's the one who left me the money. I think she would have been pleased if she knew I was spending it that way. My parents never approved of her, or of art. To this day the only pictures hanging in their house are of me and my sister as children, painted by Tulsa's leading—and only—portrait painter."

Jewel laughed, then suddenly caught sight of the clock on the wall. Four o'clock. "Oh my God, I'm late!"

"But I don't know anything about *you*. What if I want to see you again?"

Jewel fished in her purse and pulled out a business card. "This is my shop. Look, thanks for the coffee. I have to run."

Allen Prescott picked up the card and stuck it in his pocket. "I'll guard it with my life," he called out.

Jewel was halfway across the cafeteria, but she turned and smiled. " 'Bye." She waved and dashed out.

She wondered if Allen Prescott was telling the truth. If he wasn't handing her a line, he was obviously well off. Of course, there was every chance that he was handing her a line.

Still, there was something about him that she liked. He was the first man to interest her since Sascha. Not that it was anything resembling love at first sight, but he appeared to be an attractive, amusing man who could afford dinner and a couple of theater tickets.

At the very least, he could provide a pleasant diversion in her life. She hoped he would call.

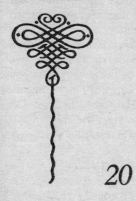

20

"Ah, so tonight is the fancy party with
Harry Harper?" Cathalene Columbier said. She had
brought a bright green feather duster to the shop and was
dusting the jewelry displays that were inset into deep wall
niches.

"Yeah, at seven. Look, if you can't stay till eight you
can close up. Just put a sign on the door: 'Emergency—
had to leave early. Come back tomorrow,'" Jewel said,
getting ready to run home and dress.

"Oh, that's okay. I don't mind staying. Jimmy's got
some big deadline . . . an article for *Rolling Stone*. He's
working all weekend. I'd just as soon be someplace else,"
she sighed.

For an instant, Jewel considered asking Cathalene to go
to the party with her. But as much as she appreciated
Cathalene, over the past weeks Jewel could not help noticing how ambitious the French woman was. Her wire rings

were selling as fast as she could make them, and Jewel suspected that Cathalene hawked them shamelessly to customers when Jewel wasn't around.

So she wasn't about to share Harry Harper, or provide Cathalene with an opportunity to dazzle him with her European charm. Jewel wanted to be the jewelry designer of Harper's eye. After months of Edward's working behind the scenes, Jewel finally had Harper's attention. She wasn't about to let Cathalene try to steal the show.

"Well, see you tomorrow then. Have a nice evening," Jewel said.

"Yes . . . you too," Cathalene sighed again.

Jewel had wanted to invite Allen Prescott to the party. He would have fit in well with the society crowd that would undoubtedly be at the Harpers'. And, she thought, it would have impressed Allen that Jewel knew these people. But Allen hadn't called her or come by the shop. So much for him and the pickup at MOMA.

"Oh, I forgot to tell you," Cathalene said as Jewel was heading out the door. "You know that guy I mentioned to you, the one named Jeb who went crazy over your work?"

"The man who bought my anodized-silver-and-lapis necklace?"

"Yeah, well, we started flirting, and he said he'd come back in a few days to see me. And, er, I thought I'd better let you know . . . I sort of let him think that I own the shop. And, er, that I designed the necklace."

"Oh?"

"Yes. I know I shouldn't have," Cathalene gushed innocently. "But he really liked me, and he liked the necklace. Then he said that if I'd designed it he'd feel obligated to buy it. So I said I had. I mean, it was only to make the sale. I'm not one to take credit for someone else's work."

"Yes, I see," Jewel said coolly, knowing for sure that she had made the right decision in not inviting Cathalene to the party. She wouldn't put it past Cathalene to tell

Harry that *she'd* designed all of Jewel's art deco pieces. "Well, in the future . . . and even to make a sale . . ."

"I know. I understand completely," Cathalene said. "But if this guy Jeb comes in, I'd appreciate it if you'd kind of act like you work for me, rather than the other way around. I really like him."

Jewel stared at her, amazed by her chutzpah, and let a stony expression convey her reaction to the matter.

"I'm sorry, Jewel," Cathalene said, now fully aware that she had stepped on Jewel's toes. "It won't happen again."

"Good," Jewel said.

Harry and Vivian Harper's penthouse on Fifth Avenue overlooking Central Park was impressive but spare, done in grays and blacks. There was nothing ostentatious about the furniture, and there was very little to-die-for art on the walls, save a large Jackson Pollock that dominated one end of the living room. There was a lot of heavy-duty jewelry though, around the slim necks and arms and fingers of the women, most of whom Jewel recognized from the pages of *Women's Wear Daily*.

"God, Edward," Jewel said, as they made their entrance. "Why am I so nervous? It's just a party, but I feel as if this is my society debut. Well, actually it is the first party like this I've been to in years—since the days when I hung around with the McNeills."

"Darlin', all those years with Sascha got you out of touch. Until you get used to this crowd you've got a right to be nervous. This room is full of people who'd as soon step on you as not. Remember what I said about puttin' on your best behavior."

"I'll be charm itself," Jewel smiled, as Vivian Harper came over and Edward made the introductions.

"Oh, I'm so pleased to meet you," Vivian said. She was blond, with a cultivated Eastern-boarding-school accent. Jewel knew, by way of Edward's gossip, that she was the daughter of a wealthy Las Vegas hotel owner and had been an aspiring model when Harry Harper married her ten years before, crowning her queen of his expanding empire. This evening, she looked the part, lovely, appealing, gem studded. "Harry's excited about your work. In fact I thought I might run by your shop next week."

"I'd love it," Jewel said, and then had an inspiration. "I also do custom work. If you have any old jewels you want redesigned . . ."

"How fabulous. What timing! My mother gave me a diamond ring of hers. It's a pretty stone, about three carats, but it's *so* boring. You know, a six-prong platinum Tiffany setting," she said. "I'll never wear it the way it is. I'd love to turn it into something fun."

"Call me," Jewel said, "and we'll get together. I'll be happy to look at it and make some suggestions."

"Wonderful!" Vivian crooned. "You're every bit as terrific as Harry said. Get a drink, Jewel, and then I'll put you into circulation. I want to introduce you to some friends."

As Vivian drifted off to greet new arrivals, Jewel whispered to Edward, "I'm doing good, eh?"

"Home run on the first ball. Since when do you do custom work?"

"The idea suddenly came to me. I want to work with precious stones, but I can't afford them. This is the ideal way."

"You're quick, darlin'. Let's get that drink and start introducin' you around."

An hour later, after two glasses of champagne and much admiration, Jewel was high on success, that of those around her as well as her own at capturing the attention of the elegant elite she was meeting.

"You're sparkling tonight," Harry said, coming over and brushing her cheek with a kiss. "I feel like a proud father. Vivian can be a tough nut to crack, and you have her eating out of your hand."

Jewel smiled. "I'm overwhelmed. I'm having such a good time. This is the first party I've been to in years."

"What? You have to be kidding," Harry said, obviously not believing her.

"I've been leading a very sheltered life. Work and motherhood."

"We have to do something about that. I want you to start getting exposure. Have you talked to Marilyn Cunningham over there?" He indicated a tall, blond, horsey-looking woman wearing extremely thick glasses. "She wants to interview you for *WWD*. You're on your way, and I think we're going to be a great team." His eyes drifted down over her body and back up to her face, holding it in his glance. He grinned, giving her a full dose of the Harry Harper charisma that had hypnotized the press over the past ten years. "Your jewels, my clothes . . . they're made for each other. Look, let's have dinner next week."

Jewel hesitated.

"It's okay. All you have to do is say 'yes.' "

"You're married. Don't you usually have dinner with your family?" Jewel asked.

"Vivian's bored by business stuff. And it *is* business between you and me. I want you to know that from the start."

Jewel smiled, relieved. "Then I'd love to have dinner with you."

"Good," he said, giving her a little squeeze around the waist. "I'll call you the first of the week."

"Well, what do you think?" Jewel asked Edward when they got home that evening. "Is he coming on to me, or not? I can't tell. I mean, he's married . . . and you told me he's gay."

"I didn't exactly say that. I heard a rumor that *occasionally* he likes to grab a fruit off the forbidden tree. But he has more than a few notches in his heterosexual belt too. My advice, if you want it, is stay cool. Be the lady he doesn't get. That way he won't tire of you."

Jewel nodded. "I'm inclined to agree. Harry and I are going to be strictly business, just like he said." She giggled. "He is attractive though. In the way that money and power make a man."

"No, darlin', I know what I'm talkin' about."

"Okay, Edward . . . but we have to make a pact. If I don't get him, neither do you."

"You're safe," Edward sighed. "Unfortunately, I'm not his type."

The next Tuesday afternoon, Jewel was alone in the shop. Cathalene was home with a devastating case of cramps.

It was a slow day, and Jewel was rearranging the displays when the doorbell buzzed. She turned to see Allen Prescott standing outside, smiling and carrying a single red rose in his hand.

She rang him in. "Well, hi. I didn't expect to see you again."

"Didn't you?" He handed her the rose. "I would have called sooner, but I've been in Tulsa. My father died. The night I met you, as a matter of fact."

"Oh, I'm sorry," she said. "Are you okay? Were you very close?"

Allen shrugged. "I loved him . . . but he never approved of me. Wanted me to become the family lawyer. I actually went to the University of Virginia law school for a year. But I couldn't hack it. Anyway, Dad had a heart condition and he smoked like a chimney. This wasn't totally unexpected."

"Even so, it's still hard. My mother died when I was a freshman in college," Jewel said. Jane popped into her mind often these days. It still hurt when she thought about Jane dying so young, without ever knowing her grandchildren.

"Yeah, you're right. It's harder than you think it'll be. In subtle ways," Allen swallowed. He looked younger today and was more casually dressed, in slacks and a tweed sports jacket. "Anyway, I wondered if you'd have dinner with me tonight?"

"I'm afraid I can't. My roommate Edward's having a dinner party, and I'm cooking. He's been letting me live with him, rent free, for ages. So I cater his parties." She deliberated a moment. "Well, actually, you could come. I mean, if you don't mind a bunch of strangers."

"With you there, I wouldn't mind at all. But would it bother Edward?" He paused. "What exactly is your relationship with this man?"

"Friends. Absolutely nothing else. And I may as well tell you right off in case you want to change your mind: I have two little girls. I'm . . . widowed."

"Hell, I can hold my own with kids. My sister has four, and I'm devoted to them. Oh, that's the other reason I'm here. It's my sister's birthday. I wanted to get something."

"Well, everything you see is for sale," she grinned.

Allen looked around for a while, praising Jewel's work. "You're really good, you know that?"

"Yes, but it's nice to have it reaffirmed every once in a while. What does your sister like? Maybe I can suggest something."

"Here . . . I'll show you a picture." He opened his wallet. Something about the fact that he carried a photograph of his sister struck Jewel as charming. And when she saw that he carried photographs of her children as well, she was struck by the sweetness of it. The sister was very attractive. Wealthy looking, well dressed.

"How much do you want to spend?"

"Doesn't matter," he said offhandedly.

Jewel started to steer him to her most expensive necklace—a highly-polished silver choker embedded with bottle green tourmalines of varying sizes—but decided not to take advantage of him.

"Do you want something for day or evening?"

"Hell, you tell me. I don't know much about that sort of thing."

"Basically, you're saying whatever I pick out's fine with you, regardless of price," Jewel said. "Aren't you afraid I'll suggest the most expensive thing?"

"You're trying to make a living—and when it comes to my sister, cost is no object."

"Most men say that about their girlfriends," Jewel teased.

"Isabel's been very supportive," Allen said seriously. "She stood up for me against Dad, kept me from getting disinherited. So I owe her a lot. We're best friends."

"That's nice," Jewel said, wondering even as she said it how she and sister Isabel would get along. "What about this engraved gold-plated bracelet? It's simple, elegant."

"That's fine. How much?"

"One fifty."

"Is that all? I told you I'd buy anything."

"But I don't *want* to take advantage of you." Jewel smiled. "And your sister looks as if she'd prefer something on the classical side, nothing too innovative."

Allen nodded. "You're a good judge of character, Jewel. I think you're right." He reached for his wallet again and put two hundred-dollar bills on the counter. "Can you gift wrap it and send it for me?"

"Of course."

"Hey, look, how much is this one?" He pointed to the tourmaline-studded choker.

"The most expensive thing I have in the shop. There's a total of fifteen carats of verdelite tourmalines in this piece. It's twenty-five hundred."

Allen took back the two hundred. "Sold. If you'll trust me enough to take a check."

"I trust you. But don't you think it's too avant-garde for your sister?"

"It is, and she'll love me for picking it out. Underneath

her conservative exterior there lurks a bohemian. She thinks I'm the only one who understands her." He wrote the check and handed it to Jewel. Her eyes nearly popped out when she saw the Sutton Place address. This guy was unattached, she knew that, wealthy—the Sutton Place address proved that he had not been handing her a line—and he liked her. He was a catch she was not going to let slip through her fingers.

"Thanks, Allen. You didn't have to buy my most expensive piece. I'd have liked you anyway."

"God, Jewel, you're refreshing," Allen said earnestly. "Not like most of the women I've met since I moved here. What time do you want me tonight?"

"Eight. I'll have the girls in bed by then."

"Then I'll come at seven-thirty. I want to meet them," he said, smiling. "See you then."

Jewel caught herself smiling all the rest of the day. To have met the eligible Allen Prescott as a random pickup? It was unbelievable. And he liked kids. Even more unbelievable.

Her luck, she decided, was definitely changing.

21

Harry Harper was deliberately soft-spoken—part of his image—and the din of Pearl's Chinese restaurant on West Forty-eighth practically drowned him out. Jewel was forced to lean forward and lip-read to catch what he was saying. So far it had been all business, as promised, and Jewel was beginning to relax.

After cracking up at one of his Seventh Avenue jokes, Jewel said, "I enjoy you, Harry. You're very funny."

Noting that she had let down her guard, he pounced. "Vivian's at our house on Martinique for a couple of weeks, with the kids. Why don't you come out to the place on Montauk this weekend? We can get a lot of work done . . . without interruption." He dipped his chopsticks into the serving platter of lemon chicken, eating directly from it rather than dishing the food onto his own plate.

"You forget . . . my shop's open on weekends. I can't get away."

268

"Sure you can," Harper announced.

"Well, it's not a good idea," Jewel said, back on guard. "I want to keep our relationship strictly business."

"Hey," Harper grinned, "that's what I've been saying all along."

"That's what you've been *vocalizing*. The look in your eyes says something else."

"I'm a natural flirt," he said. "I can't help it. Put me in a room with a beautiful woman and I'm going to be charming. But that doesn't necessarily mean I'm trying to get in her pants."

Jewel smiled, disarmed. "Look, you're very attractive . . . and I like you. It's very tempting, Harry. But every time I go the route of my emotions I crash into a wall." She took a sip of her TsingTao beer. "And I may as well be honest. I've recently met the man I'm going to marry."

"Oh? He's proposed?"

"Not yet, but I think he will."

"So you love him and you don't want to get involved in something that might mess it up," Harry said.

"That's it. Except I don't love him. I'm never going to be taken advantage of by a man again. From now on, I'm calling the shots." She paused. "That's why you're out of the question. You wouldn't let me call the shots, Harry."

Harry laughed. "God, Jewel, you're wrapping me around your finger."

"With Allen," she continued, "I think it'll work out. And he adores my kids. I'm not going to cloud it up by sneaking out to see you. And if you want me to design a collection for you because you want *me*, then let's call it quits now . . . before I daydream any more about how famous I'll get by being associated with you."

"You know I can have any woman I want," he said. "And you're right, I want you. But I can handle rejection. Don't worry. I want you to design jewelry for my spring collection because you're talented. In spite of what you may think, I don't make decisions with my cock."

Jewel smiled, relieved. "I'm glad. I'd like us to be friends. That's what I need in my life, not lovers."

"Okay, you're on. But you have a rain check."

"I won't use it, Harry."

He clamped a spicy shrimp from another platter between his chopsticks and fed it to her. "Maybe you won't. Maybe you will. I'll be around. But I won't bring it up again. Next time, you make the pass."

"Fair enough," Jewel said, smiling.

As the weeks went by, her relationship with Allen Prescott grew stronger, although what she had told Harry—that Allen would propose—was still wishful thinking. Allen never brought up the subject of marriage even though he and Jewel spent almost every evening together.

Allen adored Amber and Beryl, and they adored the attention he lavished on them. Jewel could read a bedtime story to the kids, and Allen would sit on the end of the bed, listening with rapt attention. Always, he arrived with some sort of toy for the children, and some nights he suggested that they stay home with the kids rather than go out. He knew Jewel worried about not spending enough time with them.

Allen and Edward got along well too. Edward wholeheartedly approved, which set Jewel's mind at ease even more. She valued Edward's opinion and was glad her old and new best friends liked each other.

That's how she had come to regard Allen, as her new best friend. He was comfortable to be with, funny, chatty, intelligent, caring, everything that one looked for in a friend. He wasn't much as a lover, Jewel found out after their sixth date, when she went back to his apartment for the first time. It wasn't that he was inexperienced, but she guessed that sex ranked about fourth on his list, after acquiring art, eating in top restaurants, and running his daily five miles. Sex, she could tell, wasn't a passion of his like the others. So sleeping with Allen wasn't waves crash-

ing against cliffs, but that was fine with her. She equated
love and passion with the two men in her life who had
ignited those feelings in her: Hadley McNeill, and Sascha.
But after what had happened with those relationships,
Jewel was happy to settle for friendship with Allen. Passion left one emotionally vulnerable, and she had vowed
never to allow herself to be hurt again.

Jewel knew she was on Allen's list somewhere. Allen
said she was at the top of it, but she wasn't sure whether,
if he had to choose between her and a Rembrandt sketch,
he would choose her. It didn't matter. He definitely liked
her, but Jewel fretted over whether the relationship was
leading anywhere, namely to marriage.

Then one day he announced, "My sister Isabel's flying
in tonight."

"Oh? Do you want to cancel with me so you can take
her out, just the two of you? I don't mind," Jewel said.

"No," Allen said. "She adored the necklace. She's dying
to meet you."

"Oh no. I guess I'll have to be on my best behavior,"
Jewel said.

"Not at all," Allen assured her. "Just be yourself. Isabel's down to earth, even if she did marry the richest man
in Oklahoma. Anyway, I know you two will get along.
You're a lot alike."

"Except I'm a lot poorer," Jewel quipped, dreading the
meeting. She knew exactly the purpose of it, without having to be told by Allen.

His sister was coming to check her out. This was when
she would make the club or be sent back to the minor
leagues. God, she hated Big Occasions like this. Allen had
made a dinner reservation at Le Cirque, but Jewel was to
meet them at his apartment for a drink first.

If ever making a good impression was important, this
was it. After she got off the phone with Allen, she dialed
Harry Harper and was delighted when she got straight
through to him.

"Hi, doll. What's on your mind? Montauk?"

"I thought you said *I'd* get to make the next pass."

"That's right, I forgot. Is that why you're calling?"

"Nope. I need a favor. I need a to-die-for Harry Harper to wear tonight. Dinner at Le Cirque with my future sister-in-law . . . *if* I succeed in impressing her."

"Okay. The sooner I get you married off, the sooner you'll be ready to stray. Come by this afternoon and pick out anything you want."

"Oh, Harry, I love you!"

"Would that you did, Jewel," he said.

Jewel arrived at Allen's promptly at seven, wearing a drapey thirties-style red skirt with a long, drapey top to match—Harry Harper at his most expensively understated.

Isabel Prescott Farraday was examining Allen's newest acquisition, a Carol Mothner still life, when Allen led Jewel into the living room to make the introductions. Isabel was several inches taller than Jewel, tanned, and athletically muscular. She shook Jewel's hand firmly and looked her straight in the eye. "I can't tell you how many compliments I've received on that necklace you made. Wore it to the big thirtieth-birthday bash that Floyd threw for me." She turned to Allen. "You know, I'm real sorry you couldn't make it, sweetie. All your old girlfriends were there . . . and they *all* asked about you."

Oh dear, Jewel thought to herself. *I'm in for it.*

Isabel turned back to Jewel, smiling. "Now don't you worry. Allen's old girlfriends are all married. They tried their best, but Allen was holding out. And now I understand why." She winked at Allen. "Jewel's as gorgeous as she is talented, sweetie. For once you weren't exaggerating."

Allen beamed. "I told you she was special."

"Tell me something," Isabel said to Jewel. Allen's sister now seemed less forbidding than Jewel had anticipated, with dark brown hair, pale skin, and startlingly blue eyes. "How old are you?"

Jewel paused, off guard. "Twenty-five."

"And are you ambitious . . . or is this jewelry business a hobby?"

"Anything but. I want to be the best. With a store on Fifth Avenue, then Paris, London, all over the place." She stopped, afraid that her ambition might be a turnoff.

Isabel nodded. "Well, Allen was right about you. You let it all hang out. I actually like that. But my brother wants to marry you."

So he *did* love her!

Jewel smiled and looked at Allen, and he smiled back.

"I told him," Isabel continued, "that he was crazy to pick a woman who had two children and couldn't have more. How's he going to carry on the family line?"

"I know . . ." Jewel said. "It's a real problem. Even if he adopted my daughters it wouldn't help the situation. If we married, we'd have to adopt or choose not to have more children. But, of course, we're getting way ahead of ourselves. Allen hasn't proposed to me."

"Jewel, I want to . . ." Allen said.

"Interesting," his sister interrupted. "You've got a straightforward view of life."

"Well, really I'm quite old-fashioned. I want all the creature comforts. A nice place to live, good clothes. I'm not out to raise eyebrows . . . except with my jewelry. *That* I want people to notice."

"So you'd keep working if you married Allen?"

"Of course. I've barely gotten started."

"Allen," Isabel said suddenly. "Go get me another drink, would you, sweetie?" She held out her glass.

When Allen was out of earshot, Isabel asked Jewel the question she'd been dreading all evening. "So, Jewel, do you love my brother?"

Jewel swallowed. To lie, or not to lie? "Yes . . . I absolutely adore him."

"You're hedging," Isabel said, her eyes riveted on Jewel.

"I love him very much," Jewel amended. "But I'm not *in love* with him, if that's what you mean. I love everything about him. I love being with him. Allen's one of the most wonderful men I've ever known. He's taught me so much about art, he's so enthusiastic about everything." She smiled, thinking about the day he had danced into her shop after he had bought a small Caravaggio drawing at auction. "And my girls are crazy about him."

"Well, I'd prefer you to be madly in love," Isabel said. "Allen's very special to me—he's my baby brother, after all." Allen was three years younger than Isabel. "But I've never seen him like this over anyone before. He certainly loves *you.*"

Jewel sighed. "I understand how you feel. But I don't think you'd want me to lie about it."

"No," she said quietly.

"I really believe I'd make Allen a good wife. We're very compatible," Jewel said in her favor.

Allen appeared at the door. "Is the coast clear? I have your drink, Izzy."

"Dump it out," Isabel said. "And bring out that Dom Pérignon I saw sitting in the refrigerator. I want to propose a toast . . . to you and Jewel." She smiled. "I like her, Allen. She's the best woman you ever brought home, by far."

Jewel felt dizzy. She had won the big round.

"Well, Isabel, first I have to propose," Allen said. "You've taken away all of my thunder, you know."

"Then ask her, for heaven's sake! *I'll* get the champagne and leave you two alone," Isabel said, heading off to the kitchen.

Allen took Jewel's hand. "This isn't quite what I'd planned. I was going to take you for the weekend to some cozy little inn in Connecticut. And over a candlelit dinner, I was going to drop one of the family jewels into your wine and tell you to redesign it into an engagement ring. I was going to tell you how happy I've been since I met you, and how good you are for me. I love your energy, and your drive. I love you, Jewel. So how about it? Your girls need a father . . . and I'd like to adopt them." He smiled sweetly. "Will you marry me."

Jewel was surprised to feel her eyes filling with tears; maybe she loved Allen more than she thought. He was a dream come true, after all.

"Yes . . . oh, yes!" she exclaimed, melting into his embrace.

"Oh, splendid!" Isabel Farraday came in carrying a silver tray with champagne and crystal tulip glasses. "Now that the formalities are over, let's drink to it."

"To you, Jewel," Allen said, handing her a glass. "To us."

"To us," Jewel replied, exuberant that her future was no longer in limbo. She would never have to worry about money again.

"To you both!" Isabel toasted. "And to the happiest of futures together."

Jewel Dragoumis. Soon-to-be Jewel Prescott . . . a *much* classier name. A name that would enhance her career.

And Allen had confided to her, later that night, that he was worth close to fifty million. That wouldn't hurt her career either.

22

       If Jewel managed to pull it off with Isabel Farraday, she did not fare as well with Allen's mother, the formidable LaDonna Prescott.

Heeding Isabel's advice, Jewel and Allen agreed to be married in an informal ceremony at the rambling Prescott residence outside Tulsa. On New Year's Day 1976, family and close friends, including Edward, Nushka, and a pregnant Betty Blessing Axelrod, clustered around as Allen and Jewel said their wedding vows. The officiate, an aged Episcopalian named Dr. Donavan, kept losing his place in the ceremony and, until quietly prodded by Allen, Father Donavan forgot entirely to pronounce them man and wife. Jewel looked understatedly elegant in a beige crepe de chine wedding suit designed especially for her by Harry Harper. She wore a single gardenia tucked into her upswept hair.

When the ceremony was finally over and Allen had

kissed his bride and two new daughters, the flower girls, everyone huddled around to wish them well. Everyone except LaDonna Prescott, who stood looking on from the back of the living room in stony silence.

"My mother leaves something to be desired in terms of wit and tact," Allen had warned Jewel before they arrived. "But don't worry, Isabel's gathered the rest of the relatives into our corner."

"In other words, you don't think your mother's going to like me?"

"I *know* my mother. She was from Maud, Oklahoma. Her family was large and poor. When Dad struck oil and they made it big, she quickly forgot her past. She didn't want any relatives showing up for handouts, so she simply cut them dead. Told them to get lost and stay lost. She thinks everybody in the world is after her money—and mine."

"So she's sure I'm *only* marrying you for your money," Jewel said.

"Of course. She knows you have none of your own."

"Well, how does she know that? I mean, couldn't we invent some kind of classy background for me?" Jewel suggested.

The irony was that she had already invented a new background for herself for Allen's benefit. He knew her father had deserted her at birth; she had unwisely blurted that out when they first met. To rectify the situation, she made Jane Lathem her real mother, then told him Jane had been from a wealthy steel family. But poor Jane had been disinherited, at the age of eighteen, when she ran off with the glamorous, handsome Dragoumis. Jewel spoke of growing up in various hotels in Europe (under the charitable auspices of a Great Aunt Greta, who had taken pity on Jane), while her mother resumed a promising career as a cellist. She buried Jane in Munich, not Pine Ridge, dead of consumption, not cancer, then buried Great Aunt Greta as well.

"What's the point? Mother would only hire detectives to check your credentials," Allen said. "Better to come across with none at all than go through that kind of scrutiny."

"Tell me something, darling. How come you turned out so nice, with a mother like that?"

"I'm convinced she found me under a cabbage leaf." Allen grinned. "I was always different. I read a lot, kept to myself. Got myself away from Tulsa at the earliest opportunity. Oh, I'd better prepare you for something else: Mother's bound to make a case for us moving back here to live. But don't worry. I'd never do it."

Jewel *thought* she was combat ready, but one look at the buxom, black-haired, sixty-year-old LaDonna Prescott, her countenance set in impenetrable blankness, and Jewel knew that she and "Mother" Prescott were never going to be chums.

"So you work in a jewelry store," she had said at dinner the first evening.

"I'm a jewelry designer . . . I own my own business," Jewel replied.

"Yes, that's right—I remember something about that. How much money'd you make last year?"

"Mrs. Prescott, I thought money was a forbidden subject among the rich," Jewel countered glibly. She had Allen; she didn't give a damn what his mother thought of her.

"So you're not making any?" LaDonna rejoined.

"I opened the shop eleven months ago, and I'm already turning a profit. Most stores can't even hope to break even inside the first three years."

"Isabel says you're ambitious. Are you going to spend my son's money to get ahead?" LaDonna asked, helping herself to a large slab of the roast beef that the black servant was passing around.

"Allen and I haven't talked about it, but I'm doing fine on my own. I've been making a lot of contacts lately.

Harper's Bazaar is featuring four of my pieces in their February issue. I've done the jewelry for Harry Harper's spring collection. I don't *need* Allen's money," Jewel said self-righteously. Not that she hadn't considered that his vast fortune would propel her farther, faster, but she'd never admit it. Nor would she *ask* Allen for money.

"Allen . . ." LaDonna Prescott turned abruptly to her son. "Is there anything in the world I can say to make you change your mind about marrying this woman? Jewel . . . what kind of a name is that?" she muttered as an afterthought.

"I told you, Mother . . . I love Jewel. And if you keep acting this way," Allen flared, to Jewel's surprise, "we'll take the next plane back to New York and get married there."

"Do what you want . . . but Isabel took care of all the wedding arrangements. You don't want to hurt *her* feelings, do you?" she said.

"I don't want to hurt anyone's feelings, Mother. Not Jewel's, not Isabel's, not yours. Why can't we call a truce and make the best of a situation that you're not going to change?"

"You're a fool, Allen. You always were. All right, you're making your own bed . . ."

"Whew!" Jewel said after dinner. Mrs. Prescott had retired to watch her favorite show on television, and Jewel and Allen were having coffee in the library. "That was intense. She doesn't let up, does she?"

"Nope," Allen said, putting his arm around her. "And your back was up too. Well, thank God we don't have any more meals alone with her. Tomorrow night's Isabel's party, then the wedding, then we can get the hell out of here."

"I'm sorry, darling. I'll try to be nicer. After all, she is your mother."

"It's okay. I never got along with her myself. Isabel

kept me alive in this family . . . that's why we're so close."

"Well, thank God *we* get along. I really like your sister."

"She likes you too," Allen said. "But even if she hadn't, I'd still have proposed." He kissed her. "You know that, don't you?"

Jewel nodded. "You're the sweetest man in the world. I absolutely adore you."

"Let's go up to your bedroom," he suggested. They had, of course, been given separate rooms, at opposite ends of the hall.

"Hmmm," Jewel purred, letting her hand slip down into his crotch, "excellent idea."

Over the past months, Allen had moved sex up on his list. As a lover, he didn't compare with Sascha. But he had it over Sascha in every other way. Life was getting better. And Jewel was immensely relieved that Allen was not going to let "Mother" Prescott interfere in their lives.

Allen insisted they take Amber and Beryl, along with Nushka, on their honeymoon trip to Europe aboard the *QE2*.

When he heard the plan, Edward pouted, "What about me? I'm part of the family too."

"You want to come? Allen will buy you a ticket," Jewel said seriously. "He knows how much you've helped me . . . and he really likes you."

"You're sweet, Jewel. But I think your honeymoon party's big enough as it is," Edward said. "God, everything's turnin' out so well. A year ago you'd hit the rocks. Now you're married to a guy who idolizes you. You're movin' into an enormous pad on Park Avenue. And your collection for Harry is the talk of New York."

"Yeah," Jewel said, "this is a hell of a time to go away. Somebody told me once, 'when you're hot, it's no time to take a vacation.' "

"Jewel," Edward corrected, "we all know you're a workaholic . . . but this isn't a vacation. It's your honeymoon. You owe it to Allen *and* yourself. Besides, you're going to come back from Europe with all sorts of new ideas. Getting away is good for creativity as well as the soul."

"You're right, of course," Jewel conceded. "It'll be a fabulous trip."

And it was. Traveling with Allen was first-class, but more than that. Knowledgeable and enthusiastic about everything, Allen wanted to see and do it all, from shopping and sightseeing to eating in starred restaurants. Every day was chock-full of activities, both planned and spontaneous.

After a week in London, the honeymoon party arrived in Paris and checked into a set of adjoining suites at the magnificent Bristol, on rue du Faubourg St.-Honoré. Jewel was aghast to discover that the sumptuous rooms were costing over a thousand dollars a day; she had to keep reminding herself that Allen could easily afford it. Every so often she pinched her arm hard, to make sure it wasn't a dream.

The second day they were in Paris, Jewel took Allen to a store at 40, rue St.-Sulpice. They entered and Jewel headed straight for the counter farthest back.

"Bonjour, madame," the sales clerk said, without looking at her, *"est-ce que vous voudriez quelque . . ."* Then the young woman glanced up. *"C'est incroyable!* Jewel! Is it really you? I can't believe it! Christof!" Katrina Von Berlichingen called out to the back room. "Come here . . . there is a surprise."

The reunion was everything Jewel had hoped it would be. Katrina and Christof were overjoyed to see Jewel and meet Allen. Jewel loved their shop. It resembled the inside of Taglioni's jewel box, all polished mahogany and velvet, with eye-catching, innovative jewelry.

Over lunch at Le Palanquin, a nearby Vietnamese restaurant, Jewel said, "The photos you sent me of your work don't do it justice. It's absolutely unique. Katrina, I love those necklaces you're doing in silver with the dyed emu feathers. And Christof, your geometric gold pendants are incredible. When I get a larger space, will you let me be your exclusive New York outlet?"

"Of course, with delight," Christof said. "But we did not know you were moving. We had a letter from Cathalene. She mentioned nothing."

"I'm not anytime soon. But . . ."

"Jewel's moving when we get home," Allen interrupted, to Jewel's surprise. "It's my real wedding gift to her. I found a great space on Fifth Avenue."

Jewel dropped her chopsticks. "What? What are you talking about?"

"It's my surprise. You want to be a star . . . so we're going to make it happen," Allen said, beaming. "You know that fur store between Fifty-third and -fourth? They're going out of business. I have my lawyer negotiating the lease, even as we speak."

Jewel leaned across the table and kissed her husband. "I can't believe it! But that's the best location in New York! Oh, Allen, is this really true? You're not putting me on?"

"I wouldn't kid you about something this important to you," he replied. "Forty-five hundred feet of floor space."

Christof whistled. "This is fantastic. You've hit the big time, Jewel."

"Want to hear my plan?" Jewel smiled, still dazed. "I've been fantasizing about this for years—a shop filled with little boutiques, each featuring a different designer . . . with, of course, the biggest space devoted to my pieces," she said immodestly. "There'll be the thickest carpeting, huge bouquets of fresh flowers, displays of raw gems and rock crystals, and music . . . different music to match the mood of each designer's work. And there'll be a little bar where we'll serve espresso, and Perrier—and champagne to the best customers . . ." She paused, to envision all the wealthy buyers drinking champagne.

"I'm going to have one room lit by candlelight," she continued, "to show off my most romantic pieces. And a niche for antique and estate jewelry. Oh, and a pearl room . . . with a waterfall and the sound of ocean waves. The furniture will be bamboo and shell. There'll be a cage of birds. Jasmine and bougainvillea will be growing up the walls." She paused to catch her breath.

"C'est formidable. How long have you been planning this?" Katrina asked, amazed.

"Ever since I decided to be a jewelry designer," Jewel said. "I want a store like no other. I want to be the P. T. Barnum of the jewelry business. With a place that people will love to visit. A mixture of elegance and fun. People will *love* spending their money at Bijoux." She grabbed Katrina's hand. "We're going to make so much fucking money!" she squealed, and the others laughed with her.

"You never told me about being the P. T. Barnum of jewelry," Allen said, reaching over to pick up Jewel's uneaten rouleau de printemps.

"Well, I had no idea it was going to happen so soon," Jewel replied. "The last thing I want is a stuffy, snooty little shop where everybody tiptoes around and you can't talk louder than a whisper," Jewel said. "I've been jotting down ideas for *years.* This is only the tip of the iceberg."

"I'll bet it is," Christof said. "Knowing your energy and drive. And I think we will come to New York for the grand opening. It sounds as if it will be quite an occasion."

"It will be," Jewel promised. "It definitely will be."

The rest of Jewel and Allen's honeymoon was spent taking the children around to museums, the zoo, and the bird market, seeing as much as their limited attention span would allow. They bought wonderful clothes for them at Baby-Dior, and toys to fill their new rooms at home. Jewel couldn't stop Allen from spoiling his new daughters. He insisted on buying them antique mechanical toys and par-

lor games, a theatrical set with hand-painted marionettes
clothed in silks and fur, and antique dolls, born before
1914, complete with furniture, dishware, and accessories
such as satin gowns, feathered hats, and lacy parasols.

In the afternoons, after lunch, when Nushka took two-
year-old Beryl and Amber, now three, back to the hotel to
nap, Jewel and Allen checked out the auctions at the Hôtel Drouot, the famous auction house founded in the nineteenth century. Often they strolled around the sixth and
seventh arrondissements, on the Rive Gauche, looking for
Renaissance jewel boxes for Jewel, and objets from the art
nouveau and art deco periods for Allen. On weekends,
they plowed through flea markets, especially the Serpette
and Marché Biron, which focused on furniture.

"You get to do your store any way you want it," Allen
told her. "But I want to decorate the apartment."

"Okay, that's fair," Jewel said, for she had little interest
in creating the perfect nest for Allen. He was a perfectionist, she had come to realize, and had far better taste than
she when it came to art and interior decoration. Whatever
he did to the apartment would be eclectically elegant and
creative. Best of all, she would be able to devote all *her*
time to launching the new Bijoux.

Jewel was impressed with Allen's ability to bargain and
get the best prices on things. He would visit a gallery that
interested him many times, subtly courting the owner, and
in the end, he always wound up with a large discount,
sometimes as much as thirty percent. But after the painful
poverty of her childhood and years of living on a shoe-
string with Sascha, Jewel still couldn't get used to the
amount of money Allen was spending without batting an
eyelash. It was hard to keep track of it all, and after a
while she stopped bothering to translate the francs into
dollars.

"I can't stand those people who redecorate every couple
of years to show off," Allen said. "What we start off with

is what we'll end up with. Of course," he grinned, "I can't promise not to *add* to it from time to time."

"It's your money," Jewel heard herself say often.

Before they left Paris, not only had they dined at all the great restaurants, but Allen had bought himself a priceless stash of art deco treasure: vases by Daum and Gallé and Maurice Marinot; a set of white porcelain plates painted in silver and gold by Jean Luce, and silver cutlery and a silver-and-jade soup tureen by Jean Puiforcat; an Albert Cheuret metal clock; Süe and Mare gilt-bronzed door handles for the new apartment; champlevé-enameled candlesticks by Jean Goulden; a Lalique chandelier and lighting fixtures by Rateau and Brandt and Perzel; a Benedictus knotted carpet in a triangular pattern; a wall hanging by Raoul Dufy; ornately leather-bound books by Creuzevault, Bonfils, and Pierre Legrain; and a six-leaved Jean Dunand screen with a geometric design in red and gold lacquer on a black lacquer base.

And that didn't even include the furniture that took Allen's fancy: a Pierre Chareau sofa, upholstered in a Jean Lurçat tapestry; a cubist bedroom set by Marcel Coard, in macassar ebony veneer with ivory and lapis lazuli inlay; a Eugene Printz palmwood bookcase with carved doors; an Eileen Gray carved red lacquer-and-leather chair with arms in the shape of snakes; a slinky Armand-Albert Rateau chaise longue; an alcove sofa by Pierre Lehalle; a pair of André Groult beech gondola chairs; a Paul Follot amboyna chest of drawers with the inlaid motif of a nude girl. And more, even more. Jewel could not keep track of the money he spent.

But the items that pleased Allen most of all were two he had gotten at auction for a fraction of their worth: a small Bugatti art deco bronze of a nude woman, and a painting by one of the symbolists, Levy-Dhurmier. Allen practically floated back to the hotel after those bargains had been knocked down.

* * *

On their last night in Paris, Allen and Jewel returned to Taillevent for a romantic meal à deux. Jewel had had a wonderful trip. As Edward predicted, her head was brimming with ideas. But she was anxious to get home, to start redesigning the space on Fifth Avenue that would soon be hers.

"Darling, this has been a wonderful trip," Jewel said, ebullient to be leaving for New York the next morning. "What a way to start off our life together."

"I'll drink to that," Allen said, raising his wine glass, "and to future adventures. I'm really happy, Jewel. I'm glad it's working out."

"What?" she said, alarmed. "Didn't you think it would?"

"Well, you know what they say," Allen joked, "a man tends to marry someone like his mother."

"Oh . . . you!" Jewel exclaimed. "Well, I think you lucked out . . . at least for now. I can't promise what I'll be like by the time I'm her age." She crossed her eyes and puffed out her cheeks just as the waiter appeared to take their dinner order.

Allen burst out laughing; so did Jewel. The waiter stood by, appropriately aloof, waiting for the silly Americans to come to their senses.

23

1976

Limousines jammed the block of Fifth Avenue between Fifty-third and Fifty-fourth streets. On this crisp October evening, spectators crushed against wooden police barricades, excitedly watching fur-draped celebrities—famous names of the Manhattan night scene as well as lower-profile magnates of the international money market—stream through the shimmering crystal-imbedded facade into Bijoux on Fifth. It was the store's opening night, and the show was playing to a packed house.

"So what is it?" a mink-coated lady from New Jersey asked her companion. "Some kinda new nightclub?"

"Beats me," the companion said. "Maybe they're shooting a movie."

"It's a new store," a young man in the crowd offered. "Bijoux . . . sells jewelry."

"What? All this fuss over a *store?*" an elderly woman

remarked to her twin as they passed by. "I wonder what Tiffany thinks about this."

Inside the new Bijoux, models, social dowagers, and celebrities smiled glitteringly at newspaper and magazine photographers, attempting to upstage the merchandise that nestled on silk and velvet in carved wood and beveled glass cases. The young designers Jewel had chosen to feature in her store nervously gave impromptu interviews and patiently answered the questions of the purchasing public. They were Cathalene Columbier, and Katrina and Christof Von Berlichingen, of course, as well as three designers Jewel had combed the country to find: Rody Abrams, Tom Tinker, and a talented Hawaiian known only as Leilani. Those, besides Jewel, were the stars of the show. Jewel had hired six additional behind-the-scenes craftspeople. They were in charge of producing classics, such as wedding bands and chain necklaces, as well as making the nonsigned but limited-edition pieces that she and her stars designed for the nonpareils section of the store.

"Now, admit it, it's a *fun* party," Isabel Prescott Farraday said to Jewel, after they had posed for a barrage of photographs for the news media.

"I wouldn't know," Jewel answered. "I'm too wound up. After the past nine months of twenty-hour workdays to get this place ready, I don't remember the concept of fun anymore." Jewel was decked out in a simple red taffeta Harry Harper, with ruby and amethyst Jewel Prescott jewelry adorning her neck, wrists, and hair. On her fingers she wore rings that had been made by each of her designers.

"That's a lie," Allen said, squeezing through the mob with glasses of champagne for his sister and Jewel. Although there was plenty of champagne and hors d'oeuvre, the waiters seemed unable to replenish their trays fast enough. There were hundreds of people crushed into the moss green carpeted store.

"For you, my darling," Allen continued, *"work* is more

fun than fun." He kissed his wife, then put his arm affectionately around Isabel's waist. "If my sister didn't come to town every month and let me squire her around I'd probably be a social outcast by now."

"Poor baby," Jewel said to Allen. "I promise you things will change from now on. Now that Bijoux's actually open, I can become a real human being again."

"Jewel, love!" Bijoux's preopening public relations expert, rich, blond Camy Pratt, came squeezing through the crowd to give Jewel's cheek a kiss. "Isn't this wild? I mean, it's the most successful opening I've ever choreographed. This gang absolutely adores jewelry. And all the comments I've overheard have been raves."

"I know you say that to all your clients, Camy," Jewel replied. "But God, the place is packed. How'd you do it?"

"Six months of hard labor . . . that's what it's all about. The cover article on you and Allen in *New York* didn't hurt, plus the piece in the *Times Magazine.* People have been chomping at the bit for Bijoux to open. Remember, that's what I promised . . . six months of steady build, then poof! here it is. I'm delivering."

"Allen says you cost a fortune . . . but I suppose it's worth it," Isabel said coolly. "Mother, of course, believes press agents—"

"Isabel, I'm a public relations expert," Camy corrected.

"Sorry," Isabel said. She had known Camy Pratt as a teenager at boarding school and had never liked her. "Mother believes that *public relations experts* were put on earth by the devil. But, I must admit, you do know your stuff."

"Where *is* your mother anyway?" Jewel asked Allen. LaDonna Prescott had grudgingly agreed to come to New York for the opening. Isabel felt that seeing the store in person would pave the way for improved relations between her and Jewel.

"Mother's back in the pearl room, talking to the parrot," Allen said. "She seems to like it there, although she's complaining that the waves sound too loud."

"Well, let's face it, sweetheart," Jewel said. "When it comes to your mother I'll never be able to do anything right. If I'm a failure, she'll hate me. If I'm a success, she'll hate me more."

"Then she's going to hate you more. Who are we talking about?" Harry Harper asked, joining them with his wife, Vivian, who was wearing the diamond ring Jewel had redesigned for her, as well as two other rings, a necklace, and earrings, all made by Jewel. Harry, Jewel could not help noticing, had been eyeing her all evening. She hoped his lust for her was not as obvious to his wife.

"This is definitely a smash," Vivian said, kissing Jewel on both cheeks. "But I have to warn you. Harry's angry with you."

"Oh dear, what have I done?" she asked casually, keeping her eyes on Vivian.

"Nothing yet," Harry said. "But I've heard a rumor . . . that you're going to steal Edward away from me."

"I would never *steal* him," Jewel smiled. She *had* offered Edward a job, but he had declined. "Anyway, he's very loyal to you, Harry."

"I'd better give him a raise then," Harry said. "Will you excuse us a moment? There's someone I want Jewel to meet."

He guided Jewel through the crowd to meet one of his European associates. That done, he said, "I have to talk to you alone."

"No, Harry. Not now. I still have about two hundred people to dazzle." She gave him a friendly pat on the cheek, smiled, and slipped away from him through the crowd.

"Oh, Jewel, darling!" Camy Pratt called out. "Come over here. I want you to meet . . ."

For the next hour or so Jewel spoke to so many people that she began to get hoarse. She snatched a glass of champagne from the tray of one of the circulating waiters, but the champagne bubbles made her throat tickle, and she began to cough. She excused herself from the society matrons to whom she was talking and made her way to the back of the room and out to the foyer that led to the second floor. She knew there was a water cooler there.

As she leaned over to drink, she was suddenly aware of the door opening behind her. Just as she turned to see Harry Harper, his hands brushed against her hips.

"Jewel, darling. You've been avoiding me all evening. That's not very nice. If it weren't for me, you wouldn't be here now."

"Oh? I thought I was here because of my talent. And Allen's loan."

"Ah, how quickly they forget."

"Oh, Harry, I haven't forgotten. You gave me my big break. I'll always be grateful."

"But not grateful enough."

"Harry, darling," Jewel smiled, slightly annoyed, "let's not get into that. I thought we had both agreed that our relationship is business and friendship, nothing more."

"We did agree. Once. But now I want to change the rules. You're on your own now . . . and you're more exciting to me than ever," he said, moving so close to her that she could feel his breath on her cheek. "Come on, Jewel. How about one nice, passionate kiss . . . to tide me over?"

Jewel sidestepped away from him and over to the door. "To tide you over till when?" she said, putting her hand on the knob.

"Until you come around. God, I'm mad about you, Jewel. Your success, my success. We go so well together."

"No, Harry. I've told you . . . I'm not interested," Jewel said, pulling the door open. "Come back to the party. We'll be missed."

With one hand, Harry pushed the door shut again. With the other, he pulled her to him and planted his mouth firmly over hers. Against her better judgment, Jewel gave in to the moment, too exhausted to fight it. The intensity of Harry's passion stirred something deep within her, something she did not want to acknowledge. But she pushed Harry away when his hands began to squeeze her body more urgently.

"Please, Harry. Just give up. I know you thrive on dangerous situations. But if anyone saw us . . ."

"Who the hell cares?"

"I do! You're flattering to say I'm a success . . . but this is only the beginning. I can't make mistakes now. I don't want to hurt Vivian. She's been one of my greatest supporters. And in spite of what you think, Harry, I love my husband."

"Oh? Since when?" Harry said. "One look at the two of you together and I know. Something's missing."

"Nothing's missing, Harry! Now leave it alone. I don't want to have to get mad at you." Jewel flung open the door that led back to the party. "I've told you. I'm not available."

"Want to make a bet?" Harry said, patting Jewel's buttock as he followed her through the door.

"Oh, Jewel!" Cathalene said, rushing over. "There you are. Your friend Edward is looking all over for you. His parents are here, in the cave room." She flashed Harry Harper a dazzling smile. "Oh, Mr. Harper, I am Cathalene Columbier. I have wanted to be introduced to you, but now I will do it myself. You are my favorite designer. Have you seen the kiosk with my jewelry? Would you like me to show it to you?"

Harper's eyes had been following Jewel's lithe body as she made her way through the crowd to find Edward. Now he looked at the attractive French girl, dressed tonight in emerald green silk with black feathers. "Sure . . . I'll look at your work. Who did this dress?"

"I did," Cathalene laughed modestly. "I cannot afford your clothes, so I make my own when I need them."

"Oh? You seem to be multitalented," Harper said.

"Oh yes . . . I am," she said seductively. "Perhaps we could have lunch together and talk about it."

Harry Harper smiled. "Yes, the three of us—you and me and Jewel."

"Oh, of course. Jewel," she said.

"You owe her a hell of a lot, you know. The designers she picked for this store have it made. She's already spent a fortune publicizing the lot of you. You have no idea how lucky you are," Harry said.

Cathalene lowered her eyes, "Oh, but of course I do," she said humbly.

But her mind was traveling a different circuit, making connections. The flushed look on Jewel's face and the leer on Harry Harper's as they emerged from the staircase door. Was something going on between her boss and this man?

What interesting information. It might, at some point, come in handy.

"Come on, let's get dressed, girls," Jewel said one Sunday, shortly before Christmas. "We're going for brunch with Uncle Edward. Then I'll take you to the store so you can play in the big window."

The Bijoux Christmas window display featured a Scotch pine decked out in gold bracelets with bezeled red gemstones (rubies, spinels, and garnets) or green (emeralds, tsavorites, and verdelite tourmalines). Gathered around the tree was a large family of bears, elegantly dressed and bejeweled, singing Christmas carols. The music was piped out onto the street so that passersby could hear it.

"Oh goody!" Amber exclaimed. "Will you turn on the waterfall in the pearl room?"

"Of course, darling," Jewel said as she helped her daughters into Laura Ashley dresses and black patent

Mary Janes, and fixed bows in their long, dark hair. "You can play anywhere you want."

The girls loved to visit the store on Sundays, when they could have it all to themselves. And Jewel loved it too, because she could work and be a good mother at the same time.

She grabbed the silver fox that Allen had given her for Bijoux's opening and threw it over black pants and sweater.

"Isn't Daddy coming?"

"Daddy got up early to go to an estate sale in Connecticut," Jewel said, carrying her daughter over to look in the closet. "He's buying some jewelry for the store." Allen had become so knowledgeable on the subject of antique jewelry that Jewel had enlisted him as Bijoux's official buyer of estate jewels. She had also made Allen president of the company, although he insisted that he wanted nothing to do with the day-to-day running of it.

"Oh, I wish Daddy was coming with us," Amber said.

"Well, he'll be back in time for dinner, lambie."

Since Amber and Beryl were still babies when Jewel left Sascha, they did not remember him at all. Jewel kept all the photographs of Sascha with the children locked away in a safe deposit box. She did not want them to see the album, yet couldn't bring herself to destroy it. It was more convenient to let Amber and Beryl think that Allen was their real father; she had sworn Nushka to secrecy on the subject. When they were old enough to understand, Jewel supposed she would tell them the truth. But that had always been a relative commodity for Jewel. She hadn't yet decided whether the truth would be *the* truth, or whether she'd merely say that their father had been a Russian who was now dead.

Sascha was as good as dead to Jewel. In the beginning, after she left him, he had tried repeatedly to call, but she'd refused to speak to him. He sent presents to the children that she returned unopened. Finally, he stopped trying.

He did not disappear, however. Sascha had become very successful. Tiffany had recently hired him as one of their exclusive designers, much to Jewel's displeasure. She hated Sascha and was jealous of his talent as well.

Jewel and the girls were meeting Edward at Maxwell's Plum. It was the children's favorite, because of its wonderful Hollywood set decor that included stained glass, Tiffany lamps, and several hundred giraffes, lions, zebras, hippopotamuses, and rhinoceroses, and because the waiter always gave them balloons when they left.

Edward, as always, was on time and waiting for them at the giant horseshoe bar when they arrived. On the floor next to his stool was an oversized shopping bag full of Christmas presents.

"No . . . you can't open them now, girls," he said, as they pounced on the bag with squeals of delight. "They're for under the tree."

"My, you're organized," Jewel said. "Christmas is still ten days away. I've barely done a thing."

"Well, I leave for Hawaii on Tuesday. I had to get it all done early."

"Hawaii?" Jewel asked. "I didn't know . . ."

"Yes you did. Remember the long conversation we had when I was tryin' to decide between Maui and the Big Island? And you asked Leilani, and she said definitely the Big Island?"

Jewel nodded. "It's coming back to me. There's so much stuff going on all the time, it's hard to keep track."

"Mummie?" Beryl said. "Can I have two desserts? Instead of anything else?"

"No, sweetheart. You have to have something healthy. Then you can have *one* dessert," Jewel said. "Anyway, Edward . . . I know it's not the time and place to talk about it . . ."

"But I have the feelin' we *are* going to talk about it. Whatever *it* is."

Jewel laughed. "You know I have a one-track mind:

business, and then there's business. I promised Allen he'd see more of me after the store opened. But now I'm working harder than ever."

"I don't want anything else. I'm not hungry," Beryl complained. "I want dessert."

"Me too," Amber said.

Jewel rolled her eyes at Edward. "How'd you like to talk some sense into them?"

"I have an idea," Edward said to the children. "Why don't you and Amber split a hamburger or a salad . . . and then you can each have dessert."

"Okay," Amber nodded agreeably. "You want to, Beryl?" The younger child nodded.

"What a good father you'd make. Anyway, where were we?" Jewel asked.

"You and Allen never see each other."

"Well, we go out together for all the parties and charity things. But that's business, really, for both of us. I have to chat it up with the ladies because they're the ones who keep Bijoux going . . . and Allen's always off talking art and auctions. The only time we see each other is in the car going to and from." Jewel opened her handbag, took out a pack of cigarettes, and lit one.

"When did you start on those?" Edward asked.

Jewel shrugged. "Oh, ever since Bijoux opened I've been crazed. They calm me down. I only smoke five or six a day. Anyway, what I have to talk to you about . . ."

The waiter appeared to take their orders. After much going back and forth, Amber and Beryl settled on pasta. Jewel ordered chicken salad, and Edward, grilled sole sans sauce, as he was dieting to get in shape for the beach.

"What I have to talk to you about . . ." Jewel said.

"Mummie, Amber pinched me! I don't want ska-betti," Beryl whined. "I just want cheesecake."

Jewel laughed. "Amber! No pinching, and Beryl, sweetie, try to eat what you can. You *like* spaghetti." She reached into her handbag. "Here . . . a pad and two pens. Why don't you draw until the food comes?" She turned back to Edward. *"Anyway,* I told you this wasn't the time or place to talk."

"I'm still waitin' to hear what you have to say," Edward said, leaning over to tear a page out of the pad for each girl. "I'm all ears."

"I *need* you, Edward," Jewel said. "I'm completely overwhelmed. There's a part of me that wants to do everything myself. And another part of me, a new part . . . that's beginning to realize that I can't. *Please* come to work for me . . . as executive vice president and design director? I'll pay you a third again what you're getting from Harry. And raise that as soon as I can. I know you turned me down before, but please, Edward," she said, "please, please, *please."*

Edward smiled. "I said no before because I owe a lot to Harry, and I like my job there. I also said no because we're such good friends, Jewel. If I worked for you I'm not sure what that'd do to our friendship."

"Then be my partner," Jewel said with sudden inspiration. "I'll call my lawyer tomorrow and get it all worked out. That way you wouldn't be working for me."

"You forget—first and foremost I'm a designer."

"I know. You have fabulous ideas. You can design jewelry, and work with the craftspeople to make it up. But Harry told me you manage the menswear line. He said you're in charge of practically every detail," Jewel said.

"Yes, well, I guess I am."

"You're so smart, Edward. You can do anything you set your mind to. I need someone to oversee the store. Nudge the designers. Change the look of the place from time to time to keep it fresh," she said, talking faster. "Look, the guy I hired, David Drake? He's not working out. The chemistry isn't right. I want him out before he gets entrenched.

"Oh, Edward, don't you see how perfect it would be?" Jewel continued breathlessly. "Working together. Seeing each other every day. The store's doing gangbusters business. And Allen will lend me expansion money when I need it." Jewel lit another cigarette. "I want to manufacture an inexpensive line called Bijoux Too that'll sell in department stores, then open *our* stores in all the biggest cities. And then start a direct-mail business, with a classy annual catalog and smaller monthly bulletins. Eventually, a Bijoux fragrance. And, on top of all that, I want to make real knock-'em-dead, one-of-a-kind pieces that'll be like nobody else's. But I need *time* to design, and that's what I'm lacking. I need *you,* darling. Please say yes."

"Stop! Take a deep breath. You're goin' to start hyperventilatin' any second now. You have to remember to breathe every once in a while." Edward squeezed her hand. "Look, it's very temptin', and your enthusiasm is contagious. But, Jewel, we're good friends. I'm not sure what this would do to our friendship. And I'm very happy where I am."

"But you promise you'll think about it?" Jewel urged. "This isn't a brush-off, is it? Level with me."

Edward laughed. "Calm down, darlin'. Look, I'll have to think long and hard about it. I can't give you an answer anytime soon."

"But you *will* think about it."

"Yes," he sighed. "I promise."

"Hurray," Amber, almost four, said, as the waiter appeared with their plates. "The food's here."

"What color would you like your office painted?" Jewel grinned, stamping out her cigarette.

"Jewel," Edward laughed, exasperated. "You're really too much. I don't know how Allen puts up with you these days."

"Neither do I."

In truth, Jewel *didn't* know how Allen put up with her; their life was so hectic. But she was going to change. If Edward came to Bijoux, she would have more time. She knew she was doing too much—not that she didn't enjoy every minute of it.

But Allen had made it all possible, had made it all happen so fast. She owed him everything. For his sake, she would try to tame her ferocious ambition and become a more conventional wife. Of course, that would have to be down the road a bit. First, Jewel had to make Bijoux a raging success, to repay Allen every penny he had given her to open the Fifth Avenue store.

Jewel hated being in debt to anyone, even her husband.

24

1978

When Edward finally came to work for Jewel, a full two years later, Harry Harper called her to have lunch.

They met at La Côte Basque, a block away from Bijoux.

Harry stood up as Jewel approached the table. He was dressed dashingly as always, in a charcoal gray pinstripe of his own design, with a purple silk scarf tucked casually into his breast pocket. Jewel smiled, expecting the usual suave seduction.

He surprised her. "What will you have for lunch, Jewel?" he said, coldly ignoring the cheek she presented for a kiss. "A hand? That's what you do, isn't it, bite the hand that feeds you?"

"Harry, what is it? If it's about Edward . . ."

" 'If it's about Edward,' " he mocked, resuming his seat. "Good God, Jewel, what do you think? That I can take this with a smile? It's not merely losing Edward," he said. "It's the way you did it. Buying him off."

"I did not!" Jewel snapped. "I needed a partner. Someone I could trust."

"Yes, well I thought I could trust him. And you." Harry looked at his watch. "Let's order. I have to be back at the office in forty-five minutes."

"Oh, Harry, don't be angry. You knew this would happen sooner or later. And the bottom line is, you don't need Edward as much as I do."

"I don't believe you're handing me this shit," he said. "Who says I don't need him?" He paused. "In my menswear division, Edward had carte blanche to make decisions. I wonder, at Bijoux, is he willing to let you run the whole show?"

"What makes you think I'd do that?"

"Because that's the way you are, Jewel. That's the way you have been and always will be," Harry said.

Jewel shrugged. "Well, of course, Edward understands that I'm the motivating force behind Bijoux. He understands that, from the word go. But we both know Edward's creative and professional enough to carve out his own special niche within the company. I'm not going to step on his toes."

"Well, tell him for me that we'll keep his chair warm. You'll drive him crazy. You drive everybody else crazy."

"Yes? And what's that supposed to mean? Who have you been talking to?"

Harry shrugged and remained silent.

"Oh, Harry, you knew it was only a matter of time before Edward joined me. It was a hard decision for him. And, I'll admit, I did press a bit," Jewel said. "Really, I had no idea you'd take it so hard. You're in Fortune 500 now. You have tons of people working for you." She lit a cigarette. "Look, darling, I owe you a favor. I won't forget it."

"As I see it, you owe me more than one favor. You were

scrounging around Soho when you met me. Designing the
jewelry for my collection was your springboard into the
big time. I introduced you to everyone. I got Vivian to
jump on your bandwagon."

Jewel was becoming annoyed. She had looked forward
to a flirtatious lunch, and now it turned out Harry wanted
her to kiss ass. "Of course I owe you a lot. Don't I give
Vivian discounts? Don't I bring your daughters nonpareils
every time we come for dinner? Don't I buy your clothes
exclusively?" She glanced down at what she was wearing,
a Mary McFadden, and laughed. "Oh come on, darling, is
it Edward that's really bothering you? Or is it something
else? Let's get it out in the open."

"It's you, Jewel. You're what's bothering me," Harry
said, digging a fork into the lobster that the waiter had set
in front of him. "Sometimes I think I know you, but other
times I realize I don't have the first clue of what goes on
deep down inside you. You can be candid and fair on the
surface, but I never know what's lurking underneath.
You're such an enigma that I can't let you go. Yes, I'm
pissed that you took Edward away from me. And
Cathalene tells me you're a tyrant to work for."

"Cathalene?" Jewel interrupted. "Where the hell does
she come in?"

"She's a sweet girl. I buy her lunch every once in a
while."

Jewel took a sip of her Perrier and pushed her plate of
uneaten scallop salad to the middle of the table.
"Cathalene's as sweet as deadly nightshade. You should
recognize that, Harry. I keep her on because she's talented. But I know where she's coming from. She's jealous
of me. Possibly she hates me. Mostly, I think, she wants to
be me. I see Cathalene with my eyes wide open. She's as
ambitious as I am. As far as the future of Bijoux is concerned, *she* is a limited edition."

"You're booting her out?" Harry asked.

"No, not at all. I'm waiting for her to go out on her

own. Which she'll do sooner or later. I'm sure of it. Anything I can do she'd like to do better. And she'd absolutely jump at the chance to go to bed with you. But I'll warn you . . . she won't stop at that."

"I don't believe I'm hearing this. Why are you bad-mouthing Cathalene? She's damned loyal to you."

"How do you know that? Have you already tried to get her away from Bijoux in retaliation for Edward?"

Harry shrugged. "I'm above retaliation. You say you see Cathalene with your eyes open? Then see how much she idolizes you. She'd never stab you in the back."

"Hmmm, she's already got you in her pocket, Harry. Watch out for . . ."

"Harry! This saves me the trip down to Thirty-seventh Street." A trim, fiftyish man with thick, froggy features, well turned out in a gray Armani suit, stopped at the table. He smiled at Jewel. "Sorry, didn't mean to interrupt what you were saying."

"You two know each other?" Harry said without enthusiasm. "Jewel Prescott—Neil Tavlos."

"How do you do?" Jewel said. "You own the Pierre Chance boutiques."

He nodded. "And you are Madame Bijoux. I've wanted to meet you." He turned to Harper. "Tell me if I'm interrupting. May I join you?"

"Have a seat," Harry said. He and Neil Tavlos were friendly rivals. They each wanted to buy out the other, but neither was budging.

"I hear you're launching a Pierre Chance fragrance," Jewel said. "Tell me, did you license out the name?"

"Nope. Started a whole new division to manufacture and market the stuff. Bigger profits."

Jewel perked up. Somewhere down the line she wanted a Bijoux fragrance. "Oh? I'd love to hear more about it."

"Yes, well," Tavlos reached into his wallet and handed her a business card, "call me. I'll be more than happy to tell you about it. In fact, let me take you to lunch."

"I'd love it." Jewel dropped the card in her handbag. "I'd better be going. Thanks for lunch, Harry. And don't be mad, darling. I'll pick up the check next time and we'll finish our chat." She smiled. "Nice to meet you, Mr. Tavlos."

"Neil," he corrected. "The pleasure was certainly mine."

"See you, Jewel," Harry said. "And relax. You're paranoid about Cathalene."

Paranoid, indeed! Jewel thought, as she walked back to Bijoux. The sophisticated Harry Harper was as naive as a horny teenager when it came to women like Cathalene Columbier.

But maybe he deserved her, if indeed he had offered her a job. Cathalene as a direct rival might be better than Cathalene underfoot, always trying to see what Jewel was up to, always playing up to her.

On the other hand, Harry Harper was *her* ally. Why not make Cathalene come up with someone on her own?

"Jewel, darling." Allen handed her a cup of black filtered coffee, waking her out of a deep sleep. "Room service."

"God, what time is it?" Jewel said, disoriented. Outside, it was dark; the streetlights were still on.

"Five-fifteen. But I needed to talk to you before I take off . . . since we missed each other last night." He was heading to Tulsa to visit his mother, taking Nushka and the girls with him. For some reason, unfathomed by Jewel, Amber and Beryl, now nearly six and five, liked LaDonna Prescott, and the old crone seemed to enjoy them too. Besides, Jewel didn't mind these forays home that Allen took every few months. They gave her more time to work without feeling guilty.

"When I get back," Allen continued, "I want us to get away for a holiday. We haven't had a real one since our honeymoon. And this time I want it to be just the two of us. I spoke to Nushka. She'll handle things while we're away." Allen pulled down the lace-trimmed sheet and began to fondle Jewel's breasts through her satin gown. "Christie's is having a major sale of early-twentieth-century paintings next week. I thought we could go over and play in London for a few days while I do the auction. Then we'll head to Wales or Scotland and relax." He leaned over and kissed her forehead. "And get to know each other again. We've both been running overtime."

"Sounds good," Jewel said sleepily. "But next week? I couldn't possibly . . ."

"That's what you say every time I suggest we get away," Allen snapped. "The children and I will be out of your hair for seven days. You can work the entire fucking time. But *next* week, you're going to London with me. No buts . . . just clear your schedule and do it."

"Oh God," Jewel said, "it seems like everybody's mad at me these days. I'm only trying to make a living."

"You don't *have* to make a living. You married me," Allen said. "And if you want to stay married, I suggest you try harder to be a wife. Oh shit, Jewel . . ." He put his arms around her. "I love you. But I want to see you more often. Once a week, from now on, I want us to set aside an evening to go out, just the two of us. If this marriage is going to survive, you've got to put some effort into it." He glanced at the metal art deco clock on the night table. "Okay, I have to go. I'll make all the arrangements for the trip. Figure we'll be gone two weeks."

Jewel started to protest but sighed instead. "Okay, darling, whatever you say." She raised her hand and gently stroked Allen's cheek. "You're right, we haven't spent much time together lately." Allen smiled back. "I'm glad you approve. I'd better be going. The car's waiting."

"Have a good trip," Jewel said, grabbing her silk kimono. "Wait . . . I want to kiss the girls good-bye. And Allen . . ." she said, flipping rapidly through the calendar that was implanted in her brain, "could we make it ten days instead? The catalog's due to go to the printer's on the twenty-first. I have to check—"

"Okay . . . okay," Allen said, "ten days is better than nothing."

It was a typical morning at Bijoux. After Jewel arrived at the office she spent forty-five minutes with a Texan discussing the resetting of her twelve-carat canary diamond ring into a necklace, conducted a meeting of the staff and resident designers, returned calls, and consulted with her gemologist, Erik Sanders, about his upcoming buying trip to Brazil. Then she headed over to "21" to meet Neil Tavlos for lunch.

"Jewel," Neil Tavlos said, rising from the table to greet her. "I'm so glad you called. I've been looking forward to this. You have quite a knack for what you do. I should know. The soon-to-be-*ex* Mrs. Tavlos has spent quite a bundle of my money in your store."

"Really? I keep close track of our customers. I don't remember . . ."

"She's an actress. Goes under the name of Leslie Scott."

"Oh, of course. Yes, she's mad about my collector's pieces. Oh dear. Do give her a generous settlement or I'll lose one of my best customers," Jewel said.

"Ah, for you, anything," Neil laughed. "This is the first time I've laughed over this divorce. It's been a hell of a mess. No kids—you'd think it'd be simple."

"I guess it never is."

"You been divorced?"

"Widowed. My current husband adopted my two children. I'm very lucky. Oh, by the way," she said, getting to the point, "did you bring a sample of your new fragrance? I'm dying to try it."

Neil reached into his breast pocket and brought out a small tester bottle, plain with no label. Jewel stretched out her wrist for Neil to squirt it with perfume. Then, rubbing her wrists together, she sniffed and closed her eyes to let the aroma surround her.

"Hmmm, it reminds me of early spring . . . daffodils, hyacinths, lily of the valley, and field grasses. Oh, Neil, it's delicious. I like it!"

Neil Tavlos beamed. "You've got a damned good nose, Jewel. That's exactly what we wanted, spring. We have a youthful audience for our clothes, so we wanted a young scent. In the perfume circles, they call it a 'green' fragrance."

"Yes," Jewel nodded, "I know. I've been reading up on it . . . doing my preliminary research. I already know what I want Bijoux to smell like. Rubies. The most expensive gems in the world. Rich, refined, sensual, full of history and romance." She stopped. "Oh goodness, I tend to go on and on about my ideas. You must forgive me."

"There's nothing to forgive. You're a bright woman, Jewel," Neil smiled.

Over steak tartare, they chatted lightly—mostly about the current theatrical season, as Tavlos, it turned out, dabbled in backing plays.

And later, over coffee, Neil said, "Listen, Jewel . . . I have an idea. I told you I started my own company to market our fragrance. Why don't we do yours? It'll save you a hell of a lot of money, and we're set up with distribution. You're not going to be a mass-market fragrance, neither are we. We're distributing in our shops and only the top department stores. It's all there for you, including the manufacturing."

"Sounds interesting," Jewel said casually. It was what she'd had in mind all along, but she wasn't going to be the one to bring it up. "Of course, I'd have to toss the idea around a bit with my partner, Edward Randolph. Look at the figures."

Neil handed the waiter his American Express Gold Card. "Take your time. Sit with it. It's merely an idea— one that could be lucrative for both of us."

"I will think about it, Neil. And thanks for lunch."

He took her hand, raised it to his lips and kissed it. "Jewel, you are well named. We'll do this again soon."

When Jewel arrived back at the office, she dropped in on Edward to report on her conversation with Neil Tavlos.

"We may not want to do this," she said excitedly, "but it's an option. It's fantastic, really, the way it's fallen into our laps. Bijoux, the fragrance . . . in all the top stores. What great advertising!"

Edward leaned back in his chair, shaking his head doubtfully. "How do you suppose Harper'll take it? He and Neil are rivals, even if they are cordial. And he feels territorial when it comes to you."

"Harry doesn't figure into it at all," Jewel said offhandedly. "What the hell do I care what he thinks? Business is business. That's what he always tells me."

"Okay, do what you want about the fragrance. But tell Harry yourself. Don't let him hear gossip. He's still pretty touchy because of my defection," Edward counseled.

"All right. I promise. I'll let Harry know after I've made up my mind."

"Good. When are you takin' off for London?"

Jewel looked puzzled. "How'd you know about that?"

"Had lunch with Allen yesterday. He told me he planned to lure you away on a holiday. Wanted to know if this place would survive without you. I assured him it would . . . if he didn't keep you away too long."

"We compromised on ten days. It's really a shitty time for me, but . . ."

Edward went over and closed his door. "Allen adores you, Jewel. You have to be more considerate of his feelings . . . and his needs."

"I am! Didn't you see the watch I designed and had made for his birthday? Eat your heart out, Rolex. And besides . . ."

"Look, honey," Edward broke in. "I'm not accusin' you of anything. I'm merely sayin' that the guy loves you. Maybe you love him too, but you don't show it."

"Did he come crying on your shoulder? Is that what your lunch was all about?" Jewel said, annoyed.

"No. You know Allen wouldn't do that. I'm givin' you the benefit of my observations as a longtime friend. Take it or leave it. I happen to like Allen a hell of a lot. He's a decent guy and he deserves . . ."

"Someone nicer and *more* decent than me?" Jewel snapped. "God, I *am* nice, but I'm busy. You know that; you work as hard as I do. We're building an empire here, and that takes a hell of a lot of work," Jewel said breathlessly. "Allen can't understand because he *doesn't* work. He spends all his time going to auctions and art galleries. God, we're running out of wall space. But he's not making money . . . he *fritters* it away! He tells me I don't have to work, but if you knew what he goes through in a year— well, thank God I *do* work. One of these days I'll be supporting him."

"Remember to *breathe* when you talk, Jewel. And you can lower your voice," Edward said. "I'm not attackin' you. I was merely givin' you some advice. I understand you, darlin'. And it doesn't upset *me* that you work so hard." He smiled. "Look, since Allen's away, why don't we have a drink after work? We haven't done that for ages."

"*After* work? You must be joking. If I'm going to let Allen cart me off for ten days I have to bust my ass this week. No time to relax."

"Calm down, darlin'. You're pushin' yourself too hard. It isn't necessary."

"Oh isn't it? Edward, I'd have thought you would understand," Jewel fumed. "I've still got a lot to prove. And I will."

Edward leaned back in his chair and expelled a deep

breath. "Jewel, you're a success now. What more do you want?"

"To be a *bigger* success."

Jewel and Allen went on vacation as scheduled. They spent the first part in London, which Jewel enjoyed. She visited museums and checked out the jewelry competition while Allen enriched his art collection with three prewar Russian canvases bought at auction, and a Roger de la Fresnaye and a very good Kokoschka that he acquired from an alcoholic, down-at-the-heels nobleman who was selling the family heirlooms.

Then they took a slow train through the English countryside to Wales, for a week of idyllic idling. Jewel found it enchanting—for about two days. After that the strain of relaxation began to tell on her. Allen's driving terrified her. He could not seem to get used to driving on the left-hand side of the road, and Jewel spent most of the tour oblivious to the gorgeous Welsh scenery, screaming "Watch out!" and slamming her foot onto phantom brakes, until Allen finally pulled over alongside a rolling green meadow where several dozen sheep grazed.

"Here," he said, "*you* do it."

"No, I just meant . . ."

"No," Allen insisted. "I'm sure you'd do a much better job."

So Jewel slid over behind the wheel (it *did* seem peculiar, having it on the wrong side of the car), and Allen settled happily into her former role; for the rest of the day it was he who got to scream Watch out!

They stayed in a beautiful old manor house in Llandudno, on the Creuddyn peninsula in North Wales, and made their daily forays from there. The place was called Bodysgallen Hall. It was an imposing historical mansion, a huge building with stone cottages around it that were adorned with ivy and exotic names (the Prescotts were in one called Pineapple Cottage).

From there each morning, after a hearty Welsh breakfast for Allen and toast and coffee for Jewel, they would collect a lavish picnic prepared in the kitchens—roast pheasant, hare pâté, marinated vegetables, freshly baked bread and pastries, all fitted into a wicker hamper—and roam the lush, hilly, sheep-dotted countryside. They visited woolen mills, and inspected magnificent crumbling old castles, such as Caernarfon in Gwynedd, built by Edward I in the thirteenth century to defend the outposts of his realm. They sat in colorful country pubs, drinking stout or brandy and listening to the people around them speaking the Welsh language, totally foreign from English, musical and fascinating.

When it rained, they stayed inside, bathed together in the large tub and then fell back into bed to make leisurely love. When the rain stopped they strolled out through the vast formal gardens and intricate shrub maze that were the pride of Bodysgallen Hall.

Still, Jewel was bored. She wanted to return to London for some city action.

"But sweetheart," Allen pleaded, exasperated, "the point of a vacation is to relax. To not *have* to do anything."

"Maybe you don't, but *I* do. Sitting around counting sheep is amusing for a bit . . . and it is bucolic and all that. But we've *done* it. If we went back to London we could catch some more shows."

Allen frowned. "I'd hoped that spending some *quiet* time together would get us back on track. We were very much in touch in the beginning, but it's been a long time now. Oh hell, maybe it's not worth it." Allen sat down sulkily on a stone wall. "You know I'm proud of you, Jewel," he sighed, "and of your success. But you're so busy dealing with the world at large there's no time left for anything personal. You never touch me anymore."

"What?" Jewel snapped. "We've made love every day since we left New York."

"That's not what I mean. You never take time to kiss me on the cheek anymore. Or put your hand on my shoulder. Or look up and smile at me. You treat me like a business colleague, just another person on your daily agenda. We can't go on like this," he said seriously. "At least *I* can't."

Jewel took a deep breath and sat down next to him on the garden wall. "Well, darling, let's face it. Running a marriage is a lot like running a corporation. I mean, there're so many details to be dealt with every day . . . the children, the help, money, entertaining, keeping it all going smoothly. And then there's Bijoux. I'm sorry I don't touch you enough. But I'm busy. And you're busy too. *I'm* not the only one," she sniffed indignantly. "You're always off in search of another *acquisition.*"

"So that's how you think of us? As business partners who happen to fuck from time to time?"

"No. I'm not that cold-blooded. But I do feel we're partners . . . in the best possible way. We make a good team, Allen. I don't see why you can't appreciate it and be grateful for what we have. We're a hell of a lot happier than most of our friends who flit around from lover to lover," she said. (Not that she hadn't *considered* taking a lover. But there wasn't enough time in the day as it was. How could she ever fit illicit sex into the schedule?)

Allen shrugged. "I suppose you have a point. Oh, Jewel, I'm not saying I'm not happy. I only want you not to be preoccupied about work during the time we spend together."

Jewel smiled and kissed Allen's cheek. The crisis was passing, she could tell; they had been having variations of this conversation for years now. And she knew everything would be fine if she could be more politic; she did not give in to Allen often enough.

"All right," she said, "I can handle it. From now on I'll make a real effort to leave the office at the office."

"Good, that's a start," Allen nodded. "Now what about London? Do you still want to head back?"

"No. I'm sorry, I guess the weather's been getting me down. Actually, it's quite pleasant here." Jewel slipped on her dark glasses as the sun broke suddenly through the leaden bank of clouds. "You were right to drag me away. It clears the head. And," she added, squeezing her husband's balls coquettishly, "the body too."

Allen grinned, his anger faded. "I'm sorry about the weather. Next time we'll go someplace sunny. Will you promise we'll do this more often? Or do I have to get it in writing?"

"You won't have to have your lawyer draw it up, I promise," Jewel said, in a conscious attempt to lighten her mood. "I mean . . . *look* at these roses," directing his attention toward a cul-de-sac garden of tree roses bearing a plethora of fragrant white flowers. "You know, it might be fun to have a house in the country someday. With a wonderful garden that I'll tend myself. Maybe that's what I'll do in my old age."

Allen put his arm around Jewel and pulled her close to him. "I can see us having a house in the country. I can see us having ye olde English garden. But in a million years I can't see you putting trowel to dirt."

"But I'd be a *fabulous* gardener. If I had time."

"That's what I mean. How am I going to drag you off to the country house when it's taken all this time to get you to take a vacation?"

"Well, a country house would be easier to get to."

"What? You mean you're really serious about this?"

"Yes, I mean, we could start *looking*. You know, it'd be wonderful for the children and Nushka to spend the summers in the country. Now that they're getting bigger, the girls need that balance in their life. And we'd go for weekends. Of course, that means we'll have to teach Nushka to drive." The idea of Nushka driving a car, with her squat body and short fat legs, made Jewel laugh. "Do you think she could master it at her age?"

Allen laughed. "It's not her age I'm worried about, it's whether she could see over the steering wheel. I think I'd feel safer giving them a car and driver."

They strolled around the gardens, sparkling in the late sunshine after the rain, and talked about where they would buy their country house. Allen was partial to Connecticut. Jewel favored the eastern end of Long Island. She remembered the week in Southampton before Anna was married and how much she had loved the wide, white-sand beaches along the Atlantic. She knew she was secure enough within herself and her own success to handle running into the McNeills, if that ever happened. But she was beginning to think it wouldn't. New York was a bigger city than she had given it credit for in the beginning.

"Up around Roxbury . . . over toward the western part of the state . . . is really quite nice," Allen said, re-opening his campaign for Connecticut. "It's under two hours from the city, and the traffic's nothing like the Long Island Expressway. You know, I think a country house is a great idea, Jewel. More wall space to fill," he chuckled.

Then a thought came to her. "You know, darling, it really doesn't matter to me where we buy a house." It really didn't, and if she could please Allen by letting *him* make the choice it would make him happy. After all, he'd be much more docile about being left alone for a weekend in a place of his own choosing. And there was no way that she'd have time to spend *every* weekend in the country. "I think I *love* the idea of Connecticut. And the children have plenty of friends to visit at the beach. We don't need to live there."

Allen smiled. "Sometimes you amaze me, Jewel. I was digging in my heels for a fight, and you've surrendered before the first battle."

"It's the new relaxed, easygoing me," Jewel said. "Get used to it."

"I think I could," Allen laughed. "Come on. It's tea-time."

They headed back to Pineapple Cottage, holding hands and discussing what their perfect country place would be like.

Book Two

1979–Present

25

Of course there was nothing for Allen to get used to: the new relaxed, easygoing Jewel did not happen. He began to fear it never would.

It was not until 1981, three years after their holiday in Wales, that they found the perfect country place in Connecticut—a hundred-acre farm, with sheep, weathered-wood barns, stone outbuildings that would be transformed into guest cottages, and a rambling, two-storied frame house, part of which dated to 1790. It needed massive renovation, and Allen decided to design and oversee the work himself, while Jewel continued to dig her heels into expanding Bijoux.

Jewel loved having Allen so totally occupied with his renovating and art collecting. He was as busy as she; she didn't have to feel guilty.

She entered into a deal with Neil Tavlos for the development and manufacture of her fragrance, to Harry Harper's displeasure. However, Jewel followed Edward's advice and told Harry about it ahead of time, so as not to ruffle his feathers more than necessary. Then, making Katrina and Christof partner-managers, she opened a chic Bijoux-Paris on the Boulevard St.-Germain. After that, she launched Bijoux-Honolulu with her designer Leilani, and Bijoux-Beverly Hills on Rodeo Drive with an old friend of Allen's. Plans were underway for Bijoux stores in London, Dallas, Houston, Chicago, Atlanta, and San Francisco.

Although Jewel took on limited partners for each of the stores, she still retained controlling interest. Each Bijoux had to conform to a certain look. Each had to chip in to the national advertising budget. Only the best-quality gems and raw materials were to be used, and Jewel and Edward devised strict controls. Her gemologists—there were now three—traveled the North and South American continents, as well as Africa and Asia, to buy gemstones for the Bijoux designers.

Jewel licensed a manufacturing company in New Jersey to produce her line of inexpensive designs—executed in gold and silver alloys, with synthetic stones—to be called Bijoux Too.

The catalog business took off, and Jewel expanded her office space into two more floors above the original Bijoux offices. She and Edward hired more people—to run the marketing and direct-mail divisions and to produce their own in-house advertising.

When that was all running smoothly, Jewel talked Edward into overseeing an atelier of apprentices. They worked out a program with the country's top universities and design schools to bring in the most promising students (a limit of three each year) to create jewelry in the Bijoux workshops for a summer. At the end of their stint, in late August before the students returned to school, Bijoux threw an elegant "summershow" party to display the students' work. The most talented were promised jobs at Bijoux when they graduated. Bijoux—and Jewel—received a great deal of favorable press for the program.

After that, Jewel researched and wrote a book on the folklore and reputed healing qualities of gemstones. When it was completed, her publisher sent her on a lecture tour around the country: more publicity for Jewel and Bijoux.

Finally in the fall of 1985, after several setbacks, the perfume Bijoux was finally launched, at a gala party in the gem and mineral hall of the Museum of Natural History. Sales for the fragrance exceeded Jewel's and Neil Tavlos's wildest projections. The direct-mail business quadrupled, and plans were underway for issuing monthly, rather than quarterly, mail-order catalogs. Jewel looked ahead and saw a tranquil sea. All was going so smoothly.

Except there wasn't enough time in any given day to get everything done. On the home front, Nushka continued to manage things under Jewel's erratically watchful eye. But the girls were growing up mostly without her. Amber was now twelve and Beryl, eleven. They had nearly reached their full height, did reasonably well in school, and were quite accustomed to the luxury of their lives. If Jewel failed to give them a great deal of her time, she never went back on her promise that her daughters would have everything she herself lacked in her own childhood.

Yes, the girls were given everything they wanted. But what they wanted most was a mother to be there when they needed her. Amber, especially, was beginning to resent Jewel's ambition.

One evening in year 1986, Jewel rushed home, late as usual. She and Allen were expected at a dinner party at Harry and Vivian Harper's. Before going upstairs to dress, she poked her head into the library where Amber and Beryl were doing their homework.

"Oh, hi, Mummie!" Beryl said, getting up to give her a hug. "Daddy's already dressed. He's watching the news. I wish you didn't have to go out tonight."

"Oh, I know," Jewel said, kissing her younger daughter. "Me too. But we'll have the weekend together."

"Don't you remember? I'm going to Quoque with Emily and her parents."

"Oh, that's right. Well," she said to Amber, who was still hunched over her schoolwork, "we'll do something fun, just the two of us, on Saturday."

"I have a basketball game," Amber said, without looking up, "and then the coach is taking the team back to her place for a pizza party."

"Oh? But I'd left the weekend open, to spend time with you."

"You should've checked with us first. We have lives too," Amber snapped.

"Amber Prescott! Just what do you mean by that?"

"That you never *think* to find out what we're doing. And remember? The school craft show was this afternoon. You didn't show up."

"Oh God. Oh, sweetie, I'm sorry. The day just got away from me," Jewel said. "Was it fun? Did you buy anything?"

"Yeah," Amber said. "We bought some cooking stuff for Nushka."

"Jewel?" Allen called from the stairs. "Are you going dressed like that?"

"No. It'll just take me a minute to change."

"Well, hurry it up. We're due five minutes ago."

Jewel looked back at her daughters. "Come on up and chat while I get dressed."

"Sure," Beryl said.

"I have too much homework," Amber said, turning away.

And so it went.

Edward came into Jewel's office, as was his morning custom, to have a cup of espresso and go over the day's events.

"You know," he said to her, when they had finished discussing business, "it's so ironic. Here we are, makin' money like crazy and there's no time to spend it."

"Well, you're exactly like me," Jewel said. "We both love to work. We hate the idea of vacations, and yet when Peter drags you off or Allen makes me go somewhere, it's okay. I can adjust. It's the *idea* of leaving that I hate. There never seems to be a perfect time." She went over to the wall calendar. "But you're well overdue. Set aside some time and just go. We can manage."

"Well, Peter's been talkin' a lot about Greece."

"Then do it."

"Okay," Edward nodded. "I will. Peter will be delighted. Think the place can last three weeks without me?"

"No, but we'll try. You need a rest."

Edward paused. "There's something I have to talk to you about. The time never seems right, but . . ."

"Okay." Jewel glanced at her watch. "I have a couple of minutes. Is this something serious?"

"Well, sort of," Edward said, heading over to close the door.

"Oh God, I feel a lecture coming on." Jewel buzzed Meg Higdon, her secretary, and told her to hold the calls. Then she walked around and sat on the edge of her desk, opposite Edward. "All right . . . what's wrong? Which one of the staff have I insulted this time?"

"It's not anything you've done."

"Well, that's a relief. But what is it? Why the closed door?"

"I, er, I saw Sascha the other day," Edward began, testing the waters.

"Oh? Where?" Jewel's voice turned icy.

"We had lunch, actually."

"What!" she shrieked.

"He called me."

"Sascha called *you?* Why on earth? The bastard certainly doesn't need a job." Sascha had joined Tiffany &

Co. in the early eighties, as one of their chief designers. Jewel's hatred had mushroomed since then, as he became more famous. She had been known to go through fashion magazines, tearing into shreds the pages that featured his jewelry.

"No, he's doin' great at Tiffany. Actually, he's called me a number of times over the past few years. I always put him off out of loyalty to you. But I couldn't any longer."

Edward took a deep breath. "Jewel, Sascha wants to see the girls. He wants 'em to know he's their father. He wants . . ."

"Hell, he wants to walk back into my life and mess it up!" Jewel said. "You know the girls think Allen's their father. And that's how it should be. He's the one who's been a father to them."

"They love Allen," Edward said. "They'd love him just as much if they *knew* he'd adopted them. But, honey, I think they have a right to know who their real father is. It isn't as if he's down-and-out somewhere. He's successful . . . wealthy. He and Aïna own a house in Westchester."

"How lovely for them. And thank you for sharing all this with me, Edward," Jewel said crossly. "But you can tell your friend that I don't want my daughters finding out that they're illegitimate. Sascha lied to me. He has no rights whatever, legal or moral."

"Look, don't jump down *my* throat," Edward said, getting angry. "After all this time you should be able to let go of this bitterness. Sascha loved you. He just made a mistake. We all make mistakes."

"You call lying to me, marrying me when he already had a wife, fathering two illegitimate children, a fucking *mistake?* He's lucky I didn't send him to jail for bigamy. He's lucky I didn't have him deported. I owe Sascha *nothing,* absolutely nothing. And he's not getting his hands on my children!" Jewel paused, breathing heavily. "God, I can't believe he came to you. He couldn't *stand* you. You should've heard the things he used to say . . ."

Edward stood and headed for the door. "Okay, Jewel, that's enough. Subject closed, for the time bein'. I just wish you'd think about it."

"Tell Sascha for me," Jewel seethed, "that if he ever tries to see Amber or Beryl I'll have him before a judge as fast as you can say 'double agent.' "

"Oh come on, Jewel. Be reasonable. Sascha's no spy."

"If he comes near the kids I'll say *anything* to have him thrown out of this country! You tell him that. And who do you think they'll believe, him or me?"

"You're making a big mistake, Jewel. Where's your compassion?"

"I have no compassion!" Jewel screamed. "Not when it comes to Sascha."

"You're wrong, Jewel. You've come far enough to be able to forgive him. Look at all you have now."

"If you bring the subject up again, Edward, I'll fire you," she said hatefully. "I mean, I'll buy out your share of Bijoux."

"God, you're fuckin' impossible!" Edward walked out, slamming the door behind him.

Jewel reached for a cigarette and lit it, her hand shaking with emotion.

It was the first serious fight she had ever had with Edward, but she was livid that he'd try to butt into her private affairs. She leaned back in her chair and sucked angrily on the cigarette, replaying the scene. Of course she realized that there was no rationale for her being so angry with Sascha Robinovsky after all these years. Yet the idea of his seeing Amber and Beryl, of *them* knowing the truth, caused a rage to well up within her that was totally unreasonable.

Her head throbbed with a pain that started at the base of her skull and shot hot darts up behind her eyes. Jewel leaned her elbows on her desk and cradled her head in her hands, waiting for the worst of it to pass. Then she buzzed Meg.

"Aspirin, Meg. And telephone my husband. Tell him I can't make the fund raiser for the public library tonight. I have to put the finishing touches on the spring catalog."

"Okay, Ms. Prescott. Your ten o'clock is waiting. Rita Roberts."

"What? Who's that?"

"Mr. Randolph wanted you to see her."

"Oh shit. That daughter of some friend of his. Okay Meg, you sit in on this too. But first, call and get two first-class tickets to Athens. Have them delivered to Mr. Randolph with a red rose and a note. No. Skip the note. He'll know what it's about. Okay . . . send in what's-her-name. I want to get this over fast."

Rita Roberts appeared in Jewel's office several moments later. She was startlingly tiny, yet not a midget. Her hair, obviously inspired by Cyndi Lauper, was crew cut on one side, shoulder length on the other, in shades of red and purple, and partially covered by a gray fedora. The outfit —a leopard-print leotard, several ruffled blue petticoats, zebra-striped tights, and a black coat that reached the ground—combined with her smallness to give her a comical appearance: something like Toulouse-Lautrec crossed with Jane Avril. Her makeup was a tribute to Technicolor movies of the fifties, primary colors with a bit too much yellow washed over them. Her black portfolio was plastered with stickers of Disney characters. Under her arm was a large brown Dewar's scotch box tied with string.

"Okay, come over here. I'm Jewel Prescott. Spread everything on this table. We have to make it quick."

Meg entered the room. Jewel's eyes met Meg's, high above Rita, and they exchanged a "has-Edward-gone-bananas?" glance.

"This is sure some office," Rita said as she unpacked the jewelry she had carefully wrapped in purple tissue paper. Her voice was Southern, gentle and melodic. It clashed with the fashion statement she projected. "I really appreciate your takin' the time to see me, Ms. Prescott. This is the most excitin' day of my life. I met Edward because my mother went to Mary Baldwin with his sister. That's a college in Virginia."

"Hmmm . . . yes, that's nice," Jewel acknowledged impatiently. "Please understand, I have only a minute."

"I work in reactive materials . . . titanium, tantalum, niobium," Rita explained, then apologized. "I'm sorry. I don't need to explain it to you. You mixed niobium with iolite and garnets in your 1983 collection . . ."

"It was 1984," Jewel corrected, picking up a necklace that seemed to pop out at her. The pieces—geometric shapes strung together with crystal beads—were brilliant examples of what could be achieved when certain metals were exposed to intense heat or charged with electrical current. In Rita's work, the metal's dull gray surface had been transformed into hues that glowed almost neon, yet with a subtle, ethereal beauty.

"How did you get this luster?" Jewel asked. "It's quite unusual."

Rita smiled, almost sheepishly. "Well, I tried somethin' one night. Just to be silly. I put a scrap of titanium under a pyramid that a friend had made out of toothpicks . . ."

"Toothpicks!" Meg said, scrutinizing some earrings, obviously taken with Rita's collection.

"Yeah, as long as it has the proper angles it doesn't much matter what you make a pyramid out of . . ."

"Are you trying to tell me," Jewel interrupted, "that a *pyramid* did this?"

Rita nodded. "Well, yes. I mean, I still expose the metals to heat. But first they spend a day in the pyramid. Don't ask me to explain. The pyramid just does somethin' different to them."

"Well, remind me to send you all my dull razor blades," Jewel said, flipping through Rita's portfolio. The girl had talent; Edward was right, as usual. "Okay. Your work shows real promise. If Edward can find room, you might as well try it here for a while. We'll touch base in a few months and see how it's working out." Jewel extended her hand. "And now I have to go."

Rita shook Jewel's hand, flabbergasted. "Er, thank you. Does that mean I actually have a job at Bijoux?"

"If Edward can find a nook. He'll discuss salary. It won't be much to start."

"I'd work for free! I mean it."

"That won't be necessary," Jewel said.

As Meg steered Rita to the door, Jewel called out. "Rita dear . . . do us all a favor and try dressing a bit more monochromatically. And . . . get rid of the hat."

Jewel returned to her day. She hoped Allen wouldn't be too furious about the public library benefit.

There was a quick rap on her door. "Come in," she called out, wondering where Meg was.

Mike Marshall, Jewel's newest in-house advertising director, entered, closing the door behind him. He walked over to her and planted a kiss on her cheek. "Hello, darling," he said. "I just stopped by to remind you we have to work late tonight."

"I haven't forgotten. I had to cancel a benefit with Allen."

"Oh darn. Too bad. I thought maybe we'd better work at my place again, seeing as how we'll be up so late," he said, grinning.

Jewel grinned back and stood to let him kiss her, this time on the lips, passionately. God, the guy had it. He made her springs springy again.

"I'd better tell Allen not to wait up," she whispered.

"I wish you'd tell him you won't be home at all," Mike said, running his hands down her back.

"You know I can't do that. Anyway, at the end of the month, the San Francisco store's opening. Allen's too busy to come, and Edward will be in Greece. We'll have five days together . . . more or less away from watchful eyes."

There was a knock on the door. Quickly, she pulled away from Mike, and he scooted around the desk and dropped into a chair. "Come in," she said, in her most businesslike voice.

Meg entered. "Oh, hi, Mr. Marshall. Sorry to bother you, but I have some stuff for you to sign, Ms. Prescott. The Federal Express man is waiting for it."

"Well, I have to get back to my office anyway," Mike said, standing. "You won't forget tonight, will you? Putting the spring catalog to bed?" he said, smiling behind Meg's back as he exited.

Jewel smiled back. "I won't. But let's try to make it an early evening," she said, for Meg's benefit.

No one knew it, but she had finally allotted time in her schedule for a lover. Not that she loved Mike Marshall, but there was a passionate chemistry between them. And it was so convenient, working under the same roof, traveling together.

There was excitement in the danger involved, in keeping it a secret.

There was excitement in the sex.

And there was plenty of it.

26

1987

As the years flew by, the Connecticut house had been added onto several times by Allen and had been featured in *Architectural Digest*. He and Jewel had recently remodeled and moved into a new Manhattan apartment, a penthouse-triplex on Fifth, that Allen desperately coveted because it provided much more wall space than the apartment on Park. Allen had a knack for renovation and decoration. At the weekly dinner parties they gave, guests could not stop raving about Allen's talent. He lapped up the praise, and Jewel admitted that he deserved it. Besides, she was getting her share of praise. She had won two Coty awards for her jewelry design, and the Bijoux print ads had garnered advertising honors for their originality.

As the girls continued to grow, Amber continued to grow away from Jewel. Having moved from kindergarten at the Park Avenue Christian Day School to elementary school at Dalton, they were now boarding at the Sheldon Arms School in Connecticut. There, Amber—now fourteen—and Beryl, a year younger, were near the Prescott country home for weekend visits, and far from the Manhattan high-pressured academic fast lane, of which Allen did not approve.

Allen made most of the girls' educational decisions, and Jewel was grateful that he cared so much. Every year for their birthdays he gave Amber and Beryl each a contemporary work of art that he assured them would be worth a fortune when they came of age. The girls were usually less than thrilled. When they were younger, their hearts were always set on a new bicycle or Madame Alexander doll; now, it was clothes. Therefore, it was Jewel who won kudos at birthdays or Christmas, by producing whatever it was that the girls really desired. (Even Amber could still be bought off occasionally.)

"The art will be their dowry," Allen told Jewel when she suggested that he wait a few years before giving them such grown-up gifts.

"But their rooms aren't suitable for kids their age . . ." Jewel complained. "Here I go out and buy them lace-canopied beds . . . and you give them sculptures of mashed-up cars and paintings of vulvas."

"Well," Allen was always quick to note, "according to the current art market, Amber's and Beryl's walls already contain hundreds of thousands of dollars' worth of pictures that I bought for only a few grand each. They'll thank me someday, when they've outgrown all the presents you've bought them."

Jewel had to admit he had a point but she just wished he would *sell* some things rather than buy new houses and apartments to provide additional wall space. But she did not lose much sleep over it. It took all of her energy to manage her flourishing jewelry empire.

* * *

One day, shortly after Jewel had returned from a business lunch with Edward at the Café des Artistes, he called her on her extension.

"Got a minute? I need you in my office."

"What? I thought we just covered everything in the world."

"Well, we missed this. Something's come up."

When Jewel entered Edward's dark wood-paneled office, she found Cathalene Columbier sitting across from his desk.

"Oh, hello, Cathalene. Am I interrupting?" Jewel asked. "I'll come back."

"No," Edward said, "Cathalene wants to talk to us both. She has some news."

"Oh?" Jewel came in and sat casually on the corner of Edward's desk. "What's up?"

"I was just telling Edward," Cathalene said, "that I'm afraid, after all these years, I must leave Bijoux." She was wearing a black dress with a long white aviator's scarf wrapped around her neck. Jewel realized that she could not remember having seen Cathalene wear anything but black and white for years, not since the early days.

"Oh?" Jewel said, not surprised. Cathalene had always been ambitious. What amazed Jewel was that it had taken Cathalene so long to make her move. "What are you going to do?"

"I have found myself a backer. A very rich person who believes in my talent as much as I do. My backer feels that my creativity is not being showcased enough at Bijoux . . . that it is time for me to open my own shop."

"Really? I'm sorry we've mistreated you so badly," Jewel said coldly.

"Jewel," Edward broke in, "I don't think Cathalene means we've treated her badly."

"Well, she just said that we haven't been showcasing her creativity enough. Who else, I ask you, besides Tiffany, which makes umpteen millions more than we do per year, who *else* advertises their designers like we do?" Jewel said bitterly. "When is all this going to happen?"

"I've already signed a lease for a glorious space on Columbus Avenue," Cathalene said. "I will open in a few months, as soon as we can renovate the interior."

"Columbus Avenue's prime rental these days," Jewel said. "Your sugar daddy must be very well-heeled. Who is he?"

"It's a secret. My backer wants it that way."

"Oh come on, you can tell us," Jewel said.

Cathalene lowered her large doe eyes. "No, I'm afraid not."

"It's Harry Harper, isn't it?" Jewel guessed Harry might savor stirring up trouble at Bijoux, to get back at her for never going to bed with him. After all these years, he still wanted her, and she still resisted.

Cathalene smiled. "I wish I could let you think that. But no, it's not him." She stood. "Anyway, this is my formal notice. And Edward, I want to tell you that I've enjoyed the years we have worked together. You have always been a gentleman to deal with."

Edward stood and bowed. "Why, thank you, Cathalene. Good luck. I know you'll do well. You have a lot of talent. We're sorry to lose you."

Cathalene picked up her handbag, then paused in front of Jewel. "Now that I am leaving, I can't resist telling you what a bitch you are," she said. "You've only got where you are because you married Allen Prescott. But you're selfish, Jewel. You ignore the needs of other people. You have taken advantage of me, ever since the beginning. I worked hard for you, but never once did you appreciate it. Well, now I'm going to be a big success, bigger than Bijoux, and everybody will appreciate me. Just you wait and see. Someday, Jewel *dear,* you may have to come begging to *me* for a job. And now, it gives me great pleasure to tell you good-bye . . . and fuck you."

After Cathalene had exited, Edward sat, holding his breath against the inevitable tirade that he was sure Jewel was preparing to spit out.

"God, what an ungrateful bitch! Riding my heels to success and then biting them. I *never* trusted her," Jewel said on cue. "Boy, I'd like to know who her backer is. I'll bet it *is* Harry."

Edward shook his head. "No. I'm sure it isn't. Harry's smart enough not to pit Cathalene against Bijoux. Hell, it doesn't matter who it is. She's leavin' and that's that. Cathalene Columbier with one shop is not goin' to put much of a dent in *our* market. Just wish her well and be done with it."

"Okay, Edward. You're right. I wish Cathalene every success in the world." Jewel smiled.

He looked at her skeptically.

"I *do,* darling. Believe me."

Jewel knew Edward was right; Cathalene's shop wouldn't hurt Bijoux's business particularly.

But when Cathalene had her grand opening several months later, Jewel made a point of being out of town.

Naked in bed, Mike Marshall opened a bottle of Puligny-Montrachet, to accompany the cheese and French bread that Jewel had picked up for them to nibble on. As had become their routine over the past couple of years, the lovers were grabbing an illicit hour or so at a loft on Twentieth Street that belonged to a trusted friend of Mike's.

"Ten to two," Mike said, glancing at his watch. He set the tray of food and wine on the floor and slid over closer to her. "We have time for another."

"Well, actually, no. I need to talk to you."

Mike put a finger over Jewel's lips. "Not now," he said, climbing on top of her.

Jewel was pleased that her affair with Mike had been conducted with such discretion, on both their parts. Aside from Edward, who had guessed she was having one, but not with whom, she was sure no one knew about them. At the office, it was business as usual. Jewel saw Mike alone only on evenings when Allen was in Connecticut or when they traveled together on business.

Mike had been an ultrasatisfactory lover. He was as hungry as she for money and power, and their sex—it had always been ravenous, fantastic sex—had been intensified by the heady mutual turn-on of their unabashed ambition.

But Jewel had become bored with the situation. Being with Mike was becoming more tedious than exciting for her. They had had a lot of fun, but passionate sex without love, Jewel had concluded, was beginning to pall.

Mike kept saying he wanted to marry her, but what was the point? She didn't love him and she didn't think he really loved her. Why upset the status quo with Allen and her daughters? Besides, Mike was seven years younger than she; sooner or later Jewel knew that would become an issue.

So it was time, Jewel had decided, to shed Mike the lover. But not at the expense of losing Mike the hotshot art director; he was the best.

After they had finished making love, she rolled over and lit a cigarette.

"God, I wish you'd quit," Mike said. "How many packs a day are you up to anyway?"

"Just a couple," Jewel murmured, exhaling a long trail of smoke. "I know. It's a nasty habit. I smell bad. I'll die of cancer. Honestly, I *do* plan to quit soon. Just as soon as I've finished researching and writing my new book."

"Book? What book?" he asked.

"Darling, I *told* you about it. It's called *The Power and Romance of Gems,* about all the famous gemstones that people have fought and died for over the centuries—the Kohinoor diamond, the Black Prince's ruby, the La Peregrina pearl. It's quite fascinating. Did you know—"

"Yeah, you did tell me all about it," Mike interrupted,

not particularly interested. "Hey, there's somebody I've been meaning to ask you about. My sister, Laura, in Greenwich keeps running into her. They play tennis sometimes."

Jewel took her makeup case out of her handbag. "Who? One of my customers?"

"I doubt it. She seems to hate your guts."

Jewel froze, peach lipstick poised against her mouth. "I can't imagine who you're talking about," she said, guessing what was about to come next. It was finally going to happen. The collision with the past.

"Her name's Anna Ferguson. She told Laura you two were college roommates. That you were called Madeleine Lathem then."

"Yes, it's true," she shrugged. "Madeleine's my real name. Jewel became my nickname when I was studying in Germany."

Mike nodded. "Anyway, tell me more about this Anna Ferguson. Laura says she practically has a spasm every time she sees your jewelry. I love the idea of you with enemies," he said, kissing her shoulder. "It's a real turn-on."

"Oh, it's a long story," Jewel said casually, although her heart was beginning to pound. "And terribly boring. Anna had a bad case of jealousy. Obviously she must still. We were rivals over the same boy in college, and I won. She married Randy Ferguson out of spite. She's probably been miserably unhappy ever since."

"What happened to the guy? Was it Allen?" Mike asked.

"No. Just someone I was mad about. Then I went off to Europe. When I got back we'd outgrown each other. Anyway, Mike, I don't want to talk about Anna. It's not worth the time of day." She crushed out a cigarette and lit another. "I want to talk about us."

"What about us?" Mike asked. "Are you leaving Allen?"

"No, I told you, I can't. It's too complicated. My daughters . . ." She paused. "I just think it's time for us to ease out of this. We barely have time for each other anymore, and when we do, it's so rushed."

Mike stared at her. "I thought you were happy with this arrangement. I am, except that I'd like to have you all to myself, all the time."

"Of course I've been happy. But we've been going on for a long time. And if you want to know the truth, I'm tired of sneaking around."

Mike came over to her, put his hands on her slim shoulders, and kissed her forehead. "Hey, what's this all about? I thought you loved me. I love you. I don't want it to end."

Jewel sighed. She had misjudged Mike, thinking he wanted her because of *who* she was, the wildly successful creator of Bijoux. It never occurred to her that he had been serious all those times he said he loved her. Now she had to change her tack before she made him mad.

"Well, you may as well know. Allen suspects something. And Edward insinuated the other day . . . Oh, darling, we have to lay low for a while. We can't afford for this to get around the office."

"I see," he said, hurt.

Jewel took Mike's hand in hers. "I'd feel safer if we put it on the back burner for now. Besides, I need time away from us. To sort it all out," she lied.

"I'm crazy about you, Jewel. What a team we make."

"Oh, darling, we can't think about that now."

"Okay, okay," Mike said, miffed. "I get the point. We'll cool it, if that's what you want."

"It's not what I want; we *have* to."

They finished dressing silently, Mike sulking, and headed out to catch a taxi uptown. Jewel was sure that when Mike allowed it to sink in he'd realize it was all for the best. At least she hoped so.

When they reached the street, Mike walked on ahead of her and signaled for a cab.

All of a sudden, from behind, Jewel felt a hand clamp down on her shoulder. "Madeleine?" a man's voice said.

Startled, Jewel turned to see the smiling face of Wyatt McNeill. His hair was more silver than before. A few additional lines crinkled around his mouth and eyes, but he had changed far less than Jewel would have imagined.

"Wyatt!" she managed to smile back. "What a surprise."

A taxi pulled up to the curb. Mike Marshall opened the door and called back to Jewel impatiently, "You coming?"

"No, Mike," she said. "We'll talk later."

Mike got into the taxi without saying good-bye and sped off.

"I'm rushing," Wyatt said. "Or I'd offer to buy you a cup of coffee."

"That's okay. I have a meeting."

"Are you headed uptown?" Wyatt asked.

Jewel nodded. "Back to the office. Fifth and Fifty-third."

"Then we'll share a cab. I got rid of my car and driver. I'm not in town enough to make it cost-effective."

Something about the way Wyatt said it made Jewel relax a bit. She laughed. "God, Wyatt . . . it's actually good to see you again."

Wyatt flagged down a taxi and they climbed in.

"What do you mean? Actually good to see me," Wyatt said, carrying the thread.

"Well, after all that's happened. There was a time when I prayed that I'd never see you again as long as I lived."

"I understand," Wyatt said. "I was angry. Oh, by the way, thank you for returning the money," he added. "I must admit, I never expected to see it. But then I was more than angry. You really hurt me when you left."

"I know." Jewel lapsed into silence for the next few

blocks, thinking about how young and naive she had been. "I suppose the truth can come out now," she said finally. "It would never have worked out, you and I. I felt so guilty about your family. But the real reason I broke it off when I did . . ."—she paused, playing it for all it was worth—"is that Anna found out. She flew over to Pforzheim and confronted me, just before I was supposed to meet you in Paris. She tore in, shouting, screaming . . . threatening me with everything you can imagine—"

"What?" Wyatt's face went pale. "Why didn't you tell me?"

"Anna *threatened* me, Wyatt! She made me promise to break up with you and never let on she knew. She told Hadley too, but wanted to spare Elizabeth. I'm telling you now because it's been so long. It really doesn't matter anymore."

"This explains it all," Wyatt said. "I always wondered why your and Anna's friendship ended so suddenly. Why didn't I figure it out myself? I should have guessed." Wyatt took her hand and held it. "God, what you went through. And the way I reacted . . . I wish there was some way I could make it up to you."

"Not necessary." Jewel smiled, loving every minute of the confession. "We learn from our mistakes. I was wrong to get involved with you, because of who you were. But I was so insecure then, so anxious to be taken care of. You were wonderful and loving. I couldn't help myself."

Wyatt shook his head slowly. "I wonder how Anna found out."

"I don't know."

"Anna's a complex woman—spoiled, I guess. First by me, then by Randy."

"Then they're still married?" Jewel asked, curious.

"Yes. I don't know if they're happy. They have three kids, and Anna's very much the suburban mother. Randy travels a lot. Anna doesn't have enough to do. Plays a lot of tennis. Looks good, lost all that weight. It's too bad, all this. You two were such great friends."

The taxi turned the corner onto Fifty-third. "Right up there, driver," Jewel said. "Well, here I am. It was good to run into you, Wyatt."

"You too, Madeleine. You're quite a success. I'm proud of you."

"Thanks. Stop by the store sometime and spend some money."

Wyatt grinned. "Will do. I'd like to continue our conversation. There's a lot to talk about. What about lunch next week?"

"Oh, I can't. I'm off to Paris on business, then California," Jewel said, grabbing her briefcase and brushing Wyatt's cheek with a quick kiss.

"Yes, well, I'll call you sometime," he said, realizing that she did not want him to.

Jewel looked back at Wyatt and gave him a quick wave as she headed into Bijoux. How ironic it was. After so many years Anna and Wyatt McNeill had both merged back on the perimeters of her life.

Damn! she thought, as she climbed the private back stairs to her office. She had meant to ask Wyatt about Hadley. He was the only one of the McNeills that she really wanted to hear about.

Meg Higdon, who had been promoted from Jewel's secretary to her personal assistant, handed her a stack of messages. "You look wonderful, Jewel. And you're smiling. You hardly ever smile at this time of day," she said matter-of-factly. Her boss was a hard woman to work for, but Meg had learned that the more candid you were with Jewel, the more she respected you.

"I ran into an old friend," Jewel said. "Someone I haven't seen in ages. And it went well. I vindicated myself on a certain point."

Jewel headed into her spacious office-workroom and sat down to return phone calls.

It felt good to have Wyatt back in her corner, sympathetic to what she had gone through. *Serves you right, Anna,* she thought to herself.

Jewel wondered whether Anna would forgive her someday, then decided that she really didn't give a damn.

27

1988

"I'm leaving now," Meg Higdon said. She stood in the doorway of Jewel's office, tall and leggy, with unfortunate buck teeth that kept her face from being more than pleasingly pretty. "Unless you need something?"

"No . . . no. Run along. What time is it, anyway?" Jewel asked. She was sitting at her worktable, examining a thirty-five carat pink morganite through her microscope.

"Just past six," Meg said. "I'm going to the theater tonight with Mike Marshall. I had tickets, asked him, and he accepted. I can't even believe it!"

"Hmmm, that's nice," Jewel said. She and Mike had cooled down their affair, but she had found it impossible to ditch him completely without his quitting Bijoux. Now, here was a possible solution: maybe Mike would like Meg. In fact, he and Meg were probably well suited to each

other. They both put up with her mercurial temperament
so well. "Have fun."

"Oh, Jewel, I'm really nervous. Mike makes me so
tongue-tied. We're going to have dinner after . . . at a
new French place. I'm terrified I won't be able to think of
anything to say," Meg admitted.

"You? Tongue-tied?" Jewel laughed. Meg's nonstop
chatter was a running joke around the office. "You'll be
fine."

"Oh, I hope so!" she gushed. "Well, see you tomorrow."

Jewel turned off the light of her gemscope and took the
large morganite out of the pliers. It was a nearly flawless
stone that her chief gem buyer, Erik Sanders, had brought
back from California. Next year's big promotional push
for the Bijoux stores was to feature an all-American collection. All the gemstones used by the designers had to be
mined in the United States. They would be featuring rubies, emeralds, and hiddenite from North Carolina; sapphires from the Yogo Gulch and along the Missouri River
in Montana; opals from Nevada and Idaho; pearls from
the Mississippi River area; morganite, kunzite, tourmalines, and benitoite from California; Arizona peridot;
Texas and Colorado topaz; Southwestern turquoise; Wyoming jade; red beryl from Utah; aquamarines from Maine;
Arkansas diamonds and quartz; and garnets and amethysts from all around the country.

Jewel set the pink gemstone on a black velvet tray, under the glow of the Tiffany table lamp that Allen had
given for her thirtieth birthday, an eon ago, it seemed to
her now that she was thirty-eight. She went over to the
safe and took out some eighteen-karat gold bracelets and
chokers that her craftspeople had made up for her.

Back at her desk, she sat and stared at the antique-cut
morganite sitting next to the shimmering gold. Her eyes
began to hurt, and she cupped her hands over them. Yes,
the headache was back too. She had finally gone to an eye

doctor. He had given her both glasses and contact lenses, but, so far, neither had made a noticeable difference.

It was nearly six-thirty. Jewel and Allen were having people for dinner at eight. Allen's sister, Isabel, was in town, and they had put together a small party for her, with Harry and Vivian Harper, and a bunch of Allen's friends—some art dealers and several trendy artists, including one particularly obnoxious young stud from Oklahoma, Billy Cales, whom Allen had taken under his wing.

Jewel sighed. She wished she could skip the party and get some work done, but what was the point? Allen would be furious if she missed dinner, and what to do with this stone was totally eluding her. She hadn't been able to complete a piece of jewelry in weeks, or was it months? She sighed again and stuck the tray back in the safe.

The motivating force in Jewel's life, what had kept her going all these years, was her work. When the children were babies and needed her, that had been important to her. But with Nushka and Allen around full time, the girls, now teenagers, had grown away from her. Oh, she could still talk and gossip with them about superficial things. Or, at least, she and Beryl did. Communication with Amber seemed to have closed down completely when her elder daughter became a teenager. Now that the girls had started boarding school, Jewel wrote them once a week and sent them cartoons she had clipped out of *The New Yorker* or amusing headlines from the *Daily News*. But, other than that, her daughters did not occupy a great deal of her thought.

All of her adult life, regardless of what was going on *in* her life, Jewel had always been able to turn to her designing to find fulfillment and a sense of inner peace. Working with precious metals and priceless gemstones brought her life a beauty and balance that otherwise escaped her. Creating her jewelry—not the sketches she gave to her craftspeople, but the signed, one-of-a-kind pieces that were the cornerstone of her business—centered Jewel in a way that

nothing else did. Selecting a new stone, handling it, meditating on it, deciding how to use it, was the closest thing to
a religious or spiritual experience in Jewel's life. Becoming
one with the gem, *feeling* the purest way to display it in a
new design, that was what Jewel really lived for. That
artistic process was what kept her going. She derived her
energy from it. When she was not creating she felt hollow
inside.

And that was how Jewel felt now; as if she were one of
the walking dead. Her creativity had vanished. One day
she woke up and it wasn't there. She hadn't panicked at
first, figuring she was merely tired. She even gave in to one
of Allen's vacation requests and went sailing around the
British Virgin Islands with him.

But when she returned, after a week of seasickness and
sunburn, she still had not been able to communicate with
the stones and turn them into the unique gold-and-jeweled
compositions that were her trademark. The predicament
put her in a worse mood than usual at work. Her colleagues tiptoed around, trying not to upset her. Everyone
was aware that something was wrong. No one, with the
exception of Edward, Allen, and Mike Marshall, knew
what. The dizzy atmosphere of the spiraling early days of
Bijoux was gone. There were no more peaks to scale. The
designers and staff all speculated that Jewel was bored.

And she was. Not only that, everyone around her was
annoying her more and more. It seemed as if her employees came to her only to whine or complain these days.
They needed more money, more time off, more recognition, more you-name-it.

Jewel was also seething with jealousy over Cathalene
Columbier's success. Her former designer had become
Women's Wear Daily's newest darling. Whoever he was,
Cathalene's sugar daddy had come through in a big way
for her: there were rumors that Cathalene was going to
open stores nationwide, trying to copy Bijoux's success.

Jewel was dying to know who the mysterious backer

was. She had accused Neil Tavlos, but he firmly denied it, and she believed him. He had no reason to sabotage Bijoux. From recent conversations with Harry Harper, she suspected that he knew who it was but was refusing to talk.

There was so much on her mind these days. At home, Allen was beginning to grumble even more than usual about her work schedule. He had even brought up the subject of adopting a child several times, but Jewel had quickly discouraged such thoughts. Nushka, still the housekeeper, pined away because the children were no longer underfoot on a day-to-day basis.

On Allen's birthday, Jewel had given him a dog, a King Charles spaniel, hoping it would please him and Nushka and give them something to lavish affection on. It worked, for a while. Then the puppy wriggled out of its collar one day during an outing in Central Park and ran out into rush-hour traffic on Fifth where its short life came to an end beneath the heavy wheels of a Checker cab. After that, the atmosphere at home went from bad to worse.

"Look, Allen," Jewel had suggested one night as they arrived back from a Costume Institute gala at the Metropolitan Museum, "why don't we take the girls out of boarding school? Bring them back here? Millions of children have been educated in the city and lived to tell the tale."

"No," Allen sighed. "The pressure's too intense. Especially for Amber. And I don't want to separate them. They need each other. I think the solution would be to spend more time in Connecticut, let them become day students."

"Jesus," Jewel snarled, "they're *my* children. I think I have some sort of say in the situation."

"You're the reason Amber is going through this angry phase. You've never spent enough time with them," Allen accused. "Her awe of you has turned into hostility."

"Yes, yes, blame me," Jewel said, hanging her Russian

sable in the hall closet. "I've always spent quality time with them, but no one ever gives me credit. I'm the one who's been out there in the real world slugging it out, making money, creating something. Paying for your excesses."

"Oh, please, let's not go into that again," Allen said. "You're *not* supporting me, in spite of what you think. I can sell some paintings any time I need to raise cash. Look, you've proven your point. Bijoux is a success . . . you're a success. Why can't you sit back and *enjoy* it? Relax. Let go of the reins. Give Edward more power."

"I'm going to bed," Jewel said, huffing upstairs. "I have a breakfast meeting tomorrow."

"When do you not?" Allen had muttered, heading into the library to pour himself a cognac and watch a videotape.

And so it went, life with Allen, life with everyone, these days.

Jewel replaced the painting over the wall safe and gathered up her things with a sigh.

The last thing she felt like tonight was being charming to a lot of guests.

One of Allen's friends, Tony Firstein, sat at the baby grand and launched into a Cole Porter song as the party adjourned to the two-storied Prescott living room for espresso and cognac. Jewel, in spite of her exhaustion, had gamely kept up her part of the conversation during dinner. It was a witty, congenial group, with the exception of the cocky Billy Cales. Allen seemed in especially ebullient spirits and was over by the Barnett Newman, talking animatedly with Sara Richards, an art registrar whom he sometimes used.

Isabel Farraday, who had been seated at the other end of the dinner table, on Allen's right, came over and put an arm lightly around Jewel's waist. "Let's steal away and have a little chat, just the two of us," Isabel whispered.

"They won't miss us for a few minutes, and my plane's leaving early in the morning."

Jewel led her sister-in-law into the forest green library, and they settled themselves on a rose suede sofa, under a Matisse that Allen had bought at auction. Jewel lit a cigarette, earning Isabel's disapproving glance.

"Yes, I'm quitting soon. I promise." She smiled, anticipating Isabel's unspoken comment.

"What I want to talk to you about is rather delicate," Isabel said. "And you may feel that I'm butting in where it's none of my business. But we've always been frank with one another."

What a day, Jewel thought to herself. "Of course. What's up?"

"Well," Isabel began, "for the past six months or so I've been noticing that Allen's seemed rather depressed—nothing specific, just a general mood."

"Hmmm," Jewel noted. Why was everyone always fawning over Allen? *She* was the one who'd been depressed, with her designing going so badly. But too many people depended on her; she had to exhibit strength at all times. She couldn't lapse into self-indulgence as Allen was apt to do, especially around his sympathetic sister.

"And then," Isabel continued, "he suddenly snapped out of it . . . he stopped wanting to talk to me. You know he *always* tells me everything. He became so evasive I decided to do a little sleuthing, quietly, on my own. Oh, Jewel, I'm sorry to have to tell you this, but I think you should know." She took Jewel's hand and squeezed it. "Allen's seeing someone. I'm telling you only because I'd hate to see the two of you break up. Oh, Jewel darling, I know you work damned hard. And I'm terribly proud of you, but you leave Allen with a lot of time to kill."

Allen? Playing around? Jewel couldn't have been more surprised. "Who is it? Do you know?" Jewel asked, cutting through to the essence.

"I don't know," Isabel hesitated.

"It's amazing how one learns new things about friends, the longer you know them." Jewel crushed out her cigarette, and reached into a silver case for another. "I just discovered you don't know how to lie."

"Oh, I don't know for sure. I have no solid proof. It's more intuition."

"Who?" Jewel pressed.

"What are you going to do about this?" Isabel asked nervously. "I shouldn't have told you. Allen will be furious."

"Your name won't come into it . . . *if* we have a showdown," Jewel assured Isabel. "But I think for now it's better to leave well enough alone . . . let it run its course." After all, she had been having the affair with Mike; how could she begrudge Allen? "Now tell me . . . who do you *think* it is?"

"Well, you think about it. Who would *you* guess?"

Jewel hadn't a clue. Allen saw many people without her, in his art-buying rounds. It could be anyone. No. That was wrong. There was his friend Sara Richards, who advised collectors on what to buy. Weren't they out there in the living room chatting at this very moment? Jewel looked toward the door. "I think I know. She's in there, isn't she." How could he fall in love with her, she wondered? Sara was pretty enough, in a wholesome, milkmaidish sort of way, hardly Allen's type.

Isabel nodded. "I could be wrong. It may be merely a flirtation. I don't actually know how serious . . ."

"Oh, it doesn't matter," Jewel said, getting up. "I'll never give Allen up without a fight. We complement each other too well."

Isabel smiled. "I'm glad you feel that way. I certainly think my brother's worth fighting for. But perhaps you should let *him* know you feel that way," she suggested tactfully, as she followed Jewel back to the party.

"Yes, I will," Jewel mumbled distractedly, as her eyes sought out Allen and Sara. To her surprise they were no longer talking. Sara was sitting on the piano bench next to Tony Firstein, and Allen was hunkered down over a sculpture—two heavy boxes by Donald Judd—with Brad Tobias, a painter of large, ominous abstracts that Jewel found oppressive.

As Jewel paused, looking for Harry Harper, Billy Cales came strolling over to her, wearing his inevitable paint-stained jeans with cowboy boots, a rather foppish silk buccaneer's shirt, and a Southwestern bolo tie.

"Yo, Jewel, how's it going?"

"Fine, Billy, just fine," she said, heading for the piano.

"Hey," he blocked her, taking her by the elbow and guiding her over to the floor-to-ceiling windows overlooking Central Park, "you don't like me much, do you? You're always trying to avoid me."

"Let's just say we don't have much in common," Jewel answered wearily.

"I think we do," Cales smiled seductively. "I think you're just playing hard to get."

"Believe me, with you I'm not *playing,*" she said, walking back toward the gathering. His hand reached out and grabbed hers roughly. He pulled her close to him. "Please, Billy," she sighed. "I'm not interested."

"That's not what I hear."

"And what do *you* hear?"

"That you and Allen haven't done it for years. That you race around pretty good."

"Oh?" Jewel said coolly. "Well, your information source is unreliable."

"Look, Allen's going to London this weekend. I'd like to see you," Billy said, rather boyishly. "I mean, I'm going to be working here anyway."

"Working *here?*"

"Yeah. Allen's commissioned me to do trompe l'oeil on the guest-room walls. It'll take a couple of weeks. He said I could stay here while I work. And," he smiled, satisfied, "they're going to be gone at least a week."

"They?"

"He and Sara Richards. She's going with him to the auctions."

Was that true? Jewel thought Allen was going to London only for a long weekend . . . and alone. Were Allen and Sara really *serious* about each other? Impossible.

"Come on," Billy urged, taking advantage of her hesitation. "You know it'd be real good. *I'm* real good," he bragged.

"Billy, I've never liked you and now I know why. Allen's been opening doors for you all over town. You've gotten where you are because of him. And is that how you *thank* him? By trying to screw his wife?" Jewel hissed. "Listen to me. I'll *never* give you the time of day. And I'm telling Allen what a little shit you really are. So don't count on moving in here anytime soon. Go *trompe* on somebody else. I adore my husband and I turn fierce whenever I think he's being taken advantage of." She paused, relishing every moment of telling off the young brat. "Billy, you've overstayed your welcome. Now get the hell out of here!"

"Oh, Jewel, I love it when you get mad. It really turns me on," Billy leered.

"Get the fuck out!" Jewel said loud enough so that the rest of the party stopped dead in its tracks and turned its attention to her.

Billy gave a cool but rather nervous smile, mumbled a general good-night, and headed for the door.

"Sorry, everybody." Jewel smiled. "Just a not-so-friendly misunderstanding. We were having a disagreement over cubism."

Allen came over and put his arm around her, concerned by her outburst. "Are you okay?" he said quietly. "You look upset."

"Oh, I'm okay. What a prick that guy is. Trying to stab you in the back. He thought it'd be great fun to share my bed while you're away. I sent him packing. I'm afraid you'll have to find somebody else to paint the guest room."

"Jewel," Allen said, looking at her with an odd smile, "I didn't know you were that loyal to me."

"What the hell did you think? What's going on here?"

"Oh, nothing."

"Look, my head's splitting. I'm going to say a quick good-bye to everyone and then slip upstairs to bed. I need a good night's sleep."

"Okay. But we have to talk," Allen said, looking at her seriously.

"Oh, we will. When you and Sara get back from London," she said pointedly.

Allen crossed his arms and watched Jewel as she circulated around the room, leaving a trail of smiles and kisses and good-nights. She even kissed Sara Richards on her rosy cheek.

Jewel glanced back at Allen before she left the room and was surprised to see him still standing there, studying her with an enigmatic look on his face. She blew him a kiss as she headed through the wide archway into the hall.

"Wait!" Harry Harper said, catching up with her, looking handsome in a dinner jacket of his own design. "You'll be there tomorrow, won't you?"

"What? Oh, your *show*. Of course I'll be there," Jewel said. "I wouldn't miss it; you know that."

There was a gleam in his eye. "Good. I'm glad."

She aimed a kiss in the direction of his cheek. "Well, good night, Harry. It's been a long day."

"It'll be a good show, maybe my best," Harry said, giving her a sly smile.

"I don't doubt it, darling. I can't wait."

"Me either," he said.

As she headed upstairs, Jewel tried to interpret the expression on Harry Harper's face as they parted. He looked like a cat that had just cornered a fat mouse and was waiting for the precise moment to pounce. She had no idea what it meant, but Harry was not always as subtle as he thought he was. He was definitely up to something. But what?

She supposed she would find out tomorrow.

For now, she had to take a couple of Advil and think about Allen and Sara Richards. She wondered if they were actually having an affair, or if it was merely a crush on Allen's part. As for Sara, well, *any* single woman would obviously love to nab Allen away from her. And this was definitely making her jealous. Perhaps that meant she loved Allen more than she thought.

Jewel slipped out of her clothes quickly and into a hot shower. She knew she had to completely reevaluate her life with Allen, the pros, the cons. Was it time to end the marriage? Or was she going to fight?

New York's fashion conscious—society doyennes, successful women executives, movie stars, and women's page reporters—were seated on gold chairs, slim knee to slim knee, sipping rum punch out of ceramic coconut shells. Harry Harper's fashion show was the hot ticket in town, and the newspaper photographers and television video crews were loving it.

Jewel and Edward arrived late, about ten minutes after the packed show had gotten underway. Harry's favorite model, a stunning six-feet-two black woman known as Saman, was strutting down the mauve-carpeted runway in a sassy, tangerine-dyed chamois strapless sundress, its cinched waist accentuated by a green snakeskin belt. Jewel and Edward quickly dashed to their reserved seats, applauding Saman as the colored spotlights switched to shades of yellow and magenta and three blond models bopped onstage in whimsical tie-dyed satin halter gowns with short, hooped skirts.

"Harry's in an outrageous mood this season," Edward whispered, checking his program to see if they had missed much.

"He's been in an outrageous mood for quite some time now," Jewel said, referring not merely to his clothes. She guessed that Harry harbored quiet resentment over the fact that she'd never fallen into bed with him. "I think I'd better order a lot today, to appease him."

Another model pranced down the runway, wearing black taffeta with a red-feathered overskirt and hat to match.

"What about that one?" Jewel asked Edward. "Do you think it's a bit too young for me?"

Edward rolled his eyes. "Don't be ridiculous. Harry probably designed it with you in mind. You're one of the few people here who could actually carry it off." As he spoke his eyes darted around the room, taking in friends and waving to them.

"Don't look now," he went on, "but Cathalene's over there."

"So what's new?" Jewel said. "She's had a crush on Harry for years."

Model after model sashayed down the runway to Latin American samba music, acting out the playful mood that Harry wanted to evoke with this season's collection. The audience adored it. With each new outfit, the crowd cooed and aah-ed and applauded feverishly. One of the movie stars, perhaps on drugs, or crystals, perhaps merely moved by the music, got up and danced in the aisle to the beat of the fiesta music.

At the end, all the models danced down the runway, and Saman appeared as an updated flamenco dancer, doing a cha-cha with Harry, sporting tight-fitting red Spanish dancer's pants, black snakeskin boots, and a bolero jacket. The audience whistled, clapped, and shouted spirited "bravos" for Harry's new collection. Harry took several deep bows, then broke into a Spanish dance with Saman that brought the house down.

"Well, Harry's done it this time," Jewel said approvingly. "Just when *W* insinuated that he had no new tricks up his sleeve. Boy, will they eat crow. Look, I've marked the numbers of *eight* outfits I'm going to order."

"Good. You'll have Harry eatin' out of your hand. Come on, let's make our way over to congratulate him."

As they wove their way through the crush of elegantly costumed and jeweled bodies, dodging flashbulbs while greeting friends and many of Jewel's loyal Bijoux customers, Jewel suddenly found herself eyeball to eyeball with Cathalene Columbier.

"Oh, hello," Jewel said indifferently, as she squeezed by her.

Cathalene returned an equally icy smile and put her hand on Jewel's shoulder. "Jewel, I'd like you to meet a good friend of mine, Anna Ferguson."

Jewel froze and turned to face Anna, the person she had dreaded seeing for seventeen years. "Hello, Anna."

Anna looked considerably different from the last time Jewel had seen her. She was X-ray thin, dressed in black to accentuate her pale skin. There was a sharpness to her gaunt face that aged her, although there were no visible wrinkles. Jewel searched Anna's eyes for traces of the girl with whom she had once been friends. But she saw nothing except coldness staring back at her.

Anna offered no greeting. "Jewel and I have met," she said to Cathalene, "when she was known as Madeleine Lathem."

"That was a long time ago," Jewel said, regaining her composure. "A lot has happened since then. As far as I'm concerned, Anna, the past is dead."

"Oh? Perhaps for you, Madeleine," Anna said. "I *use* the past, to remind me of mistakes I never wish to repeat."

"Oh, Anna, it's been years. What's the point?" Jewel said, wishing that Anna would let go of the hostility.

"The point is *never* to forget who's stabbed you in the back, and always to keep your back to the wall when you're around that person."

"But, Anna . . . we were so young. *Nothing's* the same

now. Don't you suppose it's time to forgive and forget?" Jewel said coolly.

"Do you think I could *ever* forgive you after what you did? Do you think I could *ever* forget?" Anna hissed. "You're scum, Madeleine—Jewel—whatever the hell your name is." Anna's dark eyes flashed with the same hatred Madeleine had seen that day in Pforzheim. "Come on, Cathalene, my driver's waiting."

Anna turned abruptly and pushed her way through the crowd, with Cathalene tagging behind. Jewel took a deep breath and looked around, trying to locate Edward. Instead, her eyes met Harry's. He was standing a few feet away and had obviously witnessed the scene. He flashed Jewel a grin of delicious enjoyment.

So *that* was what he had insinuated the night before. Harry must have known Anna would be at the show and obviously had been looking forward to the fireworks.

Jewel decided not to allow him the pleasure of her anger. She lit up with a sparkling smile and ran over to him, kissing both his cheeks.

"You did it, darling! The most exciting clothes I've seen in years." She showed him her order card. "Look, I went absolutely berserk."

"I'm glad you liked the show, Jewel," Harry said. And then he put his arm around her shoulders. "You're a good sport, kid. I thought you'd be mad."

"Oh, Harry, I had to run into her sooner or later. Now it's done. She hates me and there's nothing I can do about it. But how the hell did she get to be friends with Cathalene?"

Harry shrugged. "I guess she likes Cathalene's jewelry," he said simply. "And now, if you'll excuse me, I have to go bask in the glory."

"Well, you did good, Harry," she said with forced perkiness. "I'm proud of you."

Jewel's smile vanished the moment she turned away from Harry. Her eyes frantically searched the room for

Edward, then spotted him over in the corner. She quickly made her way over to him, avoiding everyone who might engage her in conversation.

"Let's get out of here," she seethed, grabbing Edward away from the young man with whom he was chatting. "Fast!"

After dropping Edward off at the office, Jewel picked up her car at the garage and headed for Connecticut. This weekend, of all times, was the one that the Sheldon Arms School had designated for parents, and Jewel had promised Amber and Beryl that she'd be there.

It was the last thing in the world she wanted to do now. She was livid, all the way up the Taconic Parkway, as she replayed the confrontation with Anna. The nerve of Anna, acting like that after all this time. God, the woman behaved as if Jewel had committed murder. It was so ridiculous to harbor such a deep grudge for so long, Jewel stewed, conveniently forgetting about Sascha and the hatred for him that she still carried with her.

By the time Jewel turned into the oak-lined driveway of the Sheldon Arms School, her head had begun to ache again, badly. What a week it had been. Finding out Allen had a lover, seeing Anna. And now she had to smile and play at being a good mother for the entire weekend.

Sometimes she wished it would all go away. Especially the headaches.

28

The room was blindingly bright, as if illuminated by mammoth movie strobes. Yet the intensity was comforting. Jewel did not feel the need to reach for her sunglasses. But what was she doing there, all alone? And where exactly was she? She couldn't remember.

But she knew she wasn't afraid. She was certain it was a place she had been before . . . there was a slip of memory just eluding her. It would come if she relaxed and thought of something else.

Jewel turned around slowly, but saw nothing except the light, so brilliant, so overwhelming. There was a spot near the center of the room, if indeed this was a room, that began to attract her attention, and she fixed her stare on it. Slowly the color changed, from bright orange to a pale lemon. Then green. Blue. Violet. There it stayed, and the violet light began to bathe more of the room.

Jewel had the feeling that she'd moved, but wasn't

aware of moving; she was closer to the center now, the
rich purple. She took a deep breath and inhaled the color
deeply. Such peace, such exhilaration. The place was *so*
familiar. Why couldn't she remember where she was?

She stood transfixed, waiting. For what, she did not
know. But some voice, deep from within her, told her she
was waiting. The violet light covered all now, became
more luminous. She stretched out her hands and looked
down at her arms. They shimmered with the same color as
the room.

A bed appeared. Or had it been there all along? It was
not actually a bed, but a rectangular slab that resembled
marble, yet gave way to pressure when she touched it. She
sat on it, sank into it, and breathed deeply again, beginning to feel sleepy. She lay back on the bed and rested her
body. Oh, it felt so good to lie down.

Someone came and put a cover over her. It was not
until then that Jewel realized she had been naked. The
cover was light, silky. She could see the outline of her
body underneath it. The color of the silk seemed to change
every time she looked down at it, but that did not concern
her.

Now she began to notice that the purple mist was clearing. The light changed suddenly to a warm amber-brown,
as if the room had been lighted by invisible candles.

Jewel began to hear voices, although she couldn't distinguish what they were saying. Presently, shapes surrounded the bed. People. She was no longer alone and
realized that she never had been, that they had been there
all along, but she had chosen not to see them.

Jewel closed her eyes and inhaled deeply, letting the air
sink all the way down to her solar plexus. With her eyes
closed, she could still see them, feel their soothing presence.

She opened her eyes. They smiled at her, then busied
themselves, bathing her with what looked like sponges of
bright green light. Sparks, like static electricity, darted out

from her skin. Were her eyes open now, or closed? She was not sure.

Jewel moved her mouth to speak, or tried to. No sound came. Then somehow she understood that she could *think* the question and they would understand. At least, it was worth a try.

Where am I? she asked with closed lips.

Forms parted, drifted away. New forms, no, people, drifted in. The room was crowded now. There was warmth from the energy of all the bodies.

You are all right, they all seemed to say at once, many voices melded into one, creating an echo. *You are with us.*

Jewel found the explanation satisfactory. Now she knew where she was. She *had* been there before, perhaps many times. And she felt good, so good, as if her body were being massaged by a thousand hands. *Relax, relax,* they seemed to say. *It is time to rest.*

Jewel sank into the bed, felt her body fall deep inside it, marveling at how she seemed to be able to move into and out of it.

Rest now, the voices said lovingly. *We will stay with you.*

Jewel, still not knowing whether her eyes were open or shut, sank into a deep sleep.

There was a dream, or several. She walked along a green meadow dotted with wild flowers, over to the edge of a hill, and looked down. There was a sandy beach below, and a tranquil, aquamarine sea, with huge crystalline boulders rising out of the water. It was so beautiful she took off her sandals and scampered, barefoot, down a sandy dune, across the hot beach, to the cool water. She was completely alone; but perhaps not. In the distance she could hear chanting, many voices joining into one pure note at a time. She sat down in the clear, sunlit water.

And found herself in a garden, the most ornamental she had ever seen. And odoriferous. Thousands of flowers in a palette of colors emitted their individual scents, then joined together into a chorus of fragrance. Jewel ran her hands along the soft green grass, feeling content.

You are very happy? a cheerful voice asked her, out of nowhere.

"Yes, very," she said, this time moving her lips, talking for real.

A man appeared before her. Or was it a woman? She could not distinguish the features. The body was covered by a hooded gray velvet cloak.

It occurred to Jewel to be scared, and she tested herself for fear, but found none. She felt as if she were confronting an old friend.

It is time to talk, the figure said, smiling. *Drink this.* He/she handed her a golden goblet containing a liquid that shimmered with prisms of glittery light.

Jewel accepted the goblet and drank all of the liquid, very thirsty all of a sudden. Refreshed, she sat, waiting. She could not think of questions to ask. There were no questions.

You can't stay here, you know.

"Why not?" Yes, *there* was a question. "I don't want to leave."

I know. But you must go back. You have not finished your stint. He/she laughed. *It won't be so bad. Once you're back, you'll be glad to have the chance to work things out.*

"No. I don't *need* to," Jewel said, amazed by the strength in her voice. "I don't want to."

He/she nodded, understanding. *Of course. But it has been decided. You cannot stay here, dear one, not this time. You are needed back home.*

"No . . . I *am* home," she insisted.

He/she smiled with affection, handing her a jug filled with the sparkling liquid she had drunk from the goblet. *Go and rest now . . . and drink all of this.* He/she handed her a large green emerald, unfaceted, the size of an egg. *Carry this with you. You must heal yourself quickly and get on with it.*

"With what?" Jewel asked. "What do I need to get on with?"

Your life. Your children.

"My children?" Jewel said, suddenly remembering Amber and Beryl. "Oh, yes, I forgot. You're right . . . I must go."

That is what I have been telling you. The being's face glowed radiantly, and he/she hugged her tightly. *Now, be gone with you, dear one.*

Jewel found herself back in the amber-brown room, back among the crowd. This time, though, she noticed that the bed was gone. She was standing amid a sea of smiling faces, being patted on the back, lovingly, as if she had accomplished a good deed or won a race. No one spoke, but she felt the communication of good wishes they were bestowing upon her.

Then she was back in the dazzling yellow light. It was whirling around her. In the distance she heard her friends chanting. She closed her eyes, breathed deeply, and walked into the vortex. *Maddie . . . Madeleine . . . Jewel,* she heard the chorus of voices say, *good luck . . .*

"Jewel?"

"Mummie?"

"Oh, please speak to us! Please get well."

She came out on the other side of the light. There was darkness, a long tunnel of it, then the cold fluorescence of a hospital room which Jewel viewed from above.

There were Allen, Amber and Beryl, Edward, Nushka, all looking terribly grave, all standing around a bed. Her bed. Jewel hovered above them, watching with fascination. Amber moved slightly, and Jewel was startled to see herself, lying there, head bandaged, tubes connected to her arms and throat.

"No!" she called back, changing her mind. "I can't do it. I don't want to!"

But she felt a gentle push from behind.

And then Jewel was immersed in the pain, the shrieking

inside her head. The dry mouth. The numbness of her body.

No! she said to herself. *I'm a vegetable. I can't move.*

A distant voice reminded her to drink all the liquid from the jug. She realized that she still had the container and drank from it thirstily, greedily, until the pain disappeared and she could move her limbs again. She clutched the emerald in her left hand.

"Look, Daddy! Her hand moved!" Beryl said excitely.

Jewel blinked open her eyes. Everything was blurry, but with concentration, she willed her vision to clear.

"Get the doctor, Edward," Allen said.

Jewel saw Amber first. Her oldest daughter's face was streaked with tears, full of love and caring. It had been many years since she had seen such compassion in Amber's face.

Jewel opened her mouth, and again, with great effort, she began to speak.

"I'm here," she croaked hoarsely. "I'm all right . . ."

By then the doctor had arrived and was standing by the bed. He shined a light into each of her eyes, then flicked it off and looked into her face.

"Mrs. Prescott, you scared the hell out of us," he said, smiling. He reached out his hand. "Here, take hold of my hand."

Jewel reached out and grasped the doctor's hand, not as tightly as she had meant to, but slowly her fingers wound around his, and he smiled again.

"Yes," he said, "you're going to be fine."

Jewel lapsed in and out of sleep over the next few days, awakening intermittently, able to engage in limited conversation with Allen, her daughters, and the doctors.

Nushka had been responsible for getting her to the hospital in Waterbury, it turned out, after Jewel's dinner with her daughters during the Sheldon Arms parents' weekend. After Jewel had dropped the girls off at Sheldon Arms and returned home, complaining of a headache, the house-keeper had made Jewel some tea. When she brought it up, she had discovered Jewel collapsed, unconscious, in the bathroom. Without waiting for doctors or an ambulance, the woman summoned the caretaker and they took Jewel, wrapped in blankets, by car to the hospital.

Jewel regained consciousness almost two days after her collapse. Allen had rushed home from London on the Concorde, and Edward had come up from the city to keep vigil at the hospital with Nushka, Beryl, and Amber. What had happened to her, she learned, was a cerebral hemorrhage, resulting from the rupture of an arteriosclerotic vessel. It was a fluke. The headaches she had been suffering stemmed from another cause: hypoglycemia, low blood sugar, that had never been previously diagnosed. One had had nothing to do with the other.

"You're lucky, Mrs. Prescott," the doctor said. "Only a small vessel was involved. Your prognosis is gradual but steady improvement . . . although the permanence and extent of the neurological damage can't be completely predicted for six months."

"But my whole left side is weak," Jewel said raspily. In order to maintain an airway during her coma, they had performed a tracheostomy. Although the tube had now been removed, her throat was still sore.

"It's normal for one side of the body to be affected. To me, it's remarkable that you can move your left side as well as you can. The usual course in your case is severe hemiplegia—paralysis of one side of the body. Your left side is merely weak. With physical therapy, massage, and exercise you'll be back to normal in the optimum time. Another thing to be thankful for, your speech hasn't been affected. A common side effect of a stroke like yours is motor aphasia, which is the inability to speak, or sensory aphasia, an inability to understand words."

"I have a bit of that," Jewel smiled. "But then I always did."

"You sound just fine." The doctor smiled. "Your recovery is nothing short of miraculous. I've never seen anyone heal so fast. You'll be out of here and back home to recuperate in another week. Really, it's quite amazing," he said, heading for the door. "I'll check back in on you later. In the meantime, try to get some exercise. Have your daughters race you up and down the halls a little bit." He laughed, patting Beryl on the shoulder.

The doctor thought Jewel was doing well. She wondered if he'd pronounce her crazy if she told him about the magic healing water and the large green emerald that were still given to her whenever she drifted off into a dream state.

When he was sure she was going to recover, Allen told her that she had been clinically dead for several minutes. Jewel wondered if that was when she had dreamed about the place of blinding light. The dream still seemed so vivid to her; Jewel was beginning to think it hadn't been a dream at all. She *had* gone somewhere. Wherever it was, she knew that the beings there had helped her get home, and they were helping her heal.

But why? That was always the question. Why was she, Jewel Madeleine Dragoumis Prescott, being given a second chance? Why hadn't she died and stayed dead?

In the past she might not have dwelled on the fine existential points of her rapid comeback from death. But Jewel knew, deep inside of her, that the Jewel who awoke from the coma was a far different person from the one who had lapsed into it. She was not sure how she had changed or how the change would manifest itself, but she was positive that some sort of transformation, no matter how subtle, *had* occurred.

"Here, Mummie," Beryl said, coming into Jewel's all-white bedroom with a tray, "Amber and I made you breakfast all by ourselves. Nushka's downstairs baking a pumpkin pie."

Jewel was home at the house in Connecticut the next week, as the doctor promised. Allen had arranged to let the girls stay with her and attend the school as day students, at least until Jewel had recovered enough to return to the city and work.

"Oh my, this looks scrumptious." Jewel smiled, propping herself up in bed to receive the white wicker tray. "And I'm starving. Aren't you going to eat anything?"

"We had breakfast already," Amber said. "We got up early."

Jewel laughed. "Why is it you two bound out of bed on the weekends, and on school days it's all Nushka can do to get you to school before the warning bell?"

"Weekends are more fun," Beryl giggled. "Besides we have a project."

"Shut up!" Amber warned her sister. "It's a secret."

"Aha! Keeping secrets from your old, sick mother. Shame on you."

"You'll know soon enough," Beryl said, as Amber jabbed her in the ribs.

Jewel ate her breakfast slowly. Her left hand and arm were still weak. The fingers worked well enough, but it took great effort for her to raise her left arm even half as high as her right arm. Her left leg was the same. She could walk, using a cane, but the leg dragged a bit. It was difficult for her left side to keep up with the right. The doctor assured her that once physical therapy had begun she would be set to rights within a few months. But Jewel wanted to be well now, not sometime off in the distance.

As she ate her scrambled eggs and butter-drenched English muffin, she chatted with the girls about their studies at school. With her second cup of herbal tea, she felt the need for a cigarette, but they had all been removed. No more smoking, ever. Well, it was a drastic way to quit, having a cerebral hemorrhage, but it achieved the desired effect.

There was a quick rap on the door, and Allen entered,

carrying his New York *Times* and a mug of strong black coffee. He went over to the bed and kissed Jewel on the cheek.

"Good morning," he said pleasantly. "I see you're surrounded by your trusty nursing staff."

"I am," she smiled. "They cooked me breakfast and *look* at my plate. I haven't eaten so much in the morning for years. It was delicious, darlings," she said to her daughters, as Amber picked up the tray.

"We have to go now," Beryl said. "We have things to do."

The children retreated, and Allen settled himself in a chair by the window to read his newspaper.

Jewel watched him read, oblivious to her. It was hard to believe they had been married for so many years. Looking at him now, Jewel had the sudden impression that she barely knew him. The people they had been were gone. Who was left now, she wondered?

"Allen," Jewel said after a while, "I think it's time to talk."

Allen looked up from the *Times*. "No, just take it easy. There's nothing that can't wait."

"Yes, there is. I'm feeling much stronger, and there's a lot that needs to be talked about."

Allen folded his paper, looking grave. There were dark circles under his eyes, and Jewel noticed for the first time that he had lost weight. "Okay."

"I want to know about Sara Richards. There's no point in skirting the issue. Are you having an affair with her?" Jewel asked. "Are you in love with her?"

Allen looked away guiltily, then sighed. "Oh shit, Jewel. Yes, we've been seeing each other. And yes, I thought I was in love with her. Then you got sick, and things have changed. I don't know what's going on anymore."

"But you *do* love her?" Jewel pressed.

Allen shook his head. "God, Jewel, I don't know. It's so

complicated. Part of me still loves you. But so much has gone out of our marriage. Or maybe I kid myself by pretending things were once there that never were at all." He came over and sat on the bed, then leaned down and buried his head in Jewel's bony chest. "I'm so confused. I don't know what I want. And Sara understands the situation. She's not pressing. She was terribly upset when she heard about you. She insisted we not see each other until . . ."

"Until I'm well?" Jewel snapped. "That's damned nice of her."

"Sara *is* nice, Jewel. She's sweet, and she's easy to be with. We have a lot in common. She's one of the most informed people I've ever known—about art, about many things. But I don't want to throw our twelve years out the window. We have those *years* in common. And I admire you so much, Jewel. You continue to dazzle me with your energy, even now. The doctor told me again how amazed he is by your fast recovery. You *are* a remarkable person."

Allen paused, and Jewel could see the anguish in his face. He was clearly miserable. Jewel released some of the jealousy she harbored and tried to empathize with him.

"Allen, I know I've been hard to live with . . . my obsessive work schedule and everything. But I'm going to try and change that. I know why you fell in love with Sara. I haven't been around for you to share things with, and Sara has. I suppose it was inevitable. If it hadn't been her it would have been someone else." She sighed. "I'm going through a period of self-evaluation. I don't know if I'm going to change drastically. But I know I have to switch around my priorities. I told Isabel once that I'd fight like hell to keep you. But that's changed too. I'm not going to fight. If you stay, it's because you want to stay and I want you to stay. And that . . . we've got to figure out for ourselves."

"I've never heard you talk like this." Allen took Jewel's

hand and held it tightly. "What about Mike Marshall? Do you love him?"

Jewel was caught off guard. How had Allen found out about Mike? "No," Jewel said. "We had fun for a while. It was a diversion. He *wanted* me so much. It was flattering . . . and, let's face it, you and I have never burned down buildings with our lovemaking. It's been comfortable, but you're often preoccupied."

"I'm not the only one," Allen bristled.

"I know, I know. And it's probably what happens in all marriages. There's no way to sustain the passion. That's why it's best to marry a friend . . . because when all's said and done you still have a friend," Jewel said. "What we have to decide, the two of us, is if our friendship's strong enough to keep us going."

They sat in silence for a few minutes, listening to the sounds of chickadees chirping at the bird feeder outside the window. "I don't know what to think anymore," Allen said finally.

"Neither do I," she sighed. "And there's something else that's been on my mind . . . on a different subject. Oh hell, I want a cigarette," she complained.

Allen picked up her smoking hand and kissed it. "Would you like me to get you some candy? Some sort of oral substitute?"

"If I reached for a bonbon every time I wanted a cigarette I'd weigh three hundred and fifty by the end of the year," she laughed bitterly. "No, it's going to be cold turkey for me—hold the bread and mayo." She reached over and ran the fingers of her right hand, her good hand, through his hair. "The other thing we need to talk about is . . . Sascha."

"Sascha?"

Jewel nodded. "He's popped into my mind a lot lately. I've begun to feel guilty that the girls don't know. I've been thinking about telling them. But I want to know how you feel about it, as their legal father."

"I can tell you right away. I think the girls should be told; I always have. Edward and I have discussed it at length. We even thought about telling them behind your back, but we couldn't. It's always been up to you, and you've been so adamantly against it. Tell me, what made you change your mind?"

Jewel shook her head. "I don't know really. Yesterday I was flipping though *Vogue,* and there was a Tiffany ad for one of Sascha's necklaces. It was really beautiful—chunky gold with black baroque pearls. It flashed me back to when we were together, back on Spring Street. I started thinking about him, about us, about how it ended. Hell, I started crying," she said, tears welling up again. "I don't know. Coming so close to death, you look at life differently. Maybe I just stopped hating him, all of a sudden, after all these years."

"Maybe so," Allen said. "And I'm glad. The girls need to know the truth. It'll be hard at first, but they'll adjust. We'll all adjust. When do you want to tell them?"

"Sometime after you've retrieved a photo album from the safe deposit box for me. It has pictures of them with him. That way they'll believe me."

"Would you like me to help you?"

"No thanks," Jewel said, "this is something I need to do on my own."

"I'm proud of you, darling," he said. "Really proud. And Edward will be happy. He and Sascha have become quite friendly over the past few years."

"Yes, I guessed as much." Jewel yawned. "Oh my, I think it's time for my mid-morning nap. I'm reeling from all this . . . I need my strength back."

"I'll do anything I can to help. I still care about you, darling. Enormously."

Jewel took his hand. "Thank you, Allen. I care about you too. I really do."

"Oh, Jewel. It's been years since we've talked like this. What happened to us?"

Jewel shrugged. "I guess it's the pitfall of a long marriage. We went our separate ways, then came home, slept in the same bed and called it a compatible life. It's been compatible. The question is, has it been a life?"

"Yes . . . it has." He leaned over and kissed her. "Okay, take your nap." He headed for the door, then stopped. "You never cease to amaze me. As infuriating as you've sometimes been over the years, you've never been dull."

Jewel smiled. "Thank you—if you meant it as a compliment."

"I did," Allen said, "I did."

29

       Edward drove up to Connecticut in his new BMW, to spend Sunday with Jewel and his second family. After picking apples in the orchard with Beryl and Amber, they all sat down to an old-fashioned, middle-of-the-day Sunday meal that Nushka had prepared—roast chicken with gravy, mashed potatoes, corn, and salad, followed by apple crisp with vanilla ice cream.

    "That was delicious," Edward said afterward. "But we should have waited to take our walk *after* lunch. Now we really need the exercise."

    "I'm all for taking a little stroll," Jewel said. "If you don't mind a slow one."

    Allen leaned back in his chair and stretched his arms up over his head. "Not me. The only walk I'm taking is into the library to turn on the TV. The Giants are playing Dallas today." He was a big Giants fan.

"What about you, girls? Did you finish your homework?" Jewel asked.

"No," Amber said sullenly, huffing off from the table. At fifteen, she was still going through the hormonal changes of adolescence. Now that Jewel was out of danger and recovering, Amber had, for the most part, reverted back to her old sulkiness.

"I did," Beryl said. At fourteen, she was having an easy adolescence. "But I have something else to do."

Jewel smiled. "Then it looks as if it's just us."

Jewel bundled up in a red-dyed beaver and wound a large scarf around her head and neck. They headed in the direction of a newly cleared field over to the right of the house.

"There was a plan," Jewel said quietly. "Allen was going to plant seven-year-old grapevines, right over there, in the spring. To try his luck starting a vineyard. But now, I don't know. I try to gaze into the crystal ball and it's totally clouded over." She grabbed Edward's hand, for balance. "Shit, Allen's in love with that art groupie, Sara Richards."

Edward nodded. "I didn't know for sure, but . . ." he trailed off. "How do *you* feel about it, darlin'? I mean, you and Allen have been goin' your own ways for years . . . but underneath it all I always thought you were a good couple. Allen really loves you."

"I'm not so sure, although I could probably get him to again if I really wanted," Jewel said. "I *know* how to play the game right. Trouble is, I don't know *what* I want anymore. I don't know whether I've ever loved Allen, but I like him. And we *have* built a rather impressive life together."

Jewel took a deep breath and expelled it slowly into the icy air. "Oh, Edward, there's this pressure on me. It's something new. But I feel that I've survived this damned stroke for a reason, and what the hell it is, I can't figure out." She reached out and put her arms around him. "Oh, give me a hug," and after he did, she said, "Do you ever feel like you're just walking through it all, observing the goings on, but never participating? That's how I've felt for years now . . . and I let my impatient, driven, perfectionist, bitchy side take over, because at least getting angry at people made me *feel* something. Now I don't feel anger anymore . . . but I don't know what's going to take its place."

"Jewel," Edward sighed, "I think the best thing for you to do now is get well. Get your strength back. Then it'll start sortin' itself out—what you want, what Allen wants."

"Yes, I suppose."

Edward gazed out at the field, then looked back at her. "Jewel, darlin', there's somethin' we have to talk about . . . and unfortunately it can't wait." He guided her over to a fallen tree stump. "Let's sit down here."

"Oh no. What's wrong now?" she asked, looking at his grim face.

"Look," Edward sighed, "I wish it could wait till you're stronger."

"I'm strong as a racehorse already. One that's gone a little lame, I'll admit. But I'm starting physical therapy next week, and I plan to hit the office again as soon as possible."

"Well," Edward started, looking ill at ease. His cheeks and nose had turned red in the bracing November cold. "A lot has been goin' on the past few months. Behind your back. I've only recently been brought into it myself. Then everything came to a head after you got sick. People were speculatin' that you wouldn't pull through and, if you did, that you wouldn't be well enough to run Bijoux."

"I see," Jewel said, feeling a chill run down her back, a chill not brought on by the November day.

"Cathalene's brought Neil Tavlos over to her camp, offered him a chunk of the business for some major-growth financin'. She and Anna have decided it'd be easier to deplete our operation, rather than havin' Cathalene start from scratch in her expansion plans."

"Wait. What do you mean?" Jewel interrupted. "She and *Anna?*"

"That's the other thing I found out," Edward said. "Anna Ferguson's the secret partner who came up with the money for Cathalene to go out on her own."

Jewel listened, stunned. But of course it made sense. Anna and Cathalene had been together at Harry's show. And Anna would go to *any* length to ruin her, she now realized.

"Why the hell didn't I figure it out before?" Jewel said. "Now Anna must be rubbing her hands with glee at the idea of getting back at me."

Edward nodded. "And they're workin' fast, now that you're benched on the sidelines. Cathalene's been wooin' Rody and Tom, Leilani, Rita, Erik Sanders, Mike Marshall—hell, she's offerin' them anything they want to defect. She's even tryin' to raid Tiffany—Sascha especially, because she knows how much you detest him."

"How the hell did Cathalene find *that* out?" Jewel asked. "I *never* told her about Sascha. God, that bitch!"

Edward bit his lip nervously. "I'm afraid she found out about Sascha from me."

"What? I *swore* you to secrecy!"

"I know. And I'm sorry. But, as you admitted, you've been pretty much of a bitch these last few years. There've been times when I've been completely fed up with you. Cathalene always seemed to sniff out those moments. We'd go out to lunch, and she'd be so sympathetic, so easy to talk to. We'd have a few glasses of wine . . . I didn't tell her on purpose. It just sort of slipped out. Really, darlin', I'm so sorry."

"Oh, it's okay," Jewel said, miffed, but trying not to get upset. "Let's not dwell on it. I want to hear more about the mutiny. What about *you?* Has Cathalene . . . ?"

Edward nodded. "Of course. And I must admit I was

tempted, for about fifteen minutes. But when you got sick I had a lot of time to think about it all, sittin' in the hospital. About you. About us. I've been harborin' a lot of resentment. You've been difficult and aloof, these last few years. You think if you pay people enough you can treat them like shit. But you can't, Jewel. People will take *less* to be treated decently. With politeness and courtesy."

"I never treated anyone differently from myself. I work hard . . . I expect others to," Jewel said, slipping her left hand up into the right sleeve of her coat, to alleviate the numbness.

"Yes, that's the point, darlin'. You *are* driven. I know you brought this all on yourself . . . the hemorrhage. After years of bein' so hard on others, so hard on yourself, even *you* couldn't take it anymore."

"The doctor said the hemorrhage had nothing to do with *anything,*" Jewel sniffed.

"Maybe not," Edward shrugged. "Anyway . . . I'm sorry to have to lay this all on you now. But we have a major problem here that won't go away."

"Until Cathalene has destroyed Bijoux? Well, over my dead body! I'd rather have another hemorrhage and die than let her and Anna walk in and take over everything I've worked so hard for."

Edward put his arm around his friend. "Calm down. I didn't want to upset you. I just thought you had to know what's goin' on."

"Oh, Edward, what have I done?" Jewel began to cry softly. "Shit, I've ruined everything. *I* did it. I created it and I ruined it! There's going to be nothing left. And there's no point in even trying to blame Cathalene and Anna . . ."

"Now, now, darlin', you don't have to go *that* far. Your crime is bein' hard on yourself and the people around you. But Cathalene *uses* people: me, Harry . . ."

"Harry?" Jewel interrupted, wiping her eyes with Edward's handkerchief. "What do you mean?"

"Well, I've gone this far, I may as well give you the rest. Cathalene thought that you and Harry were havin' an affair. She used to have lunch with him too, from time to time. I think she wanted him, but he wanted you. He couldn't admit to her that you wouldn't go to bed with him, so he lied. Told her you two *were* havin' an affair. That made her even madder. I mean, darlin', Cathalene has a real love-hate relationship goin' with you. She's jealous of you, of your life. In her eyes, you have everything: all the glory, all the men, all the money. And you took her for granted."

"No, I *never* took her for granted!" Jewel snapped. "I always knew where she was coming from . . . she isn't very subtle. My real mistake was not firing her years before she left with all my secrets," Jewel said breathlessly. "But back to Harry . . . how did she use *him?*"

"He was how she got to Anna," Edward explained, putting an arm around Jewel. "It seems that Anna and Vivian got sort of friendly after Harry bought the big estate in Greenwich. They ran into Harry and Cathalene, all havin' lunch at Mortimer's one day. Vivian and Anna went to their own table . . . and Harry mentioned that Anna had it in for you. Well, that's all Cathalene needed. The rest is history."

Jewel shook her head. "God, you try so hard to bury your past and it all comes bubbling up from the ground like toxic waste . . . when you're least prepared. Hell, it would've been so much easier if I'd died. Then I wouldn't have to deal with all this shit." She uttered a wry laugh. "Amber has a T-shirt that says, 'Life's a bitch and then you die.' I'd like one that says, 'Life's a bitch, but it won't go away.' "

Edward smiled. "Come on . . . it's not so terrible. I'm not goin' to desert you. We'll win. If you're willin' to loosen up."

"Oh, I'm willing, I guess. But you can't change lifetime habits overnight."

"They're not lifetime habits," Edward said. "You were sweet and vulnerable when I met you. You've toughened up, but underneath the old Jewel's still there. I know . . . I've seen her from time to time. I mean, you haven't been *relentlessly* bitchy."

"Well, that's *something,* I suppose. Look, darling, thank you for leveling with me, and for hanging in there, even when it's been hard to be my friend. You may be out of a job by siding with me and not Cathalene."

"There never was a choice really. As angry as you've made me from time to time, I could never defect. We're a team. We always have been, always will be."

Allen spent the next week in the city, leaving Jewel time alone to think. The following Saturday she arose early, after a fitful night's sleep. She showered and dressed as quickly as she could with her weak left arm. She had put off telling the girls about Sascha. Now it had to be done. Jewel was dreading it more than she thought possible.

After a short walk outside, to clear her head in the freezing dawn air, she made herself a cup of peppermint tea and took it into the library. Shivering, she turned up the thermostat, went to the desk drawer and got out the photo album of Sascha with the girls that Allen had sent up from the safe deposit box in New York. She settled herself on the sofa, with the brown leather album in her lap.

Jewel had not looked at it for fourteen years. She wished she didn't have to now, but it was too late to chicken out.

Slowly, Jewel's right hand opened the leather album and, with all the trepidation of a gladiator preparing to face a pack of lions, she looked down at the page. The first picture, an eight-by-ten blow-up, had been taken with Sascha's camera by a nurse at the hospital. There she was, with Sascha, and twelve-hour-old Amber.

She didn't know what Sascha looked like these days, but

Jewel was struck by how young she appeared. Her hair color had changed with such regularity over the past decade, after the first strand of gray appeared, that Jewel had practically forgotten what shade it had been. But there she was, with long, flowing brown hair, quite pretty actually. Maybe Edward was right. Maybe she had been sweet then.

Amber was so tiny, so angelic. It brought tears to Jewel's eyes as she remembered that day, the day of her elder daughter's birth, so many years ago. And then she allowed her gaze to wander over to Sascha's face. There he was, her burly, bearded Russian bear, with those pale eyes that had caught her in the beginning. In the picture, those eyes were focused on her. And there was such love in them.

The door suddenly burst open, and Amber and Beryl bounced into the library, wearing nightshirts and knee socks and fuzzy bear slippers. "Oh, here you are! We looked in your room but you were already up. We'd planned to make you breakfast in bed. We have a surprise for you."

Jewel closed the album quickly and smiled. "Good morning. You're both up early."

"What's that?" Beryl asked, pointing to the album.

"Oh, I'll show you in a bit."

"Can we give you your surprise now? Before breakfast?"

"Of course," Jewel said. Anything to put off telling them.

The girls rushed off and were back within minutes, carrying a large tray with a towel draped over something about a foot high and even wider.

"Close your eyes," Beryl ordered.

Jewel obliged.

"Okay, you can open now," Amber said.

Jewel opened her eyes to see, sitting on the coffee table before her, a gingerbread house, done as a replica of the very house they were living in, adorned with fantasy

touches, of course, such as candy and feathers and miniature silk flowers.

"Oh my! This is fabulous! Is this what all the secretive-
ness has been about the past couple of weeks?" She held
out her good arm, and the girls sat beside her. "I love it
. . . thank you. You did such a great job."

"We showed it to Edward last week. And he said it'd be
perfect for Bijoux's side-window Christmas decoration."

"Oh, it would. With jewelry draped all around it. I'll
take it into the city tomorrow."

Beryl sighed. "I wish you wouldn't go so soon. Do you
really think you're well enough?"

"I've got to work at getting better . . . start that physical therapy so I won't keep tripping every time I walk
across a room."

"Do you really like the gingerbread house?" Amber
asked.

"Oh, yes. I can't imagine how you did it. Look at all the
detail."

"It took a long time," Beryl said, "but we had fun."

"Well, it's just perfect. Thank you again." Jewel took a
deep breath. "Look, I have to talk to you two. About
something serious that I've never told you before."

"What?" the girls both said, puzzled by the grave expression on Jewel's face.

"Well," Jewel bit the bullet, "it's . . . about your father."

"Oh no," Beryl cried. "Is something wrong?"

Jewel shook her head. "No. Allen's fine. I mean your
real father. You see, Allen adopted you when you were
babies . . ." She opened the photo album. "Your real father is this man, Sascha Robinovsky."

Jewel heard her voice recounting the story, the story she
had pushed to the back of her mind all these years. The
girls sat still, listening, as she told them how she had met
Sascha and fallen in love with him and, finally, how his

real wife from Russia had appeared one day, with three other children. And how she had hated Sascha since then.

"I know it was a mistake not to tell you sooner," she said. "Sometimes I'd think about it and decide you were still too young to know. Then, later, it was easier not to tell you. Allen's been as much of a father as any man could be. He loves you, he's supported you."

"Where is Sascha now?" Beryl asked softly, obviously in shock.

"In New York. He designs for Tiffany . . ."

"Sascha Robinovsky!" Amber said, making a connection. "I know his work. I saw an article recently that the *Times* did on all the Tiffany designers. I can't believe it," she said, the news beginning to sink in. "All these years we've had another father—a *real* father—and *you* didn't tell us."

"Allen's been like a real father! Look, I know I was wrong. But Sascha hurt me more than you can imagine. I know I made a bad decision. But you spend your life making decisions. Some turn out good, some don't. But you live with them."

"But you *lied* to us!" Amber cried.

"I told you, I had my reasons. *Please* try and understand," Jewel pleaded. "I was very bitter . . . and hurt."

"Well, you hurt us!" Amber said. "How *could* you? No matter how you felt . . . we had a *right* to know. My God, I'm almost sixteen years old!" She flung out her leg and kicked the gingerbread house off the low table, then she stood up and crushed it under her foot.

"No!" Beryl screamed. "No, Amber! Don't ruin it! Please, *please* . . ." She burst into tears.

It was too late. The gingerbread, candy, feathers, icing, and tiny flowers collapsed into mounds of crumbs and debris on the Oriental carpet. Amber gave the tray a swift kick across the room, and it landed in the fireplace.

"I hate you, Mother!" she said. "I hate you as much as you hated Sascha! And if he's my father, then I'm going to live with him! I *never* want to see you again!" She stormed out of the room.

Beryl's sobs were reaching hysteria, and she flung herself into her mother's arms, spilling out an indistinguishable barrage of words.

Jewel hugged her younger daughter and tried to soothe her, in shock herself from the vehemence of Amber's reaction. She had known this would be hard for them to take, but she never imagined it would be this bad.

Nushka appeared in the doorway in her robe, awakened by the noise. "Oh dear, what's wrong?" she asked.

"You name it," Jewel said. "And it's all Sascha's fault." She sighed, patting Beryl's head. "No. Cancel that. It's all my fault. I've made a fucking mess out of everything."

30

Jewel returned to New York to begin her therapy, and Allen announced that any major decision concerning their marriage would not be made in haste. He and Jewel, for now, would continue living together. He would not see Sara, nor would she see Mike Marshall, which suited her fine.

Allen hired a chauffeur to take Jewel around town. In the past, she had preferred taking cabs or, on sunny days, walking down Fifth Avenue to the office. But until she improved, walking to Bijoux was out of the question.

"At my speed," she told Allen, "I'll get there just as everyone else is leaving for the day."

Jewel was conscientious about her physical therapy, and even bought two portable running tracks, one for the bedroom at home and one to be delivered to her office. She could not yet run, but after a week of therapy, she was walking with less of a shuffle. She was determined to get as strong as possible before she returned to work.

If she hadn't heard from Edward about the rumblings of mass defection at Bijoux she'd have had no inkling at all. The apartment was filled with flowers and well-wishing notes from her employees. She spoke with Meg every day, and her assistant gave no hint of unrest. Perhaps Edward had been exaggerating. Or perhaps they had merely decided not to kick her while she was down.

She would find out the truth soon enough.

The car pulled around the corner onto Sixty-eighth Street, and the chauffeur stopped in front of the therapists' offices. He came around and opened the door for Jewel.

"I can take it from here, John. Pick me up at one-thirty, please."

"Yes, ma'am," the chauffeur replied.

Jewel walked slowly to the doorway, with her cane hooked jauntily over her arm, and headed in.

"Oh, hello, Mrs. Prescott," the receptionist said. "We're running a few minutes late. Take a seat. Can I get you anything—a cup of coffee?"

"No, thanks. I think I'll get changed and do some walking around the track."

Jewel's hand was on the door that led to the gym and changing rooms when she heard a man's voice, behind her.

"Madeleine?"

It was Wyatt's voice. She turned, saying, "We keep running into each . . ." But she trailed off. It was not Wyatt McNeill.

It was Hadley.

He looked older, handsomer. Same dark brown hair, cut a bit shorter. Same dark eyes, a bit more intense. Same cheekbones, more chiseled than ever. He was dressed in faded jeans, a black turtleneck, and a down parka, looking as if he'd walked straight in from a ski slope. A pair of crutches were propped on the armrest beside him.

Jewel stared at him, stunned. "Hadley! I can't believe it. How did you recognize me? I look completely different."

"I recognized your voice first, but you haven't changed so much. Different color hair. But you're still recognizable —and beautiful."

"Except for this," she said, indicating her cane. "But what happened to you? A skiing accident?"

He shook his head. "I was riding a bus around some back roads of India. Up in the mountains near Bhutan. Hairpin turns and all that. Another bus rounded a corner into us. We went over a cliff and landed in a deep ravine. A lot of us—those who lived—were thrown from the bus. A lot of *them* walked away from the accident. But my legs got pinned under. That was two years ago. I've been in hospitals in Darjeeling and London since then. They told me I'd never walk again, but I've gotten this far . . ." he trailed off. "God, it's good to see you again. What happened to you?"

"A cerebral hemorrhage . . . stroke."

"Good Lord," Hadley said. "When?"

"Six weeks ago."

"Madeleine, I'm sorry." He shook his head with disbelief. "But you look as if you're coming along fine."

"Not as fast as I'd like," she said.

He nodded, understanding. "I take it you're married. I heard the Mrs. Prescott."

Jewel was amazed that Hadley knew nothing about her life now. Hadn't Wyatt or Anna told him *anything?* "Yes, for years now. I have two teenage daughters. What about you?"

Hadley shrugged. "Remember I told you I'd never get married. I haven't, although I lived with a woman for nine years. She worked for CARE, same as me."

"What are you doing now?"

"Healing," Hadley said with a wry grin. "That's been taking up all of my time."

"I'm really sorry, Hadley. What an awful thing to happen."

"Oh, things haven't been bad, at least not until the accident. I was really happy in India—doing something that was making a difference. You know me," he grinned.

They hadn't seen each other for so many years, yet it was almost as if they hadn't missed a beat. "Oh, Hadley, I'd love to talk to you."

"Jewel?" Linda, the therapist, appeared in the doorway. "I'm ready for you now."

"Jewel?" Hadley repeated.

"Yes, that's my name now. It's, er, a long story."

"Look, I'm leaving for Honolulu tonight. I'm going to see a kahuna . . . a healer. When I get back, I'll call you. I'd like to get together with you, catch up. There's a lot to talk about."

"Yes, there is." Jewel reached into her purse for a business card and handed it to him. "Well, so long. It's been . . ."

" . . . wonderful to see you again," he said, picking up her sentence.

Jewel replayed the coincidental meeting with Hadley in her mind for the next few days, but there was little time to focus on the possibility of their next encounter, if there was ever going to be one. Although he had seemed pleased to see her, there was a good chance, after what had happened in the past, that he would want to leave it at that.

After six weeks of convalescense it was time to return to work, and most of Jewel's time was now spent fretting over what was going to happen at Bijoux International. Jewel thought endlessly about each of her employees, analyzing their strengths and weaknesses. She considered the pros and cons of what would happen to Bijoux if, as Ed-

ward expected, many of them jumped ship to work for
Cathalene.

Of course, there were many talented people out there in
the marketplace. She and Edward could rebuild Bijoux,
and it would not be starting from scratch. The reputation
they had earned over the years would not disappear—after
all, *she* was Bijoux. But it would hurt; it would be a major
setback. A lot of momentum would be lost, not to mention
money.

Sometimes Jewel looked around her incredibly beautiful
penthouse and thought, why *not* enjoy it? She didn't have
to work anymore. She could pack it in and devote herself
to charity.

A few weeks earlier, when Edward had first warned her
about the possible mass defection, she had—momentarily,
at least—considered giving up. But that wasn't why she
had returned from the grave, as she now jokingly liked to
put it. She was going to fight. She—meaning the *new* Jewel
—wasn't going to sit back and watch it happen.

And the old Jewel, the survivor, wasn't either.

The Sunday night before Jewel was to return to Bijoux,
she telephoned Edward.

"Well, darlin', tomorrow's the big day. Are you excited?" Edward asked.

"No, nervous as hell. I can almost hear people whispering behind my back. I'm so paranoid I can even imagine
Cathalene sticking pins in a voodoo doll shaped like me."

"Ah, the old Jewel returns," Edward laughed.

"No, not completely," she said seriously. "You don't go
through something like this and come out the same. I'm
really trying to change. You know, new approaches to old
problems—and God, I have a lot of them. Anyway, I
know we have to have a meeting with everyone, get it all
out in the open. But I'd like to ease back in for a few days.
Do you think you can stall them off from the big showdown . . . at least till the end of the week?"

"It won't be easy. But I'll manage it."

"Thanks, love. And now the real reason I called. Did Sascha go to Connecticut to see the kids today?" Jewel asked. "Have you spoken with him?"

"Yes. He just called. They had a nice enough time. It was awkward, as you might imagine. They have to get to know each other."

"Did Amber ask to live with him? Did he say she could?"

"I doubt it," Edward said. "Sascha didn't mention it."

"Well, I'll quiz Beryl when I call. At least *she's* still speaking to me."

"Amber will come around," Edward assured her. "She's stubborn, like you. And fifteen's a difficult age. Give her time. She loves you very much. You should have seen her in the hospital when you were still unconscious. I think she took it harder than any of us."

"Well, I wish there was something I could say to her. But she won't get on the phone when I call. And all last weekend she stayed in her room to avoid me."

"Maybe Sascha could help," Edward suggested. "Look, he really wants to talk to you . . . to *see* you."

"No! I told you . . ."

"Jewel," Edward said firmly, "you've come this far. Why don't you take the extra step? Clear out the cobwebs once and for all. I think you both need it."

"Oh hell, Edward, I don't want to."

"You have to. For more reasons than one," Edward said simply.

"Oh shit. All right. Tell him he can come see me at the office. He can call Meg for an appointment."

"I think you should call him."

"No! Don't push me, Edward."

"Okay," Edward sighed. "I'll set it up."

Jewel's return to Bijoux was more emotional than she had expected. Everyone gathered in her office when she arrived, and there were vases of coral roses, her favorite shade, on every table. On her desk was a long, slender, rectangular box, gift wrapped and accompanied by a card signed by everyone.

"A present? You didn't have to. What is it?" Jewel picked up the box and shook it.

"Why is it," Mike Marshall asked, "that people always do that instead of opening it?"

"Oh, I'll open it, don't worry," Jewel smiled. Over the past weeks of convalescence, she had managed to gain five pounds. Although she was still very thin, the extra weight had softened her face, taking away the sharpness of the angles. There was a softness around the eyes too, and in the way she looked at people—as if she were seeing them directly now, and not through the prism of work. Everyone remarked later that Jewel looked more beautiful than ever. No one could pinpoint why.

Jewel tore the wrapping paper off her gift and found an antique black ebony walking stick with a scrolled, sterling silver head. "This is beautiful," Jewel said, tears in her eyes. "Really, I can't thank you enough. When I've finished needing it, I'll hang it on the wall above the desk. So I can beat people when I need to," she joked, hoping they would take it as such.

The impromptu party ended with individual hugs and "welcome backs" for Jewel. But she could feel eyes avoiding hers, and she knew that, despite the show of affection, this was merely the still before the tornado.

Mike Marshall lingered behind, looking as nervous as the others. "Can we talk, Jewel?"

"Yes," she smiled. "We need to. Have a seat. First, thanks again for the baskets of flowers you kept sending. They were lovely. And Edward brought over the mock-up for the spring catalog. It's fabulous. I love the idea of covering the models with muslin so you can't quite see their features, only the jewelry against the outline of their bodies. It's absolutely inspired."

"Really? I was afraid you'd hate it. It's very surreal," Mike said.

"Well, I love it. I don't think I've let you use your own vision enough in the past. I've had a hard time letting go of all the details. But that's going to change."

"Look, Jewel—"

"I don't want to talk about Cathalene and all that . . . not yet," she said. "I do want to talk about us."

Mike crossed his legs, then uncrossed them, obviously uncomfortable. "You know I'm happy to see you again. You look really wonderful."

"Thanks, Mike." Jewel picked up a glass paperweight that Beryl had made, a collage of bird pictures, and toyed with it while she talked. "Mike, I told you I couldn't see you for a while, because of Allen. Well, it's more than that. We've been, *I've* been going through the motions for a long time. You liked me so much that I was afraid you'd quit Bijoux if we ended the affair. Oh, Mike, we had some wonderful times. But there's no future in it. You know that."

"I finally figured it out," he said. "You stopped having time for me. Is there someone else?"

"No." She went over and gently closed the door to her office. "I know you've been seeing Meg. She told me she's crazy about you, and I think you're perfectly matched. But I want to know if you're serious, or—"

"I, er, may be serious," Mike said. "Does that upset you? That I was seeing her?"

Jewel shook her head. "On the contrary. I want you to be happy." She glanced at the clock on her wall. "Oh dear, I have an appointment with Erik. He wants to show me the hiddenite that the gem cutters have just finished faceting."

Mike rose and came over behind Jewel's desk and kissed the top of her head. "Welcome back," he said. "We missed you."

The rest of Jewel's day flew by, with a succession of

meetings. In each one, she tried to make contact, not gloss over what the person was saying, but listen and consider. It wasn't as hard as she had imagined it would be, quite relaxing actually. Jewel realized what a good job she and Edward had done in assembling their staff.

Edward had told her, in a brief huddle that afternoon, that Cathalene was pressing people for answers. She wanted to get everyone out before Jewel could change their minds. Not that she was entirely certain, Jewel admitted to herself, that she *could* change their minds. But Cathalene Columbier would get them over her dead body.

31

There were major fish to fry. Major fish; and Jewel had dressed for the occasion.

Even though the first fish was to be handled over the telephone, Jewel understood as well as anybody the importance of the right look to complement the frame of mind. And so she had selected, with the precision of a surgeon choosing her scalpels, a short black skirt and sweater, with a fitted deep pink jacket on top. Harry Harper, of course. The first fish demanded it.

"Morning, Jewel," Meg Higdon smiled as Jewel came in. "You're looking great."

"Thanks," Jewel said. "Get me Harry Harper on the phone, will you?"

"Sure thing," Meg said brightly.

In her office, Jewel put down her briefcase on her desk and opened the lock. She took out her appointment calendar and ran over the day. If she could get through this one, she was on her way, no doubt about it. She turned and checked her appearance in the mirror in the corner.

Meg buzzed. "I've got Harry Harper on line one."

"Put him through."

"Hi, love! Welcome back to the arena," Harry said, his voice full of enthusiasm. "Are you calling to take me to lunch?"

"Hardly," Jewel said coolly. "I'm calling to give you a piece of my mind."

"Oh? What have I done now?"

"Anna Ferguson, Harry. Ring a bell? Anna and Cathalene. Dangerous elements to mix. Especially dangerous for an old friend. Jesus, how *could* you? The two people in the world who have it most in for me and you put them together! Smart, Harry. Thank you very much."

There was split-second silence on Harry's end. "Look, this is *old* news. All right, I'm sorry. Why get so pissy about it now?"

"It may be old news to you . . . Oh, look, I'll admit I *should* have figured it out for myself. I assumed Anna and Cathalene had met each other in some random way. I forgot we had Machiavelli Harper looming around on the sidelines, looking for trouble to stir up."

"Oh hell, Jewel, it just happened. Okay, I shouldn't have. But dammit, you don't appreciate me anymore. I thought you needed a little comeuppance."

"A little *comeuppance!?* That's what you call trying to ruin everything I've worked for all these years?" Jewel shrieked into the receiver. "Don't you know what they're trying to *do* to me?"

"Look, baby," Harry sighed, "it all got out of hand. I had no idea it'd get this far. But then I didn't know how disgruntled your people over there were either, till I talked to Edward. I'll do what I can. But look to yourself a bit too, Jewel. You know the old saying, you can't break up a happy marriage."

"Oh, great," Jewel seethed; not least because the arrow had hit home. "A lecture. From Harry Harper."

"Dammit, Jewel," Harry snapped, "don't forget I've done a hell of a lot for you over the years. All right, this was a mistake, but—"

"*Mistake?* If I go down the tubes, Harry, that's some mistake! You've done a lot for me? *I've* done a lot for you too, you bastard! I've returned plenty of favors over the years. Jesus, I thought that was what friends were for!"

There was a long silence, and for a moment Jewel thought he might have hung up on her. Then his voice came back over the wire. "Look, Jewel, it was a rotten thing to do. Believe me when I say I didn't mean any real harm. You're right, I wanted to stir things up. I thought it'd be amusing to watch you gals pulling each other's hair a bit. What can I say? When I fuck up, I fuck up. I want to try to make it up to you. I'll do what I can."

"I think you're too late with too little," Jewel said sarcastically.

"Look, I'm heading out to Wyoming tomorrow. Let me take you to lunch when I get back. Thursday okay?"

"Hell, Harry . . ."

"Say yes. Come on, Jewel. I'll grovel."

Jewel found herself smiling, in spite of herself. "Oh, all right. If you promise to grovel a lot."

"I'll prostrate myself." A note of cheer came back into Harry's voice. "Hey, you're going to pull through, love. I'm not worried a bit."

"Thanks, Harry," she relented. "I certainly am."

That fish taken care of, Jewel glanced at her watch. It was shortly before eleven. She could feel her stomach muscles tightening as the clock hummed on.

Edward had not shown up. He had promised to be in her office by quarter to. She rang his private extension; he was not there. She paced, tried again. Finally she buzzed Meg.

"Where's Edward? He was supposed to be here by now."

"He's out at a meeting, I think. I'll check."

"Oh God, he's *supposed* to be here. What time do you have?"

"Eleven," Meg said. "And your eleven o'clock has just arrived. Mr. Robinovsky. Shall I send him in?"

Sascha. Right on the other side of that door. Suddenly Jewel didn't think she could do it. Where the hell was Edward?

Then she realized that Edward must have planned it this way. She was going to have to deal with Sascha on her own.

"All right, Meg," Jewel said, making her voice sound as steady as she could manage. "Send him in."

The door swung open and fifteen years vanished, melted away, in a split second. Sascha had changed, but he didn't look a day older. The largeness of him, which could have gone to fat, was all muscle now. His bushy hair was still shoulder-length, but the beard was gone. The face was more defined. And there were those eyes, the paleness now shining out from behind tortoiseshell-rimmed glasses.

For an instant neither spoke as they took each other in. Sascha strode midway into the room and stopped, awkwardly. Jewel got up from her desk and walked over to him carefully, so as not to let her weak leg betray her. She extended her hand to shake his, but instead of offering his hand in return, Sascha lunged forward, flinging his arms around her and kissing her hard on both cheeks.

"My Jewel," he said, his eyes scanning every part of her. "Since when did you get such bright red hair?"

That broke the ice. Jewel couldn't help but smile. If she were still with Sascha, he never would have let her do it. He would have insisted she grow old gracefully. But maybe not; he certainly had not aged. "Since about four months ago. Before that I was blond."

"You look different, so beautiful."

"You look good too, Sascha. You're all toned and fit." She showed him to a plush sofa by the corner windows and sat down next to him.

"I work out," he said. "Run five, eight miles every day. I was getting fat." Sascha smiled and put out his arms to indicate an enormous belly. "All day, I sit and work, sit and work. And Aïna only knows how to raise children and cook. Too much heavy food. Finally, I sent her to Weight Watchers and I joined a gym. I work out instead of eating a big lunch. I look better than when we were together, don't I?"

Jewel grinned, relaxing more. Although Sascha's English was perfect now, he still had the old accent, and she remembered how much she loved it. "You look great—but not better. You looked pretty good then too," Jewel said. All the former hatred, the reserve, the anxiety over seeing him again dissipated. Here he was, willing to meet her in friendship. Here she was, finally agreeing to meet him. Jewel had never imagined this day would come. Before her illness, she would have laughed at the idea.

All of a sudden, a wave of nervousness came over her. There was much to talk about, she was sure, but she couldn't for the life of her think what. She kept staring into Sascha's smiling face. He was obviously so happy to see her again. She could not quite decipher what *she* was feeling.

"So you've seen the girls. What did you think?" Jewel finally managed to ask.

"Nice young ladies. You have done a good job. They are both pretty."

"Well, Beryl's pretty. Amber, I'm afraid, is going through a rather awkward adolescence. But she'll come out of it soon, I hope. She's not speaking to me, because of . . . you know."

Sascha nodded. "She is a deep girl. Complex. Like you. Beryl *looks* much like you. Amber, she looks like me, but she *is* you. In her soul she is much like you. Loving, giving, but always afraid to love, to give."

"I wasn't afraid to love you," Jewel said softly.

He nodded. "Yes, that's true. But then I hurt you. I caused you a lot of pain. For that you'll never know how sad I am. It was something I would never have wished."

"Well, it's all yesterday's news, as they say. I'm making an effort now to face the past and come to grips with it. And it hasn't been easy, let me tell you." She tried to say it lightly.

"I know, my Jewel, I understand that it's not easy to see me after so many years. But I'm grateful you've forgiven me. You *do* forgive me, don't you?"

"Yes, I forgive you, Sascha." Jewel took a deep breath and expelled it loudly. "I never thought I'd hear myself say that." She glanced away self-consciously for a moment, then looked back. "But back to the girls. Is Amber going to move in with you?"

Sascha shook his head. "I think it's best for her to stay at school with Beryl. They are close. They need each other. Amber wouldn't be happy with me and Aïna. We lead a different life. Aïna's a very simple woman. Amber is used to much more. But she's welcome to visit. They both are. I would like that."

Jewel smiled. "That puts my mind to rest. I knew Beryl would be devastated without Amber. Then I was afraid they'd *both* go live with you and I'd never see them again."

"That would never happen, my dear. They love you." He got up and walked over to Jewel's worktable where she had been sketching designs to be worked up by her craftspeople, for next year's nonpareils collection. He picked up a sketch and looked at it. "Very nice," he said. "You're an excellent jewelry-maker now. You learned well."

Jewel smiled. "I apprenticed with the best. You are the best, you know."

"You have built a big business on great talent. If you

didn't have the talent, you wouldn't be the success you are." He turned and looked at her. "I've heard rumors that Bijoux is in trouble. But I don't believe it. Bijoux can be greater than ever before."

"Yes," Jewel said, leaning back against the sofa, "that's what I keep telling myself. Except I haven't quite figured out how it's going to happen. I'll know after tomorrow's meeting who's staying and who's leaving. Then we'll go from there."

"I have proposal to make," Sascha said, coming back to sit by her. "I'll come to work for Bijoux."

"What?" Jewel sat up, astonished. "You? But you're locked into Tiffany."

Sascha shrugged. "Not locked in. I want more freedom. At Tiffany, only Elsa Peretti is allowed to work in silver. I am constrained."

Jewel sat staring at Sascha. "You'd leave Tiffany and come to work for me?" Sascha nodded. "But as big as Bijoux's become, we could never do the volume of business that Tiffany does. I couldn't pay you enough."

"I would not work *for* you, my Jewel," Sascha laughed. "That would never do. But I would work *with* you. As partner to you and Edward."

Jewel bit her lip, considering the proposition. If Sascha came to Bijoux it would be a coup that would turn Cathalene and Anna green. In fact, it just might tip the scales in the big battle that was looming.

But would it work? She and Sascha, together again? Well, Amber and Beryl might be pleased. Edward certainly wouldn't object. She didn't know what Allen would think. But . . . there was a big "but."

"I don't know," Jewel said. "I mean, in the past you always tried to overpower me with your will. I'm not the same girl, Sascha. Do you think we'd end up fighting all the time?"

"Who knows?" Sascha said frankly. "But I've changed too, over the years. I'm not as much of a bully as you remember. We could try it. If it does not work . . ." He trailed off into an expressive Russian shrug. "I know a little of the problems you're facing, my dear," he said. "And I want to help you. To make up for the past."

Jewel got up and began to pace, slowly. "Does Edward know about all this?"

"I have discussed the possibility with him. He likes the idea. But we decided nothing. The decision is yours to make."

"You'd really do this for me, Sascha?" Jewel said. "Why?"

Sascha came over and took her hands in his. "There will always be a bond between us," he said. "It is very deep." He wheeled away suddenly and walked over to the window that looked out over Fifth. She heard him clear his throat. "I think I'd like working at Bijoux," he said, turning to face her again. "I think we will work well together. I won't try to make big corporate decisions that are yours and Edward's to make. Nor will I dictate what you design. But you will not tell *me* what to design. Of that I must have complete control."

Jewel nodded. "I think I could live with that."

There was a knock on the door, and Edward entered, a bit hesitantly. He looked at Jewel, then at Sascha, trying to gauge the temperature of the room.

"Where've you been?" Jewel asked. "You were supposed to get here half an hour ago."

"I had a meetin' down in the Thirties. Got stuck in traffic comin' back," he said.

"Yeah, uh-huh. Well, come on in, Benedict Arnold."

Grinning uncertainly, Edward closed the door and dropped into the stuffed white leather chair. "So," he said, "how's it goin'?"

"Sascha told me the plan the two of you have cooked up."

"You make it sound like we were schemin' behind your

back," Edward protested. "We weren't. We only barely discussed it. And it all hinges on you, darlin'."

"I know," Jewel said. "I thank both of you. But I still have to think about it. I can't commit right now, on the spur of the moment."

Edward nodded. "I understand. But don't forget the big pow-wow's at ten tomorrow. Be a good idea to make up your mind by then. If Sascha's joinin' us, I think people have a right to know before they make their final decisions. It might sway them."

"It might," Jewel said. "But this is a major decision for me. I need time."

"That's fair, my Jewel. I agree to that." Sascha got up. "And now I must be going." He shook Edward's hand and gave Jewel two more hard kisses on both her cheeks. "You call me when you decide." He looked down at Jewel again, then kissed her on the lips, more tenderly. "You don't know how happy I am to see you again. No matter what happens, I want us to be friends." Then he lumbered out of the room.

"Why do you have to think about it?" Edward asked, when Sascha was out of sight. "Why the hell couldn't you have accepted his offer right off?"

"You forget, Edward, I lived with the man for three years. He made me his fucking apprentice. How do I know he's not going to come in and start trying to tell me what to do? It *could* happen, you know."

Edward sighed. "It could. But Sascha only wants to design jewelry. Honestly, I don't think he gives a damn what you do . . . as long as he has complete artistic freedom to do his own thing. I think Sascha's askin' very little, considerin' what we'll get in return."

"Yeah, I know," Jewel said. "But I need to sort this out for myself. There's so much baggage . . . professional, personal. I just don't know." She looked at him, and for the first time that day her eyes glistened with tears. "This isn't just a partner decision, Edward. It's a personal one for me. And I've got to live with the one I make."

"Yes, darlin'," Edward said. He knew that pressing her at this point was the worst thing he could do. "You do what you gotta do." He hugged her and left the office.

Edward hoped she would make the right choice, for herself and for Bijoux. But he couldn't count on it.

Jewel was drained. She couldn't stay at the office any longer. Buzzing Meg to cancel the rest of her appointments, she shoved some papers into her briefcase and fled.

It felt strange to be going home in the middle of the day. But no stranger than a lot of things lately. She forced herself to walk all the way, through the lunchtime crowds, up Fifth Avenue to Eighty-first Street. It took enormous effort and nearly two hours. But Jewel needed to find out how strong she was.

She was in training for the big fight.

By the time Jewel reached her apartment, her left side was quivering, and she could hardly stand. She did not even have the strength to search for her keys. She rang. Shoki, the Japanese houseboy, let her in.

"Good afternoon, Miss Jewel," Shoki said, unable to conceal his astonishment. "You home early."

"I'm tired. I'm going up to rest. Is my husband here?"

"No. He out. He taking a meeting somewhere."

"Could you send up a glass of mineral water . . . and something to eat? I just realized I'm starving."

Shoki nodded. "I fix Mr. Allen good lobster salad for lunch. You want some?"

"That sounds wonderful."

She took the elevator to the third floor bedroom suite. For half an hour, she soaked in a bath as hot as she could take it. When she came out, wrapping herself in an antique chinchilla robe that had been a gift from Allen years before, she found the lunch Shoki had left in the bedroom and devoured it hungrily.

She picked up a book and settled into the pillows on the
chaise longue to read. The chaise was an art deco piece by
Rateau that Allen had purchased in Paris on their honeymoon, and she found her mind drifting back to that trip.
How long ago it seemed; how young the children were
then. How young they *all* were then.

Jewel put on her glasses and picked up the biography of
Edith Wharton she was reading. Lately, during her convalescence, she had begun saturating herself in the fin de
siècle period. And, wonder of wonders, she could feel her
creative impulse opening up again in the warm light of
that elegant era. She had been sketching new pieces that
were wildly romantic and extravagant.

She began to read, but the words would not string together and make sense for more than a sentence or two at
a time. Her eyelids drifted shut, opened, drifted shut
again. A carriage rolled by, drawn by a team of handsome
bays. A man in a top hat and tails came down the steps of
a magnificent brownstone, escorting a lady dressed in a
sumptuous evening gown of midnight blue satin. Around
her throat was a fabulous necklace of gold filigree . . .
with aquamarines and sapphires and diamonds pavé . . .

She opened her eyes, and Allen was there. He was
standing in the doorway looking at her, a glass in his hand
and a worried expression on his face.

"Hi," he said. "I didn't mean to wake you. Shoki said
you were here. Are you all right? Do you want me to call
the doctor?"

"Everything's fine," Jewel smiled. "I decided to knock
off work early."

"You sure you don't have a fever?" Allen asked, coming
over to feel her forehead.

"I just needed to relax," she insisted. "A tough morning. What about you?" She nodded at the scotch on the
rocks he was holding. "Drinking before six?"

"What?" He gazed distractedly at the glass as if he had
forgotten it, and took a sip. Then he went over and sat

down on the edge of the bed. "As a matter of fact," he said, "it's been a hell of a day."

"What's the matter?"

"Oh, Mother's worse. Isabel called. They've had to hire round-the-clock nurses."

"Oh, Allen, I'm sorry," Jewel said, not particularly sorry except for Allen and Isabel. Jewel had never achieved more than a cool truce with LaDonna Prescott.

"Yeah, well . . ." There was a flutter of strain in his voice.

"Look," Jewel said, "why don't you take a bath and relax? Then maybe we could go out for a bite and a movie later. Just the two of us."

"Yeah, sure," Allen said.

She flashed him a smile, then picked up her book again. But after a paragraph she realized that he had not moved. Curious, she took off her glasses and found that he was looking at her with an anguished expression.

"Jewel," Allen said, "we have to talk."

She laid down her book. "Okay."

Allen gulped the rest of his scotch. "I saw Sara today," he told her.

"Oh?" She must be slipping. She had not seen this coming. "Does that mean I'm recovered?" she said nastily.

"It's the first time I've seen her since—" he said, ignoring the dig.

"Well, that must have been exciting. How is dear Sara?"

"She's pregnant."

Jewel exhaled deeply. For a moment she could not respond. "Oh?" she said finally. "And do we know who the father is?"

"Sara's willing to have an abortion," Allen said quickly. "But she felt she had an obligation to tell me first."

"How moral of her." Suddenly Jewel understood. She stared at Allen, letting it sink in. She saw the streaks of gray that had appeared at his temples, and the hint of jowl that had begun to pad his once-lean chin.

"You want the baby, don't you?" she said softly. "You want a child of your own."

"Oh, Jewel, I don't know *what* I want," Allen said miserably. "I feel like a lawn mower has plowed through my brains. Yes, I would like to have a child of my own. I never thought . . ." He plunged his face into his hands with a moan. "I'm confused as hell."

Jewel got up and went over to sit beside him. She thought she should feel angrier, sadder, than she did. But the feeling that floated to the top was relief, a sort of lightness.

She put her arm around his heaving shoulders. "But you do want the baby, don't you?"

Allen did not answer. She could feel him sobbing softly.

"If you love her that much, Allen, I think you should marry her."

"But Jewel, I love *you* . . . Oh Jesus, Jewel, I never thought . . ."

"Oh, Allen, I'm not happy about this, but maybe it's the sign we needed. Maybe this is the right time to make the break—friendly, no court battles, no alimony, no bitterness. I don't want much . . . a few of the paintings . . ." Jewel paused, then added, "And I'd like the house in Connecticut. I need to spend more time there."

Allen looked up at her. His face was pale, and there were red rims around his eyes. "But it would mean we wouldn't be married anymore." He shook his head. "Somehow I thought we'd always be married."

She hugged him tightly. "Allen, you can't have us both. And she's got your baby."

"Don't think badly of Sara," he pleaded. "She never meant for this to happen. She thinks the world of you, Jewel."

Jewel smiled wryly. "I do think she could've been more conscientious about birth control."

"It was an accident. She had an IUD. Apparently it came out without her knowing it."

"Oh, Allen," Jewel said. She kissed him on the fore-head. *How gullible men are,* she thought.

Allen sighed again. "God, Jewel, I feel awful. And it's not just us. There's Amber and Beryl. They've gone through so much these past weeks. I can't do this to them. Look, I'm going to end it with Sara," he said with convic-tion. "It won't work."

"Darling," Jewel said, "you've been a wonderful father to my children. And you'll continue to be. They *love* you. And yes, it *is* going to be hard on them. But it's life . . . and life is full of change." She picked up his hand and put it in hers, examining his long, slim fingers. "I always felt bad that we couldn't have a child together, that you were being cheated. Well, now's your chance. It'll be hard, but we'll all survive."

"Will we?" Allen asked miserably.

"Look at the bright side. With Amber and Beryl around, think how much you'll save on baby-sitters."

Allen tried to smile. "Are you trying to get rid of me?"

Jewel nodded. "Yes, I think I am. Circumstances have merely brought it to a head sooner."

"And you mean it? We'll be friends?"

"Yes, darling. We'll always be friends."

Later that evening they went out to see the new Spielberg film and stopped afterward at the Ideal Lun-cheonette, a favorite of Allen's where Jewel usually re-fused to go. They ate meat loaf and potato pancakes, then walked home slowly, arm in arm, stopping to look in Madison Avenue shop windows along the way.

At home, they drank hot chocolate to warm up and then fell into bed together and made love, sharing the nostalgic sex of longtime lovers who would soon never be lovers again.

Her life with Allen was over, Jewel realized, as she lay with her hand on his naked hip and listened to his breath-ing settle into the steady rhythm of sleep. She was going to be on her own again, for the first time in many years. To her surprise, it wasn't painful. Allen would be okay; he had Sara and the baby. Amber and Beryl would adjust, after the shock; the poor girls were used to shock by now. She would survive too. Everyone knew Jewel Prescott was a survivor.

Long after Allen had drifted off to sleep, Jewel lay awake on her side of the bed. Tomorrow was crowding in on her. The first day, as the hoary cliché had it, of the rest of her life. The last of her professional life, if she did not handle the meeting perfectly.

Edward was probably right. Sascha might well be the key. But could she work beside Sascha, day after day, just to save her corporate skin?

A day ago, had anyone asked her, she would have said Arafat and Sharon were a more likely partnership. But Jewel had been amazed by her reaction to seeing Sascha this morning. All that hatred, all that energy wasted in bitterness since she had last set eyes on him! It gave her a feeling of peace to know that she could cut that loose at last, to know that she and Sascha could be friends again.

But friends were not the same as partners. Could she work with him again? Would the old patterns reemerge? And could she risk that chance? She would have to make her decision before the meeting tomorrow.

And Jewel still had no idea what that would be.

32

Jewel arose at six, having slept fitfully for only a couple of hours. But she was too keyed up to be tired. She showered, washed and dried her hair, and then spent half an hour in front of her closet, deliberating on what to wear; finally she chose a short, fitted, navy blue pinstripe suit that she had bought from Harry's fall collection. On the lapel, she pinned the heart made of opals— the one Jane had given her for high school graduation— for luck. Then she went to her wall safe and selected pieces of jewelry made by each of her designers, also for luck.

Allen was at the breakfast table when she came down. "You look smashing," he said, getting up to pour her a cup of coffee. "Dressed for total success."

"Oh, Allen, I'm a basket case. How I'm going to get through the next few hours I haven't the vaguest idea."

"No matter what happens today, you'll come out on

top. One thing you'll never be is a loser," he said, taking her hand.

"Thanks, darling." She took a few sips of her black coffee and toyed with a croissant but decided she wasn't hungry. "Allen, I'm going to call a broker today. And look for apartments over the weekend."

"Oh, Jewel, please. Not so fast. Let's not do anything until after the first of the year."

Jewel shook her head. "The girls have to be told sooner or later. I'd rather get it over with sooner. I couldn't bear having us all spend Christmas together, pretending we're one big, happy family when we aren't."

"But we will be. One big, happy family. Won't we? You said we'd always be friends."

"And we will," Jewel said. "You and I. I make *no* promises about Sara. Look, I'm being mature as hell about all this. Don't expect miracles. I'm not a hundred-percent pleased this is all happening, you know. My ego is more than a little bruised."

Allen sighed. "Oh, Jewel, I keep thinking I may be making the biggest mistake of my life."

"Maybe you are," Jewel shrugged, "but that's *part* of life. Making mistakes. God knows I've made a bundle."

"I guess you're right," Allen said. "But this morning the whole thought of losing you and marrying Sara really terrifies the shit out of me."

"Well, I'd certainly be terrified at the thought of marrying Sara Richards," Jewel said. "No, sorry, darling. I made myself promise not to be snide . . . for the girls' sake. That's the last bitchy thing I'll say about what's-her-name." She looked at her watch. "Oh dear, I'd better go. Wish me luck."

Allen got up and kissed her good-bye, tenderly. "Good luck. I love you. No matter what happens at Bijoux, I'll be here for you. I mean it. Our relationship isn't going to end just because we're getting a divorce."

"I know, Allen. I love you too," she said, grabbing her

briefcase quickly. The reality, the finality, of it all was beginning to hit her. She had to get out of there.

"Maybe after you've married Sara *we* could have an affair," she quipped, to keep from crying.

John, the chauffeur, dropped Jewel off in front of Bijoux at 9:30 A.M., but she wasn't ready to take the elevator up to her office. Instead she headed back out onto Fifth Avenue and strolled down to Rockefeller Center to see the giant Christmas tree and watch the skaters. Along the way, she stopped at a pay phone and called Sascha. He was not at work yet, so she left a message.

The morning was the coldest, so far, of the season. Jewel held the collar of her sable closed with her gloved hand and adjusted the scarf around her throat, which still bore a pinkish scar from the tracheostomy. Fifth Avenue was bustling, as always, with tourists, shoppers, and workers rushing to the office or meetings. Christmas, still several weeks away, was in the air, and Jewel tried to make herself think about what she should get for people. But her mind kept flipping back to the meeting. It was time to go back, to face everybody.

The silence was palpable as she stepped out of the elevator.

Everyone was assembled in the conference room, of course, waiting for her. She went to her office, tossed her fur on one of the sofas, opened her briefcase, and took out the papers she needed. Then she went over to the mirror to check her hair and makeup. The clock on the wall said ten o'clock, exactly. Picking up the cane her employees had given her as a welcome-back present, she walked slowly to the conference room.

They were all seated, expectantly. Edward got up and came over to greet her.

"Jesus, Jewel," he whispered as he kissed her cheek. "I thought we were gettin' together *before* the meetin'."

"I'm sorry, Edward," Jewel said. "I ran late."

Jewel studied the assembled faces: Mike Marshall and
Meg, sitting next to each other; Erik Sanders, Bijoux's
chief gemologist; Jill Cross, the marketing manager;
Charles Feldman, the display director; and the designers
—Rody Abrams, Tom Tinker, Rita Roberts, Leilani, and
Katrina and Christof Von Berlichingen, who had just ar-
rived from Paris. *All* these people Cathalene was trying to
steal away from her.

"Are you as nervous as I am?" Jewel asked with a
smile.

A polite titter of laughter rippled around the room; nervous, all right.

"I appreciate your bearing with me all this time," Jewel
began. "First, I'd like to say that there's not one person in
this room that I'd like to lose . . . not just to Cathalene,
but to anybody. Every one of you has made an enormous
contribution to Bijoux's growth and success. And anyone
who leaves will be missed more than I can say. But I also
want you to know that whoever *does* choose to leave Bijoux will not go under a cloud. You'll go because it's right
for you. And Edward and I will fully support your decision and wish you well."

How was it going? she wondered, as she paused to take a
sip of coffee. It was hard to tell. But there was a look of
surprise on most of the faces. She had caught them off
guard. Good.

"I don't expect to change anyone's mind—anyone
whose mind is already made up," she amended. "But before you hand in your resignations I'd like to talk for a few
minutes about what Bijoux will be like if you choose to
stay. Because change *is* in the air." Jewel glanced at Edward for support, and he smiled, urging her on.

"I, for one, am trying to change . . . to cool out, listen
more. But it's not going to be easy. I'm going to need
constant prodding, reminders that I'm not *always* right."
Jewel paused, as another round of laughter circled the
room, this time more comfortable, more relaxed. "So I

expect you all to fight me, every step of the way . . . except when I'm being totally reasonable, of course," she joked. "Sometimes I'll give in to your ideas. But not every time. I can't change *completely.*" More laughter. "And when I *don't* go with your ideas, it won't be because I haven't considered them up, down, and sideways.

"Okay," Jewel sighed and rubbed her hands together. "The bottom line. I'm trying to change. But you'll have to meet me halfway. I even thought I'd read some of those books on Japanese management." She smiled and put her hands together and bowed. Then she sat. "I've said part of what I want to. Before I go on, does anyone have any comments, or questions?"

"Not really," Jill Cross answered. "I'd prefer you to finish first."

"All right. Are you all agreed?"

Heads bobbed up and down.

"Well, then I have some announcements to make: some changes that will be going into effect by the beginning of the year. First, those of you who stay will be given profit sharing in the company. And at some point down the road, when the stock market's stronger, Edward and I would like to take the company public. You'd all receive stock options if and when that happens."

Jewel noted an exchange of glances. Were they coming around yet? She couldn't tell without feedback, but it was clear that no one was ready to talk.

"Next, I'm going to start taking it a little easier. Spend a lot more time in the country with my children. If you can believe it." She laughed along with the others. "There has been a very recent change in my personal life that also has an effect on the company: my husband and I are getting a divorce."

Edward, who was jotting something on a pad, looked up, shocked. Jewel smiled, to assure him that she was all right.

"Allen will be stepping down as Bijoux's president, with

my gratitude and thanks. Edward will continue as design director. But I'm appointing him CEO, to take my place." She looked at Edward. "That is, if you'll accept."

"Oh, I'll accept all right," he said. "But what about you, Jewel?"

"Since I'm going to be taking more time off, I'll step down to president. And I promise to be every bit as hands-on as Allen ever was."

She waited until the laughter died down. This was the moment, and she felt the tension buzz through her like a bowstring.

"There's one last change. The new executive VP, and our new partner, will be Sascha Robinovsky." She paused, giving time to surprised voices. "He's leaving Tiffany to join us as soon as the formal arrangements can be made." Jewel looked over at Edward. He was grinning from ear to ear, and he brandished both fists, thumbs-up.

"Sascha and I go back a long way," Jewel explained. "Most of you don't know that we were married once. That he's the father of my daughters."

Mike Marshall whistled. "God, Jewel, you're really full of surprises today."

"I wanted to tell you directly—before the gossip began. What I want you to understand, you, meaning all of my designers, is that Sascha's presence will in no way diminish the role any of you play at Bijoux. Sascha will be one of us. He'll have his own floor space, just like the rest of us. His work won't be featured in ads any more often than yours, or mine."

"Wow! This is really something," Leilani said. "Sascha Robinovsky—as part of Bijoux. It's terrific news."

"Yeah, to be around him, to see him work up close. This is fabulous," Rita said.

"Maybe," Tom Tinker grumbled. "But we've been a team. Now we're getting a star, with a capital *S*. What's that going to do to the teamwork?"

"Sascha got along well with the other designers at Tiffany," Edward said. "That's not going to change."

"I have my doubts too," Rody Abrams said. "Not that I don't think Bijoux's reputation will soar with Sascha here. But I'm not sure where *I'll* fit in."

"Sascha will push us all," Jewel said. "But I don't think there's a designer in this room who can't stand up to the heat he'll generate. Look, I'm not going to try and twist anyone's arm. Those of you who stay will do so because you want to. It's as simple as that."

"Well, I'm not leavin', Jewel," Rita Roberts said. "I love it here at Bijoux."

"Thank you, Rita. I'm really happy to hear that. But Edward and I would like to have resignations by Monday afternoon, from all those people who want to leave. You can tell us now, if your mind is already made up. Or you can let us know after the weekend . . . if you need more time to think it over," Jewel said. "Right *now* though, let's have a show of hands from those of you who're definitely staying on."

Almost immediately, Rita, Leilani, Mike, Meg, Katrina and Christof, and Erik Sanders all raised their hands. That left Rody Abrams, Tom Tinker, Charles Feldman, and Jill Cross either undecided, or ready to hand in their resignations. But that was only four people. With such a strong core group remaining, it meant the inevitable fallout defections of craftspeople and gem buyers would not happen.

That meant she had won!

Back in Jewel's office, Edward collapsed onto the sofa. "Jewel," he said, "you are some piece of work. When did you decide about Sascha?"

"About fifteen minutes before I walked in there."

"Well, darlin', you did good. *What* a morning! I must say, you handled it beautifully. I've never seen you use so much tact."

"Oh, thank you very much," Jewel said.

"But what's this about you and Allen? I can't believe it," Edward said.

"You remember Sara Richards? Well, the latest is she's knocked up. Poor Allen thinks it was an accident. Anyway, we talked the whole thing over last night. It's for the best, for both of us. You know that."

Edward nodded. "I suppose so. But I still think you're taking it awfully well."

"Thank you," Jewel said perkily. "I do too."

Jewel had Nushka bring Amber and Beryl to the city early Saturday morning so they could accompany her while she looked for a new co-op. She and Allen sat them down when they first arrived and broke the news to Nushka and the girls. Beryl took the news in shock. Amber, in anger. Nushka burst out crying.

"I'm never going to stop being your father, girls," Allen insisted, after the news had begun to sink in. "I adopted you, remember? I've helped raise you. You'll still spend time with me, here. I'll still come to Connecticut. We're going to continue to be a family. Your mother and I will always be friends. This isn't going to be a conventional divorce, please understand that."

"Nothing this family does is ever conventional," Amber mumbled.

"But there's going to be the baby," Beryl said. "This is going to be hard to get used to. I mean, Daddy, if you're our adopted father does that make the baby our brother, or half brother, or stepbrother?"

"I don't know," Allen smiled, a bit sadly. "You got me. But what makes you think it'll be a boy?"

"Well, you already have two girls. You're due," Beryl said with the unassailable logic of her fifteen years.

Even Amber cracked a smile before they all burst into tears again.

* * *

By Sunday afternoon, thanks to the soft real estate market, Jewel had found herself an apartment that she liked. It was an old, sprawling eight-room place on Central Park West, across the park from Allen. It was covered with a hideous selection of wallpaper, but it had real possibilities. Jewel knew Edward would love throwing himself into the project of making it livable.

"We can see Daddy's place from here," Beryl exclaimed with forced perkiness as they explored the empty rooms. "We could even get lanterns and send semaphore signals!"

"I don't know," Amber said. "Binoculars or a good telescope would be better. Then we could spy."

"Let's go get something to eat, girls," Jewel called out from the front hall. "It's nearly time for you to head back to school. Shall we do Chinese?"

"Yeah, I'm starved," Beryl said. She put on her camel hair coat and wrapped a gold-and-white scarf, the Sheldon Arms colors, around her neck. "Mom, I'm having a whole lot of trouble getting used to all this."

"Oh, I know, baby," Jewel said, putting her arm around her younger daughter. "We all are. Even Allen. I think we have to try to be strong for his sake, most of all."

Amber came over and unexpectedly joined in the hug. "This is all so awful. And, Mother . . . I really feel sorry for you. Daddy having a child by somebody else. It's shocking."

Jewel smiled. It was the first sympathetic thing Amber had said to her since she had told the girls about Sascha. "Well, maybe it'll all turn out for the best. I've decided to spend most of my time in Connecticut . . . and turn you into day students. I'll come into the city only two or three days a week. I can set up a studio in the guest house." She sighed. "I'm tired of working so hard. And you two will be off to college in another couple of years. I want to spend as much time as possible with you before then."

"Do you mean it, Mother?" Amber asked.

Jewel nodded. *She's getting pretty again,* Jewel thought. *She's growing out of all that.* "I'm sorry I've been such a lousy mother. I want to make up for it, if I can."

"You *haven't* been a lousy mother," the girls both said at once.

"You've just been really busy," Beryl said.

"And we're proud of you. You're such a success," Amber added.

What words to a mother's ears. Jewel smiled. "Thank you. I never thought I'd hear you say that."

"If we're going to have time to eat, we'd better get going," Beryl said.

Jewel rang for the elevator and put her arms around her daughters.

Things were finally looking up.

The atmosphere at Bijoux on Monday morning was the calm after the storm. There were smiles everywhere. She might be able to learn to like this kind of thing, Jewel thought. As long as the work got done.

Edward tapped on her door and came in. "I've got the final scorecards here," he said, holding up a couple of envelopes. "Letters of resignation from Tom and Jill. Sorry to see them go, but what the hell—nine to two, that's a big win in any league. Cathalene thinks so too. She called me this mornin', and she's pissed as hell. I wish my French was better," he grinned.

"I had a feeling they might go," Jewel said. "I'll drop them both a note and wish them well. What about Rody?"

"Oh, Rody wrestled with it all weekend, I expect. But he's stayin'. Guess he's curious about the great Sascha after all."

"Sascha's given his notice to Tiffany. He'll be joining us the beginning of February." Jewel smiled. "I guess I can start breathing again. I believe I neglected to mention that I never talked to him before the big meeting. I called, but he wasn't in. I just left a message. I didn't know till Saturday that he was in for sure."

Edward whistled. "The balls of a riverboat gambler," he said admiringly. "I'll see you, darlin'. The CEO has work to do."

A few minutes later, Meg buzzed. "Somebody named Hadley McNeill on the phone. Want me to get rid of him?"

"No!" Jewel cried. "Put him on."

"Madeleine, how are you?"

"Fine. *Where* are you?"

"In New York. Just got back yesterday. Look, Madeleine, I'd like to talk to you. Can we have lunch?"

"I'm booked. How about dinner?"

"Dinner? That's even better. You like Indian food?"

"I love it! Where?"

"How about the New Hadley Curry House? I'm staying down on Eleventh Street, and there's no better Indian chef between here and Bombay." Hadley gave her the address, and Jewel wrote it down carefully.

She was afraid it would be one of those days that dragged by, but in a few minutes she found herself at her worktable, lost in a new design. Every once in a while, when she thought about it, she was aware that she was smiling.

Hadley had a lot to tell her, did he? Well, she could give him a run for his money in *that* department.

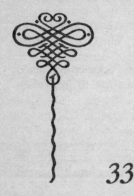

33

The limousine cruised down Park, turned west, and slid into the darker, narrower streets that made up Greenwich Village. The streets were probably no darker and narrower than uptown, Jewel supposed; but they *seemed* that way, exotic little alleys. Over the last years, she had spent very little time in this part of town, she realized. It was strange.

But what wasn't strange, these days? Divorcing Allen, yet still living with him until her place was ready. Leaving the office at five, with others still there, to get ready for dinner with Hadley McNeill. Dressing in her dressing room, while across the bedroom Allen dressed in his, then kissing him good-bye and sending him off to Sara.

"Here we are . . . number twenty-four," John said, pulling up in front of an impeccably remodeled brownstone. "What time shall I fetch you?"

"Take the rest of the evening off, John," Jewel said. "I'll take a cab home."

"Thank you, ma'am. Enjoy your evening."

"Thanks, John. I intend to."

Jewel climbed the stairs to the main entrance slowly. Before she could press the buzzer, the door flew open.

"I saw you pull up," Hadley said. "Welcome, Madeleine." He kissed her lightly on both cheeks. "A chauffeured limo, no less! Dinner's almost ready, if you can bear to eat so soon. Otherwise, I'll put it on hold."

"I'm starving," Jewel said, as he took her coat. "What are we having?"

"All my specialties . . . samosas, chapati, shrimp curry, dhal, raita . . . and chocolate cake for dessert."

"Chocolate cake? Just what part of India were you in, anyway?"

"The chocolate cake is from the Hungarian bakery around the corner," Hadley grinned. "I never developed an affection for Indian desserts."

He led the way back to the kitchen, moving nimbly on his crutches.

The kitchen was an angular, gray, postmodern room that seemed well suited to preparation of such precious new American dishes as crawfish with raspberry vinaigrette, not for the huge, homey Indian meal (pots were simmering away on all six gas burners) that Hadley had put together.

"It all smells wonderful," Jewel said. She was reminded of her first date with Sascha, when he had made a Russian meal. Was it because she was so thin that men were always prompted to cook for her?

"What a feast," she sighed. "But I'm not sure I'll make it to the chocolate cake."

"I'm glad you could come, Madeleine, er, Jewel. That's what everybody calls you now?" She nodded. "Being as you're a married lady, I was surprised you were free for dinner."

Jewel smiled but said nothing. There was no point in telling him about Allen. At least not yet.

Hadley propped one crutch against the counter and managed to choreograph the progress of the various pots using only the other. "Beer is the traditional drink with this meal, but I can give you wine, or something else, if you like."

"Beer's fine," Jewel said. "I haven't had one for years."

"In India," Hadley explained, getting two beers from the refrigerator, "we drank a lot of it. It was preferable to bottled water or soda. It mellowed out the extraordinary contradictions of the country . . . made them easier to live with."

Jewel sat on a bar stool, and Hadley handed her an Indian Eagle beer. "Are you going back? When you get well, I mean?"

Hadley shook his head. "No, I don't think so. Not to work at least. That phase of my life is over. It was starting to be over even before the accident."

"What are you going to do?"

"Don't know yet. There are a lot of options. Money's not the problem, not for a while anyway." Hadley sat on the bar stool next to her and touched his glass to hers. "Well, as they say in India, here's looking at you, kid."

They drank. The beer was cold and tasted good. Then the samosas were ready, and Hadley scooped several onto a plate for her.

"So," she said, blowing on a samosa to cool it, "tell me about your trip. How was your witch doctor? Did he help you?"

"*She.* Her name is Nania, and she's a kahuna, one of the Hawaiian healers that go back to ancient times. Anyway, the answer is, yes, she did." He swiveled on his stool so that he was facing her directly, and Jewel was surprised to see the flush of excitement in his handsome face. "You're going to have to bear with me, Madeleine, because this may sound like the ravings of a lunatic. But this is what I was talking about on the phone when I said I wanted to talk to you."

"All right," she said. "Shoot."

"Nania's incredible," Hadley continued, as he checked the rice. "I'd love you to see her. She doesn't even touch you, or hardly. She works with her hands a few inches above your body, but you can feel the energy of her hands. You can *feel* this incredible heat. Then she actually does hands-on at the more blocked, difficult spots. I swear, she brought more feeling and energy back into my legs. She helped me . . . alleviated a lot of the pain." He stopped, smiling. "Do you think I'm nuts?"

"I don't know what to think. But if you feel some improvement . . ."

"Can't you see it? Can't you tell?"

Hadley had been sitting down when she saw him last. She couldn't tell the difference, but she nodded anyway.

"I know it's a lot to lay on you at once. But just keep an open mind, that's all I ask. The whole time I was there, I kept thinking, *Madeleine! I've got to tell her about all this.* I almost called you, then thought better of it. As crazy as this sounds in person, I knew you'd probably hang up on me if I tried to hit you with this over long distance. You'd have *really* thought I was nuts." He shook his head, chuckling at himself. "Maybe I *am* nuts, I don't know. But I know I can walk better than I've been able to since that damned bus fell on me."

He picked up her hand and squeezed it. "Look, I devoted a year and a half to conventional medicine and listened to the sober opinions that I'd never walk again. They're all scared to death of malpractice. They don't like to get your hopes up. But, Madeleine, you have to hope. There's nothing else." He lowered the heat under the curry pot and gave it a quick stir.

"I've come around to all this slowly," he continued. "After meditating, searching. I can either stop here, or try to go further . . . by checking out all the healing techniques that are out there. See if they work. So people laugh. Hell, I laughed too when I took my first step out there without crutches." He threw his hands up in the air and pantomimed a little jig. Jewel laughed.

"See," he said, "you're laughing too. Isn't it great?"

"Hadley," she said, "you're amazing. But do you really believe in miracles?"

"Miracles—I don't know. Metaphysics, maybe. Nania says the scar tissue is inhibiting the healing process. She wants me to go to Brazil. Apparently the healers there are very powerful. They work for free because they claim to channel their healing energy from higher beings . . . I know, I know." He paused, picking up on her skepticism. "God, you look absolutely appalled, Madeleine. I know it all *sounds* crazy, but it's worth a shot. Over the years, I've learned that you can shut out an awful lot by being too smart."

The food was ready. Hadley busied himself with ladling it into serving dishes, which he loaded onto a tea cart. "Here," he said, "if you'll roll this into the dining room for me, I'll bring some more beer."

In the austere, gray dining room, Hadley had draped the table with a Tabriz Oriental carpet and put the place settings on top of that. Candles towered out of scrolled brass Indian candlesticks.

"This is beautiful," Jewel said. "I can't believe you did all this."

"Well, I'm not working right now . . . I had plenty of time. I find cooking relaxing—rather Zen-like." Hadley fixed a plate of steaming curry for Jewel and one for himself and sat down across from her. "I realize I've been talking nonstop. And Madeleine, *Jewel,* I want you to know how special this is—to have you here. But I'm afraid you may be beginning to regret it. Poor old Hadley, gone off the deep end."

"No, I don't think that," Jewel said. "But it's all way out of my experience. Though I'm not as against what you're saying as you probably think. But kahunas, Brazilians channeling higher beings . . . you're going to have to give me a little time."

He grinned, and held up a hand. "Take all the time you need. You still may not wind up in the same place I am. But I don't think that matters. Who knows where my head will be in a year? I might be signing up for medical school."

"I don't think so," Jewel smiled.

"I don't think so either. But I'm definitely on this, you'll pardon the cliché, voyage of discovery. I keep running up more sail, and man, the places it takes you! If you're not worried about making a fool of yourself."

That was exactly what Jewel did worry about. It had been a guiding principle of her life for as long as she could remember. But Hadley's unselfconscious enthusiasm was infectious. For the past twenty minutes Jewel had been debating whether to tell him about her experience in the hospital: her "dream" that she was now convinced *wasn't* a dream. She had not told anyone, because of her terror of making a fool of herself. But if there was anyone who would understand, it was Hadley.

"Actually," she began, "something happened to me. Something very strange . . ."

She told him everything; and in the telling it came alive for her, the warmth, the loving presence, the feeling of peace and belonging, the healing water, the green stone. How she had not wanted to come back, how the friendly beings had pushed her, gently making her see how she was needed, and what *she* still needed, in life.

Hadley listened without interruption, nodding encouragement. When she finished, his eyes were shining. He reached across the table and squeezed her hand. "Then you *do* know," he said. He grinned suddenly. "Man, aren't we a couple of space cadets."

They cleared the remains of the Indian feast. While Hadley covered the leftovers and loaded the dishwasher,

Jewel made tea and provided him with the quick version of her life since the last time they'd met. For the first time she could remember, she spoke candidly, without trying to edit and improve the facts as she went.

They took their tea into the living room. Jewel sat on the sofa, Hadley opposite her in a chrome and canvas director's chair. ". . . Which brings us almost up to the present," she finished. "Except for one little detail: Allen and I are getting a divorce."

"Oh, Mad . . . Jewel, I'm sorry."

She shrugged. "Oh, it's all wonderfully modern and friendly. We're still under the same roof for a while, till my place is ready."

"Is there anyone else in your life?"

"No, just my daughters. I think I'm going to enjoy being single again. I need the time to reflect . . . work out some things," she said carefully. "And speaking of that, I have to tell you how sorry I am about everything that happened—with your father."

A dark look passed over Hadley's face. "Yeah, it hit me pretty hard. And I'm afraid Anna's anger fed mine. She was out of control."

Jewel folded her hands in her lap. "I can't entirely blame her. Looking at it from her, your, point-of-view, what I did was . . . Oh, Had, I'm so sorry. But it happened. I can't make excuses or lay blame. I can tell you now that hurting you was the worst of it, for me—even though you had already hurt me by falling in love with that Lydia."

"A severe lack of judgment on my part," he said. "She was there, and you weren't. That's all there was to it really. I made an ass of myself. Remember? I tried to tell you that time on the phone." He shook his head. "We were all children then."

Jewel nodded, thinking back. "Anyway, I was shook up by what happened. And I was sorry to lose Anna."

"Anna's crazy," he said glumly. "Or, at least, she's unhinged when it comes to you. Hell, I was devastated, for a while. I wanted you back . . . and then I found out about you and Dad. When you're that age, you see everything in black and white. But Anna, I don't know. She's always had this complex thing going with Dad. She couldn't blame *him* for what happened. She had to lay it all on you. I think a whole bunch of raw wires got crossed in her head."

Jewel sighed, shaking her head slowly. "Well, for a long time I missed her, Hadley. Anna was a sister to me, a best friend."

Hadley came over and sat on the sofa next to her. "She's gone and there's not a damn thing either of us can do about it. She's all locked up in a thousand little compartments now, and most of them you wouldn't want to peek inside." He sighed. "I simply outgrew my hatred. Oh, there was a time when I fantasized some sort of showdown with you, where I'd tell you how rotten you were. I even started to write you. But finally I decided to just let it go. Put you out of my mind. Which I succeeded in doing until . . ."

"You ran into me?"

"No, actually, that's the weird thing. I hadn't thought about you in years. I didn't know where you were or what you were doing. Then, when I got back to New York this fall, I started seeing people I thought were you." He laughed. "The *old* you, the way you used to look. It made me think about it all over again. And I realized it was completely in the past. I didn't care anymore. As I said, we were all so fucking young."

"Yes, we were," Jewel said. "I'm glad to have had this chance to talk to you. I'm glad we can leave it all back there."

"What about now? I don't want to rush you, but what are the possibilities of us seeing each other again?"

Jewel smiled. "I don't know. I like you, Hadley. I still

find you attractive. But we're two different people now. We've both changed enormously."

"So we'll start fresh," he said. "And see what happens."

"You'd have to be willing to go very slow. There are a lot of things I'm dealing with right now."

"I'll go slow. Hell, I haven't been with a woman for nearly three years." He grinned, and she had to grin back.

"Look, I'm going to Brazil in a couple of days," he said suddenly. "Why don't you come? We can both visit the healers. It would be quite an experience to share."

"This is *slow?*" Jewel laughed, exasperated.

"Well. We could have separate bedrooms. It'd be a great place to get to know each other again."

"Oh, Hadley, I can't get away now. There's too much happening. We're having a huge party to announce Sascha's joining Bijoux. Then there's Christmas."

"But if it weren't for all that, would you go? I'm talking theoretically."

"Theoretically, I'd have to think about it. Part of my future plan is to think things through a bit more."

"Don't think too much. It's not good to ruin the spontaneity of the moment." Hadley ran his finger up and down Jewel's cheek. "Look, I know we have to get to know the people we are now. We'll take it easy, I promise. But I'll tell you this . . . when I was in Hawaii I thought about you a lot. I had this flash that we're going to be together. And that was before I knew you were getting a divorce."

Jewel shook her head. "You're impossible! I like you, Hadley, but you *may* have gone off the deep end. Besides, if we started up again, Anna might murder us both," she said. "Do you realize how furious she'd be?"

"Fuck Anna," Hadley said. "She'll self-destruct one of these days. Nobody can sustain the amount of hatred she does without having it affect them sooner or later. Madeleine, whatever happens or doesn't happen with us will have *nothing* to do with her. Remember that."

"Okay. You're right."

"Now," he said, "tell me about your daughters. I want to get to know a bit more about the competition."

They drank tea, ate chocolate cake, and talked until past midnight. Hadley kissed her lightly when it was time to go, and then he walked her out to catch a taxi.

"Life takes funny turns, doesn't it?" he said.

"Yes. Maybe one of these days I'll catch on."

"I'll call you from Brazil and see you when I get back. If you want."

Jewel nodded. A cab pulled up to the curb.

"Bon voyage!" she said, opening the door. "Good luck with the healers. I really mean it."

"Thanks." He leaned over and kissed her again, a bit more seriously, before she got into the cab.

As she rode uptown, Jewel reflected on the evening. She had no idea whether she and Hadley would go anywhere; it was too soon to tell. And she didn't know what she wanted anyway. For now though, she had to admit she felt good.

34

The café at the Russian Tea Room, on West Fifty-seventh Street next to Carnegie Hall, was as picturesque as a Paris salon of the thirties. It was a large, L-shaped private room with rich crimson banquettes, shimmering brass samovars, and carved-wood side curtains framing the windows and doorways, each with a gilded clock at the center. Its walls were crowded with paintings and drawings: costumes from *Petrushka;* a cubist picture by Braque; a Toulouse-Lautrec pastel of a couple dressed for the opera; a sketch of Nureyev by Jamie Wyeth.

Tonight the room was crowded with people in elegant dress and glittering jewelry for the gala press reception celebrating the association of Sascha Robinovsky with Bijoux. The fashionable world and the journalists who record its doings turned out in force. The air was filled with the effervescent buzz of small talk and champagne bubbles, the scribbling of felt-tip pens in notebooks, and the bright flashes and clicking shutters of cameras.

The greatest concentration of these last was in the corner where Sascha stood with his arm around Jewel. Standing shyly nearby were Amber and Beryl, dressed in creations that Harry Harper had designed for them as the cornerstone of his new line for teens.

"Get a picture of my daughters too," Jewel instructed the photographers, as she gathered them to her. "And be sure to mention Harry Harper . . . he'll die if you don't."

Harry Harper, a few feet away, pantomimed strangling himself with his own hands. "I'll kill myself anyway, Jewel," he threatened. "That's not my dress you're wearing tonight. Although you do look stunning. Much as I hate to admit it."

Jewel was done up in a short, silver-lamé-and-lace cocktail dress, and was wearing a diamond-studded silver necklace that Sascha had presented to her that evening before the party.

"A fine necklace for a fine neck," he had told her, recalling the time long ago when he had said the same thing.

"Darlings," Jewel said to her daughters. "I think you should go over and talk to Alexei and Yuri and Tanya." She nodded toward Sascha's children, sitting across the room with Aïna, who was engaged in animated Russian conversation with one of the waiters. "After all, you're half siblings. Get to know them a bit."

Amber sighed and rolled her eyes, but took her sister's hand. "Come on, Berry, let's mingle."

"They are fine girls," Sascha said, nodding proudly. "Good stock."

Jewel looked at her watch. "Excuse me, Sascha, I've got to make a call." But as she began to weave across the room, Edward intercepted her.

"This is the place to be tonight," he said, slipping an arm around her waist. "It's a smash. Everybody's here.

Except," he added, peering around the room and then lowering his voice to an arch stage whisper, *"her."*

"Who?" Jewel asked, distracted.

" 'Who?' she asks. Who else? The vanquished— Cathalene." It had been Edward's idea to invite her, along with Jill Cross and Tom Tinker, to show that Bijoux rose above any hard feelings. Jewel had balked at first, but finally came around. She could afford to be magnanimous.

"Oh, she won't show," Jewel said. "But I chatted with Jill and Tom a few minutes ago, to show how nice I am."

"Oh, I just love our new Jewel!" Edward exclaimed. "Say, darlin', we've been so crazed I keep forgettin' to ask you, what are the Christmas plans? Connecticut?"

Jewel nodded. "The girls chose me over Allen, but he may come up during the day for a bit, *alone,* at my request. Nushka's going to her family. You and Peter will come, won't you? It'll keep us from getting maudlin."

"Of course, darlin'. And what about your friend Hadley?"

"Oh, I don't know. I told you, I'm *not* rushing into anything." Jewel looked at her watch. "He's supposed to be getting back from Brazil tonight. He should have been here by now. I'm going to call the airport."

"You're not rushing into anything? Look at yourself, fretting like a mother hen."

She started to protest, then saw the expression in Edward's eyes change. She turned and followed his gaze. At the far side of the room, coming through the door, was Cathalene Columbier.

Trailing behind her were Anna Ferguson and Wyatt McNeill.

"Oh, that *bitch* Cathalene," Jewel said through clenched teeth.

"Now, now, give them a chance," Edward counseled.

"Yes, darling, all right." How bad could it be? At least the meeting with Anna was on Jewel's turf this time.

Cathalene, her hair a mass of newly permed curls,

greeted Edward with a kiss on each of his cheeks. "Don't you look wonderful, Edward! But you are always such a snappy dresser." She turned her eyes to Jewel. "Hello, Jewel," she said, giving two pecks to the air in the broad vicinity of Jewel's cheeks. "I brought some old friends of yours."

"Just to show there are no hard feelings?"

"Exactly." Cathalene smiled like a kitten and melted into the crowd.

Jewel grabbed Edward's hand. "Don't leave me for a second," she said. "Stay on my heels. I need you." Together they prepared to meet the enemy forces.

Wyatt came forward to give her a kiss, as Anna hung frostily back. "Cathalene and I talked Anna into coming tonight," he said, sotto voce. "I want to see you two friends again."

"Wyatt, this is Edward Randolph, my partner." As the two men shook hands, Jewel looked past Wyatt's shoulder. Anna, sleek in a simple, black dinner suit and a cold blaze of diamonds, looked even thinner than when Jewel had seen her last. The hollowness of her throat and cheeks made the bones of her face stand out starkly, accentuated by the tight chignon into which she had pulled back her auburn hair. Anna was glaring at her; there was no hint of friendship in her eyes. A waiter in a red tunic trimmed with Russian braid passed by, and Jewel plucked a champagne glass from the tray.

"I don't know, Wyatt," Jewel said doubtfully, taking a swallow. "I don't think there's much hope."

"Well, give it a shot," Wyatt said, giving her shoulder an encouraging squeeze. "Mr. Randolph, what about a drink?"

"Oh, I don't think . . ." Edward looked at Jewel.

She gave him a nod. "I can handle it," she said, forcing a smile.

"A drink? Why, that sounds like a first-rate idea, Mr. McNeill," Edward answered.

There was a three-yard avenue of strangely cleared space between Jewel and Anna. They faced each other across it, like two gunfighters in a Western. Then Jewel stepped forward and extended her hand.

"Hello, Anna," she said. "I'm glad you came."

Anna allowed her fingertips to brush Jewel's limply, then pulled her hand away, as if avoiding lethal germs. "Yes, well, you have quite a lot to celebrate. Getting Sascha Robinovsky to Bijoux. But then, I believe you used to sleep with him too, didn't you? You must be a marvelous asset to your personnel department."

"Can't we maintain some semblance of civility?" Jewel sighed. "We both have our grievances. Mine are more recent—your trying to bring down my company while I was laid out with a stroke. But the world's big enough for both of us. Let's give it a try. I mean, you didn't come here tonight just to pick a fight, did you?"

"Oh, that's good, coming from you," Anna said disgustedly. "You and Daddy, still plotting behind my back. And God knows what else."

"What are you talking about?"

"Daddy dragged me here tonight. *You* put him up to it."

"I've seen your father exactly once in all these years, by accident, in public," Jewel said. "Edward and I invited Cathalene out of professional courtesy. I didn't think you'd show up, and I certainly didn't ask Wyatt to bring you," Jewel said, trying to keep her temper. "Look, Anna, don't you think this hostility's gone on long enough? Aren't you ready to bury it?"

Anna's eyes narrowed. "I'll never bury it," she hissed. "I told you a long time ago, I think you're the most *malignant* person I've ever met. You're evil. And nothing's happened to make me change my mind."

That was enough. Jewel could barely keep her voice even. "I'm not evil, Anna. Doesn't hating me get *boring* after a while? If I were you, I'd try to get on with my life.

Focus on something *positive* for a change. Now if you'll excuse me, I don't think there's much point in continuing this."

As Jewel turned away, Anna stuck out her black stiletto-heeled pump, and Jewel tripped over it. With her left side still weak, Jewel was not able to recover her balance and went pitching forward toward the floor.

A split second before she landed, she felt strong arms catch her and lift her up again.

"Hadley!"

"I've been here a few minutes," he said. "But I saw you with Anna and thought I'd better not barge in. You okay?"

"Yes, I'm all right."

Hadley glared at his sister. "What the hell are you up to, Anna?"

"It's all right, Had," Jewel assured him.

Anna's eyes were burning. Her lips began to tremble, and her pale skin glowed an unhealthy red. "What are *you* doing here, Hadley?" she demanded in a voice that was tight and shrill. "What's going on between you two?"

"We'll talk about it later," Hadley said warningly.

"You've got him again!" she screamed at Jewel. "You evil slut, you can't keep your hands off my family! Why won't you leave us *alone!*" Something inside Anna seemed to snap, some imaginary cord that had been too tightly strung for too many years. With a terrible scream, she flung her glass of bourbon onto the floor and lunged toward Jewel, swinging her fists with insane wildness.

Hadley stepped between them, pushing his sister back, as Wyatt plunged hastily through the suddenly quiet crowd.

"Anna!" he said in a stricken voice. "Oh God, Madeleine, I'm sorry. Come on, Hadley, let's get her out of here. Anna, honey . . . come on."

But with a sudden twist, Anna pulled away from

Hadley's grasp. She reached to the floor and snatched up a shard of shattered glass. It cut deeply into her hand, and she raised it, dripping blood.

"At least I can make you *ugly!*" Anna shrieked, and her hand lashed out toward Jewel's face. Jewel recoiled, but the sharp glass sliced her cheek just below her right eye.

"You'll pay for everything you've done," Anna yelled hysterically, "you'll pay in hell! See if they want you now . . ."

"Mother!" Amber's horrified cry pierced the room.

Anna hesitated as her arm swung back for another strike, and Hadley grabbed it while Wyatt secured his arms around her. Anna was now sobbing hysterically as she watched her own blood trickle down her wrist and soak into the sleeve of her suit.

A waiter wrapped Anna's hand in a towel. Stumbling, sobbing, she allowed her father to steer her toward the door. Cathalene, white-faced, hurried after them.

Hadley helped Jewel to a banquette, and Sascha soaked a napkin in vodka and dabbed with it at the cut in her cheek. "It's not too bad," he said with a deep sigh of relief. "No need for stitches."

But Jewel was staring at Hadley. "Hadley, where are your crutches?"

Hadley smiled. "In Brazil." He held up the carved wooden cane he was carrying. "Next time I'll leave this there."

"We'd better get her to a hospital," Allen Prescott said, hovering nervously. Never good with the sight of blood, his face was ashen and he was trembling violently. "I'd feel better if a doctor looked at this."

"No," Jewel said. "Really, Allen, I'm all right. All I need is a Band-Aid."

Amber and Beryl had been rooting through Jewel's purse.

"Band-Aids," Amber said breathlessly.

"We found them in your wallet!" Beryl exclaimed.

Jewel kissed them. "Thank you, darlings. They've probably been there since you were babies. I don't think either of you has needed one for years. Let's hope they still work."

Hadley opened one and covered the cut.

"You'd better go help your father, Had," she said. "I'm okay. He needs you more right now."

He started to protest, then nodded. "I'll call you later."

Jewel stood up. The guests were still gathered around in shocked silence. She smiled. "And you reporters thought these press parties in the jewelry business were dull. Well, with Bijoux there's always more to it than free champagne." A wave of relieved laughter swept the room. After a moment, Jewel held up her hand. "Obviously, I can't tell you what to write. And I wouldn't try. But there's not much of a story in this little episode. Just strain and nerves gotten a bit out of hand. No harm done. There'll be no charges or nonsense like that. The real story tonight is Sascha Robinovsky and Bijoux, and the party's still going strong."

The crowd broke into applause. Sascha raised both his arms and gestured heartily, summoning people around him. "And I have plans," he boomed, "that will keep you pounding at your typewriters for weeks!"

Edward put his hands on Jewel's arms and looked at her closely as Sascha the Pied Piper drew the crowd away. "Are you sure you're all right, darlin'?"

"I don't know. How do I look?"

"You look gorgeous."

"That's the main thing, then. But I don't think I'll make it a late night."

The day before Christmas Eve, New York City was in the midst of an unexpected blizzard. The snow had begun falling during the night. Already eight inches deep, it was

still coming down in frantic, tiny flakes. The traffic on
Fifth Avenue, outside of Jewel's window at Bijoux, was at
a standstill. The icy streets had caused cars to slide into
one another all morning. Jewel was beginning to think
that she and the girls should take the train to Connecticut,
which, of course, would be a madhouse. But better than
risking the treacherous roads.

She buzzed Meg. "Meg, can you see about getting train
tickets to Danbury? I'm afraid this snow isn't going to let
up anytime soon."

"Yeah. The latest weather flash is four to six inches
more."

"How can they do this to us? With Christmas almost
here?" Jewel said indignantly. "I still haven't finished my
last-minute shopping."

"Oh," said Meg, "Hadley McNeill's just arrived. Shall I
send him right in?"

"Of course." Jewel glanced into the large wall mirror
and smoothed her hair back. Her cheek below her eye was
still bandaged.

Hadley entered the office, smiling. He brushed some
snow off his overcoat and hung it, and his cane, on the
coat rack. "Hello. Isn't this a great storm? I love New
York when it snows. Have you ever noticed how friendly
people get?" He came over and reached across her desk to
kiss her cheek.

"Hi, Hadley. I thought we had a lunch date." She
looked at her watch. "It's only eleven."

He shrugged. "I walked up from downtown. Made it
faster than I thought I would. Want me to come back in
an hour?"

"No." Jewel shook her head. "I don't feel much like
working. You're right. It *is* pretty. Of course, it's going to
wreak havoc with our Christmas travel."

"Don't look at the bad side. It'll all work out fine."

"What's the word for a male Pollyanna?" Jewel smiled.

"Hey, I'm merely in a good mood. This is the first time I've seen you alone since I got back from Brazil."

Jewel nodded, the picture of Anna's contorted face flashing across her mind.

"How's Anna doing?"

Hadley had reported from the hospital that she was heavily sedated.

"I don't know. Not great. I honestly think if she'd had a gun that night she'd have shot us both down. Anna's been on the edge for years. Not just you, a lot of things—the drinking, and the extreme mood swings. I tried to talk to Mother and Dad about it years ago, but they never wanted to see it. Now we're all having to face it. Even Randy, when he's sober enough. And who knows . . . maybe the place we've got her in now will help her."

"I hope so," Jewel sighed. "It's all such a pity. I know you said that whatever happens between us has nothing to do with Anna. But Hadley, she's *always* going to be there, hating me. I don't think I could take it."

His face clouded. "Well, let's not talk about that now. Are you hungry?"

"Not really. I had coffee and a Danish half an hour ago."

"Then want to go for a walk? Up to the Park?"

Jewel smiled. Hadley's enthusiasm for the snow amused her. "All right. But I warn you . . . I'm not a great lover of the outdoors. The cold makes my nose bright red."

Hadley laughed. "Okay, a short walk. Then we'll eat, or get some coffee or something."

Out on the street, people were darting around, carrying crammed shopping bags, trying not to slip on the icy spots. Hadley took Jewel's arm and guided her carefully across the street, to where it was less crowded. The snow had blanketed the usual cacophony, and a quiet, surreal peace had descended over the city. There were few cars on the streets now, and only a smattering of brave cabdrivers.

"I still haven't heard about Brazil," Jewel said as they headed uptown toward Central Park.

Hadley shook his head. "It blew my mind. I have a friend who's a filmmaker. We may get together and do a documentary on these people. I mean, it's incredible down there. This guy Armando just reached *into* my leg. No drugs, nothing. I was *awake,* I saw it. He pulled out this mass of scar tissue. Then he sort of smoothed it over with his hand. When he'd finished, all you could see where he'd been working was like a little paper cut."

"It's amazing—"

"And," he interrupted, "another guy, Fabio, works with light and energy. You can *see* sparks fly from his hands, from his whole body . . . like a human light bulb. He worked on getting the energy in my legs balanced and flowing. I mean, it's fucking unbelievable, what they do. God, I'd love to get you down there, to let them work on you."

"Well—" Jewel started to say.

"Look," he interrupted again, "have you thought any more about us while I was away?"

Jewel nodded. "Yes."

"And what?"

"Well, next trip to Brazil I may come too."

"Yeah?" he said. "This is looking promising."

"Calm down." She smiled. "Slow, right? Separate bedrooms and all that."

"Well, yeah, if that's what you want."

"I didn't say it's what I want. It's what would be best."

"Okay, sure, separate bedrooms. No problem."

Jewel wiped a snowflake off her eyelash. "God, it's freezing. Let's go someplace and warm up."

"Okay." Hadley broke into a wide grin. "But I'd like to remind you—in Rio, it's summer now."

Jewel rolled her eyes and pulled him out of the snow, into the nice, cozy warmth of a small café.

"Let's plan the trip over coffee," she said.

"I'd rather plan it in bed with you. I mean, Christmas is almost here. And I can tell you what I want most."

"I know," Jewel laughed. "You're absolutely relentless."

"That's me," he said, leaning over to kiss her while the waitress waited patiently to show them to a table.

MEREDITH RICH is the author of the novels *Little Sins,* *Virginia Clay,* and *Bare Essence,* which was adapted as a major network miniseries and later as a weekly prime-time series. Under another name she has published numerous magazine articles and four nonfiction books on business and health.

A former New Yorker and Virginian, she now lives in northern New Mexico with her husband, a writer and cartoonist, and her two daughters.

She is active in the movement to save the environment, and is committed to world peace.